THE BLOOD OF THE SPEAR

THE EYE OF ETERNITY

1

THE BLOOD OF THE SPEAR

MARK TIMMONY

The Blood of the Spear

First published 2021 by Ravenhawk Publishing

This edition published by Ravenhawk Publishing
www.ravenhawkpublishing.com

ISBN: 978-0-6450965-3-8 (hardback)
978-0-6450965-1-4 (trade paperback)
978-0-6450965-2-1 (ebook)

Map designed by Mark Timmony, rendered by Timothy J. Gonzales
Chapter icons by Timothy J. Gonzales
Cover illustration by Felix Ortiz
Cover design by STK Kreations
Edited by Abigail Nathan and Amanda J Spedding
Internal design by Zena Shapter

Australian English conventions, spelling, and grammar were used in this book.

To Mum and Dad, for all your support.
Thank you.

CONTENTS

GARVAND
Himath
Onea
Anvil Mnts.
Ilsaon
Helna
Dremadin
Farpoint
CYTHIS
Camore
Marisdel Forest
Rathmon
Lensara
Kyran Pass
Mundar
Latmar Mtns.
The Western Realms
Harlgate
SITHAPIA
Velonia Forest
Greycliff
Lionsgate
Elden
Whitemore
Halford
Cryned
Orlay
Soran
Sithsara
Keirmarh Forest
Banris
Aleshel
Justare
Mensara
Felsara
Highbay
The Gold Sea
Ritsarn
Isoliere
Vasara
Lakemere
Opalhis
Salstai Forest
Lubar
Borana
Nesar
Guesaybor Mtns
Lissan Desert
TREMOR-SALAYA
Serjat
Disaydos
Pinta
Karinia
Sandmark
Khemsarbis
Tarwen
Rocriaqesh
Mynar Forest
Lostar Forest
Memset
Arokesh
Lanthras
Midlan
Jarlor
Caladian Ocean
The Crescent Plains
HETAR
Escalon
Estara
Carlith
Daymor
Folase Mtns.
Sabin
Nemisdrillion Sea
Caslain Forest
Maltroy
Sulveroy
ALDANIA
Quedra
Gotoria
Barovia
Raeltia
The Amur Gulf
Tinean Mtns.
Islo
Ebron
Jarsk Forest
DAL'MERE
The Deadlands
Nesk
Jaroff
The Borderlands
Elmedrat
Dainyaia
Saysarn Peaks
The Three Citadels
Carvia
Palpora
Halaron
Fortarc

ATHMAY
The Broken Continent
MERLAI ISLANDS
Palisa Ocean
The Eastern Half
Altay
Watergrave Bay
Benor
Nayette
Massarle
Warrimon
Whitestone Plains
Lotarn
Dracolith Mtns
Tarthon
Issoud
Darlon
TOMASSIA
Balain Forest
Masin
Southpoint
Sapphire Gulf
Dothra
Oma
Vivay Plains
Elayse
Gaulen
Chaurien
Caselbar
Kia Mon Steppes
Tomaya
Altain Mnts.
Lutiad
Vadat
Kia Saya Steppes
KIA NORMA
Kia Lorda Steppes
Ki'zara
Ki'rai Forest
Daicremore
Mtns.
Andarra
Noreda
Sharrnon Bay
SULEIA
Li Mena
Malsa
Heaven's Tears
Shon'wu
Hun Zu
N
Naysa
Kituan
Dao'shen
Ban-rai
AMARIA
Nai-chan
Lo'ming
Ping Taru
Tai Goh
Waolin
Saurin'sha
Arleth'taur
Yenshan
Shi'a Li'ang
The Black Sands
The Sukmaani
Shi-Kaan
Tang-tse
Kaion
The Broken Teeth
Tisted Mtns
Hai-Sun Ocean
Ni'Zo

When the Bronze Spear returns, the Empyros will come again.
Seek Him in the sacred flame, find Him in the shadowed heart.
The forge of the morning shall be His pyre; the path of stars will light His way.
He will hold the sword of glory, wearing a crown of lies.
Born once the Saviour, and twice the Destroyer, five aspects He will claim.
Two halves a whole, the phoenix will grow, but only one will hold the seal.

- from A Rising Flame,
Addendum to the Starscroll Prophecies
Author unknown
Circa 5 A.S.

Records made during the first three hundred years after the Sundering are incomplete. Still, it is commonly accepted that the first babe born with the Mark of the Summoner after that fateful day appeared amongst the refugees in the city of Ja'rov, on the sixth day of Marcin, 2 A.S.

And she was killed by her father on the same day.

Since that time, any child born with the Mark of the Summoner on the back of their right hand has been taken by the attending midwife, and executed by the city or township authorities. And any man or woman, young or old, upon whom the Mark appears later in life, is also sentenced to death, lest the devastation wrought by daemons summoned from the Void, fall upon us once more.

- from Ci del Lathrin (Map of the Stars),
Translated by Viscount Jodar Tekmaan,
Ninth Courtier to the Shepherd Kings,
1713 A.S.

PROLOGUE

Tides of Prophecy

TAMERON'S WARDS SHIMMERED on the air as heat enveloped him, and his vision swam from the smell of sulphur until a secondary ward cleared it away. Thunder rolled overhead. He glanced up, eyeing the light show as a greater daemon struggled to push its way through the veil. Voidfire bled through the tear in the sky, purple, indigo and azure, but nothing else. The tear stabilised and faded even as he watched. The daemon – possibly one of the great Chakrigel – was too large to force its way through without a Sahrin to assist it. And no Sahrin – no Summoner – had been suffered to live in centuries to bring one forth.

He dropped his gaze, eyes adjusting to the red glow of the lava, the rock walls around him pitch black.

"Hal'iren," he said, naming the place. He eyed the walls of the volcano that now occupied the site of the once glorious city. "How far you have fallen."

Tameron had not returned since he and the others had broken free of their prisons. *Broken free* was not entirely accurate. Not when doing so required one to shed the body you were born with.

The dull ruby glow offered little in the way of illumination, but he could make out the rift, glistening in the air like oil on water. An abnormality in the natural fabric of the world. With an involuntary swallow, Tameron pushed past his fear and made his way towards the breach.

He stopped before the rent in the air, the doorway that led to his prison, and made a show of straightening his tailored long coat. Sweat broke out on his nape that had nothing to do with the temperature.

Tameron took a breath; cursing his hesitation, he stepped into the rift. And screamed.

Dragged across time and space, his body twisted, stretched. Pain washed over him like razor-sharp knives scoring his flesh. Molten light eviscerated thought and stabbed his soul with shards of ethereal glass.

Tameron screamed, his throat burning, body breaking down. But slowly, agonisingly, he pushed his will out, surrounding himself in a shield.

Then he was through the rift and the pieces of his body reasserted themselves, knitting back together around the core of his mind. He fell to his hands and knees, gasping, and waited for the pain that sizzled along his abused nerves to subside.

He'd materialised on a platform suspended in darkness, lit by blooms of bound flame that hung above it like a chandelier. His breathing finally eased when a pair of dainty feet housed in grey velvet slippers stepped into his line of sight.

"My dear Tamaarin, Lord of Shadows," came a cooing voice, "you do so like to make an entrance, don't you?"

Demara. His lips twisted in a sneer as he pushed himself up, his eyes gliding over the wide hips and ample cleavage of the short woman before him. Naturally, she was wearing water-silk that sculpted every curve, its shimmering turquoise and steel grey colouring reminiscent of the sea before a storm.

Wiping the distaste from his expression, Tameron absently smoothed the ruffles at the cuffs of his coat sleeves.

"What do you want, Diamaata?" he asked and watched her kohl-lined eyes flash at his use of her true name.

"Stop antagonising him, Demara."

Tameron shifted his gaze to the taller woman. Where Demara wore the colours of a storm-laden sea, her sister was adorned in a gown of sparkling shards. Cryshel, one of the more decadent 'fabrics' of the old world, was made of tiny crystals that traced her body like a veil of stars, hinting and tantalising, yet revealed as little as the angular eyes that bore into his own.

"Solique." He nodded to her and stared around the platform. "Where are the others?"

Ten crystalline cocoons riddled with hairline cracks stood in a scattered circle around the platform. Once they had all pulsed with the dark, violet light of the Void, now three of the tombs glowed with the soft, golden radiance of the Light of the Eye of Eternity. One more than had done so when last they'd met here.

So, another has fallen. Or found 'freedom'. It was challenging to decide which term was most accurate. And only two of the remaining eight – *seven* – were here now.

Was he late, or did the others fear to come?

"Very well," Demara snapped, glaring at Solique. "Greetings, *Tameron*. The others have already gone."

"Gone?" He spun back to her, outraged. "I am not in the habit of being *summoned* only to find I wasted a trip! Where is Sarnorn?"

"Are you blind as well as simple?" Demara spat. "*Look*!"

Voidfire raged in his veins at her insult, but he held it in check as he felt its echo in both sisters. He could take on Demara but not Solique as well. And he had no doubt they would support each other against him if it came to it, no matter their own rivalry.

Always caution in a pit of vipers.

With a thought, he released his hold on the power and scanned the platform again. The only difference was another of the tombs now glowed gold. The one next to his own…

"No," he breathed. "Sarnorn has fallen?"

"Yes." There was an edge to Demara's tone. Was it fear? "He has become the Lord of Justice in truth."

Struggling to control his roiling stomach, he hid behind nonchalance and offered her words a shrug. "He is not the first to fall to the Spheres."

Demara's laugh was tinged with hysteria. "The circle is closing, Tameron!"

He waved a hand in dismissal. "Sarnorn was ever arrogant. We must be vigilant. Avoid the same mistakes as he and you will be safe enough."

"He didn't tell you?" Solique asked, her voice calm.

"Tell me what?"

Her dark eyes met his. "The *Ne'ronsylari* has moved."

He locked his knees to keep from staggering. The Bronze Spear. But it was so much more than just a *spear*. It was an artefact crafted by the Summoners. For it to have moved from where they had locked it away–

"An Empyros has been born." His voice was a whisper.

"Yes," Demara hissed. "Or at least one who can become an Empyros. When Sarnorn discovered the Spear was gone, he made plans to set a prince of the Niskeri on its trail. An iron boar to hunt a phoenix. We do not know how far that plan proceeded. When we arrived here, his prison was already filled with the Light. We weaken further, and our doom is at hand!"

"It is only our doom if we allow it to be," Tameron drawled, gathering himself. She'd find no fear in him.

"And how will you stop it?" Solique asked, her eyes on Sarnorn's tomb.

"The rise of a new Empyros marks the turning of the Age," Demara said. "The Daemon Queen will stir as the Empyros does, and the oaths we made during the Great War will be called due!"

"Her promises were a lie," Tameron said. "As were the writings of the Ancients we followed. I will not serve her again." There had to be a way out. *Three* thousand *years and we have done nothing to escape these chains. We are all fools*!

"And how will you refuse?" Demara demanded of him. "She is a goddess!"

"Are we not gods amongst men?"

Demara snorted. "Amongst *humans*, perhaps!"

He ignored her. "The Focus Stone, the Cryndalene." *Yes, that could work*. If they could repair it, they could access power enough to sever any oaths and re-seal what should never have been opened. "If we found the shards –"

"The others are already searching for the pieces of the Cryndalene." The light from the flames above glinted on Demara's water-silk like red lightning.

"And you let them go?" The snarl that left his lips would have sent his priests cowering in terror. "This will lead to a war like nothing we have seen since the Sundering. We should all be working together!"

Demara threw up her hands. "And how could I have stopped them? We only ever listened to Sarnorn, and even then, we kicked and screamed all the way. No, I couldn't stop them, and neither could you."

"So, they are all looking for the shards, hoping to be the first to reunite the Cryndalene, the Great Focus Stone of the Ancients." His lips pressed together. Hard.

Solique shook her head. "All but for Kirana."

"What?" he rounded on her.

Solique stared at him, her eyes dark as the depths of the ocean. "Kirana wants the Empyros dead. She promised to kill Varos Korin'ad and any who came after him when he and his armies defeated us. She means to keep that promise."

"She is a fool." She was more than a fool. Kirana had been verging on mad *before* they'd been imprisoned, but now she was truly insane. "We should have locked her away like we did Dalmon."

"The Lord of Knowledge had already fallen. Kirana," Demara gestured at the tomb that held the original body of the Lady of Flame, still pulsing with its purple light, "has not."

Solique shrugged. "She thinks that if she finds the Empyros before their powers have quickened, she can offer him or her as a sacrifice to Di'shana –"

"The Daemon Queen doesn't want the Empyros dead!" he roared.

"Do you think that would matter to Kirana?" Solique laughed.

"We can stop her. If we –"

"We?" Demara gaped at him. "There is no we. Even now the others have begun searching for the shards while I stayed here waiting for you!"

"Very well." Tameron crossed his arms over his chest. "And what will you do?"

"Oh, no." Demara shook her head. "My plans are my own. I stayed to tell you this because I owe you. That debt is now repaid. You're on your own."

Tameron felt the power of the Void fill her again as she opened the rift and returned to Hal'iren without a backwards glance. He frowned in annoyance. She had shown none of the hesitancy in stepping through as he had to get here.

And her debt was not repaid until he said it was.

"My sister's nature suits her as Lady of Storms," Solique said from beside him. "She is wild and tempestuous, but as with all storms, this will pass."

"And you, Lady of the Waters? What does your nature dictate?"

Solique's smile did not reach her eyes. "The rise of a new Empyros and their bonding of the Phoenix Empyrean is the greater concern here. This hunt for the shards is a distraction, though one worthy of attention. It would not do to have one of the others gain the power to dissolve their oath while we remain bound."

Tameron glanced at her from the corner of his eye. "We should be working together."

"Perhaps," Solique said, reaching out with Voidfire to open the rift back to Hal'iren. "I will speak to Demara again. If things change, you will hear from me."

He watched her go – with the same lack of hesitation – and turned back to Sarnorn's prison. He peered into the golden light but could only just make out the shadow of the man's true body.

Shuddering, he backed away.

He needed to think. Finding the shards of the Cryndalene, the Focus Stone of the Ancients, was a prudent course of action but he was not one to rush. He worked best from the sidelines.

Yes, let the others find the pieces, and I will pry them from their cold, dead fingers.

In the meantime, he'd set his own hunters on Sarnorn's dog. This Niskeri princeling could flush out the prey, but he would be the one to catch them. Then, with the new Empyros in his grasp, *and* the reconstructed Cryndalene, the Daemon Queen would grant him whatever he wished.

Including his ascension as a god of the Void.

CHAPTER ONE

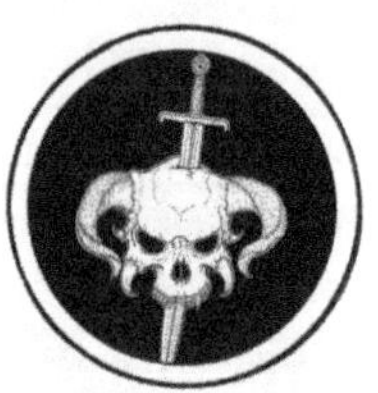

The Trial

"THE SUMMONERS HAVE been gone for three thousand years, but we deal with the remnants of their folly still," Jidara said.

Kaiel Toranth shivered as the cool touch of autumn soaked through the edges of his leather jerkin and surreptitiously eyed the others with him. The three of them stood at the bottom of a tall ridge. The granite rock face rose twenty feet before them, casting the cave at its base in shadow despite the morning sunlight shifting through the conifers, firs and the white-barked, silver-leafed moonleaf trees of the Borderland Wilds.

"That is why the Daemon Hunters exist," Jidara continued. "Since the days of the Sundering we Kas'tirien have stood as sentinels, protecting humanity from the evils the Summoners unleashed upon the world. You both have passed the Test of Mirrors, and the Long Night, where the rest of your fellow initiates have not."

Though only a Journeyman, Jidara was everything Kaiel hoped to become. She already wore the leather armour plated with the bleached bones of her first daemon kills, and now she would be conducting the Trial that would determine if he, or Rolen Etine, would become the next apprentice to Daemon Hunter Taalren.

He glanced at Rolen. They were almost of an age – Rolen being one year older at twenty. Kaiel was taller, but then at six foot four he was taller than most who lived in the Borderlands. Kaiel also had a denser musculature, gained from working in Master Milan's smithy each winter. But having trained with Rolen for the last four years, the older boy, *man*, was not to be discounted. Of the five youngsters from the citadels that had begun studying with them, only he and Rolen remained. And only one could move forward to apprentice.

The fact Rolen was the brother of Sevaani wouldn't make Kaiel any easier on him at all. He couldn't help but smile as the image of Rolen's blonde-haired sister crossed his mind, but he quickly brushed the thought aside. *Concentrate*. He'd given up too much to be here to lose focus now.

"Behind me is the entrance to the Darscene Caves." Jidara gestured to the stone doors hidden under the shadowy outcrop. "One of the original outposts of the Daemon Hunters, it is now reserved for the Trial. Within it, you will find yourself, or you will fall."

Rolen snorted.

"You have something to say, Etine?" Jidara stepped from the shadow of the ridge. Her crimson coloured hair was braided in the style of her native Hetar, the delicate copper caste chains woven through sparkled in the sunlight. The scar tracing the left side of her face did little to mar her beauty, but Kaiel found that even with her ebony skin, high cheekbones and full lips, Jidara was no Sevaani.

"Why are *you* conducting the Trial?" Rolen snapped, bringing Kaiel back to himself.

"Because Hunter Taalren set me the task."

"I am the son of the Steward of Hanore. Do the Kas'tirien think so little of me that they are too busy to be here when I win the Trial to join their ranks?"

Kaiel swallowed a groan, but Jidara merely arched an eyebrow.

"It may be that you think too highly of yourself if you imagine the Hunters even know your name," she told him. "There are no titles amongst the Kas'tirien other than Apprentice, Journeyman and Hunter. Nor are there such ranks amongst the Borderlanders that require bowing and scraping. But I am a foreigner here." She looked at Kaiel. "Perhaps I am wrong?"

Kaiel shook his head, avoiding Rolen's glare. "You're not wrong, Jidara. A Steward leads each of the citadels, but they are first amongst equals, not above them."

Rolen sneered. "You wish that were so because of your interest in my sister. My family has held the position of Steward in Hanore since the founding. You will never be good enough for Sevaani, warren-rat. You and your half-brother don't even know who your fathers are! You're not worthy of joining the ranks of the Daemon Hunters."

"Your sister knows her mind, Rolen," Kaiel said, feeling his face heat. He took a breath; he wouldn't let Rolen get in his head, not today. "And my parentage is no concern of yours."

"Applicants come from all walks of life and all realms," Jidara said. "It is the measure of your ability in the Trial that proves your worthiness, Rolen Etine, not your bloodline. The Trial is straightforward. Only one of you can imprint the bone of the Dreadlord that awaits you at the exit of the cave. From that bone, your bonesword will be forged, and you will begin the next stage of your training."

The bone of a Dreadlord! Kaiel's hand dropped to the hilt of the sword belted at his waist. He'd seen the bonesword Hunter Taalren wore strapped to his back. The massive two-hander had always been an object of fascination for the initiates whenever they'd seen its black-bone hilt and quillons. It was said the Hunters were running out of the bones of Dreadlords, given the last manifestation was four hundred years ago. And without the bone of a daemon to imprint, no sword could be forged.

"Now," Jidara said sharply, and Kaiel snapped his attention back to her. "Which god do you call upon to watch over you today?"

"I call upon Alaythias," Kaiel said, straightening his back.

Jidara nodded. "The god of the Sun. And you, Rolen?"

"I call upon Tyros, Lord of the Hunt."

Kaiel gaped at him. "The Shol'mas aren't gods!" Everything Kaiel knew about the Divine Messengers came from his ma's tales. And she'd had the Sight. She'd…

His ma.

He breathed deeply, blinking his eyes against the sudden glare. His ma had died two weeks ago, and he'd not been there.

Rolen smirked. "There are ten Shol'mas, one for each of the Elder Gods. And the temples of the Shol'mas outnumber the shrines of the Elder."

"There were *once* ten Shol'mas," Jidara corrected.

Rolen shrugged dismissively. "Well, unlike the Elder, the Shol'mas answer prayers. Is this a problem? Is there some rule that says only an Elder can be called on in the Trial of the Kas'tirien?"

"The Shol'mas were not known when the War of the Summoners sundered the land, nor did they offer their blessing to the first Daemon Hunters, but there is no rule against calling on them." Jidara eyed Rolen. "The Darscene Cave is sealed by wards. You will take no artefacts of power with you, and no power can come to your aid within; if you thought that your prayers might be answered."

Rolen let out a hiss of breath and Jidara's answering smile was all teeth.

Kaiel looked at the sharp-featured young man again. Had Rolen seriously thought he could call on a Shol'mas to help him?

"Within the cave are lesser daemons. Your training is enough to see you survive them unless you lose your focus and forget your teachings. There is no stricture against working in a team, but only one of you can imprint the bone. Remember that." Jidara turned away from them, but Kaiel heard her mutter under her breath,"Not that there'll be any teamwork from that one."

Kaiel was sure she meant Rolen. Then again, he wasn't going to let Rolen beat him. He hadn't missed his mother's final breath to fail the Trial.

"Once you enter," she stepped into the mouth of the cave,"the door will close behind you." Even in the dimness, the runic markings that formed concentric circles around a single triangle carved into the centre of the door were clear, drawn with a deeper black than the shadow that hid them."The only way out is to reach the end of the complex within and to find the bone. I will await you there."

Jidara took her belt knife and drew the tip across her left palm, blood welling dark against her skin. She placed her bloodied palm within the triangle, and the runes began to glow. The triangle turned until its point faced down, and a slash of light bisected the stone door, right through the centre of the triangle. With a rumble, the stone halves rolled into the wall of the cliff.

"May the Light of the Eye of Eternity guide you, and your gods watch over you," Jidara said, moving aside.

"The Eye guide you," Kaiel said automatically.

"I thought the gods couldn't watch us in there," Rolen sneered, but Jidara didn't respond.

The entrance was wide enough to fit a large wagon, but Rolen still made a point of elbowing past. Kaiel let him go and wrapped his hand around the hilt of his sword as the doors closed behind them.

The immediate entrance of the cave was black as pitch, but less than fifteen feet ahead dusty light shone down on old mining cart tracks. Clumps of cave weed grew where the wall met the floor, their white, grass-like stems ended in bulbs that glowed with a soft blue light.

The hiss of steel was the only warning Kaiel had as Rolen drew his sword. Kaiel jumped back, managing to get his sword free of its scabbard to parry Rolen's second slash. Training overrode his surprise, and he returned the attack, sweeping Rolen's blade aside and thrusting, using his greater reach to push the Steward's son back into the tunnel.

"What are you doing?" Kaiel spat. "We're meant to be fighting daemons, not each other!"

Rolen stepped back. "Stay out of my way if you want to get out of here alive, warren-rat. Only one of us will complete this Trial, and it won't be you!"

Kaiel followed, forcing Rolen back towards the light. Keeping one eye on Rolen's sword, Kaiel shifted his gaze over the man's shoulder to the tunnel that branched off into the darkness. Rolen took another backwards step, his mouth twisted in a snarl when a screeching cry came from the shadows and a grey-scaled skreet flung itself at him. The daemonic, monkey-like imp reached out with both clawed hands, only to be knocked aside by Rolen's blade. Then another three of the scaled vermin, eyes flashing red, were on him.

Kaiel grinned and ran past Rolen, heading further into the better-lit tunnel. Skreet were more a nuisance than a serious threat, though if a pack overwhelmed a man, they could certainly kill him. But three skreet against a trained swordsman were more a distraction than a challenge, and Kaiel was happy to take advantage of it.

He kept his eyes down to protect his night vision when a particularly pained cry from Rolen made him look back. The man was still standing, and only two skreet remained. Kaiel put on a burst of speed only to curse as an open-pit appeared before him. He stopped before he went over, his stomach twisting at the close call. The pit's sides were rough, though he was confident he could have climbed out if he'd fallen in, but the drop looked to be a good twelve feet at least and was a dead end. His eyes roved over the ground below, stopping at what seemed to be white bone. Was that a skeleton?

"Kaiel!"

He turned and only just managed to get his free hand up as the skreet Rolen had thrown collided with him. Kaiel fell backwards into the pit, the daemon on his chest, and landed with a body bruising slam. Stars burst behind his eyes, and the air exploded from his lungs. He was vaguely aware of the ringing sound his sword made as it clattered to the ground somewhere nearby.

Gasping for breath, he gathered his strength and flipped himself over, getting to his hands and knees. His head ached, but he couldn't stay on his back. There was a skreet down here.

He was still blinking spots away from his eyes when he heard the growl. It was a higher pitch than the dogs back in the citadel, more like a cat.

The skreet let out a screech and Kaiel jerked himself up onto his knees as the dycinion moved into the light, fangs gleaming.

The large, black-furred predator was created by the Summoners during the war that sundered the world four thousand years ago. A daemon and cat hybrid, it was near to size with the waist-high hunting dogs of the citadels. The daemoncats were deadly, but Kaiel had faced them before. All the Rangers of the Three Citadels had, though he'd never done so alone.

Long of limb, the dycinion crouched belly to the ground, thickly muscled shoulders quivering. But it looked thin, almost gaunt. Kaiel prayed to Alaythias that it had been trapped in this hole for some time; a weakened cat would be much easier to face than one in full health.

The cat's red eyes shifted between him and the skreet madly scampering at the wall, trying to climb out. A scorpion-like tail rose behind the dycinion, the stinger dripping with a venom that paralysed its prey so that it could feast on living flesh.

Behind Kaiel, debris fell to the floor, dislodged by the panicked skreet. He grinned. Two birds, one stone.

Still on his knees, he grabbed the skreet by the neck and flung it at the dycinion. As the yowling skreet flew towards the cat, Kaiel dove for his sword.

The cat jumped aside as the skreet flew towards it. It slashed at the lesser daemon with a forepaw, knocking it into the shadows then turned to Kaiel with a snarl.

The muscles in the dycinion's shoulders rippled, and it sprang, its tufted ears flat against its skull. Heart pounding, Kaiel pivoted and slashed down with his sword.

The dycinion twisted in mid-air, avoiding the cut, and landed on its feet by the wall. Kaiel pressed forward, sweeping his sword low. The blade sliced along the dycinion's shoulder as it whipped out a mauling paw. The sound it made was like nothing Kaiel had ever heard. It took everything he had not to drop his sword and clamp his hands over his ears. The cat pounced, flicking its hind legs around and whipping its tail towards him. Kaiel swung his sword and arched backwards. The stinger slashed the air before his face, and his sword came up to meet it, severing the tail at its middle.

The dycinion screamed, eyes flashing, and sprang at him again, claws extended. Kaiel threw himself to the side, slipping on the intestines of the disembowelled skreet. He snatched the dead daemon up by its tail and flung it back at the dycinion.

It snarled, swiping at the body, but missed. The daemoncat staggered, falling to its side as the dead skreet collided with it. Kaiel dashed forward and drove his sword into the cat's exposed throat. Putting all his weight behind the thrust, he drove the blade down. The sound that came from the dycinion was like steel scraping against steel. Kaiel clenched his jaw and pressed down. The foul feline's body thrashed under the skewering sword, hind legs kicking out before it collapsed in silence.

Kaiel yanked his sword out of the dead daemonspawn, blood splattering behind it. Red eyes seemed to track him; malice emanating from the creature even in death.

He wiped the blood off his sword on the daemoncat's torso. Left unattended, daemon blood could pit any metal it touched, weakening the steel. Kaiel sheathed the sword, his breath calming as he studied the side of the pit. Finding a foothold, he managed to lever himself up and climb the rest of the way out. His head spun as he stood; and he winced as his fingers found an egg-sized lump at the back of his skull. He'd live, but he wouldn't complete the Trial if he let Rolen get any further ahead of him.

The Steward's son was nowhere to be seen. Kaiel made his way back to the cavern and headed into the other tunnel. He drew his sword again, though he wasn't overly concerned. If there had been more daemons, Rolen would have had to deal with them first. Hopefully, they slowed the bastard down.

The dark tunnel opened into another cavern. Light from fissures above shone down onto strands of gossamer thread that covered the walls, making them seem to glow in the gloom.

He froze. *Webs*.

Small cocoons and the dried husks of tangled skreet hung trapped on the walls. Across the way, the web had been torn aside, the darkness of another tunnel revealed behind it.

Then he spotted the body of the arac'diem.

The spider-daemon was the size of a foal. It lay slumped to the side of the cavern; its eight long legs curled towards its large abdomen from which rose the torso of what looked like a small child. This one was dead, the sword slashes across the chest told Kaiel that, even if the amount of green ichor seeping from its corpse didn't. He bent towards it, peering intently at the bared fangs, like small daggers pushing out of its mouth, and noted the black venom dripping off them. The arac'diem were dangerous foes. It was rare for a Daemon Hunter to face one without being bitten, and if there was venom on its fangs, then Rolen certainly had been.

Even having killed the spider-daemon, Rolen was a dead man.

Sword held before him, Kaiel edged into the webbed cavern. He spun in a slow circle, eyes searching every cranny, but all he could see was the varying shades of white and grey web glowing in the light. No more arac'diem were present. *Thank the gods.*

Cautiously, he made his way past the corpse when a shadow behind some webbing on the ground caught his eye. He froze, skin prickling tight across his body, but the shadow didn't move. It was probably nothing, but he couldn't leave the cavern only to have another arac'diem scuttle out behind him.

Gritting his teeth, Kaiel lunged forward and hacked through the web. Silky threads rose in the air, and he jumped back with a curse, brushing his free hand hurriedly across his face and head to dislodge the clinging strands. He took a deep breath, heart thudding in his chest, but he relaxed his grip on the sword hilt when nothing attacked. He crouched for a closer look. There was no arac'diem, instead, resting in a nest of rocks, were four skull-sized eggs.

Kaiel stared.

The fluid in the unhatched egg of an arac'diem was the only cure for its bite. The rock nest was undisturbed. Rolen hadn't even bothered to stop to look for the antidote to the venom.

Without it, the man was going to die; *if* he had been bitten.

It wasn't Kaiel's problem; he had his own future to worry about.

Kaiel backed away from the nest and headed into the tunnel. There was more cave weed glowing in the dark and another, brighter light a good thirty feet ahead.

Even though Rolen had made his way through here first, Kaiel kept his sword to hand. It was a shame things had turned out the way they had between them. He understood being an older brother; Kaiel was always looking out for his younger brother, Darien. He supposed it would be worse if Darien were a girl, he'd be a lot more protective then. But Kaiel would never hurt Sevaani, and Rolen hadn't given him a chance to prove that.

Sevaani. She loved her brother. If Rolen died in this Trial… if he didn't come home…

Kaiel's chest tightened. The pain of his mother's loss was still too raw. He couldn't let Sevaani lose a member of her family when he could stop it.

Kaiel made his way back into the cavern of the arac'diem.

Gently, he prodded the closest egg with his sword . When nothing attacked or moved in the shadows around it, he grabbed the egg. It was strangely warm in his hand, and heavy. Now he just had to catch up to Rolen before it was too late.

Running back through the tunnel, Kaiel exited into a cavern more extensive than the others. The granite floor was smoothed to a mirror finish, and geometric lines and shapes had been carved into it. He recognised them, although he couldn't read the runes that accompanied the channels. It was a containment chamber, designed to hold a greater daemon.

This couldn't be part of the Trial, surely? Neither Rolen nor he could defeat a greater daemon alone. It had to be leftover from before the building of the Redoubt, back when the Darscene Caves housed the ruling council of the Daemon Hunters.

Daylight poured into the cavern from a large circular hole halfway up the other side of the room. As Kaiel's eyes adjusted to the light, he could make out stairs wide enough to fit twenty men abreast rising to a dais where a pillar of light held a long black bone. The thigh bone of a greater daemon.

Even from a distance, it was huge, easily Kaiel's own height and as thick as both of his upper arms. Once an applicant imprinted the bone, it would be taken to the Redoubt where the smiths of the Kas'tirien would craft it into a blade that no daemon could stand against.

Lowering his gaze, Kaiel saw Rolen slumped across the floor at the edge of a circular pit. Unlike the hole that had held the dycinion, this had been deliberately carved out of the bedrock. Like the rest of the chamber, the edges of the pit were smooth, and the containment lines ran directly to it.

Kaiel jogged over to Rolen.

"Rolen." Kaiel knelt beside the man, touching his shoulder. A groan was his only answer. Rolen's skin was white, the veins on his neck raised and black around the puncture marks of a spider bite. Using his sword, Kaiel cracked the top of the shell with the edge of his blade.

"You need to drink this," Kaiel said. Rolen's eyes flickered open. He groaned again. "It's an egg from the arac'diem. You need to drink." Shifting position, Kaiel put an arm under his adversary and helped him up, bringing the egg to his lips.

The rotten scent of sulphur and bad meat rose from it, making Kaiel gag, but it had to be done. One of Rolen's hands rose to grab Kaiel's wrist as he tipped the egg to his mouth.

Rolen gagged, struggling to swallow the vile fluid, and Kaiel had to clench his jaw from doing the same. At last, with spillage dripping over his chin, Rolen flung the egg away and rolled onto his hands and knees, retching, and coughing as the antidote began its work.

Kaiel stood. Now Rolen would live and Kaiel would be able to look Sevaani in the eye.

Leaving the Steward's son, Kaiel made his way to the edge of the containment cell and froze.

The prison held a single daemon – a Malkedim. Man-like in shape, it was taller even than Kaiel. Its substance was formed of violet flames, licked with tongues of gold, encased within an enormous black bone ribcage. Long, skeletal arms hung from barbed shoulders, and a horned skull floated above them, with topaz flames for eyes.

Kaiel stumbled back as the greater daemon saw him and roared.

How was he meant to get across to the dais on the other side? There was a narrow beam of stone stretched like a walkway right over the pit, but walking it would require balance and concentration, and he was confident that the daemon wouldn't just sit there passively watching him go by. The drop into the containment cell was at least fifteen feet, and while the ward runes would stop the Malkedim from escaping, it would certainly be able to reach the legs of anyone foolish enough to try and cross above it.

He made his way to the left side of the room to a ledge along the edge of the pit. It was barely wider than the walkway. Back pressed tight against the wall, Kaiel kept his face towards the pit and the roaring daemon, its flaming body casting moving shadows across the walls of the cavern. Kaiel began to edge his way across and the Malkedim moved towards him. Sweat beaded Kaiel's forehead, and he wiped it away before it dripped into his eyes. He glanced at the horned skull, meeting its topaz eyes. An overwhelming sensation of malice rippled through Kaiel, and he shuddered, tearing his gaze away.

He shuffled along, desperate to get to the other side when the ledge suddenly shifted beneath him. He gasped, stomach-lurching as part of the shelf gave way, stone clattering to the pit below. Kaiel levered his weight back when the daemon roared again and lashed out at the breach in the wards with its clawed hands.

The heat of its flames and the sharp, black-boned claws just missed him. Kaiel cursed as the daemon swiped at him again and again, its roaring grating on his nerves, a rolling wall of sound that squeezed his head. With a deep breath, he pushed all his fear into the quiet centre of his mind. Only part of the stone ledge was gone. If he was careful, he could get across it.

Without warning, the Malkedim spun away. Kaiel looked up to see Rolen at the start of the walkway. Covered with daemon gore and sweat – Kaiel was sure he looked little better himself – Rolen moved unsteadily onto the thin beam of stone.

"Rolen, don't risk it!"

Rolen shook his head. "You're not going to win, warren-rat. The daemon bone is mine!"

Kaiel shook his head. Idiot! Rolen was going to get himself killed.

On unsteady feet, Kaiel eased himself across the broken ledge. Without the daemon swiping at him, it was a much easier proposition. He looked across the cell; the Malkedim was right at Rolen now. Its roar still a droning buzz that made thinking almost impossible. The daemon swung its long arms up at Rolen, claws thudding into the beam. Rolen swayed as the walkway shuddered, but managed to keep his balance.

Kaiel gritted his teeth and continued along the ledge, pushing himself faster now the daemon was distracted, and finally reached the deep stairs that led up to the dais. He couldn't stop the grin that spread across his face. He'd won.

Then he looked over his shoulder, his stomach dropped. Rolen was hanging onto the beam, legs dangling within range of the Malkedim. Surely the Hunters wouldn't allow an applicant to die? Would they?

Only one of you will imprint the daemon bone. Jidara's words echoed in Kaiel's mind, and the white bones in the Dycinions pit flashed before his eyes.

Rolen looked up. "Kaiel. Help me!"

Then the daemon grabbed one of Rolen's legs, and the man screamed as he was dragged off the beam and into the containment cell.

Kaiel didn't hesitate. He couldn't let Rolen die. He wouldn't be able to face himself, let alone Sevaani if he earnt his place as a Hunter with the life of another. Kaiel ran out across the beam, his concern about balance evaporating. He'd never faced anything like a Malkedim before, but surely he and Rolen could handle it together. Holding his sword up, he jumped off the beam letting out a cry as he landed half on the daemon and drove his sword into its back. His momentum pushed it away from Rolen, the heat of its flaming form scorching him around his leather jerkin. Kaiel hacked down before pulling his sword back, driving the daemon further back into the pit.

Light glinted on steel to his left, and Kaiel kicked Rolen's sword back towards him.

"Take your sword," Kaiel yelled over his shoulder. "If we both attack it together, we'll stand a chance."

Kaiel turned his attention back to the Malkedim. The daemon had straightened and turned to face him. It roared, lashing out with a vicious swipe. Kaiel blocked with his sword and was shocked at the jarring impact.

"Rolen, get beside me," Kaiel called, but the daemon was on him again, herding him back as it brought its other arm around. Heat washed across Kaiel as he leant back, narrowly avoiding the talons on the end of the Malkedim's black, bone-like fingers.

"I could do with some help here!" The daemon roared again and swung forward, pushing towards him. Kaiel jumped out of the way of the slashing talons, the Malkedim's size giving it greater reach. He rolled to the side, the daemon following him. Where was Rolen?

Kaiel shot back to his feet, searching for the man. Mouth dry, he stared at the sword that still lay upon the ground. Dancing backwards to avoid a blow from the daemon, Kaiel twisted his neck trying to find Rolen and almost dropped his sword as the Malkidem's clawed hand connected with it. Pushing forward, Kaiel ducked under the arm and sliced his blade across the daemons flame-encased ribs. He didn't know if that would wound the daemonspawn, but it got him behind the Malkidem as it awkwardly tried to turn to follow him.

Behind the daemon, Kaiel finally saw Rolen atop the containment cells walls. "Rolen!" Kaiel screamed.

Rolen glanced back, guilt flashing across his face. Then the look was gone, replaced by a sneer.

With no opportunity to consider Rolen's betrayal, Kaiel turned back to the daemon in time to raise his sword. But his move was clumsy, panicked. There was a searing pain as a talon dug into the back of his hand, and he found himself flying backwards. Stars dazzled his vision as his head hit the ground. The world spun, and a blazing light flared deep behind his eyes. Ringing harmonics scoured him like lightning and everything fell silent.

Sound rushed back in and his panic swept away in a flood of adrenaline. He rolled over, pushing himself to his feet. The back of his hand throbbed; the scent of scorched hair and leather filled his nose. He ignored it, and lifted his arm to block the next blow only to realise he was no longer holding his sword.

The daemon roared. Kaiel stared, heart racing as the Malkedim brought both its arms up.

He gasped for breath, the heat of the Malkedim's flames sucking the air from his lungs. He blinked sweat from his eyes and readied himself to move when he heard Rolen's cry of triumph.

Kaiel glanced up to see Sevaani's brother holding the daemon bone in bloodied hands.

A single touch of blood imprinted a daemon bone.

Then Jidara was beside Rolen, an amulet of some sort in her hand and runes began to glow across the floor of the containment cell. The Malkedim screamed in rage, lashing out at Kaiel as an invisible force pulled it into a giant circular ward glowing in the centre of the cell.

This couldn't be happening. He'd been in the lead. He'd only had to climb the stairs to grab the bone!

What had he done?

"I win, warren-rat," Rolen crowed from the dais as Kaiel climbed the small ladder carved into the side of the containment cell. Rolen turned to the Journeyman as Kaiel approached. "He should never have been accepted to try for a place amongst the Kas'tirien. He isn't worthy."

Rage flooded Kaiel.

"He's more worthy than some," Jidara said.

"He's a cheat!" Kaiel spat, hands clenching into fists at his side. "I only faced the Malkedim to help him, and he left me there!"

"Whoever imprints the daemon bone," Rolen said, his knuckles whitening against his prize. He took a step back as though he feared it would be taken from him. "That's what you said."

Jidara eyed Rolen with distaste. "Aye, that is the requirement. It was a test Kaiel," she said regretfully. "Whoever imprints the bone. Though there is much to be said for the moral compass of our applicants, it's not what's measured here."

Kaiel let out a breath and looked away. He could have won. *Should* have won. He would have claimed the bone if he hadn't stopped to help.

He'd spent the last days of his ma's life training for this, only to throw it all away!

Rolen would join the Daemon Hunters and Kaiel would be nothing.

CHAPTER TWO

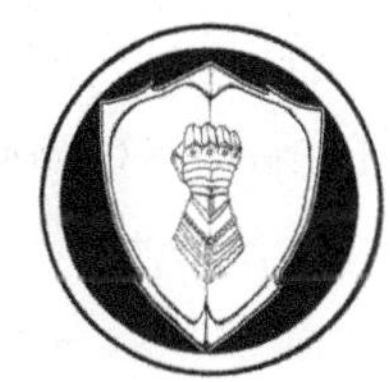

A Cold Wind

KAIEL LIFTED HIS head as the wind gusted through the forest. The surrounding pines and evergreens swayed back and forth, shifting the afternoon light across the Sonyth Road.

He bit off a curse, pulling at the brown woollen cloak that whipped over his shoulder like a flag. The wind was coming from the east. A Deadlands wind. He looked eastward, though Dal'mere – an old Summoner word for the Deadlands – was a good thirty miles away. These winds often brought with them a heightened state of readiness for the Daemon Hunters, yet living on the Borderlands did that anyway.

The forest was beautiful, but it also sheltered the strange, twisted creatures that ventured out of the Deadlands. It was against these that the Borderland Rangers had honed the skills for which they were so famed. And it was the daemons of Dal'mere that continued to give the Hunters a reason for existence. But that was no longer his concern.

Kaiel stood in the saddle, tucked the cloak under him and sat back as Lasa, the shaggy brown mare the Hanore Rangers had lent him, continued on her way home. If he'd managed to win his place amongst the Kas'tirien, he'd have received a horse of his own when he completed his time as a Journeyman. A Sarent stallion said to be bred from the famed Dominarians before they died out after the Sundering.

He sighed, giving the mare's neck a pat. Well, Lasa was good enough for him, and he'd be good for nothing other than joining the Rangers now.

He'd begun the trek home as soon as he'd left the Caves. There'd been no point in staying while Rolen revelled in his victory. It had only taken him an hour to get from the Darscene Caves to the Arch Road that ran south-east between Hanore and Sonyth, two of the three citadels built during the War of the Summoners. Tore – the third citadel – lay north of Hanore. He needed to pay attention to his surrounds, the Rangers always patrolled in groups of two, and no-one left the citadels at night.

Kaiel wasn't overly concerned about the dangers of the Borderland Wilds, but still, the blood drained from his face when he spied a flailing figure on the road ahead. He pulled on Lasa's reins, and the horse snorted in protest but halted as Kaiel fumbled for his sword. It was only as his hand wrapped around the hilt that he realised he was looking at a man fighting with his cloak in the wind.

Somewhat cautiously, Kaiel prodded Lasa back into motion but couldn't contain his grin when he recognised the brown hair and slim build of the young man. The sound of Lasa's hooves was covered by the noise of the wind in the trees, and Kaiel stopped a good sixteen feet behind the man. Cupping his hands around his mouth, he mimicked the screeching cry of a skreet.

The young man on the back of the grey mare gave a start, and half leapt out of his saddle while his horse paid Kaiel's shout no attention at all. Kaiel laughed as Simeon's deep green cloak, loose once again, lifted itself over his friend's head.

Kaiel nudged Lasa up beside her stablemate, Del, and leaned across to pull his friend free. Shorter than Kaiel by about three inches, Sim scowled at him as he pulled his cloak back under his arm.

"Ha-bloody-ha," Sim said, his brown hair whipping across hazel eyes, the left of which sported a dark bruise. "Here I am, the only one to come out to wait for you to finish your test, and this is how you treat me?"

Kaiel's grin died. He looked away.

Sim knocked his fist against Kaiel's shoulder. "You're having me on. There's no way Rolen could have beat – Eye blind me! Really?"

Kaiel scowled. "Yes. I won't be joining the Daemon Hunters."

"But… well, shit. How did that happen? How could you let that skreet-spawned knob beat you?"

"He cheated," Kaiel snapped, his anger flaring again.

Sim frowned. "Wouldn't that… I don't know, disqualify him?"

"No." Kaiel bit out the word. "He imprinted the – He got there first. That's all that matters."

"Damn it." Sim sighed. "Well, at least I didn't have money on you."

"What?"

"I said I *didn't* have money on you. No-one from the citadel would bet on the outcome. And after last night," Sim reached up and gingerly touched the bruise around his eye, "I wouldn't ask any of the Bronze Guard."

"Win too many marks from them?" Kaiel was eager to change the topic.

"There's no such thing as 'too many marks'," Sim said. "They're just sore losers."

"Cards or dice?"

"Cards." Sim eyed him. "And no, I didn't cheat."

Kaiel smiled. No, Sim never cheated, but he was very good with calculating the odds, something he claimed came from helping his father run Hanore's general store. He looked around the forest. Apart from the wind, it was quiet, but that didn't always mean much.

"I'm surprised you were waiting out here for me alone." At Sim's glance, he added, "I'm grateful, but it's not like you to venture out into the Wilds unless you're taking your turn on patrol with the Rangers."

Sim pulled a face. "Captain Daynar thought it would be safe enough as long as I didn't venture farther afield."

Kaiel nodded. The captain of the Hanore Rangers would never have let Sim out on his own if he believed there was a chance of him coming across a fist of Korda'vari this close to the citadel.

"That was before this cursed wind came up," Sim continued. "I'm sorry you lost to that daemon knob, Rolen, but at the same time, I'm happy you turned up. I'd hate to have had to make my way back to the citadel alone. Or with him." Sim sighed. "Void take me, Kaiel, the Daemon Hunters are the best fighters and trackers the Borderlands produce. Men and women have come from every realm to join them, and now Rolen Etine is going to be one? He's had it in for you ever since you and his sister started getting closer."

Kaiel kept his eyes straight ahead. "He's just protective of Sevaani, that's all."

Sim snorted. "No. Rolen's a filthy little skreet *and* a cheat. Are you really going to let him get away with becoming a Kas'tirien?"

Kaiel ground his teeth. "It wasn't cheating. Not exactly. There was a daemon, a big one. I went to help him."

"Say what?"

"Don't look at me like that! He could have died. I had to help him."

"So, what happened?" Sim's eyes narrowed.

"He…" Kaiel shook his head. "He left me when I had the daemon's attention."

"That piece of shit!"

"You'll get no argument from me on that."

Sim looked around. "Where is he?"

"Jidara's not done with him yet."

"Jidara Nesai took you through the test?" Sim was suddenly beside him, Del snorting as he dug his heels into her flank.

"Go gently, Sim," Kaiel admonished.

"How did she look? What was she wearing?"

Kaiel shook his head."She was wearing a leather jerkin and trousers, just like me, and she looked like she always does."

"She's a beauty," Sim said with a grin as they followed the road around a bend in the trees."I wonder if all the women of Hetar look like her? I wouldn't mind –"

"Stop!"

"What? I –"

Kaiel grabbed Del's reins, but the mare was cannier than her rider and was already stopping.

On the road before them, a foul black trail ran left to right.

"Borewyrm?"Sim breathed. Smoke rose from the dark stain, but the wind whipped its foul stench away.

The cacophony of rustling leaves reduced any chance they might have had of hearing the creature and Kaiel's shoulders tingled as he scanned the surrounding forest. None of the trees had been knocked over, and to their left a giant moonleaf was untouched. Native to the Borderlands, the silvery moonleafs spread amongst the forest like ghostly sentinels, beacons to the creatures of the Deadlands. Ambere resin, the addictive sap of the moonleafs, drew the creatures like a flame enticed a moth, but this tree was untouched.

"What in the Void is a borewyrm doing this far out of the Deadlands?" Sim demanded, jumping off his horse.

"Quiet," Kaiel hissed. Blind to all but the Light of the Eye, a borewyrm hunted by sound. Impossibly fast, and tainted with the corruption of the Deadlands, there was no chance two junior Rangers could survive an encounter with one. Even if one of them had been an apprentice Daemon Hunter.

Thankfully, Sim closed his mouth as he examined the stain.

A noise came from behind, and Kaiel twisted in his saddle. Most of the ground around this end of the Borderlands was flat, but outcroppings of rock peppered the landscape, thistle and brambles claiming the open sunlit ground between. Great clumps of shade deepened the forest gloom around those trees whose leaves still sat thickest, and perhaps sixty feet down the road they had just travelled was a tree whose shadow looked somehow... wrong. The hairs prickled on the back of Kaiel's neck. The shadow was deeper than the others in the forest, and though the leaves of the tree it was under swayed in the wind, the shadow didn't.

The cut on the back of Kaiel's hand from the daemon's talon began to throb. The shadow sat like a physical presence, sucking the brightness out of the air. A tendril of shadow, black and smoke-like, reached towards him, moving against the wind. In his mind, he heard a whisper but could make no sense of it. Vertigo rushed over him, his stomach muscles clenching. If he was any closer, he was sure he could fall into that shadow. It was like a window to another world, and he could hear... no, he could *feel* cries of pain, of sorrow; of a loss so great Kaiel wondered how he could still be whole and breathing in its presence.

"I can't believe how close this came to me," Sim said. "If it had crossed the road down the bend, I'd be dead." Oblivious, Sim studied the black stain across the road. "I should be back at the store earning marks and organising the last caravan to Jaroff before winter. Not traipsing around the woods and getting attacked by borewyrms!"

"Have you lost something?" The question came from the road ahead.

Kaiel jerked in his saddle. Tearing his eyes from the strange shadow, he could move again. He gasped for breath as he fumbled for his sword.

Before them stood a man dressed in the forest-green leathers of a scout. His eyes were dark, almost the same black as his hair and beard and Kaiel recognised him as one of the Bronze Guard, the mercenary company hired by Prince Alesandr Niskeri, the current Carbinah of Jaroff.

The scout laughed at their startlement.

"Sergeant Quaylin." Sim scowled.

"Did you see that…" Kaiel began, twisting back in his saddle to look at the tree once more. The darkness was gone.

"See?"

"There was a..." Kaiel swallowed, shivering as the wind gusted over them, the sunlight patterning the bark of the tree trunk the darkness had obscured. "A shadow…"

Sim straightened. "Daemon?"

"I don't know. I…" Kaiel stopped. What was wrong with him?

"A daemon?" Quaylin frowned. "There are no Summoners to pull the Daemon Queen's minions from the Void."

"Yes," Simeon drawled. "Because that's what the tradition of the Kas'tirien is all about. Hunting daemons that aren't here. You're in the Borderlands, Sergeant, the things you think are myths are real here."

"It was nothing." Kaiel shot Sim a look. "Pay me no mind."

Quaylin grunted and nodded towards Sim. "A dagger would have been little use had I been a daemoncat stalking you."

"They're called dycinions." Sim resheathed his dagger. "And a dycinion wouldn't have bothered speaking."

Quaylin smiled, then brought his right hand up to his chest in a fist. "If you'd been paying attention, as your duty requires, I'd have had a harder time approaching you unawares." He opened the flap on his glove to expose the clear skin on the back of his hand. "Borderlanders are meant to be better Rangers than this."

Kaiel copied Quaylin, and grimaced as the guardsman stared at his hand.

"It's just a scratch," Kaiel said. He looked down at the cut from the Malkidem, the wound was sore but the throbbing of a moment ago was gone, and it was a perfectly curved cut, like the crescent of a waxing moon.

"You know who we are," Simeon scoffed. "The Mark doesn't appear that quickly! Besides, you just said there are no Summoners and, more importantly –" Sim gestured at the black stripe on the road. "A borewyrm has been through here."

Quaylin looked away from Kaiel's hand towards Sim, his eyes narrowing. "Borewyrms will wait until you show me your hand, Borderlander."

Sim huffed. "Fine!" He opened the flap of his glove and waved the back of his unmarked hand at the scout. "Satisfied?"

"Yes." Quaylin nodded. "And it is the vigilance we keep in looking for the Mark of the Eye that has prevented more Summoners from plaguing us. Now..." He buttoned the flap on his own glove. "A borewyrm, you say? This far out of the Deadlands? Are you telling the same Evay tales that got you that black eye?"

"I was playing cards, not telling tales. But please," Sim gestured. "Walk across the track."

"Don't!" Kaiel glared at Sim.

Quaylin studied them both and made his way forward. Stopping before the mark, he grabbed a stick from the side of the road and touched it to the dark trail; the end began to smoke. Quaylin jerked it back.

"Is there another way across?" he asked at last, eyeing the dark stain that was at least five feet in width.

"It will be safe enough in a minute," Sim said with a snort. "The trees along its path will probably die, but the ground will recover." He climbed back onto his horse. "You've lost your armour somewhere, *sir.*"

Kaiel, still unsettled, took a moment to understand Sim's words.

The guardsman laughed. "True enough, Ravenson. But then the noise of mail and plate makes for a poor scout."

"Why are you scouting?" Kaiel asked.

Quaylin shifted his weight, watching the borewyrm trail. "His Highness has decided he should visit Sonyth one last time before returning to Jaroff next moon." He marked the sun through the towering trees. "Though I wish I could have left tomorrow morning rather than so late in the day."

"You're heading out for Sonyth *now*?" Sim stared. "You'll never make it there before nightfall!"

Quaylin frowned. "Will the citadelfolk open the gates for us?"

"I'm sure they'd open the gates for the Carbinah's guards," Kaiel said hesitantly.

Sim snorted. "No, they won't, Kaiel, you know that. Besides, what are the chances they'll actually make it there in one piece?"

Quaylin laughed. "The Bronze Guards are more than capable of handling a borewyrm, or your daemoncats. And I've yet to see a daemon this close to the Three Citadels. I'm more concerned about those clouds." He motioned to the east. "You can just make them out through the trees, but they are coming up fast."

"This wind bodes ill. Any of the Hunters would tell you so," Sim said.

"I've paid no mind to tales of daemons since well before I picked up a sword." Quaylin grinned, taking the sting out of his words.

Sim scoffed. "Unlike you Realmsmen, we live right next to the Deadlands. We know what we're talking about. Anyway, isn't that why the mercenary companies come to visit us every year? To train with the Rangers and face the dangers of the Borderlands."

"We come to fight the Korda'vari, not daemons. These Wilds may have been deadly after the Sundering, but it's been three thousand years since the Summoners created their Korda'vari foot soldiers," Quaylin said.

Quaylin was right in that the Summoners were gone, but the monsters they'd summoned still plagued the Deadlands and wandered into the Borderlands regularly.

"Well, that's the Borderlands for you." Sim's smile was all teeth. "Full of superstition and Evay tales." He looked at Kaiel and gestured at the road. "Come on. The taint's sunk far enough down. We should be getting back, *before* dark."

"I don't discount Evay tales, Raven. The forestfolk hide much truth in their fables, but some things are just stories," Quaylin said. "But before you go, how did you find the road behind you?"

"We haven't been on the roads," Kaiel said. "I've just returned from my Trial. Sim was waiting for me at the crossroad to the Caves."

"Ah, yes. The Trial of the Kas'tirien." Quaylin nodded. "How did you fare?"

Kaiel felt his cheeks redden. "I failed, sir."

"I'm sorry to hear that," Quaylin said. "You'd have made a fine addition to the Daemon Hunters' ranks. What will you do with that training now?"

Kaiel shrugged. "I don't know. Maybe I can join the Rangers."

"The Rangers will definitely take you on, Kaiel," Sim agreed.

"Or maybe you'd prefer a change?" Quaylin said.

"A change?" Kaiel frowned. "What do you mean?"

"Just that staying in the Borderlands might offer too much of a reminder of what you could have been. The Hunters frequent the citadels, do they not?"

"They do," Kaiel agreed.

Quaylin nodded. "So, maybe some space would be good. There are always the mercenary companies. The reputable ones require sponsorship to enter, it's true, but if you had a mind to try your hand with the Bronze Guard, I would be willing to vouch for you to the Commander."

"Really?" Kaiel blinked, the idea stirring something inside him.

"Yes," Quaylin said. "You should think about it. We will be passing back through Hanore before we return to Jaroff."

"You'd leave Hanore?" Sim turned to him, a strange expression on his face.

Kaiel shrugged. "Maybe. I don't know. I'd have to work out what Darien is going to do. Maybe he can come to Jaroff and find a place as a scribe?"

"A scribe?" Sim laughed. "Your brother is making plans to leave with the prince's Ciralys. He plans on being more than a mere scribe."

"What?" Kaiel knew Darien had been assisting Prince Alesandr's advisor, Ciralys Telaq, but Kaiel never imagined Darien would want to leave home. And to join the Ciralys? Half the problems – the daemons – the Hunters risked their lives to deal with came from misuse of the Light of the Eye.

Sim rolled his eyes. "I know you've been busy training to pass the Trial for the last five years, but you do realise Darien was apprenticed to Old Shany before he jumped ship and attached himself to the Ciralys, right?"

"I thought he was just helping him."

"From what I've heard," Quaylin offered, "your brother is very talented. I'm not privy to the affairs of His Highness' household but what the young merchant says is true."

Kaiel had to force himself to close his mouth. If he could think about leaving Hanore, why couldn't his little brother? Darien was seventeen after all, Kaiel had to stop treating him like a child.

"Well then, I should be on my way." Looking down at the road that was now clear of the black stain, Quaylin stepped across the distance to them. "Think about what I said," he nodded to Kaiel. "The Bronze Guard would do you well."

"Thank you, sir. I will."

Quaylin offered them a slight bow. "Now get home before the sun sets. It wouldn't do to be out after dark on a night of cold winds. The Eye of Eternity guide you."

"The Eye guide you," Kaiel replied and watched the Sergeant move on. After a moment he turned to Sim. "Let's get moving. Captain Daynar will likely be waiting for you, for us so they can shut the gates, and we need to report the borewyrm."

"What about Rolen?" Sim asked. "Do we care?"

A knot of anger flared in Kaiel again, but he squashed it. "He can look after himself."

"Good," Sim said. "What do you say we give these horses some exercise?" Without warning, Sim urged his horse into a gallop. Kaiel did the same a split second later.

The lengthening shadows turned branches and rocks on the road into dark, indistinct hazards. But the horses had walked these roads with the Hanore Rangers many times before, and memory led them without mishap.

As they rounded the last curve on the road home, racing through a treelined corridor of shadows, Lasa flicked her head with a snort, ears twitching. Kaiel motioned to Sim, and they slowed, moving to the side of the road just as two guardsmen came into view.

Clad in light armour, the guards balanced on their black mounts with the ease of long practice, steel hauberks glinting behind the leather straps of their cuirasses.

Seeing the mailed fist emblem of the Bronze Guard emblazoned on their tabards, Kaiel nudged his horse back onto the path and raised a hand in greeting.

The lead guardsman cursed as Kaiel's appearance caused his horse to stamp its hoof and snort. "Who goes there?" the man barked.

Kaiel was careful not to make any threatening gestures. Regardless of Scout Quaylin's manner, not all guardsmen were as relaxed in the Borderlands. "I'm Kaiel Toranth, sir. From Hanore."

"And your friend?" The second guardsman pointed at Sim, who had yet to move from the shadows of the trees.

"Simeon Ravenson, sir," Kaiel said, motioning a scowling Sim out of hiding. Thankfully, Sim didn't make a scene and followed suit when Kaiel raised his right fist and opened his glove to show the back of his hand to the guardsmen.

The narrow-eyed guard grunted as he and his companion presented their own hands in turn, if somewhat more slowly. A lull in the wind allowed the steady clomp of horses' hooves and the jingle of mail to announce the approach of the rest of the Bronze Guard.

"Conar!" called a commanding voice from somewhere within the squad. "What's going on?"

"Two boys from Hanore, sir!" the first guard called back.

"Then why are we stopping?"

Kaiel recognised the voice as belonging to Under-Lieutenant Hearn, even before the guardsmen moved aside to let the man through.

The Under-Lieutenant of the Bronze Guards was a big man. Taller than most even when standing, he towered over his soldiers while astride his warhorse. Bronze ribbing trimmed the lames that formed his cuirass, stretched across the imposing width of his chest. The thick, black leather-bound handle of his war axe rose above his massive shoulders, and he stared at the boys from within an open helm of bronze lacquered steel.

"They'd hidden in the trees," Conar growled, glaring at Kaiel and Sim. "We stopped to determine they were no threat, sir."

Hearn regarded them both without expression. "And you didn't notice them until you were almost upon them? They've shown you their hands?"

"Yes, sir," Conar said with only the slightest hesitation.

"Kaiel Toranth, is it not?" Hearn asked. "And Simeon Ravenson. If memory serves me Conar, they are both nineteen?" The Under-Lieutenant looked at Kaiel expectantly.

"Yes, sir," Kaiel said.

Hearn nodded."Men by anyone's reckoning, Conar, not boys.Young, maybe, but men just the same."

"Then they should know better," the guardsman said stiffly."What kind of Rangers go hiding in the scrub when real guardsmen come along?"

Under-Lieutenant Hearn stared at Conar until the silence had Kaiel shifting in his saddle."You have been with us in the Borderlands for the last two years, is that correct?" he asked Conar at last.

"Yes, sir," Conar said, eyes forward and jaw clenched.

"Then you have been here long enough to realise the Borderlands are not the quiet, broadly tamed lands of the Realms. Borderlanders are cautious because they know what is required out here to survive. The Borderland Rangers are not a mercenary company, and you are foolish to judge them as such." Conar didn't respond, and Hearn turned to Kaiel."How did you hide from my men?"

Kaiel squared his shoulders."There was no real cover to hide behind if you had been Korda'vari, or any denizen of the Deadlands, sir, so we just stepped into the shadows," he gestured behind him,"until we could see who was approaching."

"And when did my men notice you, Master Toranth?" Hearn asked. "Had you stepped forward to hail them? Or had they already seen you?"

Kaiel risked a glance at the two guardsmen in question."Well, sir, I had just stepped forward when the horses whinnied."

"Your horses gave you away?"

"Not *our* horses, sir, theirs," Simeon offered.

Hearn frowned. "Tell me, Kaiel, did you happen to see my scout, Feldar Quaylin on your way back home?"

"Yes, sir, we did."

"And did you come upon him unawares also?"

Kaiel glanced at the two guardsmen again."No, sir."

"So, Quaylin was able to note your approach and conceal himself from you." It wasn't a question. "If he had not revealed himself, would you have known he was there?"

"No, sir, not right away," Kaiel said.

"That more than justifies my decision to send Quaylin out as scout instead of you, Conar," Hearn told the stone-faced guardsman. To the other, he said, "And I expected better of you, DeMarcon, to show such a lack of concern for your surroundings in the Borderlands!"

"But the Borderlands have been safe for centuries sir –" Conar began.

"Then why are the Borderlanders trained in such stealth that even their young can hide from the Bronze Guards?"

The men behind the under-lieutenant shifted aside as the speaker pressed himself forward on the back of a white stallion. The man wore a dark blue cloak of finely woven cotton over bronzed mail.

"*Priest*," Sim hissed between his teeth.

Slight of build, the priest was almost insignificant as he came alongside the under-lieutenant. Black, shoulder-length hair framed a gaunt face of sharp lines.

"Why do they continue to stand ready if the Borderlands are safe, Conar?" the priest asked the first guardsman.

"Not now," Hearn growled.

The priest glanced at the under-lieutenant and then to Kaiel. "Your hand, Borderlander."

"They have shown their hands already, though we have lived amongst them for a year!"

"We must stand ever-vigilant," the priest said. "Borderlanders are seasoned Rangers who could match the best of the Guard, as well as *Daemon Hunters*. Where does their strength come from? They line the edge of Aldania with no eyes to watch them, and still the Carbinah does not –"

"I said, *not now*!" Hearn's tone made Kaiel want to edge his horse back, but the priest just cocked his head, his glance grazing over Kaiel and Simeon before he offered a slight smile.

"You are right, of course, Under-Lieutenant," he said calmly, but his eyes burned with anger. "Let us resume our trek; it will be well into night by the time we reach Sonyth as it is."

Hearn addressed a guardsman behind him. "Take the lead and see if you can't catch up to Feldar. Conar and DeMarcon, the baggage cart needs watching. The rest of you," he bellowed at the guards, "double-file! Stay alert! I don't want any more surprises from Hanore's Rangers, or Sonyth's!"

"I'm sorry if we've caused any trouble, sir," Kaiel offered. "It was our fault; Quaylin said His Highness was leaving for Sonyth. We should have known it could only have been guardsmen on the path."

Hearn grunted. "You did as your Rangers have trained you to do. As they have trained all men of the Borderlands to do to stay alive. Some men like to act with more surety than they own, and they usually end up more excitable than the rest of us. Get on your way," he told them, not unkindly, and directed his horse past them with a flick of the reins. "Captain Daynar will not be impressed if you miss the closing of the gates."

"Yes, sir," Kaiel said. Simeon rolled his eyes and pushed through the remaining guardsmen.

"Are you coming, Kaiel?" he called.

Kaiel raised his head as the wind gave a renewed gust through the trees. The creeping shadows of the surrounding forest closed in above them, and he shivered from more than the wind. Turning away from the trailing guardsmen, Kaiel nudged Lasa forward with his heel and continued on his way back home.

CHAPTER THREE

With Eyes to See and Ears to Hear

DARIEN TORANTH JUMPED at the sharp rap on the door and cursed. A drop of ink fell from his pen to the parchment and was absorbed swiftly by the rich paper.

"Come!"

He sighed, rubbed at his aching temples then reached for a canister and deftly cast a sprinkling of white sand over the ink stain. Darien didn't have time to re-do the entire document. He was late to finish as it was. If Master Telaq wanted him to re-do them, he'd just have to invite him back to Jaroff. He almost smiled. That would be one way to continue as Ciralys Telaq's apprentice, given he hadn't officially been asked yet–

An impatient cough interrupted his musings.

He looked up. "Yes?"

"Ciralys Telaq sent me to fetch the document you were working on, *sir*." The young man in a page's livery sneered the last.

Darien pulled back at the sight of Peitrov Chobel. One of the many young nobles serving the prince during his time as Carbinah of Jaroff, Peitrov disdained all Borderlanders as beneath him and made a point of reminding Darien of it any time they met.

"That I am *still* working on," Darien corrected, gathering himself and looking away. "I'll only be a moment. Make yourself useful and light some candles please."

Familiar with the narrow-minded attitudes of both the children and adults of the citadel that was his home, Darien often hid behind a shield of cool indifference. Since taking his position as apprentice to the prince's Ciralys advisor, he had learnt that a shield could also be used as a weapon.

The room was dark, and Peitrov cursed as he collided with a footstool, but light bloomed under his sure handling of flint and candlewick, while Darien completed the last of the messages he had been set to work on.

"Ciralys Telaq also told me to inform you that the hedge witch's girl has been around." Peitrov was back at the table, a smug gleam in his eyes as Darien looked up. He glanced over Darien's work. "You are done?"

Darien ground down the flare of panic, a reflex that had yet to die. "When did Ciralys Telaq send you with this message?"

Keeper Shany, called *hedge witch* by the prince's household, had been the only barrier between his mother and death's call. His ma had passed beyond Samantra's Veil a fortnight ago, but he still felt the panic that Shany was calling him to come to his ma's bedside.

Peitrov made a show of adjusting his fine tunic over shoulders already showing a bulk that was missing in Darien. "Earlier," he said. "I had duties that needed to be finished. *Are you done*? His Highness wants to sign those papers before he leaves this ruin."

Darien rolled up the parchment and held the scroll out, meeting the page's gaze. He had just as much right to be here as any of the city-dwelling clansmen. In fact, he had more.

The page grasped the proffered document from his hand with a sneer and made to leave the room.

"You might wish to take *all* of His Highness' correspondence," Darien said softly. "Lest you have to make a second trip."

With a snarl, Peitrov strode back to the desk. He scooped up the pile of letters and, looking Darien in the eye, deliberately knocked over the inkwell. Darien made to grab it, but it was too late. Expensive black ink spread across the table, a growing pool that mirrored the rage that flooded him. His hands clenched into fists so tight his knuckles turned white.

Peitrov laughed. "Better clean up the mess, *peasant*," he drawled. "It is all your kind are good for. Why Ciralys Telaq is playing this ridiculous game with you is a mystery, but in case you are unsure –" He leant forward and spat in Darien's face. "You are not wanted here. And if you think you are coming back with us when His Highness leaves, well..." He offered Darien an ugly smile. "It is a long trip. Accidents happen."

Darien looked pointedly at the scrolls that had begun to smoulder. "Accidents like that?"

Peitrov cursed, dropping the scrolls, and jumping back from the candle he'd leant too close to. He stamped on the scrolls with a yell, their edges blackening as the bitter smell of burnt paper filled the room.

"You'll have a hard time explaining that," Darien said, his smile as sharp as broken glass.

"It is a crime to use the Light of the Eye to attack people!"

"Says who?" It was Darien's turn to sneer.

Peitrov gaped at him. "Everyone knows it!"

"The only laws that bind the Ciralys," Darien said patiently, as though explaining to a small child, "are that they will not seek to Summon; or turn a person from their own free will. That, and the Common Law of the realm they are in." He smiled again. "In any case, why use *Asai* when your clumsiness will do the job for me?"

"I will just tell His Highness that this is how I found them." Peitrov bent to scoop up the damaged scrolls.

Darien shrugged. "You can try, but you won't be believed. I've never had an accident like this before, and I've been Ciralys Telaq's scribe for the past two years. He knows I am more careful than that."

Peitrov's expression turned ugly. "Watch your back, creep."

"Get out," Darien said in a tone that could have frozen the central well in summer.

Peitrov took a step back uncertainly, then offered a weak sneer and rushed from the room.

Darien thumped a clenched fist on the table. "The Eye blind them. Blind them all!"

The animosity of Peitrov and the other pages was nothing new. Most people disliked and mistrusted the Ciralys and those who worked with them. Even the other children, and many of the adults of the citadel, eyed him suspiciously. At least when Kaiel and his mother weren't around to–

He bowed his head as grief welled within him and dropped into his chair. He closed his eyes for a moment, then got up and grabbed a cleaning rag to throw over the spilled ink.

A storm of emotion swept over him as he surveyed the room that had been a second home. This position in the prince's household had been the most significant in his life. His education now far outstripped that of anyone living in the citadel. He'd learnt the discipline of strict meditation that opened his mind to the energy centres of his own body. That, in turn, had allowed him to become more fully aware of *Asai*, the Light of the Eye of Eternity, which formed and energised the world around them.

Now the prince's term as Carbinah of Jaroff, and the Borderlands, was nearing its end. Whatever the prince and his master had been searching for in the catacombs beneath Hanore, they had not found. So, Prince Alesandr was going to try the catacombs of Sonyth one last time before returning to the capital, Dainyaia, in the west.

Darien slid the remaining unstained pages into a leather folder to be packed away with the rest of his master's belongings. He would be leaving Hanore as part of the prince's household in the next few days, he was sure of it. And despite what those narrow-minded idiots who served the prince thought, Ciralys Telaq had not taught him the runes to truly wield *Asai*. Not yet. All he'd managed to do with *Asai* was summon light and call forth fire. It was frustrating! He'd have learnt more if he'd remained a pupil of Old Shany.

Darien shook his head. He may have learnt how to twist the reflected Light of the Eye of Eternity if he'd remained a student of the Keeper, but he'd never have learnt anything of *Asai* or the High Asairic runes of the Summoners. No, he couldn't bear to return to the witching ways of the Keepers' Covenants. Not now.

There was nothing to keep him in Hanore anymore. His half-brother, older than him by a year, would object to his leaving, but Kaiel had always been overprotective. His uncle and aunt had the citadel's only inn to run and their own family to take care of. They didn't need the added burden of Kaiel *and* himself.

Darien would sooner follow his mother beyond the Veil than stay here and never learn more.

He went to the window overlooking the courtyard. The calls of stable hands echoed up the walls of the ancient keep, but Meg – Keeper Shany's only remaining apprentice since he'd found a place with Ciralys Telaq – was nowhere to be seen. He looked to the sky, but facing west as he was, he could not see the nebula of the Eye of Eternity rising in the night sky. The five entwined rings that formed the great eye in the heavens was said to be many things, but all Ciralys knew it to be the font of *Asai*. And once his mind's eye opened – as he'd been training for it to do – he'd be able to see the Light that bled from the Eye's centre, whether he could see it in the sky or not.

It had to happen soon!

A stillness in the air raised uneasiness in the back of Darien's mind, and he pulled his attention from his wandering thoughts. Something was strange. Different.

Someone was watching him.

He leant out of the window, his skin prickling. On the crenellations of the citadel wall, a bird-like shadow – a raven? – cocked its head, as though staring at him as he leant out. There was a strange haze around the shadowy silhouette, like the shimmer of heat from the citadel's stones at the height of summer.

The shadow was so deep, it seemed to Darien as though he was looking into the Void itself. As he stared, a tendril of shadow, of darkness, reached out towards him, and a chill wrapped itself around his spine.

"Ashhhael," a voice whispered in his mind.

The skin on the back of his neck prickled, and his heart pounded so fast his torso shuddered as the shadow reached for him.

"Ashael." The voice came again and harmonics chimed in his ears.

A flash of light filled his eyes, like the quicksilver sear of lightning, and a kaleidoscope of colour – of earth, of sky, of all the stars in the heavens spinning on a single point – burst across his mind's eye, underscored with sibilant whispers like wind through the leaves of the trees.

The shadow engulfed him. Its touch was the burn of deepest cold. Darien opened his mouth to scream, but all that came out was a strangled choke, and the shadow poured between his jaws, tearing the soft tissue of his throat as it swept within him.

He clawed at his head as energy – similar to opening himself to *Asai* – swept through him. Darien struggled to control his thoughts, his actions, fighting the panic that threatened to overwhelm him. And he tried desperately to steel himself as he'd been trained.

With a flexing of his Will, he *breathed* through the energy centres of his body, his defences snapping into place around his mind, and the pain vanished with the cawing of the bird.

Darien wrestled to regain his mental balance. Only then did the raven launch from its perch and fly towards him like an arrow shot from a bow. Darien raised his arms to shield his face, and a lance of pain drove through the back of his right hand as the bird's beak hammered into it like an iron rivet. He grabbed the windowpane as he fell back into the study, and his cry blended with the sound of breaking glass as he pulled the pane off its hinge.

A flurry of black feathers and scrambling claws filled the corners of his vision as he toppled to the ground.

With the raven came the wind.

It roared through the broken window, smashing a second pane against the wall. Howling, the burst of air slammed the door shut, and neatly piled papers and quills were sent flying. Darien cried out again as small pieces of glass were flung into the air, and a bitter cold seeped through his tunic as the wind swept around the room, extinguishing the candles.

Shadows fell around him. His hand burned as though he'd thrust it into a fire, but the throbbing where the shadow-bird's beak had stabbed him quickened like a spark of frost against the pain. The whirling rush of vertigo that had accompanied the vision glimpsed in the strange raven's eye returned with bright flashes of colour that danced against the darkness engulfing him.

With a shudder, he forced his laboured lungs into calm, steady breaths, just as the door behind him was flung open and the wind dispersed.

Light streamed into the room. Confusion washed through Darien's spinning head, and strong hands helped him to sit. The deep timbre of his master's voice rolled over an unintelligible word, and a globe of light sprang into being in the centre of the room. Striding to where Darien lay, Ciralys Telaq knelt and took Darien's face in lined hands. The Ciralys met his gaze with deep brown eyes, searching past the external with the precision of long practice, and lifted Darien's right hand to examine it.

"Is he all right?" The man who had helped him sit wore the surcoat of a Bronze Guard – *Madin*.

"Yes, he will be fine." Ciralys Telaq released Darien's hand but continued to study him intently.

Darien stared at his master. What had happened? He searched his mind, but nothing stirred, there were no voices, no chilling presence. When he swallowed, his throat felt fine, as though he hadn't swallowed shards of glass only moments before.

"My lord?" the guard asked, but Telaq didn't answer.

"If you could move him to the lounge. You may go." The Ciralys got to his feet.

"Yes, my lord," Madin said. "Shall I send a carpenter with some boards for the windows?"

Darien closed his eyes as Madin helped him to the couch against the wall. The click of a flint being struck and the flaring sizzle of flame filled the silence.

"Should I call the healer?" Madin asked.

"Darien will be fine," Ciralys Telaq said. "Thank you for your help, Sergeant, if you could see to the carpenter, you can go back to your duties."

The guardsman snapped to attention and saluted. "Ciralys."

Darien closed his eyes as the guardsman left the room. The dizziness was passing, but new sensations still raced along his awareness like firing nerves. He swung his legs off the couch and placed his feet on the floor, surveying the mess in the room.

Scattered pages, shards of glass and black feathers littered the floor amid a sea of frost and scattered vellum. Darien searched the room carefully; but for the feathers, no trace of the raven remained.

"This is unexpected," Ciralys Telaq said, picking up a feather from the desk. Frowning as a fresh gust of wind swept into the room, tangling itself in the edges of the red mantle he wore, the Ciralys gazed through the broken window into the falling night.

"Well then," he said at last, moving to sit on the couch. "You should tell me what happened."

Darien took a breath and related to his teacher the events since being disturbed by the page. He wasn't sure how to describe the… *shadow*, so he said it was a bird. It was just a bird, wasn't it? And the rest? He held back a shudder. Was that part of anything at all? Had it even been a vision? Had it been real? For a reason he couldn't explain, he held his tongue.

When he explained the flash of lightning-like light he'd seen, and the harmonics ringing in his ears, Ciralys Telaq cupped Darien's face in his hands once more. A tingling rush of cold spread through him.

"It seems I don't have the leisure of choosing my own course in this matter," Telaq said. "Your mind's eye has opened."

Excitement surged through him, but Darien held his emotions in check. Never one to cower, he was suddenly apprehensive. It wasn't have supposed to happen this way.

"I have left this late, partly as you have just lost your mother," Telaq continued. "I need to discuss with you the position of an Aspirant within the Ciralys Order."

This time Darien allowed his excitement full rein, and it pushed aside the pain in his hand, as well as the stab of grief at the mention of his ma. He couldn't contain his grin.

"I see you are not opposed to the notion." Telaq smiled in return.

Darien's excitement faded as his master's words sunk in. "Aspirant? But I have been studying with you for nearly four years now."

Telaq met his eyes. "Unfortunately the Ciralys in Isoliere will not consider your time with me as any sort of official study or training, and indeed it could not be until you are Tested with a skystone, and your Circle is determined. Apprenticeships are of the Covenants of the Keepers, not part of the Ciralys methodology," Telaq said. "You have learnt much yet. Now that your mind's eye is opened you are 'Awakened', and you will have no trouble seeing empowered High Asairic runes, but you have much farther to go to truly wield *Asai*, and your name needs be entered into the *Book of Disciples* so training can begin."

Darien was silent a moment, his head spinning. "I feel quite strange."

Telaq grunted. "As well you might. Awakening without supervision is not unheard of, but it is far from pleasant when there are no masters to assist you through the transition. And spontaneous Awakenings can be dangerous."

A chill crept along Darien's spine. "Why?"

"The initial opening of your mind to the Light of the Eye can cause mindstorms, similar to those that will come if you wield too much *Asai*, or wield it for too long," Telaq said. "Also, spontaneous Awakenings more frequently occur in conjunction with the manifestation of the Mark of the Eye."

"A Summoner?" Darien's stomach twisted, and he raised his right hand. The cut was throbbing, but there were no entwined silver and gold serpents to form a Khaderneous, the symbol of the Eye of Eternity that stained each Summoner's hand.

"A Sahrin," Telaq corrected, frowning down at him. "The ignorant may well call them *Summoners*, but to the Ciralys, they will always be the Sahrin. You are unmarked." Telaq gestured at Darien's hand. "But many are the tales of men and women, as well as children, who have been killed by their family or neighbours because they manifested the ability to touch *Asai* without training. Now, hold still."

The Ciralys placed his palm on Darien's forehead.

Darien gasped as he saw his master open himself to *Asai* for the first time. Suddenly light appeared to be everywhere. Even closing his eyes, Darien could still see it, a glittering silver light at the back of his mind.

"Those who can see the Light can wield it."Telaq's voice was distant. "But untrained, you are at risk. Stare too long at the sun, and you will go blind. It is the same with the Light of the Eye."

A brief burn, like a hot coal falling on his flesh, passed through Darien's mind. As the pain faded, so too did the sensation of vertigo, and the glow of *Asai*, until everything was muted again. *Normal.*

"That will have to do for now," Telaq said, leaning back. "Once we arrive in Isoliere, a master of the Fifth Circle, the Sphere of Spirit, will test you. You should make arrangements to leave, I have spoken with your Uncle –"

"Uncle Malik?" Darien felt a flare of panic. His uncle did not approve of the Ciralys at all. "What did he say? He can't stop me from going. I'm old enough to look after myself. I –"

Telaq raised a hand, and Darien almost bit his tongue to stop the flow of words. "Peace, Darien. Your uncle was reluctant to give his blessing, it is true, but your aunt… *overrode* his objections."

Darien's shoulders slumped in relief. "Yes, Aunt Breanta would let me choose my own path."

"You will not need to take much with you, a saddle bag or two should suffice. The Palace of the Eye will provide anything more you may need once we reach Isoliere," Telaq told him. "You had best get yourself home to pack and say your goodbyes. We leave first thing in the morning."

Darien nodded. "Yes, Master."

Ciralys Telaq picked a cloak off the top of a chest. "Take this." He draped the black, richly cut velvet over Darien's shoulders despite his protests.

"You will wear it," Telaq insisted. "And we will look to a wardrobe more fitting to an Awakened of the Ciralys when we're able." He moved Darien to the door.

Darien rubbed the wound on his hand absently. "Tomorrow..."

"Yes. We will talk more tomorrow." Telaq nodded, then looked at Darien, thoughtfully. "Prince Alesandr is here for his own reasons, and I am not at liberty to reveal them. I am his councillor, but I am also a Ciralys, and *our* first loyalty is to the Scion and Isoliere. The Sundering deprived the world not only of the Sahrin but of their knowledge."

Darien frowned but held his tongue.

"Like many other Ciralys, I seek a book, a codex called the *Tome of Ascension*." His master's face was in shadow, but the entwined serpents on his Khaderneous medallion – a badge of office worn only by Ciralys – glittered as they caught the light. "That is what I am looking for in the catacombs, and Sonyth will be my last chance before we leave. I will need your help."

"Of course, Master," Darien said, thrilled to be privy, at last, to secrets of the Ciralys. "I will do anything I can. How do you –"

Telaq shook his head. "Tomorrow. You should meditate this evening once you are packed. Work on the focusing exercises I have walked you through. To wield the Asai, you must strengthen your mind and your concentration."

Darien bowed without protest and pulled the door closed. "Tomorrow," he echoed, then turned and almost collided with Old Shany.

Shany, the Keeper of Hanore, had healed, nursed, advised and scolded every person in the citadel at least once in their life. She had been *Old* Shany for as long as Darien could remember. And before Prince Alesandr had arrived in the Borderlands with Master Telaq, she had been teaching him the arts of the Keepers. Though the Keepers did not wield *Asai* the way a Ciralys did, they were a force to be reckoned with in their own right, and once joining their ranks had been all he'd ever wanted.

"Sha-Shany." Darien swallowed, his face heating at his stammer. "What are you doing here?"

Shany peered at him intently with her single eye, her white hair pulled tight against her skull. The severity of her plain grey robes relieved by an assortment of coloured shawls she wore like a mantle over her slight frame.

"I felt something," Shany said. "A wave of *Asai*. Most unsusal since it didn't feel like Master Telaq's Sphere of Hyrisere." She fixed him with her stare. "What happened?"

"Nothing happened," Darien said. "Well, my mind's eye opened."

Shany gave a grunt. "Really? That's all?"

Darien became acutely aware of the throbbing on the back of his hand, and clenched his fist. "There was a bird, a raven, I think. It flew into the window."

"A raven? Are you sure it was a *bird* you saw?"

"Yes," Darien said. "I have to go, Shany. Master Telaq has invited me to go to Isoliere with him. He's going to have my name entered in the *Book of Dsiciples*."

Shany didn't say anything, just continued to study him. With a slight shrug, Darien made to move past her when she grabbed his wrist.

Raising his right hand, she stared at the wound and then lifted her eye back to his. Without a word she laid a finger on the cut, and a searing pain blazed in the puckered flesh.

"One half the crescent, waning," she half-whispered. "More is yet to come." She produced a small jar from a pocket hidden in her robes and dabbed a scentless ointment on the back of his hand. "Take this," she said and pushed the jar at him, "and keep that wound covered."

Darien gingerly prodded the cut on his hand, but all he could feel was the smooth silkiness of unmarked skin.

"What have you done?" he demanded.

Shany made a dismissive sound. "What is necessary. Now, come along. Your brother will be back soon, you'll want to give him the news of your leaving."

"Kaiel's coming back?" Darien stomach sank.

"Yes." Shany nodded in agreement. "The Path of the Kas'tirien is not for him."

Oh no, he lost. If Kaiel was not joining the Daemon Hunters, he'd most likely be staying in Hanore. And he wouldn't approve of Darien heading off with Master Telaq.

Darien took a breath. Well, it didn't matter what his older brother had to say. He was going to Isoliere, and Kaiel wasn't going to stop him.

"Come," Shany said from the top of the stairs. "The sooner you get this over with, the sooner you can start packing."

Darien scowled; he did need to start packing. He also needed time to think about what had just happened in the room with that *shadow-bird.*

He looked at the back of his hand again. If he didn't know better he'd never guess there was a wound there.

Putting the small jar Shany had given him into his pocket, he followed the Keeper down the stairs.

CHAPTER FOUR

Night Falling

THE SUN WAS beginning to set, painting the western horizon orange and tracing it with hints of purple when Kaiel and Sim left the woods at a gallop. The wind continued to press against them from the east, buffeting them hard as they approached the open ground around the Citadel of Hanore.

The surrounding grounds were cleared of vegetation for a good two hundred yards. Kaiel's uncle claimed the forest had been kept back five hundred yards when he was a boy, but that was hard to believe given the size of the trees that surrounded Hanore now. They looked like they'd been there for centuries.

The gates were still open and the three diamond-cut crystal Sun Bells at the apex of the gates' arch – arranged like an arrowhead pointing to the heavens – sparkled with captured sunlight. Crafted by the Summoners who had built the citadel during the War of the Sundering, the bells would ring whenever daemons, or daemonkind, came close.

Kaiel slowed Lasa to a trot.

"We made it!" Sim, who was still in the lead, called back to him, also slowing.

"I've been thinking..." Kaiel said. "What happened back there?"

Sim frowned. "What do you mean?"

"What did that priest of Sarnor mean about us 'standing ready'?"

"How should I know?" Sim shrugged as both horses slowed into a walk. "No good comes of poking around in the affairs of the Shol'mas Lords."

"The Shol'mas aren't well known in the Borderlands, it's true," Kaiel said. "But they are the Messengers of the Elder Gods. They can't be that bad."

"Ha! Those priests and their Temples never let you go once they get their hooks into you. Just ask my da." Sim rubbed his chin. "What I'd like to know is where that priest came from. The Bronze Guard are sworn to the Elder God Alay'thias, aren't they?"

"Yes, the Guard follow the Sun God," Kaiel agreed. "The priest has kept to himself, mostly."

Sim grunted. "Could the King be planning to bring the Borderlands back into the fold? Maybe that's what's been going on with all these princes being made Carbinah."

"Three princes, Sim," Kaiel corrected. "The second of whom held his office before I was out of swaddling."

"That's three too many," Sim said. "And no-one has been happy about it. My da says everyone grumbles about it when they come to the store. You mark me, the Borderlanders settled here to get away from the Houses; they won't bend the knee easily."

"The scions of House Niskeri always take a term as Carbinah of Jaroff," Kaiel said.

Sim gestured at the citadel. "But none of them have spent so much time out *here*. It's strange."

"Alesandr's just picking through the catacombs, looking for the treasures every Houseborn thinks we're swimming in," Kaiel said. "It's not like it's never happened before. Mercenary companies come out here to train with the Rangers every year. They all want to find treasure in the catacombs. I suppose it's good the Rangers are so well regarded; otherwise, we'd get bandits out here too."

Sim snorted."There are bandits aplenty up around Jaroff and Raetlia."

They rode over the bridge across the dry moat and through the South Gate, onto the cobblestones of the High Keep's assembly yard. There were four keeps in Hanore, each larger than the other, and five towers. One tower for each keep, and one in the citadel's centre. That tower was home to the citadel's Keeper. It was this tower where Kaiel's younger half-brother had spent so much of his time before the prince and his Ciralys adviser had arrived in Hanore. Once the tower's everstone had been a gleaming white, or so the older folk said. Now it was a dark grey as though slowly decaying. And that decay was spreading out from the tower to the everstone of the surrounding Keeps.

Clouds gathered across the sky as early twilight fell. Men and women moved about the grounds, finishing off jobs or packing things away for the morrow. Children ran and hollered underfoot, chased by barking dogs, and Kaiel dismounted – Sim following his lead – to walk the horses in.

"Home sweet home," Sim said as they crossed the assembly yard.

"Kaiel Toranth," a man said, stepping out from the shadows of the western pylon beside the gate and Kaiel turned.

Jaric Daynar, Captain of the Hanore Rangers, was a powerfully built man, as tall as Kaiel himself, and dressed in similar leathers of brown and deep greens, his jerkin reinforced by steel rivets. It spoke in the man's favour that he'd reached the rank of captain when he was an outlander. Though mercenary companies often came to train amongst the Rangers, the citadelfolk were wary of outsiders. Jaric Daynar had arrived in Hanore fifteen years ago and had been unanimously named captain when the last had retired some five years later.

Jaric locked eyes with each of them. A day's growth of black beard against his normally clean-shaven jawline added a harshness to his stern countenance."Your Trial didn't go well?"

Kaiel shook his head."No, sir. I didn't pass the Trial. Rolen is the next apprentice."

Jaric Daynar grunted."I'm surprised."

"You're not the only one," Sim said."Rolen Etine is a cheat –"

"Sim!"Kaiel snapped

"Oh, come on," Sim protested."You're not going to let the skreetling get away with –"

"That's enough, Ravenson." Captain Daynar held up one calloused palm, halting Sim's response before it began."Daemon Hunter business is their own. It's none of ours. And I don't want to hear that you're gossiping about it to the citadelfolk who come into your father's shop either. Let Kaiel move on."

"Very well," Sim agreed, pulling himself upright in afront."I'll not bother to mention the borewyrm either then. I mean someone must have made it back from patrol with a report after all. And I wouldn't want to gossip about things that aren't my business, given as I am not a member of the Rangers."

The captain raised an eyebrow and stared at him.

"Fine." Sim gave way faster than Kaiel expected."We saw the track of a wyrm about four miles down the South Road."

"Heading which way?"Jaric directed the question to Kaiel.

"West, sir," Kaiel told him."A juvenile, I think. The wind had come up, and we didn't hear its passing. The Taint over the road faded quickly."

"Did you see the Carbinah's guardsmen?"

"We saw them." Sim's scorn was barely hidden.

"We were with Sergeant Quaylin when we saw the wyrm trail,"Kaiel glanced at Sim."He didn't believe there was any danger. We saw Under-Lieutenant Hearn and the rest after that."

"And you let them go?"

"The Eye blind me! How could we have stopped them?" Sim burst out."You know what these Houseborn are like. They kept blathering at us to show our hands as if they had never met us before!"

"Every realm has varying degrees of vigilance in watching for Summoners," Jaric said. "You know that. The cities and towns of Aldania aren't as relaxed as the Borderlands in presenting hands for inspection."

"But we aren't *in* Aldania; we're in the Borderlands," Sim said. "This is *our* home. They should bend themselves to our traditions."

"Don't be ignorant. You know Aldania claims the Borderlands." The captain eyed the darkening sky. "I'll find Captain Bruday and let him know. No doubt he'll want to go out after them, but I'll not send the Rangers out now. It will be nightfall before they reach them. The Borderlands have been quiet, though this wind..."

He shook his head and sighed. "I'll send a patrol out at first light. Thank you for your report. You'll be wanting to stable those horses and get cleaned up I'm guessing. You look a bit battered, Kaiel."

Kaiel shrugged. "Just bruised, sir."

"Once His Highness has returned to Jaroff, come see me. The Rangers could do with a man like you if you are so inclined."

Kaiel ignored the look Sim was directing at him and nodded. "Thank you, sir."

Captain Daynar left them then, heading towards the Barracks while Kaiel and Sim continued round the High Keep to the citadel stables. Not everyone in the citadel owned a horse, but those who did stabled them in the enormous two-storied building just off the west bailey, provided by Steward Etine.

Kaiel took Lasa to her stall and brushed her down before turning her care over to one of the stable boys. Night had fallen quickly, the clouds from earlier now blanketing the heavens, and Kaiel found Sim under a torch post that had just been lit.

"Void take me!" Sim cursed as soon as Kaiel joined him. "Can you believe Captain Daynar? I don't gossip. It's important to know things as a trader. Everybody knows that! What good is a trader who doesn't know what's going on around him? No good, that's what."

"I just hope those guardsmen will be safe," Kaiel said.

"More fool them if they're not! No, Kaiel. We did our duty and warned them. That's all we could do; it's not our fault if they believe they know better than us!"

"Maybe, Sim. It just doesn't feel right."

"There was nothing either one of us could've done to stop them."

"We didn't even try!" Kaiel snapped. Surprised at his frustration, he took a deep breath and clenched his jaw when Sim raised his eyes.

Turning, Kaiel started back across the bailey. Sim followed beside him, thankfully remaining silent.

"Ang!" Kaiel called, waving to a young Sola'var rolling a barrel that would have taken at least three humans to move. Taller even than Under-Lieutenant Hearn, the Var who lived beside the humans of the Borderlands were gentle giants. The Sola'var caste, one-time warriors, were farmers and labourers. They were physically similar to humans but for their size, strength and pointed ears. Large, sombre eyes filled delicately boned faces, and their large hands had only four fingers. It was the Var who had subdued the daemon hordes after the fall of the Summoners and the subsequent collapse of human civilization. And it was the Hyla'var, the elder caste of artisans and mystics, who had led them to bring order out of the devastation that followed the Sundering.

Ang gave Kaiel a half-wave but continued to the ramp that led to the catacombs below the citadel.

"At least with the Guard gone the Var will be able to come back out in the open," Sim said, as he too waved to Ang. "Aldanians have to be idiots if they can't tell the difference between the Sola'var and the Korda'var."

"We're Aldanians, Sim," Kaiel said.

"We're *Borderlanders*," Sim corrected. "Surely the stone-growths, horns and hooves of the Korda'var are fairly obvious." He snorted. "The Guard should –"

"Kaiel!"

A young woman in a dark blue dress and white blouse came towards them in a rush, blonde hair streaming behind her. Kaiel couldn't help the smile that erupted on his face, though his stomach twisted at the same time. Sevaani Etine was the most beautiful girl he'd ever seen. Beside her was Meg. Of a similar age, Meg wore dark breeches and a white blouse, her red hair pulled back in a practical braid.

"Sevaani," he said, hugging her tight as she wrapped her arms around his neck.

"Rolen…?" She stepped back to meet his eyes.

"Yes." Kaiel felt his anger flare but held it back. Done was done. "Rolen is the next apprentice."

"Your poor face," Sevaani said, reaching up to gingerly touch a scab on his forehead.

Meg scoffed. "It's just some cuts and scrapes. He doesn't have any broken bones." She paused, her green eyes narrowing. "Do you?"

"No." Kaiel shook his head.

"I expect you've had worse in sword training, although the cut on your hand looks nasty," Meg said. "He'll be fine, Sevaani. Condolences on your ma's passing, Kaiel. May Tarin greet her with open arms."

"Thank you, Meg," Kaiel said.

"May Tarin greet her." Sevaani echoed the blessing of the Elder Goddess of Nature. "I'm so sorry, Kaiel." Sevaani linked her arm in his. "I know how much you gave up to join the Daemon Hunters."

"We go where the Light of the Eye guides," he said, but the platitude felt empty.

"That, and Rolen is a cheat," Sim said.

Sevaani stopped. "What happened?"

Kaiel shot a look at Sim. "Nothing. I didn't pass the Trial. Rolen did."

He was going to have to get used to saying that. Everyone in Hanore knew he and Rolen had gone up against each other today.

Sevaani frowned and Meg locked him in a piercing gaze that was strangely reminiscent of Keeper Shany. Particularly when Shany was set on getting to the bottom of something. Usually a prank of Sim's.

"Well." Sevaani smiled at him. "Now you can join the Rangers. It's perfect. With Rolen off to be a Daemon Hunter, I'll likely take Father's place as Steward one day, and you can be Captain!"

Sim barked a laugh. "Not if he goes off to join the Bronze Guard, he can't."

Kaiel ground his teeth. Why couldn't Sim keep his mouth shut? He had to approach these things with Sevaani careful–

"Join the Bronze Guard?" Sevaani stepped back to stare up at him, gripping his arm tight. "Become a mercenary? You'd never do that, would you Kaiel?"

"What's wrong with being a mercenary?" Meg asked. "I think it sounds like a good idea."

"But Kaiel!" Sevaani tightened her grip on his arm. "You're just going to leave? What about Darien? What about me?"

"You're not promised yet, Sevaani," Sim rolled his eyes.

"I don't know what I am going to do," Kaiel said before Sevaani could respond. No, they weren't promised. He wasn't opposed to the idea, but he hadn't thought about it. Had he? Quickly he went on, "I *might* join the Guard. Sergeant Quaylin offered to sponsor me."

"The Rangers would take you," Meg said with a grin.

"I'm not sure I want to stay!"

"I see," Sevaani said, and withdrew her hand from his arm.

He cursed himself at the hurt on her face. "Sevaani –"

"No, you're right," Sevaani said with a sigh, the torchlight playing over her face. She gave him a brief smile. "The Light of the Eye guides us all. I suppose Darien will leave as well?"

Kaiel frowned."I haven't spoken to Dar."

"Ciralys Telaq is going to take him back to Isoliere; once His Highness returns to Dainyaia. Prince Alesandr mentioned it to my father this morning. Darien can wield *Asai*, and Ciralys Telaq wants him for the Palace of the Eye."

"I told you," Sim said.

"Uncle Malik won't allow it," Kaiel said. "He doesn't hold with the Ciralys or what wielding the Light of the Eye can do. Not after what happened to Ma."

"Kaiel, your ma had the Sight," Meg looked at him. "It was because she was untrained that her trances eventually killed her."

"If she needed training, why couldn't Old Shany help her?" He couldn't keep the edge from his voice.

"Because the Covenant of the Keepers doesn't deal with the deeper mysteries of *Asai*. She should have gone to Isoliere herself or found a Shrine to Samantra. It was your uncle's prejudices that kept her here and untrained."

"That's not fair!" Kaiel protested. Grief tightened like bands around his chest, and he took a deep breath. "Ma was Uncle Malik's only sister. He's been heartbroken."

Meg folded her arms across her chest. "Heartbroken, or wracked with guilt?"

Kaiel shook his head. Meg had a tendency to emulate Shany when she dealt with others, pretending to know everything. The difference was, Old Shany usually did know.

Beyond the wall of the citadel came a flash of lightning followed by thunder. Rain began to fall and the few people still out on the grounds moved quickly for shelter. Taking Sevaani's arm – at least she didn't pull away – Kaiel headed towards the Clan Keep. It was getting late, and he'd probably find Dar in their uncle's inn, housed in the first hall of the Keep. He'd talk to him about this Ciralys nonsense. Isoliere was too far away.

He'd just lost his ma; he couldn't lose his brother as well.

"I'm fine, Shany," Kaiel sighed as the Keeper kept prodding him. "I just want to talk to my brother."

Kaiel had found Darien waiting for him with Old Shany in a cushioned alcove in the Inn of the Stone Frog. Positioned beside the smaller of the inn's two hearths, the light of the flames coloured the shadow-streaked table between them in amber. Aged oak tables and chairs lay scattered across the dark flagstone floor. Cushioned benches and long trestles rested against the walls beneath frosted glass whose panes, now blackened by night, reflected flashes of colour from hanging oil lamps. The great hearth of the hall, chiselled into the shape of an enormous frog, had been banked for the night despite the chill, but the fire beside them was warm enough.

It was a quiet night in the Stone Frog, but then most of the Bronze Guard who were still in the citadel were preparing to leave on the morrow, and the few who were here for one last drink eyed Sim suspiciously; there'd be no more unwitting marks for Sim to fleece at cards or a game of kings tonight.

"Hmph," the Keeper snorted. "Your brother isn't going anywhere, not right now. What is that on your hand?"

Kaiel looked at the perfectly curved cut. "It's just a nick –"

"That is not a nick," the Keeper said, studying the back of Kaiel's hand, then she straightened with a jerk.

"Shany?" Meg said. "What's wrong?"

"Be silent, girl! Who has seen this?"

"What?" Kaiel tried to pull his hand away.

"Your wound! Who has seen it?" Shany snapped.

"Joureyman Jidara, I suppose. Lieutenant Quaylin, he stopped us on the way home."

"The guardsmen heading to Sonyth," Sim said. "You show your hand to everybody, Kaiel."

"Like we're supposed to," Kaiel growled back at his friend.

"And what did they say?" Shany pressed.

"Shany," Meg tried again. "What's wrong?"

"They didn't say anything." Kaiel gently, but firmly, extracted his wrist from her grip. "It's not the Mark of the Eye."

The Keeper shut her one eye, muttering to herself, her hand clenching something in the pocket of her woollen robes.

"You need this too." Shany pulled a tiny clay jar from her pocket and handed it to Kaiel. "Put this on the wound. And keep putting it on until it is healed."

"Shany, it's just a cut." Kaiel laughed.

"Yes. It's just a cut." She bent down, and before Kaiel could protest, she dabbed the contents of the jar onto his hand.

"Gods, Shany!" he swore. "What are you doing?"

"Don't be such a child," the Keeper said. "It's just an ointment. Leave it alone. It will wash off."

"What do you think it is?" Darien asked but the old woman remained silent, inspecting Kaiel's other wounds.

Kaiel peered down at his hand and frowned. Where the inflamed lines of the cut had been, there was now smooth skin.

"Shany," Darien pressed, his lips a thin line on his face.

"You're a clever little Ciralys," she said, stepping back from the table. "I am sure it will come to you. If not, then it is something you might like to study one day."

Darien's green eyes flared as he glared at the woman who had been his teacher before Ciralys Telaq had arrived. "Bah!" Darien waved his hand. "I don't need your secrets."

Shany laughed. "And yet you have one just the same. Keep using the ointment, both of you! You will be glad you did." She pointed at both Kaiel and Darien and then turned and made her way out of the Inn.

"What?" Kaiel looked at Darien.

Darien shook his head, and gave a half shrug. "I have a wound on the back of my hand too."

"Where?" Meg asked, peering at him.

"Shany gave me the same ointment."

"Both of you getting the same wound on the same day?" Sim drawled. He was sitting opposite Sevaani, who was on Kaiel's right. "It must be a sign."

Meg frowned. "A sign of what?"

"I don't know. That they shouldn't part?" Sim laughed.

"Exactly," Kaiel said. "How can you think of going, Dar? We're the only brother each other has. Why do you have to go all the way to Isoliere?"

"Because that's where anyone who can wield the Light of the Eye goes to train to become a Ciralys." Darien pushed away the bowl of stew he'd been playing with. "Why are you trying to make me feel guilty? You went off this morning to become an apprentice Daemon Hunter. I wouldn't have seen you again for how long? A year? Two? Three? That's acceptable, but I'm not allowed to train with the Ciralys?"

"He's got a point, Kaiel," Sim said.

"That was different. And what were you going to do if I hadn't returned tonight? Leave me a note?" Kaiel forced himself to relax his clenched hands, and took a steadying breath. "At least I would have been here, in the Borderlands. Void take me, I don't even know how far away Isoliere is!"

"A hundred leagues," Sim offered. "Give or take."

"It's where I have to go if I want to learn how to wield *Asai*," Darien said.

"You could have done that here," Meg offered. "You were going to be a Keeper."

Darien frowned. "There's a world of difference between the Keepers and the Ciralys."

"Yes, the Ciralys were disciples of the Summoners," Meg said.

Darien sighed. "I want to be a Ciralys, not a Keeper."

"Maybe I should go too," Meg said.

"What?" Darien blinked. "You can't!"

"Why can't she?" Sevaani asked. "You don't have the monopoly on who can or can't become a Ciralys, Darien."

"She's Shany's apprentice," Darien said. "Who will take over as Keeper after Shany if Meg leaves?"

"That won't be your problem, though, will it?" Sim asked.

Meg snorted. "You were Shany's apprentice before me, Darien. Why do I have to stay if you can go?"

Kaiel frowned at Meg. Growing up she and Dar had been very close, so close that there'd been a time Meg had asked Darien for his promise, which was when Darien had declared his lack of romantic interest in women and that he only saw her as a friend. They'd remained friends, but Kaiel couldn't help wonder if Meg still felt something more.

"Don't worry, Meg," Sevaani said, pulling Kaiel from his musings. "You'll join the Ciralys too."

Meg looked over at her, startled. "What do you mean? I wasn't serious."

Sevaani shrugged. "Weren't you?"

Kaiel shook his head and returned his attention back to his brother. "I can't help feeling that now's not the right time for you to make these types of decisions, Dar. Ma's just died, after all."

"I know," Darien snapped, "I was here."

Kaiel reeled back as though Darien had hit him.

"I'm sorry." Darien looked down at the table. "I didn't mean that."

"It's all right," Kaiel managed, breathing deeply. "I –"

"No," Darien made a slashing motion with his right hand. "It's not all right. I'm *sorry*, Kaiel. Ma was happy for you to have gone so far in your training, she didn't begrudge you, and I shouldn't either."

"But you had to take care of everything."

"I had help." Darien's nod encompassed Meg, Sevaani and Sim. Kaiel blinked in surprise. "And everyone else. Ma might have been looked on as… *strange*, because of the Sight, but she was well regarded. The Borderlanders look after their own."

Kaiel nodded, studying his half-brother. It was hard to see a family resemblance between them at first. He was a good five inches taller than Dar, broader across the chest and shoulders and blond where Darien was a dark. They even had different coloured eyes. But they shared the same mother, and for all that they were different – in temperament as well as physicality – they were blood.

"You know, Kaiel," Sim said. "You could always go with Darien."

Kaiel looked at his friend in surprise. "To Isoliere?"

"Why not? There are other guard companies than those here in Aldania. The Swords of the Black Sun in Hetar, or the Company of the Steel Hand. What about the Knights of Cythis?" Sim shrugged. "Or maybe the Blay Shon."

"The Blay Shon aren't a military company." Kaiel shook his head. "And with any of those you mentioned, I'd still need a sponsor unless the books were open to take on recruits."

"They're soldiers though, swordsmen, aren't they?" Sim said.

"They are indeed," came a voice from beside the table.

Kaiel turned and pushed himself to his feet in surprise. "Your Highness!" He stepped from the table and made to drop to one knee.

"Please," Alesandr said, putting out a hand to stop Kaiel from kneeling. His voice crisp with the sharp accent of the Aldanian Houses. "Such formalities have little place in the Borderlands."

A strange sense of familiarity fell upon Kaiel as he took in the prince. Though the man had been in the Borderlands for some time, Kaiel had never seen him up close. But for his black hair and clipped goatee, the prince was of identical height and colouring, with the same square jaw and blue eyes as Kaiel himself. Though dressed in the same leather jerkins and trousers as any member of the Rangers might, Prince Alesandr of the Royal House of Niskeri stood with a casual authority Kaiel had never seen anyone in Hanore convey.

"We have not had the opportunity to meet, Kaiel, what with your training and my other duties, but I have heard much of you from Captain Daynar and your brother." The prince nodded to Darien. "I am sorry I must leave on the morrow or I would have spoken more with you of the Kas'tirien."

"Of course, Your Highness." Kaiel didn't know what else to say. He'd never spoken to a prince before.

"Daemon Hunters would be the last thing he'd want to talk about, Your Highness," Sim said.

Alesandr glanced at Sim and then back to Kaiel. A look of understanding dawned on his face. "Ah, of course. Today was the day of your apprentice trials. I take it, given Master Ravenson's… tact, that you did not find a place with them?"

"I did not, Highness." It was easier to say than Kaiel had expected.

"I see. I am sure no-one can fault your dedication, whatever the results of your Trial." The prince looked around the table. "Is that what this talk of mercenary companies was in aid of? What to do next?"

"Yes, Your Highness," Kaiel said. "Sergeant Quaylin has offered to sponsor me to the Bronze Guard."

"I see." Alesandr smiled, and Kaiel was struck again by that sense of familiarity. "You could do quite well in the Guard, I imagine. As well as your brother is like to do amongst the Ciralys. My counsellor speaks highly of you, Darien."

"Thank you, Your Highness." Darien bowed his head.

Alesandr nodded. "I had come to see your uncle before I depart, is he here?"

"Oh, Your Highness!" Sella, one of the inn's maids, came running from across the room. "Please, your lordship, forgive me. Master Malik is waiting for you in the library. He told me to keep an eye out for you. I'm ever so sorry for the wait."

"No apologies are necessary," the prince said. He turned to Kaiel. "If I do not see you again, fare thee well, Kaiel. Darien, you will be ready to leave tomorrow?"

"Yes, Your Highness. I will," Darien said, not meeting Kaiel's eyes.

"Very good." Alesandr gestured to Sella. "Please, lead on."

Kaiel heard Sim snicker as Sella curtsied twice before leading Prince Alesandr away. As he moved, four guardsmen stepped out of the shadows lining the walls to take up position behind the prince.

Kaiel shivered. It was less that the Knights of the Asp accompanied the prince that proclaimed them his bodyguards – and some said assassins – so much as it was the black mail they wore. The light that struck the armour shimmered in the tell-tale rainbow hues of kharidium. Forged by the Xious'bisan of the Guesaybor Mountains, the metal was lighter and more durable than steel and could be afforded only by the great houses of the realms. Kaiel had been so intent on the prince he'd never even known they were there.

"Well," Meg said as they seated themselves again. "I suppose that settles it."

"Since when have you acceded to the whims of the Blood, Meg?" Sim asked around a mouthful of bread. "I thought Shany taught you better than that."

Meg glared at him.

"Kaiel!" Thankful for the interruption, Kaiel looked over at the bar to see the rotund silhouette of his aunt in the doorway to the kitchen.

Breanta Toranth crossed the room and grabbed him up in a hug. "I didn't expect to see you back here tonight. I'm sorry."

"Thank you, Aunt Brea," Kaiel said. "I didn't think I'd be back so soon either."

"It's to be Rolen then?" Breanta asked, and Kaiel nodded, reclaiming his seat. He moved his unbelted sword out of the way as it slid against the wood.

"What does your father think of that, Sevaani?" Breanta asked.

"I don't know, Mistress Toranth. I haven't seen him since Kaiel returned. He's likely working with Captain Bruday to ensure that the Guard are ready to leave tomorrow."

"Hmph," Aunt Brea said, brushing a strand of hair from her face. "And good riddance to them if you ask me. His Royal Highness has been far too interested in the things that go on in the Citadels for my liking."

Kaiel shook his head. "There's no law against people searching the catacombs for… What was he looking for, Dar?"

"I don't know. Ciralys Telaq never said."

"And you never asked?" Sim raised an eyebrow.

"You don't ask questions of Ciralys, Sim," Sevaani answered. "Nor of princes."

"*I* would have," Sim said. "How else do you learn things?"

"Maybe by paying attention to what goes on around you," Meg suggested.

"I do that too." Sim grinned.

"It's not just the catacombs," Breanta said as though the others hadn't spoken. "He showed up to see your mother – just after she had woken from her last trance – and *commanded* to be taken to her."

Her brow creased into the no-nonsense expression the rowdier patrons of the inn were used to seeing. "Took his time about speaking with her too, he did. If he hadn't left when he did, I was going to throw him out on his ear, prince or no!" She put her hands on her ample hips. "Two hours is more time than anyone has a right to when questioning someone as sick as your mother was!"

"Two hours!" Kaiel turned to his brother. "What was he doing?"

"We don't know," Darien said, a frown on his face.

Breanta shook her head. "Shany acted as though she'd been expecting him, and then left him alone with Mar'ee while that Bruday took up post outside the room and refused to let me enter!" She wrung her hands together. "Oh, Kaiel, I know why you weren't able to be there, and the gods know Mar'ee was happy for you, but I can't help wishing you had been."

Kaiel's grief swelled in his chest. "I wish I had been too," he said, his voice thick.

"My apologies for disturbing you all," Captain Daynar said coming up to the table. "Mistress Breanta, I was hoping you'd seen Prince Alesandr."

Accompanying Captain Daynar was a tall, broad-shouldered man. The black skin of his bald head and his bronzed armour identified him as Rowin Bruday, Captain of the Bronze Guard, and Kaiel stood again.

"Captain Bruday, Captain Jaric," he said.

"Kaiel Toranth," Rowin Bruday raised his right fist to his chest, displaying the back of his hand in greeting. Kaiel, conscious of the ointment that now hid his wound, did the same. "My condolences on the loss of your mother, and the result of the Trial."

"Thank you, sir." Kaiel pushed his sense of shame back. It would get easier. It would.

"And my thanks for bringing word of the danger my men are walking into." Rowin grimaced. "I am sure they can handle the dangers of the Borderland Wilds, but His Highness needs to know."

Sim barked a laugh but lowered his head when Captain Daynar frowned at him.

Kaiel nodded. "Of course, sir. No thanks are necessary. Anyone raised in the Borderlands would do the same."

Kaiel saw Bruday's eyes drift to Sim, but he nodded then turned to Jaric. "We need to see the prince."

"The prince is in the library with Malik," Breanta said. "I'll take you to him."

"Kaiel," Jaric said. "If you are up to it, I'd like you to join me in the morning when we send a patrol out looking for the squad."

"Me, sir?"

Jaric nodded. "You're one of the last to see the guardsmen on the road. I'll be mobilising the Rangers also – yes, Simeon, that means you – but I'll head out with a small party first. Are you in?"

"Yes, sir. I'll be ready."

"Good man." Jaric looked over to where Breanta was leading Captain Bruday to a far door. "I'll see you at sixth bell, on the green."

"I'll be there," Kaiel said.

"Well, it looks like you won't have a problem finding something to do after all, Kaiel," Meg said.

Kaiel grimaced. "Helping tomorrow doesn't mean I'm staying."

Darien got up from his place at the table. "I need to start packing."

"Dar–"

"I'll be up early to help Master Telaq, Kaiel," Darien said. "I'll see you before you leave."

Kaiel sighed, but nodded. He wasn't going to be able to change his brother's mind tonight, but if the squad of guardsmen had run afoul of the Borderlands, then the prince and his household would not be going as soon as Darien imagined.

Which would give Kaiel plenty of time to talk his brother out of leaving.

CHAPTER FIVE

The Arch of Trees

AT A SIGNAL from Captain Daynar, Kaiel and the rest of the scouting party crouched behind the trunk of a fallen tree that blocked the Sonyth road. Named for the citadel it led to, the road stretched due south from Hanore and was the same one Kaiel and Sim had travelled the day before.

Based on Kaiel and Sim's report, Captain Daynar believed the party of the Bronze Guardsmen had at least reached the Lone Trail that led to the Darscene Caves, and possibly even the Arch of Trees further south. The captain had formed a small party to scout ahead of the main force the prince would be leading. Kaiel was grouped with the captain and Oslin, one of the Bronze Guard, while Dobard Hay – an old-timer from the Rangers – partnered with Lanet, another guardsman.

They had set out an hour after dawn, although with the cloud cover there was little to mark the shifting of night to day. Captain Daynar had insisted the Rangers take the lead over Prince Alesandr's strong objection. The prince had only relented when Captain Jaric had agreed to take some of the Bronze Guard with them.

Kaiel couldn't help but believe that had he been in Prince Alesandr's place, he would have judged it more prudent that men and women local to the area lead the way. But then he wasn't the leader who'd sent a company of men into the Borderland Wilds at nightfall.

Kaiel rubbed the back of his hand absently. They had been on the road for almost four hours, but the morning shadows lingered with the sun hidden behind clouds. And the forest was quiet. Too quiet.

"Captain," Kaiel whispered, then gestured around them. "Where are all the animals?"

"Gone to ground." Jaric signalled to Dobard, who'd stopped and was looking back.

"The Arch is not that far off now," the captain said to the older man. "We stay on the road."

Dobard grunted his agreement and started out again, pulling his dagger from its sheath as he went. Kaiel followed behind Lanet, close enough that he could still make out the guardsman ahead but far enough back to be free of any potential ambush.

As the mass of moonleaf trees that made up the Arch came into view, the party stopped one by one. Larger than the conifers, firs or pines of the Borderland Wilds, the moonleafs of the Arch of Trees rose into the canopy around them like pillars erected in monument. The great trees lined the road for over two-hundred feet, growing together and twining their branches in a perfect arch, the trunk of each tree almost touching its neighbour, forming a long tunnel through the middle of the woodland.

Where once the Arch had inspired awe, Kaiel now saw it as a brooding symbol of all the dangers the Deadlands held. Its opening was a yawning mouth that led into darkness, the only light coming from the exit at the far end, like a ghostlight.

"Should we go in?" Dobard asked.

"We wait here for the prince," Jaric said. "Take Lanet and position yourselves on the west side of the road. Oslin, Kaiel and I will take the east."

They'd only just moved apart when a chilling cry sliced through the silent forest. It hung on the air, reverberating off the evergreens whose dense foliage shadowed the dull light coming from the cloud-covered sky. The whitebark of the moonleafs added a ghostlike pallor to the surrounds.

Kaiel turned back as Dobard Hay ran towards the opening of the Arch, nocking an arrow as he went.

Jaric yelled for them to take cover. Years of training came into play, and Kaiel dove to the side of the road, dropping into a crouch behind the nearest thicket. Peering round the bush, he wrapped his hand around the hilt of his sword. Tension curled in the pit of his stomach.

On the other side of the road, the captain stepped behind the broad trunk of an evergreen while Dobard still stood in the middle of the road, waiting for whatever was coming. Kaiel shifted, ready to run and grab the man, but a whistle from the captain froze him in place. Kaiel stopped, his tension increasing with frightening urgency as he willed the guardsman to take cover.

The cry came again. Closer this time. Across the road, Captain Daynar gave the hand signal for Kaiel to pull his bow. Reluctantly, Kaiel released his grip on the hilt of his sword to pull the Borderlands bow from his shoulder. Taking an arrow from the quiver, he hooked it into place and looked over the thicket.

On the road, Dobard's stance shifted as the shadows in the Arch's opening resolved, and a man dressed in the leather armour of the Rangers staggered out.

The man's face was a mass of cuts, and blood stained the dark leather of his trousers. He stretched out a hand, and Dobard lowered his bow to catch him, only to give a startled cry.

Dobard jumped back, letting the man fall. On the Ranger's back was a spider the size of a small dog. It clung to the man, knife-sized fangs gleaming with blood and venom as it raised itself.

Kaiel stood out of reflex and fell into the stance the Daemon Hunters had taught him. His heart grew loud in his ears, its steady beat slowing to a crawl as he straightened his back, drawing the nocked arrow while his mind *reached*.

He let the arrow fly.

It was as though the arachnid froze as the arrow sped across the distance, pierced its body, and knocked it off the man's back in the space of a heartbeat.

Time sped up again, and Dobard was on it in an instant, his sword flashing in the low light and cutting the spider in half, its legs twitching before curling inward.

"By the gods, what was that?" Oslin's voice was strained as he stepped cautiously onto the road beside Kaiel.

"A treewolf spider." Kaiel glanced at the man. Oslin's large eyes were wide, his face pale. "We usually don't see ones so large this close to the citadels."

"What's he doing?" the guardsman pointed as Captain Daynar took an oil-soaked rag from his pack and wrapped it around the large hump on the spider's back.

"He's killing the others," Kaiel said.

"What others?"

Jaric flicked a spark from a flint and striker onto the cloth, and set it alight. As the fire rose, the hump burst and hundreds of smaller spiders scurried out, each combusting into tiny balls of flame.

The guardsman gagged and stepped away.

"Who's the Ranger?" the captain asked Dobard.

"Ned Cunnings, from Sonyth," Dobard said, without looking up. "Lie still, man, you've been carrying a Treewolf on your back."

"Korda'vari! Two hundred, or more," Ned gasped. He struggled to get up. "They swarmed the walls... we weren't ready."

"Korda'vari?"Dobard shook his head."It's been over two generations since an attack like that."

Jaric ignored him."Check his hand, Dobard."

Dobard looked at the captain in surprise but did as ordered."He's no Summoner,"he said, holding up Ned's unmarked hand.

"How did they get through Sonyth's walls?"Jaric asked the man.

"The everstone just... it crumbled. Like it was dry clay! We cut down nearly a quarter of them."Ned closed his eyes at the memory.

"Were they organised?"Jaric pressed.

"Don't know."Ned seemed to shrink in upon himself.

"Was a Lloth'var with them?"

Ned winced as Dobard dabbed at the punctures on his back with bandages from his pack."If one of the Soulless walked amongst them, it wasn't seen. But I could've missed it,"he conceded weakly.

"What about any of the Bronze Guard?"Jaric asked."Did any of the Guard arrive?"

"The Guard? No, haven't seen them since His Highness was there." Ned jerked up."Half the citadel is in flames.You must help us. Call the Rangers from Hanore and Tore!"

"We *are* the Rangers from Hanore, Ned."Dobard rested a hand on the man's shoulder as he slumped back to the ground.

"It would be wise to send word to Tore,"Jaric said."You know Captain Kara. I need you to go to her, Dobard."

"Aye,"Dobard agreed and got up."Those bandages will hold till a Keeper can look at him, and I've given him the anti-venom."

As the captain gave Dobard his message for Tore's Ranger's, Kaiel moved over to the mouth of the Arch. Lanet and Oslin followed.

"Is it always that dark in there?"Lanet asked as he approached.

"It's just the cloud cover,"Kaiel said. Though with the events of the last day he was almost inclined to believe the shadows of the Arch were darker than usual.

"That man kept talking about the Var," Oslin said. "If they're so dangerous, why do you have them living in your citadels?"

Kaiel shook his head."When you say Var, you're thinking of Sola'vari, or the Hyla'vari. The uncorrupted. The Korda'vari are monsters; Sola'vari the Summoners tainted with powers from the Void. They were foot soldiers during the War of the Summoners, almost mindless."

"If they are mindless, how are they a threat?" Oslin snorted."Under-Lieutenant Hearne would have handled them."

Kaiel grimaced."Picture a foe as big as a Sola'var, with stone growths on its skin like armour, horns, and a raging bloodlust to kill anything in its path. Even then you're only imagining half the reality. And if Ned is even close to being correct in his count of the numbers that attacked Sonyth, and your squad met them by themselves, I'm not sure they could have survived."

"Don't underestimate the Bronze Guard," Oslin said, full of bluster.

"Don't underestimate the Borderlands," Jaric said, joining them. "If Hearne got his people to Sonyth without encountering this force, then you might find them alive. But they left late in the day and wouldn't have made it to Sonyth before nightfall."

"And you Borderlanders would have just left them outside?" Lanet demanded.

"We survive in the Wilds because we follow the rules set in place by the Founders." Jaric shook his head."One of those is not to wander the Borderlands at night, and don't open the gates after dark."

From the road behind them came a call, and Oslin glanced back. "The others are here."

More shouts announced the outriders of the Bronze Guard, and Prince Alesandr rode through the middle of the soldiers. He jumped off his mount, an elaborately armoured black war bear, throwing his reins to a squire.

"Captain Daynar!" the prince called, his regal attire catching in the dull light as he strode towards them.

Gone was the leather armour of the Rangers, and in its place was black kharidium mail covered by a black surcoat emblazoned with the Royal Crest – a charging, iron boar – in emerald and silver thread. A brooch, also in the shape of a boar, glinted where it held his sable-trimmed cloak in place.

Behind him, ever watchful, were his five Asp bodyguards in the same kharidium armour but lacking the heraldry of their royal charge.

"What's happened here, Jaric?"

"We arrived at the Arch as this Ranger from Sonyth came through." Jaric gestured at Cunning. "He was carrying a treewolf spider on his back."

"And he lives?" Alesandr asked. "Remarkable."

"The bite of a Treewolf can be fatal if not properly tended. The Rangers carry an anti-venom as a matter of course. It'll do until we can get him to the Keeper." Jaric rested his hands on his hips. "He brought word that Sonyth is under attack by a sizeable force of Korda'vari, at least two hundred strong."

"And Hearne and the others?" Bruday asked.

Jaric shook his head. "We've found no trace of them yet."

"They will be at Sonyth, surely," Alesandr said.

"Ned here didn't know anything about a squad of the Bronze Guard being at Sonyth."

"I will not give up on them until we know their fate, Captain Daynar," the prince said.

"Then we should move, Highness," Jaric said. "Sonyth needs our aid, and if your men are still alive, that's where we'll find them."

"Rowin," Alesandr called to Captain Bruday. "We rest for ten minutes, make sure the wagons are secure and the guards with the servants are aware of what we may be walking into."

"Of course, Highness," Captain Bruday said and gestured for a runner.

"Servants?" Kaiel blinked in surprise as Prince Alesandr moved away to look into the Arch. Why had the Prince brought his household? He should have left them in Hanore.

Kaiel looked back towards the wagon train that was still somewhat down the road.

"If you're looking for your brother, he stands with the Ciralys' mount," Jaric said, pointing to the horses much closer to the head of the party than Kaiel had imagined.

"Gods," Kaiel breathed. "He can't go to Sonyth. It's too dangerous!"

"We all leave home eventually," Jaric said. "And some of us go farther than others."

Meg stared out from the small window of her room on the first floor of the Keepers Tower. From her vantage she had a perfect view between the High Keep and the Keep of Hope right out to the main gates, and they had just closed behind the last wagon of Prince Alesandr's baggage train.

Darien had been on a carriage towards the front, leaving Hanore and the Borderlands to become a Ciralys. *Daemons take him.*

Well, she wouldn't stay here and rot while he went and made something of himself! They'd both been chosen by Old Shany because they could sense *Asai*. Why should he be the only one to leave and become a Ciralys?

Turning from the window, Meg crossed the short distance to her wardrobe and removed the pack she'd placed there the night before. She'd plundered the more long-lasting of Shany's stores; the hard bread, smoked ham, and some cheese. She'd also taken some of the herbs she'd gathered and prepared herself; maybe she'd be able to sell them when she reached Jaroff. Once there, she would work out exactly what she was going to do.

When she reached the capital in the west, well, then she'd present herself to a Chapter House of the Palace of the Eye and seek admittance to the Ciralys herself.

She just had to get there.

Meg opened the top of the pack and checked that everything was as she'd left it. She took out the note she'd written for Shany and turned it over in her hands, suddenly reluctant to leave. Taking a breath, Meg pushed her hesitation aside and placed the note on her bed. She paused for a moment in the small room that had been home for nearly fifteen years, then shouldered her pack and stepped out onto the wooden landing.

"I knew you were leaving."

Meg's heart leapt in her chest. "Sevaani! What are you doing?"

"Oh, Meg," Sevaani cried and threw her arms around her, burying her face on Meg's shoulder. "They've gone! I didn't expect it to happen so soon!"

"Sevaani!" She spoke more sharply than she'd intended. "What are you talking about?" She and Sevaani had never been close despite being of an age. Borderlanders tended to leave the Keeper and her apprentice at arm's length. Unless they needed something.

"They've gone!" Sevaani wailed. "Kaiel and Darien! And they won't be coming back, I *know* it!"

"Hush now," Meg said. "Of course Kaiel will come back. He won't see any fighting anyway. There are so many guardsmen with them, and over half the Rangers. He'll be back before you know it." *Unlike Darien.* She swallowed at the lump in her throat.

"No, he won't." Sevaani shook her head. "Nor will Darien. I dreamt it."

"A dream?" Meg just managed to stop her eyes from rolling.

"Yes. None of us come back!"

"A nightmare," Meg assured her. "He'll be fine. Kaiel has to come back. His idea of going off to join the Guard in Jaroff hasn't been finalised. I'm sure Master Malik and Mistress Breanta will talk him out of it." She extracted herself from Sevaani's clasp, anxious to get her out of the tower so she could get away unhindered.

"I know what you're thinking," Sevaani said. "But it's not about Kaiel leaving. Well… it is a little. But he and I, we aren't meant to... like you and Darien, we won't –" She broke off, blushing. Then she met Meg's eyes. "No, it wasn't a nightmare. It was different. I dreamt you left too, and I went with you."

"I left too?" Meg said. "I'm not going... you can't! Sevaani, it's too dangerous –"

"Don't you start on how dangerous it will be. You're no more Ranger trained than I! At least I'm dressed for it!"

And she was too, Meg had to admit, noticing for the first time what Sevaani was wearing.

Clothed in what could only be her brother's old Ranger's uniform, with a pack on one shoulder, Sevaani was infinitely more prepared for the forest than Meg was in her grey woollen dress. "I was about to change," Meg told her stiffly, then cursed as Sevaani's eyes lit with satisfaction. "All right! *I'm* going, but you're not."

"Oh, yes I am," Sevaani said, her satisfaction giving way to the air of determination she took on around Kaiel when he was being stubborn. "Because if I don't go, you won't be going either!"

"What do you mean?"

"I mean you won't get far if I tell Master Milan what you're planning."

"I'm warning you, Sevaani," Meg said, anger flaring within her. She breathed deeply, her voice swelling in her throat. "*Stay out of this.*"

Sevaani backed up a step, her brown eyes widening. "N-no. I won't."

"And you won't make anyone do anything with the Voice either, girl." Shany's words cracked across Meg from the landing above. "Not in my citadel."

Meg spun around as Sevaani gasped.

Standing in the shadows on the wooden steps above them, the Keeper had both hands on her bony hips, her single eye reflecting the light of the lamp hanging on a chain in the centre of the tower's well, glaring at her apprentice.

"What are you doing here?" Meg said, slumping. There was no way she'd get out now. She wanted to cry and then cursed her lack of control.

I will not turn into a babbling wreck like Sevaani. She straightened and drew back her shoulders.

"Waiting to see you off, that's what!" Shany snapped.

"But... what?"

Shany narrowed her eye. "What have I always tried to drum into that thick head of yours, girl?" she said. "Look around you, pay attention to *everything*. Actions speak louder than words! You're as moonstruck over Darien as she is over Kaiel! Foolish girls, chasing after men as though they will lead you to happiness. You are both of age and should know better. Hmph! Well..." She looked at Sevaani. "Some of you do know better. Still, I suppose it's not surprising. I'm lucky half the girls in the citadel aren't after them also." She eyed them both. "No. It would just have to be the two most important. Those young men are marked, and not by any of the Shol'mas either. So be warned!"

Meg's mind was reeling. "You're letting me go?"

"You're not a child anymore; I can hardly hold you back. You are going to follow that fool boy to the Ciralys. Much good it will do you." Shany walked down the steps to the first-floor landing and passed them both, continuing down. "Come on; we haven't got that much time. You won't reach them before they get to Sonyth in any case."

Meg, still reeling, only moved as Sevaani rushed after Shany.

"If you are to have your name entered into the *Book of Disciples*, Meghara," Shany continued, following the circling stairs down, "then you must demand admittance by Hedge Right. The Hedge Right of Shanaya dyn'Tian."

She held up a finger as Meg opened her mouth to speak. "Shanaya dyn'Tian. No questions, girl. If you live long enough, I might answer them. One day. The gods know you'll hear enough stories in the Halls of the Awakened once that name gets used."

She waited for the young women to join her. "The arrogance of the Ciralys will demand proof, they won't take your word for it. They'll want the *tresilian* they call the Tear of Scrying. Find a Ciralys of the Fifth Circle and ask to see the Spirit Seer. Give him this." She passed Meg a pouch she took from one of the many pockets of her robes. "It is a foul thing, and they will use it at their peril, but I warn *you*, girl. Do not attempt to use it yourself; I was lucky that I only lost an eye. Others, I have since discovered, lost far more."

Meg took the proffered pouch. It was tied with silver cording and something small and heavy, like a large pebble, sat inside the bag.

"The Spirit Seer?" she said.

Shany snorted. "The Ciralys are fond of their ranks and their titles. Each sphere, each Circle, aligns with an element, and the Spirit Seer of the Fifth Circle, the Circle of Sarmisere, is the leader of those Ciralys who are strongest with the sphere of spirit.

"Put that somewhere safe, and do not open it," Shany said. "The Ciralys are jealous of their secrets. If they believe you've touched the seals around the cording, they may take the *tresilian* and reject you out of hand."

Dazed, Meg put the pouch in a pocket.

"And you," Shany said to Sevaani, who shrank away from the Keeper's stare, only to stop and toss her head in defiance.

Shany smiled, not unkindly. "You don't know what you want yet.

Don't be so fast to throw away your future before it has presented itself. You must learn to follow your heart."

"That's what I am doing," Sevaani said.

"Oh, ho! You think so?" Shany cackled. "First, you need to learn to *hear* your heart, not what's between your legs! Young ones." She waved her hand. "You know everything. Find out where your heart is, the greatest healing comes from there."

The light from the lamp grew fainter the farther down they went, the darkness opening to swallow them like a gateway to the Void. The stairs led into the catacombs beneath the citadel, and Meg had even gone down them to the storerooms herself. But now her stomach twisted with trepidation at every step.

Shany directed them down past the landing that led to the cellars and unused rooms in the tower's roots. Stone still ruled in these lower levels, wooden stairs coming to an end above. Shany had refused the council access here, and the everstone – however black it was – was still sturdy beneath their feet. Sevaani slowed too, both hands pressed against the curving wall. Meg put a hand on the woman's shoulder in encouragement, and Sevaani grabbed it tightly.

Time stretched in the darkness, and though they'd been walking only a few short minutes, Meg was caught unprepared when Shany stopped, a wraithlike bundle of grey before them. The Keeper spoke, and a stirring caressed her mind as a spark blossomed into flame on a torch bracketed to the wall. The jewelled eyes of a pair of stone sphinxes reflected in the light, standing guard beside an unfamiliar archway.

"I've never seen this," she said. "How long has that been there?"

"Since the Tower was built, obviously. Do you think I had it built while you were asleep?" Shany said dryly. Then she asked, "Having second thoughts?"

"No," Meg said.

"Well," Shany snorted, raising an eyebrow. "It's good to see you have the courage of your convictions. You realise the amount of trouble this will cause? The Steward's daughter going missing?"

"I left my father a note," Sevaani said.

"Saying what?" Meg rolled her eyes. "That you've run after Kaiel? That will do Shany little good."

"Don't bring me into this," Shany said. "Old Taggart Lyman is going to have a hard time explaining how you two got past his closed gate, and you'd best come up with a story before you reach the Carbinah. Both Jaric Daynar and your brother –" she pointed at Sevaani, "are going to demand answers that will get back here even if you don't."

"Oh!" Sevaani's hand raced to her mouth. "I forgot Rolen would be there. He'll never let me go."

"You can always stay," Meg suggested.

"No," Sevaani said. "I'm going."

"So be it!" Shany reached into her pocket and drew out a small white stone carved in the shape of a feather. Tossing it into the air, she whispered a word. The stone feather flared a dazzling blue in the dark and transformed into a small white bird no bigger than a fist.

"A ghost owl!" Meg gave a start as the small bird flew to Shany's shoulder.

"He will lead you through the hidden way and then the forest after," Shany said. "Do not tarry, these passages are old, and the Borderlands are dangerous whether you were raised in them or not."

Meg was suddenly at a loss for words. "Shany, I…"

"On with you, girl," the old Keeper said gently. "Remember what you've learnt here. The Ciralys will disdain your witchcraft, but *Asai* flows through all things, not just what they deem it to."

Meg threw her arms around Shany, hugging her close and dislodging the ghost owl on her shoulder.

"The owl!" Sevaani cried. "It's flying off!"

A faint nimbus of light, like a halo, surrounded the bird as it flew into the dark tunnel.

"Go." Shany gave Meg a sad smile and pushed her away.

"Thank you," Meg whispered.

"Come on!" Sevaani chased after the owl.

Meg followed, running through the archway into the corridor beyond, the light of the ghost owl leading the way.

"Goodbye!" Meg called, turning back to Shany.

But where the Keeper had stood on the other side of the arch was an unbroken, black stone wall.

"Enjoying yourself looking after the horses, Darien?"

"Simeon!" He feigned surprise. "What are you doing here? Has Captain Daynar found all your hiding spots?"

"Ha, ha. Very clever," Sim grinned.

Darien looked up and levelled a stare at his brother's friend. Sim was shorter than Kaiel but still that bit taller than Darien, and the grin he gave – coupled with his black eye – lent him a roguish air. He was also one of the few people who had never been affected by Darien's stare.

"Go away, Sim," Darien said after a moment. Simeon was never completely serious in his teasing, but it prodded a raw nerve.

"Don't be like that!" Sim protested. "So why've you got horse duty?" He gestured at the white stallion whose reins Darien held. "Can't one of the guardsmen do that?"

"This is Ciralys Telaq's horse," Darien said. "As his apprentice, it's my place to take care of his things."

Sim ran a hand down the horse's snow-white neck. "So, you're really running off to the Spire?"

"Isoliere," Darien said.

"What?"

"I'm going to Isoliere," Darien said. "The Spire in Serjat is just a Chapter House of the Ciralys. The Holder of Names resides in the Palace of the Eye in Isoliere."

"Ciralys are all the same to me," Sim said. "And Isoliere is even farther north, so have fun. In any case..." He glanced away. "I wanted to wish you well."

"You're not going to try and talk me out of leaving too?"

Sim laughed. "I don't care if you go. Daemons, you have more than enough reason to want to get out of this dump. As soon as I'm able to, I'll be leaving as well."

Darien opened his mouth to reply when a shout cut over the top of him.

"Darien!" His brother's voice was unmistakable. "Dar. You can't come with us." Kaiel stopped in front of him and went on in a rush. "There are Korda'vari attacking Sonyth. You don't know how to fight, and I won't be able to protect you. You have to go back."

"Yesterday a borewyrm, today Korda'vari," Sim said. "This just keeps getting better!"

"Kaiel, stop," Darien said, ignoring Sim. "I'm apprenticed to Ciralys Telaq. Where he goes, I go. I might not be able to use a sword, but I can look after myself."

"Dar, this is different!" Kaiel grabbed him by the shoulders. "This isn't the danger Rangers normally face."

"Maybe so." Darien pulled away from his brother's grasp. "But I'm going with Ciralys Telaq. That's my place, just as you're going to go off with the Guard."

"That's not the same thing!"

Sim laughed. "It is the same thing. It's just you're heading off to play with swords, and Darien wants to go off and play with... I don't know, whatever it is Ciralys play with." He stopped short when he met Darien's glare.

"I was just trying to help." Sim raised his hands in surrender. "I'll go over and listen in on whatever His Highness is saying, then."

At the head of the column, Captains Bruday and Daynar were calling for order.

"Kaiel –" Darien turned back to his brother. "I am joining the Ciralys. You're going to join the Bronze Guard, or some other mercenary company. We've never spoken of it, yet we've both been planning it for years. I could never stay in Hanore once Shany had shown me there was that much more to the world." He raised a hand to forestall Kaiel's protest. "We're both leaving. We don't have many options as Borderlanders, but I can make something of myself in Isoliere, and you can do the same in the Guards. Don't ruin it because you're scared."

"I'm not scared," Kaiel protested, pulling himself up. "It's just... you're all I've got, Dar."

"Then don't push me away," Darien said, eager to end the conversation. "Get to Jaroff and train hard. The Palace of the Eye has an elite guard force; maybe you can get yourself a place there."

"What do the Ciralys need with guards?" Kaiel asked sceptically.

Darien laughed. "Ask some of your guardsmen friends about the Tal'desai."

Kaiel sighed, then squeezed Darien's shoulder before he moved off as Prince Alesandr called his captains to order.

"Captain Daynar," the prince said. "Are you ready to scout the way ahead?"

"Highness, I am."

Jaric saluted the prince, his fist thumping the left side of his chest.

"Very well then." Alesandr motioned and four horses were brought forward. "Take these mounts to speed you. We will make all haste, but wait for us before you reach Sonyth proper."

"Your will, Highness," the Captain of the Hanore Rangers said, and Darien watched as Jaric, Kaiel, and two of the guardsmen mounted their new steeds. At Captain Daynar's signal, the party spurred their horses forward and charged off through the Arch of Trees.

Darien swallowed past the lump in his throat. He knew Kaiel was only trying to protect him, but they had a whole company and most of the Hanore Rangers with them. If anyone needed protecting it would be Kaiel himself, not Darien.

Gathering the reins of Telaq's mount, Darien led the horse over to where his master waited with Prince Alesandr as the company prepared to leave.

It took the main party close to two hours before they finally caught up with Captain Daynar and Kaiel at a crossroads, the branches of which led to farms around Sonyth's outskirts. With them were wounded Borderlanders who had managed to flee the citadel, some in the leather armour of the Rangers, but the squad of guardsmen who had left Hanore the afternoon before were still unaccounted for.

Jaric, his face devoid of expression, gave a brief report to the prince. They'd ventured as close to the citadel as the outer walls, but the destruction raging inside warned them back to await reinforcements.

Had the sky been clear, Darien was sure they'd have seen smoke long before they reached the outlying pastureland. Like Hanore, cleared ground ringed the walls of the citadel, giving the farms that circled Sonyth a buffer that protected them from the flames. Behind those walls, black smoke poured into the cloud-covered sky. Prince Alesandr allowed detachments of the Rangers to scout the farms for survivors, but they all returned grim-faced and empty-handed.

Ciralys Telaq rode behind the prince and Captain Bruday, and Darien couldn't help but envy his calm, expressionless demeanour. His trepidation rose, chest tightening as they approached the citadel. Travelling into battle with Korda'vari was not what he had envisioned he'd be doing when he packed his master's chests. If Darien was ever to face any man, or creature, as dangerous as the denizens of Dal'mere, he wanted to do it as a fully-fledged Ciralys, not one who was barely a novice.

The scent of burning wood and the foul reek of torched flesh filled the air, and Darien gave up trying to focus until Prince Alesandr's squire blew his horn. At the head of the line, the prince raised his sword high, the dull light of the cloudy day glinting softly on the steel.

"Men and women of the Rangers and the Bronze Guard!" Alesandr's voice rang through the tense silence. "Mind your companions, 'ware the strength of the enemy and stay with your squad. We ride for Sonyth. For the Borderlands. For Aldania!"

CHAPTER SIX

Sonyth Burning

SIM WATCHED BLACK smoke billow from the burning citadel, cinders dancing across the surrounding fields like fireflies. Ash fell upon the ironwood gate that lay broken beneath rotted everstone and the glinting fragments of Sun Bells.

Screams swelled from within the citadel as the scent of blood and burnt flesh assaulted his senses, bile burning the back of his throat. Sim stood with the Rangers, trained as they were to fight the creatures that came out of the Deadlands, and eyed the Bronze Guard sure their martial order and life of obedience were all that kept them from running.

Raised in the arena of commerce by an autocratic father in his small merchant 'house', Sim had never imagined he'd join the Rangers and face the kind of fights of which Kaiel had always dreamed. When Kaiel talked of honour and glory and swords, Sim had dreamt of silver and gold and gems. Not the kind obtained by adventuring or indenturing himself in servitude to a House, but as the result of hard work and cunning. Those were his weapons, and he could wield them well. Not the sword now in the sweaty grip of his shaking hand.

Damn his father to the Void these monsters came from! He didn't have the temperament or desire to be part of the Rangers, but his father had insisted he take 'his turn'.

He was as far back in the line as he could get. If the rest of them wanted to get themselves killed, that was fine with him. They could race ahead; he'd follow, just that bit behind. He wasn't going to be fodder for these creatures. He had things to do, places to go. Secrets to uncover.

Dropping his hand to a pouch at his side, he tugged loose the leather ties and withdrew a large gold signet ring, set with a wine-red stone the size of his thumb. He imagined it must be a ruby. Carved into its surface was a raven in flight beneath a nine-tined coronet. The stone glittered like spilled blood.

He'd found the ring a month ago, hidden in a locked chest in his parents' storeroom. From the accumulated dust on the hardwood, it was apparent no-one had opened the chest in years. Unable to resist temptation, he'd set about working the old lock and delving into pieces of his parents' life before they'd arrived in the Borderlands. If they weren't prepared to give him answers about their past, *his* family history, he would find them himself. And with this ring, he had a place to start.

"What are you doing back here, Raven?"

He gave a start and dropped the ring back into the pouch as Rolen Etine and two of his toadies stopped in front of him.

Sim gave him a smile he reserved for the more annoying citadelfolk who came into his father's shop. "I'm where I'm meant to be," he said. "What are you doing? Why aren't you down the front of the line getting ready to impale yourself on the enemy?"

"Don't be flippant," Rolen snapped. "The Three Citadels stick together. You might not have any kin in Sonyth, but many of us here do."

Sim offered him a slight bow, mainly to hide his rolling eyes. "Well," he said. "I'm all set." He patted the leather satchel on his shoulder gently.

"Whatever's in that bag isn't going to help you against Korda'vari, Ravenson," Rolen jeered. "Remember your sword and try not to cut yourself with it."

Sim let his smile slide off his face as Rolen moved on and kept his hand on the leather bag. The round, fist-sized bulges in it gave him a small measure of comfort.

Without warning, a guardsman blew a horn. Cursing, Sim strove to hold back his panic and stepped forward with the men and women around him.

"Get your sword up!" someone in the line beside him called as they jogged forward, and Sim swallowed his reply.

Swords might be handy if you could use them, but he'd only paid half a mind to the old swordsman who'd tried to train him. For the most part, the younger recruits were kept to Borderland bows, the swords reserved for the Rangers proper. Most cadets would finish their duty to the citadel without ever having cause to face foes more dangerous than daemoncats and treewolf spiders.

As they drew closer, they came up against a wall of heat from the fire. Smoke stung his eyes, but the company carried him on.

Sim's stomach dropped at the wailing and cries as they entered the citadel. Shadows in the smoke became children fleeing hulking monsters. Women ran screaming, soot and blood-streaked faces drawn in masks of terror as they clasped smaller children to their breasts. The smell of smoke became underpinned with the tang of iron and faeces and Sim slipped, tripping over a wet rope. He looked down; gagged. The 'rope' was the intestines of a dead man. More bodies revealed themselves as he looked around, heart pounding. Some yet moved, but most were still. The more substantial forms of dead Korda'vari lay slumped against walls.

He stumbled, his legs suddenly weak. Ahead of them, five of the Tainted appeared. The creatures were huge, easily over seven feet tall. Red skin and dark stone carapaces made them look like fiends. How could he fight something so big? Wickedly curved black horns rose from ridged skulls. Stone-like protrusions extruded from their shoulders and flowed across their chests and legs. Sim gripped the hilt of his sword, his hands slippery with sweat. No, he couldn't fight a creature like that. Just one of them would crush him with a single blow of the axe it carried!

Sim screamed, but his cry was lost in the noise around him.

The clashing of steel erupted as momentum kept his squad moving forward, crashing into the beasts, while beside him a group of the Rangers broke off and stayed by the gates, calling to the women and the children, directing them out of the burning citadel.

Unlike Hanore, Sonyth citadel was comprised of only two Keeps, the others having collapsed into a sinkhole in the years after the Sundering. A town proper had sprung up within the protection of the everstone walls – a town of wood and stone that now burned. The crackling roar of the flames and the crashing of collapsing buildings blended in a cacophony with the screams and cries of the citadelfolk.

Sim stopped, his squad pushing past him. He turned and ran, desperate to get away. Sweat dripped into his eyes and soaked his tunic, and he stumbled as a falling beam of burning wood grazed his shoulder. He wrapped both arms around his satchel, spinning around in panic.

Which way was the gate?

Another Korda'var snarled somewhere behind him, and he ran once more, pushing along the street. Groups of men and women stood fighting together. The large blade of an axe swung out of the smoke towards him, and he ducked under it, screaming as the Korda'var wielding it charged at him. He fell over a child's body and scrambled back. A yelling guardsman crashed into the beast, and Sim was free.

Get up. Get up. Get up!

He found his feet and sprinted away.

The street was thick with Rangers, and he plunged into the middle of them to hide, pushing past people who were fighting for their lives. He cursed, unashamed at the fear driving him.

The sounds around him changed, and he looked up. He could make out Kaiel in the group ahead of him, slashing at a Korda'var. Just ahead of Kaiel was the prince, his bodyguards a blur of shadows as they engaged another of the Tainted.

Gods! He'd pushed himself towards the front of the fight, not away!

A flash of glowing red light caught his eyes, and daggers of fire flew from the raised hands of Darien's Ciralys master. Beside the old man was Darien himself, holding a staff out before him.

Sim cried out a warning as he saw a Korda'var looming in front of Darien, its fanged mouth wide as if in a roar though Sim couldn't make out anything over the noise. It swatted Darien's staff out of his hands like it was knocking aside a twig.

Darien's face lost all colour as the Korda'var drew back a jagged sword.

There were no guardsmen near to help.

Not stopping to think, Sim charged across the street. Digging his hand under the flap of his satchel, he yanked out one of the clay globes carefully packed inside and lobbed it across the remaining distance between them.

It struck the Korda'var on its stone plated back and exploded.

Light, and the roar of a giant explosion, bloomed in a wave that had him ducking for cover.

"Gods," he breathed.

Darien, his master, and nearby soldiers had been knocked off their feet by the blast.

Sim ran to Darien. Black scorch marks smeared the young man's face, and he blinked dazedly.

Relief washed over Sim and he grinned. "Sorry about that, Dar."

At Darien's blank expression, he raised his voice. "You'll be all right in a minute! That one was only a small egg." He gestured. "Couldn't let the Korda'var get you. He was aiming for your head, and I figured you'd need that if you want to get to Isoliere..." He stopped as black-clad warriors surrounded them.

Captain Daynar and Kaiel pushed their way through the Asp, who allowed them to pass at a nod from the prince.

"Dar! Are you hurt?" Kaiel grabbed his brother by the shoulders.

"The ringing in my ears is bad enough without you making it worse." Darien pulled himself back. "I'm fine, no thanks to your friend!"

"No thanks to me?" Sim gaped at him. "If it hadn't been for my dragon egg you'd be dead!"

A hand on his shoulder spun him around.

"Your what?" Captain Daynar glared at him. The man was as blood-splattered as Kaiel but less worn. "What by the Void did you just do, boy?"

"I would like to know that also," the Ciralys said from behind him.

Sim wiped the sweat off his brow with the back of his hand. "It's just something I thought might come in handy." He cast his gaze at the men surrounding him. No way out. On the other hand, no Korda'vari either.

"*What was it*?" Jaric repeated, pulling his attention back. The captain's voice was hard, and his eyes glinted in the orange light of the flames.

As surreptitiously as possible, Sim wrapped a fist around the strap of his satchel. "I call them dragon eggs," he said, falling into a practised spiel. "They're little balls of clay that pack a punch."

"In there?" Jaric said, making to grab his bag.

"Wait!" he yelled, backing into the solid presence of Kaiel. "Be careful. You could kill us all!"

Jaric thrust a finger at his chest. "That does not reassure me coming from the most irresponsible man in the Borderlands!"

"They're made of soft-fired clay," Sim said, turning the bag away from Jaric. "If you nudge them too forcefully..." He fought a smile as everyone but the captain and Kaiel took a step back.

"It's a delicate balance," he said, "but I know how to keep it secure."

"Simeon."The captain's teeth were clenched.

He sighed. "It's a mixture of quicklime, saltpetre, naphtha and... some other things."

"Are you insane?" Ciralys Telaq backed away another step.

"Yes, he is," Darien said. His tunic was scorched and black with... Sim squinted. Was that blood?

His best friend's brother pointed at the burning remains of the Korda'var hit by the egg. The top half of its body was gone, the road strewn with blackened gore and the fires that lined its legs burned an oily blue.

"Yes, he is mad," Darien repeated, breathing hard as though he was winded. "But effective."

"Effective?" Telaq scoffed. "You can't put that fire out! What Alchemist taught you such things?"

"Alchemist? No alchemist taught me. I made it myself! And the fire *will* go out. Eventually." He bent to examine his handy work.

Kaiel grabbed his shoulder. "The backroom...?"

Simeon grimaced. The 'unexplained fire' that had burnt out the backroom of his father's store a year past was indeed a result of his experiments.

"I've come a long way since then," he said, avoiding Kaiel's eyes. "And it looks as if it works pretty well to me."

Jaric rubbed his hand over his eyes. "And just what was the creation of this weapon in aid of?"

Sim shuffled his feet. "Well, originally, it was to help Ma light the stove faster. Then I thought I might be able to use it a bit differently. Maybe in mining and the like. Last time Da and I were in Jaroff, a trader mentioned that House Romale had plans to excavate the Saysarns. I had an idea that it might be useful there too." He gestured at the still burning Korda'var. "I didn't realise it would be this effective. The solution has only been mixing since early this morning. It gets stronger the longer you leave it."

Ciralys Telaq snorted. "I'm sure it does!"

"We're wasting time here," Prince Alesandr said, stepping past his guards. "You are confident they are secure?" Sim nodded. "Then this is a resource I can use. Stay alert and be careful what you throw them at. In fact, before you do throw any, call out a warning." He considered Sim. "When this is finished, we will talk more about this invention of yours."

Sim offered a short bow. "As to that, Your Highness... They are rather expensive to put together. But I suppose we could consider this a trial run."

"Indeed." The prince's gaze was cold.

"Hanore!"

A call came from behind them, and a bloodied troop of Sonyth's Rangers approached.

"Keru?" Captain Jaric said. "Is that you? Where are the rest of your Rangers? Where's Larnin?"

The patrol halted and Keru, a woman as wide as she was short, with greying hair and a soot-streaked face, saluted Jaric, right fist over heart, the back of her palm exposed and unmarked. "Captain Daynar. Captain Larnin has led over half the Rangers into the catacombs."

"The catacombs?" Prince Alesandr stepped forward.

The Sonyth sergeant's eyes widened, and she fell to one knee. "My Lord!"

Alesandr ignored the formality, waving her up. "There is no time. Tell me. Captain Larnin has gone to the catacombs beneath the ruins, you say?"

"Aye, he's following the Korda'vari." Keru glanced at Jaric. "They came out of the forest before first light. We didn't see them before it was too late. The only thing that slowed them was the gate, but the everstone crumbled almost as soon as they struck it."

"We saw," Jaric said.

"Captain Larnin sent the folk who would flee over the south wall. They were to get to Hanore."

"We saw none on the road," Ciralys Telaq said to the prince.

"No," Jaric agreed. "They would have been moving in groups along the hunting paths, not the road."

"And the squad of Bronze Guard I sent yesterday?" Alesandr said.

"Guardsmen?" Keru asked worriedly. "No guardsmen have come from Hanore until your arrival."

"We'll look for them later, Highness" Jaric said. "We fight here first."

Alesandr turned a fierce glare on the captain, then nodded. "Agreed."

Jaric gave a slight bow. "Keru, where are the rest of the Tainted?"

The Ranger took a deep breath. The troop behind her shifted, their eyes dull as more screams and howling cries echoed across the flames. "Once they were through the gates, groups of them headed off in all directions, starting fires as they went. All bar one fist – that one set out for the ruins right away," Keru said, pointing over her shoulder, back up the street.

"Simeon Ravenson," Prince Alesandr said. "You will come with us. We may have need of your eggs."

Sim grimaced and stepped forward reluctantly. "I only have a few left."

"Then you will have to use them sparingly. Ranger," Alesandr turned to Keru. "You lead."

"Yes, Your Highness!" Keru glanced at Captain Daynar, then saluted the prince. She turned and began marching up the street, her squad following.

Edging back, Sim stopped, surrounded by the rest of the men with Captain Daynar and Kaiel on one side, and a Bronze Guardsman on the other.

He sighed and let his hand fall to the hilt of his short sword, reassuring himself it was still there. Sim glanced once more at the flickering blue flames tracing the Korda'var on the ground and grinned. The first *real* test of the eggs had been a success.

He squinted through the smoky air at the back of Prince Alesandr. One thing was certain, though, he had no intention of answering any 'questions' later. If House Niskeri wanted his secret, it was going to cost them. It was going to cost them a lot.

Kaiel followed the squad up the main street. Collapsed walls and burning wood littered the road, and smoke haze obscured all lines of sight making the going treacherous. The two Keeps of Sonyth loomed high around him, dark square cliffs with tongues of flame licking the air from open windows that stared down at the broken and burning town.

The marauding Korda'vari had worked deliberately to create obstacles out of bodies and debris. Such a notion suggested more organisation than his training had suggested the Korda'vari possessed.

Keep your mind on the job. He couldn't let himself be distracted. But the elderly and children who had been hacked down played across his mind. He wasn't sure he'd ever get the stench of blood and burnt flesh out of his nose.

His step faltered, and he caught himself, forcing his back straight and concentrating on putting one foot in front of the other as Captain Jaric dropped back beside him. The pace the squad kept was light, but no-one was talking.

"How are you holding up?" Jaric asked.

"Well enough." Kaiel's answering smile was tight.

"These dragon eggs of Simeon's," the captain said. "Did you know about them?"

Kaiel glanced at Jaric, the expression on the captain's face intent as he kept his eyes moving. "He's never mentioned them to me."

Jaric grunted. "You've been doing well today."

"Thank you, sir." Pride stirred in his chest. "I haven't had much training with a sword. Even Master Taalren and Jidara only taught us the foundation forms."

"You can swing a blade," Jaric said. "These Korda'vari don't train like a human opponent might; they rely on their size and strength. You're fast, and you're strong. And you're still alive, so you're doing something right. If you're worried about where your strokes are landing, then seek the focus you find just before you release an arrow. It's hard to master in a sword fight, but if you can, you'll find uses for it in many things."

"I'll try," Kaiel said. *Light of the Eye, how do I do that*?

Suddenly they were at the end of the street, the fires falling away, and in front of them was the sinkhole.

The Sonyth Ranger halted, and Kaiel peered past the others into the enormous pit. From the edge, he could see the openings of exposed hallways leading into chambers constructed far below the citadel complex. Ramps, built by the Sola'vari when they still dwelt in Sonyth, gave access to those corridors, though here – as in Hanore and Tore – the Borderlanders had tended to leave the catacombs to the Var.

Behind them, two packs of Korda'vari broke cover from the burning buildings, roaring their challenge.

Kaiel spun around. He raised his sword and met the first Korda'var. Buoyed by the captain's advice, he kept his grip on the sword hilt firm but light and ducked under the creature's hacking chop to slice open its abdomen. The Korda'var fell back screaming, lashing out with its crude axe. Forced to retreat, Kaiel raised his sword in frantic defence, taken off-guard that his attack had been so successful. He blocked the Tainted's weapon, his arm going numb with the impact and pushed himself forward, yelling to hide his panic. He slammed his shoulder into the beast's chest, his mouth and nose filling with its unwashed, animal-like stench. It felt like he'd run into a stone wall, but the Korda'var staggered. Kaiel swung his sword around, using the strength of his upper body to add weight to his blow. The Tainted Var roared again and met the blade with a stone covered forearm, bringing its axe around with the other. Kaiel dropped, the blow whistling overhead. Panic bloomed, his heart racing as he struggled to regain his rhythm, the frenzied anger of the mortally wounded Korda'var refusing to offer him ground to recover.

The beast's knee came up, and Kaiel just managed to get his head out of the way as he fell to the ground. The Korda'var raised both arms above his head to bring the axe hurtling down, and Kaiel threw himself to the side as the weapon landed. He lurched to his feet, driving his sword up as he rose, pushing with all his strength and slicing into the underside of the Korda'var's arms as it pulled the axe from the ground. It roared and lowered its horned head, lunging forward. Kaiel staggered back,tripped and fell to the ground once more, air bursting from his lungs. The monster roared again, its features twisted with fury, its hot blood spraying over him as its axe swung towards him.

Kaiel saw the blow coming but couldn't move in time; he could barely catch his breath. He reached for the strength he needed; tried to move, and then his mind *opened*. The movement of the Korda'var slowed. The weakness in its defences appeared to Kaiel like gaping holes, and rather than waste time trying to dodge the coming blow he thrust his sword up, right through a gap in the stone plate and impaled the Tainted's heart.

It fell atop him with its crushing weight, and he scrambled to push himself out from under it as he battled for breath. He got to his knees, covered in black blood, and yanked his sword free just as Sim called across the battleground.

"Egg! *Get down*!"

Kaiel flung himself back to the ground as Sim hurled the clay ball into the midst of five Korda'vari charging from the burning buildings.

The explosion rattled his teeth. Korda'vari were sent flying, covered in blue fire and crashing to the ground like felled trees. Two were still alive, and Captain Daynar finished them off.

Kaiel got to his feet. Around him, men groaned, and two of the Asp Guard lay still on the ground, their black armour slick with blood, their own he supposed, though some was probably from the dead Korda'vari around them. Prince Alesandr stood over their bodies, his head bowed, and Kaiel looked away, grip knuckle-white on his sword hilt.

This was his first battle, but it wouldn't be his last.

CHAPTER SEVEN

Into the Catacombs

DARIEN SURVEYED THE open ground around the edge of the sinkhole. Bodies of Bordermen and Korda'vari were strewn about, lying dead or dying where they fell. Smoke still smothered the air, but the heat from the fires was easing. Or he was getting used to it.

He eyed the Rangers wandering amongst the fallen, long daggers in hand, dispatching Korda'var who still moved, calling for help when they found one of their own still alive.

"And thus, they come at the hour of our need."

Darien spun to the voice. From the street behind them, next to a Sonyth Ranger, was an old man leaning on a staff of banded oak. The Keeper of Sonyth.

"Captain Daynar, your assistance is most timely." The Keeper's voice rasped with age. His eyes were a smoky white, but he shifted his blank gaze to Prince Alesandr without error. "Your Highness." He offered a bow.

"Keeper Terias," the prince said. "You mentioned the dangers that ranged against the citadels when last I saw you, but I never expected this."

Terias smiled grimly. "Life in the Borderland Wilds is full of danger, but we have not seen Korda'vari move so boldly in over five hundred years."

"I sent a squad of the Bronze Guard to Sonyth yesterday afternoon." Alesandr told him. "Do you know of them?"

"The afternoon, you say?" The old Keeper cocked his head. "They would have made the last part of the journey at night. You must have been warned by the Hanore Rangers?"

The prince's jaw tightened. "Have you seen them?"

"No," Terias said. "And if you have not, then I fear they are lost."

"Aldania does not give up its men so easily," Alesandr said.

The blind Keeper shook his head. "I fear the turning of the Ages is upon us. I grieve for your loss but the missing guardsmen will have to wait. Your Highness, by the First Covenant of the Clans, I call on you to defend the oath of the First Lord of Aldania."

Darien blinked in surprise at the Keeper's words and watched Prince Alesandr look at Ciralys Telaq with a raised eye.

"What are they talking about?"

Darien gave a start as Kaiel appeared beside him.

"Lower your voice," Sim hissed at Kaiel from Darien's other side before asking, "Well?"

"His Highness is being asked to honour the oath sworn in Serjat after the fall of the Var Imperium," Darien said. "The High Houses swore to defend Athmay from the Sahrin, should they return."

"House Niskeri was not present at the First Covenant, nor have they been ratified to uphold its tenets in their predecessor's place," Jaric said, joining them. "I'm surprised the Keeper isn't aware of this."

But Alesandr raised his right fist to his heart. "As a Prince of House Niskeri, holders of the Ivy Throne, I acknowledge my duty to defend Aldania and all its environs."

Terias cracked a skeletal smile. "That will do."

"One of the Sonyth Rangers said Korda'vari entered the catacombs. What are the Tainted Var looking for?" Telaq stepped beside the prince. "And how could they hope to find it? It's a maze down there."

The Keeper lowered his head."They are led by someone who knows the way," he said."A daemon struck Sonyth last night also, and claimed a host."

Claimed a host? Darien's heart leapt as he thought of the shadow-bird.

The guardsmen behind Darien murmured, but Captain Bruday silenced them with a look.

"A daemon?" the prince scoffed."Surely, you jest! There have been no daemons on Sobia in over three thousand years!"

"That is not entirely true, Your Highness." Jaric stepped forward.

"Not *entirely* true?" Ciralys Telaq repeated, turning to the captain.

"Dal'mere once housed the last bastion of the Summoners," Jaric said."The Veil is thin there, which is why the Kas'tirien still exist."

"You have seen a daemon?" the prince asked.

"The Kas'tirien do their job well," Jaric said."There's been no full manifestation in centuries. But that doesn't stop would-be Bloodlords from seeking out the places where *Des'maadr* still seeps through the cracks between our worlds, poisoning the land. The things that are stories to anyone living north or west of Jaroff are real dangers here."

Alesandr stared at Jaric."Very well, so this person has become a nomen. But if you know this, you could have killed it, surely? A nomen's danger lies in our inability to detect them."

"Only those without the ability to see and wield *Asai* are made nomen," Terias said.

Alesandr frowned."So, not a nomen then. Whom did it take?"

"It has possessed my apprentice."

Darien gasped.

"Even the most promising students can be tempted by the power of the Void."

Though Terias addressed Alesandr, Darien was sure his words were meant for him.

"It was Di'shana, the Queen of Daemons who tempted and enslaved the Sahrin," Ciralys Telaq said. "And She has slept in the Void since her forces were defeated in the War of the Summoners."

"What makes you believe She sleeps, or forgets, any more than we do?" the Keeper asked solemnly. "Not all servants of the Void are born power-hungry monsters. Some are tricked, others *tempted*. Her daemons still seek a way for her to consume this world." Terias sighed. "Highness, please come. Time is of the essence."

The old Keeper shuffled to the edge of the sinkhole and stepped onto a rough-hewn path that descended from the lip and spiralled along the inside wall to a broken tunnel.

Alesandr motioned to Captain Bruday, and the Bronze Guard fell in behind him.

"We did not reach the catacombs this way when last we visited," Telaq said as they followed the Keeper down the narrow path. "And those catacombs were spread out below the ground outside the citadel's walls. Does this path lead to catacombs under the citadel itself?"

"It is the duty of the Keepers to hold the secrets of the catacombs safe," Terias said. "It would be our failure were we to allow people into the catacombs proper."

"'The catacomb's proper'?" Telaq snorted. "I've just spent three years in the catacombs beneath Hanore; I assure you I explored them thoroughly. And what of your Var? Do they burrow beneath this citadel as they do in Hanore?"

"The Sola'vari took many of the children and elderly to safety when the Korda'vari attacked," Terias said. "And I dare say you only saw the parts of the catacombs Keeper Shany opened to you. You can only see this path because I have revealed it."

"Enough, Telaq," Alesandr said before the Ciralys could respond. "I would very much like to see what has been kept hidden from me."

Darien followed more carefully, forcing himself to concentrate as he descended the steep path. The pit opened on his left in a vertigo-inducing drop. Wind whistled around the sheer walls and tugged at his limbs. He couldn't help looking into the open hole, but just as quickly averted his gaze. The light from the sky only fell so far before meeting darkness, and in that glance, he could make out no bottom at all. He almost cried out with relief when they reached the opening of the catacombs, and stepped into the dark tunnel, and away from the yawning chasm behind him.

On either side of the entrance stood winged lions carved from onyx; the messengers of Garnavaar, the Elder God of Earth. As a Ciralys, Darien knew the source of his own power lay not in the hands of the gods, but in *Asai*, yet he still had a healthy respect for the gods that ruled the elemental spheres the Ciralys touched.

He followed the prince and Telaq past the statues, the light from the entrance growing fainter as the hall opened upon widely spaced stairs that led deeper underground. Dark openings were spaced intermittently either side of the immense passageway, and shadowy alcoves held ghost-white everstone statues that had to have been crafted by the Sahrin.

"Darien," Telaq said quietly. "I would speak to you."

Darien stepped to the side with his master as the others filed past.

"You recall I spoke last evening of the *Tome of Ascension*?" Telaq said.

Darien nodded. "Yes, Master, but I don't know what it is."

"Few outside the Ciralys do." Telaq glanced around before he continued. "*Asai* is not just the Light of the Eye, it is also the runes, the language that, powered with the Light, creates changes in the world around us. The Sahrin could look at a tree and see the runes that shaped the *Asai* that formed it; its *name*. They could see these runes everywhere. Ciralys can use the runes the Sahrin shared with us, we can see them when they are empowered with the Light, but we cannot *see* them in the natural order of the world around us. That is why we seek the Tome.

These books are said to be a codex of every High Asairic rune the Sahrin ever recorded. We have not had access to a *Tome of Ascension* since the Sundering. We need to find one to unlock the secrets the Sahrin never thought to share outside their own order."

"They didn't teach us everything?" Darien asked.

"We do not know," Telaq said. "But if we can find a copy of the tome, perhaps we could unlock the secrets that allowed the Sahrin to see *Asai* everywhere."

"And you believe it is in the Borderlands?"

"Ciralys seek signs of it wherever we go, and the catacombs of the Borderlands' citadels are some of the few places built by the Sahrin that remain standing. Keep your eyes open while we are down here."

"Yes, Master."

Telaq nodded and moved away. A moment later Darien felt a tingling of *Asai* and light flared above them as his master summoned a sunglobe. Murmurs filled the hall as the shadows were pushed back to pool at the edges of the stairs like dark puddles. The light revealed walls of rose marble riddled with sparkling veins of gold and framed by pillars of viridian everstone that supported an arched ceiling glittering like glass. Darien couldn't help but be surprised, though he tried to hide it. Did halls like this reside in the catacombs under Hanore?

They all stopped as the Keeper came to an abrupt halt.

On the stairs lay the bloodied remains of two Korda'vari, and between them a third body, slimmer than the Tainted Var, but too elongated to be human. Sharp-edged hooves protruded from the long, black leather kilt that covered its legs; clawed fingers curled at a gaping hole in its chest cavity. Darien covered his mouth. He could make out the floor through the hole in its chest.

"Is that a Lloth'var?" Prince Alesandr asked, disbelief painting his tone as his Asp guard drew closer to him.

"Yes," Jaric said.

"I thought the Lloth'var never left Halaron,"Telaq said.

"You're misinformed."Jaric crouched before the slaughter, studying the scene with a composure Darien envied."While it isn't a common occurrence, thank the gods, it's not unheard of."

"Surely only a Blay Shon of Amaria or swordsmen just as accomplished could defeat a Lloth'var. What is down here that could stand against a Shadowstealer?"the prince asked.

"A power far older than the one you seek,"Terias said, stepping around the bodies."The Keepers are not the only line of defence for the secrets we help hide."

"What are the others?"the Ciralys demanded.

"There is only one other,"Terias said.

Alesandr gestured."Then lead us on to this apprentice of yours –"

The prince was cut off by a howling wail that rose out of the darkness.

The cry ended as suddenly as it began, and the troop remained still in the silence.The flickering of the torches and the glow of the sunglobe dimmed inexplicably, and Darien folded his arms around his chest to hide the shaking of his hands.

Without warning, one of the Asp Knights sprang forward. The darkness beyond the ring of light enveloped him completely, and the clash of steel meeting steel rang loudly as bestial snarls filled the air.

Captain Daynar called for the torches to be brought to the front, and Ciralys Telaq's sunglobe spun ahead to reveal a Korda'var fighting the prince's bodyguard. The beast was bigger than any of the Korda'vari Darien had seen outside and wore finely crafted black chainmail over the plate-like stone that grew on its body.

It parried the furious blade of the Asp Knight and bellowed its battle cry. Sparks flew as the prince's elite scored a blow on the monster's stone-plated arm. Its terrifying roar reverberated in the tunnel, and Darien stumbled back amongst the mingled Guardsmen and Rangers. He couldn't stop his body from shaking, and Kaiel's warning that it was dangerous out here echoed in his mind. His brother was right, damn him. Darien wasn't a soldier. He wasn't even wearing armour! Closing his eyes, he reached for *Asai*, the silver light flooding his mind and filling him with energy. But there was nothing he could do with the power that flowed into him; none of the minor teaching cants he'd learned could protect him from the fury of the monster before them. He had no proper training. Darien could call flame and air, he could mould light, but he couldn't help here. He stepped back again, jostling himself sideways and letting an armoured member of the Rangers move into the space before him like a shield.

Darien breathed deeply, trying to steady his nerves when a rune unlike any he'd encountered floated past his mind's eye.

Startled, he released the *Asai* he'd been holding, and the burning flick of the energy seared his mind in backlash.

He was jolted out of his reverie as arrows shot past his head. Most missed the Korda'var as the archers sought to avoid the prince's knight, but as one raised its arm to bring a massive sword down on the man before it, an arrow pierced it through a gap between its plated fist and stone vambrace. It dropped the weapon, bellowing in pain, and ripped the arrow from its wrist. The knight took advantage of its distraction, punching his sword through the Korda'var's exposed neck before it could attack again. The horned beast gurgled and then collapsed, its mail armour ringing as it hit the ground in the sudden silence.

Prince Alesandr gestured, and two more knights sprang forward, their black silk and leathers gathering shadows around them as they disappeared into the hall, while the third went to check on the knight who'd engaged the Korda'var. Captain Daynar came forward to inspect the corpse, dropping to one knee and running his fingers over its armour.

"This is kharidium," he said.

"Where in the Void did they get that?" Captain Bruday demanded.

"The forges of Halaron burn once more," Keeper Terias said wearily.

"Then why all the rusted swords and mail on those beasts outside?" The Captain of the Bronze Guard was incredulous. "Even if their armourers could forge kharidium the Xious'bisan are the only source of the metal, and they wouldn't trade with such as these!"

"Who knows what the Ants would do?" Jaric said. "Before the Sundering, the Korda'var hordes had master armourers with access to the same knowledge as those of the Realms." Jaric got to his feet. "And they're kin to the Var whose imperium ruled the Broken Continent for over a thousand years after the Sundering. Be grateful this is all we've seen."

A shout came from the ranks behind, and Darien flinched. But instead of more Korda'vari descending on them, a globe of pure white light soared through the air, coming to rest directly above him. There it began to spin and cast down a soft glowing radiance.

"Darien," Ciralys Telaq said. "Move away."

He obeyed his teacher without question, but the light moved with him.

"That," Jaric said, "is a ghost owl."

"Shany," Darien whispered. Ghost owls were a thing of the Keepers. He peered over the heads of the company to the stairs behind them, and Captain Daynar pushed through the soldiers as three newcomers came into view.

"Talien!" Jaric barked, causing the young man to pull up short. "I believe I left you outside the walls to assist Berrat and Arlun with the survivors."

The gangly young man went red. "Yes, sir, you did."

"Well?" Jaric said.

"Sir?"

"What are you doing here?"

"Present your hands!" Prince Alesandr spoke before Talien could reply.

The newcomers quickly raised their right hands for inspection.

Jaric looked them over. "They're unmarked," he said. "Now tell me why you're here."

"Sir, it's Meg, sir. And Sevaani." He glanced at the young women beside him. "I… I couldn't stop them. They were going to come in no matter what! I thought it best if I came with them to make sure they were all right."

"Stop bullying him, Captain." Meg stepped forward, the light of the ghost owl settling on her flame-coloured hair. Her eyes searched the crowd. "He wasn't going to let us come in here by ourselves. You should be proud of him; he helped us."

"He did, Captain Daynar," Sevaani said, clutching at Meg's shoulder. "If it weren't for Talien that monster would have… would have –" Her voice broke.

"Sevaani?" Kaiel said.

"Kaiel!" she cried and pushed through the party, launching herself into his arms. "Thank the Elders! It was horrible!" Sevaani's face froze as she took in the remains of the Korda'var behind him and she let out a shriek.

"Sevaani!" Rolen Etine pulled his sister out of Kaiel's arms. She blinked in surprise then clutched at him, burying her face in his shoulder.

"Captain Daynar." Prince Alesandr was unamused. "What is the meaning of this?"

"Your Highness," Jaric said. "I'll send them back to the surface."

"No, you won't," Meg said in her best imitation of Shany. "I didn't trek all this way to be sent back now." She set her feet apart, her hands on her hips.

Darien made his way up the stairs. "Meg, what are you doing?" he asked urgently. "It's dangerous here. People are dying!"

"I… I'm going to Isoliere too," she said.

Darien stared at her; his mouth open.

She blushed. "I have Shany's blessing!"

"Get your people in line, Captain Daynar!" the prince snapped. "We have no time for this."

Jaric offered him a bow. "Your will, Your Highness."

"No," Meg said, standing straighter. "I am not a member of your Rangers, Jaric Daynar and I will not be ordered about as if I were!"

"You are a subject of Aldania!" Captain Bruday roared. "And a Prince of its ruling House has spoken!"

Meg opened her mouth, protest written along the lines of her face when Keeper Terias spoke. "She is an initiate of the Witching Ways; she may be of assistance."

"My sister isn't, though!" Rolen said indignantly. "She shouldn't be here at all."

"Keep to the back," Jaric sai. "And if the odds we face are overwhelming, *run*!"

Meg's face went blank, but she gave a swift nod of acceptance. Darien stared. Meg was coming to Isoliere too? Part of him wanted to scream in outrage – this was *his* dream, *his* plan, but he pushed it back. Meg was his friend. It would be good to have a friend in Isoliere. Wouldn't it?

"Your Highness." Captain Bruday called, gesturing at Keeper Terias, who had begun to make his way down the stairs.

"Get the men together," Alesandr ordered. Surrounded by his Asp Knights, he stepped into the darkness leaving the others to follow.

CHAPTER EIGHT

What Lies Beneath

THE SHADOWS WERE heavy in the corridor, but Sevaani's blonde hair caught the light, and Kaiel's attention, like a beacon.

He slowed, letting others jostle him aside. What was Sevaani doing here? *Why* had she left the citadel? He was worried enough about Dar heading north, having to cross two realms to reach Isoliere. Now he had Sevaani to worry about as well?

He smiled briefly. Sevaani was a more attractive prospect to worry over, he had to admit, but he didn't know if he and Sevaani still had a future. He was leaving Hanore to join the Bronze Guard, or even the Ciralys guardsmen that Dar had mentioned, and that was no life for a young woman like Sevaani. He had to set her straight if they ever got–

Someone knocked into him from his left.

"Sorry." His apology was automatic, being so much bigger than his friends had made him wary of hurting others.

"You will be, warren-rat."

Rolen Etine spun Kaiel around, his face marred with anger. "What is Sevaani doing here?" he hissed.

Kaiel ground his teeth. The last person he wanted to speak to was Sevaani's brother. "Don't try me, Rolen. You only won in the Trial because you're a coward."

"Prove it!"

Kaiel's breath left his lungs as Rolen's fist slammed in his stomach.

"That's right," Rolen sneered. "You can't, can you? And even if you could, no-one would believe *you* over *me*." Rolen pressed him tight against the wall. "What is my sister doing here?" His breath was hot as he glared up at Kaiel's face.

Kaiel pushed himself upright and shouldered Rolen back. "Sevaani showing up is no plan of mine."

"I told my father he should never have allowed her to spend as much time with you as he did. You've had her wrapped around your finger for years. You're as bad as that snake of a brother of yours, both of you cosying up to your betters –"

"Our *betters*?" Only his anger hid his surprise. "You're not my better, you coward! Neither of us is Houseborn!"

"Even growing up a bastard you had the citadel fawning over you. If I hadn't taken matters into my own hands, you would have been a fucking Kas'tirien as well. My family has held Stewardship over Hanore since the Sundering! We *are* your betters. And now you've dragged my sister into danger."

"I haven't dragged her anywhere." Kaiel's anger turned cold, and his hands closed into fists. "No promises have ever been made between Sevaani and me, and I have *never* compromised her honour. Say it again, and you will never finish your training!"

Rolen's laugh was ugly. "Try it, warren-rat." He made to yank Kaiel down by his collar, but Kaiel didn't shift. "Stay away from her."

"Is there a problem, Etine?" a Ranger asked from behind.

Rolen glared at the man over his shoulder and pushed himself away from Kaiel. "No problem."

"Then keep moving!" Kaiel, his eyes still on Rolen, recognised the roar as belonging to old man Joron, Captain Daynar's second.

"Stay away from her!" Rolen growled again before shoving his way back to his position at the front.

Kaiel took a deep breath."Eye blind me!"

"He givin' you trouble?"Joron asked, watching Rolen leave.

Kaiel glanced at the older man."Just surprised me is all."

"Surprised?"The old Ranger offered a half-laugh."Maybe you need to stop being so trusting and borrow some of your brother's wariness. Rolen Etine is a bad seed."Kaiel looked at Joron, and the man shrugged. "The boy smells off to me, and I'm not the only one to think so."He spat to the side."In the meantime, you'd best do something about his sister, because whether you want it or not, I'd say there is a promise she means to get out of you."

"*What*?"

Joron's laugh was full this time."It ain't for nothing she and Meg have followed you two boys here."

Kaiel craned his neck over his shoulder again. For a moment, his eyes met Sevaani's, and then she lowered her head. He wasn't sure what he was doing, or where he was going; he couldn't take her away from her family.

Could he?

Joron left Kaiel to his thoughts, and the walls grew taller as they continued. The columns girding their sides soared higher, supporting a ceiling hidden in shadows. Before them the hall widened into a yawning darkness the Ciralys' light did little to banish.

Somewhere down the corridor, a blood-chilling cry erupted, different to the wail they'd heard earlier.

"What in the name of the gods was that?"someone asked.

The cry came again, and the ground rumbled. Members of the Bronze Guard muttered, their officers urging them all back into line while the Rangers exchanged looks but remained.

"The Korda'vari have woken the guardian." The Keeper's voice carried clearly in the high-ceilinged hall."Come, we have little time."

For all that he was blind, the old Keeper moved quickly, stepping without hesitation as he made his way into the dark while Kaiel moved along with the others in his wake.

"Be alert!" Prince Alesandr called as he followed the Keeper.

Kaiel was caught up in the crowd as the Bronze Guard marched down the corridor at pace. He tried to catch sight of Darien but was forced to keep his attention on the men and women ahead.

Around them a misty light pushed back the dark, pulsing behind panels of glass that ran in long stripes along the walls and another roar sounded from somewhere ahead. Swallowing with a suddenly dry throat, Kaiel tried to focus as they continued forward.

The corridor ended abruptly, and Kaiel blinked as he stepped into a chamber of dazzling light. Noise washed over him. The clashing of swords joined the roaring, grunts and bestial cries of the Korda'vari they had been searching for.

The immense chamber spread out before him in a perfect circle. Wider than the Ranger's assembly yard back in Hanore, it was lit by an enormous, glowing lattice buried in the ceiling high above. Alcoves with statues of lean, graceful figures in alien armour dotted the curved walls, and racks of glinting weapons were ranged beside the alcoves.

"Dragon!" Captain Bruday cried, panic lacing his voice as he entered the chamber behind Kaiel.

Kaiel finally turned his eyes to the fight in the centre of the room and froze, his blood running cold.

On a raised platform amongst gems and gold, raged an enormous lizard-like skeleton, its bones carved with runes and peppered with gems. On the floor before it was an ivory box, inlaid with gold-worked runes. The box's sides had unfurled like a flower opening to the sun, and a black gem pulsed within, releasing a dark mist that sent questing tendrils to the skeleton above it, wrapping around its bones like ivy.

"Guardsmen. Attack!" Bruday shouted.

"No!" Terias called, raising his staff. "The bone drake is not our enemy. The Lloth'vari seek its possession!" But his protests were ignored.

Kaiel's heart was pounding. What was a dragon doing here? There were no dragons in the Borderlands! He'd read of them, and the creature battling the Korda'vari could have matched those descriptions but for the fact it was a skeleton. There were no scales, no flesh. It was *undead*. Bones that framed the shape of its wings clattered as they rose in the air behind its massive body while its long tail lashed back and forth, sweeping the panicked and mewling Korda'vari from their feet. As Kaiel watched, the bone drake snapped its great horned skull forward, opening its huge jaws and releasing a river of flame to strike those before it. Tiny arcs of lightning sparked along its bones, setting shadows in the room flickering as though they were caught in an electrical storm.

"Rangers!" Captain Daynar raised his voice against the din. "For the citadels!" The Bordermen answered his call. Kaiel gritted his teeth, ignored his sweaty palms and drawing his sword, joined the answering cries from the Rangers around him and ran into the madness.

He slashed his sword across the back of the first Korda'var, momentum pushing him forward. The Korda'var roared and turned, swinging its axe. Kaiel parried, his blade shuddering.

He swore, moving to block another hacking swing as the Tainted bellowed. Kaiel ducked under the blow, and pulled a long dagger from his belt. Shifting his stance, he brought his sword around with all his strength. He met the Korda'var's chop with jarring force and twisted, following his momentum around to slash his dagger across the creature's unprotected throat. The Korda'var fell back, blood flying, and Kaiel yelled in triumph.

Another of the twisted Var took its place. Kaiel met the beast's sword with his own but stumbled, heart hammering. The Korda'var swung again, pushing its advantage. Kaiel managed to bring his sword up, only for the Korda'var's strike to send his blade spinning across the floor. The

Korda'var roared, jumping forward, bashing him with a stone-covered forearm, knocking him to the ground. It raised its sword to strike.

Kaiel rolled, scrambling out from under the blow, his head ringing. Desperation washed away panic, and he heaved himself up, looking around wildly for another weapon. His dagger would be of little use by itself, but the room had racks of weapons against the walls. The Korda'var roared again, and he dodged, taking the edge of the sword against his left flank. Pain sliced across his side. Clenching his teeth, he made for the racks, grabbing the first weapon he reached.

His hand wrapped around an old battle spear. The blade on its end was as long as Kaiel's forearm, the body made from a surprisingly light metal. He spun back to face the charging Korda'var and blocked its blow with the shaft of the weapon. The metal vibrated slightly as it met the sword but stopped the blow cold.

Kaiel twirled the spear in his hands and silently thanked his Kas'tirien trainer for insisting he learn to use a quarterstaff.

He jammed the butt against the Korda'var's exposed wrist, making it drop its sword. Kaiel twisted his torso, spear held with both hands, blade pointing out, and swung it forward to meet the Korda'var's charge.

The blade sank through the creature's stone breastplate with shocking ease, piercing its heart like a dagger plunged into snow. The lack of resistance caused Kaiel to stumble, and the weight of the dead Korda'var almost dragged the spear out of his hands. Shaking himself, Kaiel pulled the spear free of the still-writhing body.

The blood on the spearhead disappeared, and a pulse of golden energy travelled down the pole and into his hands. His chest relaxed; his laboured breathing eased. His heart slowed its frantic pounding.

The spearhead shone bronze in the light. Tiny runes revealed themselves, inscribed along the sharp edge of the blade and continuing down the haft, which was made of a black metal Kaiel had never seen in the smithy. The pole showed no signs of damage, even where struck by the Korda'var's sword, and was no heavier than an oak staff.

Its length fit him perfectly.

In the centre of the room, both the Rangers and the Bronze Guard battled with the Korda'vari. Tightening his grip on the spear, Kaiel charged back into the fray.

Darien stumbled as he entered the chamber and *Asai* flooded his mind, its silver light framing his vision. The Light of the Eye blazed in the crystalline lattice on the ceiling. It hummed, vibrating in his bones. Darien clenched his hands, his nails digging into his palms. He tried to force his mind to stillness, only to stop when he spied the bone drake on a dais below the lattice. But it was the box before it that clawed for his attention. It was a Daemonartis Trap; he was sure of it. They'd been used in the War of the Summoners to catch and hold daemons of enormous power. And this cube's sides were white, traced with runes of gold. It had been used. And now it was open.

Captain Bruday called to the Bronze Guard, and he was aware they ran to face their foes, but he couldn't take his eyes from the horror before them.

His life was in danger. *Everyone's* life was in danger. Dragons were incredibly powerful; even the Sahrin had existed with them in an uneasy peace.

Darien's attention was wrenched away by a shadow sliding across the light of *Asai* that shone in his mind, like a cloud passing before the sun. He turned to his master, but Telaq was already stalking ahead as a Lloth'var stepped out from behind the Korda'vari.

Unlike the soldier caste of the Korda'vari, the Lloth'var had no stone armour sprouting from its skin. It was as tall as the Korda'vari it commanded, but lean where they were broad. Elegant where they were clumsy. Controlled where they were wild. Its crimson eyes glowed from an elongated, leonine face of chiselled beauty painted with malice. Razor-sharp teeth filled its mouth behind blood-red lips that split in silent laughter. A long, slim sword of black metal drank the light, stretching out from a gauntleted fist. Ebony scale mail covered its torso.

A chill sprung across the back of Darien's neck, moisture vanishing from his throat like the light absorbed by the Lloth'var's sword. He couldn't help but stare. The prowess of the half-daemon Lloth'vari was legendary. Swifter than any human or Var, their daemonic beauty and strength made a lethal combination few could match.

"Ciralys." Captain Daynar stepped over the bodies of the Korda'vari before them. "Stand back." He raised his sword. "I'll face the Shadowstealer."

Telaq hesitated and then laid a hand on the captain's sword, tracing upon it a line of runes that flamed along its length before settling into a dull red glow. The Captain of the Rangers nodded his thanks, then faced the Lloth'var.

The world exploded into motion.

Darien couldn't help but be impressed as Captain Daynar became a whirlwind of spinning steel. The Lloth'var countered every slash of Jaric's blade, its black sword hissing as it met the *Asai*-touched steel. They both moved fluidly, circling each other as though in a dance, their steps pulling them back and forth across the entrance to the corridor where Darien stood with Meg and Sevaani huddled close behind him.

The Lloth'var moved like a snake, its body twisting, its black blade meeting the sword of the Captain of the Hanore Rangers who was displaying a skill Darien had never imagined he possessed.

Shadow struck fire, the black sword snapping out at each thrust of the captain's glowing red sword. They both pressed forward, Jaric giving way to the twisted Var's inhuman strength when an arrow hit the Lloth'var in the back, causing it to stagger. Jaric struck without hesitation, his sword lashing out and severing the creature's left arm.

The Lloth'var screamed, its cry exploding like breaking glass, and it leapt towards the captain, who spun aside.

Impossibly, the Lloth'var moved even faster than before, elegance discarded as it hacked at Jaric in a fury. Its assault forced the captain back against the edge of a doorway. It struck at him in a blur until suddenly Jaric dropped to one knee, the half-daemon's sword striking above his head and embedding itself in the corner of the entrance. Jaric rolled out from beneath it, swinging his sword and taking off its head.

Behind him, Sevaani screamed as the Lloth'var's body fell twitching to the ground.

Captain Daynar stepped back, careful to avoid the black blood that gushed from the monster's neck. He wiped his blade on its black silk tabard, and steam rose from the cloth.

The cacophony of steel and screams, and the rallying calls of Bronze Guard sergeants brought the small group back to the danger they still faced. The ground rumbled as the bone drake roared again, its fury and flame striking Korda'vari and humans both.

"Darien," his master called. "Stay here. I must assist His Highness."

Prince Alesandr was across the room in a knot of Korda'vari, his black-clad bodyguards tight around him, swords ringing in defence of their lord. Their protective circle tightened as one of their number fell under the attack of the Tainted.

Ciralys Telaq stepped towards the group, raising both hands. His aura flared with the glow of *Asai* as he cast runes in the air. Before him, light twisted into fractals of ruby flame, bursting forth to engulf the Korda'vari surrounding the prince.

Their stone carapaces were no protection against the *Asai*-born flames that devoured them like parchment, and they fell back, their shrieks forcing Darien to cover his ears.

Asai pulsed around him. The temptation to reach out, to open his mind's eye to the Light of the Eye, had led many of the Awakened to ruin. He would not burn himself out.

Beside him, Sevaani and Meg held each other. Meg was struggling to hide her terror, and he cursed his lack of training.

Ashael.

The voice rolled through his mind like a tolling bell. The *same* voice he'd heard the afternoon before. He winced as the wound on the back of his hand flared in pain. Bile rushed to the back of his throat as fear lanced through him.

Darien.

No, no. This wasn't happening. It wasn't real! He opened his eyes, but in his mind, the voice spoke again. Foreign syllables growled in his head.

Rage washed through him – not his own – and light flared in his mind's eye again as the voice, the *thing*, in his mind reached for *Asai*. His panic became terror as he was suddenly filled with power.

Darien.

In his mind flashed an image of himself within a circle, runes he'd never seen at each cardinal point. His hand fell upon the rune placed in the north and–

His body stood abruptly. He couldn't stop himself. He fought for control, but nothing he did made any difference. Sweat beaded his forehead as he was walked out of the corridor, stopping just past the threshold. His heart thudded in his ears, his face hot with effort as he struggled to stop whatever had taken control of him. He watched, an outsider in his own mind, as he crouched and, with a finger trailing *Asai*, traced a circle. Fear gripped him, and quickly drew the runes he'd seen at their allotted points, and then fell back on his heels in the circle's centre. He trembled as he lifted his hand to his face and blinked, in control once more. Darien pushed himself to his feet, but a pulse of heat knocked him back to one knee.

Energy burned through him.

He fell forward; right hand slapped down on the north rune, and he spoke a word he'd never heard before.

Asai washed through him and into the glowing rune. His throat burned as though fire trailed from his mouth. Each of the runes blazed crimson and rose from around the circle, spinning in place. They spun faster and faster and then flew out into the battle.

The spinning runes sliced through Korda'var after Korda'var, like discs of vermilion light, maiming, and distracting, setting alight each beast it passed through, laying them open to the swords of the Bronze Guard and the Rangers.

The Light of the Eye surged through him, empowering the runes he had drawn.

Bok cha nak crasa. The voice rolled through his head and suddenly released the *Asai*.

Darien fell forward, the floor racing to meet him, and he began to shake from the backlash of *Asai*

"Darien!" Meg cried out, but he couldn't turn his head.

"What was that?" Sim said excitedly. "What did you do? That was brilliant! Why didn't you do it earli –"

"Simeon!" Meg turned on him.

"What?" he scowled at her.

"Now's *not* the time!"

"I just want to know what he –"

"And I'd like to know why you're back here with us instead of out there with the Rangers!" She pointed to where the Rangers and the Guard were facing the bone drake, rallying around Prince Alesandr.

"Someone had to stay back and make sure you were safe," he said.

Darien had a wild desire to laugh, but all that escaped his scorched throat was an unintelligible moan. He had been forced to wield more

Asai than he'd ever done before. A mindstorm would come upon him; he just prayed it wouldn't burn him out.

"Help me move Darien back into the corridor." Meg placed her hand on his forehead. "He's burning up."

Darien wanted to protest; could feel his shaking lessen already, but his tongue was thick in his mouth. Meg and Sim grabbed his arms, helping him find his feet as the bone drake roared again and the room trembled.

"No!" the Keeper called, stumbling out from the archway behind them. "The Great One is not our enemy. It is the Lloth'var. They are turning him!"

Enough!

Darien closed his eyes in despair at the voice. But Sevaani's whimper and Simeon's gasp made him open them. Everyone was staring at the bone drake.

Upon its dais, the skeletal frame of the undead dragon rose above the gathered soldiers. The blue glow in the eye sockets of the horned skull turned red. Flickers of black lightning played over its bones, wrapping it in shimmering shadows as its long neck snaked forward to regard the prince. Two Asp Knights pushed themselves in front of him.

Foolish mortals, the bone drake hissed. *You have lost. The bone drake is now mine, and with it, the treasures your Summoners so thoughtfully left behind.*

"No," Terias said, his voice steady but thin before the undead dragon. "You cannot have them."

And who will stop me, little Keeper? You? It is your own who betrayed you to me. The daemon-possessed drake lifted a giant foreclaw, something impaled on one of its talons.

"What is it?" Terias asked Ciralys Telaq, who had moved to stand beside him.

"The body of a young man," Darien's master said in a strained voice

"He is dead?" the Keeper asked.

Yes, it is dead. The drake shook the body free; it hit the floor with a wet thud. *Your own apprentice turned on you for the merest suggestion of power,* the bone drake hissed. *Humanity's greed has ever been its undoing. You were given refuge in paradise only to bow before those who would take it from you like wretches before their betters.*

"You are only a servant to powers we have defeated before," Terias said, his voice thin but strong. "Daemons will not be granted a foothold in this world again!"

A figure moved at the edge of the bone drake's dais, and Darien made out his master among the gems and gold, his right-hand clutching something behind his back.

"The Princes of *Des'maadr* will not –"

The drake raised its head to the ceiling and roared. Two of the statues in the alcoves lining the chamber crashed to the floor as the ground heaved beneath the daemon's rage, wisps of flame seeping from its massive jaws.

You have spent centuries culling any who possess the Mark of your Summoners from your race and believe the petty power of a Ciralys *and a* Keeper *can stand against us? You will not be allowed to take the* Tome of Ascension *from this place.*

"Telaq." Prince Alesandr stepped forward. "Is what it says true? The Tome is here?"

"Your Highness –" Telaq began, stepping back from the dais.

"This creature, this child of madness lies," Keeper Terias said. "It sees your thoughts and twists your innermost desires –"

The drake snarled and batted the old man away, smacking him across the room.

You know nothing, the daemon sneered. *Had I free rein, I would make the pain of your deaths a lingering torment.* It shook its skull. *Be thankful I do not.*

"Guardsmen. Swords up!"

Darien didn't recognise the man who stepped forward, but the ranks of the Bronze Guard obeyed his orders.

"Wait!" Telaq cried. Darien stared in horror and stumbled forward. His master joined the Asp Knights before the prince as the drake opened its enormous jaws. Ruby flame belched forth, and Telaq raised his hands.

Asai blazed, runes twisting at his master's command. The power Telaq raised was like nothing Darien had ever seen, and in his mind, something rolled as if in recognition.

The Guard and the Rangers screamed and fell back as heat and flame washed over them, the pile of gold melting at their feet. Beneath the raging torrent, Telaq and the prince and his knights, stood safe, a shield of energy sparkling in a cascade of sapphire webs that forced the flames aside.

When the flames died, the bone drake reared back as its prey stood unharmed before it.

"Save the prince!" Telaq shouted, and the Asp knights grabbed their lord by the arms, hauling him back across the room.

You. The daemon's voice rolled through Darien's skull. It leant forward, studying Telaq intently. *You are no novice of the* Outer *Circle*.

His master opened his mouth as though to speak, but the bone drake's skeletal tail lashed forward. The blade-like tip pierced Telaq through the chest, sweeping him off his feet and bringing him up to its red gaze.

"Master!" Darien screamed.

What are you?

"Kill it!" Prince Alesandr broke free of his bodyguards, running at the drake with his sword bared. The company moved forward with a roar, but it was Kaiel who reached the drake first.

Darien stared at his brother in horror. What could he do with a spear? No weapon would ever hurt a dragon that had lived past its death and was now possessed. But Kaiel pulled his arm back and threw the spear.

It flew true. The bronze blade impaled itself in the breastbone of the daemon-drake.

An ear-piercing scream filled the chamber. Golden light flashed from the spear, and the black lightning of possession that had wrapped itself around the drake's bones unravelled. The undead dragon reared, bone wings snapping out, as blue-tinged sparks flashed along its bones.

Asai flashed across Darien's vision as the bone drake struggled wildly against its weakened possession.

"Well, that's done it," Sim said. "We're all going to die."

Sim opened his satchel and pulled out one of his eggs.

"What are you doing?" Darien asked. "You can't use those in here."

"That thing is still alive." Sim pointed at the bone drake. "If I'm going to die, I'll do as much damage to that as I can before I go!"

Without another word, he ran up behind the guardsmen yelling, "Get down!" and lobbed the egg at the writhing bone drake.

The drake swung its head at Sim's shout, the crimson glow in its eye sockets flaring as the small ball of clay arched through the air to smash against its ribcage.

The egg exploded in a burst of azure flame, the shockwave knocking over the guardsmen who surrounded the beast.

Darien shut his eyes against the blast, only to open them again as blue flames engulfed the creature, its cry of rage and pain rising as it burned.

Bits of bone fell from it as fire raged along its body.

Men fell back from the conflagration as the drake flailed on the dais, its skeleton falling apart. Captains Bruday and Daynar were calling for order amongst the chaos.

With an effort, Darien picked himself up as Meg and Sevaani huddled behind him, and staggered towards the body of his teacher, crumpled in a heap on one of the piles of treasure surrounding the dais. Molten gold hissed and flamed around his robes, filling the air with the stench of cooked meat.

His throat tightened at the blood and torn flesh, sweat prickling his brow, but he couldn't turn away. The wound in Telaq's chest was a gaping hole – the dragon's tail had punctured all the way through. Blood ran from his master's mouth, his eyes shut.

Darien lowered his head.

"D... Darien."Telaq's throat worked as he tried to swallow, and blood pumped from his mouth.

"Master! You mustn't move, the Prince –"

Telaq's eyes rolled in his head. He tried to speak again, but his voice was lost behind a gurgle. He reached out, and Darien leant forward to clasp his hand. His master spat blood from his mouth, pulling Darien to him.

"Go... Ciralys... still!"The man shuddered, and then he was still.

Darien stared at him, unable to breathe when he became aware Telaq had passed something to him. Darien looked down to find a large, red-tinged shard of crystal in his hand.

"Telaq!"

Startled, Darien slipped the jewel into a belt pouch as Prince Alesandr's came up behind him.

The prince's face was white with rage, but his anger wasn't directed at Darien.

Alesandr's eyes flicked to his and Darien bowed his head.

Without a word, Alesandr strode to the still-burning remains of the bone drake, ignoring the heat Darien could feel twenty feet away. The prince went to the huddled form of Terias, who had made his way to the centre of the dais, beneath the burning arch of the dragon's enormous ribcage.

His Highness stopped beside the Keeper, and Darien stared. The old man was still alive, slumped beside the lifeless body of his doomed apprentice. The prince grabbed the Keeper's robes and yanked him up. "Is this what you expected?" His voice was clipped.

"I..." Terias shook his head weakly. "No. I did not expect *this*. The drake was the *guardian*. I... I did not expect the Lloth'var would have a daemon, a soul-eater, with them."

Alesandr spat. "Had you bothered to tell us the slightest part of the 'secrets' you invoked me into helping you protect, let alone the nature of your guardian, we might have been better prepared."

"You have no idea what I have lost here tonight, old man, but I *will* leave with something!" He let the Keeper slump back and straightened.

A rasping laugh shuddered through the apprentice's corpse, and Darien, who had made his way over to the crowd gathered behind the prince, stumbled back. The cadaver sat up with jerky movements. Red flames filled its eyes.

"You will take nothing, princeling." The corpse lurched to its feet, its voice rolling and sibilant. "We would not leave such power available to you pitiful wretches." Its blackened hand grabbed the Keeper by his throat, lifting him from the ground. "Your lives are like the blink of an eye. Always building, always moving forward and forgetting the past; forgetting your origins. You are sheep, fodder for the great Lords of the Void and nothing more."

The animated corpse closed its fist, and Terias began to choke, his skin hardening like marble beneath the hand; the change spread over him like water running across a sloping floor.

"Stop him!" Alesandr roared and one of the Asp Knights darted forward. His sword slashed at the corpse's arm, only to bounce off as though it had struck stone.

Looking around, Alesandr grabbed the spear Kaiel had cast so effectively against the daemon drake. The prince threw it at the possessed corpse, to no avail.

The body of the apprentice laughed again, a grating sound that sent shivers down Darien's spine as the marble spread over the Keeper's face and his struggles ceased.

The cadaver released its hold on the statue that used to be a man.

"The Queen of Daemons calls once more," the apprentice hissed through a cracked and blackened mouth. "And your Empyros, your prophecies, will not save you!"

The light embedded in the ceiling flickered, and the corpse dropped to the ground, the red flames in its eyes winking out.

Alesandr screamed his frustration.

"Your Highness," Captain Bruday said, approaching cautiously, holding the spear Alesandr had just thrown. "We should leave this place."

"Kaiel Toranth," Alesandr said, taking the spear from Bruday and striding out from within the dragon's ribcage. "This was the spear you threw at the drake?"

Kaiel stepped forward. "I –"

"Before you threw the spear, we could not touch the creature," Alesandr continued over the top of him. "Where did you get this from?" The spear in his hand was old, the wooden shaft was rough and worn, the blade chipped and pitted.

"My sword broke, Your Highness," Kaiel said, his blond hair matted with sweat. "I was near one of those racks by the walls. I just grabbed the first thing I could find."

"Indeed." Alesandr tossed the spear to Kaiel, who caught it.

As Kaiel's hand closed over the spear, a chime rang. A ripple of gold light travelled its length, and the shaft became black as obsidian. Runes that Darien couldn't make-out ran up and down its length, and the chipped blade on top became an elegant length of honed bronze.

Murmurs ran through the surrounding company

"So," the prince said, his voice soft. "A *bronze* spear." His gaze became considering. "Toranth," Alesandr said at last. "Toranth. I am no scholar of the Blood to study how names can change over time, but that could almost be Taaren'th..."

"Your Highness, no!" Darien stepped forward in shock. A muttering rose at the mention of the previous House to rule Aldania; one said to be descended from the blood of the Last Empyros, leader of the Summoners. "We have no ties to the old Blood. Our family has lived in Hanore for as long as anyone can remember. Our ancestor was a founder!"

Alesandr eyed him. "We shall see."

The flickering light above them faded. Whatever had powered the crystal lattice must have gone with the true death of the bone drake.

"Captain Bruday." Alesandr stepped back from Kaiel. "This man is to be held under guard."

"What?" Kaiel looked around in confusion. "But, Your Highness, I haven't done anything!"

Bruday motioned two guardsmen who took up places on either side of Kaiel. Darien wanted to speak, but self-preservation held his tongue.

"Your Highness." Captain Daynar came towards them. "This man is a member of my Rangers. On what grounds do you hold him?"

"Of your Rangers? Only yesterday he was an applicant to the Kas'tirien. I am holding him on my authority as a Prince of the Realm," Alesandr said. "A prince, I might add, that you Borderlanders are all still subject to!"

Jaric spread his hands. "As Captain of the Hanore Rangers, Kaiel is my responsibility –" He stopped as Alesandr held up his hand.

"Kaiel Toranth holds in his hands the Bronze Spear, a weapon crafted by the Summoners and bound to the Blood Mark of the House to which it is a Crest; a *dead* House.

"The spear," Alesandr continued, "disappeared from House Niskeri's Arliel Vault nineteen years ago. And now I find it here, in this man's hands. I find that very interesting, and I wish to speak to him of it.

"His brother also," the prince said to Captain Bruday, and a pair of guardsmen herded Darien to stand beside Kaiel. "I wish to speak to them both of treason."

CHAPTER NINE

The Blood of the Spear

THE SPEAR STOOD like a line of shadow, the flickering flame of the torch barely reflecting off its wooden haft. It had been thrust blade-first into the ground near the centre pole of the prison tent, right between him and Darien. He wished he'd never picked it up.

Kaiel pulled his knees to his chest and rested his forearms atop them. He wanted to stretch out, but the chains linking his wrists to his ankles weren't designed to offer comfort. What he really wanted was to be back in Master Milan's forge. There'd been a time – before he'd been chosen to study under the Kas'tirien – that he thought he'd become a smith himself. He enjoyed the physicality of the work in the forge, the heat, the shaping of metal. The feeling of creating something real, something solid. Like these chains that kept him prisoner, confined in this tent.

He sighed, glancing over at Darien who had somehow managed to sit cross-legged.

Kaiel listened but couldn't make out any noise from the camp. Sim, Meg and Sevaani had been by earlier and tried to gain access, along with Captain Daynar, but the guardsmen outside had refused them entry. Under the orders of Prince Alesandr.

Maybe Sim had the right of the Houses and their lords. If he'd done something wrong in Hanore he'd at least have had the chance to speak before being put in irons, but Prince Alesandr hadn't allowed that, nor would he turn them over to Captain Daynar's custody. It's not as though Jaric, Captain Daynar, would have let them go, but he certainly wouldn't have had them bound up like criminals either.

The march of booted feet announced sentries passing the tent again.

In a way, Kaiel was almost glad to be in the tent rather than roaming the camp on watch. Night had already fallen by the time they'd reached the surface. The smell of smoke still hung in the air, though most of the fires devouring Sonyth had been put out. Some of the surviving citadelfolk were shifting through the smouldering remains, looking for possessions, and searching for family and friends.

Though he and Darien had been held at the back of the troop, they had easily overheard Captain Daynar's argument with the prince over his decision to set up camp outside the breached walls of the citadel. But Captain Daynar's protests had fallen on deaf ears. The prince, who had been informal amongst the Three Citadels during his extended stay, had been replaced by a scion of House Niskeri whose word was law, and the Borderlanders quickly – if not a little resentfully – were made to obey.

Kaiel stifled a groan and tried to move again. His buttocks were going numb, but short of lying on his side, he couldn't move. Darien was sitting straight-backed with his hands folded in his lap, eyes closed, oblivious to the world.

"I'm sorry, Dar," he said quietly.

"It's not your fault, Kaiel."

Kaiel jerked up, chains rattling. "I thought you were asleep."

"How can I possibly sleep while I'm in chains?"

Kaiel grimaced. "I'll get us out of here, I promise."

"This isn't your fault," Darien repeated with a sigh. "Though I'd like to know how you think you're going to get us out."

"I didn't do anything. The prince will see that," he said, trying to convince himself as well as his brother.

"This isn't about *you*, it's about that spear – and who he thinks our family is."

Kaiel stared at the spear. "Well, it's what killed the dragon, or whatever it was, isn't it?"

"That and Sim's 'eggs'." Darien lifted his head. "Did you–?"

"No," Kaiel said, knowing what Darien wanted to ask. "He used to go off to the mire sometimes, you know, to the fire pools out past the Rock Giants. Do you think that's what makes it burn?"

"More than likely," Darien agreed. "We aren't here because you killed the bone drake, this is about the spear. And the fact that it only looks like that –" he nodded at it, "when other people touch it."

"I don't understand it," Kaiel said.

"When you held it, it didn't look old and plain. That's not the same spear you threw at the drake. And having heard the talk on the way out, you were felling Korda'vari like they were straw dummies."

"Not that. I know it changes," Kaiel said. "I don't understand *why* it does when I touch it. Anyway, what about you?"

"What about me?"

"Those fire blades. I saw them. And they didn't come from Ciralys Telaq either."

"I... I don't..." Darien dropped his head. "It just *happened*."

"But you said you weren't learning any magic!"

"*Asai*. There is no such thing as magic. And of course, I'm learning it. Just..." He shifted, the shackles around his wrists rattling. "Just not that. I must have read the runes in one of Ciralys Telaq's books."

Kaiel moved again and groaned. "Gods, I wish they'd take these things off." He tugged at his chains, still unable to get comfortable. "I *will* get us out, Dar, I promise."

"Oh, stop it. Unless you can change our bloodline, I can't see what you're going to do."

"We aren't Blood," Kaiel protested. "Nobody in the Borderlands has a House."

"I wouldn't be too sure about that," Darien said. "Some of the more recent additions to the citadels must have been Houseborn before they ended up here. But it's our blood the Prince is interested in. Unless it's just *your* blood."

"Meaning what?"

"We don't know who our fathers are, but they aren't the same man." Darien bit his lip. "Maybe it's his blood in you that's the cause of this."

"There's one way to be sure," a voice said from the door flap.

Kaiel swung his head around as Prince Alesandr entered the tent. The prince had changed out of the battle-scarred armour of the day, and in its place he wore a long, black, velvet coat with a high collar, tight in the waist and arms. The boar of his House was worked in silver thread over his heart, matching the embroidery on the turned-back cuffs. Beneath it, a green silk doublet caught the light of the torch above black moleskin leggings that were tucked into tall leather boots; the buckle of his belt glittered with dark green gems in the torchlight. Alesandr looked every inch the prince he was, and Kaiel couldn't help but be aware that he was battle-stained and weary in comparison.

Kaiel swallowed as Alesandr plucked the spear from the ground and tossed it lengthways at Darien.

Kaiel flinched as Darien, unprepared, raised his hands to protect himself and the spear bounced off his wrist. A line of golden light flashed along its length, and the blade became bronze, the haft obsidian.

"It would seem the common thread is your mother's blood, not your father's," the prince said. He picked the spear up, again it transformed into a plain old-looking spear, and he thrust it back in the ground. He stood in front of Kaiel and looked at the back of his right hand. Alesandr said nothing at sight of the unmarked skin, then moved to Darien and inspected the back of his hand.

"So." Alesandr stepped back, folding his arms across his chest. "Neither of you bear the Mark of the Eye. Are you House Toranth; or is it in fact House Taaren'th?"

"Your Highness," Kaiel said. "We are no House. There are no Houses in the Borderlands."

"And yet the sacred weapon of House Taaren'th, Highlords of the Clan of the Bronze Spear, once the rulers of Aldania, responds to you." Alesandr absently rubbed his thumb over his right palm. "Of course, the other question, and perhaps just as important, is how the spear ended up here in the first place."

He paused for so long, Kaiel wondered if he was actually asking a question. He opened his mouth to say something when Alesandr continued.

"The First Commander of my father's armies never believed those punished for the desecration of my family's Arliel Vault were responsible for the spear's disappearance." He grimaced at the memory. "Are you familiar with the Arliel Vaults?"

Kaiel shook his head, but Darien answered.

"It is a shrine next to the ancestor tree of a House."

"More or less." Alesandr nodded and began to pace the small length of the tent. "House Taaren'th fell to House Niskeri five hundred years ago, and despite some outbreaks of rebellion, we have retained the Ivy Throne ever since." He stopped pacing, facing the black wall of the tent. "I have spent most of the four years of my term as Carbinah of Jaroff here in the Borderlands. You folk are well versed at keeping things from outsiders. For centuries, the Ciralys, amongst others, have searched what's left of the Sahrin's citadels, never imagining the things they seek could truly be hidden from them."

He turned to Darien. "You have been in my household for nearly as long. You knew what Ciralys Telaq and I were seeking, did you not?"

"No, Highness," Darien said. "My master rarely explained his actions to me. He spoke to me of the *Tome of Ascension* yesterday, but nothing else."

"And you?" Alesandr's face was a mask as he addressed Kaiel. "Did you know what we sought?"

"I don't know about any of this. I picked up the spear because I lost my sword."

"No doubt the spear chose you. I am told it is the way of these things." Alesandr leaned down. "There is such a resemblance between us; it is remarkable."

He reached a hand towards him, and Kaiel was thrown back, pain flashing through his skull.

Alesandr clutched his hand, staring at him white-faced. "What did you do?"

Kaiel groaned, unable to answer. Breathing hard, he struggled to sit upright.

Alesandr held the palm of his right hand out before him, the light from the torch dancing over the silver lines of an old scar, like a brand of weighing scales, in its centre. Kaiel blinked.

"Strange," the prince murmured, closing his palm into a fist. "The Shol'mas Lord, Sarnorn, wants the spear. He told me so when I was just eleven years of age. When he branded me his *servant*." Alesandr's lips twisted on the last and Kaiel wondered if the prince even remembered he and Darien were here. "He wants the spear, and *I* need one who can wield it." Alesandr took hold of the spear again, studying its aged brown wood. He swung it around, and the cold prick of the blade pressed against Kaiel's neck.

"Have you ever had a knife held to your throat, Borderlander?" Alesandr asked. "Been told that *justice* would be served and that if you did not serve it willingly, you would fall victim to it?"

The spear tip pressed harder, and Kaiel held his breath.

"After a time, you would *beg* for mercy; you would do anything to have that knife removed. Offer anything to avoid the tip slicing your skin and spilling your life out into the footnotes of history. But *justice* is rarely partnered with mercy."

The spear was withdrawn, and Kaiel took a gasping breath.

"For years, I have been a pawn, though by birth, I am a prince." Alesandr laughed, seeming to mock himself. "As, I suppose, are you. The blood of kings, different though they are, flows through our veins." He offered Kaiel, and Darien, a bow. "But we can all be so much more than what is expected of us. I am no piece to be moved on a sareis board." His smile did not quite reach his eyes. "It has been foretold that your bloodline, will be the downfall of House Niskeri; that you will destroy my father's realm."

"Highness, no! I – we..." Kaiel's voice was hoarse. He cleared his throat. "We want nothing like that. What could we do? We are Borderlanders!"

Alesandr shook his head, ebony locks as dark as Darien's falling over eyes just as green. "I will not stand by and see my family brought down." He crouched before Kaiel. "Understand that this is not personal. I do not doubt that on your own you would do what you say. But you are not alone. We all dance in the Light of the Eye. Such roles as yours and mine are not solitary, to be hidden from the world. We stand on the pages of history, and our audience watches every move we make. It may not be fair, but that is irrelevant."

Alesandr stood. "Have you ever considered how you might kill a god?"

Kaiel gaped at him. "A god?"

Alesandr turned the spear in the light. "Well, a Shol'mas Lord, but they claim there is little difference." The gems on his belt buckle flashed. "No? You haven't thought of it? Well, I have." He ran a finger over the edge of the spear's blade. "I have tried to find some way out of this. Some loophole that may serve us both, but justice will not be denied. Luckily for you, justice is a double-edged sword, and I can wield a sword like a blademaster of the Black Sands." The prince's smile made Kaiel's skin pebble. "You and your spear will be my sword."

Alesandr cursed as he cut his thumb on the point of the blade.

"Careful, Your Highness," Darien said. "Such an accident could be seen as a bad omen."

"Really?" Alesandr snarled. "For your brother or me?"

Darien shrugged. "It is usually the wielder of the sword who gets cut."

Alesandr threw his head back and laughed. "Gods, you sound like your Master, I shall miss his counsel." He tilted his head, considering. "You will also stay, Darien, and make sure your brother does as he's told."

"How do you expect to murder a Shol'mas Lord?" Darien asked. "I've never known a messenger of the gods to come when called."

"Oh, he will come. He and I have a special relationship." Alesandr studied his thumb, then hefted the spear. "I will keep this with me. Try and get some rest. We will be leaving for Jaroff tomorrow."

"But what about Sonyth?" Kaiel said. "We have to help the people here! You can't just leave them. You're their prince!"

"Yes, I am; when they want me to be." Alesandr's eyes darkened. "I will send word to Ebron when we reach Jaroff. High Prince Benevar is always looking for something to do. Trouble in the Borderland Wilds is just the thing to keep him occupied."

"That will take too long," Kaiel protested.

"Then maybe you Borderlanders will tread more carefully next time before insisting you are not part of Aldania!" Alesandr turned on his heel and strode from the tent.

As the door flap fell, it was pushed open again, and one of the guards entered.

Kaiel straightened as he recognised the man. "Oslin?" The man had been with Kaiel in the scouting party that very morning, but there was no hint of friendliness on the guardsman's face. Pulling the lone torch free of its iron bracket, Oslin left just as quickly as he'd arrived.

The darkness that fell inside the tent was complete. No hint of light shone through the thick fabric of the walls, though cooking fires and torches must have been lit.

"What do we do now?" Kaiel muttered.

"Weren't you going to get us out of here?"

Kaiel ignored the sneer in his brother's tone; instead, he asked. "Is he god-touched?"

Darien barked a short laugh. "Alesandr? No. I fear he's very much sane."

"I can't kill a god!'

"He doesn't want you to," Darien said. "He wants you to kill a Shol'mas Lord."

"It's the same thing!"

"No, Kaiel, it isn't. No matter what their priests might like to claim."

"I– wait." Kaiel motioned Darien to silence as a noise came from outside, and then realised Darien wouldn't see his gesture in the dark tent. Thankfully, his brother stayed silent.

Yes! There it was again. A tearing noise from the curtain behind him. He turned, his chains clanging in the dark. Against the blackness of the tent wall, he could just make out a line of grey light. It was a tear! And it was getting bigger.

"Kaiel," Darien whispered.

"Be quiet!" a voice hissed. The tearing resumed, and the opening grew large enough that night sky sparkled clearly on the other side. The man outside was a large shadow, briefly outlined by the ethereal light of the Span that crossed the northern heavens. The dull flash of light on the bronze piping on his broad shoulders told Kaiel he had to be a member of the Guard, but his face was in shadow.

"Who are you?" Kaiel asked, keeping his voice low.

The flap of the tent wall fell back, and the man was hidden in the darkness of the interior. "Rowin Bruday, Your Grace. I've come to get you out of here."

"Captain!" Kaiel half whispered. "Wait, what did you say?"

"I said I've come to get you out of here," Bruday repeated in a whisper. "Hold out your wrists."

"He meant the 'Your Grace' part," Darien drawled.

"I'm no Grace," Kaiel protested. "Why does everyone think I am the lord of a dead House?"

"Because you wielded the spear, Your Grace." Bruday's voice was gruff. "It's the *Ne'ronsylari* you found, the Bronze Spear; we have books on it back in the barracks in Jaroff. Not that we keep them out in the open, mind, but all sworn members of the Guard know what it looks like. Void take it!" he cursed. "I can't see a thing in here." He let go of Kaiel's chains, and light filled the tent as he pulled a small, glowing, stone, half the size of a clenched fist, from a belt pouch.

"Where did you get a sunstone?" Darien demanded. "Only the Great Houses can afford such things, and you have no Ciralys in your company."

Bruday snorted. "The Guard has been around since the fall of House Taaren'th, my lord. We have coin." He reached out for Kaiel's chains again. "Quickly, Your Grace, we must hurry."

"We're not lords," Kaiel spat in frustration and then bit his tongue. "Sorry." He lifted his arms, presenting his manacled wrists. "But we're not."

"The Niskeri is right," Bruday said, pulling out a key that fit the lock on the chains. "Only the Taaren'th blood could wield the spear the way you did, killing that possessed bone drake." He bent to the chains at

Kaiel's ankles. "I thought for sure we were all dead when I saw that thing." He smiled. "You're a true Prince of House Taaren'th, all right."

"Captain," Kaiel hissed between gritted teeth. "That's treason! You are oathbound to House Niskeri."

"Ha!" The captain of the Bronze Guard piled the chains on the floor quietly. "I am not, none of the Guard are." He moved over to Darien. "When the Iron Boar threw down the Bronze Spear, we were directed by the last true king to take our oaths to the Shrine of Alay'thias. The commanders swore the company in before the Sun God, as mercenaries, until the Bronze Spear rose again." He grinned. "And now it has."

"And how did this king know this would happen?" Darien asked.

"The Shaluay still guided the Old Clans then," Bruday replied.

"Shaluay?" Kaiel said.

"A Starbinder," Darien muttered. "A seer," he explained as Kaiel opened his mouth to ask.

"So, what does this all mean then?" Kaiel asked Bruday, who was picking up the sunstone.

The captain's eyes shone like black stones in the light. "It means the Bronze Guard is yours, and your brother's, Your Grace."

"What?" Kaiel yelped, and Darien thumped him on the arm.

"What's going on in there?" one of the guards outside called.

"Void damn it!" Bruday hissed.

"What's the problem? Isn't the Guard 'ours'?" Darien asked.

"The Guard only learn our true history after they have been with us for five years!" Bruday said. "Oslin and Regor outside haven't –"

The tent flap was pulled aside. Bruday dropped the sunstone and grabbed the first guardsman's wrist, pulling him in.

"Regor! What is –" Oslin began, and Kaiel dashed over, pulling him in behind his partner. Oslin stumbled inside, the helm he'd been holding falling to the ground with a clang. Kaiel winced at the noise before reeling back, pain blossoming, as a fist made contact with his face. Out of reflex, he swung his fist into the man's gut, cursing as he made contact with the chainmail.

Oslin pushed him back, and he tripped over a still-kneeling Darien, landing hard on his shoulder. The young guardsman reached for the sword at his hip. Kaiel grabbed the chains that had bound him and pushed himself off the ground. He bunched the heavy chain around his wrist and swung it at the man's head. It collided hard, but it was the crunch of bone that stopped Kaiel, as the short end of the chain holding the heavy manacles followed through and smashed into the back of Oslin's unprotected skull.

The guard fell to the ground.

"No!" Bruday got up from where he had finished easing Regor, incapacitated, to the ground and bent over Oslin's body.

Kaiel couldn't breathe.

"Is he...?" Darien reached out a hand and touched the man's neck. He sat back. "He's dead."

Kaiel turned and emptied the contents of his stomach onto the floor, his legs suddenly weak, the wound on the back of his hand burning.

"Well, that's done it," Bruday said gruffly. "There's going to be trouble."

"You helping us escape wouldn't have caused trouble?" Darien said, laying his hand on Kaiel's back. "Are you all right?"

"Killing a man isn't the same as killing those daemonspawn you have here in the Borderlands," Bruday said. "If I'm not wrong, you've never killed a man before?"

Kaiel shook his head. Turning around, he was unable to bring himself to look at Oslin's lifeless body.

"We need to go," Darien said.

"Yes," Bruday agreed. "Before more guards come."

"They didn't." Kaiel stopped and cleared his throat, spitting into the ground. "They didn't know about... about the spear?"

"Too green," Bruday said. "They have another two years yet before they take the final oaths. Well." He looked down. "Two years left for Regor."

Kaiel clenched his eyes shut.

"Where did they put the spear?" Bruday asked.

"The prince took it with him when he left." Kaiel opened his eyes again.

"Void take him!" Bruday swore and then bent to retrieve the sunstone. "Well, it can't be helped. I'll see if we can't somehow *lose* it for him on the way back to Jaroff."

"That won't be easy," Darien said, getting to his feet. "He's not going to let it out of his sight. Not when he needs Kaiel to wield it to kill Sarnorn."

"I don't know about killing a Shol'mas or anything of the like, be we'd best get you two out of here now." Bruday pulled aside the hole in the tent, the light of the moon and the Span entering the darkness.

"Run for the trees," he told them. "Make your way to Jaroff, but whatever you do, *don't* go back to Hanore. You will be putting the lives of your family and friends at risk if the prince thinks you've gone back there."

"We're to make it back through the Borderland Wilds by ourselves?" Darien said. "We're better off at the mercy of the prince!"

"It can't be that bad," Bruday snorted. "The Rangers only travel in pairs."

"In pairs, armed, and only during daylight! Weren't you here when word came back that twenty of your men had been slaughtered?" Darien said incredulously.

"That was the Korda'vari," Bruday said. "We've dealt with them."

"There are more dangers out there than just Korda'vari," Kaiel said distractedly. He raised his eyes to gauge the position of the stars.

"You must go, now," Bruday urged, the light of the moon glinting off his bald head."It will be bad when they find Oslin and Regor, but I will straighten it with the Commander back in Jaroff."

The crunch of booted feet on the ground had Kaiel spinning as two sentries rounded the corner of the tents.

"Who goes there?" one of them called.

"By the Eye," Bruday hissed. "Run. I'll lead them the other way! Alaythias be with you!"

Kaiel grabbed Darien's arm and pulled him across the field towards the forest as the Captain of the Bronze Guard ran back the other way. Beyond the first line of trees, he pulled Darien to the left, heading north-west. As soon as the sun was up, the trackers amongst the Rangers would be able to pick up their trail; but whether they'd tell the prince was another matter. Hopefully, that would give them enough time to gain some distance, so they could work out what to do. But shouts came from the camp as the alarm sounded, and Kaiel's hopes fell as barking filled the night.

Darien laughed mirthlessly."What do we do now?"

Kaiel paused. His legs were still shaking, and his pulse thundered in his ears."This way! If we can get around the camp and cross back to Sonyth, we can cover our scent with the ash and smoke of the fires."

"Will that work?" his brother's voice was close behind.

"I hope so," Kaiel muttered.

"What?" Darien was already panting.

"I said 'yes'!"

Moonlight fell through the branches, casting a patchwork of black, grey and silvery half-light across the uneven terrain. Kaiel picked his way as cautiously as he could without slowing. The wind had picked up since they had been confined to the tent, and it was cold. They had a long trek to Jaroff, and winter already stalked the Borderlands. They'd have to get to Tore for supplies first. But questions were bound to be asked by the Captain of their Rangers, and he didn't have any answers. Borderlanders were notoriously private and wary of drawing the attention of the Houses. If they believed he and Dar would bring the prince and House Niskeri down on them, they would turn them over in a heartbeat.

He kept them moving, trying to keep one ear on the pursuit and the other listening for any nocturnal predators, of which the Borderlands had many. And the smoke and fire of Sonyth's sacking would surely attract the most dangerous.

He turned his head, watching for signs of pursuit, and stumbled over a tree root, crashing to the ground.

"Kaiel?" Darien panted, reaching down to grab his arm.

"I'm okay." He pushed himself to his feet. "I'll get you out of here, Dar. We'll head to Ebron. From there we can find a ship to take us somewhere else. I don't know, the Eastern realms, maybe?"

"What are you talking about? I'm going to Isoliere," Darien said between deep breaths.

"You can't, Dar. Alesandr will know you're headed to the Ciralys. He'll be able to find you –" He broke off as a bird call whistled through the night.

"Was that a redbreast?" Darien peered around them.

The whistle came again.

"It is," Darien said. "Why is a redbreast issuing a mating call at night?"

"It's Sim." Kaiel grinned.

"What?"

"It's Simeon! It's our hunting call." Kaiel got up. "And the only bird he can mimic."

"And how many bird calls can you imitate?" Darien asked.

"Six." Cupping his hands over his mouth, he sent out the hoot of a ring-necked owl.

There was a moment of silence, and then the redbreast called again.

"This way." He gestured through the dark trees.

"Wait." Darien grabbed his arm. "Do you trust him? *Really* trust him? He's not going to be waiting with Alesandr and a troop of guardsmen, is he?"

"Sim, siding with the Blood? No," Kaiel scoffed. "Sim would never do that. Come on."

He made his way deeper into the forest, only stopping to send out the call of the owl and wait for Sim's response, to make sure he was heading in the right direction as the barks of the dogs still chased them.

"He's up ahead," he said to Darien, and broke into a run, stumbling between the trees into a grove.

Moonlight lit the clearing, and Kaiel paused at the line of the trees. Darien came up beside him, his breath pluming into white clouds in the chill air.

"Where is he?"

"Wait," Kaiel said. Taking a breath, he stepped into the open. Across the grove a figure also moved, stepping out of the shadows.

"Kaiel?" Sim's whisper was loud in the stillness of the night, but Kaiel whooped at the sight of his friend and ran across the grass to meet him.

"Thank the gods," Kaiel laughed. "Tell Dar you didn't bring anyone with you."

"Kaiel –" Sim began when another figure stepped out of the trees behind him.

Kaiel instinctively took a step back, only to stop as the moonlight fell on Captain Daynar's stern countenance.

"You've stirred up a ciret's nest, boy," Jaric said dryly. "How did you get out of your chains?"

"The dogs!" Darien hissed. "I hear them! We have to go!"

Kaiel swore. "We'll never get back to Sonyth to hide our tracks."

Captain Daynar turned his head and trilled a whistle. "We've brought horses."

From the dark trees, a tall black stallion came to his call. Kaiel's eye widened as he recognised the captain's horse, Celaridus, and behind him came his own mount, Lasa, and Sim's Del.

"We?" Darien asked.

Behind the captain came two more horses, carrying riders leading a sixth horse.

"Who is –" Kaiel began.

"Meg," Darien said as Meg appeared on the back of a chestnut dun mare.

Kaiel frowned, but then the light of the moon fell on a bay mare, with white socks, ridden by a young woman with golden hair and the breath left his lungs.

"Sevaani." He stepped forward, but a chorus of barking rose in the distance behind them.

"There'll be time for questions later," Jaric said, swinging up onto the stallion. "Quickly! Mount up, both of you. We ride."

CHAPTER TEN

Through the Night

DARIEN BENT OVER the neck of Waro, a cream-coloured gelding, to avoid tree branches as they followed Jaric. Moonlight cast wide beams between the trees and paired with the light of the Span – the ring of sparkling skystones that belted the globe – offered some visibility to the ground beneath their feet.

He kept his eyes on the horse in front. Questions chased themselves around his head, but with a palpable urge to put as much distance between himself and the prince, he had no time to pursue the answers.

And the prince was the least of his concerns. He couldn't outrun whatever was in his head.

The night shifted as they ran, the Moon passing Her zenith and beginning Her fall across the sky, stretching the shadows before them. There'd been no further sign of pursuit in the hours since they'd left the grove thanks to Simeon. He'd fallen behind, only to return a short while later with a wide grin. Darien's enquiry as to what he'd been doing fell on deaf ears, but Jaric's terse demand revealed he'd covered their tracks with wolfsbane. Darien wasn't surprised, and none of them could feign unhappiness that the hunting dogs of the Rangers would be laid low, unable to lead their masters after them for a time.

Adrenaline had long since faded and the cold night air intruded through the blood and sweat that soaked Darien's clothes. The cloak his master had given him the night before was gone, probably left in the tent, and the events of the past two days beat upon him, leaving exhaustion in their wake.

He had no idea where they were or where they might find shelter. Life in the Borderlands didn't lend itself to the exploration of your surrounds unless you were a member of the Rangers. And neither Kaiel nor Jaric had mentioned recognising any landmarks yet.

Given the time they'd been travelling, if they'd been on the road, they'd have reached Hanore by now, surely. The citadel of Tore was still another eight hours north from there. He wasn't sure he'd be able to ride much longer and was about to say so when a cry came from behind.

"Sevaani!" his brother called out. The horses milled about as they pulled up short for the Steward's daughter, who had fallen from her saddle.

"Are you all right?" Meg said, dismounting her horse, Helese, and knelt beside Sevaani, brushing hair back from her face. "Does it hurt anywhere? Have you broken anything?"

"No. I don't think so," Sevaani said, getting shakily to her feet with Meg's assistance.

"You're exhausted," Meg said. "We all are."

"Kaiel," Jaric called. "We need to scout out somewhere we can rest."

"But Sevaani –" Kaiel protested.

"I'll help her," Meg said. "She'll be fine. Maybe a little bruised."

Darien expected Kaiel to argue, but his brother nodded.

"This way." Jaric motioned ahead, and they set off slowly.

Darien slid off Waro and helped Sevaani into a sitting position while Meg passed her a square of cloth to wipe her face.

"I'm sorry," Sevaani said, her face downcast. "I don't know what happened."

"Don't fret," Meg comforted her. "We've been riding half the night and walked most of the day. You're tired."

"Come on," Sim urged them. "We can't stay here, and we have to keep the horses moving. We may as well follow Kaiel and Jaric."

"*Captain* Jaric," Darien corrected, but Sim just grinned.

Sevaani sighed. "Couldn't we just stay here? Maybe make a fire? I'm so cold."

"I told you this wasn't going to be easy," Meg said, climbing onto her mount.

Sevaani's jaw tightened. "I know, Meg."

"Sim!" Kaiel's call came out of the darkness.

"Gods, Kaiel. Don't shout out here at night. You'll bring every dycinion for miles around," Sim muttered. "You're the one who's always telling *me* to be more careful."

Darien gazed into the darkness, tension crawling across his back. It was easy to forget other dangers when you were running from one in plain sight, but the Borderlands were made up of as many hidden threats as visible ones. That reminder was suddenly like a rock in his stomach. He turned back to the others and helped Sevaani remount Cloudchaser.

Kaiel stepped out of the trees ahead. "We've found a place. Some broken walls and pillars. There's no roof, but the ground is clear."

"Pillars?" Sim asked. "It's not Lovers' Stand, is it?"

"I think so," Kaiel said.

"Void! We're on the other side of Hanore!"

"Watch your language, Simeon," Meg chided.

"You're not my mother, Meg," Sim said and turned back to Kaiel. "When did we pass Hanore? We could have stopped there. Steward Etine would have protected us."

"No," Kaiel said. He moved his horse beside Sevaani's. "We can't go home." He glanced at Darien. "Not until the prince has given up on us."

"And when will that be?" Darien asked, climbing back onto Waro's saddle. "In any case, I am *not* going home."

"You can't still expect to go to the Ciralys?" Meg said with a frown.

"I want to know why the prince is so interested in you both, but let's set up camp first," Sim suggested.

Darien sighed and nudged Waro through the trees in the direction Kaiel had come, the others following. It only took them minutes to reach the clearing that held the cluster of broken old walls and the pillars that Sim had identified as 'Lover's Stand'.

They corralled the horses in a space protected by three hip-high walls of creeper-covered stone, and Sim walked to the middle of a dais.

"Is this Lover's Stand, Sevaani?" Sim asked arms spread wide. "You and Kaiel can be the new Marus and Renee."

"That's not funny, Simeon." Meg glared at him. Sevaani ducked her head, her golden hair falling across her face like a curtain.

"But it fits, doesn't it? Except, of course, in the story, it's Renee who's from the Warrens and Marus from the High Keep." He stared out into the dark. "Pretty soon we'll be surrounded by a pack of dycinion or more Korda'vari. How many will you be able to take down to protect Sevaani before we all die, Kaiel? Didn't the Rangers find a dozen dead dycinion when they came looking for the lovebirds the morning after they'd run away?"

"And no sign of Marus and Renee." Kaiel looked around the clearing cautiously. "Maybe this wasn't such a good idea."

"It's not like we had a choice," Darien said, wrapping his arms around himself as the wind gusted through the forest.

"What a surprise you'd be the one to draw the comparison with our plight to a fable with such an unfortunate end, Simeon," Jaric said.

Sim grinned. "I was just mentioning it because –"

"Don't," Jaric said. "Get some kindling. We can risk a small fire."

Sim rolled his eyes and left the dais to gather wood from the edge of the forest. After a moment, Kaiel joined him.

Sevaani and Meg sat together on the dais and Darien took himself to the opposite side. His head still ached, and his throat was dry. All he wanted to do was sleep.

Kaiel and Sim returned before too long and set about moving rocks into a ring to hold a fire on the platform.

"Something to light this with would be good," Sim muttered unloading an armful of branches.

"You don't have your flint? Isn't in your bags?" Meg asked. "Don't all the Rangers take flint with them when they go out of town?"

Sim glared at her. "I would have my flint if I had my *satchel.* Do you see my satchel anywhere? That's right!" He slapped his palm to his head. "I was barely able to grab my bag when you came to fetch me; you were in such a rush..." His eyes went wide. "My eggs! They were in the satchel. Void *damn* it!"

"Your eggs? Those little explosives you were using today?" Meg asked. "You're better off without them, Simeon Ravenson. Those things are dangerous. It's a wonder you didn't get yourself killed."

"Well, now they're in the hands of the Guard!"

"Enough," Captain Daynar said from beside one of the pillars. "There's nothing we can do about it now." Crouching at the edge of the piled wood, he took a flint and striker from his pouch. A tiny finger of flame soon danced on the twigs, quickly growing into a fire. Standing again, he took a water skin from a pack.

"Here," he said. "Each of you take a mouthful. We'll see what we can do about getting supplies in the morning." Jaric sat again before the flames, his eyes catching the orange light. "What did the prince want with you?"

Darien pushed his weariness aside, settling before the fire also. "He believes Kaiel and I are the scions of House Taaren'th."

"But your name is Toranth," Sim said.

"Names change over time," Jaric said, frowning. "Taaren'th may have changed to Toranth. Or it may have even *been* changed."

"Been changed? Why?" Meg asked.

"Because House Taaren'th were the lords of the Clan of the Bronze Spear." Jaric took the water skin as it completed its way to him. "That's it, yes? Alesandr believes the spear Kaiel used is the *Ne'ronsylari*."

"That's what Kaiel was using?" Sim said. "The *Ne'ronsylari*, the *Bronze Spear*. That was one of the weapons crafted by the Sahrin during the War of the Summoners."

"You mean like those stories about the Golden Hammer and the Jade Bow?" Meg asked.

"Yes," Jaric said. "The *Deon'adrin* and the *Seia'tolni* are among those weapons created by the Summoners. It's said each of them was bound to the blood of the Summoner who wielded them." He looked at Kaiel. "Only a direct descendant of the Empyros could use the spear. To anyone else it would just be a *normal* spear, I suppose."

Kaiel looked at him, and Darien met his brother's gaze reluctantly.

"What?" Jaric eyed them both.

"It..." Kaiel took a breath. "When the prince touched it, it changed."

"How did it change?" Jaric was suddenly as still as if he'd come across a sleeping borewyrm.

"The whole thing *changed*. It turned into an old spear with a rusty blade."

"Did he give it back to you?" the captain asked. "Did it change again?"

"Umm, no. He gave it to Dar."

"And what happened when you touched it, Darien?"

"It changed back to the way it looked when Kaiel held it," Darien admitted.

"Then it *is* true," Jaric said.

"What's true?" Meg asked.

"Kaiel and Darien are scions of House Taaren'th, descended from the bloodline of the last Summoner," Jaric said. "The Taaren'ths held the Ivy Throne for an age before the ambition of House Niskeri pulled them down."

"Don't be ridiculous." Meg was sitting straight, her eyes wide. "Darien and Kaiel aren't Blood."

Sim laughed. "They're not! It's some scheme of the Houses." He nodded at Darien. "Although I could believe you're Bloodborn easily enough. You have that –" He clicked his fingers searching for the word, "arrogance. Yeah. You have their arrogance about you."

Darien felt his stomach twist, but he kept his mouth closed. If it *was* true, then he had the blood of the Sahrin running through his veins. He ran the fingers over the wound on the back of his right hand, hidden beneath Shany's ointment.

"Well, Kaiel certainly likes battle enough to be mistaken for being Bloodborn," Sevaani said.

"What?" Kaiel raised his head.

"I saw you today, Kaiel, you... You enjoyed it." It sounded like an accusation. "All that killing."

"Sevaani!" Meg turned to her, her surprise evident. "What are you talking about? He was protecting us."

Sevaani looked away.

"Well, I don't believe it," Sim said.

"Nor do I," Meg said. "You can't be Blood."

"All of this will have to wait until later," Jaric said. "Our priority is to get to safety." He eyed Sim. "Good job with the wolfsbane, but they'll be after us all again by morning. And Rolen Etine will be leading them, most likely."

Sim groaned.

"I suspect, Kaiel, that you were planning to head to Jaroff?" Jaric asked. "Prince Alesandr has a speakstone," the captain continued. "He'll have certainly sent word to the guard in Jaroff to be on the lookout for you both."

"But the Guard is ours," Kaiel said. "They'll help us."

"See?" Sevaani muttered.

"Kaiel!" Sim barked a laugh. "You can't believe this rubbish?"

Kaiel shifted under their stares. "The Bronze Guard, they're… sworn to us. Well, to House Taaren'th."

"What else happened?" Jaric leant forward.

"There isn't much more to tell," Darien said, silencing his brother before he could speak. "Captain Bruday came to us after the prince left, told us the Guard had once been sworn to House Taaren'th, and the last Taaren'th passed their oath to the Shrine of the Sun Lord."

"And they're swearing fealty to you." Jaric arched an eyebrow. "Just like that?"

"Not 'just like that'." Darien stared at the captain. "The Shrine was to hold the oath until a scion of House Taaren'th returned. Kaiel's use of the spear was the sign."

Kaiel stared into the fire. "Captain Bruday said a Starbinder warned the last Taaren'th king to send the Guard away to wait for us. How could they have known?"

Jaric studied the night sky. "They saw it in the stars. In their visions."

"The *stars*?" Sim smirked.

"You wouldn't know much of them out here," Jaric said, "but the art of the Starbinders was once highly respected."

"Why not now?" Sevaani asked.

"Because most of the Order was lost in the chaos after the Sundering."

Sim snorted. "If the stars are so all-knowing, then how did those Starbinders get caught in the Sundering?"

"Everyone got caught in the Sundering, boy." Jaric's words held no heat, but they were sharp.

"The Shaluay Starbinders are not to be trusted," Darien offered, wrapping his arms around himself as the autumn wind blew through the trees. "Their aid is never free, and their foretellings are rarely what they seem. Or so the Ciralys say."

Meg stirred. "All I know of the Shaluay is that those who survived the Sundering went mad and started the stories of the Empyros' return."

"Those are great stories!" Sim said. "The Saviour and Destroyer, the destined hero to save us from the Daemon Queen. Except, you know, for the whole Summoner part."

"The Prophecies of the Empyros are more than stories," Jaric said. "They're warnings of what's to come. The Ciralys and the Covenants may disparage the Shaluay Starbinders as manipulative, but every court in the realms has scholars who know those prophecies by heart. And they all come from visions of the Shaluay Seers." He looked up, gazing at each of them in turn.

"Do you know them, Captain Jaric?" Sevaani asked. "Do you know what the prophecies say? The signs?"

Jaric hesitated, Darien could almost see the thoughts turning in his head.

"I know of them. I know enough to hope I never live to see the Veil between worlds torn open, or the day another Empyros like Varos Korin'ad walks the world once more. I know the Evay believe them. And they were here long before humankind came to Sobia."

"The Evay?" Sim scoffed. "They're the biggest liars around."

Meg glared at him. "Shany told me a lot about the prophecies of the Shaluay. We're coming to the turning of the seasons. It's now that all things come to a close and a new pattern begins."

"Well, I know little of the prophecies," Darien said. The conversation was making him uncomfortable. "But I'm still going to Isoliere."

"Dar." Kaiel sighed. "I told you, Prince Alesandr knows you're heading to the Ciralys. He'll find you if you go there."

"Find me, and do what?" Darien rolled his eyes. "The Ciralys don't answer to Aldania or any realm. Besides, they'll be after you too for the guard's death. What was his name, Olwyn?"

"Oslin," Kaiel said with a stricken expression, and Darien bit his tongue.

"I'm sorry, Kaiel," he said. "I know it wasn't on purpose."

"What happened?" Jaric asked, and Kaiel explained how the Bronze Guards, juniors in the order, had heard Captain Bruday unlocking their chains and had come to investigate. He stumbled over the beginning of the fight, and Darien explained the rest.

Jaric shook his head. "The death of another is never something to take lightly, but you didn't seek it, Kaiel. Take solace in that. But it certainly begs the question, will the Guard – who are not privy to the information of the older guardsmen – still follow Kaiel and Darien?"

"Captain Bruday would," Kaiel said.

"If Bruday were caught helping you escape, the prince wouldn't leave him in a position to command anyone," Jaric said. He eyed Darien thoughtfully. "It *would* be easier to head to Serjat," he suggested at last.

Sim cocked his head. "I've always wanted to visit Serjat."

"You have?" Meg raised an eyebrow.

"The Palace of Merchants is there," Sim said, as though that explained everything.

Jaric grunted. "Yes, it is. And so is the Crystal Spire. Darien, you can seek admittance to the Ciralys there."

"Really? He doesn't need to go to the Isoliere for that?" Meg asked.

"You may petition for admittance to the Ciralys at any of their Chapter Houses," Jaric said. "If you're successful, they'll send you on."

"You think that's wise?" Kaiel asked. "Dar, it would be better if you came with me. You don't know that the Ciralys can protect you from Alesandr, or if they'd want to. We need to go somewhere he'd never find us."

"Kaiel," Darien sighed. "Stop it. I'm joining the Ciralys. Isoliere, even

Serjat, are both far enough away from Dainyaia that I'll be in no danger from the prince."

"Don't we need to get word back to Hanore?" Meg looked around the group. "If Prince Alesandr thinks House Taaren'th still lives, he'll go after Master Malik and Mistress Breanta, and your cousins."

"You're right," Jaric agreed. "We must get word to Etine; the Steward will protect them. The Stewards of Hanore have planned for your discovery for centuries."

"What?" Sim said.

"You knew?" Darien felt his eyebrows raise.

"I'd been told the Toranths were of an old bloodline from before the Sundering," Jaric said. "That's all. Each Captain of the Rangers is told, and the Steward knows because it was his line that saved your family during House Niskeri's rebellion."

"*I* didn't know," Sevaani said.

"You're not your father's heir," Jaric said. "Although with Rolen now swearing to the Kas'tirien that might have changed."

"This is my life, my family," Darien cut in. "Mine and Kaiel's. Why does anyone have a right to know secrets about us that we don't?"

"The fewer people who know any secret, the less risk it might be revealed," Jaric said. "You would've only been told if you had a need to know. As you do now."

"So how do we get to Serjat," Meg asked before Darien could respond. "If we don't go to Jaroff and take the trade roads?"

"We can sneak around them. Head to the River Asp and find a boat heading north on the Torsaen?" Sim offered.

"That would take us too far west," Jaric said. "Once he's returned to Jaroff, the prince can summon the Vash'kiri. We do *not* want a gryphon rider on our trail."

"Shouldn't we try to do something they won't expect?" Meg mused.

"Let's see," Sim made a show of thinking before slapping his thigh.

"I know! How about we go to Tore, grab a boat and head east on the Murk, into the Deadlands." He paused. "Although we'd have to leave the horses I guess."

"The Murksay river is hardly worthy of the name," Jaric said. "And you'll not find it on any map. Though some of the Tore fishermen say it goes all the way to the Sukmaanai Swamp. It would be a worthy plan if it could get us to Exile Point."

"You're not serious," Darien said. "No-one ventures into the Deadlands. And from what I've read, Exile Point is full of cut-throats and corsairs!"

"It's the best way to get out of the prince's grasp," Jaric told him.

"No," Sim shook his head. "It was a jest!" He scrambled to his feet. "We can't go that way. It's suicide. No-one who goes into the Deadlands comes out the other side!"

"Sim's right," Meg said. "We can't risk that. It would be beyond foolish."

"Do you really think I'd take you to such a place? And through Dal'mere no less?" Jaric was unamused. "No, we should head to Ebron. We could find passage on a ship to Serjat from the City of Towers. But let's get some sleep. We'll speak again in the morning."

"I'll take the first watch," Kaiel said, getting to his feet.

Darien raised his gaze to the night sky as the others settled themselves. The Span flickered in the clear night sky, its shining stones stretching across the heavens east to west. He rubbed the wound on his hand and considered the things he'd learned that day. The revelations about his supposed House were useless; claiming a dead House would be more trouble than it was worth. And the bloodline of a Sahrin? He didn't know what he could do about any of it, but if Prince Alesandr wouldn't be a pawn on a playing field, then neither would Darien.

CHAPTER ELEVEN

The White Road

THE EVERSTONE PLATFORM was cold. Meg rolled onto her side, trying to get comfortable, but one side was as hard as the other. Letting out a breath, she gave up on the idea of sleep.

It was still dark in the forest, but the sun was lighting the eastern horizon. Through the gap in the canopy, the soft glow of the Span turned from silver to gold, glittering in the rising sun. Shany said the Span was *Asai* manifest on the physical plane; and that the Ciralys, and the other orders that wielded the Light of the Eye, paid a fortune for those stones that fell to Sobia. They called those skystones the Tears of the Eye.

The others lay like shadows against the white slab. Sometime during the night, the little fire had gone out, and the scent of smoke, bitter and pungent, hung in the air.

Meg wrapped her arms around herself. She tried not to shiver, but these were the last days of Ohrin, the tenth month, and winter was stretching its cold grasp over the land. In fact, she counted the days in her head; it must be the first of Novin today. It was winter already. What a lovely time to be traipsing through the Borderlands. Do they celebrate the Turning at midwinter's eve in other realms? They'd have to, surely? It was her favourite of the festivals. All the white flames of burning moonleaf wreaths, lit as prayers to the Elder God Alay'thias, Lord of the Sun, to light His way back from the Void to bless the land in the coming year. Well, her favourite besides the spring celebrations in Marcin, for the Lady Tarin and the harvest.

Meg took the cloak she had bundled up to use as a pillow, shook it out and wrapped it around her shoulders, pulling it tight. The thick wool was cold, but it halted the seeping chill. She got to her feet, stamping them softly to get her blood moving.

The forest was quiet, a mass of velvet shadows in which the white trunks of the moonleafs, and the pale light of their leaves, stood out between the dark bark of the evergreens like spectral wraiths, watching them as they slept. Meg could make out the black of Jaric's stallion, Celaridus beside Cloudchaser, the russet bay mare with the white socks Sevaani had been riding, and the indistinct shades of the others in the half-light around them. Thankfully no skreets had made their nest nearby, or they'd have had no rest at all. She frowned; she hadn't seen any skreets for the last week. Could it be the pests had known something was stirring close to the citadels? Quietly, she stepped off the everstone and onto the forest floor.

"Meg?" The whisper came from Sevaani's huddled form.

"Yes?" she said quietly.

"Where are you going?"

"I'm just stretching my legs. How are you feeling?"

"Cold," Sevaani said. "And sore." She sat up. Sevaani's face was pale in the dark; her bright eyes shadowed as though they'd been outlined in kohl.

"That's to be expected," Meg said. "You fell off a horse. At least there were no broken bones."

"Meg… what's going to happen to us?"

"I don't know," she said and swallowed against a sudden lump in her throat.

"I didn't expect it to be like this." There was the quiver of unshed tears in Sevaani's voice.

Meg sat back down, pushing her own fear away. "If you said that around Shany, she'd tell you that nothing is ever the way you expect it's going to be."

"I have *dreams,*" Sevaani said. "And none of them showed all those horrible –" Her voice broke. "Horrible, Korda'vari. Or Kaiel... and all that blood. He could have died, but it didn't scare him at all." She wrapped her arms around herself, shuddering. "He *liked* it. The killing. He wasn't scared at all."

"I wouldn't say he liked it," Meg said. "You know Kaiel; he's always been chasing the Kas'tirien, playing with swords and practising. And he was fighting Korda'vari. It's always a matter of them or us."

"But the dream was different," Sevaani insisted. "And now he and Darien are of the *Blood*."

Meg sucked in a breath. Gods, how had she forgotten? Kaiel and Darien believed they were of the Blood. And so did Captain Jaric. It couldn't be true, but who had their fathers been?

"I can't face him, Meg," Sevaani said, pulling her attention back. "Every time I look at him, I see all the blood..." She buried her face in her hands.

"Oh, Sevaani," Meg sighed. "Then, what do you want to do? You came all this way determined to be with Kaiel, and now you can't even look at him?"

"You can hardly talk, you're here chasing Darien," Sevaani cried. "All I dream of now is a white road! I am sore and hungry and *cold*. I didn't come following Kaiel. I mean, he was here, in the dream but I would never have left Ma and Pa to follow a boy. It was the dream. I had to come."

Meg's cheeks burned, and she ducked her head, but it was still dark. Sevaani couldn't have seen her anyway. "I'm not chasing Darien."

"Really?" Sevaani wiped the back of her hand across her eyes. "Then, what are you doing?"

"Well, I... I suppose it could look like I am following him, but that's not why I am here."

Sevaani stared at her, and Meg felt her cheeks heat again.

"I'm seeking admittance into the Ciralys." She cringed at the defensiveness in her tone.

"Truly?" Sevaani said. "Can you even do that? You're a witch."

"It's not that different," Meg muttered. "Darien was an apprentice witch before Ciralys Telaq arrived too. The art of the Covens follows an external path rather than the internal discipline of the Ciralys. It's a different process, with a different price to be paid, but they both require the ability to perceive *Asai*, and I can do that."

"A price?"

Meg stared out into the forest. "Shany says a balance must be kept." She had no notion of what the price might be.

"So, you're not chasing Darien?" Sevaani pushed. "Is that because he's of the Blood now and you're just an orphan?"

Meg's lips pressed together in a tight line. "That's what Prince Alesandr wants us to think, but I don't believe it." *I won't believe it.*

"I think it's true," Sevaani whispered, her cheeks were wet. "There was always *something* about Kaiel... and the dreams. I wish I could go back home."

"How are you going to do that?" Meg asked, carefully biting back the sharp side of her tongue. This was precisely why she hadn't wanted Sevaani to come in the first place. As soon as the woman had seen a real fight, she wanted to run home.

"I'm not," Sevaani said. "I said I *wish* I could."

"Sevaani." Captain Daynar moved out of the shadows of the trees before them. Meg gave a start. Had he been on watch? How long had he been there?

"There's no going home for any of us," Jaric said. "Not yet."

"That's *not* what I *said*."

Meg was sure that had Sevaani been standing, she'd have stamped her foot.

"You've helped Kaiel and Darien run from the prince's justice." Jaric stepped onto the dais. "Prince Alesandr won't let that go, or I don't know the Aldanian Blood."

"Why won't you *listen*? I know I can't go home, but not because of anything you've said. I can't go because I know we have to travel on the *white road*!"

"What 'white road'?" Jaric frowned.

"That one!" Sevaani pointed north-east into the woods.

Meg followed the direction of Sevaani's outstretched hand and stared.

No more than a hundred paces from the dais, in the orange-gold light of dawn, a path of gleaming white everstone stretched out into the forest in a perfectly straight line, trees, moonleaf and birch bordering it like pillars.

"Gods," Simeon groaned. "What's all the yelling?"

Kaiel rose also and moved to Sevaani's side.

"Kaiel, don't!" She shot to her feet.

"Sevaani, please..." Kaiel's hurt was painful to Meg. She wasn't without sympathy for Sevaani's feelings, but this was becoming tiresome.

"That's a *Renimor*."

Meg gave a start to find Darien beside her staring at the white road.

"This must have been a Ley Hub before the Sundering," Jaric said, coming over, his leathers dark in the brightening light of day.

"Don't the stories say these white roads could take you hundreds of miles, leagues even, in the blink of an eye?" Sim asked.

"They used to," Darien said. "They aren't easy to find now. The

Sahrin were able to travel the *Renimor*, the Ley Paths at will, but they only appear at dawn and dusk to the eyes of those unable to summon, making them hard to find."

"It could be the perfect way to put distance between ourselves and Prince Alesandr," Meg offered, turning away from Sevaani.

"Where will it take us?" Kaiel stood, still watching Sevaani.

Darien grimaced. "I don't know. I didn't even know one was so close to the citadels."

"It'll go to another Ley Hub," Jaric said. "If this one is near Hanore, another must be near Tore or Sonyth."

"Or at the bottom of the Nemisdrillion Sea," Sim protested. "I know the stories too. These Ley Paths crisscrossed the continent *before* it was split in half during the Sundering!"

"It's more likely the Summoners linked the citadels with white roads," Jaric suggested.

"I don't care where it goes, as long as it's away from here," Darien said. "We need to get out of Prince Alesandr's reach."

Kaiel moved closer to Sevaani, who promptly walked to the other side of Meg and Darien.

"Sevaani," Kaiel said. "What's the matter? What have I done?"

Oh, for the love of Tarin! Meg barely stopped her eyes from rolling. Kaiel though was seemingly oblivious to everything else going on and stepped towards Sevaani, his hand outstretched.

"I'll help you, Darien," Meg said. She was not getting in the middle of *this*.

"No. Kaiel," Sevaani put up her hand. "Please don't."

"But why?"

The confusion in his voice was plain, and Meg cursed under her breath. This was not going to be a pleasant trip with those two. Maybe she *should* say something–

Kaiel cried out, a dagger now jutting from his upper arm.

"Kaiel!" Sim shouted, pushing past Meg.

"Whore!" The shout came from behind them. Meg turned to see Rolen Etine stepping out from the trees; his face caught in an ugly snarl directed at Sevaani. "You have dishonoured our House!"

"Rolen!" Jaric stepped forward, but the Kas'tirien-in-training was faster. Rolen stepped onto the marble dais, grabbed his sister, and pulled her against him. A second dagger was in his hand, flashing silver in the morning light as he pressed it against her throat.

"What are you doing, lad?" Jaric stopped, his hands held out and away from the sword at his belt. "That's your sister you have there."

"I'm making sure the warren-rat," he spat at Kaiel, "doesn't get away before the prince arrives."

"Void take me," Simeon swore, kneeling beside Kaiel, who held his arm tight against his side as blood soaked his sleeve. "What is this rubbish about Houses? We're *Borderlanders*!"

"My line has been Stewards of Hanore since its founding, *outlander*!" Rolen sneered.

"You've been admiring His Highness a little too much, Rolen," Meg said. From the corner of her eye, she could see Jaric edging closer to the young man.

"Stay where you are!" Rolen glared at the captain. "You're as much to blame. You've betrayed the trust of the citadel. You helped him and his witchborn brother escape!"

He spat at Kaiel, eyes wild. "You stay right where you are," he hissed as Sevaani gripped his forearm so tightly her fingers were white.

"You're not going to hurt your sister, Rolen," Jaric said.

"Why not? She's no good to us now, soiled as she is! She's probably already carrying the traitor's spawn!"

"I am *not*!" Sevaani snapped her head back and connected with her brother's face. He cried out, and she broke his grasp.

"How dare you!" she screeched, turning on him in a fury. "I am not pregnant! I –"

"Whore!" Rolen yelled again, blood streaming from his nose, and backhanded her. Sevaani staggered, and he grabbed her tunic, the dagger in his right hand back at her throat.

"You're a pig, Rolen!" Meg snapped. "Calling your own sister a whore. Drop that dagger and –"

"Get off her!"

Meg blinked. Kaiel had jumped to his feet and was at Rolen's right, the dagger still lodged in his arm. His face was flushed red and Captain Daynar's hand axe was gripped in his fist. Before she could open her mouth, Kaiel roared and swung the axe at Rolen. Kaiel's expression of rage turned to one of shock, and he seemed to yank his torso back, pulling the blow, but it was already too late. The sharpened steel cut through flesh with a dull *thwack*, severing the arm that held the dagger at Sevaani's throat, just above the elbow.

Sevaani screamed, and Rolen's cry followed as he staggered back, falling to the ground.

"Don't move!" Years of training at Shany's side pushed Meg past her disbelief. She rushed over the dais, reached for the dagger in Kaiel's arm, and pulled it out in one quick movement. "Hold your arm as still as possible."

Kaiel looked at her as though he couldn't understand what she was saying, the axe falling from his hand.

"Get the horses, Sim," Jaric shouted behind her as Meg dropped to her knees beside Rolen who was screaming on the ground.

"I'll stop the bleeding, but I cannot do more," she said. Gods, this was a mess.

She brushed the thought aside and, taking a deep breath, opened her senses to the life of the earth around her. Though not as potent as the healing of the adepts of the Elder Goddess Tarin, or the Ciralys of the First Circle, the witchery of the Keepers healed well enough. Leaning forward, she stopped Rolen's incoherent cries and thrashing with a hand to his sweat-sodden forehead, then reached for his arm. Her hands flashed, incandescent, the bones glowing through the skin, and she pressed her palms hard against the stump. Rolen screamed again, and the stench of burnt meat filled the clearing. Meg moved her hand to his torso, expecting to find the axe to have cut into his side, but the leather armour was unmarked by anything other than blood.

Meg let go of the power she'd been holding and fell back with a gasp, her whole body shaking as the light fled her hands. She leant forward; head bowed."I'm sorry,"she said to Rolen."It's the best I can do. Shany will be able to do more."

Rolen twisted his head aside. "Too late," he said between breaths. "Too late!"

From beyond the moonleafs surrounding the dais, barking rose in the forest.

"The prince is here!"Jaric called."Get to the road!"

Staggering to her feet, Meg grabbed Sevaani's arm and pulled her towards the horses. Meg stopped Kaiel with a warning glance as he reached out to Sevaani, and he flushed, looking away.

Jaric helped Sevaani into her saddle as Meg mounted her horse. She moved it to Sevaani's side, grabbing her reins and leading them both towards the white road.

"Hurry!" Sim called, already on the road with Darien. "You're all fading away!"

A shout came from behind them. Meg turned in the saddle; patches of sunlight marked the bronzed armour of soldiers moving through the trees.

"Ride!" Jaric yelled, and she urged her horse into a gallop, holding tight to the reins of Sevaani's horse.

From the road, Darien shouted a warning. The whipping whoosh of arrows came from behind them, and dark shafts fell, littering the white stone.

"Halt, in the name of the prince!" someone called out behind them.

"Don't stop!" Jaric commanded, and Meg yanked her head back around as they pushed their horses onto the white road of the Summoners.

There was a lurching sensation as her horse stepped onto the perfectly cut stones of the road. Sounds from the forest and the pursuing guardsmen faded away, and the morning sun cleared the trees to the east. It washed over the road, turning it into a blazing strip of light and the dais disappeared – along with the Bronze Guard – replaced by a view of unbroken forest.

"Where in the Void are we?" Sim's shout had an edge of panic to it.

Meg took a deep breath to steady her nerves. The road stretched into the forest from the southwest to northeast, where no road had been before.

"We head northeast," Captain Daynar said, sounding a lot calmer than Meg felt. "Let's see where that takes us."

"Where it takes us?" Simeon's voice rose.

"Enough, Sim." Jaric's voice was flat. "We can't go back, so let's get on with it."

"Anything you say, Captain," Sim said, turning away and muttering under his breath.

"What did you do, Kaiel?" Beside Meg, Sevaani had dismounted and was staring pale-faced at Kaiel. "You cut off Rolen's arm. Oh, gods, I'm going to be sick." She dashed to the side of the road, heaving.

"Good thing we haven't eaten anything recently," Sim said.

Meg glared at him as she slid off her horse, but she had to admit he was right.

"Kaiel," she said in warning as he made to approach Sevaani. "Stay away."

"But I didn't mean to do it," he said, clutching his arm. "He had a dagger at her throat. I... I –"

"That was an excessive way to stop him, Kaiel. You need to learn more control." Jaric's voice was flat. "Show me your arm."

Kaiel sucked in a breath as the captain examined his wound, but Meg had trouble feeling sympathy. What was happening to them all? A day out of the citadels and they were being pursued by the Carbinah of Jaroff – a Prince of House Niskeri no less – and attacking each other!

"I don't believe the bone is broken," Jaric said. He nodded at the axe. "You should keep that given you don't have a sword, just remember it's more used to chopping wood."

Kaiel looked down at the bloodstained axe. "The Kas'tirien say a dagger is as good as a sword when it's all you've got."

"Evidently," Jaric said. He turned to Meg as she joined them. "Did Shany show you her trick?"

"She did. Stand still," she said to Kaiel and took his arm in her left hand while placing the palm of her right hand above the wound. Closing her eyes again, she reached out to the world around her with her mind and pulled a thread of its energy to her. An emerald light pulsed beneath her palm and she lowered her hand, her fingers sinking into his flesh. He cried out and tried to jerk back, but she was ready and held him firm. "I said, don't move," she muttered. She concentrated and then pulled her right hand back and let him go.

"You'll need to bandage that," she told him briskly, swaying. "The damage has been healed, and the cut will close over naturally."

Kaiel swung his arm out, testing it. "Thank you."

"Meg," Jaric said, watching her closely. "Are you well?"

She offered a half-smile. "I've never done that without Shany present. I think... I just need food."

He grunted. "Food and water are both priorities, but each horse has a pack with travel rations. Enough to last us a week."

"If we ever get out of here," Simeon sniped. "What do we do after a week? There's no food on this road. And look at this!" Taking his dagger, he tossed it towards the forest only for it to clatter to the ground as though striking a glass wall at the road's edge. "You see?"

"Calm down," Jaric said. "These roads were well used in the Age of Glory."

"The Age of Glory?" Simeon stared at him. "That was almost four thousand years ago!"

"The Summoners built them to move people across the world quickly," Darien said, studying the road. "There's a stone archway somewhere near the Crescent Cities, on the border of Hetar. It stands on a hill, and you can see through it clearly, but anyone who walks under it never comes out the other side."

Sim glared at him, his fists clenched. "You knew that and let us come in here?"

"The Ley Paths are not the same thing." Darien shook his head. "It's said there are some still used in Tomassia and Cythis. If this one had broken when the world cracked, we wouldn't have been able to enter it."

"Then we'll be able to get out of here?" Sim said. "The sooner, the better. The light's all wrong in here."

"I agree," Meg said. She could make out the sun through the trees, but it had a strange, tin-like edge to it, as though it were a reflection rather than the source of light. And around them, sounds seemed to hold a peculiar, hollow echo.

"We'll get out," Jaric said confidently. "Can you ride?" he asked Sevaani, who nodded in response. "Good. Meg, stay with her, please."

Meg bit her tongue. Someone needed to keep an eye on Sevaani she supposed. She had no siblings herself, but if she did she'd like to think none of them would ever call her a *whore*. Sevaani didn't even seem upset! It must be shock.

And as for Kaiel's response… Blessed Tarin! She repressed a shudder thinking of what he did to Rolen. Maybe Sevaani is right to avoid him?

No. It had to have been the heat of the moment. Kaiel had never been a bully or cruel. It wasn't in his nature. Sevaani was wrong to say he enjoyed the violence of battle. The *adrenaline,* yes, Shany had explained that sort of thing to her. But not the blood.

Meg climbed up on her horse after she'd helped Sevaani onto her own and eyed the empty forest around them. She closed her eyes and reached out with her senses the way she had been taught, looking for the threads of life. They were there; if they hadn't been, she wouldn't have been able to do anything for Kaiel. But they were like a slow-moving pulse. She stretched further, straining to reach beyond the road and the barrier enclosing them. Suddenly there was a blossoming of golden light across her mind's eye, but it passed too quickly for her to grasp. Sighing, she opened her eyes just as Sim, having moved on ahead, called out. She kneed her horse forward.

Something flashed past them in the forest. Meg pulled her horse up short as the others called out in surprise.

"What was that?" Sevaani's voice trembled

"Nothing to cry over," Meg said before she could stop herself. "Sorry." She looked away from Sevaani's offended stare.

She snapped her reins and trotted towards Simeon. Again, something flashed by on either side of the road.

"We're moving!" she cried. She urged her mare onwards, and again the trees of the forest blurred by.

"It's the power of the Sahrin," Darien said. "We travel a few steps on this road and tracks of forest pass us by."

"How fast are we going?" Sim asked.

"There's no way to tell until we get out of here," Jaric said.

"And when's tha –"

"When we get to the next Ley Hub," Darien said.

"How do you know that?" Sim growled.

"Because it makes sense." Darien shrugged. "We entered through one; we'll be able to get out at one."

"Really?" Sim urged his horse forward. "Then why does no-one use them? Why aren't these Ley Hubs marked on maps?"

"They are on maps," Jaric said.

"They've not been on any I've looked at."

"That's because you only look at maps of trade routes," Darien pointed out.

"I do not!"

"Older maps, from the early years of the Var Imperium, mark where Ley Hubs are," Jaric said. "Your father has one in the High Keep, Sevaani."

Sevaani shook her head. "I don't know."

"Oh, he does," Jaric said. "I've seen it."

"I just want to know where we're going. We can't just keep running." Sim threw his hands up in exasperation.

"We're going to Serjat," Jaric said.

"Through the Deadlands?" Sim scoffed, and Jaric just stared at him. "Fine! But if we all get killed, I want you to remember this wasn't my idea!"

Meg rolled her eyes. "I'm sure none of us are likely to forget that."

"Let's go," Jaric said. "The sooner we move on, the sooner we'll find a way out."

They fell into line behind the captain, with Kaiel taking up the rear.

Jaric clicked his tongue, and the black stallion began to trot, slowly building speed. The others followed suit, the trees on either side of the road becoming a blur as they raced past.

"Excellent, they've entered the *Renimor*."

He leant over a table that depicted a map of the Broken Continent in sparkling stones. The light that shone through the blue-tinted lattice of his prison walls – so different to his first prison at the end of the War – was fractured, leaking through the runes he had spent the last thousand years inscribing onto the supposedly unbreakable solae from which they were formed.

He shook his head. *Unbreakable*. So much of what they had once believed to be true was a lie.

Every shard of solae, that eternal, crystalline substance that contained him, every fragment of it he had been able to gouge away, had given him something to work with. For what was *Asai* but the key to the building blocks of the universe? And solae was matter, just like everything else.

With a smile, he considered the placement of the pieces on the map, as though it were the field of a sareis board. All life was one great game. Position and reposition. Attack and defend. Action and reaction.

He tapped a finger on the crystal half-mask that hid the lower portion of his face. The mask was a manifestation of his true prison.

He studied the Silver Boar, cast blue in the sapphire light of his 'tomb', for that was what his brethren had intended this prison to be, his final resting place. But in the end, they were just as trapped as he.

"You have been too clever for your own good, Sarnorn." He chuckled. "Revealing your pieces before they are in position is foolish, even for you. But, as you did it first…"

His eyes narrowed as he considered the board, then reached over and moved another piece to the other end of the *Renimor* he had opened for the companions. *Yes, just there*. They would exit to the Hub right by the Tower. His prison-tomb.

Straightening, he surveyed the board again and smiled.

CHAPTER TWELVE

Directions

THE SUN MOVED across the sky, and the forest surrounding the Ley Path changed with every step. The only sound was the hard, ringing clomps of the horses' hooves upon the stone.

Darien couldn't judge how far they'd travelled, the trees blurring at each step left little room to gauge distance accurately, but if the position of the sun was anything to go by, they were already coming towards the end of the day. Yet it felt as though they'd been riding for an hour. The monotonous blending of the world around them offered little distraction, and he worried at the events they left behind. The death of his mother, and then of his master; the horrifying power of the possessed bone drake, and the supposed heritage he and his brother shared. But most of all, his thoughts kept turning to the fight with the Korda'vari. To what he'd done.

He could barely recall the runes he'd drawn, let alone the sounds that had torn themselves from his mouth, and his mind and body still ached from the *Asai* that had roared through him without control.

How had he been able to do any of that in the first place? Who, or *what*, did that voice in his mind belong to?

Taking a breath, Darien stilled his turbulent thoughts and turned his attention to the Light of the Eye of Eternity. Though it was day and the nebula of the Eye could not be seen, it was alight in his mind's eye. He let the Light fill him and his body began to tingle; the fine hairs at the back of his neck prickled against this cloak. With another breath he grasped the energy with his will, and wielded it like a quill, drawing in his mind *aleth*, the first High Asairic rune.

The rune glowed silver and bright before his mind's eye, its sharp edge neat and unwavering. As he studied it, it began to turn of its own volition, moving in three dimensions.

He let go of *Asai*, and the rune vanished.

Well, there was nothing wrong with his ability to draw on or wield the Light of the Eye. No daemonic force reached out to grab hold of his will for its own nefarious purpose.

Maybe he could find answers with the Ciralys, but if a daemon had tainted him, he'd never pass their tests. Would he?

Sim called out, and Darien gave a start; it took him a moment to get his bearings.

When he looked up, he saw a pair of rampant lions carved in brilliant white marble just ahead of them. The statues framed a shimmering in the air, beyond which aged paving stones led away from the Ley Path, disappearing into the forest.

Darien pushed his worry aside as they all moved forward, crowding around the lions and looking out into the forest in silence. Beyond the edge of the path sat another cluster of ruins. But where the pillars around the dais of Lovers' Stand had stood tall, stretching into the leafy canopy, these were broken and lay sunken on the forest floor around a central platform.

"Are these ruins near Tore?" Sim asked finally.

"I don't know," Jaric said.

"Well." Sim shrugged. "It's a way off this road, and who knows where the next will be. I say we take it."

"We must have put enough ground between the prince and us by now, surely," Meg said.

"We've only been in here, what? An hour?" Kaiel said. "And we've travelled fifty miles? I say we keep going!"

"That's not a bad idea," Captain Daynar said.

"But we don't know where this goes," Sim protested.

Darien glanced at Sim. "We didn't know where it led when we ran onto it, either."

"If it helps us get farther from Prince Alesandr, I say we keep going," Meg offered. "I mean, we can always turn around and come back if we don't find a way off."

"Can we?" Sim demanded.

"Yes, Simeon," Sevaani said. "We can." Without another word, she tapped the side of her horse with her heels and started down the road.

"Oh, right," Sim said. "It's okay when it's the daughter of the Steward who decides upon reckless courses of action, but if I do it, I'm the worst person in the world."

"Come on, Sim," Kaiel said. "Let's go."

They started walking the horses down the road. Darien looked up, through the blurring canopy of swiftly moving trees, to eye the sun as it raced across the sky. It would be night before they knew it, but then he supposed that wouldn't last particularly long either. He couldn't comprehend the artistry of the Sahrin, to be able to craft such a thing as this White Road. Invisible to the eye, and untouched by the forest around it, moving through time like an arrow. Even if the Ciralys only held a fraction of the power that the Sahrin had wielded, he had to join them. He *had* to. If this thing in his head stayed quiet, and if the Ciralys of the Fifth Circle didn't sense it within him maybe he'd be able to find a way to get rid of it himself.

He released a shuddering breath, his stomach a knot of anxiety.

As soon as they stopped, and he had a moment to himself, he'd start to work through the mental exercises Ciralys Telaq had taught him. He'd follow the steps to quieten the constant babble of thought, and when his mind was still, he'd search every corner for the thing that had violated him. And when he found it, he'd rip it out!

He turned his head as Meg's words floated back to him from where she and Sevaani were talking with Jaric Daynar.

"Meg, don't be foolish," the captain said. "We'll find a way to get both you and Sevaani back to Hanore."

"I'm not foolish." Meg's voice was cool. "I'm no longer Shany's apprentice. I'm going to Isoliere to take the test for admission into the Ciralys."

"Are you sure, Meg?" Darien asked. "What's the citadel going to do for a Keeper if you're gone?"

"She has Shany's blessing," Sevaani said.

Darien stared at Sevaani and closed his mouth. It wasn't that he didn't want Meg to come to Isoliere, but Meg… well, their friendship hadn't been the same since he'd refused her offer of a promise.

"Ah, I don't mean to interrupt," Sim called from where he was at the front with Kaiel. "But I think we might be heading east. You know, into the *Deadlands*."

"Not this again, Sim," Meg sighed.

"I realise navigation probably wasn't high on the list of skills Old Shany was teaching you," Sim said to Meg, wearing his most innocuous 'merchant's smile', "but I'm fairly sure that if the sun is there behind us – and *setting* – then we're heading east. Now," he made a show of thinking, his index finger tapping his chin. "What is east of the Wilds?"

"We aren't going into the Deadlands!" Meg said. "We're going to go to Ebron." She looked at Captain Jaric. "Aren't we?"

Jaric studied the sun through the trees. "Making our way north to Ebron would be wise, but I think Sim is right."

"Thank you," Sim said. "We need to go back to those lions and get off this road."

Darien looked back over his shoulder. He couldn't even see the lion statues anymore.

"There's no going back, Sim." Sevaani's voice trembled.

"Of course there is!" Sim scoffed. "We just turn the horses around and walk back until we see the lions. They can't be that far away." Sim peered past Darien. "Can they?"

"Are you sure you want to do this, Sevaani?" Jaric asked her. "We can get you to Tore. Captain Kara will see you back to Hanore. Your father will protect you from the prince."

"No." Sevaani shook her head. "He can't afford to make an enemy of House Niskeri. The citadels live free of Aldania because we're no trouble. He'd have to hand me over to Prince Alesandr as leverage over Kaiel. But I'm not going back to Hanore."

"I don't understand what's come over you all," Jaric said. "What's this about, Sevaani? If you're chasing after Kaiel –"

"I'm not!" Sevaani's face was bright red. Darien looked to his brother, but Kaiel was staring pointedly in the other direction.

"Really?" Jaric pressed. "Then how long have you been dreaming?"

"For a long time, Captain," she said stiffly.

Darien frowned. "So, you want to come to Isoliere too?"

"What I want isn't part of it, Darien." Sevaani shook her head. "If I could dream what I wanted into existence, then I would be –" she stopped abruptly and took a breath. "My dreams are real."

"I believe her," Meg said. "She… well, she knew things. That I was leaving when I hadn't told anyone else."

"That wouldn't have been hard to deduce, Meg," Jaric said with a raised eyebrow.

"What does a gold rose mean to you, Captain Daynar?" Sevaani asked.

Jaric stared at her. "What?"

"I dreamt of you before you arrived in Hanore," she told him. "Of you and a gold-coloured rose. It was dying. Each of its petals falling away."

Jaric stared silently at her, his expression as blank as stone. Darien watched the man and wondered what nerve Sevaani had touched.

"Well then," Jaric said at last. "Where will you go? What are you planning to do?"

"She can come with us to the Ciralys," Kaiel said. "They must know about dreaming. Maybe she can become a Ciralys too?"

"I'm not a Ciralys," Sevaani told him. "But we're heading in the same direction; I know that."

"We're going to need to do some planning," Sim said. "Or are we just going to walk on this road until we drop?"

"We go on," Jaric said. "We accomplish nothing standing around."

Darien nodded. There wasn't much else they could do.

Eyes closed, Darien sank his awareness into the stillness of his mind. The gentle rocking of Waro, even the rhythmic *clip-clop* of the horses' hooves on the everstone road, all aided his trance. The inky blackness of no-thought swum before him and he walked the razor's edge of awareness while focusing on nothing at all, gently brushing aside any stray thought that sought his attention or sound that pulled at his calm.

Time lost meaning as he floated in that space within, the part of every human that breached the veil of manifestation. Everyone possessed this centre, but few ever found it.

Gently, yet with a relaxed, lazy intent, he stretched out with his senses.

There was no foreign presence here, no Voidborn power. He floated within the stillness, waiting.

It had taken him months to reach a point where he could meditate without the intrusion of his unquiet mind. It was one of the first things Ciralys Telaq had taught him, for it was within this centre that the Light of the Eye of Eternity would shine, a reflection of the light that bled from the nebula in the night sky. And it was from here that he would wield *Asai*. That the Light did not shine here now didn't concern him. He didn't seek to touch *Asai* now, but to find whatever presence had seized control of him in the catacombs beneath Sonyth.

It could have been minutes, or it may have been hours before he noticed the shimmer of movement at the edge of awareness. There'd been a time when such an event would shatter his calm and return him to his conscious mind like a slamming door, but he'd trained hard these last four years, and he held steady. The thing tickled the edge of his floating thoughts, a glimmer of violet flame, the swish of shifting sand. He waited, even as some part of him felt his stomach clench and sweat break out on the back of his neck, but these were peripheral distractions, and he was stronger than that. The sound came again, along with the feeling of something moving, like the coils of a snake slowly unwinding, just out of the corner of his eye. Slowly Darien turned his awareness towards it, patiently, painstakingly, he let not a single edge of urgency arise, not a blade of focus. He reached out with his mind and–

"Are you asleep?"

Darien jerked in his saddle, his heart-pounding. "Gods!" He glared at Meg. He had been so close to discovering what was inside his mind. "Void damn it!"

Meg reared back. "There's no need to be like that."

Darien's heart was still racing. He'd almost had it! Light of the Eye, was this what he had to look forward to all the way to Isoliere? No peace, no privacy. Meg everywhere he turned, making him feel guilty that he couldn't feel for her the way she felt for him.

She sighed. "Aren't you talking to me now?"

"When did you decide you wanted to be a Ciralys?" he snapped, and almost bit his tongue.

"Dar," she said and nudged Helese alongside Waro. "I thought you might be happy having someone from home at the Palace of the Eye."

"I want to get away from home, Meg, not be reminded of it. Who's going to take your place in Hanore?" Gods, he couldn't hold his tongue. This wasn't her fault!

"Why do you care?" she snapped. "If you're so desperate to leave, what does it matter to you who'll be Shany's apprentice?"

"That's two citadels now who need an apprentice," he said. What was *wrong* with him. He sighed, breathing deeply and tried to moderate his tone. "Shany must have known something was going on; I can't believe she let you go."

"Yes, because this is all about Hanore and the people you're discarding! Are you too good for me now?"

"What?" he blinked.

"Now that you're Blood?" she said. "Are you too good for the poor little orphan girl from the Borderland Wilds?"

"I've never treated you like that, Meg!" This was ridiculous. He needed a minute to himself.

"Ever since you apprenticed to Ciralys Telaq, you've had no time for m – your friends."

He caught her pause and raised an eyebrow. "I've been busy learning, Meg," he told her. "Being an apprentice to Ciralys Telaq wasn't an idle position or one I was looking for. It was new and challenging, and I had little time for myself, let alone for anyone else."

Silence fell between them, the forest continuing to shift in a dizzying blur as the horses walked the road.

"How are you feeling?" Meg asked finally.

"What?" He felt the blood drain from his face.

"I saw the backlash you suffered after casting those runes yesterday. A mindstorm. That's what the Ciralys call it, isn't it?"

"Yes, that's right." He wanted to laugh in relief. The backlash, the mindstorm, not the presence in his head. He supposed it had been a mindstorm. A minor one, and hardly surprising after wielding that much *Asai*. He shifted in his saddle, looking away. "And I feel fine, thank you."

"I was impressed," she said. "I wouldn't have imagined the Ciralys teaching such things to an apprentice."

"I read it in one of his books." Darien felt his stomach turn.

She eyed him for a moment then looked away. "Well, we're lucky you did."

"Come on," he said to her after a moment. He gave Waro a nudge with his heels. "Let's catch up to the others."

He could get away from Meg and her questions by putting others between them, but he couldn't get away from whatever nestled in his head. Solitude would have to wait.

"You cut off his arm," Sim said. "I know Rolen is a horse's arse, and that he stole the Kas'tirien apprenticeship from you, but did you have to cut off his arm?"

Kaiel glanced over his shoulder. The others were some distance behind them. "I didn't mean to," he said, turning back around.

"Just remind me never to get you angry."

"I don't remember what happened, Sim," he whispered. And it was true. He didn't even remember picking up the axe.

"I just told you. You chopped off Rolen's arm."

"I know that!" He took a breath as Sim raised an eyebrow. "I just... It just happened."

"Rolen's not my favourite person, so you don't need to explain it to me. Sevaani, on the other hand... although if he was my brother and had called me a whore, I'd have cut his arm off myself."

"She won't even talk to me."

Sim shrugged."I think that bird has flown."

Kaiel sighed, marking the sun through the trees. It was moving fast; it would be night in the next hour at this rate.

"Kaiel? You're still planning on following Darien to Serjat, aren't you?"

"There's not much else I can do. He's not going to stop in Ebron."

Sim shook his head."And neither should you. The City of Towers is still part of Aldania, my friend. The more I think about it, the surer I am that you're going to need to run farther than that."

"I know."Kaiel gritted his teeth."But if I can just stop Dar from racing off to the Ciralys, I mean if can talk him into taking a post as a scribe, then –"

"Fat chance of that," Sim scoffed. "Your brother is set on being a Ciralys. He's not going to settle for being a scribe."

"And Prince Alesandr knows that," Kaiel agreed. "How hard a time do you think His Highness will have tracking Dar down once he joins the Ciralys?"

"I'm fairly certain the Ciralys bow to no kings, but political maneouvering can make strange allies." Sim glanced at him. "You're not going to claim whatever's left of this House? You'd be Blood then."

Kaiel laughed. "Who'd believe I'm a descendant of the Blood of a Great House? A dead House. *You* don't even believe it." He shook his head. "How did this happen? All I did was pick up a daemon-cursed spear!"

"It's not that I don't believe you." Sim wore an uncharacteristically serious expression, his dark eyes hooded as he looked at Kaiel. "It's all just a little like an Evay tale to me, you know – a poor young shepherd discovers he's the lost king to a realm in peril."

"I'm not a shepherd," Kaiel muttered.

"You know what I mean." Sim waved a hand. "I just don't trust the people who are spinning you this story."

"You don't trust Captain Daynar?"

"Maybe, I don't know," Sim said. "But who is he? Have you wondered that? He's not Borderlands born."

"I picked up the spear, Sim," Kaiel said. "It changed in my hands."

"It could have been picked up by anyone."

"It didn't change for the prince or any of the guards that picked it up. Just me and Darien."

"Well –"

"What about our name? Toranth? It is fairly close to Taaren'th, isn't it?"

"Depends on how you pronounce it. And anyway, what about that? How come you're the Highlord of the House and not your Uncle Malik?"

Kaiel frowned. That was a good point.

"Exactly." Sim reached over from the back of Del and clasped Kaiel on the shoulder. "I don't trust the Niskeri. They were bannermen to House Taaren'th and turned on them to steal the Ivy Throne. No Prince of the Niskeri is going to back a Taaren'th."

"He doesn't want me to be a lord," Kaiel protested. "He wants me to kill one of the Shol'mas."

"Void take me, Kaiel, that's just crazy!"

"I'm here, aren't I?" he said, his chest tight. "I *ran* from Prince Alesandr."

Sim grimaced. "I know. I'm sorry."

Kaiel met his eyes and gave a tight smile.

"It's a good thing you aren't going to chase a House name," Sim said after a moment. "I'm not sure I could be friends with a lord. The Blood are always looking down their noses at us."

Sim smiled. Kaiel tried to smile back, but his attempt was half-hearted.

"What if you can't change Darien's mind?" Sim asked.

"He said something about the Tal'desai," Kaiel said. "Maybe I can join them?"

"The Talda-what?"

"Tal'desai," Kaiel repeated. "They're the guardsmen of Ciralys."

Sim scoffed. "Keep me away from rubbish like that."

"What else can I do? Dar's all I have left. I can't go back to Hanore, and Jaroff is just as bad, not least because that's where the Bronze Guard have their barracks."

"You could always come with me," Sim said.

"Where are you going?"

"I don't know. At least, not exactly. See, I found this in a chest in my parents' attic." Sim fished something from a small pouch, glancing over his shoulder. He hissed at Kaiel who was about to do the same and then reached over to hand it to him.

The gold ring gleamed in the sunlight, and a ruby, the size of Kaiel's thumbnail, flashed wine-red fire around an etching of a raven. Kaiel peered at the crest. The raven was in flight below what looked like a nine-tined coronet. "You *found* this?"

"Yes. I found it," Sim said, looking him in the eye.

"What is it? Do you know how much it'd be worth?" He handed it back to Sim.

"I have a fair idea." Sim snorted. "I don't know what it is, other than a signet ring, I suppose. Nor do I know why my father had it. But I'm going to find out." He put the ring back in the pouch.

"Here you are getting your back up about the fact that *I* might be Blood, and your father has a signet ring in his attic?"

Sim scowled. "It's not the same thing."

"Oh, really? How's that?"

"Because I don't want to be a lord! I just want to find out what my parents are running from."

Kaiel didn't pursue the illogic. Instead, he asked,"How are you going to find out what it is?"

"Well, Ma and Pa came from Tremor-Salaya. And if it's a signet ring, then it'll be hereditary. Serjat is as good a place to start tracking down the origins of the crest as any."

"And then?" Kaiel asked. "You'd be safe going back to Hanore. I'm sure Prince Alesandr wouldn't bother you."

Sim raised an eyebrow. "Really? Because Alesandr wouldn't suspect me of knowing where you're headed? No," he said. "Hanore isn't somewhere I can return to any time soon either. And why would I want to? I've always wanted to get out of there as much as Darien. But I want out to make coin." He grinned. "Now that the prince knows about my eggs, he's not going to leave me alone; or rather House Niskeri won't, and I won't become indentured to someone else when I can make my own way."

"What about your parents? He won't go after them?"

"They don't know how to make the eggs," Sim said. "Besides, my father can talk his way out of anything." He paused. "Don't you want me to come?"

"What? It's not that." Kaiel said. "It's just... I wish I were able to go home and see Aunt Brea and Uncle Malik again. But now I can't."

"You will, one day," Sim said. "And they'll be fine; Steward Etine will take care of them. If it's true the Stewards have been keeping your heritage a secret for so long, they won't give it up now."

Kaiel eyed his friend. "I hope you're right."

"Me too."

"Other than the loss of his arm, he'll be well, Your Highness," the field surgeon said.

"I am glad to hear it." Alesandr gripped the haft of the spear so tightly he imagined it would snap at any moment. They had been in these cursed ruins for nearly half a day, and the longer they tarried, the greater the distance between himself and the Taaren'th brothers became.

"There is one thing," the surgeon said.

"What is that?"

"The young man is insistent on going with Your Highness to track the fugitives."

"That is commendable. His sister has been taken by the traitors after all. He has a duty to see to her safe return."

"But, Highness, he is suffering from shock. He needs rest and time to adjust."

"Adjust to a missing arm? How do you do that? No, these Borderlanders are built of hardy stock. If he wants to come, then we shall allow it. You will attend Rolen Etine, and make sure he *adjusts* while we continue the hunt."

The surgeon bowed and Alesandr left him, crossing the ruins to where the captain of his bodyguard still inspected the site of the Taaren'th brothers' disappearance. A column of marble carved with the High Asairic runes of the Summoners had been found at the edge of the dais. Under his direction it had been lifted upright and brushed off so the runes could be properly read.

"If there were nothing to be found before, Olan, it would not have miraculously reappeared now," Alesandr said. "The runes tell us where the Path goes, not how to get on it."

The Asp knight bowed, his black silk surcoat absorbing the sunlight.

"We need to move. They get farther away from us all the time!" Alesandr bit off the last and clenched his jaw, taking a deep breath.

Olan nodded. The man was young for a captain's rank in the Asp but he had been part of Alesandr's personal retinue since the death of his older sister and had saved him from assassination twice. When Alesandr had reached his majority and had to assemble his own guardsmen, Olan had been his first choice to captain the Asp Knights assigned to him.

"There is something here, Highness," Olan said, his eyes narrowing. "A touch of *Asai*, I would say, but not that of the Ciralys." The Asp were all chosen for their sensitivity to the Light of the Eye.

"That is hardly surprising," Alesandr said. "The Ley Paths were made by the Summoners after all."

Olan shrugged. "Of course."

"Tomassia is the only realm with active Ley Hubs! How did they get on a *Renimor* here?" Alesandr spat in disgust and gestured sharply at the column. "This indicates the Ley Path runs all the way to Amaria. We need to follow them."

"Through Dal'mere?"

"Are you scared, Olan?"

The knight grunted. "Dal'mere is a death sentence, Highness. For you just as much as anyone else, but I live to serve."

"Peace, friend. You are right, but if I remember the maps correctly, there may be another way..." Alesandr smiled. "Get the others mounted. Send a runner to the Guard on the road and get them marching to Citadel Tore. And send a Fist to Hanore as well. They are to hold the brothers' aunt and uncle. If we cannot find the boys, perhaps they will be of use."

CHAPTER THIRTEEN

The Deadlands

NIGHT FELL FASTER than Darien or any of them had expected given they'd only been travelling the Ley Path two hours. At least it felt like two hours. It was hard to judge when both the sun and the landscape moved so quickly. But within a matter of hours, the sun rose again as the blurred trees surrounding the road suddenly gave way to broad, black plains and wide streaks of luminescent white.

Sim had been correct. The road travelled directly into Dal'mere.

Darien supposed it wasn't surprising. After all, Dal'mere had once been the Atresian Plains, the cradle of human civilisation on Sobia. It had held the most significant cities and libraries, even the fabled Halls of Governance. That the Summoners – the *Sahrin* – would seed the realm with Roads that let people travel quickly from one place to the next made perfect sense; although how they were accessed and where they were to be found would be helpful to know. But that was one more thing lost in the Sundering.

The Ciralys claimed that it was here, in the Deadlands, that the Summoners had unleashed the cataclysm known as the Sundering, breaking Athmay into two halves, and leaving a ruin of the Atresian Plains. The once fertile fields had become poisoned ground, black as the space between the stars and riddled with a white phosphorescence that stalked unwary explorers and could kill with a single touch. The people of that time had called it Dal'mere, the Deadlands. A place where the Veil between worlds was so thin that the Daemon Hunters spoke of pulsing lights in the sky as daemons tried to find their way back into Sobia.

Naturally, Sim had been beside himself when Jaric announced they'd walked into Dal'mere, but given they were moving so fast – and none of the Deadlands' poisons seemed to be affecting the White Road – they'd all decided to push on.

That decision had left Darien with little time to find the solitude he needed to meditate, and he was not going to try again until he was sure of his privacy. Their stops had been brief and given they were confined to the road around them, there was no privacy, but as they'd walked, he'd slowly allowed Waro to edge to the side – Sim just ahead of him and the women just behind. Stretching his neck to look around as unobtrusively as possible, Darien decided this was as 'private' as he was going to get.

He reached into his pocket and withdrew the shard Telaq had given him in the catacombs. Though the crystal lay in the shadow of his torso, the sun already past its zenith behind them, light gleamed off its lines, its ruby hue flashing as he turned it in his hand. It fit snugly in his closed fist. Its edges were rough, and though ovoid, it was clearly a shard of a larger piece.

He had no idea what it was.

It had to be important for Telaq to pass it to him with his dying breath, but it was a mystery to Darien.

His desire to hold it to the light of the sun was outweighed by his desire to keep it hidden.

Cautiously, Darien opened himself to the Light of the Eye of Eternity as Telaq had taught him, and the silver light of *Asai* filled his mind. Breathing in, he could feel the world around him as though he was suddenly connected to everything in a vast web, and he looked down at the shard.

Staring at the crystal, his eyes lost focus and something *shifted* within him. There was a rushing sensation, and the crystal filled his vision. Its ruby tones, deep like blood, began to lighten, to shift, glowing from within as though licked by tongues of flame.

He could feel the thing in his mind *roll*, and fear caressed his back like cold fingers.

Darien held his breath, terrified the voice would speak again, his awareness racing through the rooms of his mind. But there was nothing.

"What have you got there?" Sim's voice startled him.

Void take him! Darien closed his fingers over the shard and with a small flick of *Asai* caused it to fade from sight. His time working with Old Shany hadn't been a complete waste. He'd learnt many useful things as her apprentice; they just couldn't compare to the power of the Ciralys.

"Nothing, Sim," he said, making an effort to speak calmly. "What do you want?"

Sim eyed him for a moment then shrugged. "There's something up ahead, and the captain wants us all together." He looked back at the women behind Darien. "Come on, you two."

"What is it?" Meg asked.

"I don't know," Sim said. "But if you come along, we can all find out."

"There's no need to be rude," Meg said.

Sim raised a hand to his chest and let his mouth fall open in a little 'o'. "Me? Rude? I'd never be so cal –"

"Oh, shut up, Sim," Darien sighed and pushed Waro forward to catch up to his brother and Captain Daynar.

The terrain changed. Suddenly, rocky cliffs of black stone rose around them, what looked to be a river began to flow beside the Ley Path, the sky was reduced to a thin strip far above, and in the air, gossamer threads caught the light.

A spider web? Here? They'd encountered no wildlife on the Road, not even birds. How did a spider get in here? It was then that he realised he could hear the flowing gurgle of moving water. He could *hear* the river.

Looking around more closely, he could make out strange lines running along the invisible wall Sim had discovered when they first stepped onto the Road. Fine lines, like the cracks in broken glass.

With a nudge to Waro, Darien moved towards his brother and noticed the canyon walls did not rush past him. He could see every crevasse and shadow in the rock as though time was once again moving the way it should.

Darien shivered, feeling the full chill of autumn for the first time since they'd escaped onto the Ley Path.

"What is that?" Sim's voice rose behind him, and Darien looked up. The webs were becoming thicker as they moved farther down the corridor. A strange, chittering sound came from the ledges above, and there was the odd splash of displaced stones tumbling into the water beside them.

"Tarin, lend us grace."

Darien looked back as Meg called on the Elder Goddess of Nature to see her pointing at rope sized strands of spider web that stretched like a net between the canyon walls, decorated with giant cocoons of silk dangling over the water.

"Light blind me," Sim muttered, looking at the web. "Suddenly I'm not too happy about killing all those treewolf spiders. What if mama treewolf made this?"

"There aren't any trees around, Sim," Sevaani observed. "Whoever made this is a different species."

"*Who*?" Sim grumbled. "It's a 'what', not a 'who'."

"Look!" Kaiel pointed. At the top of the cliffs ahead of them, stood three hulking silhouettes.

"Korda'vari," Jaric said.

"I *hate* this," Sim muttered. "First spiders, now Korda'vari! I thought you said this road was safe?" He grabbed a bow from the packs, deftly strung it and shot an arrow at the figures above.

"Simeon!" the captain yelled, but it was too late.

If Sim had one talent, outside of wringing your last copper from you and getting into trouble, it was marksmanship. He was one of the best archers in Hanore, and his aim was, as ever, true.

One of the Korda'vari fell, an arrow protruding from its neck.

The beast landed in the ropes of web strung across the canyon and over the Ley Path, its journey to the river halted not far from the canyon's roof. Its companions howled like wolves, raising their fists above their heads. One threw a spear but it, too, tangled in the web. The Tainted peered down before giving one hooting call and moving out of sight.

"I'm not sure I like this." Kaiel kept his head raised, searching the web above when Meg shouted.

"Spider!"

From the canyon walls to their left emerged a crystalline spider, easily half the size of the dead Korda'var. Its eight thin legs were at least five feet in length, and its body reflected light like glass.

Moving deftly along its silken web, it approached the dead Var and sank its large fangs into the Tainted's back, before it began to cocoon the body in white strands.

"I suggest we move," Jaric hissed. "Before it comes after us."

"Do we go forward or back?" Meg asked, a quiver in her voice.

"At least if we go back, we'll be returning to the area where the road still works," Darien said.

"What do you mean 'still works'?" Sim demanded.

"We can't go back!" Jaric pointed behind them, and they turned to see a swarm of smaller, glittering spiders.

"At least they aren't as big," Kaiel said.

Darien turned on his brother. "They're the size of rats!"

"I meant they're not as big as the one up top."

"There's more!" Meg screamed.

Darien looked up to see more of the smaller spiders dropping towards them.

"Move!" Captain Daynar shouted and then they were galloping, their mounts whinnying as heels dug into flanks.

But as fast they were moving, the spiders were faster, some dropping off the web, spinning their threads to lower themselves to the road ahead.

Hooves flashed as Kaiel directed Lasa over a spider that had landed in front of them.

Darien peered ahead, the canyon was dark, but the webbing above them gave a soft glow, and he could see more daylight ahead. And more spiders.

Captain Daynar, on his black stallion, pushed past Darien with a flaming brand in his hand. Standing in his stirrups, Jaric waved the open flame over the web, and it caught fire in a whoosh of noise. Masses of the smaller spiders began to back away from the flame travelling up along the web, but more began dropping to the road.

"You know that fancy fire thing you did in the catacombs under Sonyth?" Sim called to Darien. "That would be handy here!"

Darien felt the blood drain from his face, but before he could respond, a roar echoed from above.

The two remaining Korda'vari were shadows atop the edge of the canyon. Darien narrowed his eyes as he saw them wrestling a dark silhouette to the lip of the cliffs.

"Look out!" Jaric called.

A massive stone boulder was pushed over the edge of the canyon, smashing into the web. Unlike the body of the Korda'var Sim had shot, the great stone tore a vast swathe of the web off the canyon walls as it came crashing down. Darien stared. Some part of the Ley Path's energy field must still have been active because the stone struck an invisible ledge in the air and rolled past the road and into the river running beside it.

Beside Darien, Meg gasped. He looked up to see still more of the spiders descending, moving to escape the flames that were spreading across the web above them.

Sevaani urged Cloudchaser forward and jostled Sim's mount. Already spooked by the spiders and the fire, Del reared in panic and Sim, not seated properly, fell from the saddle.

"Sim! Watch out!" Kaiel shouted, swinging his axe and slicing into a spider. Sim got to his knees, then cried out as a spider landed on his back. He reached behind himself, knocking the thing off.

"Gods, Sim!" Sevaani cried. "Have you been bitten?"

Sim had his left hand against the back of his neck; his face screwed up in pain.

"Let me see," Meg said and made to get off Helese.

"Not now!" Jaric shouted. "Kaiel, get him on his horse and get out of here!"

Kaiel leaned down and helped Sim up onto the horse while Darien held Del's reins.

"I don't feel so good," Sim said, and his eyes rolled back.

Kaiel caught him as he fell and had to pull him off Del's back and set him in front of himself.

"Oh, gods, is he dead?" Sevaani cried.

"No," Meg said. "Not yet. But we have to get away from here."

Without another word, they let the horses have their heads and galloped out of the web-strewn section of the road. Darien eyed the canyon walls; still, they remained the same as if they were moving at normal speed, and no-one else seemed to notice anything. They raced down the road, escaping the smell of burning web. Darien glanced over his shoulder, but no wave of enraged spiders followed.

When they reached the end of the canyon, the walls fell away, stretching out behind them into a line of cliffs that travelled the length of the land north to south. The river beside the road widened into a concourse that continued to run east through a green forest of twisted trees and sickly scrub, spreading out across the north-eastern horizon, the line of the White Road running across the top of the water like a bridge.

"We can stop here," Meg called. Reining Helese to a stop, she jumped off the mare's back and went directly to Sim. She put her hand to Sim's forehead. "He's already burning up."

"Can you heal him?" Sevaani pressed her hand to her face.

"I don't know," Meg said.

"You have to try!"

"I will." Meg took a breath. "Kaiel, get him down."

Darien dismounted and came to help his brother lower Sim to the road. Meg knelt beside him and brushed Sim's hair from his neck, revealing a spider bite that pulsed an angry red.

Kaiel stifled a curse.

"Kaiel," Darien put his hand on his brother's shoulder. "Meg will do what she can, but she's no Shany."

Meg flashed him a look of irritation and cupped Sim's face in her hands. She closed her eyes and began to chant. Darien didn't recognise the words, they were not High Asairic, but a gold light seeped from the edges of Meg's eyes. Darien frowned and shifted his sight, opening his mind to the Light of the Eye. His eyes widened at the glow surrounding Meg's hands as she lowered them over the wound on Sim's neck.

Darien was going to speak, to question her on what she was doing when Meg took a gasping breath and sat back on her heels, the golden glow fading.

"That's the best I can do," she said, panting as though she had been running.

"What have you done?" Jaric peered over her shoulder.

Darien studied Sim. "He's not breathing!"

"He's *asleep*," Meg snapped. "I placed a stasis charm in the wound. He *is* breathing but very slowly. I'm hoping it will hold the spread of the venom and buy us time to get him to a healer."

"Do you think we might find one in Exile Point?" Kaiel asked Jaric.

The captain considered for a moment and then nodded. "I imagine so, and corsairs would need to be healed, no doubt." He knelt beside Sim. "How long can he stay like this?"

Meg sighed. "I don't know."

"It's okay, Meg," Kaiel said gruffly. "Thank you."

"Captain," Sevaani sat on Cloudchaser off to the side looking out across the waterway and the sickly green trees that marched across the horizon ahead of them. "Where are we?"

Darien turned from Sim and joined the captain as he made his way over to Sevaani.

"Gods," the man let out a breath. "If I'm correct, that's the Sukmaanai Swamp. We've crossed the Deadlands. Six leagues in a day? Two days? I don't know how long."

"Six leagues?" Meg joined them. "Six *hundred* miles. That's impossible. It would take a month to travel that far on horseback, and we haven't even stopped, not really."

"And yet, here we are," Jaric said.

"The Summoners could cross the breadth of Athmay by stepping through a hole in the air," Darien said. "I think you could say we took their version of the long way."

Jaric grunted. "Let's get Sim onto a horse; we should see where this road's taking us."

"These are all the boats you have?"

Prince Alesandr stood in the morning light as the sun rose over the forest, a commanding figure dressed in black silks and emerald kharidium mail. The iridescent metal was not something she'd seen often, but Kara Ferin, Captain of the Rangers of Tore, recognised it quickly enough and it made her uneasy.

She had met the prince several times before; he'd even taken up residence for sixteen months in Tore, as he had in Hanore and Sonyth. He was always courteous in his dealings with the citadels – unlike his brothers during their tenures as Carbinah. The way they had treated Ma'ree Toranth… She turned her thoughts away from *that*. But Alesandr had never been so cold as he was now. Commanding, yes, but in a gentler way that fooled you into believing he was just like everyone else. But he wasn't, and the instinct to respond to the authority he exuded wasn't something she was familiar with.

She didn't know what had happened with the Toranth boys or Jaric Daynar, but this was going to cost Tore and the whole Borderlands. She was sure of it.

Kara stood at his side, her leather armour still blood-splattered from a pack of Korda'vari that had thrown themselves at the walls of the citadel the night before, and she set her jaw, ignoring the desire to make herself more presentable before the Bloodborn prince.

"Yes, Your Highness, these are all the boats."

At his silence, she continued. "We're only a small town, as such things are reckoned in Aldania, and the Murk is no place to sail. The rapids to the west make following the river to Jaroff impossible, and east are the

Deadlands." She shook her head. "Dal'mere is just as dangerous on the water as it is on land. We never go far. A handful of men range to the west to fish, that's all."

Alesandr's face was dark. "The old maps indicate the *Renimor* that passes through what you Borderlanders call Lover's Stand, goes all the way to the north-eastern coast of Dal'mere. It did, in fact, travel all the way to Shi-Kaan in Amaria before the Sundering. And seeing as you cannot tell me how they got onto the *Renimor*, I have little choice but to follow them by river."

Kara paused. The Ley Paths were legends. The old maps marked them, but no-one had used them in centuries, and certainly no-one had ever heard of a Ley Hub at Lover's Stand! It was fool's talk. But she wasn't about to tell a prince that, not when he had the son of Leman Etine whispering all the secrets of the Borderlands into his ear. That Rolen was somewhat delirious, missing an arm and spewing vitriol against Kaiel and his own sister, didn't seem to bother the Niskeri Prince at all.

If it were up to her, she'd let the Deadlands take them. The citadels didn't need this kind of attention! But if Halaron was stirring, and last night's attack, not to mention the force the prince said had attacked Sonyth, seemed to indicate it was, then the citadels needed to be ready. And they needed allies.

"Your Highness, it's madness. The Deadlands are not safe. It's a death sentence to go in there."

"And yet, if I cannot get onto this *Renimor* I have little choice!" he snapped.

"Your Highness, this is a mistake," Kara tried again, her stomach tight. Gods damn him! If he died on this fool's journey, the King would demand answers! "I can't imagine Jaric Daynar assisting anyone running from justice. If Kaiel Toranth is truly a traitor –"

"You doubt my word, Captain?"

"No, Your Highness, it's just –"

"We will leave the rest of the Bronze Guard here," the Prince spoke over her. "I am commandeering these vessels in the name of House Niskeri. I expect their owners to accompany the force that will fit on the craft." His eyes flashed an emerald green in the morning light.

Kara took a breath and bowed. What choice did she have? "Your will, Highness."

CHAPTER FOURTEEN

Echoes and Visions

BITTER WINDS SWEPT across the open expanse of water as the canyon fell behind them. The river bled into a body of water Darien was sure was wider across than all three of the Borderlands citadels if placed side by side.

Vegetation flourished around the waterway, though its colour was sickly, and a foul stench of rot filled the air so thoroughly that even the wind couldn't alleviate it. Bare twigs reached between grey-green foliage, raking the sky like bony fingers, while trails of white-green moss hung from dark, bent branches, populated with crows and other, stranger birds.

The world outside the bounds of the Ley Path was no longer a blur as they moved, but it was shifting around them with increasing speed the farther away they moved from the canyon of crystal spiders.

Darien held his arms tight against his body, seeking warmth from the chill wind and the fear that pressed his mind. The fear the meditative techniques Telaq had imparted, failed to keep at bay.

At the edges of his thoughts, the *thing* whispered to him, and in response his stomach twisted like the eels that kept surfacing on the river. The inner calm of the Ciralys eluded him, broken as it was by both anxiety and a fierce pain that was suddenly stabbing at the back of his hand again. His mind's eye had opened, yet nothing was any clearer. Everything was the same, and he was useless!

Even Meg, with the witchery of an apprentice Keeper, had been more useful in helping Sim than Darien had. Her training with Shany had advanced far beyond his own. His education had begun anew when Ciralys Telaq had taken him on. And it wouldn't be completed for years once he was admitted to the Palace of the Eye in Isoliere.

But what were his prospects of being accepted by the Ciralys now? All he had was the crystal his master had thrust into his hands as he died and a voice in his head!

A voice that *shouldn't be there.*

He'd been a fool to dismiss what had happened when his mind's eye had opened. When the dark, shadow-bird had attacked him. He'd wanted to believe it a side effect of his Awakening – an event that should have been conducted under the supervision of the Masters of the Fifth Circle. He should have spoken to Master Telaq about it right away instead of brushing it aside. Shany wouldn't have been waiting for him if it was nothing, but she hadn't pressed him and he hadn't wanted to look into it further.

Had he continued learning under Shany, he would have been defended from any sort of daemonic possession by the Bond that witches chained their apprentices with; had he been in the Palace in Isoliere, his own defences would have been honed in dedicated study and practice, and he could have defended himself.

But he'd had a spontaneous Awakening, and now something was amiss.

At night, the nebula of the Eye of Eternity lit the heavens far to the north. But day or night, its light was always a presence in the back of a Ciralys' mind.

He could open himself to that silvery Light. It was a basic exercise that all Awakened must master. For only when an Awakened was filled with the Light of the Eye could the runes of *Asai* be taught. And without those runes to direct and give form to the power, it was uncontrollable. Lethal.

Many Awakened had died attempting to wield *Asai* with their minds alone. Or worse, blinded themselves to the light of *Asai* altogether. Darien could do little with the few runes he had picked up. Yet in the chamber of the bone drake, he'd spoken runes he'd not learnt and wielded power that should have been beyond him.

And lived.

Something had stepped forward and moved his body like a puppet.

"Darien."

He flinched at the call.

"Darien?"

He spun in his saddle, and Sevaani stumbled back. "What?" he snapped, his heart racing. Gods, this was becoming a habit.

"I... I just wanted to see if you were well. You've been very quiet."

Darien grimaced. "Sorry. You startled me is all."

"Did you ever imagine you'd leave Hanore like this?" she asked, moving Cloudchaser up beside him. Captain Jaric was at the back of the line, and Meg and Kaiel were in front, looking after Sim, who his brother still supported in his saddle.

"No," Darien shook his head. "I'd thought I'd be travelling with Ciralys Telaq. Maybe heading to Ebron and finding passage on a ship, I don't know. But I never imagined this."

"I didn't either." She sighed.

"You mean you didn't dream this?" he winced at the bite in his tone.

She blushed and shook her head. "No, I didn't dream any of this."

"This dreaming doesn't seem very helpful, does it?"

"I don't know," Sevaani said. "Some things are clear, and others are less so."

"Like knowing you will never return to Hanore? Pity you didn't know Rolen was going to put a knife to your throat, you might have avoided it." Gods! He was snapping at everyone who tried to talk to him.

Her eyes flashed."Or warned you about the voice in your head?"

Darien felt the blood drain from his face and Sevaani clasped a hand over her mouth.

"Oh, Darien," she said."I'm sorry. I didn't mean, I..."

"What *did* you mean?" his voice came out in a rasp.

A look of concern crossed her face."No-one else knows, Darien. I swear to you."

"I don't know what you are talking about."

"I've dreamt of you," she said, her voice low. "I've seen it in my dreams."

"Seen what?"

"I see you, but it's not you, it's..." She struggled to find the words, her face pale."Do you remember those stories we were told as children? About the Bloodlords, with the gnarled hands and hunched backs, red eyes and bones of babies around their neck?"

He squeezed his jaw so tightly, his teeth hurt.

"Those are just children's stories," she told him, seeming to also reassure herself."I know the reality must be different. But I… I dreamt of you, standing in a field of bodies that stretched all around." Her knuckles were white as she clenched her reins."It was dark, and the night was filled with howling creatures, and black tears in the air with angular, glass-like tentacles reaching out of them and..." She faltered.

Darien could only stare as she squeezed her eyes shut. He didn't want to hear this, but he had to know."And?" he whispered.

She took a breath. "And an army of Korda'vari, all bowing to you." She met his eyes."You looked just as you do now, but on your shoulder, wrapping around your neck was a... a *shadow*. Your eyes weren't your eyes anymore." She bit her lower lip."I could hear it speaking to you, *through* you. And at your feet, directly before you, was Kaiel. Dead. His throat was slit, and you were holding a bloody dagger in your hand."

He tried to scoff, but no sound came from his mouth. He was sure icy fingers stroked the back of his neck.

"But I had another dream too." Her hands finally relaxed, blood flowing back into the skin."You were standing in front of a door of black stone; at its centre was the seal of the Eye of Eternity –"

"A Khaderneous,"he said.

"Yes! But this was huge, and the serpents were wrapped around a giant pearl."

"Wisdom,"he murmured.

"You stood before it," she continued."And I could see your aura. It was... it was..."

"What?"His eyes narrowed.

She smiled."It shone like the sun, Darien. Brighter than anything I've ever seen. And there was no shadow around you, the one I saw in the other dream was gone. In this dream, you raised your hand, and the door opened."

"And then what?"

"I don't know,"she said, dropping her gaze."I don't know what any of it means, but I thought I should tell you."

"You won't,"he began and stopped. Tried again."You won't..."

"I won't tell anyone,"she said."But maybe someone could help you, Dar."

"Help you with what?"Meg asked.

Panic flared through him. He hadn't even noticed Meg drop back to join them. What had she heard?"Did you want something?"

"I'll go check on Simeon,"Sevaani said into the silence that followed.

"Are you still angry?"Meg asked, strands of loose red hair streaming in the wind.

"You shouldn't be here, Meg," he said, fumbling for something to say and instantly wished he could take the words back. "It's dangerous."

Anger suffused her face. "I shouldn't be here? *Me*? But it's okay for Sevaani to be here? If I believed you cared, you might be able to brush me off with that answer. The Gods know I would have been thrilled by that show of concern once. But you don't care at all, you selfish little warren-rat!"

"You of all people can hardly call me a warren-rat!" He snapped, stung by the insult. "And you've chased me around ever since you began studying in the Keeper's Tower. Why would this be any different?"

"I may have 'chased you around', but that was because you were in the same position as I was. Learning the same things. There was no-one else I could talk to in the citadel who would understand! Gods, I could genuinely believe you *are* Bloodborn, you are so arrogant. Everything is always about you. I don't know why Kaiel puts up with you, brother or no!"

"For the same reason you do, I'm sure," Darien muttered.

"And more fool me!" she spat the words at him. "This might be hard for you to believe, but I have a gift too. And why shouldn't I take a chance to make something of myself, and it? Why shouldn't I go to Isoliere and seek training and a life outside of the Borderlands? Everyone in the Three Citadels is trapped there because their ancestors broke from the Clans centuries ago. Ask Kaiel, who has no gift, how hard it is to get out! You don't know, do you? And what's worse, you don't even care." She shook her head. "There is a whole world around you, Darien, if you bothered to notice it."

"You've never shown any interest in becoming a Ciralys before," he protested. Gods he wanted this to end. "You didn't even speak to Telaq about it."

"I'm not a complete idiot!" Again, she spat the words. "This is the sort of rubbish I'd have had to put up with from you for the last three years if I had! Shany knew I was leaving. She even told me what to do when I reach Isoliere."

"Oh, and what a fine example she is." He should stop. None of this was fair to Meg – or Shany. "Happy to remain a Keeper when she could have been a Ciralys!"

"She's a witch, Darien!" Meg said. "She's spent more years immersed in the craft than we've been alive. The Ciralys would never have accepted her. And why would she want to join them? A Keeper was all you aspired to be before the prince and his pet Ciralys arrived!"

"You never asked me what I aspired to be," he protested. "You were too busy hoping I'd become – that *we'd* become something we're not."

She fell silent and regarded him strangely. "Well," she said at last. "Better I come to my senses late than never. And you're not stopping me. I've left Hanore now, and I won't go back. I *will* take the Test, and if the Circles reject me, so be it." She tilted her head. "But that's not going to happen. I have Hedge Right, so you're going to be stuck with me for some time yet, Darien Toranth."

Then, to his shock, she burst into tears and flicked Helese's reins to rejoin Kaiel and Sevaani.

Darien bit his tongue. The presence moved like a shadow in his mind, and he steeled himself against it, breathing deeply. He wrapped his hand around the shard in his pocket, holding it as though it was a talisman.

He'd never been like this before. Not to Meg, or his friends. He just needed to get this thing out of his head!

He suppressed a shudder as visions of the dreams Sevaani had related crossed his mind. Dream-reading was something the Fifth Circle might know of in their studies of the Sphere of Spirit, Sarmisere. His natural leanings had been towards Hyrisere, the Sphere of Fire more commonly called the Third Circle, and he knew little enough even of that at this stage of his training.

He breathed in through his nose and out through his mouth and closed his eyes.

After a few moments Darien opened his eyes again and blinked.

Before them, the river had disappeared into a wall of trees. The trunks were thick and gnarled, growing right out of the water. Braided through the branches before them were the skeletons of three enormous snakes, their skulls painted red. Dark, crude pennants dangled from their bones.

With a wince, he opened his fist. He'd been gripping the shard so tightly it had left a deep crease across his palm. Carefully putting the crystal away, he took a deep breath and urged Waro down the road to join the others.

"Is that the Sukmaanai?" he asked his brother.

"Yes," Kaiel said, glancing over his shoulder to Darien while still supporting a comatose Sim.

"The road keeps going, straight through it like it did the trees in the Wilds," Sevaani said, gesturing at the wall of trees before them.

"Those snakes don't look welcoming," Darien offered. He looked at Meg, but she kept her eyes focused straight ahead.

"Captain Daynar thinks they're territory markers for the skreet," Kaiel said.

"The skreet?" Darien looked over the bones again, feeling uneasy. "I didn't think they were that smart."

Kaiel grimaced. "Compared to a human, they're not. But we haven't seen any yet." He peered into the trees. "There has to be land in there, somewhere."

"As long as this road offers us a way out and we can find this Exile Point the Captain has spoken of, we'll survive." Sevaani said.

Darien sighed. "What about Sim?"

Kaiel shook his head. "No change."

"We'll find Exile Point." Jaric finally joined them at the place the Ley Path entered the trees.

"Have you been there before, Captain?" Meg asked.

"I haven't," Jaric admitted. "But while it's not on many maps of the realms, its location isn't a secret to everyone. The Broken Teeth, hundreds of tiny islands between the north-eastern edge of Dal'mere and the south-coast of Aldania, have become a haven of sorts for the corsairs that terrorise trade on the Nemisdrillion Sea and the Gold Sea. Exile Point is significant because it's the home port of the Drowned Blades, and the closest thing to a capital these thieves have."

Darien frowned. "You know a lot about it."

"I wasn't always Captain of the Hanore Rangers."

"But you know about a secret pirate port?" Meg said.

"Exile Point has quite the reputation amongst sailors," came a voice from the trees.

As one, they spun around. Darien's fist was wrapped around the hilt of his belt knife as Captain Daynar drew his sword while Kaiel gripped his axe in a fist, his other arm still wrapped around Sim.

"Who's there?" Jaric called. "Show yourself!"

The water beside the road began to splash. Darien turned, startled, as the water rose, sculpting itself into the shape of a man. Intricate detail etched every inch of the water form, from the embroidery on his robes, to the gemstones at the belt around his waist. Long hair flowed to his shoulders, and an angular half-mask covered his lower face.

"What *is* that?" Meg's voice trembled.

"A sending," Darien said.

Meg glanced at him. "A what?"

"A sending, a thought form that the Ciralys use to communicate across vast distances. They usually bend light to give themselves form, I've never heard of it being done with water."

"He is the Master of the Swamp," Sevaani said. "I… I dreamt of this."

"That is unexpected," the water form said. "I did not know you had a Dreamseer amongst you."

"What do you want?" Jaric demanded.

"I wish to help you." The figure spread watery hands. "You are all tired and hungry, and your companion quite ill. Come, continue down this road. The next Ley Hub is not its end, but I strongly recommend you leave the road there. People who continue down the broken Ley Paths tend not to find their way out."

"Why would you help us?" Jaric asked.

But the water image had begun to lose its shape, sinking back into the river. "Come. You will find sanctuary here for the night." The sending seemed to look at Kaiel. "And I would speak with the scion of Varos Korin'ad in more depth."

CHAPTER FIFTEEN

The Master of the Swamp

KAIEL FELT HIS blood run cold at the water man's words, the skin across his shoulders prickling as it shrank against him. "I'm not a Summoner."

Around him, the shadows of afternoon deepened as though a cloud passed over the sun. A call that was almost a word came from the trees beyond, and the unmistakable hooting of laughter answered.

Captain Jaric took his eyes off the river and faced him. "I told you before; House Taaren'th was founded from the bloodline of Varos Korin'ad, the last Empyros of the Summoners."

"But –" Kaiel floundered.

"It doesn't make you or Darien a Summoner." Jaric faced the swamp and the White road that led directly into it. "We're left with little choice here," he said. "Let's go."

Kaiel looked at Darien, but his brother had already turned Waro and was following the Road into the trees. Kaiel shifted his grip on Sim; for such a bag of bones his friend was heavy. But he wouldn't leave Sim behind, and they couldn't tie him to the back of Del when they had no rope.

"Come, Kaiel," Captain Daynar called.

Kaiel sighed and used his knees to turn Lasa around and followed the others into the swamp.

Nobody spoke as they entered the shadows of the trees, although the exchange of glances told Kaiel they'd all noticed the world around was no longer moving at a blur. Tendrils of mist drifted around them, and wisps of light offered an eerie backdrop to the splashes and dripping water that echoed across the stilted atmosphere of the Road. Waterlions, creatures he vaguely recalled hearing of in the adventure stories of his childhood, appeared between the tree trunks that rose from the murky water, and in the branches above, great black snakes slid over hanging limbs while chittering calls rose all around.

Kaiel peered into the half-dark surrounding them, warily eyeing the strange flowers and plants that glowed in phosphorescent blues and greens. Sevaani had expressed her delight at the flowers until a large, yellow winged insect landed on one, only to have the petals snap shut around it, trapping the thing. She had turned away, her face ashen.

Darien attempted to light their way by calling a flame to dance over his palm, but the infestation of bugs attracted to its brightness, even through the wall of the Ley Path, had him release the fire, returning them to the mercy of the swamp's ghostlight.

"Can we trust it?" Meg swatted something on her arm. Her plain woollen dress was as dirty and soiled as Kaiel's trousers and tunic, but it was the circles under her eyes and the way her hair lay in oily strands about her head that spoke of her exhaustion.

"I don't know, Kaiel," Jaric said.

Darien shook his head. "Not for any of you maybe. He only wants to speak to the 'Scion of Varos Korin'ad'."

"And who is that?" Meg asked. "Kaiel, or you?"

"It's not me," Kaiel protested.

"It hardly matters right now, does it?" Darien said. "You're all acting as though we're going to get out of here. As if we'll not only make it to the other side of this swamp but that whoever lives in Exile Point will be disposed to assist us rather than cut our throats."

"Would it be better to do nothing and act as though we are already dead?" Jaric didn't raise his voice, but his tone was icy.

"Hope is what keeps all people going, Darien," Meg said tiredly. "If you lay down in defeat then you've truly lost."

"I was meant to be on my way to Isoliere by now," Darien muttered. "Not stuck in a swamp with a Shol'mas Lord looking to play me like a piece in whatever game he's engaged in."

"Why do you believe you're a pawn? And that this Master of the Swamp is a Shol'mas Lord?" Jaric stared at him, the glow from a nearby clump of hanging blossoms illuminating the hard planes of his face.

"Why don't you?" Darien shrugged in exasperation. "Sarnorn is after us at one end, and this Master of the Swamp stands at the other? It hardly seems coincidental. Who else but one of the messengers of the Gods could do this?"

"If Alesandr is right, Sarnorn wants you and Kaiel, not us," Meg pointed out.

"Then let's hope you don't all get caught in between," Darien sighed.

They fell silent after that, the peculiar ambience of the swamp, its odd sounds, shifting shadows and clumps of humid air blanketing them in a strange pall.

The Ley Path cut straight through the Sukmaanai and the sky above darkened, not that they could see much of it through the dense canopy. Kaiel couldn't even make out the Span to orient himself.

They'd been walking for at least an hour when Sevaani called out. "Look, there are those lion statues, like the ones we saw after Lovers' Stand."

They crowded around the lions that framed a faint shimmer in the air. Beyond was a platform, almost identical to Lovers' Stand, but where that had been in the middle of a forest, this was surrounded by swamp. And all the creatures that called it home.

"Will it be safe to leave the road?" Meg asked.

"I was just thinking the same thing," Kaiel said. "In here, the Deadlands couldn't touch us."

"Except for the spiders," Darien said. Kaiel looked at his brother, but Dar was staring through the doorway.

"I think we have to risk it," Jaric said at last and directed his stallion between the statues.

Meg and Sevaani looked at each other for a moment before moving off the road after the captain, leading Sim's horse with them. Darien followed, and Kaiel brought up the rear.

The platform was circular and at least twenty feet in diameter. With Jaric's help, Kaiel lowered Sim to the ground and dismounted, his legs stiff from the prolonged time spent in the saddle. Meg and Sevaani gathered the horses and tethered them to the broken pillars that rose around the edge of the platform and began brushing them down, while Darien was standing at the edge of the dais looking out into the dark.

"Dar?" Kaiel called. "What is it?"

"There's something out there." His brother's voice was spectral in the dark.

"What is it?" Kaiel joined him.

"I don't know," Darien shook his head. "*Something*. It's too dark to see."

"So, where is this Master of the Swamp?" Kaiel asked. "He wanted to talk to us, didn't he?"

"Your guess is as good as mine," Darien said and turned away.

"It's a good question, Kaiel," Jaric said. "However, we're stuck here for now." The captain gestured behind them; the entrance to the Ley Path was gone.

Kaiel looked back at Jaric. "What do we do now?"

"We wait until morning and make a decision then. I'll take first watch," Jaric said. "We shouldn't let caution fall to the wayside, even if we're entering a trap knowingly."

"Is that what it is?" Sevaani had stopped brushing Cloudchaser to listen, but the captain didn't answer.

"I'll take second," Kaiel said. Jaric agreed and moved to the edge of the platform that backed into the swamp. The rest of them gathered by Sim, who had been laid out in the middle wrapped in the captain's cloak, a backpack placed under his head like a pillow, to wait out the night.

Darien stood in a hall of mirrors.

Soft mist hid the floor beneath his feet, and the light came from a source he couldn't find. Looking at the mirror closest, he gasped. A velvet over-robe of inky black was draped across his shoulders. Silver runes graced the cuffs of the sleeves and circled the high collar at his neck. Pinned to his left breast was a Khaderneous medallion, the entwined serpents made of multi-coloured skystone.

The skystone loops of the twinning serpents sparkled and reflected the light in a brilliant splay of prisms. A hole opened in his stomach. Each Ciralys was attuned to one sphere, and that sphere manifested in the colour of their skystone. Green for earth, yellow for air, red for fire, blue for water and pearl for spirit. He'd never heard of... *opal* amongst the skystones used by the Circles.

His gaze lowered, caught by the sheen of the inner robe; he wore a cassock of dark grey damask silk, his waist cinched by a belt of deep violet scales. Soft, black leather boots covered his feet.

He ran his hands over the robes. The travel grime was gone from his face, and his hair had been cut close to his head.

His green eyes flashed in the mirror.

Darien looked away and studied his surrounds more closely; he marked mist above and below. This wasn't real; it couldn't be. He shivered. Had the thing in his head taken control of his thoughts? Was he trapped in his mind?

To his left lay darkness and to his right lay light; it was apparent in which direction he was supposed to walk. Scowling, he turned to his right.

He straightened his robes, unease still flickering through him, but he pushed it away and willed his legs to move.

The mirrors formed a corridor, but in a single step, he was at their end. He walked into a circular room. Thin crystal columns, veined with sapphire light, reached high to a ceiling lost in the mist. In the room's centre stood two full-length mirrors in ornate frames of silver. The floor was made up of tiny squares of black and white tiles, forming a mosaic of concentric circles. This was a dream, it had to be.

The blue glow from the pillars flickered eerily, tinting the swirling mist the same colour. Taking a deep breath, Darien stepped in front of the silver-framed mirror on his left.

The robes he now wore in his reflection were crimson. Sharp-edged runes with wicked curls and strange tails flicked across the edges of the sleeves and along the high collar with a fiery light. Dark runes, wet with blood, marked both his cheeks and trailed down his neck. His eyes were narrow and his face, though his own, had a strange cast of viciousness to it, of cruelty. His skin had a maggot-white pallor and above his right hand glowed the Mark of the Eye. The sign of the Sahrin, of the Summoner, pulsing a dull vermillion.

In his fist was an obsidian dagger that dripped blood. On the ground, at his feet–

No! He spun away.

It was the dream Sevaani had told him of. That's all it was, and he would not look. He *couldn't*. He didn't want to see his brother dead!

He turned back slowly, careful to keep his eyes off the lower half of the mirror and recoiled. The image in the mirror had changed again.

Dark clouds rolled behind him and at his shoulder stood Kaiel. His throat was slit in a gruesome caricature of a grin. His eyes were glassy and unseeing, and his hand was reaching to rest on Darien's shoulder.

Crying out, Darien spun away, falling to his knees as bile seared the back of his throat. He bit his lips against the heaving of his stomach and tried desperately to block the image from his mind.

He breathed deeply; sweat beading his brow. He would never, *never*, do something like that, not of his own volition.

The laugh that left his throat verged on hysterical but was muted against the mist. He closed his eyes.

That image wasn't him as a Ciralys; it was him as a Bloodlord. A sorcerer of *Des'maadr*, controlled by the daemon he already feared was in his mind.

He opened his eyes and found himself before the second mirror.

In this reflection, he was still wearing a cassock and overrobe, but there was no red, no cruelty. No blood.

The robes were those he was wearing now, and his face was much the same but for a sense of calm, of authority and confidence.

Above his right hand floated the Mark of the Eye, rendered in lines of gold and silver light.

He struggled to his feet.

There was a sense of freedom in this image that he very much desired. No-one would tell this man what to do; no *thing* would invade his mind without his consent.

If only he could reach that place. Become that person.

But a Sahrin? No, surely not. To be a Summoner was to have the entire world hunt you down. He would never be able to escape. He rubbed the back of his right hand, feeling the unhealing cut under Shany's ointment.

This was a dream. It had to be – a cruel parody designed by the thing inside him.

He tried to laugh but choked on a sob. How could he possibly fight a creature in his mind?

"You use the only weapon you have." Darien immediately recognised the man who stepped out from behind the silver mirror.

He was taller than Darien, but not quite as tall as Kaiel; Darien studied the stranger without any sense of surprise.

The man, if indeed he was human, cast no reflection in the mirror. But unlike Darien he was dressed in the robes of a Ciralys, a dark blue mantle draped over the shoulders of his silver, silken robe. No Khaderneous medallion rested on his chest, and the lower half of his face was hidden behind a crystal mask, while long brown hair was pulled away from eyes which were untouched by age.

"You use your Will."

"My Will?" Darien said. "You are the Master of the Swamp?"

"You may call me, Anith'eal," he said with a bow of his head.

"That is the tongue of the Sahrin. It means... Seeker of Knowledge?"

"Very good." His eyes travelled over Darien. "Although this is interesting. I did not expect you to be wearing these robes."

"Perhaps it is a manifestation of something you've read."

Darien kept his expression neutral. Was this a dream?

"Yes, it is a dream," Anith'eal answered him. "Although you will have to take my word for it. I know your suspicious nature will wonder next if I am a trick of the daemon dwelling within your mind. I am not. Nor does it have the power to control you. Not yet. That will only come with time."

Darien swallowed, his mouth dry. "Can you remove it?"

"I could." Anith'eal said. "But I won't."

"Of course not," Darien sneered. "Why would you help me? I am nothing to you."

"This is true," the man agreed. "You are nothing to me. But that is not the reason." He clasped his hands behind his back and began to circle the room. "You have enormous potential, Darien. Not only for who you might be, what you might become, but because you hold a shard of the Cryndalene."

"A what?" Darien regarded him warily.

"The crystal your teacher passed you." The mask hid his mouth, but Dairen was sure he smiled. "You are wise to hide that, and you should continue to do so. Many would kill you to possess it."

"But not you?"

Anith'eal's eyes flared silver. "I would dearly love to possess the shard, little man, but one mere fragment of the Cryndalene would not break me out of my prison." He took a deep breath, and the light receded from his eyes. Darien strove not to shiver.

"It is time to change the game," the Master of the Swamp said. "The Eye of Eternity stops for no god, or man, though some would plot towards such a goal regardless. So." He gestured. "In the mirrors, you saw what could be. All men are offered a choice in life. Some recognise it; most do not. Every action they take, every response they make, changes the path they are walking. Sometimes by a few degrees and sometimes completely. You hold part of the key to humanity's future in the shard. It is one piece of ten, and all of them will be needed to face what is coming. If you fall to the daemon inside you, you will doom us all. If you can fight it off, even rid yourself of it – and that is possible, though no Ciralys in this age could manage it – then we stand a chance."

"A chance at what?" Darien was becoming dizzy as he moved to keep the Master of the Swamp in his line of sight. "If it is so important this daemon be gone, *help me.*"

"A chance of *survival.*" Anith'eal stopped before a mirror. "If I give you the answers, what do you learn? Your third eye opened before you were properly prepared. As a result, a daemon has sunk its claws into you. It's enough to make one believe in destiny, is it not?" He tilted his head."What I *will* do for you is grant you a ward that will act as a buffer. It will give you space and time to learn, but it will not hold forever, so be warned." He reached into a pouch at his waist. "And take this." He tossed Darien a small flap of brown leather no larger than the size of his palm.

Darien caught it, turning it over. There was an opening at the top, revealing it to be a bag, and a long cord was stitched into it at one end so that it could be tied around a belt or a wrist. Opening himself to *Asai* revealed small runes lining the seams, moving like drops of water, disappearing and reappearing as he turned the bag, but he could sense no trace of *Asai* on it.

"The bag will keep your shard safe from prying eyes and give you a more secure place to hide it."

Then the Master of the Swamp opened himself to *Asai*, and Darien felt a torrent of power pour into the man. Anith'eal raised his right hand and traced a rune on Darien's forehead.

He spoke in an unfamiliar tongue, and Darien screamed as fire roared through his veins.

Kaiel was alone.

Beneath his feet was a crest carved into flagstones, but so worn by age and the tread of countless feet that he couldn't make out anything other than the shape of a kite shield. Above him, mists wreathed the sky. He moved forward.

His footsteps sounded hollow, and the sensation of being watched crawled along his nape. His hand went to the hilt of Captain Daynar's axe, and he slowly turned a full circle, peering into the mist. Where was he?

The mists rolled, and before him, he could make out battlements that rose like sculpted shadows. Frowning, he walked across the yard.

A dark shape loomed out of the mist to his right, and he stopped. Cautiously, his hand still on the axe, he made his way towards it and collided with an invisible barrier.

He pressed his palms against the empty air. It was as though he pressed them against the expensive clear glass Sim's father had installed in his storefront windows back in Hanore. He peered through the barrier, and the shape revealed itself to be an intricate frame of wood and steel that glowed with a blue-white light.

Within the frame, a man clothed in red had been bound by his wrists and ankles. Kaiel's blood ran cold.

He struggled for breath. Was that Darien?

No, it couldn't be.

But the slight figure, and the way the dark hair fell from the bowed head, all screamed at him that the man tied to the frame was his brother.

From the right he heard the stomp of marching feet, and into view came a troop of soldiers in black surcoats over mail that glittered like stars.

Kharidium. They were wearing mail made of silver kharidium.

Soldiers stopped before the frame in front of Kaiel, but his height allowed him an unimpeded view over their heads.

At an unseen signal, they all snapped to attention. A man as tall as himself stepped from the mist and walked down the line. His armour was also made of kharidium, but where the soldiers were only wearing mail, this commander wore plate. The pauldrons on his shoulders swept up in sharp edges, traced with gold filigree that glowed. On the breastplate, more lines of golden light followed the man's torso, glowing like a sunglobe. A white cloak graced his back, held in place on each shoulder by ten-pointed stars of gold and diamond.

His was as commanding a presence as Prince Alesandr, and across his back was a large sword. Its hilt was a sculpted dragon's head, jaws opened wide to clasp the blade, and an enormous sapphire lay in the eye socket.

"Today is a great day." The commander's voice rang across the courtyard, and Kaiel's head jerked back. The man had removed his stylized helm, and blond hair glinted like the gold on his armour.

He was looking at himself.

"We have at last captured the Bloodlord whose Korda'var horde has laid Aldania to waste. Whose hands are soaked with the blood of the innocent and who, had we not stopped him, would have opened the Ninth Gate, allowing our world to be overrun by daemons of the Void," the other him said to the gathered crowd. "Unlike most men, he cannot be sentenced to death; the Lichlords of the Crescent Cities have given us ample proof that death is no obstacle to power. But with the assistance of our Ciralys allies –"

He gestured to the side, and the mist revealed a redheaded woman in ornate robes of gold. Kaiel barely recognised her, but it was Meg who stood at the head of the Ciralys. Gone was the grubby-faced orphan who had been Darien's shadow, and in her place was a beautiful woman with the bearing of someone used to command. She nodded in acknowledgment of the commander.

" – with the assistance of our Ciralys allies," the other Kaiel continued. "There is a prison to which he can be exiled. Not since the Summoners betrayed their people has so treacherous an enemy walked the land." The other Kaiel's gaze swept the soldiers before him.

"'Ware the Bloodlord!" Meg cried out, her voice sharp with authority.

Even as she spoke, the man – Darien – shackled to the frame raised his head and Kaiel gasped.

His brother's face was a twisted mass of hate and bruises, and his eyes glowed red beneath blood-caked strands of black hair. He opened his mouth and darkness fell from it like smoke as he spoke in a tongue that tore at Kaiel's ears like claws.

The men beyond the barrier fell to their knees, screaming, and behind Meg, the Ciralys staggered.

Kaiel's other self let out a roar and wrenched his sword from his back. Lunging forward, he plunged it into Darien's belly. There was a flash of light, and the sapphire eye of the sword glowed blue, sparking with energy that flared along the blade, and Darien screamed.

"Now!" the other Kaiel cried, looking his brother in the eye. Behind him, Meg rallied and drew runes in the air that trailed a vaporous light. Kaiel's other self yanked his sword from his brother's torso and stepped back.

"Farewell, brother," the man whispered, the words ringing in Kaiel's ears.

Darien snarled and struggled against his bonds, spitting a mouthful of blood that splattered across the kharidium breastplate, sizzling like oil on a hot pan.

"Step back, Kaiel!" Meg said, and golden pinpricks of light, expanding as though devouring the air itself, formed an oval-shaped door behind the frame holding Darien; a gaping maw of writhing and bucking darkness. Screams and howls rose from the Void and a burning wind barrelled out from its depths. The other him stumbled as the gate moved to encompass Darien. Blood-curdling laughter echoed out of the gate as glass-like shards, writhing like tentacles, reached to pull Darien into their dark embrace. Then the braided frame of the gateway snapped shut, and his brother was gone.

"Quickly!" Meg said, running forward. "Get the breastplate off him, now!" Two men in kharidium mail pulled daggers to cut through the side straps and remove the other Kaiel's armour.

"I told you not to get too close!" Meg's voice was cold. "He's not your brother anymore."

Kaiel's other self raised a hand, stopping her words, and he pushed aside the breastplate the soldiers were taking from his chest. The blood

Darien spat had eaten through the armour. Light reflected off the wet tracks upon his other self's cheeks. "He will always be my brother, Meghara. *Always*."

The mists swirled and obscured Kaiel's view. He fell to his knees as the barrier disappeared, his head ringing and the scar on the back of his hand burning.

"You said you'd look after him, Kaiel," a voice from behind said, and he staggered to his feet in shock.

"Ma?"

Mar'ee Toranth stood before him, wearing the white shroud in which all dead were sent to the flames. Her hazel eyes filled with sorrow. "You said you'd look after your brother," she repeated. "You promised. You let them take him. You killed him, Kaiel." The mist whirled around her, covering her from view. "You killed him, and you've doomed yourself." She disappeared, and Kaiel stumbled after her, falling to his knees once more.

"I didn't, Ma. I didn't!" His back heaved as sobs tore from his throat. "I'm sorry I wasn't there to say goodbye. I *do* promise, Ma, I do! I *will* look after him. I won't let him go to the Ciralys. I won't!" He crawled into the mist, searching wildly for her.

"Ma? Ma! Come back. Ma!"

"She is not here, Kaiel."

He twisted around, his hand finding the hilt of his axe. A man ambled towards him dressed in silver robes, a navy mantle embroidered with eagles and hawks over his shoulders. Long brown hair was pulled back off a face whose lower half was covered by a crystal mask.

"There is no need for that." He gestured at the axe. "This is only a dream."

The mists swirled around him. "Who are you."

"You may call me Anith'eal," the man said. "I am the Master of the Swamp."

Suddenly on his feet, Kaiel took a step back.

"Nothing would give me greater pleasure than to speak with you in the flesh, but that is not possible at this time," the Master said, folding his hands together within the deep sleeves of his robe.

"Why not?"

Anith'eal raised an eyebrow then smiled briefly. "I am not as free as you might expect." He gestured around them, and the mists parted to reveal a latticework dome of glowing sapphire before it was obscured once again. "But that does not concern you. We must speak quickly before others notice and try to interfere."

"Interfere with what? And what others?" Kaiel tightened his fist around the hilt of his axe.

"That is the question, isn't it?" Anith'eal stared at him intently. "Justice can be very narrow-minded at times, and the pieces Sarnorn plays with require a broader field."

"Sarnorn? The Lord of Justice?" Kaiel sighed. "I don't understand any of this. I saw... I saw Dar –" He choked.

"That was a vision of one possible future, Kaiel Taaren'th. A glimpse of what might be. A warning, so heed it well," Anith'eal said. "This Age of Man has come to an end."

The silver light of Anith'eal's eyes darkened. "Knowledge has become stale, and those who once searched for more are hampered. They measure what they know against what legend tells them was once possible. All the while, culling those who could offer them more. My brethren and I have much to answer for."

Anith'eal sighed. "I am effectively removed from the world here." He gestured to the mists surrounding them. "Yet I can help you still."

Kaiel stared. "Why would you help me?"

"Because we stand at the precipice of a new age." Anith'eal swept his arm wide. "And humankind has fumbled in darkness for too long." The blue stones on the leather cord in his hair flashed, and he paused, his head tilted as though listening to something. "I am sorry; one of your companions became belligerent."

"They're here?"

"They are in the dream too; or rather, I am in their dreams."

Kaiel shivered. "What do you want of me?"

"Ah, here is where I step on Mykiel's toes. I shan't be popular." A throne-like chair of gold and onyx coalesced behind the Master of the Swamp, and he sat. "You will soon find yourself facing a choice, and the world will hang in the balance. You *must* choose, and your personal feelings of loyalty cannot sway you. You will be offered the choice of being true to who you were born to be or to deny it. One path leads to death – your death – and if you die, the world will fall to the Daemon Queen and the Void, forever. You will pay a heavy price if you choose to be true to yourself, but you will live, and so will the world. Do not allow humility to guide you into passivity." Anith'eal stared at him sternly. "I know, this is all very vague, but free will cannot be underestimated, and if you are to survive, you *must* be your own man."

"Are you talking about my bloodline? That I must raise House Taaren'th?" Kaiel asked warily. He couldn't think what else it might be.

"That is but one step before you. The ashes flare even now, but the Phoenix must rise before it can fly once more." Anith'eal regarded him and the scar beneath Shany's ointment on his hand suddenly flared with pain. "I have broken many of my brethren's rules tonight, and I must bid you farewell. Do not be blinded by what you hope to be real, and what *is* real, Kaiel. Hope, while necessary, is by its very nature a wish. Do not spend gold on what hard work will get you for free."

The mists swirled around them, obscuring Anith'eal on his throne.

"Wait," Kaiel called, pushing aside his exhaustion. "You haven't answered my question. What others?" No answer was forthcoming and Kaiel shook his head. "Then please, Sim is hurt. You must help..." But the hall faded from view.

CHAPTER SIXTEEN

A Cold Welcome

KAIEL WOKE WITH a start. The weak light of early morning accentuated the gnarled trees bending over the platform, and a rhythmic, barking drone – frogs? – fell silent as he sat up. Breathing deeply, he waited for his heart to slow its pounding.

His muscles ached as though he'd been working sword forms all night. His tunic was soaked with sweat beneath his leather vest. It was difficult to imagine it was winter; the mist that circled the trees was cold, but there were strange patches of humid air and a rank stench, like rotten eggs, that saturated everything.

The bent trees of the swamp marched into the water around the shore, and trailers of mist drifted across the mirror finish of the lake to caress a broken tower rising from its centre. Wet stones glistened in the morning light, and green moss crawled up the tower's body like a rash, straining for the broken battlements at its crown. Dark, empty windows stared out across the lake in silence.

Kaiel shivered and looked for Darien.

His brother lay curled on his side, arms wrapped around his chest as though warding off the morning chill. Kaiel sighed, slumping, as the others stirred.

Jaric sat bolt upright. His eyes settled on Kaiel and then moved to Darien, staring at him for a moment before returning to Kaiel.

"Who has the watch?" he asked.

"You didn't wake me?" Kaiel's voice was hoarse.

Jaric's lips twisted. "I fell asleep."

Meg groaned, pressing her palms on her forehead. "Agh. I feel like death," she said, her eyes still closed.

"Dar." Kaiel reached over to his brother. "Dar, wake up."

Darien rolled over, and Kaiel blinked. For just a second, he could have sworn his brother's eyes gleamed red. But there was nothing to cause alarm, no bruises, no glowing eyes; just the same old Dar, frowning up at him.

"Time to get up!" he said.

It was just a dream. And I promise, Ma, Darien will never go to the Ciralys. Never.

He slapped Darien on the arm, earning a groan from his brother, but he didn't care.

"Sevaani?" Kaiel said as Jaric bent over her still form. She awoke with a gasp, and the captain caught her shoulders in both hands, slowing her ascent. "It's all right," he told her as her eyes scanned the dark trees wildly.

"What happened?" she asked.

"We fell asleep," Jaric said, shaking his head.

"Blessed Tarin," Meg groaned, sitting up. "I had the strangest dream. It seemed so real. I don't remember much of anything. I remember a man in silver and blue, with a glass half-mask over his mouth and a huge table that was a gigantic map."

"A crystal mask?" Sevaani asked.

Meg looked at her and Sevaani gave a small smile. "I dreamt too."

"I had a nightmare," Kaiel said. "I –" He stopped, not looking at Darien. "It was nothing."

"I don't know if I dreamt or not," Jaric said. "But I feel like I've drunk an entire barrel of your uncle's Tomassian brandy."

"What about you, Dar?" Kaiel asked, half afraid of the response.

Darien looked up. In his hands was a dark piece of cloth. "What?"

"Did you dream last night?" Kaiel repeated.

"Yes," Darien said, dropping his eyes. "I dreamt."

Kaiel studied his brother, but when Darien offered nothing more, he got up.

The sky beyond the twisted canopy was getting lighter. Kaiel's shirt was still damp and sticking to his skin. He'd have liked to wash it, but from the smell of the swamp, he'd be better off waiting until he found cleaner water. He leant over the side of the platform, cupped his hand in the water and brought it up to his face, sniffing, but couldn't tell if the water was bad.

"Kaiel! You're not going to drink that?" Meg's screwed her nose up, and he let the water drop back into the still surface.

"Be careful of that log," Sevaani said. "It's drifting closer."

In the dim light, Kaiel could only just make out the large shape in the water. "That's not a log," he said, grabbing his axe.

"What is it?" Jaric turned.

"Light!" Kaiel called out. "We need light!"

Fire gathered in Darien's raised palm, its orange tendrils sending shadows flickering all around them.

Kaiel set his feet as the creature lunged out of the water. Much larger than the log it had first appeared to be, it exploded from the lake, jumping onto the dais with a roar. Dirty water ran down a hide of pallid green scales, and great tusks gleamed like steel as giant fists lashed out.

"Look out!" Jaric warned, but the creature wasn't aiming for Kaiel and went for one of the panicking horses. Darien cried out as it skewered Waro with its tusk and hurled the screaming horse into the lake.

Kaiel hacked out at the creature with his axe, but it was fast and dodged his blow. Beside him, Jaric slashed at it with his sword, but the steel made no impact on the hide, and the beast jumped back into the lake, diving under its surface.

"What is it?" Sevaani cried.

"A tusked skreet," Kaiel said, naming the daemon.

"Oh, Darien," Meg reached out a hand. "Poor Waro."

Darien didn't reply, pale-faced he stared at the the body of his mount, Waro's thrashing slowing as blood filled the water around him.

"It's going to come back," Jaric warned.

"Are you sure?" Sevaani asked.

"Skreet aren't water creatures, and it will have to come up for air if nothing else. Meg, move the bags to the middle of the platform! Sevaani, stay with Sim."

Kaiel shifted his attention back to the water; the light from Darien's flame was fading as he moved to help Meg shift their gear. The swamp was silent.

The seconds stretched like hours. Knowing the daemonspawn was somewhere under them made Kaiel's skin crawl. He tightened his grip on his axe just as Jaric called a warning. The water next to Del on the far side of the platform heaved. The horse screamed, rearing, but the tusked skreet was too fast, and Sim's mount followed Waro into the lake, a large black stain billowing into the water as the enormous skreet jumped after it.

Beside Kaiel, Jaric cursed and jumped into the lake.

"Captain!"

"We can't fight it from up here. The water will slow it some!" Taking a breath, Jaric dived beneath the surface.

"We need to get Sim out of here!" Kaiel looked back at the others.

"We've got him," Meg said, already positioned by Sim's comatose form.

Kaiel nodded and waded into the lake. He searched for Jaric in the murky water and found the captain just as a boulder-like fist battered into the man. Jaric fell back, then came up spluttering.

"Its belly!" Jaric said, coughing. "Get under the water and stab the daemon. Watch out for the tusks!" Without waiting for a response, the captain dived below once more.

Taking a deep breath, Kaiel followed. He'd swum in rock pools amongst the small, offshoot rivers to the south-east of Jaroff but had never been in a body of water this deep. The light from Darien's flame did little to illuminate the swirling mud, but through a rush of bubbled water he made out the shadowy bulk of the creature lunging forward, tusks stabbing towards Jaric.

Kaiel tried to yell a warning, but the sound was blunted, and bubbles of air escaped his mouth, letting brown water in. He kicked his feet off the muddy bottom and thrust the blade of the axe at the monster, willing with all his might that the sharpened edge might bite hard. Unexpectedly, the blade sank into the creature's hide like a hot knife into butter. Kaiel almost lost his grip on the haft as the beast jerked towards him, away from the shadow that was the captain.

Its tusks moved through the water like twin scythes, and Kaiel pulled the axe free to bring it up in defence. The water hampered his movements, but the steel blade of the axe shimmered in the cloudy water and sliced through one of the tusks and into the creature's snout.

He kicked back to avoid the other tusk and the momentum of the creature, pushing himself towards the surface, lungs burning. Breaking free, he took deep, lungfuls of air and swept his axe through the water around himself in a panic.

Fear played at the edges of his mind, but adrenaline gave it no foothold. He dived again. The silence in the water was unnerving. The beat of his thundering heart pounded in his ears. He couldn't see the creature, but there was something… There! He raised the axe again just as the monster barrelled into him.

Kaiel twisted away, but the weight behind the creature's attack pushed it onto the keen edge of the axe, driving it diagonally into the scaled torso.

It thrashed wildly, clawed nails slashing at him like knives. He almost lost the axe, his hands burning from strain when a pulse of energy raced through his body.

Kaiel clasped his left hand over his right and steadied his feet on the muddy lakebed, then he twisted away, dragging the embedded axeblade through the creature's torso. More blood bloomed in the water like spilled ink.

With a cry, he pushed hard from the bottom and broke through the muddied surface of the lake. He made his way to the platform and heaved himself out of the water, breathing hard.

"What did you do?" Jaric called. Relief washed through Kaiel as he saw the captain by Meg and Sevaani, with Sim between them. The captain was still alive, though his face was marked with a grimace of pain.

"I killed it," he said, relieved the was captain safe.

"I know that!" Jaric snapped. "How?"

"Are you hurt?" Kaiel struggled to his feet. "I can't see any blood."

"There is none." Jaric lifted the edge of his tunic, and the sparkling iridescence of his mail caught the light. "No punctures either, but I'll be black and blue underneath."

"You're wearing kharidium?" Kaiel reached out, the links shining in the morning light. "Where did you get that?"

"Not now," Jaric said through clenched teeth, gripping his side. The morning sun brightened the swamp. "How did you kill it? That was a tusked skreet." Jaric pointed to the split carcass of the massive beast now floating dead in the water. "I couldn't even graze it."

"I don't know." Kaiel pushed his wet hair from his eyes. "I just did it."

"Kaiel," Darien said from his other side. His brother grabbed his wrist, pulling him back from the others."Your hand. Don't forget to put Shany's ointment on," he said in a low voice."It could have washed off in the water. Do you still have yours?"

"Yes." Kaiel took the small ceramic jar from his pouch, the pot was wet – his clothes were soaked through – but the cork stopper was still secure. He pulled it out with his teeth."There's not much in here," he said."Will this last until the wound is healed?"

"It should." Darien wrapped his arms around his chest."I don't think we'll need it for much longer."

Kaiel dabbed the ointment over the scab on the back of his and tucked the tiny pot away as Sim's voice rose in anger.

"Leave me be, Meg!"

Kaiel spun, his mind finally registering that Sim was awake.

"Simeon Ravenson, I will spank you if you don't sit still!" Meg said, pushing him back as he tried to rise.

"By the Void! All right! Just let me sit upright."

She eyed him suspiciously."You're not going to try to stand?"

"No!"

"You." She pointed at Kaiel."Make sure he doesn't get up."

"You're awake! How do you feel?" Kaiel couldn't help but grin and crouched next to Sim.

"I feel fine!" Sim protested. Then he looked at Kaiel and lowered his voice."I feel as weak as a newborn cave-goat. No!" He motioned furiously."Don't *say* anything."

Kaiel frowned but kept silent.

"Void damn it," Sim groaned."What happened to me?" He began to get up, but Kaiel put a hand on his shoulder."And where in the Void are we?"

"You got bitten by one of those spiders. Don't you remember?"

"Maybe?" He shrugged."It's all kind of blurry, like a dream." His eyes went wide."Blind me, but did I have a dream!"

"You too?"Kaiel looked over at Darien."Mine was more a nightmare."

Sim patted at his waist pouch and pulled out the ring he had found in his parents' attic. He sighed, inspecting it for a moment before putting it away again."Where are we? Is this the Sukmaanai?"

"Yes."

"Hmph. It's not so bad. A bit wet."He looked around."Seems pretty tame to me."

Kaiel gave a half a laugh."I suppose. Tame enough for tusked skreets."

"A tusked skreet?"Sim scoffed."Don't go telling me Evay tales."

"Morning friends," a man's voice called out from the other side of the dais.

Kaiel had his axe up and was on his feet in the same movement. Two men in dark armoured leathers and crossed harnesses – holding more daggers than he'd find in the Ranger's armoury – stepped from behind the trees where the Ley Path had been. Their hands rested on the hilts of short swords; trousers were tucked into calf-high black boots, and the brown cotton shirts they wore were similar enough to be a uniform.

"Good morning,"Jaric said, stopping beside Kaiel.

"Don't get many strangers around here."

Jaric nodded."I can imagine. We're looking for Exile Point."

"Glass Bay," one of the men said, spitting into the water. He spoke without menace, but Kaiel's fist clenched just the same."Ya won't get far callin' it Exile Point. People who live there don't like that name much."

"Imagine that,"Sim said."So, it does exist."

Jaric ignored Sim."And you are?"The captain's tone matched that of the speaker.

The leader gave a bark-like laugh.

"We're ya escorts,"he said, at last, spitting into the water again. The man was about Darien's height, but where Darien was slim, this man was stocky. Brown hair hung in a warrior's braid down his back, and gold gleamed at his left earlobe. His square face was dominated by a large, hooked nose that had been broken more than once. At an unseen signal, more men appeared amongst the trees.

"That's good of you," Jaric said. Kaiel could see the captain's eyes taking in the numbers, but his face gave away nothing. "We've had some trouble. A tusked skreet seemed to think our horses were breakfast."

The hook-nosed man spat into the water again. "Lucky to have gotten out of that in one piece. Targ ain't one to let an easy meal go."

"We proved not to be so easy," Jaric said.

"The only way ya'd have gotten out alive is if Targ had decided to go after somethin' else."

"He didn't. That's what's left of him." Jaric pointed at the carcass floating in the water, the bodies of the two horses not far behind.

One of the men stepped forward. "Gods!"

Kaiel looked around uneasily, but no-one said anything else.

Hook-nose swore. "Targ was a fucking watchdog! This swamp is riddled with skreet clans, but they wouldn't cross ole Targ. They'll be coming now." He swore again. "The Old Lady is gonna be pissed."

"Only because they killed it," the round-faced man beside him said. He stood taller and leaner than the leader, his shaved head shining in the morning light.

"Yeah, she's gonna be pissed with that too. Ya hands. Let's seem 'em."

They all raised their right hands, and the man did the same, the others around him following suit.

The hook-nosed man nodded. "I'm Maris. This is Huji. How in the Void did ya get through this daemons-cursed swamp?"

"And the Deadlands," Huji said. His hand tightened around the hilt of his short sword.

Maris grunted, looking at their tattered and worn gear. "Not dressed for travellin', are ya?"

"We were hoping to buy provisions in Glass Bay," Jaric said. "And passage to Serjat."

Maris let out a full-throated laugh and Huji offered a dark scowl.

"Glass Bay ain't no port," Huji growled. "We don't have merchants and boats for trade out here. This is the end of the world." He gestured around them. "This is where you Realms folk dump your unwanted. You'd have been better off killin' us, 'cause we're gonna have –"

Maris clapped his hand on the taller man's shoulder, cutting him off. His smile didn't reach his eyes. "Huji is still new to Glass Bay. He forgets that at times." He looked around the group. "Ya gonna be coming back to town with us. The Old Lady is gonna want a word with ya."

Huji's eyes were gleaming. "If there's a way through the swamp –"

"There ain't," Maris said, a dagger suddenly appearing in his hand, its edge pressed against Huji's throat. "That's the whole fuckin' point of why the Realms call this place *Exile* Point. Not to mention the daemonspawned skreets! The only way ya gonna see outside is by submittin' to the captains and followin' orders. An ya time is runnin' out. Ya got it?"

Jaw clenched, Huji nodded. Carefully.

Maris held the dagger at the man's throat for a moment longer before nodding. He turned away. "Sometimes, the new ones find it hard to adjust."

"Look out!" Sim shouted, and Maris spun as Huji, short sword in hand, lunged.

Before the man could strike, an arrow took him in the neck, knocking him down with a splash into the water.

"Ya know better than to turn ya back on him," one of the men said from the trees.

"Shut up, Rykan." Maris kicked the dying man in the head with a sickening crunch that had Kaiel's skin crawling, and then bent down to gather his sword and daggers.

Maris straightened; the dead man forgotten. "I'd ask ya for names, but the Old Lady will get 'em out of ya soon enough."

"I take it you mean the First Captain,"Jaric said, and Maris went still.

"How does one of the Blood know about the First Captain?" he asked softly.

Jaric shrugged."I'm not of the Blood, but I've lived on the shores of Nemisdrillion. I know the Drowned Blades choose one captain to lead them. That captain is the First Captain."

Maris grunted. "Not many outside Glass Bay who know that much."

"How did you know we were here?"Jaric asked.

For a moment Maris' eyes flickered across the lake to the tower rising from this centre. Then he looked back at Jaric."We got a message."He gestured at Sim."Can he walk? Or is he gonna to have to ride? Ya ain't going to be able to get them horses into the Bay."

"How did they get'em here in the first place?"

Kaiel looked up to see the bowman, Rykan, watching them.

"We came by the White Road," Sim said, holding on to Meg as she helped him up.

"The White Road?" Maris spat."Fucking Evay tales. Keep ya secrets then, they won't do ya any good in front of the Old Lady."

"What do you mean we can't take the horses to Glass Bay? Don't you have horses?" Sevaani asked.

Kaiel looked at her in surprise as she stepped up beside him.

"Ya'll see!" Rykan cackled.

"We have horses," Maris gave the bowman a sour look."We use'em to patrol the coast. But Rykan's right. Ya ain't going to be getting them into the Bay proper. Not today at any rate."

"We'll take the horses as far as we can then,"Jaric said.

Kaiel didn't like the way Rykan was studying the horses. Ranger trained mounts were highly sought after, right across Aldania, and even to the Realms beyond. If they left the horses, he had a strong suspicion they'd never see them again.

Maris pointed at Sim."What's he got, it ain't catchin', is it?"

"No!"Meg said."Nothing like that. It was just a spider bite."

"I'll help him get on Lasa,"Kaiel said, moving to Sim's side.

"Where's Del?" Sim asked. Kaiel pointed back into the swamp. He hadn't thought Sim could get any paler.

"Ya big enough for it, that's for sure,"Maris said, watching Kaiel."We can handle big boys here."He fondled the hilt of his sword."Watch ya step."

Kaiel nodded. He had no intention of starting anything.

"Gonna make for an interestin' day."Maris grinned."We ain't had no visitors since that merchant wreck last storm season."He looked them over as though assessing cattle."Might be ya'll last longer."

"There ain't as many of them," Rykan said. "The girls are pretty enough."

Kaiel froze, his back stiff and ground his teeth as Sevaani stifled a gasp.

Captain Daynar put a hand on his shoulder in warning."How far to Glass Bay?"Jaric asked.

Maris shrugged."We'll get ya to the Old Lady by midday. Once we get down the cliffs, we'll leave ya horses with Norly." He nodded to a tall, nondescript young man with mousy hair. "He'll see 'em to the stables."

Norly nodded; the man was bristling with daggers.

"The rest of ya,"Maris called, looking around."Ya try anythin' an' ya'll see how we deal with troublemakers. That was a lesson Huji was too thick to learn, but I have a feelin' ya won't be the same."

"We don't want any trouble,"Jaric said.

Maris grunted."This way,"he said, and led them onto a path between the trees, right where the Ley Path had been the night before.

CHAPTER SEVENTEEN

The End of the World

THEY FOLLOWED MARIS away from the lake and the broken tower in a single file, the other men disappearing into the murk around them. The farther along the path they travelled, the straighter the trees grew, and mud made way for firmer ground as the waters receded.

Darien shivered, and for a moment he wished they'd stayed in the swamp until a passing scent of decaying vegetation made him reconsider.

He wrapped his arms around his chest; the pack on his back, while annoying, offered some warmth, and kept the wind off the back of his damp shirt. But it made him think of Waro, and he swallowed as he thought of the gentle horse's violent end.

His hand dropped to the black pouch at his waist. Even crushing the material, he could not feel the crystal shard within it. Nor could he sense the thing – daemon – in his mind.

He sucked in a breath as his stomach twisted. He was possessed. The Master of the Swamp had confirmed it. But was the dream real? The pouch at his belt meant it was. What was he going to do? And how long would the ward Anith'eal put on his mind last?

The Ciralys would never accept him when they found out. It would be the end for him. But Sevaani had dreamt of two futures for him. Did that mean he wouldn't die? That he could either fall to possession or purge the daemon?

Purge the daemon…

It was impossible. Anith'eal said so, but how much did anyone really know about what the Summoners could or couldn't do? Maybe if the ward in his mind held long enough for him to find a *Tome of Ascension*, he could find a way out of this mess and be admitted to the Ciralys.

An increase in daylight heralded their exit from the trees, and Darien lifted his face towards the sun. But the small warmth it offered fled before an icy wind that whipped across a short field of waist-high grass.

"Keep moving," Rykan growled behind him. "Haven't you ever seen grass before?" He gestured after Captain Daynar, who had made his way to a small rise, leading Celaridus. "Glass Bay's that way."

"At last!" Sim said from the back of Lasa, Kaiel walking by his side. "I hope you have gold, Captain, because we all need winter clothes."

"Why would Captain Jaric buy you anything?" Meg snorted.

"Not *me*," Sim said with a wink. "Us."

"There aren't any merchants there, Sim," she said. "Apparently."

"Oh please. There are merchants everywhere. Not all of them are as skilled as me and my da, but they'll be there. Mark my words," he said blithely. "Anyway, it sounds as though Captain Daynar knows his way around this place. We should ask him."

"How *does* the captain know so much about Glass Bay?" Sevaani asked.

"Why don't you ask the captain?" Simeon said.

"Ask me what?" Jaric said as they crested the small hill.

"Sevaani wants to know how you know so much about this Exile Point," Sim said as she glared at him.

"I don't know much," Jaric said. "I've spent some time in Ebron. The Drowned Blades, who make their home in Glass Bay, are well known on that part of the Nemisdrillion Sea."

Sevaani frowned. "Will thieves and murderers really help us?"

Jaric looked at her and then over at the men behind them. "Stay close together," he said at last. "We'll need to keep our eyes open."

Darien considered this, fingers still tight on the pouch at his waist. He eyed Maris and the rest of his men; they weren't like Rangers at all, and not just for their accents.

The wind changed and blew a gust of brine in his face. He wrinkled his nose, but the smell was not unpleasant, just surprising. He followed Jaric and Maris over the rise and caught his breath.

The far side of the hill dropped down to the edge of a cliff. Beyond, encompassing everything from east to north to west, moving as though it were alive, was the sea.

"Gods," Meg breathed as she and the others came up behind Darien.

They stood gazing at the vista and Darien shivered. In that moment the world opened into a place far larger than anything he'd imagined. They had truly left the Borderland Wilds behind.

Meg and Sevaani hurried after Captain Jaric, but Darien trailed behind, staring out at the sea as waves broke across the beach below, the booming of the water like distant thunder. He wanted to sit at the edge of the cliff and watch it for hours. Sim and Kaiel were waiting beside him, each with their gaze locked on the horizon.

"Come on," Kaiel said after a minute. "We need to stay with them. The sea won't go anywhere."

They made after the others, following Maris east along the edge of the cliff.

"Colum!" their hook-nosed guide called out. On the path ahead of them were four men and two women, all wearing the same brown shirts under dark leathers as their guides. Each looked hard and capable, holding long daggers or curved swords respectively. The man in the lead was older but no less imposing. His dark hair was laced with grey, pulled back from an unshaven, scarred face, and his broad shoulders strained under a crimson silk shirt and black leather vest.

"Maris." The man, Colum, nodded as they approached. "So, there was someone there? And they have horses."

Maris flashed a grin that didn't reassure Darien. "Aye. And... well. They killed Targ."

The people before them muttered, and Darien eyed them warily.

Maris grimaced then gestured towards Jaric. "This one wants to see the First Captain."

"Maris," Colum eyed him. "Where is Huji?"

Maris spat. "He broke. Rykan had to put him down."

Colum was silent then looked to Jaric. "All right, we'll take you to see the First Captain. If she doesn't want to see you, then you'll be having an interview with her son. And that will be a long wait as he's not yet returned to port."

"Winter is upon us." Jaric turned his face northward as though testing the wind. "Trade will be dying down before the first storms. I imagined Corwyn would be out trying his luck on the last ships of the season." The men behind Colum shifted, but their leader stared at Jaric blankly, eyes like flint.

"I'd tread with care when you speak about the *Crow*," Colum said.

After a moment, Jaric nodded.

"It's a two-hundred-foot drop, straight down to the beach," Colum continued, "so watch where you put your feet. And lead your horses carefully. Maris told you that you won't be getting them into Glass Bay?"

"He did," Jaric agreed. "Norly is to look after them."

"Look after them?" Colum's brows rose.

"For a price," Maris added hastily.

Darien didn't recall any mention of coin being needed, but Captain Daynar didn't object, so he kept his mouth shut too.

Colum just grunted in response, then stepped off the cliff onto a narrow switchback path.

They took care following the corsair down. Darien had to keep his eyes lowered to stop himself from staring at the sea. Even then, he found himself looking upon it as often as he could. At the cliff's base, large flat-topped shelves of wave-sculpted granite offered an uneven path above the sand. The tall, thin man with the daggers, Norly, took the reins of the horses, and Kaiel helped Captain Daynar gather the packs.

"I'll be back for you, boy." Darien heard Jaric whisper as the man patted Celaridus' neck."And if you need, you know the way home."

Darien hid a smile. It was true. The horses the Rangers rode were distantly related to the Dominarians of legend. If Celaridus got tired of waiting, he could lead the rest of the horses back to the Wilds, although getting through Dal'mere might be a problem.

They finished their goodbyes, and Norly and a woman from the other group took the horses, then they all followed the other corsairs out across the shore. Rockpools filled with an abundance of seaweed, multi-hued shells, and tiny darting fish, dotted the granite stones that formed a meandering path along the coast. They led all the way to a headland of smooth, dark rock that jutted at least three miles into the sea.

The wind continued to batter them, sea spray keeping them damp, and Darien was shivering when they finally reached the base of the sheer-sided headland. Maris pointed up at a cave that stood a good twenty feet above the tidemark.

"That's the only way into Glass Bay by land," he said.

"We climbed down just to climb back up?" Sim said, breathing hard. "That's a little stupid, no?"

"That wall is volcanic rock," Maris said. "The rocks atop are sharp an' thin. Ya'd be cut in half in ten steps, but if ya like we can take ya back up an ya can have a go."

"Really?" Sim scoffed. "You have tools, and you know how to use them." He pointed at the chiselled hand-holds up the rock face to the cave. "Why not just smooth a path out?"

"Don't be foolish, boy," Colum said as some of the other men laughed. "There's a nest of skreet at the top of those cliffs. Not even a squadron of Cythis Knights would dare go near them."

"That too," Maris said, with a grin at Sim.

Colum sent one of the men to scale the handholds on the cliff face. He disappeared into the dark opening of the cave, reappearing to throw a rope ladder down for the rest of them.

"We're not going in there, are we?" Sevaani asked.

"If you want to see the First Captain, you are," Colum said.

Meg pushed Sevaani forward. "If you could go into the tunnels under Sonyth chasing after Kaiel, and with all the Korda'vari around, you can climb into a cave."

"Korda'vari?" One of the men behind them scoffed.

"You're hemmed in on this stretch of coast by the sea on one side and Dal'mere on the other, and you scoff at Korda'vari?" Jaric said.

"I don't know nothin' about Dal'mere. It's them skreets that keeps us here. Korda'vari are for children's tales," the man spat.

"Don't you worry none, girl, I'll look after you," another leered, and Kaiel lurched forward.

"Enough!" Colum's bark cracked over the crash of the waves. Jaric had put his arm out to hold Kaiel back, though it was clear to all that Kaiel allowed himself to be stopped. Strong as Captain Daynar was, he couldn't have held Kaiel back so easily if he had honestly been trying to get to the man.

Maris eyed them. "Ya from the citadels, are ya?" He rubbed his chin. "Never thought they were much more'n stories. There's always some fool like Huji, every decade or so, who thinks they can get through the swamp and make it to 'em. They never come back." He shook his head. "I don't s'pose ya ever heard about anyone like that?"

"Can't say I have," Jaric said. "Few Borderlanders have even heard of Exile Point, let alone of someone stumbling into one of the citadels after leaving the Deadlands. Of course, if you really want to know, we'll need to find a Kas'tirien."

"A Daemon Hunter?"

The captain nodded. "If anyone comes through Dal'mere, they'll be found by one of the Kas'tirien first."

"I said the swamp, not Dal'mere." Maris protested. "What do the Deadlands have ta do with it?"

"The swamp backs onto the Deadlands." Darien couldn't keep the incredulity from his voice. "You must know that."

"The skreet keep us busy enough without worrying about what might lay beyond," Colum said. He gestured to the man who had ridiculed Sevaani. "Go ahead and tell Danyl that the First Captain has guests."

The man spat and climbed up the rope ladder, disappearing into the cave.

Colum turned his grizzled face to Sevaani. "You're up after your friend." He pointed at Meg. "Just follow the walkway." He motioned to another man, who climbed the rope ladder and crouched at the top of the ledge.

They followed one by one.

The cave proved to be the entrance to a tunnel, and somewhere in the darkness below, the hiss of seawater spoke of an opening to the sea. A rough-cut wooden bridge, attached to swaying rails of rope, stretched across an open expanse to steps cut into a ledge. They climbed up into another tunnel whose walls bore the marks of chisel and pickaxe, smoothed away in parts, and left rough and raw in others. Torches on long poles with black iron frames stood at intervals, illuminating the way as darkness pressed around them. Darien couldn't tell how far they climbed, but his legs had begun to burn, and his palms were scratched from the jagged stone walls.

It was hard to judge time in the dark, but he was sure they'd been climbing for at least ten minutes when the tunnel twisted away to the left and led them out into daylight on another ledge of stone the other side of the headland.

The cliff was at least three-quarters of the way up the side of a giant, volcanic crater filled with seawater so still that it reflected the sky as though it were a mirror.

"Welcome to Glass Bay," Maris said behind them.

Darien blinked.

At the southern wall, a waterfall tumbled from the rim of the crater into the bay. Clustered in a wide semi-circle below it, a safe distance from where the falls poured into the bay, a mass of ships were lashed together, some large, others small, stretching out over the water. A forest of bare masts rose above them, and ropes slung between, while tracks of wooden planking, piers and jetties poked like outstretched fingers all around. Small fishing craft and larger, sleeker vessels moved across the quiet waters, their wake somehow disappearing after leaving a short trail of whitewash behind.

And in the centre of the falls was a massive outcropping of stone, upon which sat a fort built in the style of the Var Imperium.

Towers rose gracefully around a central keep poised over the harbour like a hawk on a high branch; its position making it impregnable to attack. Another rope bridge was its only connection to the carved path on the wall that led to the ships one-hundred-and-twenty feet below.

"It's a floating town," Sevaani said.

Colum pushed his way out of the tunnel behind them and grunted. "I hope your story is good," he told them. "If the First Captain doesn't buy it, you'll be spending a lot of time here."

They followed the cliff path around the inner wall of the crater, heading towards the waterfall and the boat-town below. The sounds of industry echoed across the bay. Below them, fishermen and women hauled their morning catch up onto the docks, where others sorted it into waiting barrels in a flurry of chatter and catcalls. Children ran across ramps and climbed the rope rigging on the masts like monkeys, barked at by dogs that jumped around beneath them.

The path descended towards the bay as they neared the town of ships. It was a careful climb down steep steps carved into the side of sheer walls until they finally reached a plank that led a short distance to the floating town.

Ramps, planks, and ladders crossed the lashed-together flotilla-like streets. The motion of the boats was unsettling, a gentle, rolling movement rippling through the whole town like a sheet in a breeze. The groan of shifting wood, and the slap of water against hulls merged with the churning thunder of the falls in the background, and the smell of salt, damp, and tar permeated everything.

Townsfolk stared as they followed Colum, clambering over decks and around piled boxes, ropes and cloth; the women – and Sim – muttered as they stubbed their booted toes on pieces of wood and iron attached to the decking for some purpose Darien couldn't begin to fathom. They all became mindful of the square holes cut into the decks that opened into dark holds below after Kaiel almost fell into one.

Women with babies stood at doors, or in small groups. Others draped themselves at glassless windows in various stages of undress. More sat with men working at carving wood, mending nets, or sharpening swords, and they all eyed the group suspiciously. The more daring of the children ran around them, following in a gaggle behind.

Darien, the skin on the back of his neck crawling at the attention they were receiving, took everything in, careful never to make eye contact with those staring at them. The town – he wasn't sure that was the correct term for the chaos around him – was filthy and rough, and reminded him of the Warrens of Hanore. The clothes the people wore were garish, and in strange styles, mostly made of fabrics that were not the cotton and wool he was used to.

He was concentrating, watching his step as Colum led them across one ship after the other, when a hand snaked out from behind a curtain of coloured glass beads and latched onto his arm in a steel-like grasp, jerking him to a stop.

An old woman, wild-haired and with a mouth only half-full of yellowed teeth, had hold of his wrist in a gnarled claw of a hand.

"You!" she hissed, foul breath wafting across his face. "Darkling Child of the Waning Moon." Her other hand darted out, a nail stabbing at the hidden wound on the back of his palm. "I've been waiting for you."

"Get off him, Bertha!" Colum growled, yanking Darien away.

The crone shrieked with laughter and gave Colum a mocking bow. "Told you they were there, milord. Yes, yes, told you I did!"

Colum spat and pushed Darien along. "Stay away from the townsfolk, boy."

Darien didn't protest, the back of his hand tingling where the woman had poked him. He looked back, and she grinned before retreating into the cabin, the glass baubles clicking against each other in the movement of the deck. "You want to know, boy?" she called from beyond the coloured curtain. "Come see Bertha! I can tell you!"

He stumbled after the others who had stopped the next deck over, the men of their escort laughing.

"Looks like he's caught old Bertha's eye," one said, while another, who wasn't laughing, eyed him suspiciously and made a gesture to ward off evil.

"Who was that?" Meg asked.

"Bertha is harmless," Maris said dismissively. "She takes care of the sick and speaks the weather."

"What did she mean, she told you we were there?"

Maris spat onto the deck and didn't answer.

"What did she want with you?" Meg asked Darien.

"I don't know."

"Well, what did she say?"

"Nothing." He shook his head. "Nothing that made any sense."

Colum continued across a few more ships before turning towards the waterfall on the south wall of the bay. Here, the wood of the boats were older, stained with time and peeling paint. New wood, lighter in colour, spread around them like patchwork.

They finally came to a ramp leading off the boats and onto a switchback cut into the cliff right beside the waterfall. The thundering torrent made conversation difficult. Firm ground beneath their feet again was welcome, and Darien leaned a hand against the stone to steady himself as they climbed.

As they made their way back up the crater, Darien noted the sun was climbing towards its zenith. It was a good fifteen-minute climb up, zigzagging along the path, and Darien's legs were shaking from exertion by the time they reached a ledge with the outcrop the Var fortress perched on. Looking behind him, he saw his brother was practically carrying a very silent Sim up the last turn of the path.

A rope bridge stretched across the dizzying drop from the wall of the crater to the ledge. Without giving them a moment to brace themselves after the climb, Colum motioned them to make their way to the imposing Keep.

Deafened by the thundering roar of the water, Darien crossed the bridge quickly, praying to all the Elder Gods that his shaking legs didn't give way on him.

On the other side were six men, guards dressed in leather armour, wearing the same red as Colum instead of the browns of Maris and his crew. The two guards in the centre of the line stood with crossed tridents, barring their way forward.

A tall, lean man walked from beneath the portcullis, a gold chain that tied his white hair at the nape of his neck flashing in the light. He crossed his arms over a chest draped in silk, a fur coat falling from his broad shoulders, and eyed them coldly.

"Lord Danyl," Colum said. "These are the ones Bertha told us about. They've come out of the swamp. From the Borderlands they claim. And Maris says this one," Colum pointed at Jaric, "knows about the First Captain."

The older man's face remained expressionless, but his eyes darted over them, lingering on Kaiel before shifting to Captain Daynar.

"Knows what about the First?" Lord Danyl's voice was strangely accented, as though he spoke with a stone in his mouth, but his words were exact, like those of the Bloodborn.

"I know the leader of the Drowned Blades is called the First Captain," Jaric said. "That's all."

"The Nine Realms refuse to acknowledge Glass Bay, or the First Captain, as a legitimate power. But you, from the Borderland Wilds, come asking to see her?"

"I've not always lived on the Borderlands," Jaric offered an enigmatic smile.

"I see," Lord Danyl said. He lifted the palm of one hand – every finger of which wore a gold, gemmed ring – and the guards raised the crossed tridents. "Come." He strode back into the fortress.

"After you," Colum said to Jaric. The captain eyed the man carefully before he stepped under the gate and into the bailey.

Darien eyed the gateway and took one last look over his shoulder at the boat-town below before stepping into the dark.

CHAPTER EIGHTEEN

The Consequences of Actions

THE COURTYARD WAS compact, the dark stone of the fortress slick and gleaming from the spray that misted the air. Kaiel wiped water from his face and glanced at Sim, but the thunder of the waterfall reverberating through his chest discouraged speech.

Lord Danyl led them up a flight of broad steps directly into a great hall. Light streamed in from the entryway and slanted down from tall windows that lined the walls above it. Kaiel's eyes widened at the seamless stonework. It was the work of Sola'vari craftsman he was sure. He'd known the Var Imperium, which had arisen in the wake of the Sundering, had reached far across the Broken Continent. He shouldn't be surprised to find they had an outpost on the northern coast of the Deadlands, but after traipsing through the haphazardly constructed ship town below, it had been the last thing he'd expected.

However, the beauty that graced the Three Citadels was missing from this fortress that perched above the shackled ships of Glass Bay. The walls were clothed in bright silks that spoke heavy-handedly of wealth, hiding the bas-relief sculptures that poked out at odd places where sections of cloth did not meet. Nets hung across the ceiling with oil-lit seaglass orbs ranging from blue to green to clear. A wooden gallery lined the first floor of the hall, the men and women standing on it dressed in red leathers, the fists of their right hands grasping wickedly pointed tridents.

The churning roar of the waterfall faded as they made their way into the hall, replaced with jeering and the loud talk of a crowd that must have numbered in the hundreds, packing the hall from wall to wall. Beside him Sevaani made a sound of disgust, covering her nose with her hand. The odour of tight-packed humanity washed over them, co-mingling with the smell of burning pitch from the wall torches and the cloying scent of damp straw beneath their feet. Voices bounced over the crowd, and a ripple of movement spread as Lord Danyl led them down the centre of the hall. Weathered faces of tanned skin, some much darker than others, watched their group with hard eyes. Daggers bristled at waists, and the least threatening expression that Kaiel could make out was that of curiosity.

He looked over the crowd, careful not to meet any eyes for more than a moment, only to stumble as his gaze fell upon a tall man lounging nonchalantly against the wall to his left. It wasn't the black silk in a room of hardened leather and rough linen that caused Kaiel to pause, but rather the blue of the man's skin.

"Eye blind me," Sim whispered. "A Sander!"

Simeon's whisper was not a whisper at all, and Kaiel winced as the Amarian's eyes narrowed.

"Be careful with your words," Captain Daynar said, somehow pitching his voice below the babble around them. "Not all the names you know for the peoples of other realms are ones they'd call themselves. Most Amarians would draw steel at such an insult. You're lucky the Blay Shon has more control."

"Blay Shon? A *blademaster*?" Sim asked, and Kaiel just shook his head. "How could he hear me from here?" Sim muttered.

Kaiel craned his neck, looking back. His eyes swept over the Amarian once more, taking in the warrior's topknot that spilled from the centre of his shaved head. As the man pushed himself from the wall into a slanting ray of light, the hilts of twin blades rose above the man's shoulders.

For a moment Kaiel feared the man had taken exception to Sim, but rather than approach, the Amarian made his way along the wall and exited through a door at the far end.

"No. Please!" A strangled cry came from the head of the crowd, pulling Kaiel's attention."I didn't steal nothin'. It's lies!"

The crowd booed around them, hurling insults that had Sevaani's hands move from her nose to her ears.

"Quiet!"A man's voice cut across the hall and the crowd settled back into mutters and scoffs.

"I am sure it is a mistake, Nayral," a woman said. Her voice had a strange smoky quality, and her words rolled in an unfamiliar accent, but they were delivered precisely in the style of a Bloodborn."Just as it was a mistake last time. And the time before that."Her voice hardened."And though you are intimately familiar with the salt cages already, they seem to have been of little assistance in helping you curb your ways."

The crowd suddenly gave way, and Kaiel found himself ten feet from a dais occupied by an enormous wooden chair carved with waves, sharks, and octopi. Upon the chair sat the woman who had spoken. Her hair was white with age and pulled back in a long plait revealing a distinct widow's peak. She lounged on the throne, confidence radiating from her eyes as much as her posture, leaving no doubt as to the command she wielded. Her long legs were stretched out before her, clad in red leather and knee-high boots of black; her red silk blouse caught the light beneath a red leather vest embroidered with gold thread.

On the steps before her knelt a man in little more than rags, weeping. His hands were tied behind his back and his face – mottled with bruising – was pressed against the flagstones by the fork of a trident wielded by a guard.

"I'm sorry!" the man, Nayral, Kaiel supposed, wailed.

"Oh, so you are sorry now?" The woman, the First Captain, tsked. "First you are innocent, and now you are sorry. Well." She sat up. "I am sorry also. Sorry, you ever turned up on my fucking doorstep, you shit-flinging skreet!"

Her booted foot lashed out, kicking him in the mouth. Blood splattered the stone, and the man wailed.

The skin on Kaiel's shoulders tingled at this display, and he tried to swallow past a suddenly tight throat. Beside him, Sevaani grabbed his arm, her fingers digging into his flesh.

"Glass Bay is not Massarle," the First Captain continued calmly. "We do not have laws. People here fit in, they do their work and contribute to our home or –" She gestured to the side, smiling down at the crying man. "They pay the price."

Kaiel felt his mouth open in surprise as a Var, covered in tattoos of black and red ink, stomped forward, a great stone block in his massive arms.

What was a Sola'vari doing out here?

"No!" Nayral let out a hair-raising screech, blood bubbling from his mouth.

The First Captain gestured, and the guards yanked Nayral from the floor. The Var dropped the block on the dais beside him with a thud.

"You were given your chance," she said. "You have not been out of the salt cages a month, and you were caught stealing, again!"

Her eyes flickered over Kaiel and the others. "Theft is indeed no great crime here," she said, laughter and a few jeers rising from the crowd around them. "If you are unable to look after your own possessions or your own neck, then you get what you deserve. But you did not steal in town. You snuck aboard one of the bloody Drowned Blades and got caught in the fucking captain's quarters!"

The voices in the crowd rose once more, spitting insults and ridicule, and Kaiel's already tight throat went dry.

"And that is bad luck for you." The captain ignored the tumult, her face hard as stone. "If you were out at sea, then you would walk the short walk, and that would be that. But when the ships are in port, then it becomes *my* problem." She sneered. "And you have caused me trouble one time too many!"

One of the guards slipped a dagger between Nayral's hands and severed his bonds. Grasping the prisoner's left wrist, the guard, flat-faced and dull-eyed, jerked Nayral's arm up and held it down over the stained block. The other guard, a strong woman with as little expression as her partner, kept Nayral's other arm behind him and pressed a boot firmly on his lower back.

The woman in charge held her hand out, and the Var who had brought in the stone block placed the hilt of a gleaming short sword in her palm.

The hairs on the back of Kaiel's neck prickled. The sword was not an axe, but in his mind, he could hear the dull thwack as he took off Rolen's arm.

Sevaani must have as well because she suddenly let go of his arm and moved as far away as she could within their tight-packed group.

Iron fingers gripped his shoulder.

"Whatever you are thinking, *don't*," Darien hissed in his ear.

Kaiel tried to swallow again. Sweat was dripping down his back. Why was it so hot in here?

"Darien's right," Jaric said. "This isn't the citadels."

Kaiel shook his head. He couldn't focus on their words.

Nayral howled as the woman raised the sword, the crowd calling out.

And just as the sword was about to fall, Kaiel lurched forward. "Stop!"

The woman arrested the fall of the sword, and the crowd fell silent.

She stared at him in shock, but the expression quickly twisted into something else.

"Hold him, Grazat!" she barked.

Kaiel raised his hands, but the Var was faster, moving across the distance in two strides. Grazat's arm snapped out, his sausage-thick fingers closing around Kaiel's throat.

He clasped the Var's wrist with both hands as he was lifted off the ground. The screaming Nayral scrambled back from the block, breaking the hold of the distracted guards. The man barrelled into the one on his left, knocking him to the ground.

Kaiel struggled, his vision exploding into sparks of colour, and he choked as the Var's hand closed tighter around his windpipe.

"Stop him!" the woman commanded as Nayral stumbled to his feet.

The Var twisted his head, and Kaiel sucked in a breath as his grip loosened, blood thundering in his ears – but Grazat didn't let go.

The woman picked up the fallen trident, stood, and hurled it at the little man as he ran for a door.

The sharp spikes punched into Nayral's back, and he fell onto the ground with a cry.

The guards he'd managed to escape, ran forward and pulled him up between them, the trident still lodged in his back.

The white-haired woman stalked forward. The sword in her hand shone in the light.

"No-one runs from me!" Her words crackled with rage, and without ceremony, she thrust a foot of steel into Nayral's gut.

The crowd roared behind Kaiel and blood bubbled over Nayral's chin.

She pulled the sword back and stepped away as Nayral slumped between the guards. Turning, she gestured, and a spindly, ebon-skinned man in a white tunic scurried forward.

"Take the parts you want for your studies, Domak'eesh," she said, returning to her chair. "And when you are done, call for Ahsih. She can feed what is left to her spine-hogs."

A grumble ran around the room at this announcement, but Kaiel, both hands straining against the massive paw of the Sola'var holding him, barely noticed. It felt like his head was going to burst from the pressure. His lips tingled, and his hold on the Var's wrist slipped, his vision darkening.

"Lord Danyl," the woman said, her voice cold. "You have brought us guests? Grazat." She waved a hand. "Do not kill him. Yet."

The Var released his grip and Kaiel fell, his knees buckling. His arms were too weak to catch himself, and he crashed on the stone floor, pain exploding across his shoulder, his lungs bellowing for air.

"Yes, First Captain Nataya," Danyl said from behind him, his tone oily. "Please forgive the intrusion. I did not realise that philanthropy ran so strongly amongst them, or I would have waited until Nayral's sentence was over."

Kaiel breathed hard, his legs shaking as Sevaani and Sim helped him up. They managed to get him to his knees, the burning in his lungs abating. But the pain at his neck and along the muscles in his shoulders protested every move he made.

Nataya's gaze raked him as he blinked the stars from his eyes. "Mercy is rare in Glass Bay," she said, her voice and expression icy. "I am not sure any of us would recognise it after so long, no?"

"Indeed." Beside him, Danyl offered her a shallow bow. "First Captain, these are the ones Colum's men found in the swamp."

The First Captain regarded Lord Danyl, a flicker of distaste crossing her face. "The ones Bertha told him of this morning?"

"Yes, First Captain," Danyl agreed.

Kaiel raised his head as the First Captain studied them. Her fingers drummed on the arm of her chair and on her hands, rings of precious stones flashed multi-coloured fire as the noon sun caught them in its light.

"Who are they, Colum?" Nataya asked the man-at-arms who had followed them in.

With an effort, Kaiel got a foot under him to stand.

"Stay on your knees!" the First Captain's voice lashed out. He froze.

"Apologise!" Darien hissed behind him.

"I... uh, am sorry your, um... Your Grace," he managed to rasp.

"Colum?" Nataya said again, ignoring Kaiel.

"They say they are Borderlanders," the grizzled veteran said.

"And you believe them?"

"Aye."

"Because you would not bring them to me armed if they were hired by one of the captains to launch a coup." Her mouth widened into a smile, but her eyes remained cold and expressionless.

The armsman was unshaken by her accusation. "You know me better than that. Besides –" Colum nodded at the curtained wall behind her, "the Tridents can take them."

Kaiel looked over and gave a start as he took in more guards standing to either side of the throne. Unlike their fellows in the entrance hall or the one who had held Nayral, these two, a man and a woman, wore unrelieved red leather – the same colour as the First wore and of the silk-covered wall they stood before – and they melded into the background. They reminded Kaiel of Alesandr's Asp Knights, a checked menace just beneath the surface waiting to be unleashed.

"Borderlanders?" she spat. "In the name of the Elders, how did they get through Dal'mere let alone the skreet in the swamp?"

"We –" Jaric began, but the First Captain raised her hand cutting him off.

"More important is *why* you would even try?" Nataya tilted her head.

"Very few people choose to come to 'Exile Point' voluntarily. And those that do try their luck by sea, not the Deadlands."

"Bertha says the Master of the Swamp brought them," Colum said.

At this pronouncement voices in the crowd behind them rose once more.

The First Captain was on her feet. "Grazat!" she barked in a sudden rage. "Court is over. Get them out."

The Var didn't say a word, but the folk in the hall began to make their way out, protests and catcalls rose from their midst, but none lingered. Soon only Colum, Lord Danyl and the Trident guards remained, along with the Var and their own small group.

"The fucking Master of the Swamp!" She glared at Kaiel. He shifted uncomfortably under the weight of her stare. "And from the Borderlands? What made you so eager to risk a trip over Dal'mere to get here?"

"We didn't have many choices when the White Road appeared," Sim muttered.

"White Road? A *Renimor*?" She leaned forward. "Where?"

"It's gone now," Jaric said before Sim could open his mouth, "but it left us at the tower in the swamp."

"Convenient." She sat back in her throne, her voice loud in the empty hall. Captain Daynar's hand was like a weight on Kaiel's shoulder. "And what were you fleeing, to run into the Deadlands? People who go into Dal'mere do not come out."

"The Kas'tirien do," Sevaani said.

"Daemon Hunters." Nataya's lips twisted. "Gullshit. And if you went in *before* the prisoner of that cursed tower reached his fucking hand out to pull your strings, then you had to have been desperate!"

"Prince Alesandr didn't leave us much choice," Kaiel said.

"The Niskeri?" The First Captain went still.

"That means the Realms," Colum said.

"I know what it means!"

Jaric stepped up beside Kaiel. "We left the prince in the Borderlands. No-one in the Borderlands knew a Ley Path, a *Renimor*, was there, and I doubt Alesandr will either."

"Nothing that crawls out of the swamp is harmless! That fucking tower is to be avoided at all costs, and *still* that decaying old cunt inside it meddles in our affairs!" She stood, glaring at Kaiel. "I have enough to deal with. Winter is on my doorstep, and I have a town full of captains who want my seat. I do not have time to be fucking around with Houseless, cave-goat fuckers being chased by a Realm!!"

Her sword was out of its sheath again and pointing right at Kaiel. "And if you believe I will not get every last secret out of your cock-sucking mouth, one way or the other, you are mistaken!"

Kaiel swallowed, his eyes tracking the length of the gleaming steel in front of him. "I... I didn't –"

"What makes you believe he knows anything?" Captain Daynar demanded.

"Because his is the only conscience amongst the lot of you that speaks loud enough to move him to action," Nataya said, the corner of her lip curling. "He will be the catalyst for your adventures. The one being chased."

"We're not being chased!" Kaiel blurted. "We can't be. Prince Alesandr would have had to return to Jaroff by now. I left the spear; he can have it!"

"Kaiel!" Sevaani's reprimand was whispered, but in the silence of the hall, it was as loud as a scream.

The First Captain's face was tight. "Spear?"

Kaiel cursed himself and shut his mouth, refusing to answer.

The First narrowed her eyes. "Very well. Grazat take the skinny one." The Var turned, reaching for Darien.

"No!" Kaiel cried out, quickly moving in front of his brother. "I found a spear in the bone drake's hoard. In the catacombs under Sonyth.

Prince Alesandr thinks it means I am the heir to a dead house. But I'm not –"

"That is enough, Kaiel." Jaric grabbed his shoulder, pulling him back. "These young people are from the Borderlands; they offer no harm to you or yours."

"And yet a prince of the Blood wants you! Grazat, the brother."

"He wants *me,*" Kaiel said and pushed himself in front of Darien again. It was the truth, after all and he wouldn't let Dar be hurt for it. No-one could believe that he was who Alesandr claimed he was. "He thinks I'm the Blood of House Taaren'th."

"House Taaren'th?" Nataya repeated, waving the Var back. Her eyes moved from Kaiel to Darien. "And you two are brothers?"

"You wouldn't know from looking at them, would you?" Sim offered, only to grunt as Meg moved to his side.

The First Captain gestured, and the guards in the room stepped forward. "Grazat, take him to the salt cages." Nataya pointed at Kaiel.

"No!" Sevaani cried.

"He doesn't wield *Asai,*" Jaric protested. "There's no need for you to put him in a cage of corusite."

"I have found that corusite can... encourage those within its grasp to mend the habits that have led them there." Nataya offered them a thin smile.

"You didn't have much success with Nayral," Sevaani said defiantly.

"You can go with him if you like!" the First screeched, her civil demeanour vanishing.

"Sevaani," Meg hissed urgently, and the other girl bowed her head, glowering at the floor.

The guardsmen surrounded Kaiel, and his arms were pulled behind him. He struggled, heart racing, and was rewarded with a backhanded blow from Grazat. Stars burst across his vision, and his head rang like a struck bell. His left eye throbbed as though it was about to burst from its socket.

"Kaiel!" Sevaani clutched at him, only to cry out as she was elbowed back by one of the trident-carrying guardsmen.

"Bastard!" Sim snarled, and Kaiel tried to turn his head as more of the guardsmen stepped forward, their tridents lowered.

"Sim," Meg's voice was strangled. "Put the dagger down. What is wrong with you all?"

"Wise words," Nataya said, seated on her seawood throne once more.

"Kaiel." Captain Daynar stepped forward, and the guardsmen reluctantly let him close. "Stand as close to the centre of the cage as you can, do you understand me?"

"What?" Kaiel's stomach twisted. What was a salt cage?

"A night in the cages will not kill anyone who does not wield *Asai*." Nataya laughed. "You are lucky you are not all joining him."

By Kaiel's ear, Jaric growled something unintelligible and stepped back. The guardsmen took his place, and Kaiel's arm was wrenched back again. Hard.

"I should hang the lot of you and be done with it," the First Captain said.

"There's no call for that," Jaric said. "I tell you again. We're no threat to you or yours."

"No threat?" Nataya shouted. "You have arrived here, *overland*. A feat generally considered impossible. How long will it be before some ambitious captain in the Drowned Blades decides to search for this Ley Path so they can bring a force overland and attack me from two sides? And you are being followed. What shall I do when a prince of House Niskeri locates the harbour of the Drowned Blades?"

"Killing us won't stop that," Jaric said.

"But it will fucking make me feel better!" the First spat at him.

"The prince doesn't have the assistance of Anit – the Master of the Swamp,"Darien said, speaking up.

"And *that* is another reason I should hang you all now. I do not trust that bastard tower fucker not to bring more here!"

"We have gold,"Sim offered.

"Gold?"Nataya raised an eyebrow."Really?"

"Enough for a room down in the, um, town, and passage on a ship," he told her, and Kaiel recognised his tone as the one he used when he haggled with folk in his pa's store."We'll be out of your hair before anyone can arrive. If we're not here, well, you can hardly be held accountable."

"You miss the point,"she hissed."And I can *take* anything you have." She lay a finger over her lips."So perhaps the real reason you are being chased is because of this gold?"

"No,"protested Sim."It was from the hoard –"

"Take his bag,"she said.

"Wait!" Sim made to struggle but, more prudently than usual, stopped when the trident spears pressed against his chest.

A guard dropped the bag at her feet. It landed with a distinct jingle.

"Lovely,"Nataya said."I will keep this to hand over to the prince you stole it from if he comes looking for it. If he does not come, well. I will just keep it."

Her smile was cold, and Kaiel shrunk beneath her gaze.

"Take his axe and escort him to the cages."She regarded Kaiel coldly.

"*I* will keep his axe,"Jaric said.

The First Captain's eyes narrowed, but she gestured, and the guard passed Kaiel's axe to Captain Daynar."And tell Domak'eesh he is not a subject for his experiments."

"And the rest?"Colum said.

"Take them to the Sea Lion. They can wait there until I decide what I am going to do with them."

"Kaiel." Darien's voice was strained, and Kaiel twisted his head to look back at his brother, ignoring the pain in his neck.

"I'll be all right, Dar,' he said, but his brother's eyes were on the First Captain.

"You see?" she smiled. "He will be all right. Take him!"

She gestured again, and Kaiel was hauled around and marched to the door the Amarian had disappeared behind. Anxiety twisted his stomach once more, but the pain of his arm being pushed up the centre of his back distracted him.

"We'll be back for you, Kaiel!" Captain Daynar called out. "Stay in the centre of the cage. The centre!"

Kaiel threw his head back as his arm was wrenched behind him again and caught a glimpse of a girl watching from the gallery above. As he was pushed through the doorway, all he was left with was the impression of dark brown hair and copper skin.

The gaudy silk hangings of the hall gave way to the clean lines of unornamented Var stonework, and glass orbs that sat in iron brackets filled with fire oil. Kaiel's heart raced, and he struggled against the guard. By the Eye, he was a fool!

"Where are you taking me?"

One of the guards at his back shoved him. "Keep your mouth shut."

"Like the First said, you're going to the salt cages." The guard in the lead looked back, eyeing him. "You're a big one, ain't you? Well, your size ain't gonna do you any good here. The salt cages treat all men equal. Unless you are a wielder." The guard spat to the side. "The cages aren't nearly so kind to them."

Kaiel stared at him. *What are these cages*?

At the end of the corridor, he was led down a steep set of stairs, the shadows cast by the intermittent glass orbs were long. It was hard to judge distance, but he didn't think they'd gone far before he was pushed out of the stairwell and into another corridor that switched back beneath the one above.

The guard in front suddenly stopped, and Kaiel grunted as he collided with the man.

"Watch it, Derni," the guard in the lead said, scowling over his shoulder briefly before turning back. "What business do you have here, Amarian?"

Kaiel sighed in relief as the grip on his arm lessened, and he moved his shoulder, working the muscles. The guards behind him shuffled uneasily, and he peered ahead. Blocking their way was the tall, black-clad form of the Blay Shon.

This close, Kaiel could make out the five-petalled lotus crossguard of both swords rising behind the man's shoulders. Only a jisana bore the lotus, and only the blademasters of Amaria carried them.

Even in the Borderlands, they had stories of the blademasters of Amaria. The tales of the Knights of Cythis paled in comparison beside those of the Blay Shon of the Black Sands.

"Lihon came to fetch me from the storerooms," a woman said from behind the Blay Shon.

Kaiel tore his attention away from the swords and met violet eyes.

Tanned skin offered a striking palate against the snow-white lustre of her hair, pulled back and bound with pearl-studded pins. The light of the tunnel shimmered on a gown of sea-grey silk and two black panels, stitched with silver thread depicting the night sky, decorated its front. At her neck, a sizeable, sapphire-hued stone sat on a black metal torque, with strange pulses of light moving in straight lines around it.

"He told me visitors had arrived, and that they had come through Dal'mere." She smiled. "I am Iana," she said to Kaiel. "And this is Lihon. You are?"

"A prisoner of the First Captain," the lead guardsman said before Kaiel could reply.

"Oh, Caldo, there is no need to be like that," Iana said with a smile.

"My name is Kaiel Toranth, my lady," Kaiel said. The guard, Caldo, looked back at him with a scowl.

"Is it true you have come to Glass Bay through the Deadlands?"

"Yes," he said.

"Your journey must indeed be a tale," Iana said, excitement lacing her voice, "and one I would very much like to hear. To the best of my knowledge, any who enter Dal'mere do not come out."

Kaiel shifted on his feet, uncomfortable under her regard. "The Kas'tirien do."

"The Kas'tirien? You are from the Borderlands." She nodded as though it was what she expected. "Which citadel?"

"Hanore," Kaiel said. "You've heard of the citadels?"

"Yes, though I have only visited Tore. The Borderlands are quite beautiful considering how dangerous a land it is they neighbour. But surely, you who has been raised a Borderman would not enter the Deadlands lightly." Her violet eyes bore into him. "Why would you and your friends risk such a journey?"

"We had little choice," Kaiel said. Captain Daynar's words of caution flittered through his mind, but her eyes caught him. "I'd left the spear in Prince Alesandr's camp, but he still chased us."

"Prince Alesandr?" she said. "Why would he chase a Borderlander?"

"He said Darien and I are the Blood of House Taaren'th. Only we can use the spear."

Her eyebrows rose at that. "What spear did you leave?"

He shouldn't speak, she was a stranger, but he couldn't stop himself. "The Bronze Spear, from the bone drake's hoard. I didn't mean to pick it up. It was just there, and I needed a weapon."

"Gullshit," Caldo said. "He and his friends stole gold from a prince of Niskeri, and that prince is following them here."

"We didn't steal anything!" Kaiel protested.

"He does not lie," Iana said.

"Witch." Muttered a guard behind him, but Iana did not respond.

"Why is a young man, just arrived in Glass Bay, a prisoner of the First?" Iana asked. "Why are his companions not here also?"

"They weren't so stupid as to interfere with the First's justice." Caldo nodded at Kaiel. "He did. He's to be kept overnight in the salt cages."

It was Iana's turn to frown. "I see." The points of light dancing on her torque seemed to flash faster for a moment. "I see. Be sure to stay as close to the centre of the cage as you can."

Caldo snorted. "He's too big for that to work."

"Perhaps, but it will help nonetheless." She took a breath. "Very well, I will not keep you. I shall return tomorrow when the First releases you, to check on how you fared during the night."

Kaiel frowned. *Void take me, what* are *these cages*?

The lady swept past the guards, the Blay Shon, Lihon, still eyeing Kaiel waited a moment before following her.

"Storms boy," Caldo said. "You sure attract trouble."

"What do you mean?"

"You get yourself in the First's sights with that foolishness you pulled upstairs, and now you got a witch interested in you."

"A witch?" Kaiel twisted his head, trying to look back down the corridor. "She, I mean, the Lady Iana, she's a Keeper?"

The guards laughed darkly, and Caldo shook his head. "Worse, boy. She's a Shaluay."

At the east end of Glass Bay, where the boats were older and less well repaired, a long stretch of planking connected the flotilla to a small pier. Tucked into a fold of stone that reached out like a curtain raised for privacy, the pier led to an ill-kept shack.

Lord Danyl stopped at the closed door to that shack and glanced behind him, peering across the darkening waters at the ship-town. Satisfied he was unobserved, he took a key from his belt and opened the solid door just as a clap of thunder announced the arrival of the storm that had been building all afternoon. He moved inside as the rain fell and pulled his fur-lined, sealskin cloak closer around his wiry frame as the wind rattled the salt-smeared windows.

Such storms were common enough on the northern coast of Dal'mere this time of year. He had been awaiting the arrival of this particular storm for weeks. *This* storm marked the change of season. The Drowned Blades had already returned to take shelter in the bay while the winter storms conducted their yearly dance across the Nemisdrillion. Not all of them, but most. The boldest would brave the sea for a little while yet, looking for the merchants who continued their crossings in the name of commerce and profit. But the rest would remain here, drinking and whoring, dicing and murdering each other. And he'd have no choice but to rub shoulders with them. To conduct business with the captains; all the while avoiding a knife in the back as opportunists sought to overthrow the First, or to position themselves closer to her with his permanent removal.

His lip curled. *Feral bitch. They are welcome to the murderous wench*!

Twenty years ago he'd been one of the most powerful men in Cythis. Then the cursed Stone King – a filthy *Summoner* – had risen to power and begun binding the noble Houses under his rule. If that void-cursed Summoner *had* been the next Empyros, and Danyl had chosen to stand against him… But the bastard had not been. And the Knights of Cythis had killed the fool before he'd consolidated his power. The Summoner had fallen to the Paladine's sword.

And everyone who had allied themselves with him had been condemned. They had stripped him of his earldom and had dumped him in the Thorn for execution.

But he had not risen to Earl in his own House by chance. There had been enough warning for him to call in the favour that had saved his life. The execution had been cancelled when his cell was found empty. He dearly wished he could have seen the face of those cock-sucking Knights when they had opened that door.

Another crack of thunder split the heavens, and he jumped.

Fool. It is not the thunder that has you ready to piss your breeches. Do it now and get it done! You cannot return the whelp to the egg once it has hatched.

Maybe he would have been better off dying or calling in a different favour.

He scoffed. Truth be told, this outcome was not without its benefits.

Making sure the door was closed securely behind him, Danyl crossed the short space and pulled an old tarp off a stack of crates. On the worm-ridden wood rested a black palm-sized bowl. Its basin swallowed the small light of the room as though it was made of the Void itself.

This was his chain. His prison. And he had walked into it willingly enough.

Jagged veins of garnet crossed the basin, and he ran his finger over the runes that traced the bowl's lip like the scrawling death throes of a spider.

He took a deep breath.

From his belt, he pulled a dagger made of bone and drew it across his left palm. He balled his fingers into a fist and let the blood drip down, pooling in the centre of the bowl. The garnet veins pulsed as his blood was absorbed. He shuddered, his skin prickling as the cut healed over leaving a long, red scar. Prying a dark stone from the setting of one of his rings, he dragged the gem along the blood on his palm before dropping it over the bowl.

The dark stone fell no more than a handspan before it stopped, hanging in the air just above the basin. Danyl spoke the words he'd memorised so long ago.

The temperature in the room fell with each twisted syllable. Frost crackled across the dirty windows behind him, and his breath came in plumes.

The bloodied gem burst into black flame.

"Why do you call?"

The voice grated across his senses, deep and sibilant, and Danyl wrapped his arms around his body, tight, to stop his shaking.

"A gr-group of travellers have come. From Da-dal – Dal'mere."

The burning stone rolled in the air. *"And?"* The voice affected disinterest, but something lurked beneath it. Excitement?

"Th-they sp-peak of a bo-bone drake. One of-of the boys... they s-say th-they fought it!"

The black flames flared high, and Danyl threw his hands up with a cry.

"A hunter comes," the voice rolled through Danyl's skull. *"Open the way."*

Danyl let out a sob as the flames winked out, and the gem fell into the bowl with a ping. Tears burned in his eyes, freezing to sharp shards of ice before they could fall.

No. Danyl moaned, deep in his throat, but there was no escape.

He tried to unbutton his shirt, but shaking fingers impeded him. With a snarl, he yanked the panels of cloth apart, and small seed-pearl buttons went flying. His skin was corpse-white in the dark, and his heart pounded so fast his chest shuddered, shaking the traces of violet scarring that reached out from his breast like a spider's web caught in a breeze. With a cry of defiance, one that was weaker than he would have liked, he pushed through the bitter cold and shrugged out of his coat and shirt. Hesitation to obey was death.

Panting, he grasped the bowl, the skin of his palms freezing to its surface. Lifting it level with his chest, he began to speak once more, each word sending tendrils of ice down his throat.

With his whole body convulsing, he closed his eyes. The shards of his frozen tears sliced his pupils. Crying out, he pulled the bowl towards himself with all his strength. And burst into black flame.

He made to scream, his mouth opened as wide as it would stretch, but no sound issued forth as the bowl sank through his chest. No crackle or hiss was made as the flames engulfed his heart and raced along his veins, burning – each vein pulsing dark beneath his skin like a candle behind a paper shade.

Danyl felt every agonising lick of the Voidfire as it leeched the energy of his soul. And then his body twisted, stretching, transforming until thought was ripped away and he became a living gateway to the Void.

CHAPTER NINETEEN

Hunted

WARPED GLASS COVERED the portholes, barely rattling as the storm battered them. No draft made its way inside the Sea Lion to shift the low hanging weed smoke, and seaglass lanterns turned that smoke into a haze, tinting it orange and spreading shadows like an eerie twilight. The inn – and Sim was not even sure that it qualified as such – was full of people who eyed them with either curiosity or hostility. He'd been confident they'd find trouble here, but Jaric had faced down the first drunkard to approach them. The man had been missing an ear as well as most of his teeth from what Sim could tell, and a barmaid had arrived brandishing a cudgel threatening them both if they began fighting. The rest of the patrons had left them alone. Mostly.

The communal galley of the inn buzzed with conversation, and an old man with a pipe kept playing tunes Sim didn't recognise. Bench seats along the curved walls held cushions of mismatched fabric of varying shades of'dark', their colour lost in the half-light. Rough-hewn planks, worn smooth with age and use, were crafted into plain tables and chairs that were scattered haphazardly across the reed strewn decking – reeds stained with things Sim didn't care to focus on too closely. Didn't they ever clean here? Then again, maybe fresh reeds weren't easy to come by out in the middle of nowhere.

Back in Hanore, this crowd would have dispersed with the coming of the storm, seeking comfort in their own homes and beds. But here in this strange ship town no-one appeared to sleep. Men and women, young and old, as well as cats and dogs, came and went regularly. And most of them thronged around the tables of dicing and cards Sim was itching to join. It was the perfect place to recoup some of the coin he'd lost to the First Captain when he opened his big mouth.

He ground his teeth. Why, by the gods, had he done that? He *never* offered coin freely. Did that spider bite do more damage than he'd thought?

He rubbed at the puncture marks at the bottom of his neck, then pulled his hand away. It wouldn't do for Meg to notice, she'd start at him again about needing more rest, and then Sevaani would start worrying if he was sure he was all right. He was. He didn't even *remember* the bite. Or what happened after. He could have died and he'd never have known what was happening. He shivered.

"Are you well, Sim?" Meg asked.

"Never better!" He gave her a grin he reserved for the older ladies of Hanore who visited his father's store. The ones who thought he was a troublemaker.

Meg narrowed her eyes at him in suspicion, and he looked away. Eye blind it! I need to be more careful.

But it was true. He *could* have died. And he'd worried about being killed in some stupid patrol with the Rangers. Never from a spider bite!

It was enough to make him lose his appetite. Almost.

He had to be more careful in future. Now they just needed to get out of here.

As interesting a place as Glass Bay was, Serjat was where he'd start finding the pieces of his parents' past. Start making his own coin.

They just needed to get Kaiel, and they could go.

If they could get him out of those salt cages. Who'd ever heard of *salt cages*? Still, Captain Daynar seemed to know what they were, and they didn't sound good.

Ah, daemon shit. They *had* to get Kaiel out of there.

"We have to get him out of there, Captain Daynar."

Sim gave a start. Had he been speaking out loud?

Jaric sighed. "Sevaani, I'm as concerned as you are, but what can we do?"

"We can't just leave him there!"

"Fine time for you to start caring," Sim scoffed. "You've wanted nothing to do with him since he saved you from Rolen, now you can't leave him behind? As if we would."

"Sim!" Meg glared at him. "He cut off her brother's arm. That's not easy to forget."

"Sure, but Rolen had a knife to her throat and he called her a… well, you know. What kind of brother does that?"

"That doesn't matter," Sevaani said, shaking her head. "Kaiel is from Hanore. He's one of us. And we *do not* leave ours behind."

"You heard the captain. We aren't going to leave him behind." He glanced at Jaric. "Right?"

Jaric gave him a level stare. "That's what I said."

"Simeon, he's your best friend," Sevaani said. "You can get him out. You can get into the fortress."

"Me?" Sim's voice chose that moment to squeak, and he felt his cheeks heat. He cleared his throat. "How am I meant to do that?"

Sevaani glared at him. "If you could make your way into Mistress Dovene's kitchen and steal an entire tray of sweet cakes, you can get into that fortress and get Kaiel out!"

"Will you keep your voice down?" he hissed. There were far too many people eyeing them for his liking. His lips tightened; well, watching the girls. They were all still dressed in the same swamp-stained Borderlands gear – except for Meg in her dress – they had started out in days ago, but they had managed to find somewhere to wash their faces and straighten their hair. Compared to the other women in here, painted up, brassy and all hard-eyed, they were somehow... fresh? Daemons take them, he'd never really thought about it before, but both Sevaani and Meg were beautiful. He dropped his hand to the dagger at his belt, and he cast a scowl at the people around them.

"That was you?" Meg stared at him, open-mouthed.

"What was me? Oh, Mistress Dovene. Yes, yes. How did you know that, Sevaani?" he glared at her, then shrugged. "But it doesn't matter; it was a long time ago. I've changed."

"It was last summer!" Meg rolled her eyes.

"Exactly."

"Simeon –" Meg began, but Sevaani interrupted her.

"Surely someone with your skill can get into that fortress?"

"Getting into Mistress Dovene's kitchen didn't involve crossing a bridge in front of twenty guards without being seen!" Sim hissed.

Sevaani waved a hand dismissively. "It's night; they won't see you in the dark."

"Enough," Jaric said, staring at each of them in turn. "Stop acting like children. This isn't Hanore. There are more dangers here than you realise."

"The Borderlands are dangerous too," Meg said defiantly.

"And you know those dangers," Jaric agreed. "They're ones you've grown up with. But here you could step outside and get stabbed by a ten-year-old for your purse."

Sevaani scowled at the captain but sat back in her chair. Sim suppressed a sigh. She wouldn't let something like this go so quickly. She surveyed the room and shuddered as her gaze travelled over the drunks, and the glass-eyed men and women staring into space. From the stain around their mouths, he was sure they'd been chewing Black Lotus leaves. He barely suppressed his own shudder at that.

"Where's Darien," she asked, suddenly turning her attention back to the table.

"He's 'meditating'," Sim said and picked up the last crust of his bread to wipe up the remains of his meal. It was fish chowder, apparently. None of them, except Captain Daynar, had ever eaten fish before they'd left the Borderlands.

He eyed the untouched bowl that had been ordered for Darien.

"Oh, have it, Sim," Sevaani said, pushing the bowl over. "You probably need the food after that spider bite."

"Darien needs to eat too," Meg said, then dropped her eyes back to her bowl.

"We all need to keep our strength up," Jaric said. "Food on long sea voyages isn't always appetising."

"Salted beef and hardtack become surprisingly tasty when hunger is the alternative," a female voice said behind them. "Although that is hard to remember once you are back on land."

Sim looked over his shoulder and forgot all about the eyes sizing up Sevaani and Meg. Behind them stood a woman who was like a high tale come to life. The grey silk of her gown glowed in the hazy light. Her hair, white as the moon, cascaded over her shoulders, held off her face by pearl capped pins. And at the base of her neck, framed by a high collar glittered a large blue stone, the size of an egg.

Was that a sapphire? How had she not been killed for a jewel like that in this town?

"My lady," Jaric said, rising from his seat to offer a half bow. Sim rose also.

"You!" Sevaani gasped, and the woman arched one platinum eyebrow.

"Me?" the woman asked, and Sevaani coloured.

"I'm sorry," she said. "It's just, I've seen you before..." Sevaani trailed off, and Meg turned a thoughtful gaze on the stranger.

"A dream?" Meg asked, and Sevaani nodded. The woman watched them thoughtfully.

"Ah, g-good evening, milady," Sim said into the silence. He stumbled over the words, but his embarrassment was momentary as his eyes drifted back to the sapphire.

"Please." The woman gestured them back to their seats as the others made to rise. "Do not get up. I am interrupting your meal." She looked around the table. "Though I believe you are missing someone."

"Darien stayed in our room," Sim said. "But I'm not sure you'd say we're *missing* him."

"Simeon," was all the captain said and Sim grinned.

"You know us, my lady?" Jaric asked.

"Everyone in Glass Bay is speaking of you and your arrival through the swamp." Her smile glittered in the dimness of the taproom. "But no, it was not Darien of whom I spoke. I met your young friend in the fortress."

"Kaiel!" Sevaani jumped from her seat. "Is he well?"

"He was well when I saw him, though somewhat bruised. I dare imagine he does not fare so well now." She smiled in what Sim supposed was meant to be a reassurance at Sevaani's choked cry. "He will suffer no permanent harm from the cages, but he will not find the experience pleasant."

"We didn't catch your name, my lady." Jaric's face was blank.

She smiled.

Simeon felt as if she'd caressed his cheek with her hand.

"Forgive me," she said. "I am Iana Sabay, and this is Lihon of House Tang."

Sim blinked as the Amarian stepped out from behind her. A black silk coat fit snugly over his broad shoulders, while the smooth blue skin of his shaved head was darker in the orange light, and his top-knot hung straight behind his back.

"The Sander!" Sim exclaimed.

Iana smiled. "'Sander' is a common enough term for outlanders to name Amarians," she said to Sim. "But it is often construed as an insult by the people of the Black Sands."

"Your pardon, milord," Sim said to Lihon and offered the big man a bow, much like the one he'd seen his father offer Sevaani's mother back in Hanore. "I meant no offence. I... err... I'm Simeon Ravenson. I often open my mouth without thinking. That's Captain Jaric Daynar, and these ladies are Sevaani Etine and Meghara Carin."

Meg rose to her feet beside Sevaani, who ran her hands over her rough and dirty clothing, eyeing the rich silk that clad the newcomers.

"Please." Jaric gestured to the spare chairs at the end of the table. "Join us."

"Thank you." Iana sat as Lihon held out a chair for her. "I had not expected to find Borderlanders in Glass Bay."

Jaric nodded. "I didn't expect to find a Shaluay Starbinder here either."

Simeon's mouth fell open, and he snapped it shut, retaking his seat to hide his surprise. Shaluay. That wasn't a sapphire at her neck; it was a cora'stone! He made a sign of warding against ill luck, then grimaced and lowered his hand.

"Shaluay?" Sevaani asked. "But you never leave the Starcradle."

Iana laughed. "The Shaluay do not leave Arleth'taur often, but it is not unheard of." She smiled. "I am impressed you all survived the trek across Dal'mere," she said. "And not a little curious as to why you would even attempt it. Kaiel told me of an encounter with a daemon possessed bone drake?"

Sim jumped as a cry rose from the far end of the taproom, and chairs crashed to the floor as two men went for each other's throats.

"The Borderlands edge Dal'mere," Jaric said after the commotion died down. "Daemons still find their way out of the Void through tears in the veil all across that cursed land."

"Yes," Iana agreed. "It is a dangerous place. Tell me, what did you do to have a Prince of the Realm chase you into it?"

"He believed treason had been committed and wasn't prepared to wait for any sort of process by which a defence, and the proving of innocence, might occur," Jaric said.

"There was no treason against Aldania," Sevaani put in. "Kaiel and Darien have never left the Borderlands until now. But that spear was strange. The prince thinks it has something to do with House –"

"His Highness didn't explain his reasoning to us," Jaric interrupted firmly.

Sim snorted. "No, he just chained them up. We should have left Darien for him. Surely one brother is as good as the other. What?" He fell silent under the weight of the stares of both Meg and Sevaani.

"What is this spear?" Iana asked. "It seems to be of significance."

Sim eyed the others, but they all had their mouths closed.

The Shaluay smiled. "Perhaps you will tell me later?" She gestured at Jaric, rings on her hand glittering. "You are a Captain of the Rangers? It is rare for a Borderlands Captain to leave his post."

"It's not unheard of," Jaric said.

"Hanore has always looked after its own," Sevaani offered. "Captain Daynar is doing his duty helping Kaiel and Darien. We're all family in the Borderlands."

"That is very sensible," Iana said. A thoughtful expression crossed her face. "The families in the Three Citadels date back to the Sundering, do they not?"

"Most, milady," Sim agreed. "Some, like my own and the good captain here, are more recent additions. It takes a couple of generations for that stain to be forgotten."

"Simeon!" Sevaani glared at him.

"What? It's true. Just because *House* Etine doesn't like the citadelfolk's prejudices being spoken about out loud, doesn't mean they aren't real."

"Enough, Sim," Meg said in her Keeper's tone, and he snorted but said no more.

"And is your family one of the founding families, Sevaani?" Iana asked in the silence that followed.

"Only a handful of the families that live in the Three Citadels are founding families," Sevaani said, her gold hair glinting red in the lamplight. "My family is one. Kaiel and Darien's another. Though most have lived there so long as to make little difference. We tend not to speak of it." She looked pointedly at Sim.

Iana nodded thoughtfully. "There are old bloodlines in the Borderlands."

"No older than those that can be found elsewhere," Jaric said.

She gave a soft, tinkling laugh. "Just so. The bloodlines of the High Houses and many others are spread far over the Realms. But none have been exposed to the same conditions as the bloodlines of the Borderlands."

"Conditions?" Sim arched an eyebrow. "You mean poverty? No, I suppose few of the High Houses could claim to have experienced that."

"You would be surprised," the lady said. "Not all High Houses are rich in coin, but I was referring to different conditions." She gazed at each of them in turn. "In the fortress, I had heard that Prince Alesandr believes Kaiel is of the Blood of House Taaren'th?" she asked. "That line is believed to have been stamped out by House Niskeri, but I would not be surprised to find it true."

Sevaani sat up. "Your pardon?"

Jaric frowned. "You'll find very few families in the Borderlands have held onto their histories, or blood marks, my lady."

"Please, you must all call me Iana," she told them. "If that is true, it is a shame. For instance, the name Toranth is reminiscent of an older diction. The inflections have drifted somewhat from the original form over time, or by purpose. Toranth could very well be Taaren'th of the first kings of Aldania."

"Could be," Sim said flatly. Kaiel might have opened his big mouth but he wouldn't.

"You're mistaken... Iana," Jaric said from his corner of the table. "There are no clans in the Borderlands. And even if there were, it wouldn't matter. The Realms barely acknowledge the Clans these days."

Iana locked gazes with him. "House Niskeri rules the Clan of the Iron Boar and takes it as their symbol. And there were once many clans in the Borderlands. When the last of the Sahrin drove the daemonic hordes into the land that became Dal'mere, the Clansmen stood at his side."

"You mean the last Empyros?" Sim leant forward.

"This is a history the Borderlanders no longer consider relevant," Jaric said, cutting him off.

"You live at the edge of civilization, face the remnants of the War of the Summoners, and don't consider it relevant? Our history on this world is very relevant, especially the history of the Borderlands. So much has been lost." She shook her head, then smiled. "If I am offending, please forgive me. That was not my intention."

"Are you a historian, Lad– I mean, Iana?" Sevaani asked.

"The stories say the Shaluay were many things, even Dreamers," Meg said, and Sevaani flashed her a look. "I suppose historians could be counted amongst their numbers. Though I thought most of the Starbinders had died out. In the Sundering, I mean."

"The Sundering struck the Order very hard," Iana agreed. "But Arleth'taur still stands and a small circle of my sisters remained to carry on our work. It has taken us a long time to find our feet; I pray we are not too late."

"Too late for what?" Meg asked.

"*Cine mi'or*?" Lihon spoke before Iana could reply.

Sim looked at the man. Was that High Asairic?

Iana glanced at her companion but continued. "That we are not too late to resume our work in the world. It has been many years since we were present to assist the Clans of Humanity, and there is still a great deal of resentment that our healers were not there to work with the Shrines during the Age of Chaos."

"It's the year thirty-nine forty-eight," Jaric said. "It's taken you nearly four thousand years to rebuild?"

"To our sorrow," she said sadly. "While the Starcradle was largely untouched by the Sundering, key... artefacts were lost to us. We seek these still. And other factors slowed our efforts. But the tides are turning. The Winter Solstice is approaching, and the hinge of the Ages swings on its axis." She glanced again at Lihon. "And so, we return to the world of men."

"This seems a funny place to start." Sim couldn't help himself.

"On the contrary," Iana said. "But for Serjat and Isoliere, and of course the Dreamholds which are not accessible, these farthest reaches of the Var Imperium are the last possible repositories of the knowledge of the Summoners. Knowledge that will be sorely needed should they return."

"Many scholars have visited the citadels over the years to study the ruins also," Sevaani said.

"But none of them ever found what they were looking for," Meg said. "What are you looking for, my Lady?"

"Knowledge that would see us all protected," Iana said.

"Have you found it?" Sim asked.

The Shaluay offered him a small smile. "It is rare that we set down a path without finding something."

"What have you foun – Ouch!" Sim glared at Meg.

"Is it true Prince Alesandr is establishing his Household in Jaroff after his term as Carbinah is complete?" Iana asked.

"He's doing what?" Sevaani straightened.

Still scowling, Sim shook his head. "We've had the dubious honour of hosting each of their Royal Highnesses of Aldania, playing at Carbinah of Jaroff. I can't imagine Alesandr being any more likely to settle there than his brothers." He picked at his bread. "Why he'd want to stay in that hovel is beyond my comprehension."

"There are plenty of reasons why His Highness might move his court to Jaroff," Jaric said. "Niklai is heir to the throne and Pavyl is now occupied with the King's navy; what better place for House Niskeri to put one of their own than where he might keep an eye on the High Prince of Ebron?"

Iana tilted her head. "House Sarentis is a sworn vassal to Niskeri; the High Prince's autonomy has never been questioned."

"Four High Princes rule territories in the name of House Niskeri. They are, for all intents and purposes – and in fact, once were – kings." Jaric said. "The House that holds the Ivy Throne has always been watchful of the High Princes. But I'm not privy to the prince's council."

"An interesting line of speculation nonetheless," Iana said. "However, the reason I came to see you tonight is that I understand you are seeking passage to Serjat?"

"You have a ship?" Sim was careful to keep the eagerness out of his voice.

"I have an arrangement with one of the captains. Once we get your friend Kaiel back, I believe we could all find passage together."

"That's a very generous offer, Lady Iana," Jaric said. "May I ask why?"

She shrugged. "You need to leave, Captain, and I have a way, is that not enough?"

"For help from a Shaluay? I don't believe so."

Sim narrowed his eyes. The man was going to lose them the first ship they'd come across.

"I go where the stars lead me, Captain. And I do not believe you will find a more trustworthy ship than the one I have found for myself and Lihon."

"And you just happened to be going to Serjat?"

"Captain Daynar –" Sim began, but Iana stopped him.

"It is all right," she said. "It is convenient; I will grant you that. I did not plan to go to Serjat, but I can certainly take a detour along the way if you wish to join me."

Jaric sighed. "Thank you. We need to collect Kaiel from the fortress, but yes, I'd like to accept your offer."

"I am sure we can persuade the First to return Kaiel to you in one piece," Iana said.

Behind them, another cry rose. Sim stared as a man fell off his chair, a dagger jutting from his throat. The table he'd been playing goh'ja at was overturned, and a heavily built woman was lunging at another man as a barmaid and two others pushed through the milling crowd with cudgels out.

"Oh, dear," Iana said rising, her silent blademaster getting up behind her. "I believe it is time I retired to my room." She nodded at Meg and Sevaani. "You young ladies might like to do the same. I will speak with you all again tomorrow. Goodnight."

"Goodnight, my lady," Jaric said, and the rest of them followed suit. "Finding our rooms sounds like a good idea."

"Why do we have to leave?" Sim asked, his eyes on the fight that was pulling more of the spectators into it. "Why did she? That blademaster could have taken on every man and woman here and not received a cut."

"Because a Blay Shon will only fight when he has to, and we'd do well to follow that example," Jaric said. "Unless you feel you're recovered enough to hold your own if the fight comes to you?"

With a smirk, Sim stood, and then grabbed the edge of the table as his knees nearly buckled. He looked at the captain who arched an eyebrow. Sim's smirk turned into a scowl. He pushed himself upright. "You're likely right," he said to Jaric. "It's probably best we keep our heads low."

"Very wise." Jaric nodded in agreement, his lips twisting up.

Sim scowled again and let the man lead him out of the common room.

Smoke obscured the low ceiling of the galley, stale and unmoving, much like the men and women who lay slumped over tables and chairs. Some people stirred, but those that did appeared to be chewing their tongues. Black Lotus addicts; Darien shook his head. He'd heard of the leaves from his time as an apprentice to Shany, but they'd never seen it in the citadels. He moved past them quietly and up the laddered steps to the closed hatch. The Sea Lion Inn was sleeping, and he was careful not to attract attention. This town was like nothing he'd ever imagined. For all the posturing the folk of the Three Citadels made at being 'free of the rule of the Houses', they held to the mores of the Realms more tightly than he'd imagined.

The others had returned hours ago, and he'd feigned sleep so Simeon would take himself to bed in the room they shared. He'd waited a good while once Sim's snores had filled the small cabin, listening to the thunderous storm outside and the rain hammering the ship's walls, before he'd risen and snuck out. Jaric would never let him see the old woman, Bertha, alone, and he had no intention of speaking to her with anyone watching over his shoulder. This way, none of them would ever know.

He made his way cautiously up the step ladder to peer out the hatch.

Rain still fell, and he could barely make out the new cabins being built on the giant ship's upper deck. The town had no street lamps, but then he supposed, it didn't have streets either. Dull flames sat in coloured seaglass orbs, hanging on vine-like ropes that drooped from masts and over railings. Each offered small pools of light that illuminated little in the deluge. He imagined that few of Glass Bay's inhabitants would be concerned with pickpockets or knives in the back. Not when he was sure any one of them could play the part of an opportunistic attacker.

He climbed onto the deck and made his way across the wet wood, instantly drenched in the driving rain. Canvas snapped like whips in the darkness, and shutters rattled against makeshift frames where portholes had been widened into windows proper. Darien picked his steps carefully as he made his way across bridges made from planks, counting the yawning darkness of water-filled spaces between the ships, and looking for the small boat on which Bertha had grabbed him that afternoon. It would have been a difficult task in daylight, given how confusing ships were, it was almost impossible in the dark. But he kept moving in what he thought was the right direction.

His hand still throbbed from where her nail had pressed against the covered scar. How had the old woman known it was there? Maybe she hadn't, but he'd sensed something around her, and that was enough to tweak his interest.

He came to a stop before a ship, little different to the rest but for its size and shape. The rain soaking through his clothes set him shivering, but he was sure this was the right spot. As he made to step onto the deck, pale blue wisps of ethereal light began to glow along the edges of the vessel. His skin crawled as a primal warning wrapped itself around his spine.

In the end, it was force of will that pushed him forward. If he was going to be a Ciralys, he could not be halted by fear; Ciralys didn't let emotions dictate their actions. That was the way of the herd and the

Ciralys, by virtue of their ability to wield the Light of the Eye, needed to be stronger than their base responses.

He clenched his jaw to stop the rattling of his teeth, to no avail. Taking a breath, he walked across the plank onto the ship, and the pouring rain suddenly became a drizzle.

The wind also softened, though his soaked clothes did little to ease its chill bite.

Somewhere behind him, a crash echoed in the night; voices rose in anger, and a woman shrieked in protest, before falling away to leave his heart racing.

Gathering himself, he made his way forward.

Light leaked from behind the canvas that covered the door to the companionway, a curtain that pulled aside as he approached. Warm air puffed over him, and he fought the urge to run into its embrace, his shivering increasing as the cold around him tightened its grip.

"I've been waiting for you, boy," a voice called from below. "Come in, come in!"

He looked in cautiously; the light of a small lamp lit the cabin, and a fire blazed in an iron dish beneath a chimney that was obviously not original to the ship.

The old hag, Bertha, sat swathed in blankets before the flames, another chair directly opposite her. He was halfway down the ladder without realising he'd taken a step. The curtain dropped with a clicking flap, and her laugh – more a cackle – brought to mind tales Old Shany used to tell during midwinter nights of the Lady of Death, Samantra's aspect of the Crone. Stories that would send them running for their mothers.

Bertha reminded him a lot of Shany, but where Shany was solid with the strength of the witching ways, there was a wildness to this Bertha that made his skin crawl.

"Come in, come in," she cackled again, her mouth lined with age.

"Warm yourself by the fire. I knew you'd come." Her stare pierced him. "Yes. Saw you in the Dream! Saw *it* call you on the White Road. I felt the Taint on you. I can almost see the shadow coursing through your blood." She peered up at him. "Come over here."

He was transfixed. The energy that crackled around Bertha was strange, off-putting. It was not *Asai*, of that he was certain.

"I said, sit down." The voice that spurted from her mouth was deep. Glottal. His stomach rolled as his blood went cold, and to his horror, the *thing* surged in his mind.

"No, no, no!" Bertha snapped, her voice normal once more. "We don't do that. I've told you before!" She smiled at him, the flames of the fire flaring beside her. "Come, you don't need to be afraid. We need to talk, and the one who swims in *my* veins cannot hurt you."

Darien stumbled to the chair, a small part of him grateful for the heat of the fire as he stared at Bertha, mind racing. "What are you talking about?" he rasped, his throat dry. "What's swimming in your blood?"

"The same thing as what's swimming in yours." She shifted, turning to the fire. The veins in her neck pulsed black beneath her paper-thin skin, branching off like a tree bare of leaves before fading again. "We can see it, you know. There's no hiding it from us. Whatever you have done to push it back, there's no escape. Once a host is chosen, you meld, or you die."

"I don't know what you mean." He strove for firm ground.

"Ha! You do." She leant forward, pinning him with her gaze. "You can't fool me. I have lived in a constant battle for more years than I care to remember. You might be strong enough to remain in control, but your sanity will be the price."

"But the Master of the Swamp put a ward on –" He bit his tongue.

"Those *things* can do nothing." She sat back. "What did he promise you?"

Darien scrambled after his stumbling thoughts. "Nothing was promised, but surely –"

"But nothing!" Her left hand clawed at the armrest, splinters of wood curling under her nails. "Even if he were not bound in his crystal tomb, he could do nothing. The Imanarg – know what they be, boy?" she asked, and he shook his head.

"Bloodlords," she cackled. "Slaves to a mature csitargon. And they will already be hunting you. The ward will fade, then you will fight. If you win, you die. If it wins, you meld; and if you come to a draw, then you have this to look forward to." She gestured to herself, her laughter bordered on hysterical. "Mad! Unwanted. Alone. But!" she wagged a finger at him. "You have been Marked. And that might make all the difference."

Darien took a breath. "You said to come to you. That if I wanted to 'know' I should come to you." He shivered in his wet clothes despite the heat in the room. "Well, I'm here. Tell me what I want to know."

"You have no idea of what I speak, do you?" Her gaze narrowed. "You have some training; I can sense *Asai* about you, though I can no longer touch it myself. How can you be ignorant?"

"You can see it?" He stared at her hard. If she could see *Asai* but was possessed like him… "You are one, aren't you? A Bloodlord."

"I am no slave! Come. Let us see." She grabbed his wrist, pulling him towards her. A small knife dropped from the sleeve of her ragged blouse, and she nicked his palm.

With a cry, Darien lurched to his feet, snatching his hand to his chest, but she was paying him no attention. The skin around her eyes darkened, and the white of her eyes flooded with blood as she gazed at the drop that had fallen to the table from his hand.

"Ah! You are from the Borderland Wilds!"

"What an astounding observation," he drawled. "This entire town knows where we're from!"

She cackled again, and then words that hurt his ears rolled out of her mouth. Hard edges of sound rumbled from her throat and were spat across the table. His blood shivered and broke into tiny droplets lifting into the air. Spiralling, they circled each other and began to glow like wine-red fireflies.

She studied them, then snatched one from the air. Holding it between thumb and forefinger, she stared at it for a moment, then put it in her mouth.

Panic bloomed in Darien. Shany had always warned of the power of blood, that it could be used to bind and harm as well as to heal, to track and find the person from whom it came. He lunged forward, his hand slapping down through the spiralling, ruby droplets. They pierced his skin like shards of broken glass. He turned his hand over, Bertha cackling madly. His palm was riddled with tiny ruby shards that sunk into his flesh.

"Witchborn," Bertha said, her voice harsh and accented once more. "Trained as well... but forgotten? No. A master came. I cannot see him. He is powerful. Removed. You let them take your knowledge of the Craft, freeing you of your vows so you could learn of the Outer Circle. Oathbreaker. You cannot be freed from such oaths as that! Your Keeper should have known better." She paused. "Maybe she did? The Mark, the one you hide, show me."

"Release my blood!" Darien backed away on shaky legs.

"Bah!" She spat a glowing red jewel at the fire. It popped and crackled as it was consumed, and she spun to face him, hair wild. "Done! Show me the Mark!"

She lurched forward and grabbed his wet coat as he made for the door. Wrinkled hands with sharp nails grabbed at his right wrist and pulled it towards her. The smell of rotting teeth filled his nose, and he gagged. A thumb brushed against the spot the shadow-bird's beak had cut, and the scar hidden by Shany's ointment flared, silver light pouring from it into Bertha's blood-filled eyes.

She screamed and fell back. On all fours, she scurried to the corner of the room.

"Too bright, too bright! Child of the Moon! No, no, no! It comes." She clutched her knees and moaned, rocking backwards and forwards, hair hiding her face. Suddenly she sat upright, as if attached to a string, her eyes now blackened pits. "The Hunter comes. Beware the Hunter, child. Beware the Garendai!"

She began to scream again.

The noise pierced Darien's ears, and he stumbled back to the steps. The scream kept increasing in volume, bursting through his skull. Terror spiked his blood, his heart pounding so hard he expected it would burst from his chest.

He couldn't be found here.

Darien stumbled up the step ladder and out into the cold night.

The curtain dropped noisily behind him and muffled the screaming. He was surprised to find the decks around the ship still empty. In Hanore, such a commotion would bring half the citadel out like a flock of geese.

He stumbled over the gangplank and onto the next deck, then the one after that. He climbed up rope ladders to the taller ships and scrambled down planks to those that sat lower. The rain had stopped, but the wind still howled through the alleys created by the boats. The clouds above parted to reveal a crescent moon, light reflecting off the myriad puddles and wet wood.

Darien paused when he reached a higher deck, and something made him turn. He stared across the dark shadows towards the bay. He could just make out the silhouette of a man in the shifting light of the moon, standing four decks away. He waited for a moment, eyeing the figure, and was about to move on when a flash of violet blinked from the shadowed face.

The hairs on the back of his neck rose. No man had glowing, violet eyes. He was still panicked, off-centre after seeing the old woman. He was a fool! No crazy old hag in this collection of hovels could know anything about him!

Darien turned back towards the man again and bit his lip. He was gone.

He peered into the night, and the man crossed out of the shadow of a ship and into the light of the scythe moon. The way he held himself was off.

Instinct warned Darien to move, and he dashed across the gap between the ship he was on and the next, moving quickly towards the bulk of the Sea Lion.

He twisted back. The man was crossing the decks, following him.

On shaking legs, Darien quickened his pace, leaving all efforts at stealth behind. He slipped on a plank, arms pinwheeling as he caught himself and stumbled forward to the next ship. He caught his booted foot on a brass bar in the darkness and fell to his knees with a cry. A dog barked and he pushed himself up, palms stinging.

Darien's legs were like water, but he willed them to move. The wind rose again, and more dogs howled in the night. His heart skipped a beat as the shadows shifted around him, but it was only the seaglass orbs swaying in the rigging above.

Another howl filled the air, and the skin across his back tightened.

That was not a dog.

Darien looked again. Slipped again. He caught himself before he fell between the boats, heart pounding, scanning the night behind him.

There. A silhouette in the moonlight.

The man was matching, if not gaining, on him.

Turning south, he made his way forward, the dark bulk of the cliff walls rose ahead, and the churning rumble of the waterfall grew louder.

Darien lurched into a half run towards the Sea Lion, and behind him, the strange man pursued.

CHAPTER TWENTY

A Kindling Flame

KAIEL HUDDLED IN the centre of the cage. Arms locked around his knees, he shuddered as wave after wave of nausea wracked him. The cage was large enough that he could have stood, but his legs had given way hours ago from the... resonance? Was that the right word? Darien could've told him. Captain Daynar and Lady Iana had been right. The middle of the cage was more comfortable – he almost laughed – than leaning against the bars. He'd done that when his legs failed him earlier, stumbling hard against the red, pitted metal. His left shoulder still burned from the contact, but the headache had faded.

His stomach twisted again, and he was thankful he hadn't eaten since the day before.

He breathed through the sensation and raised his head.

The cavern was sizeable. At least thirty feet across and fifteen feet high. The walls were detailed in carvings sculpted by the Var. Black iron stands held torches that cast flickering shadows, giving them a strange sense of movement. In the first panel, tall elongated figures walked across the walls to the Var who huddled on the ground on all fours. In the next, those same figures placed their hands on the Var, some of whom were depicted now as standing. Kaiel recognised the scenes, he'd spent enough time with Ang back in Hanore to be familiar with the Var's tales of the Ancients, and how they had gifted the Var – the People – with intelligence beyond their previously crude limitations.

Beyond the light of the torches at the cavern's far end, maybe another sixty feet away, the waterfall thundered into the bay. He was surprised it wasn't louder; but something about the acoustics of the cavern softened it to a dull roar.

Scattered around were wooden tables and benches, and collected in the back-right corner of the cavern just across from him, were racks and shelves filled with jars and bottles. On a large bench before those was the corpse of the man Kaiel had tried to save. He kept his back to that corner of the room.

How could he have been so stupid? Even if Sim and the others had backed him up, he couldn't have stopped a hall full of people. And it had been none of his business anyway! But...

Another wave of nausea hit him, and his abdomen clenched painfully. His stomach muscles felt like they had been pounded repeatedly with Master Milan's hammer over an entire afternoon of work in the forge. He groaned.

"Would you like some water?"

The question came from behind him, and he jerked his head around, cursing as another wave of nausea swept over him. He rolled back as strained muscles failed to offer support. A flash of panic had him thrusting out an arm to stop himself from falling. He couldn't hold back the cry of agony as his hand brushed the bar; it was as though a red-hot bar of molten iron had lanced his flesh. But the support of something solid – even briefly – was enough to stop what would have been a more painful sprawl against the daemon-cursed metal.

She moved around the cage. Torchlight lapped over black leathers and deepened the red of her silk blouse to the colour of fresh blood. Dark hair was pulled back, and a widow's peak framed her face like a heart. He'd seen her before, standing on the balcony overlooking the hall as he was being led away.

She dropped to her haunches and peered at him. "You don't look well at all."

"W-who are you?" Kaiel struggled to straighten himself.

"I'm your new best friend."

"What?"

"I'm here to get you out."

Kaiel straightened, swallowing against the warm wetness that stuck in the back of his throat. "Did Captain Daynar send you?"

"Daynar? The Sithapian? No, he didn't send me." Dark eyes studied him. "Corusite doesn't usually affect those who can't see the Light of the Eye, at least not so strongly." She leant forward, a hand dropping to the dagger at her hip. "Are you a wielder?"

He straightened. "No!"

"Show me your hand."

Kaiel wanted to scowl but didn't have the energy. Thankfully Dar had reminded him to apply more ointment that morning. He raised his right hand to his chest and closed his fist, presenting the back of his hand to her.

After a moment, she nodded, and Kaiel let his hand drop.

"I've never seen anyone blind to the Eye so sick from corusite before," she said.

"These cages get used often, do they?" he half snarled as his stomach twisted yet again.

"Yes, they do."

"I was trained to sense it," he said, mouth dry. "You have water?"

She cocked an eyebrow but pushed a water skin through the bars. "Trained to sense *Asai*? In the Borderlands?"

He fumbled at the stopper. "I trained as a Kas'tirien," he said, finally getting the plug out and took a swallow of the warm water.

"Daemon Hunter?" She laughed. "And I swim with the mer'ay." She eyed him again. "Show me your teeth."

Kaiel lowered the water skin. "What?" his head felt like it was filled with Aunt Breanta's toffee. "I'm not a horse."

"Funny,' the woman said. "Your teeth, Borderlander. I want to see if you're an Ambere addict."

"Ambere? The resin from the moonleaf trees? Borewyrms eat that stuff, not people."

"You'd be surprised. Now show me your teeth or I will leave you in here to rot."

This time Kaiel did scowl, but he peeled back his lips to show her his teeth.

She grunted. "Well, they aren't stained."

"Ambere is medicinal. It'll kill you if you ingest too much of it."

"Not right away it won't," she said. "And it will make this shit life bearable for a few years before it does. Or so I'm told."

"Oh, really?" he said. "How about you show me *your* teeth."

"Don't get smart with me; I'm not the one inside a corusite cage."

"Or what?" His eyes started to droop and struggled to sit upright. "You'll leave me in here to rot?"

She laughed. "Don't pretend you don't care. I promise you that you will care in the morning very much. Especially if you're like this halfway through the night."

"Halfway?"

She laughed. "It's at least another five hours before the fortress will stir."

"Captain Daynar will get me out." He shook his head and wished he hadn't as pain knocked against his temples. "My friends won't leave me."

"I'm sure they won't," she agreed, the flickering light of the torches playing over the planes of her face. "But one of your friends has already handed over a sack of gold to get you released, and it didn't work, did it?"

"The First Captain said she'd let me out tomorrow."

"And you believe her?"

"Why would she lie?"

"Why wouldn't she?" the woman hissed back at him. She took a breath and smiled. "Do you really want to spend another eight hours in here?"

"I should just trust you? Why are you helping me?"

"You talk a lot, don't you?" Exasperation snapped in her tone, accompanying her glare. "It's not so much helping you as it is fucking with the old woman. She thinks she's all-powerful here, but she's not, and I am going to remind her of that."

"What will it cost me?"

"Cost you? I'm offering to get you out of here and you're worried about the price?"

"No-one does anything for free," he said. "Not in this place." He had learned that much from Sim at least.

"Anyone else would be begging to be let out." She considered him. "When the old woman finds you gone tomorrow, she will scream herself hoarse. She'll be worried over which captain can reach into the very heart of her power to pluck a prisoner out. Especially one who has a prince of Aldania chasing him."

"And where am I to go?" Kaiel growled. She was going to get him killed. "To my friends? We'll all be hanged when she finds us!"

She grinned. "You're right. You would be if you were staying here."

"I'm not leaving without my friends." He shook his head again, gritting his teeth against the dizziness that followed.

"That's very honourable of you," she snorted. "What makes you think you have a choice?"

This was beginning to worry him. How had she gotten in here? "I'll call the guards," he said.

"There are no guards down here. No-one escapes the cages, that's why I'm doing this."

He gritted his teeth. "No. I have no wish to be killed because of whatever game you're playing."

The woman stood, and Kaiel frowned. The light of the torch fell upon her face. She was just a girl.

"Gods, I have never met anyone as stupid as you," she spat. "No wonder you're sitting in here. The First Bitch is not going to find you! I have a boat waiting to take you out of the bay and up the coast. You'll be set ashore six miles from Ebron."

"Tell me why you're doing this," he insisted. "Who are you?"

"I've told you why. My name, if you need one, is Zaria." She pulled a key from a pocket and hefted the padlock on his cage. "Now you need to stop talking."

"I'm not going to help you," Kaiel said. Gods, this was like a dream he couldn't wake from. Ma, what do I do?

Her hand dropped to the dagger at her waist, wrapping around the hilt. "I can make you move."

He sighed. "No, you can't. That dagger can do a lot of damage, but you'd still have to drag my corpse out, and that would leave a trail."

She clenched her jaw, rage flaring in her eyes. But she didn't move. Just stood there, watching him through the bars as though he were an animal she was unfamiliar with.

"You haven't thought this through, have you?" he said gently.

"Shut up," she snarled.

Kaiel stared as her eyes suddenly brimmed with tears. If he'd have to guess, he'd say she was younger than Meg. She was still a girl. "How old are you?"

"Old enough to kill you!" The tears didn't fall, though Kaiel was sure that had he been out of the cage, the dagger she gripped would have found its way through his neck.

"I don't doubt that in this place," he said

"What? You don't kill in the Borderlands?" she arched an eyebrow.

"We kill the creatures of Dal'mere, Korda'vari and sometimes daemons. Not people."

She turned away, blinking. "I should just leave you here."

He closed his eyes as nausea returned and groaned.

"Are you sure you don't want to come with me?"

"I *can't* leave my friends," he said, then paused. Sim wouldn't let her leave; he'd work at changing what she wanted so that it suited *him*. What if he... "If you can get my friends out as well, I'll go with you."

"That's too many people." She stepped back from the cage.

"But that would make the First wonder, wouldn't it?" he suggested. If Zaria could get him out, maybe she could get all of them out.

She was silent, and he raised his head.

"Are your friends as stubborn as you?"

"Is everyone in this town as crazy as you?" He wished he could take the words back as soon as he spoke.

"I'm not crazy!" Eyes blazing once more, the dagger was now in her hand. "My Pa and I are going to change things. He promised. It's my gran who is craz –"

"Gran? The First Captain is your *grandmother*?" He struggled to stand. "Why would you do something like this to your own family?"

"Because she killed my *mother*!" This time the tears did fall, and Kaiel choked as his own ma came to mind.

"I'm sorry –"

"Shut up! If we're going to do this, I have to think." She sheathed her dagger and unlocked the padlock on the cage, swinging the door back. The pitted metal screeched at the movement and Kaiel winced, but Zaria paid it no mind. "Lonah is going to want more Black Lotus to carry you all out. Shit!"

"You're giving someone Black Lotus leaves?"

"I'm surprised you've heard of it in the Borderlands. It's as valuable as gold coins here, and the Drowned Blades make a pretty penny shipping it across the Nemisdrillion." She stared at him. "What? You said you were prepared to pay."

Kaiel suppressed any further sign of disapproval. These people were certainly different. He took one painful step, and then another, and he was out of the cage. He felt the difference immediately, and his body was awash with pins and needles, as though blood flow had just returned to it. The ache in his head receded. His legs were shaky, though, and he lowered himself to the ground before he fell over.

Zaria leant over him and wrinkled her nose. "When was the last time you bathed?"

"Yesterday morning, in the swamp." He took another mouthful of water from the flask.

"Well, I guess that explains it. Can you walk?"

Kaiel pushed himself up. He was weak, but his legs were steadier, and he gestured back at the door to the cavern. "Let's go."

"Not that way." She made for the waterfall. "We'd never get past the guards at the bridge."

His stomach tightened. "Are we going to jump?" He could swim, but he had no idea how high up they were.

"What?" she looked at him as though he were mad. "Into the bay? Not likely. Even if we survived a three-hundred-foot drop, it's full of tiger carp. We'd be devoured in minutes. There's a path behind the waterfall the First uses to come and go quietly. Follow me closely. We can't take a torch; the light would be seen."

His brow furrowed – tiger carp? – but he followed her past the Var carvings on the walls. The sound of the waterfall increased as they drew closer until it was a roar that almost drowned out everything else.

"Follow closely!" Zaria yelled, snapping her fingers in his face to get his attention. She moved to the western wall, and out of the cavern by a path carved into the cliff face.

The stone was covered in a slick coating of water but was still miraculously free of moss or slippery patches. Either that or he was just lucky – and given recent events, he was not confident that was the case. The path was tight, twisting and turning back upon itself as it made its way down to the bay below. The night's darkness was barely relieved by the light of the moon as it battled the remaining storm clouds that crossed the sky. Thankfully, Zaria paused at each bend in the path to help him navigate the turn in the dark.

He had no sense of time as they made their way down. But for the odd patches of ghostlight, and the rushing of the water that underscored the drumbeat of his heart in his ears, it was as if he was falling through the Void. In the dark, he couldn't tell how wide or narrow the ledge he was clinging to might be, and even sweeping one foot out – carefully – to find the edge, gave him no sense of security. When Zaria stepped away from the wall, Kaiel's heart jumped. Reflexively, he reached out to grab her. But she remained standing and shrugged him off. They'd reached the bottom. Gingerly, he pushed himself away from the wall, his muscles tight and legs shaking again. With care, he tried to match her step for step as they moved beyond the curtain of the waterfall.

The water before them rippled with paths of reflected nightlight, ending in a dark bulk of black that held circular windows of orange light. The night was quiet but for the wind and roar of the waterfall, which continued to diminish as Zaria led them to another stone ledge that sat just above the waterline and followed the curve of the cliff around the bay.

"We're lucky it's been raining," she said over her shoulder in a whisper.

"Why is that?"

"Keep your voice down!" she hissed back at him. "Sound travels over water."

Kaiel's ears burned at the censure, but he was too busy putting one foot in front of the other, to retort.

"The town never really sleeps," she continued. "If the storm hadn't hit, there would be eyes everywhere and the night fishermen would be out setting their cages."

"They fish with cages?"

"The ones who are after pike crab do." She lifted her arm and pointed. "See that big ship." She pointed at the dark bulk that had the windows of orange light. "That's Debrov's inn, the Sea Lion. Your friends will be there."

The path followed the curve of the crater, hidden in the shadow of the massive four-storied hull of the Sea Lion – the only boat this close to the waterfall. As the crater stretched away, faint pools of light illuminated the smaller ships of the floating town and the start of the trail to the fort.

"Will there be more guards?" he asked, eyeing the large vessel as they came to its edge. It was almost as if it was wedged against the wall of the cliff.

Zaria scoffed. "There are no guards in Glass Bay, except the Tridents, and they keep to the Fort and the First."

"How is the peace kept?"

"You have guards in your Borderlands? Well, this is no city with laws and nobles, and the rich who can't protect their own gold."

"We don't have guards in the citadels," he said, frowning. "But we aren't crim –" He stopped abruptly.

"Criminals?" she said without rancour. "People here can either protect themselves and what's theirs, or they can't. That's the law. Those who can't don't last long and the rest balance themselves out."

She leaned out from the path towards the side of the Sea Lion. Kaiel tensed, but then she straightened, gripping the rung of a rope ladder.

Zaria smirked at him. "You thought I was going to fall, didn't you?" He pressed his lips together, willing his heart to slow its thumping as she gave a soft laugh. "Drylander. I've done this before. This ladder will take us up to the deck of the Lion," she said. "I'll go first, once I'm up a bit I'll stop so you can grab the ladder. Understand?"

"Yes," he said, although he wasn't at all sure.

"Good. Don't fall."

Zaria raised a foot onto a rope rung and gave a small almost jump. The rope ladder swung back out into the shadow of the Sea Lion, and she deftly climbed about ten rungs before stopping and looking back at him.

"Your turn," she whispered in the dark.

Kaiel took a breath, shaking his head to shift the last remnants of vertigo from the cage and reached out for the ladder. It took him two goes to find the side of it. His jump was a little too forceful, and Zaria hissed as he sent the ladder swinging. He flailed, hitting the side of the Sea Lion loudly, struggling to gain his footing. No other sounds arose though, and Zaria motioned him to follow as she flowed up the rope ladder with the same ease as the children he'd seen swinging from the rigging that morning. He was more careful, hands holding tightly to the rough rope until he finally reached the top.

The large deck stretched either side of them. Kaiel eyed the forecastle behind them, piled with timber and a rough framework.

Zaria snorted. "That's going to be a stable."

"You have horses here?" Kaiel asked, surprised.

"No. Where in the Void would we go? Debrov believes we could use donkeys, or some such, to move things, wood and the like from up the coast." Her derision was apparent. "The First is letting him build it, but no-one knows where we're going to get donkeys from."

Kaiel thought of the horses they'd had to leave with Norly when a howl rose in the air.

He lifted his head, his skin pebbling. "What was that?" His hand went to where his axe should have been, but came away empty.

"I don't know." Zaria had her dagger in her hand and moved back, closer to Kaiel.

"Do things come out of the swamp?" he asked.

"The skreet do all the time. But they usually come over the falls, dead. Although now you've killed Targ they may start to come closer." She peered into the darkness. "But skreets don't sound like that."

The howl came again, and a voice cried out in answer.

Kaiel moved to the railing. He picked out the shadow of someone running across the planking between the ships. Whoever it was, they were moving fast, heading towards the Sea Lion, when they ran into a pool of moonlight.

"Darien?" Kaiel said.

His brother raised his head as he scrambled up the step ladder.

"Kaiel!" Darien stumbled towards him. "Run!"

From the dark ships behind Darien came the shadow of another figure. Its gait was somehow wrong. It moved in a crouch, torso leaning forward as though balancing a weight behind it.

Its eyes glowed purple.

Kaiel grabbed Darien by the arm and pulled him back.

The thing chasing him straightened, shadows rippling around it, and it *stretched*. Its torso and legs thickened, horns curled from its head and a frilled collar, like a thorn-spike lizard, flared around its neck as a tail whipped out behind it.

The creature opened its jaws and roared.

Relief washed through Darien. His brother was Kas'tirien trained. He'd be able to handle whatever was chasing him. He gave a start as a woman behind his brother screamed, noticing her for the first time.

The thing behind him roared again, and the woman dropped down the hatch Darien had been running towards, slamming the trapdoor behind her. He grabbed the handle, but the deadbolt had been thrown.

He banged his fist on the wood, but there was no response from within.

"Dar." His brother's voice was tight. "What in the Void is that?"

"I don't know!" he cried, still tugging at the door. "Gods. She's locked us out!"

"What? Let me try."

Darien stepped back, careful to keep his brother between him and the thing with the purple eyes, his hands shaking.

"Zaria!" Kaiel yelled. "Let us in!" But the hatch remained shut. "Is there another way in? A door?"

"It was locked when I came out," Darien said. He looked over Kaiel's shoulder. "It's coming!"

The wind gusted through the alley of the ships, bringing a cold mist of water with it, splattering against hulls and across the deck. The creature shook its horned head, the crest-like frills around its neck flaring as it roared another challenge and stepped forward. The clouds moved across the sky, and the light of the moon glistened off black scales and razor-sharp talons.

"That's not a Korda'var, is it?" Darien's voice was tight.

"No. That's a daemon." Kaiel swore. "I don't have my axe or a sword!"

The daemon crouched; the muscles of its powerful thighs bunching before it sprang, leaping halfway across the deck in one bound. Darien stumbled back, running to the shadowy construction at the end of the deck, Kaiel close behind him. The structure was dark, but the slats of the unfinished roof allowed the moonlight to bathe it in shadows of black and grey. The half-light and the cloudy sky made the darkness move, flickers of ghostlight dancing in the corners of his eyes.

"Stay in there," Kaiel hissed. "I'll hold it off!"

"How?" Darien couldn't keep the scorn from his voice.

"Just stay back!"

Darien ducked behind the first partition, though it offered no real protection. If, *when*, the thing finished with Kaiel, it would find him quickly enough. Guilt flashed through him at the thought but he didn't know what he could do!

He watched Kaiel grab a broom lying against a half-built wall. His half-brother put the bristled head under one arm and pulled the handle free. Kaiel let the straws fall away and faced the daemon stalking towards them. Darien didn't doubt his brother's ability to fight another man, but this was a daemon.

Darien peered around the half-finished construction and jumped as his hip pressed against the wood. Something had burnt him! Like a hot coal. He patted his hand down his side and hissed as he brushed the pouch the Master of the Swamp had given him. He couldn't feel the shard within, but the bag radiated heat.

The daemon roared again, and Darien gave a start, heart racing, the pouch forgotten.

Where had it come from? I can't leave Kaiel to face it alone. I *can't*.

He took a breath and stepped out of the stall.

His brother stood in the moonlight in a fighter's stance; broom held diagonally across his body, gripped in both hands. The daemon crouched before him, its tail swaying back and forth, violet eyes fixed unblinkingly on Kaiel. Large, diamond-like protrusions sprouted from its shoulders and across its arms. White markings travelled in right angles across its torso, stark against its black scales, while a dark smoke leaked from it like steam.

Clouds passed over the moon, and as the light dimmed, the daemon struck, lashing out faster than Darien's eyes could follow.

Kaiel ducked and the creature's diamond-bright talons passed over his head. It hissed and swung its other arm, but Kaiel slapped it aside with the broom.

Kaiel was *fast*.

The daemon's cry of rage pierced the night, and, in a blur, it slashed at Kaiel with both arms, talons spread wide. It tried to knock aside the long handle of the broom with one, following through with the other but Kaiel blocked both blows even as the broom snapped in two.

Clouds continued to move, altering the fall of the moon's light. Kaiel shifted his feet before lunging at the daemon, battering it with blows from both halves of the broken broom shaft. The daemon fell back under the fury of Kaiel's attack, and his brother swept the pieces of wood forward, following each strike with a second, one after the other. Kaiel moved fluidly, and Darien couldn't help but be impressed, urging him on silently, fear prickling across his skin.

Where Darien had spent his time in the study of books, Kaiel had been on the practice field, training to join the Daemon Hunters. He watched his brother flow from form to form, the broken shafts of the broom always meeting the daemon's scale-covered forearms, deflecting its talons, driving it back.

Then Kaiel tripped, and the daemon roared, lashing out and slicing him across the chest, knocking him back.

Darien cried out, and the daemon swung its head in his direction. Without warning, it sprang towards him, releasing a blood-curdling hiss.

Panicked, Darien grabbed for the first thing he could find and flung it at the daemon's head.

The bucket was empty, but the daemon roared in anger as the wood smacked against it.

"Dar!" Kaiel was picking himself up. "*Get back*!"

"*You will die, humans,*" the daemon hissed at them, tail flicking behind it. "*Child of the Moon, Sunborn, your blood marks you both for death.*" Its eyes flashed bright, and its teeth gleamed in the moonlight. "*But the destruction you wrought on Lord Azkarshun's avatar has ensured your end will be painful.*"

It roared again, its crest flaring.

Voices rose from the nearby ships.

Kaiel stepped in front of Darien. "Who is Lord Askashon?"

The daemon hissed as Kaiel mispronounced the name and slashed at him with its talons.

"*You defied the Bonelord, servant*!" The slithering hiss of its voice deepened in rage.

"I'm guessing it means the daemon that possessed bone drake," Darien said, breathing heavily.

The daemon growled and lashed its tail at Kaiel, sweeping him off his feet.

Darien cried out again as Kaiel hit the ground, but his brother rolled back to his feet, managing to get the makeshift batons up as the daemon attacked him again.

Kaiel was tiring, slowing as he kept the daemon at bay. His makeshift weapons no more use against it than wooden swords were against the practice dummies of the Rangers.

"Boy!" a voice called from across the deck. Darien spun around. The woman who'd been with Kaiel peeked out of the hatch. "Here!" she cried and tossed something at him.

Moonlight flashed along the steel length of the dagger as it arced through the air to land at his feet. Darien blinked, and she dropped back down the hatch, pulling the trapdoor behind her. No doubt locking it again as well.

He picked up the dagger as his brother exploded into motion. Kaiel's attack managed to splinter both batons against the daemon's scaled forearms.

Kaiel paused in surprise; the pieces of wood he was now holding looked like stakes. The daemon howled in triumph, but Kaiel flipped the weapons, adjusting his grip. His brother raised them both in the air and brought them down with all his might on the daemon's chest.

The daemon screamed in pain, and its backhanded blow sent Kaiel crashing into a stall with such force, the wooden planking cracked.

The daemon ripped the stakes from its chest, bellowing to the sky.

More voices rose in the distance, but the daemon was stalking towards his dazed brother.

Panic, and a sense of helplessness that infuriated him, gripped Darien. He longed to reach for *Asai*, to send it blasting towards the daemon in a ball of flame! But he didn't know *how*.

Get up, Kaiel. Get up! But his brother didn't move.

He looked desperately over the ship, but the deck was empty. The daemon towered over Kaiel and raised its arms.

Darien tightened his fingers around the hilt of the dagger, his heart beating like a drum, and lurched forward in a half-jump, half-stumble, to stab the daemon under its raised arm.

The sharp steel of the weapon met no resistance as it sank deep into the exposed underside of the creature's flank.

The daemon roared in pain and lashed out at him with a heavily muscled arm.

He raised his hands protectively. His right palm exploded in a burning pain as it was sliced open by the daemon's talons, and it then retreated into the shadows of the empty stables, away from Kaiel, clutching its side.

Darien pushed his pain aside and crouched beside his brother. "Kaiel! Look at me. Kaiel!"

Kaiel's eyes focused on him with agonizing slowness. "Dar?"

"Come on, get up. We have to run!"

Desperation warred with frustration as Kaiel groaned and tried to get to his feet. His right arm was black with blood. Darien couldn't make out the wound, but as Kaiel tried to put weight on his arm, he cried out in pain.

"What is it?" Darien said, searching for the daemon in the shadows.

"My shoulder." Kaiel groaned and sucked in a breath.

The daemon hissed in the darkness and Darien jumped, his pulse racing. People were gathering on the opposite ship, he could make them out in the torchlight, but they were milling about, hesitant to come across.

Kaiel groaned again and got to his knees. "Go," he said, panting. "I'll distract it. Find Captain Daynar."

The daemon rent the night with a wild cry, and Darien flinched as something silver struck the wooden post beside them. It was the dagger.

He didn't know how badly he'd wounded the creature, but obviously it wasn't enough to stop it.

Violet eyes glinted from the darkness, and the daemon stepped into a shaft of moonlight.

Where before it had moved with casual grace, it now moved with deadly intent. It had been playing with them. Now the game was over.

"Dar, go!" Kaiel got to one knee, but Darien couldn't move. He was mesmerized by the glowing, purple gaze of the daemon. Shadows whipped around it as though alive, and his skin prickled as power laced the air.

The daemon could use the Light of the Eye? That was impossible!

Rage crashed over him like a firestorm. He would not stand here and wait for this creature to take him out!

"Run, Darien!" Kaiel was angry, but Darien didn't care. They would *not* die here!

He reached down to help Kaiel and his sliced palm met the open wound on Kaiel's shoulder. Their blood mingled.

The pouch at his side flared, heat burning through the cloth of his trousers.

Vision fled as *Asai* filled his sight. Energy blazed in his mind's eye.

The light of *Asai* flickered across his soul like white-hot tongues of flame as floodgates opened.

He had no time even for terror as a titanic boom cracked like thunder across the ship-town and a column of fire, jagged like lightning and brighter than the sun, fell from the heavens right upon them.

CHAPTER TWENTY-ONE

Under the Cover of Night

DARIEN LANDED ON his back, and his breath left his lungs in a rush. Orange light danced across his vision, and a great racket filled his ears. A fire had engulfed the half-built structure on the deck of the Sea Lion. In the night sky gulls were screeching, their white-feathered bodies orange in the glow of the flames. And every dog in the town was barking.

He tried to sit up, but it was as though his bones had left his body and his blood was aflame. Was this a mindstorm? He rolled onto his side, unable to suppress a moan. Only Ciralys who wielded so much *Asai* that it pushed their very limits suffered a mindstorm. He had almost succumbed to one in the catacombs under Sonyth, but the *Asai* that had flooded him then was a trickle compared to... what *had* just happened?

"Dar?" Somewhere beside him, Kaiel coughed. There were voices over the crackling of the fire, and footsteps sounded on planking as people scrambled onto the deck of the Sea Lion.

"Kaiel!"

Darien glanced to the side; pain lancing his skull. He closed his eyes, wanting to curl into a ball. Instead, with effort, he raised his head. Sim was running towards them with Captain Daynar and an Amarian, presumably the one Sim noticed in the fortress.

"Here," Kaiel croaked.

Darien pushed himself upright. Nausea swept over him in a wave and passed just as quickly, replaced by cold shivers that chased the heat across his body.

"What happened?" Sim crouched beside them. "How did you get here? Don't tell me Darien got you out."

"He was already here when I returned," Darien said, teeth chattering.

The girl Kaiel had been with reappeared at Captain Daynar's side. "Summoners take it!" she spat. "This is a fucking mess. I told you to be *quiet*, Borderlander!"

"Who are you?" Jaric demanded.

"Zaria?" a woman said before the girl could answer. Beside the Amarian, a short woman stepped forward. Silver chains over white hair sparkled orange in the firelight, but it was the black panels embroidered with stars on her gown that told Darien what she was as much as the cora'stone at the base of her neck. Shaluay.

"What are you doing here?" the Seer asked.

"Lady Iana." The girl, Zaria, said. Panic flashed over her face, but she hid it quickly, shrugging. "I heard the commotion so I came to see what was happening."

"Really?" Iana said. "And did you bring Kaiel with you?"

"Who?"

"The Borderlander you were just chastising," Sim said at Kaiel's side.

"Zaria."

Another stranger. Darien pushed himself to concentrate as a man, this one dressed in black, climbed onto the Sea Lion. Tall and straight shouldered with a strange curved sword sheathed at his side, his dark hair pulled back to reveal a widow's peak that was a mirror image to the girl's.

"Papa!" The girl wilted under the man's stony gaze.

"Captain Desrin; Corwyn," the Shaluay said. "I did not know the *Crow* had returned."

"We docked in time to see a... lightning strike... hit the Sea Lion."

The man's dark eyes swept over them, and a shiver danced down Darien's spine.

"Have you seen Lonah?" Zaria asked.

"No," Corwyn said. "The signal for a pick-up had been left in place, but there was no sign of him. The signal was yours?"

The girl nodded reluctantly.

"What have you done?" he stepped forward.

Beside Darien, Kaiel struggled to his feet. "She saved me from the cages," he said, swaying. Sim steadied him. "She's going to get us all out of here. On a ship."

"Be quiet! Fool, Borderlander," Zaria hissed. Her eyes swept the crowd.

The corsair, Corwyn, looked from one to the other. "He was a prisoner?"

"It's just what we had talked about," Zaria protested.

"You were not meant to get involved!"

"I wanted to help!"

The corsair captain drilled them all with black eyes. "Your hands, strangers. I want to see them."

Panic bloomed in Darien, and he looked at the back of his right hand. He let out a breath in relief. He raised his hand with the others, displaying the clear skin.

"My stables!" cried a voice Darien *did* recognise. Debrov, the innkeeper, thumped up onto the deck, cudgel in hand. "What have you done to my ship?"

A whistle blew, and men and women appeared with buckets and started bringing water up from the bay to throw over the burning timber.

"Kaiel," Captain Daynar said. "How do you feel? Did you stay in the centre of the cage?"

"I've never been so sick in my life," Kaiel muttered. "My arm hurts, and my chest."

"Looks like it's stopped bleeding." Jaric inspected the torn shoulder. "And you, Darien? Are you unharmed?"

"I'm fine," he said, waving the man's concern away. He flexed his cut palm, it stung some but didn't seem as deep as he'd first imagined.

"What were you doing out here?" Sim said. "I thought you were in your room?"

"A daemon was chasing him," Kaiel said before he could answer. "Are you sure you aren't hurt, Dar? What about your hand?"

"A daemon?" Sim drew back, looking at Kaiel. "Are you sure you're feeling okay, Kaiel?"

"Tell them, Dar," Kaiel looked at him.

Blood still pounded in Darien's ears, and he just wanted to sleep. "It was a daemon," he said through gritted teeth.

The Amarian stepped towards them. "Are you certain?" he pressed in precise, yet accented, common.

"I know daemons," Kaiel said. "It couldn't have been anything else."

"Where did it go?" Sim asked, looking around.

"I..." Kaiel glanced at Darien and hesitated. "It has to be dead. There was a – I don't know. A bolt of lightning? It landed right on top of us. On it. Now it's gone."

The Amarian straightened, and something in his manner made Darien glance up to catch him exchange a look with the Shaluay. The Starbinder nodded at some unasked question, and the man moved off to the burning stables.

"Zaria," Kaiel said. "We need to get out of here. Now. The First is sure to come down to see what's happening." He swayed on his feet, and Sevaani pushed through the crowd to help Sim keep him steady.

"You need to lie down, Kaiel," she said to him, eyeing Zaria in such a way that the girl laughed.

Kaiel looked at Sevaani in surprise. She blushed, lowering her gaze.

Darien shook his head at the two of them and winced at the flash of pain behind his eyes. Beside Captain Daynar, Meg folded her arms across her chest.

"I'm not helping you up," she said, her tone oddly neutral. "Neither of you should be moving right now."

"Captain Desrin," the Lady Iana said. "I had planned to come find you when the *Crow* docked. I would like to arrange passage for myself and these companions."

The corsair's stare had Darien shivering once more, but the Seer did not quail.

"It seems your daughter had a similar idea," she said. "But whatever your plans were, they are likely to spoil if she and the prisoner she helped escape are still here when the First arrives." She looked up to the fortress behind them.

The corsair lifted his head also, his face hardening. Darien followed his gaze to see a line of torches making their way down the cliff.

"Balard," Corwyn called. A man stepped up beside him. Grizzled in face and thick of limb, the man was a head shorter than the captain but held the same menace Darien had seen in the hunting dogs of Hanore's Rangers.

"Captain," Balard said.

"I am taking the Starbinder and her friends back to the *Crow*. Take someone and get their things out of their rooms, discreetly."

Balard spat to the side and nodded. With a gesture, another slighter man joined him. They'd begun to make their way across the deck when the Amarian returned. Balard eyed the warrior but didn't protest as he followed.

"Debrov, stop your caterwauling." Corwyn tossed the man a pouch.

"I wasn't here, my daughter wasn't here, and you don't know where this lot have gone."

"But all these people..."the innkeeper protested but quickly pocketed the pouch just the same.

"You can deal with it," Corwyn said. "You know too many secrets for the First to press you too hard."

"And if I break?" the fat man said with a scowl.

"My mother won't live forever, and I will be the next First." The corsair's eyes glittered in the firelight. "I suggest you don't break."

After a pause, Debrov lifted his hands in defeat. "Very well."

"I'll help Balard, Papa," Zaria said.

"No, you won't."

"But Papa!"

"If you disappeared now, the First will know you were involved."

"No!" she cried. "Don't leave me again. You promised!"

"Zaria." The man sighed and pulled her into a hug. "I wouldn't have to if you hadn't gone freeing the First's prisoner. I will be back, and when next the *Crow* sails you will find a berth with her crew."

"But Gran –"

"Leave your grandmother to me." He kissed the top of her head and pushed her away. "Now get back to the Fort before she gets down here."

She nodded, lowering her eyes.

"Zaria!" Kaiel called.

"What, Borderlander?"

"Thank you."

"Didn't do it for you," she snapped back but softened it with a smile. Then she was gone over the side of the Sea Lion.

Gritting his teeth, Darien managed to get to his feet while cradling the hand that had been sliced open by the daemon's talons.

The corsair captain faced the Shaluay. "We need to go now if you want to leave without the First stopping us."

"The last we knew Kaiel was locked away in the fortress and we were getting him out tomorrow," Daynar growled. "What's he doing here?"

"This is none of my doing, Captain," she said calmly. "But we need to take our chance before we lose it and are in worse straits."

"Kaiel, Darien." Jaric whirled on them, face hard. "Can you walk?"

They both nodded.

"Very well," Jaric said, mouth tight.

Captain Desrin strode off the Sea Lion. Men and women scrambled to get out of his way, some spitting and throwing curses as the group following him pushed their way through the crowd. Five more sailors from the *Crow*, at least Darien presumed that's who they were given the corsairs lack of concern at their appearance, surrounded them as the crowd thinned. Eyes followed as they made their way across ship decks and planks towards the docks. The muted voices of the people faded as they left the glow of the burning framework on the Sea Lion, but the barking of dogs and the raucous calling of disturbed birds still filled the night.

"You can't possibly believe the First won't be told we were escorted to your ship," Captain Daynar hissed. "Look at all those people! They all saw us. Saw you!"

The captain of the *Crow* looked over his shoulder, dark eyes glinting as they caught the light of a nearby torch. "She'll hear something, but people who call Glass Bay home will be wary of saying too much against a captain."

"Unless the speaker is another captain."

The men around them tensed, hands falling to the hilts of swords and sabres as another band stepped out of the darkness.

Darien gingerly touched his forehead, the ache of the mindstorm still throbbing in his skull. He stepped closer to the others, Meg and Sevaani doing the same. Kaiel and Captain Daynar took position on the outside of the small group, while Sim and the Shaluay stayed behind them.

"Remay," Corwyn drawled in a bored tone. "Poke that nose of yours into business that isn't yours one too many times, and you might find it gets bitten off."

A woman laughed and stepped into the light. Short hair shone red in the torchlight, and gold hoops hung at her ears. Her nose had been broken more than once, and now resembled a beak.

"Who are your friends, Desrin?" she said as if they were the only two present.

"New recruits."

"A Shaluay is joining the *Crow*?" Her eyes widened, but her lips curled in a dry smile. Corwyn didn't say anything, and the woman's smile broadened. "I noticed you aren't helping with the fire over on the Sea Lion."

"There are plenty of people helping Debrov," he said. "He doesn't need me."

She laughed. "Could it be that your friends might be the ones who started the fire?"

"Oh, do you think?"

"Why don't we just ask the First?" She smiled lazily. "Let's see what Mummy thinks of her little boy running off with these ones."

"I'm busy, Remay," Corwyn said. "Play your games with someone else."

He made to step past the group, but a large man with a beard whose jaw was working at chewing something, stepped in his path.

"You'll be wanting to move, Dek."

Darien tensed at the corsair's tone. The big man, Dek, spat and grinned. The teeth he had left did not reflect white in the torchlight. Corwyn's sailors unsheathed their blades, and their opponents followed suit.

Remay laughed, her voice rough and husky. "This will be fun."

"You don't want to do this, Remay," Corwyn told her without looking away from the man in his path.

"Oh, but I do." She smirked. "It's been a long time coming, but I knew if I watched you long enough, you'd slip on your decking eventually. I've already sent for the First." Her hand dropped to a short sword at her waist. "I just have to keep you here."

"Oi, cap'n!" The squat man, Balard, came towards them, dragging a taller, fleshy man with him. "I caught this pufferfish tryin' to sneak past ye all. Thought ye might be wantin' a word wit' him."

Balard's thick arm was wrapped around the man's neck, bending the taller man down to his own height. The man gripped the corsair's arm tightly, his face darkening to match the colour of his red hair, stumbling as he was pulled along.

"Norlan!" Remay called out. "Let him go!"

"Nice catch, Balard," Corwyn said.

Without warning, Corwyn grabbed the bearded man by the shirt, bent forward and *yanked* Dek's face down – hard – onto the crown of his head. He then pushed Dek away, and the big man fell back, senseless. His crewmates cried out, but Balard's voice rang over the din.

"Ya'll be wantin' to stay where ye are." Balard pulled Norlan forward. "Or this one'll pay the price of our passage."

"Stop!" Remay gestured to her crew, and they held their place. "Get your filthy Cythian hands off my brother."

The squat man laughed. "Ye need to be talkin' to the cap'n if ye want that. Right sneaky sendin' your brother out behind a man to go tell tales." Balard tightened his arm around Norlan's neck, causing him to gurgle. "But can't expect much else from ye lot. Bunch of useless cuttlefish."

The corsair bared her teeth. "Cuttlefish poison is not so easily survived."

"Know a lot 'bout poisons, don't ye," Balard said. "Small wonder ye cap'n the Dead Rose."

"Enough, Balard." Corwyn turned to Remay. "Get your worthless deck crawlers out of my way."

"Let my brother go," she hissed at him.

Corwyn's smile was all teeth. "Your brother is your biggest weakness."

"And your daughter is yours!"

His smile darkened, and Darien shivered. "That's why she is with my mother. Now, fuck off back to your stinking ship and keep your mouth shut."

"Or?" she thrust her chin out at him.

"Or next time I will let Balard kill him."

"Is that wise?" Jaric stepped forward.

"Stay out of this, stranger," Remay hissed.

Jaric ignored her. "Once you release him, she'll be free to go to the First."

"And she will," Corwyn nodded. "Like I said, there'll be some talk, regardless."

"But your daughter?"

"Needs to plan more carefully," Corwyn said. "My mother won't hurt her granddaughter, though she will be punished just the same."

"I will make your life a living hell, Desrin," Remay spat. "I will watch you bleed."

Corwyn ignored her. "Norlan's coming back with us to the *Crow*. Have a boat ready to catch him; he'll be thrown overboard as we leave. Now get out of my way!"

For a moment Darien thought she might refuse, but then with a wordless snarl she stepped back out of the torchlight, and her crew followed.

"Balard," he said. "With me. The rest of you keep moving."

The *Crow* was moored at the farthest end of the boat-town. Draped with running lights in seaglass orbs, it blocked the view of the moonlit bay as its three-decked bulk rose before them. A long plank of wood led up from the pier to the deck, the crew up top talked and joked in the dark.

"Welcome back, Captain," a voice called from the shadows of the deck. It was soft and light, Darien couldn't tell if it belonged to a woman or a young boy.

"Get her ready, Erin," Corwyn said. "Balard will be up shortly to sort the rest out."

"We ain't staying then," Erin's voice was expressionless, but Corwyn paused.

"You'll get to see your ma next time, lad. We're running quiet too. Get on with you."

"Aye, sir," came the reply. A series of three short, sharp whistles sounded, and the rest of the shadowy crew stopped talking and running feet pattering over the deck as lights went out over the side of the ship.

"Jab'l," Captain Desrin called to another. The woman stepped over, short dark hair framing a roiling tattoo of *something* on her right cheek. "Take this land walker –" Corwyn gestured at Norlan who had been dragged up the plank by Balard, "and throw him back to his friends when we set sail." Remay and her crew waited at the end of the plank, hands still on the hilts of their swords. "I don't particularly care if he lands in the water."

A squeal came from under Balard's arm, and the woman smiled, the tattoo on her cheek seeming to slither as she did. "Yes, Captain."

Corwyn Desrin led them across the deck, past one of three enormous masts and through a door that led into the upper galley. The room inside was gloomy, and bolted down tables and benches lined the walls. They followed him through to a short hall that ended at a door carved with sea creatures Darien had only ever seen in books. Fish with dorsal fins and rows of razor-sharp teeth looked ready to leap from the wood. In the door's centre was carved a great octopus with staring eyes and grasping tentacles, its multiple limbs wrapped around the vicious fish and reaching up to crush a ship that rode on the sea above it. Corwyn pushed the door open and gestured for them to enter.

Iana led them into the dim interior, the Amarian following directly behind her.

"We could use some light in here, Balard," Corwyn said as the others moved into the stateroom.

Darien winced as he bent his neck to pass through the door, grateful when he was able to straighten again on the other side. His back was aching, and his hand – though the bleeding had stopped – was stiff and stung whenever he moved it.

Within the cabin, intricately designed lanterns had their vent tops twisted open. Exposed to fresh air, the luminescent algae within brightened, chasing the shadows into corners, the light as powerful as any flame.

The room they revealed was large. A wall of diamond-paned windows looked out across the bay, but velvet curtains, bound top and bottom to polished brass rails, were quickly pulled shut. A large table of oiled rosewood, bolted to the floor, sat before them covered in charts that were rolled open and held in place by wood and brass pegs. More chairs were positioned around the room on a plush rug of dark red wool. Darien could make out small brass clasps poking through the carpet that presumably held them in place. Black and crimson cushions covered benches around the sides of the room, filigreed cabinet doors underneath. Another table, with three small chairs, was pushed against the left wall, and a bed was built into the wall behind them.

The Shaluay glanced around and took a seat at the smaller table, her dress sweeping the floor. She gestured at the other chairs beside her.

"Kaiel, Darien, sit. Ladies, you can take the bed. Do you have any more chairs?"

The corsair eyed her for a moment before nodding at Balard, who had followed them in with their bags once he'd handed Norlan over to Jab'l.

The first mate left the room, returning with folding chairs that he handed to Daynar and the Blay Shon.

"They're ready up top, Capt'n. Ye want I should lead the *Crow* out?" Balard said.

Corwyn grunted. "No, Balard, I will take the helm. Tell Tren to castoff." He looked them over, his face blank. "Best you take the time to get your stories straight, I want answers before I take you anywhere." He then followed Balard out of the room, closing the door behind him with a click.

Jaric tried the handle. "It's locked."

"It doesn't matter," the Shaluay said. "Lihon, if you would?"

The Blay Shon immediately took up guard at the door, and the lady fixed her gaze on Kaiel. "Now, tell me what happened."

Kaiel opened his mouth, but before he could utter a word, Darien spoke.

"Who are you?" he asked, looking at the Shaluay.

"Darien! Don't be so rude," Sevaani said.

Darien put a hand to his forehead. His head was throbbing. "I'm sorry. We haven't even been introduced, yet she appears to know both mine and Kaiel's names and is asking about things that are none of her business."

"She's a lady," Sevaani said.

"She's a Shaluay," Meg said.

"I can see that," he said past a clenched jaw. "Only a fool would dare wear a gown with those panels, let alone a fake cora'stone around her neck. But why should that matter? The citadels have never bowed to the Houses or any Orders of the Realms."

"Don't be so ignorant," Captain Daynar said behind him. "You were quick enough to bow to Ciralys Telaq when he came to Hanore. Lady Iana is helping us, and while it's wise to be wary of help from strangers, this particular help is getting you on a ship to Serjat. A little courtesy isn't too much to ask, given your adventure brought a daemon to us."

"Us? I don't recall you being there at all, Jaric Daynar," he said through gritted teeth.

"Dar," Kaiel said, putting his hand on his shoulder. "I met her in the fortress. She helped me. Maybe she can help us now, too?"

"At what cost?" Darien asked. None of them understood.

"What do you mean?"

"I mean…" He took a breath. "The Shaluay do nothing without an ulterior motive."

"What a dreadfully pessimistic view you have," Iana said.

"My views are generally built from experience," Darien said.

"And you have dealt with many of my sisters in your time, have you?" she raised an elegant eyebrow.

Sim snickered behind him, and Darien pressed his lips together. "The Shaluay always seek a price for their aid."

"When such aid is sought, yes," Iana agreed. "But we are negotiating no contract here, and my aid – such as it is – is offered freely and without constraint."

"Dar," Kaiel said again. "It's all right."

"And if it isn't," Sim said, "you can tell us all that you told us so."

Darien didn't have the energy to argue. He gestured to Kaiel, who began to relate all that had occurred since he'd been dragged away by the First's guards in the fortress.

"I am surprised at how strongly you were affected by the corusite," Iana said, tapping a finger on her lips as Kaiel finished his tale. "And the daemon was chasing Darien?"

Kaiel grimaced and nodded, glancing at Darien.

"You told us you were resting," Captain Daynar said, his voice hard.

"Meditating," Sim said from the bed beside the Meg and Sevaani. "He said he was meditating."

"And if I'd told you anything else, you would've tried to stop me," he said to Jaric, ignoring Sim.

"Glass Bay may appear safe when surrounded by your friends and people with swords." Iana turned her violet eyes on him, "but it is not. You are lucky the storm kept the decks clear. If there was a daemon present, then there must be a nomen in Glass Bay."

"A nomen!" Sevaani gasped. "I thought the daemons were locked away in the Void."

"Nomen are human, not daemon, although some may wish they were – fools making a fool's bargain. The price is always higher than they believed, and the power gained is never as much as they heard offered. This is too remote a location for a daemon to have just been waiting here for you." Iana looked at Darien once more and cocked her head. "Where did you go?"

"I'd gone to see the old woman," Darien said, offering no more.

"The old woman?" Jaric asked. "Nataya?"

"No," he shook his head.

"The old woman who accosted him when we first arrived," Meg said from her perch beside Sevaani on the bed. Darien looked at her and stopped in surprise. She'd discarded the coat she'd been wearing. Gone was the plain, grey woollen dress she had worn since they fled Sonyth. In its place, she wore a butter yellow dress of fine wool, and a soft blue velvet over-robe styled like a long coat.

She met his gaze with the same lack of expression with which she had spoken to him earlier, and he looked away.

"Yes, that's right," he said.

"You went out at night without telling anyone where you were going?" Jaric folded his arms across his chest. "I thought better of your sense of responsibility, Darien."

"Oh, really? You have a sense of responsibility enough for all of us," he snapped back in turn, stung by the man's condemnation and then annoyed at himself.

"Until you start acting like the adult you claim you are, it looks like I need it," Jaric said, shaking his head.

"Please. What is done is done." Iana pulled his attention back to her. "Why did you go to see her, and what did she say to you?"

"It wasn't so much what she said as what I felt," Darien said. He rubbed his forehead, the headache pressing behind his eyes. "Actually, it was probably a combination of both."

"And?" prompted Sim.

"And it's none of your affair!" He bit off as his head throbbed. "Least of all that of a Shaluay Starbinder!"

"I am afraid I must disagree," Iana corrected him coolly. "If you are to travel with us, we must know why the daemon was after you. And where it came from."

"Kaiel told you why," he said, taking a breath and trying to respond calmly. "It was sent by the daemon that possessed the bone drake we encountered under Sonyth, its 'Bonelord', to kill us. The story the First Captain was so quick to dismiss was not a fabrication."

"Which begs the question of just what is a Daemonlord doing in this realm?" Sim asked.

"A Daemonlord?" Kaiel's eyes widened.

"What else could possess a dragon?"

"The Lloth'var had a Daemonartis Trap, I saw it in the catacombs," Darien said. "The daemon that possessed the bone drake was released from it."

"Yes," Iana agreed. "The Kas'tirien would know if a tear large enough to allow a Daemonlord through had opened. It sounds like it was a csitargon that was released. They are minor daemons, though they come in many varieties and can rise high in the Void, if they survive. One caught in a Daemonartis Trap would have to have been snared during the War of the Summoners. And to have drawn the attention of the Sahrin, it would have to have been powerful."

"Why would it want to kill Darien and me?" Kaiel's confusion was evident. His head probably pained him as much as Darien's did, though his brother held his temper better.

"Most of the records of what occurred in the War of the Summoners were lost," Iana said. "The daemon that possessed the bone drake said it served a mistress?" Kaiel nodded. "What did the old woman, Bertha I presume, say, Darien?" the Shaluay's voice was gentle, but her lavender eyes caught his own.

Darien met her gaze and felt a pull behind it, a compulsion. The desire to tell her everything came over him. "She said I was being hunted." He relaxed into the sensation; he did not fight it. This was like a mind exercise Ciralys Telaq had been training him in. When he stopped struggling against the compulsion to speak, he was able to relate only the things he wanted her to know. "She was crazier than she appeared on the street."

"A lot of people are madder than they look," Meg offered, and Iana moved her eyes, releasing Darien.

Relief washed over him as the compulsion melted away, but he was careful to keep his expression clear.

"Why did you go see her?" Iana asked. "If you suspected she was crazy."

"Because I felt an echo of *Asai* around her. I wanted to find out for sure." He hedged.

"And she wanted nothing in return?" Iana pressed him.

The cut on his palm flared in pain as his fingers dug into his clenched fist. He opened his hand, blood pooling slowly in the re-opened wound. "Maybe, but it quickly became apparent that she'd have nothing rational to impart. I left before we got that far."

Iana reached to take his hand, inspecting the wound in the lamplight. "Take off your shirt."

It was Darien's turn to raise an eyebrow.

"I am going to use the cloth as a bandage," she said. "You, Kaiel and Simeon have new clothes as well as the girls, your shirt won't be missed."

"New clothes?" Kaiel said. "I don't understand."

"Kaiel, your mother taught you better manners than that." Sevaani glared at him.

"What?"

"When you're given a gift, you say 'thank you'," she said in disgust.

"Thank you for the gift, Lady Iana," Kaiel said through gritted teeth. Sevaani sighed and whispered in Meg's ear.

"You are welcome, Kaiel," Iana said with a half-smile. "None of you are dressed for winter; I am surprised you have not caught your deaths. Fevers plague these coasts, and sailors like to share them more than most. And I couldn't present you to the High Conclave of the Ciralys still wearing the clothes you left the citadels in."

"You know the Ciralys High Conclave?" Darien looked up.

"I do," Iana said. "Though it has been some time since I last visited the Spire. Your little group intrigues me, and I would like to see the end of your journey. And as we are going in the same direction, I am more than happy to assist you."

"You believe there's more to this, don't you?" Jaric said.

Iana shrugged. "Perhaps, but we don't have all the pieces yet, do we? I could be of assistance to you."

The ship rocked.

"They've castoff," Jaric said.

Outside came a muffled cry, followed by a splash, then shouting that faded as the movement of the ship increased.

"That would be Norlan," Sim said. "Well," Sim grabbed his pack from the pile on the floor. "I can understand Prince Alesandr wanting you two, but this possessed bone drake thing is just strange. Could it have known about House Taaren'th also? I mean, it did have the spear after all."

"Can we please stop talking about that?" Kaiel slumped in his chair, rubbing his forehead. "Dar and I are just... we're just *us*! House Taaren'th died a long time ago."

"You'd abandon those men and women of the Bronze Guard who've waited centuries for your return?" Jaric asked.

"No, but I'd like to know why they've waited," Darien said.

The captain frowned.

"Aldania has done well enough under House Niskeri," Darien continued. "Why must a dead House be resurrected?"

"It has less to do with Houses and thrones than it does the return of the Sahrin; or more specifically the Empyros," Iana said.

Darien froze at her words. He glanced at Kaiel and saw his brother rubbing the back of his hand, and it took all Darien's strength not to do the same.

"And the Ciralys, or the Watch of whatever town the poor bastard is born in, will kill him before he can summon anything," Sim scoffed.

"If that were so, then why is there a prophecy about the return of an Empyros?" Darien said. "Can it just be turned aside by ending the line of Varos Korin'ad?"

"Who can say?" Iana's lips moved in the briefest of smiles.

"How soon will whoever sent it, know the daemon failed?" Jaric asked.

"It already knows its assassin failed," Iana said.

"How did you two get away from it?" Meg asked. "It was a *daemon*; how did you kill it?"

"I don't know," Kaiel said. "That lightning strike must have hit a barrel of oil."

"A barrel of oil," Iana repeated.

"What else could it have been?" Kaiel offered an awkward laugh. "I don't have the spear anymore."

Darien stared at his brother. He'd never heard Kaiel lie before; but then, maybe he didn't know what happened. He almost snorted. The Eye take him; he *didn't* know what happened!

"Well, you are fortunate you did not get splashed with the oil yourselves," Iana said. Darien was sure she didn't quite believe the story Kaiel had offered. "Burning oil is dangerous."

"They were also lucky lightning chose to strike when and where it did, or they'd be dead," Lihon said from the door.

"Well," Iana said. "Dawn is still some way off, and sea travel, while easy on the feet, can be tiring in other ways. And Corwyn will want his answers yet before we can all get some rest.

"If you will allow it," she said to Jaric, "I will deal with the captain. There is much we should keep to ourselves."

Jaric pressed his lips together, considering. "I don't mean to be ungrateful, Lady Iana," he said at last. "But I'd like to be present for any negotiations that involve us."

"That is not unreasonable," she said. "Let us discuss what we will say to Captain Desrin."

Kaiel moved out of his seat for Captain Daynar. Darien watched his brother motion at him with a nod, and got up to follow.

"What is it?" Darien asked. Kaiel winced and looked back at Lady Iana, but she was paying them no mind. "What?" Darien repeated more quietly, frowning. Kaiel looked pale and dark circles were gathering under his eyes. Had those been there before the daemon had attacked them? He couldn't recall.

"It's just," Kaiel began, giving a furtive look around. "That thing, the daemon. It was after both of us, wasn't it?"

"I think so," Darien said. "It found me first but the things it said…"

"What I mean is –" Kaiel looked around again and took a breath. "If it found us here, in the middle of nowhere, then it could find us anywhere."

"I suppose so?" This was not like his brother at all.

Kaiel let out a breath and pushed a hand through his hair. "My point is that maybe I was wrong. Maybe you *should* go to the Ciralys."

Darien blinked. He hadn't expected this from Kaiel. "I'm glad you think so."

"And I think I should come too."

"What?"

"I have to, Dar," Kaiel said. "If daemons are after us, for whatever reason, then we have to stick together."

Darien closed his mouth. Kaiel did have a point, but before he could agree, Lady Iana called to them.

"Kaiel, Darien. Let me look at those wounds," she said as Captain Daynar rose from the chair Kaiel had vacated for him. "I suggest the rest of you get what sleep you can. It is a long way to Serjat."

CHAPTER TWENTY-TWO

Written in the Stars

SEVAANI SHIVERED AS she took in the carvings on the door to the captain's cabin. There was something about the monster reaching its tentacles to capture the unsuspecting ship above that put her on edge. It also made her look at the open expanse of Nemisdrillion Sea with no little amount of trepidation.

She brushed the thought aside and ducked her head to enter. The curtains over the diamond-paned windows had been pushed back, though you couldn't see much past the salt-smeared glass, and daylight flooded the room, just falling short of the bed in which Kaiel and Darien lay.

Within hours of leaving Glass Bay both men had been complaining of a headache, then succumbed to a fever before they both collapsed. Lady Iana directed Lihon and Captain Daynar to move them onto the bed so she could inspect them, but the Starbinder had been unable to rouse them. A brief confrontation with Captain Desrin had ensued over the concern that Kaiel and Darien had brought an illness onboard. Still, Lady Iana had managed to reassure him and the crew, and they'd moved into another cabin a floor down, leaving Kaiel and Darien to recover.

At Captain Daynar's insistence, someone had always remained with them, and it was Sevaani's turn to relieve Meg and take over the watch.

"Any change?" Sevaani asked, looking at Meg who was dozing in a chair that was pegged to the floor. The reason for those pegs had become apparent when the *Crow* had left the tranquil, protected harbour of Glass Bay and made passage into the waterways of the islands Captain Daynar had called the Broken Teeth. Not to mention when she'd passed those islands and entered the sea proper. The storm that had hit Glass Bay was still circling, and out on the open water it had whipped the waves high. While not a pleasant experience, Sevaani had found her sea-legs, as they were called, quickly. Unlike poor Meg.

After a night of her leaning over the railing, Sevaani thought they might have to add Meg to same bed as Kaiel and Darien, but Lady Iana had given her a strong-smelling tea that seemed to cure Meg's vomiting if not her seasickness.

Meg opened bleary eyes and sat straighter in the chair. "No. It's been nearly two weeks, and they haven't moved at all." She glanced at Sevaani. "I wasn't asleep all morning."

Sevaani smiled gently. "I know. However, I wouldn't blame you if you had been. Why don't you go lay down in one of the bunks below? It's my turn to keep an eye on them."

"Who would have thought that leaving home would be so adventurous?" Meg said, rubbing her hands over her eyes.

"Not me," Sevaani said. She looked at Kaiel, lying peacefully on the bed. The way he was now she could almost forget some of the things he had done. She looked away.

"Really?"

"What?" Sevaani turned back to Meg.

"You didn't know we were going to have an adventure like this when we left Hanore? Because you seem to have been dreaming quite a bit lately."

"Not really," Sevaani returned. "I dreamt that you were planning to leave, that you *would* leave, and I dreamt that once I walked a white road, I would never go home. That's all."

"That's all?" Meg pulled a face. "That seems like quite a lot. What about the dream you had of Jaric?"

Sevaani waved her hand dismissively. "That was a long time ago. I didn't know then that my dreams meant something."

"But you remembered it."

"Yes," she pressed her lips together. "I did."

"Why didn't you ever come to Old Shany about your dreams? She could have helped you."

"I didn't want to. And I didn't really know what was happening. It was only when Kaiel failed the Trial, and I caught you planning to sneak out of the citadel that I knew there was more to these dreams than I'd imagined."

"So, what's going to happen now?"

"I..." Sevaani looked away from Meg. "I don't know."

"But you knew Lady Iana was going to be in Glass Bay."

"No," she protested. "It wasn't like that. I recognised her from my dreams, yes, but I didn't know we'd be in Glass Bay when I'd meet her. How could I? I hadn't even heard of that place before we arrived in the swamp."

"So, you don't know if the Ciralys will take me in?" Meg asked, her voice suddenly small.

Sevaani blinked. Was Meg... worried? *Meg*? She was the most confident young woman Sevaani knew. Even Captain Daynar listened to her when she spoke. She – daughter of the Steward of Hanore no less – didn't even warrant that concession from the Captain of the Hanore Rangers. Now Meg was asking her about the future.

This was why she didn't like to talk about her dreams. People would want to know more. Great Tarin, *she'd* want to know more too if the shoe had been on the other foot. But the truth was she had no idea. She couldn't even choose what she dreamt about. They were dreams. They just happened when she fell asleep.

"No, Meg, I'm sorry. I don't know. But you have Shany's hedge right and that… that thing she gave you."

"I don't even know what it is!" Meg said, frustration and worry clawing through her voice. "What if it's not enough? I can't go back to Hanore now. Prince Alesandr will surely be looking for me."

"Not nearly so much as he's looking for Kaiel and Darien," Sevaani offered. "And Shany would protect you. So would my father. The Borderlands don't hold with the Blood. You know that."

Meg snorted. "They would if Prince Alesandr brought the Royal Guard to our gates. No. I just have to keep going forward no matter what."

"What are you going to do?"

Meg shrugged. "Shany said to find the Spirit Seer. I will do that. When Darien is being presented to… whomever, I'll slip away and ask for directions." Meg stood, paled as the ship chose that moment to move beneath their feet. "Gods, sea travel is awful."

Sevaani's stomach was tied in knots, though she wasn't sure if it was because of the unknown before her on her own journey, or in sympathy of Meg's plight.

"You don't have to go to Isoliere, you know," she told Meg. "You could stay with us. You don't have to follow Darien. You know nothing will ever come of it."

Meg went bright red. "Yes, I know," she said with a quiet dignity Sevaani had never heard from her before. "And believe me or not – he certainly doesn't – but he is *not* the reason I'm going. I have a dream too. Not like your dreams, but I can see the light of *Asai*. I could stay in the Borderlands and learn the witching ways from Shany; I already know how to bend *Asai* in small ways, to aid healing, to make a fire or summon light. But it's not the same as the art of the Ciralys. Even

Shany admits that. No," Meg shook her head. "Darien isn't the reason I'm going, Sevaani. Besides, where would we go? Are you going back to Hanore? I thought you said you'd never see the Three Citadels again."

"That's a curious thing to say."

Sevaani and Meg both gave a little start as Lady Iana entered the room. The Shaluay Starbinder was dressed in a steel grey gown whose skirts were slashed with charcoal panels. Silver embroidery edged the waistline and neck of the dress, and her white hair was pulled over one shoulder and pinned in place by a diamond comb, the stones of which appeared to catch the light in time with cora'stone at her neck.

"Lady Iana," Sevaani dropped into a curtsey, feeling as though she was still wearing the soiled Rangers garb that she'd first met the Lady in, not the fine wool Iana had so generously gifted her before they left Glass Bay. "We didn't see you there."

Iana waved them both up. "Please, girls, I have asked you to call me Iana."

It was Sevaani's turn to feel her cheeks colour, and she murmured, "Yes La–Iana."

"I'll take my leave," Meg said. "I need some air."

"Is the tea helping, child?" Iana asked.

"Yes, thank you. I still feel… ill, but I haven't been sick again."

"Well, chances are there is nothing left for you to empty from your stomach. Get some fresh air, and be sure to drink. I have left a flagon of water in our room." Iana smiled.

"Thank you. I will." Meg glanced at Sevaani and back at Lady Iana, then left the room in a rush, leaving Sevaani alone with the Shaluay Starbinder.

Sevaani turned to watch Lady Iana go over to the bed and lean over Kaiel. She placed a hand to his forehead, then lifted the blankets and checked the back of his right hand. Sevaani almost gasped. What if this illness was some, some manifestation of the power of a Summoner?

But no, they were both ill, and she had dreamt a true dream of Darien, two dreams of Darien, and he had not had the Mark of the Eye on his hand.

Lady Iana nodded and pulled the blankets back over Kaiel before she moved to the other side of the bed and repeated the process with Dairen and then straightened.

"Are they well, Iana?" It felt so strange calling this woman by her first name. She was a Starbinder. A woman of power, if not one of the Blood itself.

"Yes, I believe so," Iana said.

"Do you know what's wrong with them? What illness this is?"

Iana pursed her lips. "I do, but it is strange. It is not an illness at all in fact, but a side-effect. A reaction."

"A reaction? To what?"

Iana gestured at the boys. "I believe they are both suffering from what the Ciralys term, a mindstorm."

"But surely, if that were the case, then only Darien would be unconscious?" Sevaani frowned. "Kaiel is not a wielder."

"No, as you say, he is not. But there is a… resonance around those who can wield the Light of the Eye of Eternity. It is noticeable around Darien. And it is noticeable around Kaiel, but that could be from how close he was standing beside his brother when the daemon was killed."

"So, Darien invoked a cant? To kill the daemon?"

"I think whatever happened was less structured than that," Iana said, the strange points of light on the toque that held her cora'stone moving in different directions. "More akin to the type of wielding done by the Keepers, more instinctual. The quant field was roiling when we came on deck in the aftermath of the lightning strike. But I suspect that was not lightning at all but pure *Asai*, called upon in an hour of desperate need."

"The quant field?"

Iana smiled. "An energy field that the Light of the Eye travels upon. It is like an invisible ocean that surrounds us completely. It is this field the Ciralys change when they use their High Asairic cants."

"And the Shaluay can see this field?" Would she be able to see this field too?

"It is not a matter of seeing it so much as sensing it. And being able to manipulate it."

"The Shaluay use *Asai*?"

It was Iana's turn to shake her head. "Not in the way the Ciralys do. But come, you never answered my question."

Question? Sevaani cast her mind back but couldn't think.

"You told Meg you knew you would never be returning to Hanore?" Iana prompted. "What struck me in that statement was the certainty in your tone. Many people may think they will never return to the place of their birth once they leave, but you seemed to know this as unequivocal truth."

"Yes," she said. "It seems silly, now, to say this to you. I mean you are a Shaluay, you see the future."

"Not all Shaluay see the future," Iana told her. "Some are Seers, born with the gift, and others must utilise the tools we are taught. But much has been lost since the Sundering. Are you a Seer?"

"Oh no, nothing like that." Sevaani put up her hands. "Kaiel and Darien's mother had the Sight. It killed her."

"Killed her? She was not trained?"

"No," Sevaani shook her head. "She never left Hanore. She would slip into trances and not come out of them for weeks at a time. The boys would look after her, feed her broths and water but Shany – the Keeper of Hanore – said that after such repeated abuse, her body just gave up."

"That is unfortunate." Iana looked both the brothers over again. "But if you are not a seer, how do you know you will never return home?"

Sevaani took a breath and met the woman's eyes. "Because I dreamt it."

"Ah, you are a dreamseer then?"

"I don't know. I think so. Yes." What was she doing? "I have dreams, and they come true."

"Do all your dreams come true?"

"No, not all of them," she admitted. "Only some do."

"How can you tell one dream from another?" Iana looked at her curiously. "Surely you have dreams that are just that. Dreams."

"Yes, I do have normal dreams," Sevaani said, "though they're rarely as memorable. And those dreams never have the golden light surrounding them."

Iana raised an eyebrow.

Sevaani felt her nerve fleeing, but she gathered her courage and ploughed on. "My true dreams are edged in gold, and it feels like I'm watching those dreams happen with my own eyes. It's like I'm there."

"I see." Lady Iana tapped a ringed finger against her lips.

"I dreamt of you too," Sevaani blurted out.

"You did?"

"Yes." You may as well tell her all! "I didn't know who you were, a Shaluay, but I dreamt of your sapphire – the cora'stone. And I dreamt of the Sea Lion."

Iana gave a slight smile. "The cora'stone is not a sapphire, though it looks like one. It is not a gemstone at all."

Sevaani blinked. "What is it?"

"That is a secret only the Shaluay know."

"I dreamt that. That I am going to be a Shaluay."

Iana nodded, then asked. "How much do you know of our order?"

"I don't know anything," Sevaani admitted.

"But you want to join us?" Iana's face was expressionless.

"It not like that. I don't have a choice," Sevaani said and then blushed at her words.

"Despite what our detractors say," Iana drawled, "the Shaluay do not force others to join our ranks."

"No, it's not that," Sevaani shook her head. "It's the dream. It was a true dream that showed me I would be a Shaluay. The true dreams are always true." *Then what do I make of that dream about Darien? Two true dreams? Either he kills Kaiel, or he's a symbol of hope. Yes,* all *my dreams come true, don't they?*

"No choice? So, your fate has been set in stone? And how does that make you feel?"

"I..." Sevaani stopped. How did it make her feel? Hopeless? Scared? "Frustrated," she said at last. "But it also feels right. That this is what I need to do."

"Yes," Iana said, "as I mentioned to your Captain Daynar we Shaluay are not as numerous as we were before the Sundering. Perhaps we should sit? The boys will be quite well, and their fever has abated. Now we wait for them to wake."

They made their way over to the chairs before the large desk under the windows. The sun was warm against the late autumn chill.

Sevaani waited for Iana to take a seat before taking the one opposite.

"Novices to the Shaluay are taught many things, one of which is the history of our order and the history of humankind," Iana began. "Did you know that humans are not native to this world of Sobia?"

Sevaani blinked. "Not native? Where did we come from?"

"Humanity originated on another world, called Erth." Iana smiled. "It was a shock to me also, and I did not believe it either. You will be shown proof of this when you are admitted to the Cradle of the Stars. Suffice to say, this world is very different from our own, and the history and achievements we earned there have been forgotten here on Sobia."

"What achievements?"

"Or records tell us that humanity once flew between the stars."

Sevaani gaped at her. "But why? How has this been forgotten?"

"Because the truth was no longer necessary," Iana said. "Because the men and women who had the innate spark to become Wielders, discovered how to use it. And then the old ways were abandoned." Iana shrugged. "Human nature is a fickle thing. Offer someone power over their fellows, and you have an equal chance to find a tyrant as you do a noble leader."

"The Summoners?" Sevaani asked, suddenly feeling chill despite the warmth of the morning sun.

"No, or at least not at first. The Sahrin fell to corruption much later," Iana said. "The Shaluay did not integrate into this new world well. They were men and women who held on to the old ways of Erth, to older ideals and, more importantly, the history and the knowledge our species had gathered over countless centuries, and at great personal cost. They kept safe the heritage of our ancestors for future generations." Iana looked back to Sevaani. "That is what you will be swearing yourself to if you join us."

"I understand."

Iana smiled. "You don't. But you will."

Sevaani looked down at her hands, clasped in her lap. "No, perhaps, I don't. But I will be a Shaluay." She looked up. "Whether you accept me or not, I do know that."

"Oh, I will take you to Arleth'taur," Iana said. "And not because the order can use as many new members as will come to us, although that is certainly true. No, I will take you because you are a Dreamseer, and you have a gift that is leading you to us."

Behind them came a groan from the bed. Sevaani gasped and stood, turning to go to Kaiel and Darien when Iana grabbed her by the wrist. Sevaani looked back, her eyes meeting the Starbinder's. She felt as though the woman was looking into her soul.

"Joining the Shaluay means different things to different people, child, but one thing we all accept, however hard it may be, is that the knowledge we safeguard and the powers we have access to, change us. And not just the colour of our hair."

"Our hair?" Sevaani raised her other hand to her blonde hair.

"Because of this, all novices give up ties to their past, including relationships."

Sevaani felt the blood drain from her face, and Iana let her wrist go. "I don't–"

"You will need to say goodbye to your young man." Iana nodded towards the bed.

Stricken, Sevaani followed her gaze to see Kaiel, tossing under the blankets. "But he's... he's only just waking."

Iana relented. "Not this instant. But you will need to do it before we arrive at Serjat."

"So soon?"

"There is never a good time for these things," Iana said. "Oh, child, do not cry."

Sevaani was shocked to find the woman was right as a tear rolled down her cheek.

"The Shaluay are not celibate, but there is no marriage amongst us. Not with the outside world. You are leaving all you know behind, do not leave a thread to hold you – or Kaiel – back from what the stars have in store for you." Iana cupped Sevaani's cheek. "We have at least another fortnight on this ship, child, and I urge you to make the break before we reach Serjat. Once we arrive, I do not know how long our paths will remain linked to theirs."

CHAPTER TWENTY-THREE

The City of Forever

MEG'S HANDS TIGHTENED on the rail. Though she had found her sea legs weeks ago, heavy swells still set her stomach churning. As she stared at the view, the movement of the ship settled into a dull discomfort in the back of her mind, and stomach.

The rising sun ignited the city on the port side of the ship, painting it an inferno of reds that faded into orange. Lining the coast of the enormous bay were more buildings than she'd ever seen. She couldn't imagine how many people must live there. Where did the food to feed everyone come from?

In the water there had to be as many boats as there were buildings behind them. And above the city drifted large... objects, with a nimbus of light twinkling along their sides. Given their size and the distance they were from her, she judged they might be twice the size of the *Crow*. They had to be the vessels of the Aerynai. She'd heard Shany tell the young ones tales of the avian race back in Hanore. Large of eye and feathers for hair, their elders were even said to grow wings. They were as mysterious and as exotic as the Evay. Could those be the aeries they retreated to when the world was broken in the Sundering?

A thrill coursed through her and she couldn't contain her grin.

Glittering towers of white stone rose high, catching the morning sun. Wider, squat-looking buildings below, of different coloured brick, pock-marked the morning glow like dark stains. The floating vessels caught the light of morning and flashed it back at the sun like twinkling stars. But it was the sparkling tower in the city's centre, stretching high above all else, that kept drawing her gaze.

"What is it?" she breathed.

"The Crystal Spire."

She gave a start and looked up to find Captain Desrin beside her. Her face heated. How long had he been there?

The captain was dressed in unrelieved black, and his long dark hair was pulled off his face and clipped in a tight knot at the back. Though his face was in shadow, the sun-darkened skin of his neck was almost ochre in the morning light. He moved beside her and clasped the rail firmly, swaying unconsciously to the movement of his ship.

"The Spire at dawn is a sight to behold," he said, gazing towards the city. "On the morning of the summer solstice, just as the sun lifts itself above the horizon, the tower flashes with a blinding light."

"On the Festival of Li'aria?" Meg stared at the Spire. "I've never understood why the Goddess of Fire is worshipped on the day her son Alay'thias burns longest."

"You follow the Elder Gods?" he asked. "If so, then my advice would be not to say so too loudly in that city."

"But the Elder Gods have shrines in Serjat, surely?"

"Aye," Corwyn said. "But the Temples of the Shol'mas hold sway here, as they do in most cities these days." His face was a mask as he stared across the bay. "Is it not strange the Shol'mas came to us after the Sundering as 'messengers' of the gods, only to take their place in the hearts of humanity?" He offered her an unsettling grin. "Who would not follow a being they might touch and see rather than one who answers no prayers?"

"In the hearts of humanity. But not all who walk this world are human," Meg said, thinking of Shany's teachings. "And the adepts of the Elder Gods can work as many miracles as the priests of the Shol'mas."

"Yet they don't." He shrugged. "And in Serjat they celebrate the Feast of the Shol'mas Lord Kirana, Lady of Flame. But to answer your original question of why Li'aria is celebrated on the day that marks the turning of her son's cycle, I'd advise you never to underestimate a mother's love," he said. "Or her grief. We acknowledge that grief, so she does not set the world alight in her pain."

Meg scoffed. "Astrologers have known for centuries that the Elder Gods have little to do with the rotation of Sobia around the sun."

He gave a half-smile. "Spend your life on the sea, and you will come to know the Elder Gods permeate all aspects of the world we live in. In any case, no-one knows why the Spire flashes. Something leftover from the Summoners, no doubt, but it is magnificent, and blinding if you are standing too close."

"I've never seen anything like Serjat," she admitted, turning her face back into the wind. Meg knew the captain hadn't been happy to be back out on the sea when he'd only just made dock in Glass Bay. They'd had to stop in a cove west of the Bay to take on freshwater and gather supplies, and he'd made that displeasure known. Oh, he hadn't been rude, he was very polite – for a corsair – but Corwyn kept to his crew, only answering Lady Iana's questions and attempts at conversation when he must. Meg hadn't expected he'd be so philosophical about the Elder Gods. But then, as he said, he'd lived his life on the sea, and the stories all agreed that sailors and superstition went hand in hand.

Stray strands of hair escaped from the thick braid she had taken to wearing, whipping across her eyes. She pushed them aside, wincing as her nails scraped the sunburn on her cheeks. Her pale complexion had not fared well on the voyage across the Nemisdrillion Sea, and while she was perversely glad to have had the chance to travel by sea, she was equally sure she never wanted to set foot on a boat again.

"I didn't know the Aerynai had aeries here," she said, watching one of the floating vessels drift away from the city, heading north. "Do they move around much?"

Corwyn laughed. "Those are not aeries," he said. "They are skyships. Aeries are much, much larger and they are rarely seen in the Realms."

"Skyships?" She couldn't stop her mouth from gaping. "But they are so big!"

"Some are," he agreed. "But most are no bigger than the *Crow*."

The ship leaned towards the water as it made a sharp turn, and the blood rushed from her head as she swayed against the rails, her stomach-turning. She drew a deep breath of the cold air and closed her eyes. Corwyn shouted something towards the helm, but she missed the words.

"Come," he said. "Look at this; it will help take your mind off the motion."

She gritted her teeth but didn't protest, despite a sudden panic that if she moved away from the rails, she *would* make a scene – all over the scrubbed deck. But she let Corwyn take her arm and lead her to the starboard rail.

He pointed across the water, but the direction was unnecessary.

Half a mile away, a massive column of dark rock broke out of the sea, crowned with intricately carved crystal sculpted in the shape of enormous waves. The waves were layered in hues of sapphire and turquoise, edged along their tops with moonstone. The sculpted waves were built one atop the other and seemed to crash and break around towers – their walls a dusty rose that bled into white as the sun continued to rise. Each building was capped with a dome sparkling in the sun. And statues of lithe, nude female bodies with the heads of lions stood in eternal vigilance, their hands clasping massive tridents of gleaming steel along a flight of wide steps that lead right into the sea. Even the terns that wheeled above did not land upon them.

The ethereal beauty and grace, visible even from this distance, could only have been crafted by the Summoners.

"Is it a shrine?" she said. "It must be." She leant over the rail, trying to trace every nuance of its confounding architecture.

"The Shrine of Taluun, son of Sharenesh, the Elder God of the Water," Corwyn confirmed. "Don't fall overboard."

Meg straightened and felt her face heat. She wasn't a child.

From the corner of her eye, she caught a flash of gold and turned just as Corwyn threw a coin towards the shrine.

Her mouth fell open. In Hanore a gold coin, of any mark, would feed a family for a month, for *two* months – not that she'd ever seen one – and he just tossed it into the sea? He grinned, his white teeth flashing against his swarthy skin and the heavy stain of his beard.

"Your face." He chuckled, and she snapped her mouth shut. "I'm sorry I shouldn't laugh." Still smiling, he gestured at the shrine as the ship sailed past. "The coin is a tribute; all ships offer it as they come and go for a blessing of good fortune. Others, fishermen and the like, will offer a tribute of their labours."

"But the Elder Gods weren't worshipped here?" She looked back at the shrine.

"The temples of the Shol'mas tried to have the Lady of Storms installed as patron of the seas. But fisherfolk and sailors, well, they are stubborn, and none cared to risk offending Taluun when they are subjects of his dominion daily."

"So, you all just throw things at him?" She arched an eyebrow.

"The Lord of the Sea has wide nets and catches all that is cast at his shrine." His eyes tracked the shrine as it fell behind them. "Or so it is said. If he doesn't, then there is a lot of coin on the seabed beneath us."

"I am sure it is all put to good use." Iana joined them at the rail. "Taluun's shrine is one of the richest in Serjat."

The captain offered the Shaluay a terse nod. "Mistress," he said, all traces of mirth gone. "The sea is cruel; you will find those who cast tribute to Taluun's priests do so for practicality rather than to see the adepts who serve him live in comfort."

The lady smiled. She was wrapped in a violet cloak edged with ermine, clasped close at her throat. The wind picked silver-white strands of her hair and flung them out like pennants, but the rest lay secure against her head, held in place by silver and diamond combs that glittered like ice in the morning sun.

"If you will excuse me," Corwyn said. "I must go and make sure all is ready for docking."

Meg was not surprised that the captain didn't stay. He never remained in Lady Iana's presence any longer than protocol demanded. Protocol, from a corsair. She didn't understand these people at all.

"Where is your cloak?" Iana asked. "You will catch a chill out in this wind, child."

Meg looked out towards the growing city once more. "The cold seems to help with seasickness."

"I am sure seeing Serjat for the first time makes it worthwhile," Iana said. "It is quite a sight, is it not?"

"I can't believe it's so big," Meg said as they moved to the prow. The small blocks of colour she had seen from afar slowly resolved into buildings that flowed one into the other.

"I imagine it is very different to the world you know," the Starbinder said.

Meg remained silent, the towers rising higher as they neared, and the forest of masts grew denser in the bustling harbour. Smaller fishing vessels darted between the anchored ships as they made their way back out to sea, having already brought in the first haul of the morning.

"Are you sure you wish to pursue this path?" the Shaluay asked, breaking the silence.

"I've come this far," Meg said, still looking towards their destination.

The bright light of early morning washed the colours of the city clean, dampened only slightly by the haze of chimney smoke that drifted in the air between the rooftops and the skyships floating above. "There's nothing back in the citadels for me, and much better prospects here."

"But you do not have a sponsor," Iana pointed out.

"I have the Keeper's pledge of Hedge Right," Meg said, with forced confidence.

"Ah, yes."

Meg's stomach tightened; and not from nausea. "They won't acknowledge Shany's request?"

Iana moved her shoulders beneath her cloak. "The Ciralys like to tell tales of how we Shaluay always act from hidden motives," she said. "But secrecy has long been their way also." She looked at Meg, "What is your Sphere? Do you know?"

"My Sphere?" The Spheres of *Asai* determined what elemental energy a person was most strongly aligned with. "No, I don't know. The Keepers use a reflection of the Light of the Eye; they don't use *Asai* itself."

"But you have used *Asai*," Iana stated.

"What?" Meg shook her head. "I haven't. I haven't been trained."

"Regardless of whether or not you have been trained, you have used it." The Shaluay looked out across the bay again. "There is a resonance around someone who has wielded the Light of the Eye."

Meg opened her mouth but caught herself before she spoke. When had she used *Asai*?

"Shany said that Hedge Right would have me accepted by the Ciralys." If she had been wielding *Asai*, she'd find out soon enough.

A corner of Iana's mouth curled in amusement, but she accepted the diversion. "Hedge Right is an old custom and one that is no longer used. Why would they pay attention to a Keeper of a remote citadel in the Borderland Wilds?"

"Because I have potential?" Meg bristled.

Iana arched an elegant eyebrow. "Child, the Ciralys have become arrogant – more arrogant – over the centuries since the Sahrin fell. They are not what they once were. Though," she said with a wry smile, "that can be said of us all."

The Starbinder gazed across the city. "Their war with the Temples of the Shol'mas built them a reputation the Realms still fear, and they have learnt to wield it like a sword. Those applicants who come to them today, do so with a sponsor. Or with a large contribution to the coffers of the Palace of the Eye in Isoliere."

"Are you trying to scare me off?" Meg's anger raised its head at Iana's words. She'd worked so hard at containing her fear, but Iana's words were battering her defences like the Korda'vari at the walls of Sonyth. Meg had left Hanore for Darien, thinking, *hoping*, he'd be different away from the citadelfolk who'd shunned him. But now, she was thinking about herself, her own dreams, her own future.

If she didn't care about *him*, did she really want to carve out a place for herself in a world where she'd still be near him?

"I am not trying to scare you." Iana smiled gently. "Nothing I have said is a lie or an exaggeration. You *do* have potential, I see it also, but will the Ciralys see the same? Or even care? They are not renowned for their charity."

Meg straightened. She had the pouch Shany gave her when she was leaving Hanore – it was hidden at the bottom of her bags, even now. That was her bargaining chip. Given as a *gift*, not charity, and it would buy her a place. The rest would be up to her, and if she could navigate the fractious waters of citadel politics, the way all Keepers were trained to do, then she could do the same with the Ciralys, surely.

"What would you have me do?" she asked the Starbinder. The tension left her shoulders as her resolve strengthened. "Find passage back to Ebron and then back to Hanore? Prince Alesandr will still be looking for us. Hair like mine isn't easy to hide on the Borderlands, or in Aldania." She gestured at her red braid.

"You could join the Shaluay," Iana suggested.

Ah, so that was it. "Don't you already have Sevaani for that?"

"The Order of the Shaluay Starbinders was once as large as the Ciralys, and the role we played in the Realms was similar, to a degree, though our agenda is very different to the one the Circles embrace."

"What do you mean?"

Iana stared at the city. "The Ciralys were once more concerned with the Path of Ascension," she said at last. "They kept themselves separate from their fellows, sitting at the feet of their teachers, the Sahrin. They removed themselves from worldly concerns and strove to focus on the Eye of Eternity, on finding that place within themselves that reaches past the veil of manifestation. The Shaluay have ever been more concerned with protecting humanity."

"Protecting us? From what?"

"From ourselves." Iana's laugh was dry, and a chill, biting wind snapped the sails above their heads. "Humanity is its own worst enemy. We have forgotten so many things, including where we came from. It is the Shaluay's directive to preserve that knowledge, and to guide our people back to themselves as best we can."

"What have we forgotten?" Meg was curious. Shany had mentioned the Shaluay to her many years ago, but she recalled no details, and everything Darien had related, which was little enough, was painted with his master's bias.

Iana glanced at her and smiled. "Many things," she said. "But nothing I can speak of, not without your formal oaths to the Estay Matrix."

"The Estay Matrix?"

"The cornerstone of our order," Iana said. "An ancient artefact, but that is all I can tell you."

"So many secrets."

"Secrets are necessary." Iana continued to gaze at the harbour. Behind them, sails were being lowered, and the ship was slowing. "Do the Keepers not have secrets also?"

"Yes," Meg said, brushing loose strands of hair from her face. "They do. But I've never seen Shany dangle them in front of people like a carrot before a donkey."

Iana nodded. "I dare say your Keeper never had to dangle anything in front of you to interest you in the Covens, did she? And do not listen so closely to young Darien. The reputation the Ciralys have been so quick to spread about the Starbinders stems from misunderstanding and, to a degree, jealousy. It was the Shaluay who first stood at the side of humanity when they tied themselves to the Sahrin. It was my sisters, and those few brothers called to serve, who aided the world during the Sundering. We had spread ourselves across the Realms to protect what we could and were caught in the storm."

"But if you tried to warn everyone, why are the Shaluay so distrusted?"

"It was because we *didn't* warn people. Not until it was too late. Our Sight was blinded, and we did not see the Sundering coming. We didn't see what happened and we still don't know exactly. To this day, the seers of my order have only been able to catch glimpses of the events. The fabric of reality at that point in time is too turbulent to see clearly. But my order saved as much of humankind as we could, while with the passing of the Sahrin, the Ciralys replaced the knowledge they lost with temporal power."

"You dislike the Ciralys, then."

"Not at all," Iana disagreed. "We Shaluay have enough to do shepherding our own order without concerning ourselves with the Ciralys. We are not in competition."

Meg considered her words. "Why are you rebuilding now?"

"We have always been rebuilding."

"Three thousand years seems a long time to rebuild anything."

"You are right; it is." Iana pushed herself from the railing. "We can talk more later," she said. "If we have time. But consider my offer, please. The Ciralys are not the only option open to you." She looked back over her shoulder.

Following her gaze, Meg saw Sim burst onto the deck.

"I told you I could smell land!" he said, nimbly dodging sailors.

Kaiel followed behind him, hastily pulling on a coat. "The captain said we'd reach Serjat this morning, *that's* how you knew there'd be land." He nodded to Iana and Meg. "Good morning," he said, and Meg smiled at him in return.

Both Kaiel and Darien seemed no worse for wear after the illness they had suffered on leaving Glass Bay. Whatever it was seemed to have passed cleanly, and both were back on their feet.

Captain Daynar and Sevaani came out on deck a moment later, with Darien bringing up the rear. Meg was watching Darien when he saw the Crystal Spire for the first time. He stilled as his gaze took in the shining tower, and her chest went tight as she saw the excitement that came over him.

"Serjat, the City of Forever," Jaric spat over the side of the ship as he reached the rail. "Home of corruption and dishonour."

Iana tsked. "Come now, Captain. Is that so different from any other city?"

"I suppose not," Jaric admitted. "But my father died in the Culling, here. You'll find I rarely have anything pleasant to say about the place."

"Really?" Iana eyed him. "Your accent sounds more Sithapian to me."

Jaric grunted. "I *am* from Sithapia. My father and his family were not."

"So that's where you're from." Satisfaction radiated from Sim.

"What's the Culling?" Sevaani asked as she peered ahead of them. "Gods, it's so *big*! Meg, could you ever imagine it would be so huge?"

"Of course it's big," Darien said, but his tone held a trace of excitement.

"It's the centre of trade on this side of the Nemisdrillion Sea. It was built before the Sundering and survived. It's magnificent."

Jaric snorted. "Do you have plans for lodgings, my lady?" he asked, ignoring Sevaani's question.

"There is an inn on the main market square that will suit us," she said. "But I must visit the Shrine of Orthias first. Then, tomorrow, I will take you to seek an audience at the Spire."

"Tomorrow?" Darien protested.

"The Spire will still be there, and you will be refreshed from your journey," Iana said. "Surely you can wait one more day?"

Meg missed Darien's reply as the crew on deck began to move like a nest of disturbed ants. Kaiel and Sim joined them as they were pushed out of the way by sailors dashing around the forecastle.

Jaric grunted, and Meg braced herself against the railing. A small cutter was making its way towards them. Its mast flew a flag of navy blue, with eight silver stars forming a circle around an anchor in its centre.

"The harbourmaster's lackey." Jaric nodded towards the small ship. "Look at the pirates run."

"Captain," Iana said reproachfully, and he just shrugged his broad shoulders.

"How do we get past?" Sim asked, peering intently at the cutter as it came closer. "Surely the harbourmaster has descriptions of this ship?"

"Which is why an assistant is coming to visit," Jaric told him. "You watch. This won't be the first time the *Crow* has visited Serjat."

The cutter pulled up alongside the *Crow*, and a small pouch was tossed down to its crew. An officious-looking man in a navy coat peered inside it. Nodding, he motioned, and the cutter hoisted its sails, moving away.

"That's going to cost you," Jaric said to Iana.

"Did we just buy off the harbourmaster?" Sim asked.

"Who can say if the coin makes it that far." Captain Daynar stared at the boat. "It could just be the harbourmaster's assistants who take the money and look the other way, or it could be the harbourmaster himself. In this city, I'd put my money on the harbourmaster."

"The Houses allow it?" Meg said.

"They're in on it," Jaric growled. "Though they go to great lengths to keep all such *agreements* behind closed doors."

"What of House honour?"

"What of it?" He snorted. "If you don't get caught, then there's nothing to stain your honour."

"You're not serious?" Sevaani was scandalized.

"Aldania is somewhat more..." Iana paused, "*rigid,* in their view of how these things operate."

"How did that boat know we were here?" Sim pressed. "There must be hundreds of ships in this harbour. And there are more coming in. How did it know to come to us?"

Jaric snorted. "As I said. This ship would be known. Most ships sail into port before being approached. Others –" His face was blank. "They'll already have arrangements with."

Captain Corwyn strode over to them. "We will be making our way to the lower port to let you off."

"We cannot go to Middle Harbour?" Iana protested.

"No." His face was expressionless. "This is an unscheduled run; we risk much if the Sea Lords of the Eight notice us. We usually prepare visits to a harbour like Serjat in advance. By going to the lower port, we can leave faster."

"Why's that?" Sim asked, and Meg, standing beside him, pinched his arm. "Ow!"

"The lower ports are at the southern end of the city." Corwyn pointed. "And closer to the open sea given the curve of the bay."

"So why did we come up here just to go back?" Sim asked, rubbing his arm and shooting a glare at Meg.

"We came to pay tribute to the Shrine of Taluun, for safe passage," she said.

"Sharenesh is the God of Water." Sim pointed out, still glaring at her.

"He is," Darien said. "Taluun is his son, the God of the Seas."

"Are you sure you cannot take us to Middle Harbour?" Iana persisted.

"I am sure," Corwyn said sharply. He pointed across the water to a great ship, at least ten decks tall, with many, many gun ports along its length. "That is the *Sea Hawk*, the first ship of the Imperial Navy. I will not take the *Crow* past her. Her crew are also familiar with us, and I want to be away from here as soon as possible. Now, if you will excuse me, I have preparations to oversee." He stalked off.

"Imperial Navy?" Sim's eyes were fixed on the massive warship. "Serjat doesn't have an emperor. Does it?"

"Not anymore," Jaric said. "Serjat, and Tremor-Salaya itself, is ruled by the Eight. But this was the heart of the Darvelanian Empire two thousand years ago, capital of the Shepherd Kings. The Lords of the Nine Fiefs came much later, but some names stick."

"Nine Fiefs? You said eight lords rule."

As much as it irritated her, Meg admired Sim's ability to ask questions of anyone. She could ask questions with the best of them, but she usually held herself back from doing it publicly.

"The Eight rule *now*," Jaric said. "There were Nine, once."

"What happened to the Ni –"

"Sim, come and help me get the bags." Kaiel grabbed his friend by the arm, pulling him away.

"But I wanted to know more about Serjat," Sim protested.

"We'll be there soon enough," Kaiel said.

Jaric sighed. "Simeon could join the Temple of Dalmon."

"He's more Tameron's get, I'd wager," Lihon said, who'd appeared silently behind them.

"Then the Lord of Shadows had best watch his pockets," Jaric said. He addressed Iana. "Will docking at the lower port change any of your plans?"

"We're not going to Middle Harbour?" the Amarian growled.

Meg felt her eyebrows rise in surprise as Iana ignored them both and turned to Sevaani. "You should do it now, child."

Meg looked at Sevaani. Do *what*?

Sevaani looked stricken, but the Shaluay turned away from her.

"No, we're not going to Middle Harbour," Iana said, picking up the conversation as though there had been no interruption. "Corwyn is concerned about the presence of a naval warship in the harbour." She turned to Jaric "It will only take us half an hour or so to reach the market district, but the Packs shouldn't cause us any problem so close to the border of the Middle City."

Meg watched Sevaani's eyes following Kaiel as he and Sim crossed the deck. Then she took a breath and started after him.

What on earth was going on?

A sudden roll of the deck sent nausea washing through Meg again, and she grabbed the railing. Swallowing hard she faced the chill wind once more and focused on the calls and clamour of industry floating across the water as the *Crow* came into port.

"Kaiel?" Sevaani called out to him, and he turned to face her just as the ship rolled beneath them. Sim disappeared down the hatch to the galley, and Sevaani heard a loud thump, followed by a stream of invectives rising from below deck. A month spent on a ship crewed by pirates had done nothing for Simeon's language, but that thought fled as the deck rose beneath her, and she fell forward. Onto Kaiel.

He grabbed her, his grip firm and familiar, and part of her ignored her suddenly racing heart to marvel at how strong he was, he barely moved to keep his balance. He had fully recovered from whatever malady had struck him and Darien down as though being unconscious for a fortnight was nothing.

"Oh, I'm fine." Sim's voice came from behind. Looking over Kaiel's shoulder, Sevaani saw his head pop out of the hatch. Sim's eyes widened as he spotted her in Kaiel's arms.

"Don't mind me," Sim said, ducking back down the stairs. "Daemonspawned boats..."

Sevaani pushed herself away from Kaiel, her cheeks hot, and pulled her shawl more firmly around her shoulders, certain that every member of the crew was watching them.

She cleared her throat. "Kaiel, I, uh, I wanted to apologise... There is no need to look at me like that!" The great ox was staring at her as if she'd grown two heads! This was a terrible idea.

"What? No, Sevaani. Please, I'm not looking at you like anything." He gave a helpless shrug. "I'm just surprised is all."

Well, she hadn't spoken to him since that morning he'd saved her from Rolen, chopping his arm – no, she wouldn't think about that. It was just too horrible. She still couldn't believe that her brother had pulled a dagger on her or spoke to her the way he did. If Kaiel hadn't... if he...

She stepped past him, moving to the starboard railing. She looked across the water at the white-stone mansions sprawled over the hills and cliffs on the northside of the harbour. Serjat might very well be the oldest city in the world, but surely it was the biggest too. Kaiel stepped beside her, silent.

"I..." She took a breath. Oh, why did Lady Iana insist she do this? She glanced at him out of the corner of her eye.

She took another breath and turned to face him. "I'm sorry for the way I have behaved towards you. What happened with Rolen, it...." She swallowed. "It was very confronting. I know you did it to save me, I mean, I know that's how you rationalise it –"

"You think I wanted to chop his arm off?" Kaiel asked, very loudly. "This isn't an apology at all, is it?"

"Keep your voice down," she hissed, glancing over her shoulder. "I don't *know*. Maybe not cut his arm off, but *something*. I can't help but wonder if some part of you wanted to do that to him. He beat you in the Trials, and –"

"No." He shook his head, frowning at her. "How can you think that of me? You know me, Sevaani."

"I thought I did!" She felt her face colour as a deckhand looked over at them. She turned away from Kaiel, leaning on the railing. "I thought I knew you, and then... then..."

"And then what?"

"And then I saw you fighting the Korda'vari in Sonyth." She shuddered as the memories assaulted her. "You enjoyed it, Kaiel, I saw you."

"Enjoyed it? I was fighting for my life! For your life, for all of us. Sevaani, look at me." Reluctantly she turned her head and met his eyes. "I didn't enjoy it."

"I think you did," she said. "I think there's a part of you that enjoyed it. The adrenaline, the excitement."

"Excitement? Maybe, but it's not as though I am having fun! Gods, Sevaani I don't have time to think about anything except coming out alive. And with the way it's been since Sonyth, that usually means someone has to die." He ran his hands through his hair in frustration. "You think I *enjoyed* it?"

Sevaani sighed. "This isn't going how I wanted." He was right. Tarin help her she *did* know him. That was what made this so hard. He was a wonderful, caring man and one day he'd make some woman a loving husband. It just wasn't going to be her.

The morning light glittered on his gold-blond hair as she looked at him.

"I'm sorry for what I did to Rolen." A look of shame crossed his fine features. "But I didn't plan to do it. He had a knife to your throat, Sevaani! And the things he was saying. I didn't think; maybe I should have. I just had to get you away from him."

"I know, Kaiel, I remember what he was saying. But this isn't about all of that. I don't know why I even brought it up. Please believe me; it *isn't* about that."

"What's it about then?"

"I wanted to apologise to you for the way I've been acting. And to, to explain something." Her mouth was suddenly dry. Gods. *Just do it, girl*!

"Back in Hanore," she said, "we spent as much time together as your training, and my duties would allow. And I liked – *like* – you, a lot, but..."

"But?" His expression was closed to her.

"We can't be together, Kaiel." It came out in a rush. But there. It was done. Oh Tarin, why didn't she feel better? She kept her eyes on his. "There is no future for us, Kaiel."

"Because of what I did to Rolen?"

"No. I told you, this isn't about that." She reached out a hand to him but let it fall. "We both want different things and are walking different paths."

"Couldn't we make it work?" While his expression was closed, she saw the hurt in his eyes.

"Kaiel." She reached up with her right hand and cupped his cheek. "No, Kaiel. You're staying with Darien, and I... well I am going with Lady Iana. I can become a Shaluay."

"You didn't even know what a Shaluay was a month ago!"

She let her hand fall. "No, I didn't." She shook her head. "You all laugh at my dreams, but they're real, Kaiel. I knew Meg was leaving to follow you and Darien –"

"She was following Dar, not me."

Sevaani tossed her head. "Yes, you're right. But you were both heading in the same direction. I dreamt that. And I also know I'll never return to Hanore."

"You could go home if you wanted," he protested, "Your da would protect you –"

"No, Kaiel. I can't."

He was silent for a moment. "So, we're over."

It wasn't a question, but she nodded anyway. "Yes, Kaiel, we are. I should have said something before, but I didn't know what to say –"

"You did say something. In your own way." It was his turn to look away.

"Kaiel, I'm sorry."

"It's all right, Sevaani." He smiled, but again, it didn't reach his eyes. The chill of the wind cut through her.

"We're still friends?" She asked into the silence.

Friends? Gods, how would that work, you stupid girl.

Kaiel cleared his throat. "Of course, we're still friends."

"I'm glad," she said, and made an awkward half-step towards him, arms raised to hug him, but he stepped back from her. She let her arms fall.

"I should go check on Sim," he said.

That hurt, but what did she expect. "I'll talk to you later?"

He nodded stiffly and left her by the railing. She watched him go, then clasping her shawl tightly once more, made her way back over to Lady Iana and the others.

CHAPTER TWENTY-FOUR

The Mark of the Raven

EXCITEMENT RUSHED THROUGH Sim as he stepped onto the old stone pier of the lower port. Burly dock workers went about their business in a riot of curses, yells, and chatter as he and the others spilled off the gangplank. The shades of the dockers' suntanned skin were of such variety that more than one realm must have been represented amongst them. Wagons rumbled along the street of the lower port docks, drivers screaming curses as they weaved through the throng of workers that swarmed like ants into buildings the size of barns.

The noise was incredible; never had Sim imagined that so many people in one place would cause such a racket. The noise all rolled into a droning buzz, interspersed with sharp shouts and whip cracks.

He looked at the others. Kaiel was staring wide-eyed, a faint frown marring his golden features. Meg's head was turning every which way. Sevaani stepped closer to Captain Daynar as stevedores jostled past. And Darien, of course, was frowning at the crowds.

Sim grinned so widely his cheeks hurt. None of them understood. They were standing in the greatest city in the world, and it was all just a loud and unruly crowd to them.

But he had come home.

Hawkers called out to passers-by, while wagons dotted the roadside, variously offering old vegetables – definitely past their prime – and an overwhelming variety of seafood, which filled the air with a pungent odour and squawking gulls. The vendors all had truncheons and appeared as much to guard their wares as sell them, lashing out at rag-wearing children who got too close. Across the road, women hauled baskets of bread and bundles of clothes, stepping around piles of horse dung and over streams of dirty water as they went about their morning's business. Other, more scantily clad women, their faces luridly painted, whistled, and exchanged catcalls with the dockworkers, while men in the uniform of what Sim assumed to be the city guard, walked in pairs up and down the road.

Serjat thrummed with life. He wanted to throw himself into it and wallow like a pig in a sty. He stepped forward, staring at the women across the road, only to be stopped by Jaric, who clapped a firm hand on his shoulder.

"You'll want none of that," the captain said. "Your mother would kill me if I let you anywhere near those women."

"What are they wearing?" Meg asked. "You can see her –"

Sim laughed as she clamped her mouth shut, her face the same colour as her hair.

"Yes, you can," Iana agreed. She stepped forward, and Sim couldn't help but be impressed by the way the crowd parted for her.

"Child," she called, a bronze coin arcing from her hand. It was snatched out of the air by a grubby fist, extending from what he had taken to be a pile of rags.

The rags moved, revealing the legs and arms of a boy that Sim judged to be no older than ten.

"Yes, lady?" A white smile flashed from a dirt-stained face.

"I need a rickshaw," Iana said.

The boy looked at the Starbinder, eyes widening as he took in the torque around her neck.

Sim had seen that look before on the mischief-makers back in

Hanore and grabbed the neck of the boy's shirt just as he made to run, pulling him up smartly. The boy squealed in protest, his head disappearing into the stained shirt and his arms following as he worked to free himself.

"No, you don't." Sim grabbed an arm through the soiled fabric. The boy's head reappeared, and he started yelling and thrashing in Sim's grip.

"Stop that." Iana reached out and caught the child by the chin.

"Let the boy go," Jaric said. "I can find you a rickshaw."

"I ain't no boy!" the urchin said. "Let me go, ya bastards!"

Sim paused and took a closer look at the... boy. The elfin-like features *could* belong to a girl. But how could you tell under all that dirt?

"Do you have a name?" Iana asked.

"I ain't telling ya, witch! And I'm not a *child*. Let me go!"

"Where I come from, all ten-year-olds are considered children," Sim said.

"I'm not ten! And ya wouldn't last a night where I'm from!"

Sim laughed. "Where's that? The sewers?"

Iana held up a silver coin silencing whatever protest had been coming next.

The coin was marked with the nine-tined crown of Serjat. Sim wanted a closer look at that coin. He'd only ever seen the Ivy marks of Aldania.

The girl eyed the coin like a starving wolf. She backed away some, glancing around at them warily but didn't run.

"The coin's yours, if you want it," Iana told her. "But I have a task for you first."

The girl's face took on a mulish cast. "What task?"

"She looks just like you do when you're caught out in one of your pranks," Meg said, looking over at Sim.

"I do *not* look like *that*!" Sim said, indignantly.

"I don't look like no pansy!"

"Meg insulted *me*, not you, gutter rat."

"If you don't want the coin..." Iana said over the top of him.

"What did ya want?" the girl scowled. "I ain't going with ya, though. I ain't gonna disappear like Joey and Ven and the others."

"I mean you no harm."

"Ya one of them witches," the girl said. "Ya got the star pendant. I know yas. Ya take the children to the temple and theys don't come back!"

"What does she mean?" Sevaani asked with a frown.

"She means the Shaluay are recruiting off the streets," Jaric said, folding his arms across his chest.

Iana shot him an irritated glance. "We do not do that. We run orphanages as part of our charitable work, but we do not sweep city streets to fill them."

"Ah, yes, and once you feed a child in need, you have an advocate for life." Jaric drawled.

The Starbinder ignored him, returning her attention to the girl. "I am not going to hurt you, but I do need your assistance." She held up the coin again. "This for you now and I have another after you've helped us."

The girl eyed the coin again, and then she snatched it out of Iana's hand with a speed that had Sim whistling.

He caught himself and scowled. "Is this necessary?" he said, folding his arms across his chest. "I'm sure –"

"What do ya want?" the girl interrupted, the coin disappearing into the rags she was wearing.

"What is your name, child?" Iana said.

"Cassi," she said.

"Cassi, I am Iana." She got a stiff nod of wariness in return. Iana turned to them. "I need to go to the Shrine of Orthias, can you take my companions to the Cockatrice Inn in the Market District? I will join you there this afternoon with the other coin."

"What about ya question?" Cassi eyed her.

Iana nodded though she seemed distracted to Sim.

"You're throwing away good money," he protested. "Captain Daynar's been here before. I'm sure he can find the way to this inn."

"I've not been here since before you were born, Simeon," Jaric said. "And I never spent much time outside of the High City."

"Lihon and I will re-join you as quickly as we can," Iana said. "Give my name to Semhar, the innkeeper, and he will give you a room."

Cassi snorted. "All the inns are full, what with the Light of the Eye visitin'."

"The Scion of Isoliere is here?" Darien exclaimed.

"It's what the guards say." Cassi eyed him. "All the inns are full of people come from outta the city ta see him."

"That is interesting," Iana said.

"Does it change anything?" Jaric asked.

The lady shook her head. "No, it doesn't."

"Will we still be able to see the conclave?" Darien's face was creased with a frown.

"Tomorrow," Iana told him. "Lead them carefully, Cassi, and there will be another coin for you."

The girl nodded warily, and Iana and Lihon gathered their packs and headed off into the crowd.

"All right," Jaric said, looking to Cassi. "Do you know the Cockatrice?"

"Shouldn't be hard ta find," Cassi said. "Middle City is that way." She pointed north-west.

"You just reek of confidence." Sim put his hands on his hips and faced Jaric. "Let's go; we don't need her."

"Ya gonna pay me?" Cassi demanded.

"Sim is the most tight-fisted person in Hanore, and he's not going to pay you," Kaiel laughed.

Sim glared at him. "I am not! I just don't trust street urchins. The ones in Jaroff would as soon slit your throat and steal your coin as help you."

"This isn't Jaroff, Sim," Meg said.

"The witch promised me another silver ta take ya ta the Cock. Ya want me gone, give me the coin now."

"The name of the inn was the Cock*atrice*," Sevaani said primly.

"Like she'd know the difference," Sim said.

"Leave it, Sim." Darien rolled his eyes. "Let's go."

"So long as she doesn't lead us into one of those Packs and rob us all." Sim shook his head.

"I ain't a Pack mate!" Fury twisted Cassi's face. "Ya take that back!"

"Go away, little girl." Sim turned to Jaric as a weight slammed into his back, knocking him to his knees.

"Take it *back*!" Cassi's voice came from above him and blows rained on the back of his head. He lifted his arms to push her off, only to hold them over his face as she split his lip with a well-timed punch. "I ain't no *Pack mate*! Take it back!"

"I know you've never been out of the Borderlands in your life," Jaric growled, "but try and contain your enthusiasm and stop acting like a half-wit and apologise to our guide."

Sim put a hand to his lip and winced. "You pack quite a wallop for such a little thing."

Cassi bared her teeth.

"All right!" He rolled his eyes. "I don't believe this. I apologise for calling you a 'Pack mate'."

The glare vanished, and she gave a sharp nod. "Come on," she said. "Get ya stuff before it gets nicked."

Sim narrowed his eyes. Two youngsters had sidled up to their belongings during the excitement.

Sevaani pulled her pack close to her chest with one hand and grabbed Meg's arm with the other, while both boys dashed back into the crowded street.

"Stay close," Jaric said and motioned for Cassi to lead the way.

Cassi led them north along the docks. Throngs of people grew thicker as the sun rose. Carts and wagons clogged the street with small regard for pedestrians as their drivers brought their loads to the waiting ships or took them away for sale. Sim kept twisting his neck, trying to take everything in.

He had no idea where Cassi was leading them, but he didn't care. This was Serjat!

Those ships filling the harbour – lining the Lower, Middle and High docks – were the lifeblood of the Gold Sea. Goods from Saurin'sha, Naysa, Jardin and Cryned arrived from the East to filter through the Western Realms from here. And when those same ships left again, they were filled with gold, silver and bronze from Calmed, and the Guesaybor Mountains; with precious gems from Hetar, and with wools, silks and velvets from Lanthras and the Crescent Cities. This city was everything he'd dreamt of when he joined his father in the markets of Jaroff or sat at the counter of their store.

He was never going back to the Borderlands. *Never*!

Cassi stopped abruptly, jarring him from his musings. She scanned the busy road as though looking for something.

"What is it?" Jaric asked.

"Feels like..." She bit her lip. "Feels like someone is following us. Following *ya*."

Sim looked around at the shifting masses of dockworkers, caravan drivers, merchants, and other city dwellers."How can she possibly tell?" he asked Kaiel beside him.

"I've never seen so many people in my life, Sim. Look at the size of that bridge." He pointed at a stone-wrought structure, easily fifty feet across, that arched over a canal that flowed through the docks to the sea.

"Don't point," Sim hissed.

"I *can* tell," Cassi said. "Livin' in the Lower City ya learn, or ya Pack fodder." She eyed Sim as if daring him to comment.

"I believe you, but there's no point looking around," Jaric said. "Let's keep moving; just stay close. If you lose someone or get separated, call out."

Cassi frowned darkly, but she led them on.

Sim eyed the guards standing in pairs at either edge of the arching stone bridge. Short swords lay against their legs as they propped themselves up with halberds. He imagined their crimson surcoats, edged in black fur, would offer little in the way of warmth over the steel links of chain mail showing at their sides. But by the looks of the padded sleeves of the dark shirts and their leather-clad legs, they'd be warmer than he'd been traipsing through Dal'mere.

"Why are those guards dressed differently to the ones we saw at the docks?" he asked.

"'Cause they're Middle City guards," Cassi said, as though it was obvious.

"So then," he said, "there must be three sets of guards? Lower, Middle and…" He paused. "Upper?"

"High," corrected Jaric.

"Close enough." Sim nodded.

Cassi's eyes were still on the crowd, but she shook her head. "There are *four* Guards in the city," she told him. "We got the Lower City guard called the Coppers; the Middle City guard – who we call the Steels on account of how they're the strongest of the lot; then we got the High City guard, the Golds. But it's the Seekers who run the lot of them from the Courts of Law. An' ya don't wanna run into a Seeker."

The crowd parted briefly, offering a view of coloured stalls and striped awnings lining the street at the other end of the bridge.

"So, this is the market district," Sim said. "The inn can't be far off."

Cassi laughed. "Dat ain't the market."

"Are all these crowds normal, or are these people in the city because the Light of the Eye is here?" Darien asked her.

"This ain't busy," Cassi disagreed. "Summer's worse. You can't hardly move then."

"Who is the Light of the Eye?" Sevaani asked.

"The most powerful man in the world," Darien said.

Jaric grunted. "To some, perhaps."

"He's the head of the Ciralys," Meg explained, shooting Darien a glare.

"Oh," Sevaani said, clearly unimpressed.

"What's he doing here?" Sim asked.

"Ciralys business," Jaric said firmly. "And you'll not want to stick your nose into that."

"He's here because of some rebellion in Sithapia," Cassi said disinterestedly.

"Sithapia?" Jaric stopped. "What's happening in Sithapia?"

"I don't know, do I?" she said. "But the Princess Heir is in the Spire."

"Princess Andraste? She's here in Serjat?" Jaric looked as though he'd just been punched.

Cassi shrugged his hand off her shoulder. "I don't know what her name is."

"Captain?" Kaiel said. "Are you all right?"

Jaric looked away, his face going blank. "I'm fine."

Sim met Kaiel's gaze and gave a slight shrug. He had no idea what that was about.

"Let's get to this inn," Jaric said. To Cassi, he added, "Quickly."

She surprised Sim by saying nothing; instead, she dove into the flow of the crowd, dragging them along in her wake. They passed more guards in crimson and sable, but Sim only caught a passing glance of them as Cassi pulled them up the road, weaving through the swirls and eddies of the crowd. She led them along a street that lined the start of what must have been the Middle City docks. The warehouses that lined the western side of the road were in no better repair than those in the Lower City; yet with distinctions like Lower, Middle and High, he'd expected that such things as appearance would matter. All the buildings were blurring together when Cassi veered left, and they entered a thoroughfare filled with even more people.

This street was broader than any he'd ever seen. Giant poplars, gnarled with age, spread their branches over the road on either side of the street *and* down an island in its centre, and still, there was more open sky than shade.

"Gods," Kaiel said open-mouthed.

More stalls lined the sides of the roads, grouped around the trunks of the trees, and behind them, shop fronts occupied the ground floor of each building. The air had the scent of packed humanity on its shoulders, mixed with smoke and the aroma of cooking. People hawked their wares next to each other, their skin colours ranging from pale as snow to burnished copper and ebon. Singing players added to the din, and jugglers and acrobats attracted crowds as coloured balls, and scantily clad men and women leapt into the air.

He expected more than one fight to erupt from the raised voices and insults as Cassi led them along the street, and he eyed the flashes of crimson guards, always paired, amongst the crowd.

"Did you ever expect it to be like this, Dar?" Kaiel asked.

Darien was staring ahead. Sim followed his gaze and took in Crystal Spire ahead of them."That is incredible," he said.

"It's just a tower," Cassi said dismissively.

"That –" Darien gestured at a round, stone structure up the street, "is just a tower. *That...*" He pointed at the Spire. "That is the work of the gods."

"It's the work of the Summoners," Jaric said shortly.

"You don't find it impressive?" Sim looked at the captain in surprise. "Daemons, even *I* find it impressive!"

"It's certainly that," Jaric agreed. "But it's a monument to what the Summoners left behind, not those who now claim it."

"What do you mean?" Darien frowned.

"He means the Ciralys can't even fill the place," Cassi said.

"How do you know that?" Meg asked.

"Because the Summoners built it." Cassi looked surprised. "Just like they did the Courts of Law, the Palace of Merchants, and the High Seat of the Eight."

"And the docks of the High City, and the countless other structures that surround us, just like the ruins back home," Jaric told them.

But Sim was already bored with the talking and had stopped listening. He looked up and down the street, trying to spot the work of the Summoners amongst the wood and stone constructions, only to stumble as he was pushed from behind.

"Sorry," a voice said. Sim scowled, dropping his hand to his left hip and froze.

His pouch with the ring in it was gone. He spun around as a slight figure in dirty, tan-coloured clothes, ducked into the crowd.

"Stop!" he yelled. "Thief!"

"Sim, what is it?" Sevaani asked.

"My pouch! He stole my pouch!" He pushed past the people around him.

"Ya won't catch him," Cassi called after him.

Sim ignored her. He hadn't almost died from a spider bite to lose his parents' signet ring now! He pushed through clots of people on the road, a series of cries rising behind him as he knocked baskets out of arms and shoved people aside to get through.

"Damn it!" he swore. He twisted between more people idly going about their business before jumping up onto the base of a statue. He vaguely recognised the stone beneath his hands as everstone but paid it little mind as he scanned the heads of the crowd along the street.

There! A boy in tan ducked into an alley across the way.

He jumped off the statue and barrelled his way across the street, not even bothering to apologise. If none were willing to help a stranger, then he'd be damned if he was going to say sorry.

The alley slid between a pair of small two-storied buildings with bright windows full of goods, and he ran into its mouth and almost fell over the boy.

Sitting on his haunches, his back against the wall, he was working at the knot Sim had tied into the string with dirty fingers.

"Watch it!" the boy snarled, looking up.

"Watch it?" Sim snapped back at him, breathing hard. He hadn't run far at all to be this winded. Void damned spider bite! Sim stretched out his hand. "Give me back my pouch, you thieving little skreet!"

"What pouch?" The boy stood, hands disappearing behind his back.

"The one you have in your hands!" Sim clenched his fists.

"What, this?" The boy's hands came back around, and he slashed a dagger at Sim's face.

Only the training he'd paid half attention to in the Rangers kept him from losing an eye as he reflexively bent back. He ducked under the dagger as the thief swung it again, then stepped in close to swing his right leg around and swept the boy's legs out from under him.

The thief fell on his backside. Sim folded his arms over his chest in satisfaction. But the boy's reflexes surprised him, and the thief was back on his feet and running down the alley in a heartbeat.

"Daemonspawn!"

Sim gave chase, leaping over puddles and stacked crates that the boy pulled down to slow him.

The end of the alley was looming up ahead, a brown brick wall with streaks of charcoal across it when the boy slipped and sprawled face-first across the dirty ground.

Sim slowed to avoid the same fall.

"Doesn't look like you have anywhere to go now, does it?" Sim smirked as the boy got to his hands and knees. "All this trouble for a pouch and you don't even know what's in it?"

"You chased me for it, din' ya?" The boy smirked.

Sim's eyes narrowed. "Give it to me."

"Here ya are." The boy tossed the pouch. Sim snatched it out of the air.

"What have you brought us today, Nev?"

Two more youths approached from around a corner at the end of the alley. Both held cudgels the length of Sim's forearm.

The cutpurse, Nev, shrugged. "He's an Outlander. Swords won't give a toss. An' –" He eyed Sim. "He's got sumthin in that there pouch he dinna wanna lose."

"Watcha give it back ta him for?" jeered one of the youths.

Nev kicked a stone at his feet.

"Ya gonna get a beatin'." The older boy's face darkened behind the grime, and he kicked out at the younger boy.

"Hey!" Sim protested, then snapped his mouth shut. What in the Void was he doing trying to protect the little skreetling who had stolen from him?

The other youth, who'd missed fewer meals than his friend, laughed. "Don't worry none," he said, stroking his club threateningly. "Ya kin get a beatin' too if ya want."

"Give us that pouch!" The skinny boy flashed a snarl of missing teeth at him.

Sim closed his fist around the pouch. "No."

Hopefully, these two couldn't run as fast as the pickpocket.

"Sim!" Kaiel was at the mouth of the alley and his lip curled in a half-smile.

"Down here!" he called. He grinned at the would-be thugs. "It's not very smart, leading someone down here to rob them. You already took my purse on the street."

"If he wanted to rob ya, ya wouldna felt nothin'," Skinny said. "Ya's worth more than ya coin."

"What?" Sim didn't understand.

"They was gonna sell ya to the Black Birds," Cassi said behind him.

Kaiel loomed larger than usual in the small alley, and he was suddenly very glad of his friend's imposing size.

"What's going on?" Kaiel asked, eyeing the boys with the cudgels.

"Does Phaelon know ya on his turf?" Cassi pushed past Sim fearlessly.

The pickpocket eyed the older boys uncertainly. "Ya didn't say nothing about the Pens."

"Shut up!" The fat boy whacked him on the side of the head.

Kaiel pushed Sim back. "Leave the boy alone."

"Ha! That's what I said," Sim offered, but no-one was paying him any attention.

"Phaelon knows." Skinny licked his lips nervously. "He set us da test himself!"

"Leave it out!" Fatty shoved him.

Cassi sneered. "Phaelon getting desperate? This lot ain't da sort he'd want. They're friends with the witches."

Skinny went pale and Fatty spat, turning on the pickpocket.

"Ya trying ta get us killed?" he screeched, jowls at his neck quivering. "Phaelon will put *us* in da Pens!"

"What are the Pens?" Sim whispered out of the corner of his mouth.

"It ain't my fault!" the boy shouted. "I didn't wanna do it anyway!"

"Come on," Cassi said, backing away.

"I'm gonna kick ya," Fatty said, menacingly. "An' den ya can see Phaelon in that one's place!"

"No!" The boy dodged the blow from Fatty's club, punching Skinny in the gut as he tried to snatch his shirt, then slipped behind them and around the corner at the alley's end.

"Ya little shit!" Fatty called, his face turning so red Sim expected him to collapse. "I'm gonna get ya! Come on!" he called to Skinny, who was moaning as he staggered after him.

"What was *that*?" Kaiel asked.

"A mistake," Cassi said, her expression pensive.

"What are the Pens?"

"*Slave* Pens," she said, turning and heading back up the alley. "An' ya lucky them weren't used ta baiting, or ya'd have been on ya way ta the Black Birds."

"*Slaves*?" Sim said. "But only the Amarians and the Liss have slaves!"

"Don' know where ya heard that. The Crescent Cities don't mind them none." She shrugged. "Just one more thing we gotta watch for. Lucky for me the Black Birds have better uses for us in the Lower City."

Sim walked over to the corner the thieves had disappeared around. The alley stopped no more than ten paces from the edge of the building, and a small hole in the wall, bordering the ground, opened to a dark tunnel beyond, a rusted grate lying to one side. On the keystone of the arch was an engraving. He made his way over to it.

"Sim?" Kaiel called.

"Just a moment," he said, leaning down to peer at the carving.

What he had first taken to be a thief's mark to indicate territory was an intricately carved crest that had obviously been there a long time.

He stared at the stone. Before him, above an entrance to what he imagined was the sewer system, was a raven in flight with a coronet above its head.

Sim's hand tightened around the ring in his pouch, its heavy edges pressing through the soft leather, adrenaline firing through his veins.

He didn't need to take the ring out.

The carving on the ruby was identical to the one on the wall before him.

CHAPTER TWENTY-FIVE

Found

NIGHT FELL OVER the city as Darien perched by the window. Sunstones lining the main street ignited, their light steady and strong, and the flickering flames of candles and torches also appeared in windows across the rest of the darkening city. But his attention was always drawn back to the Crystal Spire, and the lights behind its walls, sparkling like fireflies in a glass jar.

Once a subdued Simeon had returned, Cassi had led them without any further adventures up the long street Captain Daynar had recognised as Falcon Road. Two members of the Middle City Guard had gladly gone on their way when Kaiel told them the stolen pouch had been retrieved. They'd eyed Cassi with suspicion, but she'd held her tongue before them. She hadn't, however, held it as she led them on, lashing Sim with harsh words about chasing thieves and wandering down alleys.

Darien had read of the city in the books Master Telaq had given him. Serjat liked to proclaim itself the oldest city still standing since the Sundering, but Isoliere, the city-state ruled by the Ciralys, was older. And much of the beauty that had been found in Serjat before the fall of the Var Imperium had long since been cannibalised by its inhabitants.

But little had prepared him for the inn the Shaluay Starbinder had sent them to. On the outside, the Cockatrice rose a good forty-five feet above the main square, its façade clean and imposing, was set off the square beyond a small garden and wrought iron fencing. On their arrival, the mere mention of Lady Iana's name had seen them escorted to an enormous suite of rooms that took up the entire third floor. High ceilings and expansive windows graced the main sitting room, and finely carved furniture the innkeeper claimed came all the way from Tomassia was artfully placed to be both inviting and serviceable. Darien had never seen anything like it. Nor had any of the others, except perhaps Captain Daynar who didn't even blink as they were shown in.

Behind Darien, on the plush and finely covered lounge chairs, the silence of his companions – though welcome – was palpable. Iana had arrived at the inn with Lihon late in the afternoon, her face a storm cloud. She had said little to any of them. Even Kaiel, who had received some small training in sword work from the blademaster during the voyage, hadn't dared ask her stern protector the cause of her ire.

Cassi, on the other hand, had no such compunctions.

As soon Iana had swept into the rooms, the urchin had launched herself at the Shaluay, demanding the rest of her payment. Iana had considered her carefully and then handed over the coin she'd promised and held up a third.

"What's that for?" Cassi asked, eyeing the coin warily.

"If you would stay," the Shaluay had said, "I will give you more."

Cassi's eyes had narrowed. "Why?"

"Because you were right," Iana said. "Something has happened to your friends, and I am waiting for a guest who might tell me what that is."

The Starbinder had refused to say more, but Cassi had stayed, sitting near the women and as far away from Simeon as she could, while Iana ordered food to be brought up to the rooms.

"How is it you have these rooms kept for you when the city is filled to the brim with Blood and visitors hoping to see the Scion?" Sim asked, absently holding the pouch he'd rescued from the pickpocket.

"The Shaluay Order owns the inn. These rooms are kept for use by the senior Starbinders," Iana had said, sitting in a high-backed chair by the fire.

"How did you know it wouldn't be occupied by someone else?" Meg looked up from a leather-bound book.

Iana met her eyes. "Because the stars suggested I would be returning here in the month of Deson, and I requested they be kept for me."

"Oh." Meg lowered her head.

Not long after, Lihon had taken Kaiel and Captain Daynar down to the walled courtyard behind the inn to observe their sword work, and Darien had moved from the couch to take up a position at the window seat, looking out at the Palace of Merchants and the Crystal Spire that glittered in the distance. What he would do tomorrow would change his life forever. He wanted that. But he was scared for it too. He'd never expected fear of the unknown to enter his mind.

His mind. Now there was an amusing distinction.

He stretched his awareness along the edges of the ward the Master of the Swamp had placed upon him. It gleamed in his mind's eye, but he could not make out the runes that moved in concentric circles, both clockwise and counter clockwise, at its boundary. Runes that were fading. He strained to sense the daemon, but could find no trace of it. He took some small measure of comfort that if he couldn't detect its presence then surely no-one else would either.

As much as he wanted to go to the Spire now, to present himself to the Ciralys and seek admittance to the order, he was terrified of what would happen. Why the Void-cursed man wouldn't remove the thing was a mystery. But that he could – or claimed to – did give him hope. He would find a way to get rid of it, and when he did, he'd learn everything he could and go back and bring that rotting tower down on that bastard's head.

He gave a soft sigh. No, he wouldn't do that. Being a Ciralys and being free of the csitargon would be enough. As long as this ward held, and he was able to pass the Test to gain entrance. If this daemon did end his chance at joining the Ciralys, then he would find that spear and use it to kill a Shol'mas, just not the one Alesandr wanted dead.

He sighed again, and his breath stained the glass. What could he do? What could anyone do?

Darien's answer lay within the walls of the Spire, he was sure of it. And safety from the Houses of Aldania. No House – or dynasty – of any Realm, crossed the Ciralys.

A clattering of hooves on the paved road below drew his attention. A carriage pulled by a pair of matched horses stopped before the inn. A woman, wrapped in furs, alighted from the carriage with the assistance of a footman. There were street-lamps all around the square, but they didn't cast enough light for him to make out the colours of the coachman's livery.

As they crossed the neat flagstones of the path below, the woman lifted her head, and Darien jerked back.

"What is it?" Meg came up to the window to stand at his shoulder.

"Nothing," he murmured.

"Do you believe it's true that most of the Spire is empty?" she asked. "None of the lights inside go very high up the walls."

He turned to her. "What?"

"It's true," Cassi said, appearing beside Meg. The young urchin more closely resembled the girl she had claimed to be since she'd bathed at Iana's insistence. "The lights never go no higher than da tenth floor."

"Ten floors," breathed Meg. "How tall is it?"

"Jase said da city planners reckon it's eighty stories. But I don' know if dat's a real number."

Darien smiled.

"Who is Jase?" Meg asked.

"My friend. He disappeared too." She frowned darkly. "He said dat they reckoned the Ants could probably build as tall, but not outta glass."

"The Ants?" Meg raised an eyebrow.

Cassi nodded. "The Ants."

"She means the Xious'bisan," Jaric said.

"Never heard of 'em," Cassi muttered. "Da Eight asked da Ants to come to build a tower taller, but da Ciralys did'n like dat too much an' made 'em go away."

There was a knock at the door, and the maid who had been clearing away plates moved to answer it.

"Made them go away?" Jaric asked. "That doesn't sound right."

"If your young friend is talking about the war that nearly destroyed the city five hundred years ago, then she is correct," came an imperious voice from the open door.

"Elsa," Iana said, getting to her feet. She crossed the room and hugged the older woman whose white hair was twisted into a bun laced with strands of glittering stones.

Darien recognised her as the woman who had arrived in the carriage below.

The Shaluay took the woman's hand and led her into the room.

"I'll keep the cloak," she said as Iana made to take it, wrapping it around her shoulders more tightly. "I feel the cold more than I used to."

"Milady?" the man at the door said. His short, dark blue jacket had orange-striped sleeves, and his black trousers were tucked into high leather boots. A small crest Darien couldn't make out was sewn onto his jacket above his heart.

"I'll be fine, Evyn," she said, without looking at him. "You go downstairs and get yourself some supper."

"Yes, ma'am." The man gave a bow and closed the door behind him.

"So," the old woman said. "You had to choose rooms up all those flights of steps, and then summon me?"

Iana smiled and sat next to her. "It is good to see you."

"Hmph. Let me look at you." Iana took the aged hands between her own, raising them to her face. Darien couldn't help but stare when he realised she was blind.

"Just the same," Elsa said. "You *still* haven't aged. If only you had found me when I was a girl. Who else do you have here?"

Iana smiled. "This is Lady Elsa," she said.

The old woman scoffed. "I'm no 'lady'."

"Stop it," Iana told her, taking her hand once more. "Lady Elsa is a Shaluay."

"Only just." Elsa shook her head. "You have been gone too long. We have missed you, Firstbinder."

"You know why I cannot stay." Iana smiled sadly. "Without the Estay Matrix, the Wells will remain silent."

"Oh, aye." Elsa pursed her lips at that, then turned her milk-white eyes on Darien. "You still haven't told me who is here. Who is the one that shines?"

Darien frowned at that, but Sim jumped up from his seat and took Elsa's hand.

"I do believe that would be me," he proclaimed and bent over her hand. "Simeon Ravenson, at your service, milady."

"Ravenson?" Elsa smiled lightly. "Indeed, you are, but no. I meant him." Again, her blank gaze moved unerringly back to Darien.

"How can you see him if you're blind?" Meg asked.

"And another!" Elsa exclaimed without answering. "Truly, Iana, what have you been doing?"

"What do you see, Elsa?" Iana asked.

"That one –" She pointed at Darien, "*shines*. But there is a... division. I don't know how else to describe it. Master Ravenson, you will be trouble. And she –" Elsa nodded in Meg's direction. "*She* is not meant for us."

Elsa turned her head. "But the one hiding by the window, now she has the Gift, though it's hazy. But you would already know this, Iana." She frowned, her blind eyes moving disconcertingly. "Dreams," she said at last. "This one dreams true."

Sevaani's eyes went wide.

"And the little one –" Elsa stopped abruptly. "Child, come here." She beckoned Cassi, who tried to hide behind Sevaani.

"It's all right, Cassi," Iana said, trying to coax her out.

"You don't want to get too close to that one," drawled Sim. "She bites."

"I do not!" Cassi jumped out from behind Sevaani and launched herself at him, but Elsa's hand lashed out and gripped her wrist fast.

"Oh my. I hope I live to see this match," Elsa said but did not let go of Cassi's wrist. "However, you are far too old to be acting the way you are. Sit."

Cassi was rigid, her shoulders tensed as though she might flee, then she lowered her eyes and sat beside the older woman.

"Good," Elsa said. Her blind eyes found Iana without error. "This is the one?"

"Yes. You were right, Cassi," Iana said. "Something is happening to the children, and others in the Lower City. It is not of the Shaluay's doing, but our tenets direct that we help the children we can." She paused. "Lady Elsa is a Starseer –"

"*Retired* Starseer," the old woman said.

Iana smiled. "You cannot retire from the Sight."

"I can try," Elsa grumbled. "But it seems as though I am being called back to service."

"You still reside as an advisor to the Jakora, don't you?" Iana said. "That doesn't sound like retirement."

"Ha! All the old man wants to know is if the sea winds will be favourable or not, and that doesn't take a Seer!" She drummed her nails on the armrest. "We will need to work from the ground up here."

"I imagined so." Iana took the girl's hand. "You have no reason to trust me, but if you want it, I can offer you a place with Elsa."

Cassi stared at the older woman, her eyes narrowing.

"Do not think because I'm blind, that I cannot see," Elsa said with a snort. "If you stay with me you will be put to work."

"I ain't afraid o'work!" Cassi said, taking her hand back and shooting Sim a glare as though daring him to speak.

"I hear a 'but', behind your words." Elsa folded her own hands in her lap and waited.

"Well…" Cassi glanced at the others in the room. "How do I know I won't disappear like my friends?"

Elsa nodded sombrely. "A fair consideration. You don't know me, but I wonder, do you recognise this?" From a pocket, Elsa handed the girl a small lacquered plaque. Darien peered at it as Cassi turned it over in her hands. The circular plaque was no bigger than her palm, bordered in silver, with the emblem of an anchor embedded on a surface painted with blue and orange stripes.

The girl looked up. "House Jakora."

"That's right," Elsa agreed. "Are you familiar with House Jakora?"

Cassi nodded reluctantly.

"I can't see you, child," Elsa said. "Do you know of the Jakora?"

"Yes," Cassi murmured.

Elsa sat back. "Then you know too, that the Jakora do *not* deal in human slavery, let alone stealing children from the streets."

Cassi looked at the old woman biting her lip.

"House Jakora retains my services," Elsa explained to her. "If you would come with me, I promise you we will find your friends. But I warn you; it may be dangerous too."

"I ain't afraid," Cassi said, her reluctance seeming to have vanished at the revelation of who the old woman worked for.

Darien raised an eyebrow. It appeared this House Jakora had a reputation amongst the poorer of Serjat's citizens that it was enough to overcome the girl's natural wariness.

"Good!" Elsa clapped her hands sharply, and Cassi jumped. "Because I don't work with cowards; nor do I work with fools. We will find your friends," she promised as she took Cassi's hand.

Cassi bit her lip for a second and then nodded.

"It's settled then," Iana said, leaning back.

"Ah." Cassi shifted on her seat. "What do I gets paid?"

Meg chuckled. "She sounds just like you," she told Sim, grinning at his scowl.

Elsa ignored the exchange and turned her head towards Iana. "You know about the orphanages?"

"What is happening?" Iana's voice was grave. "The High Adept of Orthias refused to see me."

Elsa ran her hands over her lap, smoothing the folds of her dress. "I don't know when the rot set in, but something is happening in the city. I hear scales sliding over sand in my dreams, and crows peck at the ruins of the Well. You have not yet been to the Complex, have you?"

"No," Iana said. "Children have been disappearing, and Cassi seems sure that those who are responsible wear a star sapphire, a cora'stone."

Elsa was grim. "I, too, have heard this but have been unable to verify it given my position within the Shaluay these days."

"It's true!" Cassi huddled in the corner of the couch. "Da witches took 'em!"

Elsa grimaced. "That is what the Lower City is calling us. Evyn has told me of graffiti appearing on the walls around the Well. Harad has it removed, but there are many people in the city talking of it."

"Harad?" Iana went still. "Why is Harad in the Complex?"

"He was posted there when he failed to attain the rank of Firstbinder," Elsa said primly."As you would know had you been at Arleth'taur. Harad is a Senior Binder now, and I believe the Starmaster felt this posting would be a... consolation prize, I suppose, when Maron passed."

Iana got up and walked to the window."I did not know."

Elsa snorted."I know the Estay Matrix is important, but we need you back in the Cradle. I fear –" She stopped, pressing her lips together.

"Tell me," Iana said, turning back to her.

"This is business of the Collective, and it has been a long time since I sat at its table," Elsa straightened."Very well. I believe what Cassi has said is true. Harad is in league with the gang lord Phaelon, and the orphanages we ran are either abandoned or have been turned into a flesh market."

Iana's face was stone.

"I don't understand," Sim said."You're talking about slavery? That's what Cassi said about this Phaelon. But isn't slavery illegal?"

"The old laws strictly forbid it," Elsa said,"but you will find it in many places and under many guises. Phaelon is a murderer and a bully who has risen to prominence since the Eight removed the Ninth Lord. He does not understand the subtleties of the throne he has claimed, so he hacks and slashes. Slavery is something he understands, barely, and he has the means to participate in it."

"Throne? He's a king?" Sim sat up straight.

"Serjat doesn't have kings," Darien said.

"Not like others, no," Elsa agreed. "But the Eight rule just as completely in their way."

"So," Iana's voice was thoughtful."Harad is working with Phaelon?"

"No," Elsa said, her face tight."Phaelon *thinks* he's working with Harad."

"What have you seen?" Iana's question was more command.

"And what would you do about what I have seen?" the old woman snapped. "You have removed yourself from Arleth'taur while you seek the relics. You are not there; you do not see the Starmaster as she ages, and other factions take what power from her they can –"

"I have been away for some time; it is true." Iana's tone was unrelenting. "But I have studied the Shal'ashay and know the Sequences; the reigniting of the Wells is our greatest priority and has been since the Sundering. The turning of the Age approaches. As a Firstbinder of the Order, I hold your oath, and you *will* obey me."

Darien glanced at Sevaani. What was she getting herself into joining the Shaluay?

Elsa slid off the couch to her knees and bowed to Iana. "Mistress."

Iana relaxed her pose and moved forward, helping the older woman back to her seat. "I must know, Elsa," she said gently and sat opposite the seer.

"I have no proof," Elsa said. "But I believe Harad's cora'stone has cracked."

Iana didn't move. "Because he breaks the tenets?"

"Amongst other things." Elsa took a breath. "Twenty years ago, when Phaelon's interests became more widely known, Harad went to the Undercity to try and stop him."

"By himself?"

"No." Elsa cocked her head. "No, there was a party of Cythis Knights here, Knights of the Flame. And... and a priest of a Shol'mas Lord."

Iana's face was as cold as the diamonds in her hair. "What were they doing here?"

"I do not know," Elsa said. "It was said at the time they wished to arrange to see the Starmaster, to heal the breach."

"Only the Paladine could instigate such a thing," Iana said, her eyes narrowing. "And the priest? Which Shol'mas?"

"Kirana," Elsa said.

"The Lady of Flame," Iana said.

"The Knights of Cythis don't follow the Shol'mas," Kaiel protested. Darien looked over at his brother. "They follow the Elder Gods if any at all."

"And what is between the Shaluay and the Knights?" Darien asked.

Iana looked at them as though she'd forgotten they were in the room.

"A long and unpleasant history," Iana said. "Go on, Elsa."

"When he returned from the Undercity," Elsa continued, "so did the priest but without the knights. And Harad... was different. I called on the Second Senior at the time, but she refused to see me. I have tried to find Harad's Signature amongst the Swarm, but there is a darkening at its heart here in Serjat, and I feared to approach it."

"I have felt it too, but there are no active Wells to bind the Swarm, so it cannot be delved. And I have no time now." Iana moved to the hearth.

"You are not staying." Elsa sighed with resignation.

"I cannot." Iana shook her head. "It is now more important than ever that the Estay Matrix be restored."

"And after three thousand years, have you narrowed down its location? Surely a Firstbinder should be here to deal with this?"

"And risk my own stone? You know I cannot. Until I have returned the Matrix to Arleth'taur, the Starmaster is vulnerable, and we are unable to compel more than one oath at a time. If what you have said is right, then I fear Harad's tainted stone has spread." She walked back to the couch and took Elsa's hand. "You must stay isolated from the rest."

The old woman laughed. "Easily done. Harad dismissed me from active participation himself."

"You will take Cassi with you." Iana went to the table and picked up a small chest bound in silver and gold, which she'd brought back that afternoon. "Teach her the rudiments, and if she is suitable, you have my permission to Initiate."

"Initiate? Outside of Arleth'taur?" Shock coloured Elsa's voice.

"It is necessary," Iana said. "What you need is in here." She brought the chest over. "Including an unbound cora'stone. Guard it well."

"And what Setting does she take?" Elsa's hands fluttered atop the chest.

Iana smiled at the girl who was watching the exchange suspiciously. "Cassi is a fighter," the Starbinder said at last. "She may suit the Wardens."

The girl peered at her suspiciously.

"Cassi." Iana sat on the girl's other side. "Elsa will give you shelter, and she will train you in what you need to know, to help us find your friends."

"Ya never said..." Cassi began then bit her lip.

"Said what?" Iana prompted.

"'Ow much I'll be paid." Cassi folded her arms across her chest.

Iana gave a faint smile. "You will receive an allowance, food, a safe bed, and an education."

"Why?" Cassi demanded.

"Because the Shaluay owe you, and your friends," Iana said, the glint in her eyes hardening. "And I intend to see the debt repaid."

Darien gazed again at the Crystal Spire, blinking as the rising sun was reflected off its walls. Today he would stand in the presence of Ciralys masters and take the Test of Attunement. His name would finally be entered into the *Book of Disciples*, and he would never again be subject to the rule of anyone but the Conclave, and the Scion of Isoliere.

His brother traipsed into the room, laughing as he returned from the practice the Blay Shon was putting him through in the courtyard. Again.

"Dar." Kaiel came over and thumped him on the shoulder. "Have you eaten?"

"No, he hasn't," Meg said from the table in the middle of the sitting room. Simeon, Sevaani and Captain Daynar were seated with her.

"I'm not hungry," Darien said. And he wasn't. Cheese and fruit – oranges and grapefruits, mandarins, and avocados – had been generously piled on a silver platter, along with bread and jars of honey and jam. Just looking at the food made him queasy.

"Leave him alone," Sim said through a mouthful of food. "He has his underclothes in a knot about the Ciralys."

"Don't worry, Dar." Kaiel squeezed his shoulder. "I'll be speaking to the Captain of the Tal'desai when we get there."

"Are you sure you want to do that, Kaiel?" Jaric asked.

His brother nodded. "I have to, sir; I'm not going to leave Dar alone."

"I'll hardly be alone," Darien sighed.

"See? He won't be alone," Sim said, stuffing even more bread laden with jam into his mouth. "And besides, Meg will be staying with him." He raised an eyebrow. "Will they let you share a room?"

Meg glared at Sim, but before she could retort, Iana joined them. Darien blinked. She was dressed in a gown of violet damask with the same black, constellation-embroidered panels as on her grey gown. It was cinched at the waist by a silver cord that sparkled with diamonds, echoing the pins that flared around her head. At her neck sat the cora'stone in its strange torque.

Her eyes flickered to Kaiel, "You'll need to finish getting ready, Kaiel," she told him. "We will be leaving shortly. I've hired a coach to take us to the Spire."

Kaiel nodded. "Almost done."

"You don't all have to come," Darien said as his brother left the room.

"Are you prepared to say your farewells now?" she asked him, her violet eyes knowing.

Darien opened his mouth. He choked as his throat went dry and turned it into a cough.

"So, this is goodbye?" Sim said.

Meg looked around the table. "It is, isn't it?"

"Then, I suppose I should mention that I'm not going back to Hanore, either." Sim brushed his hands off on a linen napkin.

"And where will you be going?" Jaric asked, dark brows raised above blue eyes.

"I'm not sure; I figure I'll find some work here. I'd like to take a closer look at the Palace of Merchants, that's for sure."

The captain frowned. "You'd leave your parents? With no word to them that you're alive and safe?"

"Well, you can take word back for me, can't you?" Sim protested.

"I..." The man clenched his jaw. "I'm not going back to Hanore either."

"What?" Sevaani's mouth dropped open.

"Oh, I see." Sim crossed his arms over his chest. "It's all right for you, the Captain of the Rangers no less, to abandon the citadel, but I can't choose my own path?"

"But you *have* to go back, Captain," Sevaani said, ignoring Sim. "Who will command the Rangers? We –" She broke off with a stricken expression then shook her head. "*They* need you."

"There are any number of Rangers who can take over," Jaric told them. "I don't want to go, but I have to find out what is happening in Sithapia."

"Who cares about Sithapia?" Sim said.

"So, Iana was right?" Meg asked, watching him closely. "You *are* from Sithapia."

"Yes," Jaric said. "And I need to go back. Once I've found the princess."

"You know a princess?" Kaiel said, returning to the room.

Jaric pressed his lips tight before he spoke. "I was a Knight of the Gold Rose," he said. "I know Princess Andraste."

"Oh, come on," Sim groaned. "You know we don't have any idea what a Knight of the Gold Rose is!"

Jaric sighed and walked to the window overlooking the city square, gazing out.

The Starbinder eyed Jaric expectantly, but when he made no move to answer, she said, "The Knights of the Gold Rose are Sithapia's royal guardsmen."

"I knew it!" Sim said.

"Knew what?" Kaiel asked Sim.

Darien inspected Kaiel as his brother made his way back into the sitting room, tugging at the high-collared coat Lady Iana had provided. Kaiel's coat was identical to Darien's, but for the colouring. Both were embroidered at the cuffs and hemmed with a fox chasing a crescent moon, but where Darien's was black wool with silver thread, Kaiel's was honey-brown wool with bronze thread. They also had matching silk shirts, trousers and knee-high boots. The clothes must have been expensive – he'd never worn silk in his life – but he was in no position to refuse them. And the Starbinder had provided Kaiel with a sword, allowing him to retire the axe he'd been using.

"I always suspected the captain was one of Niskeri's Asps," Sim said. "I might have been wrong about that, but he *is* a knight of an elite order."

"You thought I was a Knight of the Asp?" Jaric turned from the window, incredulous. "Did you pay no attention to the personal guards of Prince Alesandr?"

Kaiel looked between the two of them, confusion written plainly on his face. "I still don't understand,"

Sim ignored Kaiel, gesturing at the captain. "You can move pretty quietly when you want to. Always jumping out of the shadows when you least expect it."

"Bah." Jaric waved his hand and returned to staring out the window. "If you paid more attention to..." He stopped. "Darien. How long has that man been watching the inn?"

"What man?" Darien suppressed a sigh; he just wanted to go to the Spire.

"That man, down by the lamppost. How long has he been there?" The captain didn't point; he didn't need to.

"I don't know." Darien frowned, there was something strange about the man. "I'm sure he wasn't there before."

The man was dressed in black, and though the sun was high enough to light the enormous square below, his face somehow shadowed. In the corners of his mind, Darien felt the csitargon stir.

There was a commotion outside the door to the suite, and blood-curdling screams rose from the floor below.

Lihon, who had been in the other room, was suddenly in the doorway with both jisanas drawn.

"Everybody get back from the door," Iana said, standing as Sevaani and Meg got up from their chairs looking confused.

"What is it?" Sim asked. "What's happening."

"Daemons," the Blay Shon said, his silver eyes glittering. "Get back."

As the blademaster spoke Darien felt the hairs on the back of his neck prickle, and he turned just as the door to their suite exploded inwards, and sharp splinters rained into the room like a hail of tiny arrows.

In the open doorway stood a creature from nightmares.

Horns sprouted from a ridged cranium and its massive body only just fit in the confined space of the stairwell. Dark red skin covered a heavily muscled frame, and long arms ended in clawed hands that matched its clawed feet. Unlike the daemon in Glass Bay, this creature wore an intricate harness that attached pauldrons to squares of plate mail that covered its chest, running down to the leather guards over its massive thighs. In its hand, a curved blade with a jagged edge gleamed.

It opened its mouth and roared, swinging its sword.

There was a silver flash, and the scent of burning hair filled the air as the sword smashed against a translucent shield.

Darien flinched. Iana stood in front of the breakfast table, wrists held up and crossed before her. She had pulled back the sleeves of her gown to reveal black bracers, white runes glowing across their surface.

Lihon stalked forward, matched blades held lengthways before him. At an unseen signal, the Shaluay dropped her arms, and the shield winked out.

Lihon dove into the gap, swords spinning. The clanging of steel filled the room.

Darien moved back, and Sevaani helped Sim up from where he'd crashed through a small table to the ground. Kaiel unsheathed his sword and stepped forward.

Darien could hear shouts coming from the floor below and two smaller, scaled bodies pushed into the room on either side of the larger daemon. A jabbering filled the air, the daemons yipping and growling, a hair-raising counterpart to the clash of steel. Inhuman grunts rose from the massive creature as Lihon's swords sliced past its defensive parries, separating scales from flesh.

The smaller daemons flanked the larger one. They wore no armour, red scales shimmering in the light. Crouching beside their brethren, gibbering and screeching, they raised small crossbows on spindly arms and took aim.

"Get down!" Iana called. She swept a hand at their attackers. From the rings on her fingers, blazing beads of light shot across the room to strike the daemons. They squealed but did not fall back.

"Help me!" Meg called over her shoulder to Darien. She was trying to drag the couch around to act as a barrier, as Jaric and Kaiel tried to edge around the raging daemon and the whirling blades of the Blay Shon.

Darien lurched forward, grabbing the arm of the couch and heaving it over.

"Lihon, move back!" Jaric called as he jumped to avoid one of the blades. The Blay Shon gave no acknowledgement but neatly stepped away from the door, drawing the daemon with him, its long tail lashing the air. Jaric and Kaiel rushed the smaller daemons who pointed their crossbows toward Darien and the others. The black bolts flew across the room, but the shots had been taken with more haste than care and embedded themselves into the back of the couch.

His brother swung his sword at the smaller daemon on the right. Between its horns, a frilled crest flared as it hissed. Kaiel's blade hummed like a wasp and shattered the crossbow the daemon held. The tip of the sword dragged along the chest of the creature, a thin trail of blood appearing in its wake. The daemon's scream pierced the air, and its larger kin stumbled, opening its side to Lihon's swords.

Darien's eyes were drawn to the Blay Shon as he moved in circles around the daemon. His blades gleamed in the light, singing as they slashed through the air. The daemon matched the dance of the blademaster, his two-handed sword catching the jisanas along its length. Its greater strength pushed the blademasters' swords back, and Lihon followed the circular motion through, spinning away and exposing his back to the creature, which roared. But Lihon continued moving, pirouetting, his blades whirling. Without warning, the daemon's jagged-edged sword went flying across the room, slicing the back off a chair as an axe might split a block of wood.

The daemon screamed in rage.

Still moving within his circles, Lihon followed the turn of his blades and, in a whirlwind motion, brought them around again and took the creature's head from its neck.

At the death of the larger daemon, the smaller two dropped the pretence of their humanoid forms falling to all fours and lunging at their attackers like dogs.

Kaiel thrust his sword at one of the daemondogs, piercing its neck. He fell forward, pulled off balance, and barely turned aside in time to avoid the snapping jaws of the creature. As Kaiel recovered his footing, Jaric and Lihon finished the other.

"Get the bags!" Iana shouted as she knelt over Sim. Lihon stepped over the carcass of the dead daemon and dashed down the stairs.

Darien followed Meg, stumbling over the broken chair and giving the sizeable sword of the daemon a wide berth.

"The man watching the inn is gone!" Jaric said, back at the window.

"You believe he was involved?" Iana asked.

"I don't know," Jaric said, frustration darkening his tone. "Look!"

Screams rose from the street below.

Darien was passing the bags to Meg when the window to the bedroom shattered, and a creature of dark scales and leathery wings flew inside.

He stumbled back and threw the bag in his hands at the daemon, terror washing over him. Ebony claws slashed, tearing the pack apart. The daemon straightened, midnight wings folding behind its back like a shadow, and Darien stared. It was the man who'd been standing beneath the lamppost in the street.

"Dar!" Kaiel called from the other room, but he couldn't move. The daemon's eyes were whirling pools of twisted amethyst, glittering brightly against the void-like black of its scales.

"The Shard." Its mouth didn't move, but the voice was clear in Darien's mind. It stretched out a clawed hand, palm up, talons cutting the air. *"Give it to me."*

Of its own volition, Darien's hand moved to the pouch at his waist. He tried to scream but had no control over his own body.

Just as his fingers curled around the crystal shard his master had given him, a silver blur past in front of him, and the daemon's hand dropped to the floor.

Kaiel jumped in front of Darien as the daemon let out an ululating cry of pain, its wings snapping out behind it.

"Don't look at its eyes!" Iana warned from the doorway.

The daemon cried out again, and Darien staggered as Kaiel thrust his sword at it, scoring it across the arm. Kaiel ducked as a wing snapped forward, whistling through the air.

Darien scrambled back as his brother twisted his blade, bringing it up under the retreating wing and sinking it into the daemon's torso.

With an eardrum-bursting screech, the daemon exploded into pieces of fluttering darkness that flocked together and flew out the shattered window.

"What in the Void was *that*?" Sim said weakly from the doorway.

"Are you hurt, Darien?" Meg put her hand on his shoulder.

He shook his head, unable to speak.

"You just dispersed a Vak'nar," Iana said to Kaiel, eyes narrowed. "How did you do that? What did you *do*?"

"I don't –" Kaiel blinked as though coming back to himself. "What happened?"

The Shaluay's eyes moved to Kaiel's right hand as he rubbed the back of it with his left. Darien had to bite the inside of his cheek not to rub his own scar, thankful that both their marks were still hidden. Though Shany's ointment would not last much longer.

Lihon returned to the rooms. "There are dead maids and serving boys up and down the stairs, and that screaming is calling the Middle Guard to the inn as we speak. We must go now unless you want to be dragged before the Courts of Law."

"We can't go anywhere," Sevaani protested, white-faced. "We have to help the innkeeper."

"We go now," Iana snapped. She turned to Lihon. "Is the carriage in the courtyard?"

"Yes, but the boy was terrified. He ran when he saw me with my swords."

"But where are we going?" Sim asked.

"Where we had planned," Iana said. "Darien and Meg still have appointments with the Ciralys."

CHAPTER TWENTY-SIX

A Fork in the Road

MEG FOLLOWED THE others as they fled the inn and spilled into the courtyard at its rear, her heart pounding. Ahead of her, Captain Daynar cursed. The carriage was gone.

The buildings that lined the laneway kept the courtyard in shadow, and she pulled the thick cloak Iana had provided tight around her shoulders. Her stomach roiled from the carnage she'd seen as they left the inn and she took deep breaths of the cold morning air, trying to calm her nerves.

"Keep moving," the Starbinder said. Meg stared at her. What about all people inside, the guests and servants, people she had known – well at least the innkeeper and his wife – all dead.

"Nothing can be done for them now, girl," Iana said sharply. Meg gave a start. Had she been speaking out loud? But no, Iana was looking at Sevaani, who was pale-faced and shaking.

"No!" Iana raised her hand as Sevaani opened her mouth. "There is no time for this." The Shaluay stalked out of the courtyard's open gate. Sevaani looked stricken, and Meg put her hand on her arm, but Sevaani said nothing and followed Iana.

Well, Meg pursed her lips. *At least she's not screaming.*

The southern end of the alley that ran alongside the Cockatrice opened out onto Falcon Road. The sounds of the city echoed faintly down the corridor between the buildings. Iana led them in the opposite direction, and the street they came out on was quiet in comparison; people walked its footpaths oblivious to the commotion in the square, the screaming too far away to raise alarm. But if she stopped for even a second… the blood in the stairway flashed across her mind's eye, and the screeching call of the daemons filled her ears.

Meg pushed the image away with effort.

"Where are we going now?" Sim asked. "Shouldn't we find the guards?"

"Don't you prefer to avoid the guards?" Meg said, grateful for the distraction.

He scowled. "Not when someone's trying to kill me, I don't."

"We do *not* want to talk to the Middle Guard." Iana scanned the street. "We are going to the Spire."

"Why don't we want to talk to the Guard?" Sim said. "I'm the last one to want to call the attention of any sort of authority, but daemons in the city is something they should know about."

"The Guard will detain us," Iana said, irritation lining her voice.

"But what about those people?" Sevaani's voice wavered. "Don't you care what happened to them?"

"I care more than you know!" Iana turned, violet skirts whirling. "But there is *nothing* I can do for them now." Then she was striding down the street ahead of them.

"But wouldn't the Guard help?" Sevaani asked the others.

"Cities are different," Jaric told Sim. "The Guard are here to help citizens and keep the peace. But when it comes to daemons?" His face was hard. "You go to the Guard with word of daemons when an entire inn has been slaughtered – a slaughter you managed to survive – and they'll start looking for a Summoner amongst you. They'll lock us up faster than you can finish speaking."

"They wouldn't believe us?" Sim said.

"Would *you* believe it?" Jaric looked at him pointedly.

"No." Then with a shrug, he said, "Come on. Lihon has a carriage."

"That's not a carriage," Meg said, frowning at the covered wagon.

"The driver has finished his morning run, and is willing to take us to the Spire," Iana told them. "We should avoid being seen on the streets, and this will be much faster than walking."

"What is that smell?" Sevaani said as she climbed into the shadowed interior. "What was he carrying in this thing?"

"Milk," Sim said. Meg wrinkled her nose at the sour odour. "Be grateful it's not summer."

The wagon began to move as soon as Lihon jumped in. The inside was gloomy, but not dark, the light of the morning sun brightening the plain linen stretched over the arching ribs that formed the roof and walls.

Meg leaned back against a wooden rib and closed her eyes. The rocking of the wagon was almost as bad as that of the *Crow*. She pushed the swell of nausea aside, unsure if it was from the motion, the attack, or what she planned to do when they arrived at the Spire. She wanted to take a deep breath, but the smell inside the wagon was cloying.

Sevaani slid beside her. "Are you well?" she whispered.

Meg nodded, offering Sevaani a smile, and praying to whatever god was listening that she'd leave it at that. She patted her shoulder bag. "I have the *tresilian* Shany gave me."

"Will it be enough?"

"She believed so." Meg bit her lip. "And I have to believe so as well. All I need to do is find a Ciralys from the Fifth Circle and claim Hedge Right."

"Are you sure?" Sevaani persisted. "How does Shany know these things? The Keeper has never left the Borderlands, has she?"

Meg glanced at Darien, who had his eyes closed as though he was meditating. "I don't know," she said. "But I'm doing this."

Sevaani gripped her hand."At least stay with us. Lady Iana can surely get you presented as well as Darien."

Meg felt her eyes widen and panic gripped her. "Please," she whispered, eyeing the others."I know what I have to do. I don't want another argument about it. It's better if I just slip away and follow Shany's instructions once we are all inside. Please don't say anything."

"I won't." Sevaani's smile was sad, and Meg choked back an unexpected welling at the back of her throat.

"Why shouldn't you look for a different life outside the Borderlands? Darien isn't the only one in Hanore who has talent. Just…" Sevaani paused, her eyes roaming towards Kaiel. She took a breath and suddenly she was gazing intently into Meg's eyes. Sevaani squeezed her hand again."Be sure what you are doing is for yourself."

"I am." Meg had to push the words past a tight throat. After a moment, Sevaani nodded.

Meg took a deep breath and cursed as she almost retched. Retrieving her hand, she wiped her eyes with the back of her palm and closed them again.

Breathing through her mouth only, she tried to focus on the rumbling of the wagon's wheels over the cobblestones of the street.

She let the rhythm of the wagon lull her.

Meg opened her eyes as the wagon came to a stop.

Why were they stopping? The stiffness of her neck told her she had dozed off.

Sim had untied a leather cord holding a linen panel in place and was peering outside."I think we're here,"he said.

Meg swallowed and tried to clear the fog of drowsiness from her mind.

Lihon exited the wagon, and Captain Daynar followed. Sim made to join them, but Iana stopped him with a raised hand.

"Let Lihon check it is safe," she said, and Sim sat back with an impatient sigh.

The Blay Shon pulled aside the cloth door a moment later. Iana nodded, letting Sim jump past her, out onto the sunlit boulevard.

Meg climbed out behind Sevaani, shielding her eyes with her palm. The sun was higher in the sky, and she judged that it was no more than an hour from noon.

Behind the wagon, the street stretched east, lined with old trees set before richly appointed shopfronts, and beside it stretched a tall wall of gleaming white everstone. The great blocks used to construct it merged seamlessly; neither age nor weather had marked them, and as clean as if they had just been laid. Meg stared. She had never seen so much everstone in one place.

"This way," Jaric said. She turned around, her throat dry.

At the end of the road, men and women in varying colours and styles of clothing were milling about a pair of enormous gates. Guards armoured in white enamelled steel stood at either side, while others herded the crowd into lines. They all wore intricately crafted armour. She could see stylized etchings around the eye slits of the helms along with the opening that revealed the wearer's nose, mouth, and chin.

No. Not enamelled steel. That was white kharidium.

"Who are they?" she breathed, realising she was looking at more wealth than she'd ever imagined back in the Borderlands.

"The Tal'desai," Lihon said, coming around behind them. "The personal guards of the Ciralys."

Iana walked up to one of the guards whose silver-etched helm had a white horse's tail hanging from it.

"Captain," she began but was interrupted by a balding man of dark skin and middling years.

"Lady," he barked, stepping out from his place by the gates. Meg blinked, shocked at the man's tone. He was dressed in grey robes with a white mantle over his shoulders, clasped together by a Khaderneous medallion, its skystone white like a luminescent pearl. "The line starts down the street."

"Ciralys," Iana said, nodding. "I need to speak with the Scion."

"Of course you do." Sharp, brown eyes roamed over Iana, and then took the rest of them in. "Everyone behind you would say the very same thing. You will have to wait your turn."

Iana didn't even glance at the queue, and Meg smiled. The Starbinder could give Shany a run for her coin.

"I believe you will find that the Scion has time for me," she said. Reaching her hands up, Iana shifted her cloak to reveal the torque and cora'stone at her neck.

The Ciralys raised an eyebrow. "A star sapphire will not speed you past the other petitioners!"

He reached to seize the cora'stone, and a spark of violet light leapt from the stone to his hand. The Ciralys fell to the ground with a shriek of pain and Tal'desai instantly surrounded the group, halberds lowered.

"Don't point that thing at me," Sim said. "I didn't do anything."

Lihon's blades were in his hands, and he stepped up beside Iana as Jaric pulled Simeon back.

"Hold!" The shout was loud. Even the petitioners in line behind them fell silent.

It was the Tal'desai with the silver-etched armour and horsetail. He flicked a hand at one of the guards, who bent to help the gasping Ciralys.

"We have no quarrel with the Blay Shon," the man said.

"Nor I with you," Lihon replied. "But you hold arms against my Lady."

"You follow the..." His eyes swept over Iana and darted to the Ciralys. "The *Lady*?"

"I do." Lihon nodded.

Meg clenched her hands, her fingernails biting into her palms as the guard captain stared hard at the blademaster.

"Stand down, Captain." The Ciralys was red-faced and wheezing. He brushed his robes down over his legs as he got to his feet and offered a stiff half bow to Iana. "My apologies... err, Sister," he said, sounding as though he was being strangled. "The embassy from the Star Cradle was not expected to arrive like... that is –"

"An embassy from Arleth'taur is expected?" Iana's face was neutral, but Meg caught something in her tone.

"You are not from the embassy?" the Ciralys asked, his surprise evident.

Iana pursed her lips. "We are not." She turned to Lihon and Jaric, lowering her voice. "I hadn't planned on seeing any of my sisters, but we must proceed. I can only hope Lorelia is not the ambassador." Addressing the Ciralys once more, she said, "I am Iana Sabay."

The Ciralys bowed his head. "Josin Schumar, of the Fifth Circle. Welcome to the Spire, Lady Iana. The embassy from the Arleth'taur is due shortly, do you wish to wait for your sisters?"

"No," Iana said. "This is not business that directly involves the Shaluay. There is no need to wait for the embassy."

Ciralys Josin considered this for a moment. "Very well. Please." He gestured to the gate, "I will escort you to the Hall of Voices."

"Ciralys, the Blay Shon," the captain said. The Tal'desai had lowered their spears, though they still eyed Lihon.

"What about him?" the Ciralys snapped.

"I cannot allow him to enter the Spire while armed with jisanas."

"*You* cannot allow? You forget your place, Captain!"

"My place is that of Holder of the Gate. By that right, none may pass my station who could harm the Ciralys, and a Blay Shon –" he nodded to Lihon, who returned it with barest of acknowledgements, "could harm many before the Tal'desai could neutralise him."

Ciralys Josin eyed the twin blades in Lihon's hands. "My Lady, is the Blay Shon your protector?"

"Lihon is a friend." She put her hand on his arm. "But yes. He is currently in my employ." At her motion, Lihon sheathed his swords.

"A Starbinder is entitled to have a guard, as is the representative of any great House or Dynasty," Ciralys Josin said. "Captain, open the gate."

"And the others?" Iana asked. "Do my companions have to give up their swords also?"

"They are not Blay Shon, my lady," the captain said. He gave a slight bow, and the white stone panels of the gate swung inwards.

A commotion arose from the crowd and more Tal'desai, impassive behind their white helms, formed a line to keep them back.

"Gods," Sim said.

Seeing the Spire from a distance did little to prepare Meg for seeing it up close. She craned her neck to spy its summit.

"You stand before one of the wonders of the world," Iana said.

"I've never seen anything..." Sim began. "I mean, I never imagined..."

"It is magnificent," Iana agreed, gazing at the Spire. "And never quite what you expect."

Clear quartz walls rose from the ground without break or ornamentation. At its base, facing the drive, a platform of broad everstone steps led up to a perfect circle cut into the crystal wall. Its size was overwhelming, and Meg almost missed a step as they made their way towards it.

She glanced at Darien, who was staring straight ahead, his hands clenched at his side. Not quite as calm as he'd like them all to believe.

She smiled.

To the left were a collection of buildings, the columned palisades of white marble, rather than everstone, were the only indication the Summoners had not constructed them. No, she corrected herself – the Sahrin. The Ciralys never refer to the Sahrin as Summoners. She'd have to get used to that.

"What are those buildings?" she asked.

"They are the barracks of the Tal'desai," Iana said.

"They don't live in the tower, um…" Kaiel gestured ahead of them. "The Spire?"

"The Tal'desai do *not* live in the Spire," Ciralys Josin agreed, arching an eyebrow in distaste as he glanced over his shoulder.

Sevaani grabbed her arm. "Look at the gardens!"

On the opposite side of the drive was a display of ponds and streams twisting between evergreens and grey-barked trees with amethyst leaves. Flowers bloomed in beds and twisted up around columns, while brightly feathered birds sang and darted between statues that peeked out behind foliage or stood on display in the middle of pools.

"Oh, yes, lovely," Sim grumbled acidly. "Void take me, no-one would believe we were almost killed less than an hour ago."

"Shh!" Sevaani hissed.

Lihon dropped back to walk beside Sim. "A time and a place, Ravenson," the blademaster said quietly.

"What?" Sim said. Meg recognised the innocent tone he adopted from his time working behind the counter at his father's store.

"Learn when to hold your tongue, or you may find you don't live long enough to build the fortune you seek," Lihon said without looking at Sim at all.

"Believe me; he knows exactly what he's saying," Meg said as they began up the marble steps. "Sim's always been one to stir the pot. And the more nervous he is, the more his tongue runs away with him."

"Then, caution is a worthy lesson to learn."

Sim scowled but didn't say another word.

Reaching the platform, they made their way through pockets of people gathered in groups of two or more. On either side of the grand circular entrance, twin statues of the guardians of Vasharviel, the Elder God of Air, floated in pillars of blue light. Each crafted into the shape of a man, both statues lifted great swords to the sky, framed by wings extending up from their backs. Across the eyes of each stretched a blindfold so intricately worked that it looked to Meg like real cloth. She and the others slowed at the sight, but Ciralys Josin spared neither statue a glance and led them into a cavernous entry hall.

Meg braced herself as they passed from sunlight to the more subdued light of the interior, expecting *something* as she entered one of the greatest seats of learning in the world. But she felt nothing.

Inside the Spire, the walls rose smoothly in straight lines, defying the angled outer walls. Stationed around the entrance hall were pairs of Tal'desai standing back to back, still as stone. Men and women in different coloured robes and mantles, all sporting Khaderneous' medallions, stood alone or in clusters, addressing petitioners, while young men and women in servants' uniforms moved about the hall.

"Look at that!" Sim said, pointing at the floor.

A mosaic of the Khaderneous – crafted in silver and gold tiles – stretched beneath their feet, its entwined serpents wrapped around a black stone centre.

"Is that real gold?" Sim whispered from the corner of his mouth.

"Keep your hands away from it," Darien hissed. "Or I swear, by the Eye of Eternity, I will gut you!"

"Ease up, Dar," Kaiel said, placing a hand on his brother's shoulder.

"I was just asking," Sim said with a grin.

Meg opened her mouth to reply, but the words died on her tongue. She didn't have time for Sim and his stirring.

Shany had said to find the Spirit Seer. But who was the Spirit Seer, and where did she find him or her? She couldn't ask Ciralys Josin. That would draw everyone's attention. There were doorways on either side of the long hall, free of people, but where did they lead?

The further they walked, the closer they came to a pair of golden doors at the end of the hall.

She slowed her steps, falling back, her heart pounding.

If she didn't do this now, it was back to Hanore she'd go. Or join the Shaluay, and there was something about that she liked even less.

Ciralys Josin had paused before the doors and was speaking to another Ciralys whose mantle was also white. The Ciralys eyed Iana, then opened the doors and disappeared inside. Ciralys Josin motioned them all forward.

Meg edged back into the crowd as the others went through the doorway. Her heart was drumming in her ears.

Just as they all passed through the doors, Iana looked back. Meg caught her breath. But the Starbinder only offered her a small smile. The Lady turned away without drawing any attention to the fact that Meg was no longer with them.

The tall, golden doors swung shut, and the Tal'desai crossed their halberds before it, barring the way to those left outside.

CHAPTER TWENTY-SEVEN

The Disciples of the Spheres

THE CRYSTALLINE WALLS of the Hall of Voices soared around them, glowing with a soft inner light. Evenly spaced pillars of coloured everstone – yellow, green, red, white and blue – edged the room, supporting a ceiling that somehow showed open sky.

Darien had to force himself to keep walking.

The Hall was filled with robed men and women in mantles identifying the Circle they belonged to – the element in which their gift was strongest. They stood arranged on tiers that cascaded down the sloping floor of the room like giant steps, descending to a centre dais where a woman dressed in white faced seven Masters, one of whom was dressed in robes of silver, sitting on the only chair in the room.

He was a slight man with thinning, dark hair swept back off his face. His presence was in no way commanding, but after many nights listening to his own teacher's tales, Darien recognised the crystal circlet holding the Khaderneous on the man's brow. Together with the silver robes and no mantle, he was easy to identify as Karlon Bahlestian, the Light of the Eye, the leader of the Ciralys and Scion of the city-state of Isoliere. Behind him stood another man, clearly not a Ciralys, in scarlet and amber robes that rippled as though aflame. Darien stared then quickly moved his gaze back over the assembled Masters. Panic gripped his chest, and he sucked in a deep breath, a trickle of sweat beading his temple. He was going to be sick.

Traditionally, all applicants to the Ciralys went to the Palace of the Eye in Isoliere to be presented to the Holder of *The Book of Disciples*. And here he was, a Houseless nobody from the Borderlands without even his own master to present him. Who was he to stand before the most powerful man in the Realms and ask for admittance to the Order?

Should I claim House Taaren'th? He firmly put *that* thought aside. He wouldn't falter now. There was nothing to be afraid of but fear itself.

Darien delved inward, searching again. The ward placed by the Master of the Swamp still held. He let out a breath, only to give a start as a hand patted his shoulder.

He half-turned to see Kaiel offering a smile of encouragement, and he nodded back. Regardless of whether Ciralys Telaq was at his side or not, his brother was – something he'd never thought would happen. He was going to be accepted into the ranks of the Aspirants. As long as the ward held.

The Ciralys who had admitted them returned and gestured for them to move onto an empty tier at the back. "Her Royal Highness has the floor," the man said softly to Iana.

"Her Royal Highness?" Jaric said.

Ciralys Josin levelled a disapproving stare upon the captain. "Princess Andraste of Sithapia."

Jaric stood rigid for a moment before melting back behind the others.

"Highness." The voice was loud and came from a Ciralys in bronze coloured robes. His mantle was edged in silver, marking him a master, and he stood at the Scion's right, a position of some authority. "We have spoken to your uncle's emissary. The Regent wishes nothing more than your safe return to Sith'sara."

"Prime Councillor Feraan." The princess had her back to them, but her voice, laced with frustration beneath its cultured tones, was clearly heard and Darien eyed the man with interest. The Prime Councillor led all the Ciralys in the Spire; at least he did when the Scion was not present. "Torimun may claim he is regent, but he is no blood of mine. The man murdered my parents and wants me back in Sith'sara under his control so he can claim the Rose Throne for himself."

A murmur rolled around the gathered Ciralys, and a man dressed in costly silks stepped forward at the bottom of the tiered platforms. "Prime Councillor, that is an outrageous accusation. And utterly without merit." He bowed to the gathered council, then stretched a hand towards the princess. "Your Highness, you accuse your uncle of regicide! You cannot genuinely believe the Regent could be capable of such a vile act. No." He waved his hand through the air in a gesture of denial. "No, it must be the madness of grief –"

"How dare you presume, Tarsec deKahn." The frustration in the princess' voice fled before an icy fury. "Your sycophancy clearly shows where your loyalties lie. You hold your position because of the trust my father, the Ardhel, gave you, and you dare tell his daughter that she is *mad*?"

"Your Highness." Tarsec shook his head. "My only loyalty is to the Rose Throne."

"Your loyalty has ever been to yourself," the princess said.

Darien was impressed. She had dismissed the man without once looking in his direction.

"Scion," Princess Andraste said, nodding at Karlon Bahlestian. "We cannot wait any longer. We *must* have an answer to our petition."

"Highness." The Prime Councillor arched an eyebrow. "You do not speak to one of your subjects here."

The princess drew herself up. "Nor do you speak to one of your Ciralys."

Behind him, Sim snickered. "I like her."

"I have been in this city awaiting a decision on whether or not

Isoliere will assist me for three months, and all the while, my people have been without an Ardhel. It is untenable!"

"Your people have a lawful regent."The bronze-clad Prime Councillor matched her tone for tone."You have been unable to support your claims of foul play. No." He shook his head to ward off her reply. "We have listened to your petition, and we have heard the Regent's response. You have asked us for a ruling, and so you shall have it."

"And that ruling is?"

"It is –" He stopped as the Scion raised a hand. A frown crossed the Prime Councillor's face but was quickly smoothed away. "It is to be presented before the Conclave tomorrow." He finished smoothly.

"I see." The princess bowed her head, though Darien suspected it was not in respect. "Thank you, Eminence." She gave a short bow to the seated Scion and stepped off the dais. Beside her gathered a set of guards, each with a different coloured rose embroidered on a tabard covering glittering mail. The escort took position to either side of the princess, and she made her way up the sloping path to the golden doors, facing them at last.

Raven-dark hair was pulled back by a silver diadem. Her eyes, cold yet compellingly vulnerable, never left the door ahead of her as she made her way past the crowd of watching Ciralys without a second glance.

The Ciralys who had led them into the Hall whispered in Ciralys Josin's ear.

Josin turned to Iana. "The Master of the Records has allowed your petition to be heard, Lady. We will –"

On either side of the aisle, heads turned towards the doors as a large woman in stately red robes struck an ornate staff of jet and gold upon the floor.

"Light of the Eye." She bowed to the Scion. "The Sun holds the day, but behind the light of the Moon, it is the Stars who lead all that are lost in the night. She comes, a Daughter of Eve, the Voice of the Speaker of the Stars. Her Excellency, Shaluay Arais Minashi!"

"By the Void," Simeon hissed. Two Amarians marched into the audience room before an old, blue-skinned woman. Swathed in furs over a black cassock panelled with silver constellations, she leant on the arm of a younger woman.

Darien stared; there was something about the younger woman that was different.

As the party passed, the old woman turned her head, piercing silver eyes pinning Darien where he stood. Her gaze flickered briefly over Iana, and a small smile crossed her lips. She continued down the stairs, flanked by the lean, silk-clad warriors who both wore jisanas on their back.

Darien's eyes met those of the Shaluay's assistant as she passed, and he blinked.

Unlike the other Amarians, her eyes were not silver; they were an ordinary brown. And her skin was a much paler blue, almost mottled, compared to her companions and Lord Lihon's.

He risked a glance at Lihon. The normally impassive blademaster's face was stone-like, his jaw clenched.

The Ambassador's blademasters wore the same black silk jacket and trousers as Lady Iana's companion, but where Lihon's topknot was threaded with amethyst and gold, the newcomer's hair was threaded with jade and copper, between violent slashes of dark red that brought to mind dried blood.

As they passed, one of the Blay Shon, a scar running down the left side of his face through a darkened eye, gave Lihon a measuring stare that made no attempt to hide its hostility.

If they had not been in the Crystal Spire and surrounded by both Ciralys and Tal'desai, Darien might have been concerned. But a glance at Lihon, while not reassuring, convinced him a challenge was not going to be issued.

"Your Excellency," Prime Councillor Feraan said, stepping forward as the Amarian reached the dais of the High Conclave.

"Excellency?" The Starbinder's voice was a rasping whisper the acoustics in the hall made audible to all. "Surely we are like family."

Ciralys Feraan peered over his patrician nose, his pursed lips the only sign of his displeasure. "But of course." He offered a shallow bow. "Welcome, sister."

The Shaluay returned the bow with the help of the woman at her side.

"We were not expecting this honour so soon after you arrived in Serjat," Ciralys Feraan said.

Arais waved a withered hand. "What we have come to witness is at hand," she said. "The Stars have spoken."

The Ciralys masters stirred, but the Prime Councillor of the Spire did not turn. "Will you offer us the wisdom of the Stars, sister?" he asked.

The ambassador chuckled. "Wisdom is earnt, not given, brother," she said. "But if you would leave your palaces and your servants, you would be welcome at Arleth'taur."

The Prime Councillor offered a tight smile. "Perhaps."

Arais gave a slight smile and, clutching the arm of her attendant, shuffled back to her waiting escort.

"Now, my Lady," Ciralys Josin said, and stepped onto the stairs leading down.

Iana motioned for Darien, and he turned, pausing. "Where's Meg?" he asked.

Sevaani stared at him, her blue eyes hard. "She didn't come in with us."

"Come, Darien," Iana said. He hurried down the steps after her.

"Your Grace," Ciralys Josin called. "A Firstbinder of the Shaluay comes before the Conclave this day. I present Iana no'Rylak Sabay!"

Darien's legs trembled as a murmur raced across the assembled

Ciralys. He kept his eyes firmly on the Scion, searching for some reassurance this would be all right.

But the man who sat on the only chair in the hall offered no welcome. His eyes held a cold calculation, and Darien's hand moved to clasp the shard in its pouch at his waist. The man in the silver robes of the Scion of Isoliere did not give the impression of a benevolent ruler. Unimpressive physically, he held about himself an cold air superiority similar to that of the haughty servants in Prince Alesandr's household.

Darien bit the inside of his mouth and took a steadying breath.

He lowered his eyes, focusing on the silvery light of *Asai* at the back of his mind. Taking a deep breath in and out, he raised his head. His eyes fell on the Ciralys Master dressed in forest-green robes; her emerald mantle bordered with silver and clasped together by a Khaderneous of green skystone.

She was the Earth Keeper, identifiable by the colours she wore, head of the First Circle. The woman had a solid presence that belied her slight build, and her startling topaz eyes were locked on Darien.

He blinked. The sheen of *Asai* glittered all around the room, and he quickly turned his mind away from the Light of the Eye. He had not meant to embrace it, but in his distress, *Asai* had flooded him, opening his Sight.

"Welcome, Lady Iana," Prime Councillor Feraan said formally. Darien took a deep breath, closed his mind's eye and chided himself to pay attention. "You do not come with the Embassy?"

"Greetings, Masters." Iana bowed before them. "I do not. I was unaware an Embassy had been sent. Nor indeed that the Scion –" She gave him a half bow in his direction, "would be present when I began my journey here."

"Then perhaps you would like time to meet with Ambassador Arais to avoid any... conflict, in what brings you here?" Feraan asked pointedly.

"That will not be necessary, Prime Councillor," the Shaluay

Ambassador said. "The Speaker of the Stars knows why Firstbinder Iana has come before you. Our purpose does not conflict."

"The stars must indeed be smiling upon you." Feraan's mouth twisted ever so slightly. "What brings you to the Crystal Spire, lady?"

"I was in Glass Bay recently when I came upon a party of Borderlanders seeking passage to Serjat. One of your own was amongst them, and I offered to bring him to you," she said and gestured at Darien.

Darien straightened his shoulders and met the eyes of the man standing behind the Scion. A wave of heat washed over him at the contact, and he struggled to pull his gaze away.

"Really?" Feraan studied Darien. "You found one of ours in a pirate den? The Shaluay may have no compunctions in associating with such outlaws, but the Ciralys do."

"People often find themselves where they need to be." Iana smiled. "The Awakened and his companions would have had a trying time leaving Glass Bay. I do not share those difficulties and simply aided where I could."

Darien swallowed as the Prime Councillors' eyes narrowed at this. "That was gracious of you. Milady."

"It was no bother." Iana's torque glittered at her neck. "Talent is precious, as the Shaluay well know. I am happy to help, given the circumstances."

"I do not recall any Awakened being given leave to visit Exile Point," the Prime Councillor declared.

"I am not an Awakened, Master," Darien said, annoyed at the odd way the Shaluay had introduced him.

"Oh." Iana looked at him. "But your mind's eye has opened, no? I apologise, I suppose he should rightly be called apprentice?"

The Prime Councillor of Serjat studied Darien. The man engaged *Asai*, his aura flaring, as the onlooking Ciralys murmured around them. "Who are you?"

"I –" Darien cleared his throat. "I am Darien Toranth of Hanore, Your Eminence. I am apprentice to Ciralys Telaq, advisor to Prince Alesandr Niskeri, Carbinah of Jaroff."

Feraan glanced at the masters gathered beside him, and the man in the white mantle of the Fifth Circle lifted one shoulder in a shrug.

"I am not familiar with a Ciralys of that name," the Prime Councillor said. "Nor do I recall that we had resumed the archaic practice of taking *apprentices*."

Darien felt the blood drain from his face. Not familiar with the name? How could that be? Briefly he recalled the daemon possessed bone drake claiming Telaq was not part of 'the Outer Circle', but he pushed it aside.

"Do not be so hard on the boy, Feraan," the Master of the First Circle said drawing Darien's attention back to the room. She stepped forward, her voice clear and rich. "It is not unheard of for an exceptionally talented applicant to be taken as an apprentice before they can be brought to Isoliere."

"Perhaps, but it is unheard of for a Ciralys we do not *know* to be appointed an advisor to a prince of Aldania – and to take an unregistered apprentice." The Prime Councillor stared at Darien. "Or am I wrong? Has your Master Telaq indeed sent your name to *The Book of Disciples*?"

"No, Your Eminence," Darien said. "Master Telaq was going to present me himself. He said I am ready for testing. He told me to come here as he –" He swallowed. "As he died."

"*Died*? Before or after you ended up in Exile Point?" Feraan waved his hand as Darien made to answer. "Do you have his Khaderneous to support your claims that this man was indeed a Ciralys?"

Darien opened his mouth.

"Well?" demanded another Master in the blue mantle of the Fourth Circle, Maestrisere, the Sphere of Water.

"No," he said, his cheeks tingling as the blood drained from his face.

They weren't going to accept him. He had come so far, and they weren't going to let him in.

"Test him."The dry whisper came from the man standing behind the Scion.

"What?" Ciralys Feraan looked startled.

"Test him," the man repeated.

Hope welled where a moment ago, a yawning pit of nothing had been ready to engulf him. Behind the seated Scion, the man in the red and orange robes smiled broadly.

"If he has been trained as he says, then let him find his Sphere," the man said.

"This is a matter for the Circles, not a priest of the Shol'mas. We know of no Telaq!" Prime Councillor Feraan snapped. "Whoever has been advising Prince Alesandr is lucky they no longer draw breath, or they would have been facing many questions. As for this one." His brown eyes scored Darien like knives. "We are not in the Chamber of Seeing."

"The Chamber of Seeing is comfortable, and certainly traditional, Feraan," the Earth Keeper offered. "But we can perform the test ourselves."

"Ewynn." Feraan turned to glare at the woman. "You go too far!" The voices around them grew louder.

"Test the boy."

The Hall fell silent.

"Your Grace?" Ciralys Feraan's face was once again impassive, but his eyes tightened in annoyance as he turned to the Scion.

"Test him," the Scion repeated.

"But –"

"If he passes the Ladder of Lights, he will be taken to the Chamber of Seeing, as tradition dictates," the Scion declared.

"Yes, Your Grace." The Prime Councillor bowed. "Mistress Ewynn," he said, his face barely able to contain its mask of neutrality,"as you are so eager, perhaps you can lead the applicant?"

It took Darien all he had to keep from shaking.

The Earth Keeper smiled at Darien in what he supposed was a comforting way, but he could offer her nothing in return.

"We shall need a skystone." Ciralys Ewynn smiled at the Master in yellow robes. The Sky Lord of the Second Circle, Darien guessed, his stomach tight with knots."Master Chelim, if you would be so kind?"

The master moved to the end of the dais without a word. A liveried servant opened a gold-bound chest, and the Sky Lord took a milky stone from it that shone as it caught the light.

Darien's eyes widened. A Skystone. Master Telaq's books said some claimed them to be solidified *Asai*, and they were used in the first Test a Ciralys applicant underwent to find his or her natural Sphere. The stone would then be used to craft the rings of their Khaderneous.

"Raise your right hand," Ciralys Ewynn said to him.

Darien unclenched his fist and presented the Earth Keeper with the unblemished back of his hand. Shany's ointment was still working, though he was sure the cut was healed by now. Ciralys Ewynn took his hand, turning it over. She took the precious stone from the head of the Second Circle and placed it on his palm.

She looked him in the eyes. "Many can see *Asai*, but few have the strength to let it flow through them. This will show us if you have that fortitude." She closed both her hands over Darien's own, wrapping his fingers around the cold stone."And which Sphere you are aligned to.

"Take a breath." She breathed in as he did."And let it out. When you are ready, focus on the stone and reach for *Asai* through it. Do you understand?"

He was not sure he did, but he nodded just the same.

"Good. Your aura is strong." She closed her eyes and breathed in.

Darien could sense the *Asai* she was holding, like the warmth of the summer sun. "Now, reach out to the Eye of Eternity."

Closing his eyes, Darien reached for *Asai* with his mind. But this time, rather than reaching for the Light, he let his mind sink to the stone in his hands. It thrummed in response.

Startled, he almost pulled back, but the Earth Keeper's hands tightened around his own. Instead, he allowed his awareness to fall into the crystalline matrices of the stone. All was still, the noise of the chamber falling away. Suddenly *Asai* filled him, moving through his body with every beat of his heart, escaping from his lungs with every breath.

"Now, let it go," the Ciralys' voice came from far away. "And open your hand."

Darien reluctantly let the light recede from his mind. He slowly opened his fingers to reveal the stone in his grasp.

The Earth Keeper let go of his hands. "Child, I am sorry," she said and let go.

Darien peered at the skystone. No longer a milky white, the stone was now many colours rather than one to indicate his elemental affiliation; red and green, blue and yellow, lined with veins of silver and gold, flashed in the light of the Hall.

"What does it mean?" he asked in a hoarse whisper.

"It means you cannot be trained as a Ciralys," Ciralys Feraan declared.

"I can touch *Asai*," Darien protested weakly as a roaring filling his ears.

"But you do not have a Sphere from which to find your foundation," the Prime Councillor said. "You are a Catalyst. You can hold *Asai*, but you will find it difficult, if not impossible, to direct it. As such, you have value to those masters whose research requires such assistance as your... *gift*... can provide. But if that does not appeal to you, you can choose a ritual Blinding and join the Erlain. That way, you will not be a danger to yourself, or at risk from other, less scrupulous, wielders of *Asai*." He turned to the Scion. "Is that sufficient?"

Darien swayed. The Erlain had once been Ciralys but had burned themselves out. That they resided in Isoliere as servants was deemed a charity, but he could not imagine being around those who could wield *Asai* every day when he could not.

He had to do something. *Anything*. This couldn't be the end!

"It is you who are blind," the Shaluay Ambassador said. "And I have seen enough. For many years you have mocked the Shaluay and Arleth'taur. To you, we are a dying order, and yet you sleep in your own grave." She ignored the outraged murmurings of the gathered Ciralys. "We had hoped that things would be different, but perhaps they truly cannot be changed. The Stars speak true, and the sands cannot be stopped once the glass is turned." She took the arm of the young woman by her side and bowed to Iana. "Choose your path well, sister."

Iana bowed in return, and the Ambassador turned her back on the Scion and the High Council. The voices of the gathered Ciralys rolled around the room as she exited the Hall.

The Prime Councillor's eyes remained on the doors as they closed behind them. "As ever, the Shaluay do little to ingratiate themselves with others."

"Did you expect anything more?" demanded an older woman dismissively. She was dressed in vermillion coloured robes and Darien presumed she was the leader of the Third Circle.

"This morning's audience is over," the Scion spoke, waving his hand as the Shol'mas priest straightened from whispering in his ear.

The gathered Ciralys moved towards the archways around the edges of the room, ignoring the golden doors.

"My Lady Iana." The Scion motioned, and Tal'desai guards moved forward, gathering his friends. "We are most grateful for your charity in bringing one of ours to us."

Iana bowed in acknowledgement.

The Scion's eyes had a strangely reptilian cast to them. "I am interested in hearing more of how you found this young man from the Borderlands in Glass Bay. Please –" He gestured to the masters still on the dais. "While we discuss where best to place our young friend, rooms will be provided for you all."

"Your Grace is most kind," Iana replied, but her eyes were on the priest beside him.

"It is no trouble," the Scion said, his own eyes on Darien. "I am overjoyed that a Catalyst is amongst us once more."

CHAPTER TWENTY-EIGHT

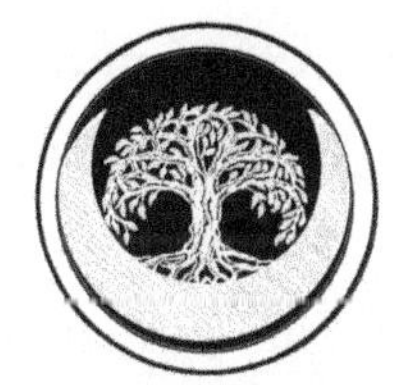

Hedge Right

THE GOLDEN DOORS closed, and Meg considered running forward and begging to be let in. Instead, she closed her eyes and quashed that desire, breathing deeply. The crowd around her was muttering, and Meg opened her eyes, sure everyone in the line was watching her.

She almost sagged with relief to find that no-one was paying her any attention at all. Turning away from the doors, she slipped past the front of the line on shaking legs. Pressing her lips together, she smoothed the embroidered panels of the green dress provided by Lady Iana, using the motion to press down on her thighs and willed her legs to stop trembling. Taking a hesitant step forward, she lifted her head.

There's no time for fear, she told herself, and Shany's laughter echoed in her head. *There is* no *time! Keep walking and pay attention to where you are going.*

She came to a halt as she spied one of the corridors leading off the main hall.

On either side of the archway were statues, almost as large as those floating at the entrance to the Spire. But these guardians were female, *naked* females at that. They stood at attention, their heads, like those at the Shrine of Taluun, were those of a lioness, glowering in watchful menace at anyone who came to their threshold. Above them, at the apex of the archway, was another Seal of the Eye, the serpents twining around an orb of swirling indigo.

She peered down the corridor, only to give a start when her eyes fell on the Tal'desai standing on either side of the doorway. Looking away, she moved further down the enormous hall until she spied an unoccupied bench of plush velvet cushions and sat. Across the hall from the corridor with the two leonine statues was another, framed by winged serpents. She noted the Tal'desai this time but kept her attention on the statuary. The serpents, like the lion women, were carved with stunning artistry and rose from a mass of coils to tower above the doorway, rainbow-feathered wings stretching out from beneath their great diamond-shaped heads. Above them, the Seal of the Eye of Eternity was again stamped into the wall, its rings wrapped around a ruby, glowing red like fire.

Fire.

Meg got to her feet and made her way through the crowd until she came to the next corridor. Ignoring the human guards completely, she stared at the statues on either side of the arch. Winged lions of black marble, bigger than horses, stood regally before her, their golden wings rising high behind their heads, reaching for the sky. Nestled in the Seal above was a giant emerald.

"Earth," she breathed.

That was it.

Each corridor was marked by one of the elements; the Guardians of that Elder God stood before it. But did that mean the halls led to areas of the Spire reserved for the Ciralys of those elements – Spheres?

Behind her, the petitioners muttered again, their voices rising in protest. She looked back to see those at the head of the queue being turned away from the closed door. Why did they all need judgements from the Ciralys? The Ciralys had a reputation of wisdom, but couldn't people sort out their own issues?

She supposed that if they could, Keepers would not be needed so much either.

Focus, Meghara! You'll never get anything done if you stand around 'umming' and 'ahhing' all day, girl!

She took a deep breath. She'd come this far. Had left the others, just as Darien was going to do on the other side of those doors. And if he could do it, so could she!

The line of petitioners ran along the south side of the Spire, leaving the rest of the corridor free for moving foot traffic. Excusing herself once more, she ignored the protests of the people she elbowed her way through and went to find a Ciralys.

Looking around, she had no trouble identifying the men and women who could wield the Light of the Eye. She rolled her eyes at her foolishness. Of course, they'd be easy to find. They *lived* here.

Straightening her spine, she gathered her courage and headed towards a solitary Ciralys in white robes. He was standing with his hands folded in front of him, the Khaderneous medallion on his chest made of simple ceramic, and painted with blue enamel. He appeared for all the world as though he was trying to stay awake.

"Excuse me," she said, approaching him.

The Ciralys did not reply.

She lowered her head, embarrassment colouring her face, then gritted her teeth. She would never act like this in Hanore, and it wasn't the time to start now. Ciralys were just men and women. Meg had been raised amongst folk free of the strictures of the old Clans. She would not be cowed by their trappings now when she'd been around it for little more than a day!

"I'm very sorry to keep you from your nap, but I said, '*excuse me*'." She glared at the young man.

He blinked, and she felt a crawling sensation at the nape of her neck as people stared.

"Yes, *you,*" she said, impatience – and some fear – pushing her on. "I am very sorry to disturb you, but I would like to speak to the Spirit Seer."

The man, a good head taller than her, looked a little dazed. "What?"

"You are a Ciralys, aren't you?" she said, she studied him more closely. He was young. "Maybe you could point me in the direction of someone who could actually *help* me."

"Can *I* help you, young lady?" an imperious voice said from over the young man's shoulder. "Gerun, return to your meditation."

An older, ebon-skinned man with more silver in his hair than black, stepped forward, a Khaderneous with entwined serpents made of pearl-toned skystones on his chest. "I presume you have a good reason for disturbing one of the Awakened?"

"Awakened?" Meg's confidence wilted, but she kept her spine straight as she met the older Ciralys' eyes. The white mantle on his shoulders was bright against the dusty red cassock he wore, and the luminescent, pearl-like Khaderneous flashed in the light.

"Yes," he said, "as indicated by the lack of a mantle around his shoulders."

She took in the young man's plain white robes.

"All petitioners to the Spire are informed that those Ciralys found in the halls without a mantle are not to be disturbed," the older man continued firmly.

Meg swallowed. "I apologise," she said. "I was not made aware of that."

"Really? And who was it that admitted you into the petitioner's queue?" he asked, a bushy white eyebrow rising.

"No-one –"

"No-one?" the second eyebrow rose to join the first. "I cannot believe the Tal'desai allowed you in here without instruction from the Ciralys at the Gates."

"Well no, but he went on with the others through the golden doors." She was flustered.

"I cannot get you into the Hall of Voices if your dawdling has locked you out." His eyebrows lowered. "You will have to wait for whoever you are with outside."

"No." She shook her head in frustration. "I don't want to wait for them. I am looking for the Spirit Seer."

"The Spirit Seer?" His eyebrows rose once more. "The Spirit Seer does not see anyone outside of the Circle."

"But I have to see him," she said, mortified as tears flooded her eyes. "Shany said that I had to present my case for Hedge Right to him. That he'd remember her. That he'd listen..." She bit her lip.

The Ciralys sighed, and she wanted to crawl into a hole.

"Now, child, there is no need for tears," he said. "Come sit yourself down and catch your breath." He took her by the arm and led her to an alcove half-hidden by a potted fern.

He motioned for her to sit on a bench of rosewood, and offered her a square of white cotton.

"I'm sorry," she said, taking the cloth and dabbing her eyes. "I don't do this."

"You don't interrupt meditating Awakened? I should hope not." He offered her a grandfatherly smile, so different to the stern-faced expression he had presented a moment ago, that she couldn't help but smile in return.

"No, never," she said.

"Well, then there is hope for you yet. I am Rocend Arbenuto." He offered her a small bow. "Ciralys of the Fifth Circle."

"The Fifth Circle," Meg repeated. "The Sphere of Spirit. Then you'd know the Spirit Seer?"

Ciralys Rocend gave a half-smile. "I do."

"I'm Meghara Carin; Meg," she said. "But I don't know if there's any hope for me. Shany told me to come to the Spire and to ask for admittance by Hedge Right. But I only have the vaguest understanding of what *that* is, and no idea who to talk to about it if I can't see the Spirit Seer as she said."

"I cannot recall the last time Hedge Right was used to admit an aspirant to the ranks of the Awakened. And certainly, jumping past the Holder of Names is not the right way of getting it done."

"Who?"

"The Holder of Names is responsible for *The Book of Disciples* and all the Aspirants in the Palace of the Eye. Child, how much do you know of the Ciralys?"

She studied the twinned fingers in her lap. "Of the Ciralys, not very much," she muttered. "I'm from Hanore; I've only ever seen one Ciralys in my life."

"Hanore," he said thoughtfully. "Isn't that a village in the Borderlands Wilds?"

"A citadel," she said.

"Of course. One of the... Three Citadels?"

"Yes."

"And this Ciralys told you to come to the Spire and ask the Spirit Seer to admit you to the Testing by virtue of Hedge Right?"

"No, Ciralys Telaq never had cause to speak to me. He was too busy with the prince, and Darien was his apprentice," she told him. "My mistress, Old Shany, the Keeper, told me to go."

"Keeper? So, you were apprentice to a witch?"

"Yes."

"Well, that makes some sense. Hedge Right was established in the Age of Chaos to allow men and women schooled in witchcraft or sorcery to leave their covens and masters and enter the ranks of the Ciralys." He looked Meg in the eye. "I do not believe it has been called on for centuries, and I am surprised that any Keeper still recalls it. Most Ciralys do not."

"You do," she pointed out.

"Yes, members of the Fifth Circle, along with our brothers and sisters of the Second, tend to study history and tradition, if with somewhat different ideals."

"I don't understand," Meg said.

"Nothing for you to worry about," he said. "Tell me, had your mistress another apprentice to take your place that she would send you here?"

"No, Darien was her apprentice also, but he joined Ciralys Telaq as soon as he arrived in Hanore," Meg said. "He always thought he was the more talented. But Shany believed differently. She told me..."

"Yes?"

"She said that if I was to follow Darien... if I was to follow him into the Palace of the Eye, then I was to ask for the Spirit Seer and tell him that Shanaya dyn'Tian demands I be accepted for the Trials, by Hedge Right."

"Shanaya dyn'Tian." Rocend reared back as though she had tried to slap him.

Meg caught her breath. "What is it?"

"It can't be," Rocend said. "If she is the same... Surely there can be only one Shanaya." He eyed her in suspiciously. "What does she look like?"

"She's old," Meg said. "I don't know how old, but she was old when she first took me in and hasn't changed. Shany has white hair and, oh, I don't know. She's as tall as me, maybe a little shorter. Why? What's the matter?"

"And her eyes?"

"Eye," Me said. "She only has one eye, and it's blue."

"By the Gods."

"Who do you suspect she is?"

He focused on her as though seeing her for the first time. "Come."

He turned and strode down the corridor, barely pausing for her to follow him.

"Where are we going?"

"I am taking you to see Joram Banhere, head of the Fifth Circle."

"Will he let me see the Spirit Seer, do you suppose?"

Rocend snorted."The head of the Fifth Circle *is* the Spirit Seer, girl."

Meg stopped as her mind tried to catch up with what was happening.

"Are you coming?" Rocend asked over his shoulder. Taking a deep breath, she ignored her suddenly racing heart and followed the Ciralys.

As they walked, men and women paused to bow to the Ciralys, and Meg smothered a groan. They were servants. She could have asked any of them for assistance rather than disturb a meditating Awakened. Although there was the possibility they would have been more likely to call the Tal'desai, she supposed, than to help a nobody like her. She ground her teeth. She needed to pay more attention. To *everything*.

They passed tapestries whose colours broke the monotony of the walls of frosted crystal. She was sure they were works of art, but it was unlikely she'd recognise any scenes of historical significance.

They had almost reached the large circular entrance when the Ciralys turned to ascend a curved staircase. From a mezzanine balcony, they proceeded down another corridor. More Tal'desai stood guard at the entrance, but they didn't so much as glance at her in the presence of a Ciralys.

After the chatter below, the quiet here was foreboding. The few Ciralys they passed eyed Meg with open speculation. Ciralys Rocend was hailed by men and women in mantles of varying colour. He nodded in reply but didn't stop.

An uneasy apprehension worked its way into Meg's bones as she pondered the importance that had been given to Shany's name when they rounded a sharp bend in the corridor and stopped.

The path went no further, falling away into the body of the Spire, with a small wall of marble to guard against the sudden drop. To their left extended a platform on which sat a dais of black everstone flecked with gold, somehow balancing a sizeable oval ring of the same material. Within the ring, colours swirled like oil on water, rippling and refracting.

"Oh!" she gasped, tearing her eyes away as her skull began to pound.

"This is a Gateway," Rocend said. "It will take us to the upper levels of the Spire."

"I heard no-one could get up there," she said, raising a palm to shield her eyes against the shimmering light.

"Not the higher levels," he said, stepping onto the dais. "This will take us to those floors we still have access to." He raised an eyebrow. "Unless you would like to walk the stairs?"

"How many flights are there?" she muttered.

"You have no fear of disturbing an Awakened, yet you hesitate to use a Gateway? Come," he said. "It is no harder than stepping through a door." He walked forward and disappeared through the twisting curtain of colour.

Meg took a breath. *Come on, girl,* she chided herself. *You wanted this*! She stepped onto the dais and – closing her eyes – walked through. For a brief moment, she felt a rushing sensation as though she was caught in a gale; then she stumbled out into another hall.

The tall walls of the Spire rose before her just as they had on the other side of the Gateway, but where that corridor was awash in light as the sun reached its midday height, this corridor was bathed in cold shadow.

Breathing hard, she clutched a hand to her breast and gaped at the dizzying view offered through the crystal wall. Below wandered a walled garden that was more intricate than she'd imagined when she'd seen it from the ground. And beyond it stretched the other side of the city.

More towers and buildings filled every inch of land between the Spire and the curving line of the city wall. It was a big job for the Rangers to man the walls surrounding Hanore; she couldn't imagine how many men and women might be needed to patrol the walls of a city the size of Serjat.

"You'll have time enough to look at the view later," Ciralys Rocend said. "If you are admitted to the ranks of the Aspirants."

"If?"

"If," he repeated and strode off along another curving hall.

Unlike the halls below, no Tal'desai stood sentinel here. She supposed they were too deep within the Spire for guards to be needed. She lifted the hem of her skirt to keep up with Rocend as he entered yet another corridor that stretched into the Spire. Again, statues graced the archway beneath a Khaderneous wrapped around a massive pearl-like orb. The figures were identical, a woman in flowing robes with her arms raised, each palm laid against her eyes to hide them from sight, or to hide the world from hers.

Meg hurried after Rocend, who paid the statues no mind, and she stared as the corridor opened before her into a round hall with an impossibly high ceiling. Balconies jutted from the walls overlooking a great dais in the hall's centre, its floor inlaid with glistening mother of pearl. Ciralys walked in and out of more corridors that stretched from this central hub. Again, some called out to Ciralys Rocend, and he waved in their direction but still did not stop, leading Meg around the dais and entering the hall directly opposite.

Servants walked past them. They never failed to bow in Rocend's direction, but they took her in with poorly hidden curiosity.

Her anxiety continued to grow, but she had no chance to voice any more questions as her guide stopped before a set of double doors set with polished moonstone and knocked.

"Be mindful of yourself in here, young lady," the Ciralys said. "You are being accorded a very rare honour for one who is not a Ciralys, let alone an Aspirant or an Awakened."

She straightened, a flare of spirit responding. "I am always polite," she said, and then blushed as he raised an eyebrow.

"Do not embellish anything Shanaya has told you," he said. "Keep to the facts as you know them, and you might very well get your wish of admittance."

"But don't I have to take a test?" she asked.

"There will be Tests," he assured her. "But they will come later." He turned back as the doors opened.

Dressed in dark velvet and grey damask silk, a dusky-skinned man stood in the door with a scowl that he smoothed from his brow before he offered Rocend a shallow bow. Dark eyes raked over Meg as he straightened. "Ciralys Rocend." His voice held an unfamiliar accent. "You are not expected today."

"Yes, Hazhend, I know." Rocend stepped past the man. "Unfortunately, a matter that requires the Seer's attention has come upon us."

Meg followed close behind as Hazhend interposed himself between Rocend and the room.

"A matter that you cannot deal with, Master?" his singsong accent held steel. "Is it not your duty as First Seer to deal with all matters for My Lord?"

"Do not try me, Hazhend, not today," Rocend said, and the kindly older man who had sat Meg down in the alcove not a quarter of an hour before was gone, replaced by one used to being obeyed.

Hazhend paused. "The Seer has not been well –"

"The Seer is not so ill as you imagine, Hazhend," came a voice rustling with age from beyond a pair of intricately carved doors at the far side of the room.

The servant eyed Rocend then sighed. "Please do not tire him."

"Of course," Rocend said. He beckoned Meg to follow, and they crossed a room of rich furnishings and passed through the carved doors.

Crystal spheres filled the room beyond, glittering as they reflected light from a wall that offered a view across the city. The air was filled with the sweet smell of an incense she didn't recognise, but she did recognise the scent of the herb it was trying to mask. Briar rose.

In the middle of the room was a large bed, and an older man was lying in its centre.

Hazhend's objections now became clear, and she schooled her face as Shany had taught her. If briar rose was being burnt to ease his pain, then his time must be very close.

Joram Banhere was old. In fact, he might be the oldest person she'd ever seen. A white mantle edged in gold thread draped his thin shoulders. Skeletal hands rested atop the bed's overlay; each finger adorned with two rings but for the small finger of his right hand. His Khaderneous medallion had the same luminescent pearl rings as Rocend's. His skin was wrinkled, and he was bald, save for a wispy, white beard that still grew from his cheeks. Dark circles deepened his blue eyes, adding to their sunken appearance, but Meg could tell he was alert.

"Seer," Rocend said, bending over the bed, taking the gnarled hand the man raised.

"My friend." His voice was rough, but still stronger than Meg expected. "You spend far too much time in the Halls and not enough time here."

"There is much to do, my Lord Seer," Rocend said with what sounded like genuine regret. "Even more now the Scion opened our doors to the Shol'mas."

The Spirit Seer gave a sigh, which quickly became a choke.

"Master." Rocend frowned at Hazhend with concern.

"The healer is meant to be back." The servant grabbed the chains of the small brazier of briar rose and waved the smoke into the Spirit Seer's face.

"What are you doing?" Meg was shocked. "Get that away from him!"

She pushed the servant aside. Leaning forward, she reached behind the Seer's back and lifted him. At once, the coughing eased.

"Put pillows behind his back to keep him upright," she said. "And get me some tarmen, *black* tarmen. We need to heat his chest to help reduce congestion."

"Oh, ho." The Spirit Seer gently patted her arm and waved the others back. "It is not –" he wheezed. "It's not –"

"It is not fluid on the lungs," Rocend said, his tone hard.

"Who is this you bring to me?" The Seer coughed, still holding onto her hand. "Thank you for your concern, child, but my affliction is not one herbs can cure."

"What of the adepts?" she pressed. "Surely Serjat houses a Shrine to Tarin? Or the Shol'mas, there must be a Temple to Solique here?"

Hazhend hissed.

"Meghara," Rocend said, with frost in his voice. "You are unaware of the politics between the Temples and the Ciralys, so I will put your question aside as –"

"Do not scold the girl, Rocend." The Seer waved the admonishment aside. "It is a reasonable question, and our Scion does not share our prejudices where the Temples are concerned." He turned bright eyes to Meg. "Had we asked, an adept of the Mother would no doubt come, or even one of my brothers or sisters of the First Circle."

"Really?" Rocend's tone spoke disbelief.

"Perhaps." The Seer gave a weak smile. "Your name is Meghara?" he asked, and she nodded.

"Yes," Rocend said. "She has asked for admittance to the ranks of the Aspirant by way of Hedge Right."

"Hedge Right?" The old Seer's eyes widened. "That is a stone which has been left unturned for many years. But admittance into the Ciralys is not within your purview, Rocend."

"No, my Lord, it is not," the Ciralys said. "Nor would I even be aware of her petition had she not tried to disturb Gerun during his meditations."

"You had him in the main corridor again?"

"His focus needs work, and Gralian was occupied with the Audience," Rocend said.

"And why is she here?" The Spirit Seer coughed again, but the fit passed quickly.

"In the course of her explanation to me as to why she was disturbing Gerun, she said she was sent to ask you for admittance."

"She asked for me by name?" Joram studied Meg with sharp eyes.

"Not by name, no. By title," Rocend told him.

"Then I do not know you," the Seer sighed, nodding to himself. "At my age, memory is not always reliable."

"Your memory is better than my own," Rocend scoffed. "But while she did not ask for Joram Banhere, I do believe it is *you* she was looking for."

"Why is that?" the Seer settled himself against the pillows Meg had stacked behind him.

"Because the Keeper who sent her, her teacher, told her to tell you that she claimed the Hedge Right of Shanaya dyn'Tian."

"Shanaya!" Joram sat forward, startling Meg, and grabbed her wrist in a surprisingly firm grip. "Is it her? Is it really her?"

"My Lord!" Hazhend moved between them. "Please! You must not strain yourself."

"I do not know if it is her, Joram," Rocend said soothingly. "But Meg told me with no prompting that the Shany who teaches her has no left eye."

"Ha." The Seer fell back against his pillows. "It is her. I know it!" He smiled at Meg. "How is she? I have not seen her for over a century."

"A *century*?" Meg gaped at him. "You can't be that old."

Joram laughed and began to cough once more.

"Girl," Rocend said, his voice terse. "By the grace of the Light of the Eye which we wield, Ciralys are long-lived. Joram Banhere is near three hundred years old."

"But that means Shany would be..."

"Three hundred and twenty-eight." Joram smiled. "I have always had a thing for older women." He winked at Meg. "Is she well? Happy?"

"Um, yes." Meg was confused. Shany was, had been, a Ciralys? Could you *stop* being a Ciralys?

"Where are you from, child," Joram said.

"Hanore," she said, still reeling.

"On the Borderlands? Yes, yes, of course. She was always going on about the Starscroll Prophecies of the Shaluay. But the Chapterhouse in Aldania searched for her. They made inquiries."

"Joram." Rocend put a hand on his shoulder. "You know she did not want to be found. But we still do not *know* if this Shany is our previous Spirit Seer, or someone using her name."

Meg bristled at his suspicion of Shany, but she bit her tongue.

The Seer nodded. "But it fits." He looked at Meg. "Are you her kin?"

"No," she said. "I'm an orphan. Shany took me in when my parents passed because I showed an aptitude for the witching way, even though she already had an apprentice. Darien is somewhere below, with Lady Iana, asking for admittance. But Shany said you wouldn't believe me, so I was to give you this." She reached into the bag still slung over her shoulder, taking out the pouch Shany had given her. She tried to work the knot at the strings, but a chime rang, and the cord sparkled with light. She dropped the small bag onto the Seer's bed, startled.

"A Trigmenis Lock," he said. "Rocend, would you?"

The other Ciralys picked up the pouch and drew a series of runes in the air above it. The runes pulsed with light and the skin on Meg's forearms prickled with gooseflesh. A light enfolded Ciralys Rocend, and there was an answering resonance deep inside Meg.

Rocend spoke a word she didn't understand. The knotted string holding the pouch closed flared once and then disappeared.

"Shany likely told you not to open the pouch?" Joram said.

"Yes," Meg said. "She said you would know if the knot had been tampered with."

He smiled. "She warded it."

Meg stared at the bag in Ciralys Rocend's hand.

"What is in it, child?" the Spirit Seer said.

"I don't know. Shany never told me, she just said this would prove my claim."

"Then let us see. Rocend." He nodded, and the Ciralys gave the open pouch back to Meg.

She took it hesitantly, as though it were no longer the same construct of rough brown wool she had carried from the Borderlands. Then, clicking her tongue at her foolishness, she tipped the pouch up and a small glass ball, no larger than a human eye, fell onto her palm. It was filled with rolling clouds that flashed, brightened by an inner light, as though they held a storm deep within.

"It can't be." Rocend stepped forward.

"The Scrying Eye," Joram said. Meg placed the orb in his outstretched palm. "I have not seen this since Shanaya left." There were tears in his eyes. "There can be no doubt."

"No," the younger Ciralys said, his eyes never leaving the orb.

Joram laughed and struggled not to cough, waving Meg's concern away.

"What is it?" she asked as he caught his breath.

"This is a *tresilian*." He rolled the small orb on his fingers. "An artefact created by the Sahrin, and one of the cornerstones of the teachings of the Sphere of Spirit."The Scrying Eye caught the light and winked in his hand."This is what truly makes a Spirit Seer."

"Then I am glad to have returned it to you," she said, not knowing what else to say or how this might affect her in their eyes.

Joram nodded, still looking at the Eye. "You say she had two apprentices? She could never abide teaching when she was in the Palace. She was always too preoccupied with her research."

"Well, Darien stopped being her apprentice when Ciralys Telaq arrived," Meg said.

"Ciralys Telaq?" Rocend asked. "Who is Ciralys Telaq?"

"He is, was, the advisor to Prince Alesandr."

"This prince was in the Borderlands?" Rocend said.

"He was the Carbinah of Jaroff. The Carbinah, by tradition, rarely ventures into the Borderlands," she said. "But he and his brothers before him had each spent some time amongst the Three Citadels. Prince Alesandr more so than the others."

"I am not familiar with Ciralys... Telaq?" the Seer frowned. "An unusual name. Did he know Shanaya?"

"Know her? Well, he knew she was the village Keeper, but they never spoke unless they had to. She is, well." Meg paused. "But she's only a Keeper. That is, no-one ever thought her a Ciralys." She gave a hesitant laugh. "If it's true, Darien will be furious."

"Darien is the other apprentice?" Joram asked. "He is down in the Hall of Voices? And his Ciralys Telaq is also here? Rocend, we should ask to speak with him."

"No! I mean, you can't. Ciralys Telaq was killed by a bone drake – the possessed bone drake – under Sonyth."

"A *possessed* bone drake?" Rocend's tone spoke volumes, and Meg bridled. She was not a liar.

"Child," Joram said, "You had best start at the beginning."

"My Lord," Hazhend protested. "You need to rest."

"No," the Spirit Seer's voice was firm, his eyes fixed on Meg. "From the beginning, please, Meghara."

"And this Shaluay is in the Hall right now," Joram Banhere said as Meg finished.

"Seer," Rocend said. "This is all very unusual."

"Yes, it is," the Seer agreed. "Could Shany have been right?"

"Right?" Meg looked between the two men.

"You say the Bronze Guard have acknowledged these young men?" Joram asked.

"They acknowledged Kaiel," Meg said. "But Darien was there too. You could speak to him at your leisure once he's admitted into the order."

Joram and Rocend exchanged a look.

"What?" Meg asked, a chill pricking her spine.

"Child," Joram said. "If Darien is as strong as you say, I fear he will not be admitted into the order."

"But why?"

"Rocend." Joram did not meet her eyes. "It might prove advisable if you were to make some enquiries as to where Meg's friends have been placed."

"We – *they*, are staying at the Cockatrice. Or were." Her distress was rising.

"I don't believe they will be leaving the Spire just yet," Joram patted her hand. "Although Karlon will find holding the Shaluay a challenge." The Spirit Seer closed his fingers over the Scrying Eye. "I believe it best we make moves to accept your application, under Hedge Right, before anyone learns you were a member of the party in the Hall.

"Hazhend, please send for Secretariat Chumena, tell her the Spirit Seer would speak to her about Hedge Right." Joram smiled. "Unlike her superior, the Holder of Names, she is not one of Karlon's lackeys and will accept Meghara's name for testing."

CHAPTER TWENTY-NINE

Things Left Behind

KAIEL STARED AT the tapestries that adorned the walls of the suite of rooms within the Spire. Low tables of pale woods inlaid with obsidian and mother of pearl were sat between matching sets of chairs and couches in the centre of the room, holding platters of food, but Kaiel had little appetite.

Dar wouldn't be joining the Ciralys. They'd be able to go home. If home was still safe. He grimaced. Well maybe not *home*. In fact, not home at all. They'd need to find somewhere else to hide. Maybe Cythis? The martial prowess of the Knights of Cythis were renowned, and no daemons found fertile ground there.

Darien sat on the edge of one of the small, squat chairs and stared at the wall ahead of him. Unlike the crystal that formed the outer shell of the Spire, these walls were everstone, lined with quartz pillars that glowed with light. In that light, he was paler than usual to Kaiel's eyes.

His brother hadn't said a word since they had been escorted out of the Hall of Voices. He must be in shock. Kaiel wanted to reach out to him, but it was likely best just to leave him be.

The others had arranged themselves around the room. Sim was sitting as close to the table with the food on it as possible. Sevaani sat beside Darien, and Lady Iana stood studying a tapestry on the far wall while Lihon stood by the door, his arms folded across his chest.

Kaiel wanted to ask him about the Blay Shon who had escorted the old Amarian into the Hall. But Lihon had a haunted expression on his face, similar to the one Darien wore, so he held his tongue.

Captain Daynar was preoccupied, but he met Kaiel's eyes and offered him a half-smile.

Kaiel sat back in the chair carefully, unsure whether it would hold his weight, when he froze.

"Where's Meg?" He hadn't seen her since they arrived.

"Meghara seeks admittance into the Ciralys," Iana said, still studying the tapestry. "Remarkable. This is Abelaan's *Warlords*, a depiction of the last council of the Sahrin, who led the fight against the Daemon Horde in the War of the Summoners. I thought it was lost, though I shouldn't be surprised to find it amongst the Ciralys."

"Are you sure it's wise to, you know, say things about them?" Sim asked around a mouthful of food.

"Simeon," Sevaani complained. "How can you eat?"

"I didn't get to finish breakfast, remember? We got *interrupted*."

"What do you mean about Meg?" Darien said to Iana.

"You knew Meg left Hanore to join the Ciralys," Sevaani told him. "She didn't have your training by Ciralys Telaq, but Shany told her of an old tradition called Hedge Right. If she's successful, she'll be sent to Isoliere to take the Test."

"If?" Sim looked up. "And if she's not, will she become a..." He glanced at Darien and trailed off.

"It is unlikely she will be made an Erlain," Iana said, sitting down next to Kaiel. "She left us before we entered the Hall and won't be tarred with the same brush Darien's application has been. Although I dare say, she'll have troubles of her own, being a witch's apprentice."

"You mean she can be admitted because she was training to be a

Keeper?" Darien was incredulous. "A Ciralys trained me, and they are threatening to make me Erlain if I do not become this, this *Catalyst*!"

"If what I recall of the Ciralys' doctrines is correct, you cannot *become* a Catalyst, you *are* a Catalyst," she told him calmly. "That Shol'mas priest also seemed to have some say in the matter. That is highly unusual – and worrying, given Elsa's revelations about the priest of Kirana's interference in my own order." She said the last almost as an afterthought.

"She's not going to be accepted." Sim swallowed his mouthful of food.

"Why do you say that?" Sevaani asked, indignantly. "She is very gifted."

"It doesn't matter how talented she is," he told her. "You saw the way they looked at us."

"What do you mean?" Kaiel frowned at his friend.

"Like we were traipsing Borderland muck all over their precious crystal floors." Sim waved his hand at their feet. "I don't care how educated they are; they're all snobs."

"You are painting all Ciralys with a brush that only a few deserve," Iana commented.

Sim snorted, rubbing his hands on his brown trousers. "You are too used to people bowing and scraping when you walk by."

"Simeon!" Sevaani was scandalised.

"What? Oh, don't look at me like that!" he said. "What I meant was that the lady doesn't have quite the same perspective we do."

"As *you* do!" Darien snapped. "Don't include me."

Kaiel hid a smile, relieved to find there was still some fire in his brother.

"Don't include you?" Sim gaped at him. "You should be feeling it the worst. You're the one they rejected!"

"I was not –" Darien stopped as someone knocked at the door.

Kaiel jumped to his feet, but Jaric and Lihon were already positioning themselves between their seats and the door.

"I don't believe that will be necessary," Iana said. She looked pointedly at each of them as they still wrapped their hands around the hilts of their swords. "Please get the door, Lihon."

The Amarian nodded, and Jaric moved back to lean against the wall as the door opened.

Standing in the hallway was a woman dressed in white over-robes, a hood covering her face.

"Can I help you?" Lihon asked.

She pushed the hood back, and Kaiel stared.

Ice blue eyes sat above high cheekbones; whose sharp planes were softened by full, red lips. Glossy auburn hair fell over her shoulders in waves, and the woman held a self-possession that matched Iana's.

"I am seeking Lord deOrlay," she said, her voice cultured and precise.

"Your Highness," Jaric said, stepping forward and dropping to one knee before the woman.

"*Lord*?" Sim said, his eyebrows climbing up his forehead.

"It *is* you," the woman said, but her expression was not pleased.

"Princess Andraste," Iana said, standing. "Please, come in."

Kaiel tore his eyes away from the princess as she entered the room and glanced guiltily at Sevaani as they all rose from their seats, but she was paying him no mind.

Behind the princess, a swordswoman in black velvet and leather followed, an unadorned sword at her hip and an intricately embroidered rose in gold thread on her tabard.

"A Knight of the Gold Rose," Lihon grunted, and Kaiel gave a start.

She was a knight? She was older than the princess she guarded, but not by much; her eyes a darker blue, hair black and her face – though striking – harder.

Lihon stepped forward again, but at a motion from Iana, he allowed the knight in.

The princess stopped before Jaric. "Erika saw you as I left the Hall; I did not truly believe her I –" She broke off, struggling for words, and then she slapped him.

"Captain!" Kaiel stepped forward but held himself back as Jaric raised a hand, the princess's handprint red on his face.

"You abandoned us!" she said through gritted teeth. "We trusted you, relied on you, and you left –" This time the captain grabbed her wrist as she made to hit him again.

"Take your hands off her, traitor!" growled the knight, stepping forward as Jaric rose to his feet, but Lihon interposed himself between them.

"You know me better than that, Erika," Jaric said, wincing.

"I believed so once," the knight said, her face tight with anger as she glared up at Lihon.

"Unhand me, Jaric," Princess Andraste said, her tone cool and remote. "We are not in the training room now. You overstep yourself."

"You can't just come in here and order people around," Kaiel said.

The princess's eyes raked over him dismissively. "You have farm boys to protect you?"

The captain released her wrist and stepped back. "Your Highness –"

"Your *Majesty*," bit out the knight.

"I have not been crowned yet, Erika," Andraste said to her guard.

The line of Jaric's mouth tightened. "When?"

"Four months ago," Andraste said, rubbing her wrist. "Though I hardly imagined you would care, given your abandonment of your post."

"Why are you here?" he said, ignoring her accusation.

"Because Erika saw you –"

"No." Jaric raised a hand gesturing at the walls of the Spire. "Why are you *here*, in Tremor-Salaya?"

Andraste's lips tightened."You would have heard, at least, the end of my audience with His *bastard* Eminence."

"Is this the way the future Ardhel of Sithapia conducts herself?"Iana asked from her seat on the lounge, and Andraste's back stiffened."We have not been introduced, and you barge in here and assault one of my companions? The royal privilege you take as your due does not extend to private rooms in realms that are not your own, except by dint of common courtesy."

"I –"the Princess began, only to stop as her face coloured.

"Don't mind her," Sim said, grinning."She has a way of doing that. I'm Simeon Ravenson,Your Majesty."He gave a flourishing bow.

Kaiel felt a flare of *something* at his friend's easy manner before the princess but pushed it aside.

"My apologies,"the princess said, glancing around at them all."I am Andraste duCerin, Prime of House duCerin, of Sithapia."

"Your Highness,"Iana said, still seated, and gracefully nodding."I am Iana Sabay of the Shaluay."

"I am sorry, Lady Iana," Andraste said, returning the smile, if somewhat stiffly."I did not mean to come, and certainly not so rudely, but it was such a shock to hear Uncle Jaric was here –"

"*Uncle*!"exclaimed Sim."You're a prince?"

"No, I am not,"Jaric growled.

Andraste's brow furrowed. "They do not know you are a Rion of Sithapia and Prime of House deOrlay?"

"What's a Rion?"Sim asked, eyeing Jaric.

"The equivalent rank in Aldania would be a Highlord,"Andraste said. "But he is also my teacher, and a close friend of my... my father's."

"A friendship he does not deserve,"the knight said.

"Erika,"the princess said,"please don't."

"She is right, Andra,"Jaric said."I left that behind a long time ago."

Andraste arched an eyebrow and glanced about the room."Who are your companions, Lord deOrlay?"

"Andra, what has happened? Why are you here." Jaric ignored her question, pressing her again.

"I am here because my parents were murdered!" she flung at him."If I had not fled when I did, I too would be dead!"

"Or wedded to Rhodri," the knight said.

"I do not understand." Jaric's expression was tight."How were they murdered?"

"By Torimun's treachery and that of the Covens!" Andraste's voice was strained."A pack of wolves – *wolves* – took them, and their guards, as they fled an ambush in Velonia."

"But you have no proof?" Jaric said."That is what the High Conclave said."

"The High Conclave is in my unc– Torimun's pocket!"

Kaiel was struck again by her beauty as tears threatened to spill from her blue eyes. He ducked his head, certain his thoughts were written across his face.

"That is a serious accusation," Iana said.

"And one you know better than to say aloud," Erika scolded.

"Oh, it doesn't shock me." Iana grimaced, waving a hand."For every man of integrity, there is one without it, and the Bloodborn are no different. I am sure you only speak so in front of strangers because you are overwrought and..." She glanced at the captain,"amongst friends."

Andraste gathered herself."Your generosity is very kind, Lady Iana. I do apologise for imposing," she said,"but Lord deOrlay, I fear you are needed by the Rose Throne once more."

"Andra." Jaric took a breath."It grieves me to hear of Andre and Selambra's death. But I have obligations elsewhere."

"You have *obligations* to Sithapia." Her tone froze the blood in Kaiel's veins."You are Defender of the East and First Lord of the Golden Rose. You are the supreme commander of the armies of the Rose Throne." She took a deep breath. "I know you have been gone for some time. That you abandoned your post for a... a *whor* –"

"Milady," Erika warned, putting a hand on her shoulder.

Andraste paused, her lips pressed tight. "Your past indiscretions are excused," she said at last. "The throne has need of you."

Jaric closed his eyes. "Your Highness. My heart aches –"

"No," she said, a hand raised in denial. "No. I will *not* have you refuse me!"

"I can do nothing else," Jaric said, his face tight. "I cannot be forsworn."

"You already are!" Her voice was cold with anger. "Your oath to the Rose Throne was taken as a child. What of your people in Orlay?"

"Your father absolved me of those oaths before I left," he told her gently.

She reeled, and Kaiel wanted to reach out to her. "No. No, he couldn't have. He would have told me."

"What happened between your aunt and me was a private matter," Jaric said, his face closed. "Your father would not have said a thing."

"Without you..."

"You have Erika beside you, a Knight of the Golden Rose," Jaric said. "The Order will support her, surely?" He gestured at the knight.

"I cannot call on the support of the armies," Erika said, begrudgingly. "Torimun has the Brothers eating out of his hand. We barely made it here without being caught. Four men lost their lives to protect the Ardhel."

"Who are you sworn to?" Andraste was watching him like a shrike hawk.

"I am the Captain of the Hanore Rangers," he said.

"A Ranger Captain? In Hanore?" Erika asked. "Where is that?"

"The Borderlands Wilds," Andraste said, frowning. "You kneel to House Niskeri?"

"Ha!" Sim snorted. "That'll be the day."

"Then, I don't understand." She eyed Sim. "The Borderlanders do not hold with the Clans or the Houses."

"That is true," Jaric agreed. "But I have sworn to protect Hanore to the best of my ability."

"Then why are you not there?" she flung the accusation at him.

"Because I am making sure these young people survive."

She turned her gaze on them, and Kaiel could not meet her eyes. "These children?" she said after a moment. "They mean more to you than your own home?"

"Hanore is my home now," Jaric said firmly.

"So, *I* am to be left to the mercy of the Ciralys my uncle has bought."

"I told you," Erika said urgently. "I have a way out of the city!"

"And where do we go then?" Andraste asked, weariness colouring her voice. "If the Ciralys will not help, then no Realm will. It will be worth more to a House or Dynasty to hand me over to Torimun than to finance a civil war to reclaim the Rose Throne."

"Surely there are Houses in Sithapia who would rally to your cause?" Iana asked.

"First I must get to them." Andraste sank gracefully to the nearest chair. "My dear uncle Torimun has ever had a talent for cultivating allies." She shook her head. "But these are my burdens. I cannot stay. We must leave this crystal prison before the Ciralys hand me over to Lord deKahn."

"You don't have to go. You can come with us." The words left Kaiel's mouth before he realised he'd opened it to speak, and he snapped it shut again, almost biting his tongue.

Sim snickered, and Sevaani arched an eyebrow, folding her arms across her chest. The princess gazed at him in silence, and he lowered his gaze.

"Thank you, but I –" A fierce knocking on the door interrupted her.

The Blay Shon stepped past Erika and opened the door.

"*Harsee*." Lihon's tone had Kaiel's hand on the hilt of his sword.

"My Lord," a woman speaking accented common said from the other side. "I have urgent message for Firstbinder from Ambassador Arais."

Lihon stepped back, and the mottle-skinned aide of the Shaluay Ambassador stepped into the room. Kaiel stared as the blademaster turned his back on the woman without a word.

"Lord Lihon?" he said. "Aren't you going to tell her to come in?"

"One does not speak to dirt," was the cold reply.

Jaric stepped forward to pull the woman into the room.

"I am the Firstbinder," Iana said, without a glance at her companion. "What is your message?"

"Lady, I called Yuanel," she began.

"Dirt is given a name?" Lihon spoke his question to the wall, but Yuanel's jaw tightened though she didn't reply.

"Yes, Yuanel?" Iana said, as though Lihon had not spoken.

"My mistress send warning." Her eyes never left the floor. "She say Scion see potential of young Aspirant who Test today. She say Scion position is precarious, bought with family influence, not strength with *Asai*. He make bad alliances. My mistress warn you, flee city, now." Yuanel still did not raise her eyes, but her urgency increased. "Scion not suffer powerful applicants. His Tal'desai have been told young master must be removed."

"What?" Kaiel's hand did fall to his sword this time.

"Someone was bound to want to kill him eventually." Sim shrugged.

"Shut up, Sim," Kaiel said.

"Please, Kaiel." Iana frowned. "How does Shaluay Arais know this?" she asked Yuanel.

"My mistress know many things," the Amarian told her.

"And we're to believe her?" Darien said, white-faced.

"Darien is right," Jaric said. "Who is this woman? And why does her mistress send us a warning?"

"I am *harsee*,"Yuanel answered as though that explained everything. "I not know why mistress send warning." Still, she did not look up. "If wish to live, must act now."

"Act?" Iana said. "What action does Arais believe we should take?"

"Erika and I best take our leave," Princess Andraste said.

"She tell me lead out of Spire, through catacombs,"Yuanel said.

"You know a way out?" The princess exchanged a glance with her knight.

"If we can get out, we have a chance of making it to the ship," Erika said.

"Shaluay Arais show me where to lead,"Yuanel agreed.

Outside the door, voices were raised.

"What's that?" Sim said, getting to his feet.

Lihon opened the door to the clash of steel.

"Renar!" Erika ran over. "The men are fighting Tal'desai!"

"They here,"Yuanel's voice became anxious. "We go now."

"Sim, get back from the door," Jaric commanded, pulling his sword from its sheath.

"We will come with you," Andraste said.

"You cannot," Jaric said. "It is too dangerous."

"Too dangerous?" Outrage blazed in her eyes. "Those are my guards out there fighting the Tal'desai coming for *your ward*!"

"Why are they fighting for me?" Darien was shaking.

"They aren't, boy," Erika snarled. "If they saw armed Tal'desai coming here, they would have assumed they were for Her Highness."

"Keep your bickering for later." Iana turned to Yuanel. "Can we still get out with the Tal'desai already here?"

"Yes, Lady," she said.

"We trust our lives to a *harsee*?" Lihon spat.

"I may be half-Amarian," Yuanel said, her tone biting. "But why *lu'salar* think he above *harsee* only sands know."

Lihon's swords left their sheaths. "*Nus kar*! *Anksheen nai sune* –"

"Enough!" Iana said, stopping the Blay Shon in his tracks. "If you can get us out of here, we need to go now," she said to Yuanel.

The half-Amarian gave a shallow bow and moved to the door.

"Sevaani, Sim, follow her," Iana directed. "Your Highness, if you wish to come, you are welcome, but we go now. We have no time to return to your apartments first."

"I took nothing when I fled Sith'sara," Andraste said, her blue eyes flashing. "I *am* Sithapia. That is all I need."

"That won't keep her warm at night if she's on the streets," Sim muttered to Kaiel.

"Very well," Iana said, silencing Sim with a glance. "Kaiel, take your brother."

From the hallway came a blood-curdling bellow.

"We must go now!" Jaric called.

"Come on," Kaiel said to Darien as the others filed out the door.

"No." Darien sat back down on the couch.

"What do you mean 'no'?" Kaiel demanded, the fighting outside was louder now.

"If I am not to be trained as a Ciralys, to read High Asairic and wield the Light of the Eye, then they can take me," he said.

"Don't be a fool. Come on!"

"No. I have nothing else, Kaiel. Nothing!"

"You selfish little –" Kaiel bit his tongue. In two strides, he was at the couch. He pulled Darien off the seat by his shirt. "You have me. And you have your life! How do you think I'd feel if I left you here to die?"

"I don't care!" Darien cried.

Kaiel cursed. "You know, Sim would tell me to leave you here, and maybe he'd be right. But I can't because I *do* care!" He grabbed Darien's arm. "I'll wrench your arm out of its socket if I have to drag you, but I *will* drag you if you don't come willingly."

"Don't worry about your promise to Ma," Darien said, his eyes dull. "I'll tell her it was my fault when I see her beyond the Veil."

Kaiel punched him.

"Kaiel, *now*!" Jaric called, as Darien fell back with a cry.

"Stand up. I didn't hit you that hard, but next time you speak about Ma like that you won't get back up." Kaiel stretched his hand down to his brother. "Is this the only way you can become a Ciralys? A wielder? You're just going to sit back and let Meg beat you?"

"Shut your mouth!" Darien snarled, pushing his hand away and getting to his feet in a rage.

"Well, that's what it looks like." Kaiel let his hand fall. "I'll be sure to let her know you bowed at the first sign of pressure."

"There is no other way to be a Ciralys!" Darien snapped and stalked past, his hand at his lip.

"Maybe there isn't," Kaiel said with a sigh. "But at least you'll be alive."

CHAPTER THIRTY

Old Halls, Buried Secrets

SIM DIDN'T LOOK down the corridor at the fighting. He had no illusions he'd be able to assist whoever was holding the Tal'desai back, and he had far too many concerns about keeping himself alive to want to try. He was a planner, not a fighter. He could hold his own but he'd rather he was never in a position like this to begin with.

And all because someone wanted to kill Darien.

"Don't look back!" he shouted at Sevaani as she stumbled in front of him. He grabbed her arm and pulled her to her feet, pushing her after the Amarian.

"Those men are dying for you!" the princess said at his shoulder, outraged.

"No, they're not. They're dying for *you*, and that's fine with me as long as I get out of here!"

"Pfft!" Andraste scowled. "You are not worthy of the concern Lord Daynar has for you."

"You hardly know me, and you've already reached that conclusion?" He flashed her a grin that was all teeth.

Ahead of them, the Amarian pushed past a servant dressed in brown and lifted a tapestry revealing a slim opening in the everstone wall.

"Here," Yuanel said, and Sim herded Sevaani forward with a firm shove.

Where the outer corridors were elegant, carved from crystal and everstone, the passage was made of bare stone, lit by sunstones in iron sconces along one wall.

"Where are we?" Sevaani said.

"No idea," Sim said, and Yuanel pushed past to retake the lead.

"We wait for the others," Lihon said from behind.

"We hurry!" Yuanel cried.

"We *wait*!"

Sim grunted, knocked into the wall as the Blay Shon reached past him to grab the half-caste's tunic.

"Lihon!" Iana said sharply.

"Void take it! Watch what you're doing," Sim glared at Lihon, but the blademaster's attention was locked on Yuanel.

The half-caste's face was blank, but her eyes sent a shiver down Sim's spine. He dropped his hand to the hilt of the short sword at his waist, but then Lihon let her go. After a moment, they all shuffled forward with the knight, Erika, holding the tapestry and waiting for Kaiel and the others.

"Where are they?" she raged.

"They will be along," Iana said calmly. Sim looked at the Shaluay. She wasn't even out of breath.

"I cannot wait," the knight said. "My priority is the defence of the princess."

As she spoke, Darien stumbled into the small passageway with Kaiel and Jaric close behind. Sim narrowed his eyes. Darien's lip was swollen.

"Quickly!" Jaric said. "Only one man holds them back!"

"No!" Andraste protested.

Erika rounded on her. "We knew this might happen. They give their lives for you and Sithapia."

Andraste gave a sharp nod, but she didn't look happy. Sim would never be a guardsman. Giving your life for someone else? There wasn't enough gold in all the realms.

"Come,"Yuanel pressed, moving forward.

They ran along the narrow passage.

"Where are we?" Sevaani asked as they passed more slim openings, some hidden by tapestries on the other side and others with iron-bound doors.

"In the servant's ways," Erika said. "The Spire is riddled with them."

"You have been here before?" Jaric brought up the rear.

"We've been *guests* here three months," the knight said. "I've had a lot of time to explore."

"How far do they run?"

"I followed one passage as high as the tenth floor of the tower, it stopped there as all the public ones do," she told him.

"And below?" the captain pressed.

"Below are the kitchens. Under that are a series of furnace rooms and the storerooms. Anything else is locked."

"You can't pick a lock?" Sim asked.

"It's not a trait I look for in my knights," Andraste's interjection was icy.

"Locked *and* warded," Erika snarled.

"The Ciralys keep pre-Sundering artefacts in the vaults below the Spire. They would be well protected," Iana said. "How far are we going, Yuanel?"

"Down, Mistress," their guide said from the head of the line.

A clattering on the stairs behind brought a shout from Jaric. "They are here!"

Steel rang, echoing against the stone. A man cried out, and Sim ignored his own advice and looked over his shoulder.

"Keep moving!" Andraste shouted as they hit another long passage, wider than the ones above.

Sim faced forward just as something shot past his ear, skidding off the wall.

"Crossbow!" Jaric yelled.

"Get down!" Iana spun around and raised her arms.

A pulse of energy, and a sudden blast of heat made Sim duck with his hands over his head. Sevaani screamed. He looked back. Kaiel and Darien, white-faced, were both pressed tight against the walls of the passage as rotating bands of light sped up the steps behind them.

Iana lowered her arms, the bracers on her wrists alight with glowing symbols. "We must hurry."

The passage opened into a large stone room of high, arched ceilings and long wooden tables. Men and women dressed in the servant's livery of the Ciralys, the Khaderneous emblem on their uniform, looked up in surprise.

"Your Highness!" one man said as they slowed. "Are you lost?"

"I –"

"Come!" Yuanel called. She had not stopped moving when they entered the hall and was already at an arched doorway on the other side.

Sim pulled Andraste away from the startled servant before she could say anything. "Best not tell the *servants* where we're going," he hissed, and she yanked her arm away.

"I had no intention of doing anything of the sort!" she snapped.

A female voice cried out. That wasn't Sevaani.

He saw a serving girl staring at them in horror, and servants looked up from their chores as the group followed Yuanel into a warm and fragrant room. The kitchen.

"Who are you?" a large woman demanded; her hair hidden behind a cloth hat.

"Don't stop!" Iana said as Sevaani slowed.

"You ain't supposed to be here! The Seneschal is gonna hear of this! Bella, get the guard!" The woman wielded a wooden spoon like a sceptre, and the way she shook it at them as they passed through the kitchen reminded Sim of Mistress Breanta. An unexpected wave of homesickness washed over him. Pushing the emotion aside, Sim offered the woman a grin and followed after Sevaani.

They left the kitchens by the far door and made their way down a ramp into another cavernous room, low-ceilinged and crisscrossed with dark beams. Sunstones were used more sparingly here, and long shadows crept around corners. Sacks were stacked against one wall and barrels on the other, wooden doors opened into darkened rooms, and closed doors were marked with small signs that advised of their contents.

Yuanel stopped at a big, iron-bound door at the ramp's end and pulled a key from her pocket. The door opened stiffly, but silently, and she gestured for them to follow her into the long, dark corridor beyond.

"Lady, you light?" the Amarian asked, panting.

Iana nodded. Her cora'stone ignited with a white-blue flame.

"How are we going to get out of here?" Sevaani asked.

"We go catacombs," Yuanel said, leading them on.

"The catacombs?" Sevaani said, wide-eyed. "Like back home?"

Sim gave a start as she grabbed his hand, squeezing tight.

"The Summoners built the Spire with the assistance of the Xious'bisan," Iana told them. "It is said that as high as the Spire reaches to the heavens, so too does it sink into the earth. But I understood the lower levels, like those above, were inaccessible."

"Are we sure she knows where she's going?" Sim said.

"Mistress show me," was the reply.

"We don't have much choice, now," Princess Andraste said. "And I don't intend to stand here waiting for the Tal'desai to catch up."

"Uh, Sevaani?" Sim lifted the hand she was gripping. "I'm kind of fond of my hand."

Sevaani glared at him and let go as though he'd grown thorns.

"What?" Sim said at Kaiel's frown, rubbing his hand.

The corridor was long but not as narrow as those above the kitchen. Large grey stones were fitted together smoothly, and the air was dry. More doors lined either side, but no markings declared what lay behind them, and Sim had the impression that they had been shut for a very long time. "Are you sure the Sahrin built this?" he said as they moved along silently. "It looks pretty plain to me."

"Most of the rooms in the Spire were rebuilt after the Sundering," Princess Andraste said, as though it was something he should have known already.

He chose to ignore her tone. "What happened to the rooms that were here?"

"You ask a lot of questions." She glared at him.

"If you don't know the answer, Your Highness, you should just say so."

"Sim!" Jaric growled but said no more.

They'd only walked a hundred paces when they stopped at another door, this one set into a wall that crossed the corridor at an angle. Again, Yuanel took a key from her pocket, and the door swung out on squealing hinges.

"I hope no-one's out there," Sim muttered.

Through the door, they walked onto a ramp a good ten feet wide that spiralled around an empty shaft, with only a knee-high balustrade at its inner edge. Soft light bled off crystalline pillars, and beams of light fell from high above, traced in the air by hanging dust.

"This is the centre of the Spire," Iana said, her voice echoing. "How does my Sister know her way here?"

"I not know, Mistress," Yuanel said softly. "We go down. Quickly."

Iana eyed their guide expressionlessly. "I would like to speak to Shaluay Arais very much when this is done."

Sim stepped over to the edge, looking down. The shaft fell away into nothing. "There's no bottom!" he said and jumped as his voice boomed in the shaft. Everyone froze, and he winced as the sound faded.

"Be quiet!" hissed Andraste, glaring at him.

He opened his mouth to respond when the slamming of a door came from somewhere above.

They all looked up the stairs. The silence stretched, and Sim smiled. "Nothing to worry –" A hair-raising chorus of hacking barks cut him off.

"What is that?" Andraste hissed.

"Daemondogs," Sim said.

"Run!" Iana commanded.

Yuanel led them down the sloping curve of the ramp. Tall statues of everstone and crystal stood sentinel in alcoves along the wall, but Sim barely had time to take them in as they ran. Closed doors marked the entrance into different levels, and Sim got dizzy as they went around and around, following the spiral deeper. The light dimmed as they descended, and only the bright glow of Iana's pendant lit their way.

Above, the daemondogs' distinctive barks stopped but they didn't dare halt to listen for any sounds of pursuit.

"How do you know that was a daemondog?" Andraste pulled at Sim's arm, her breath coming in gasps.

"Because we were attacked by them this morning."

"There haven't been any daemondogs in the Western Realms since the Sundering!" she protested.

"There are now," he said between breaths as the ramp levelled out onto a granite floor.

"This can't be as far as it goes?" Sevaani said. "We're trapped!"

"No, look." Kaiel pointed ahead.

The light from Lady Iana's cora'stone showed Yuanel standing before a pair of doors.

"Thank the Gods," Sim said as they approached. "What are you waiting for? Let's go!"

He reached past the Amarian to open the door.

"No!" Yuanel shouted. The Amarian grabbed Sim and flipped him onto his back, pressing him into the floor with a knee on his chest.

"Get off the boy now, *harsee*." One of Lihon's blades was touching Yuanel's chin. She let go of Sim's arm.

"Now, get up," the Blay Shon said, and Yuanel slowly rose.

Sim rolled onto his knees as soon as she got off him. He rubbed the back of his head and glared at the Amarian. "You could have knocked me out with a move like that!"

"I sorry," Yuanel said, but she was looking to Iana. "Door warded."

Iana walked to the door and raised her hand, as though searching. Her rings flashed, and lines of violet lightning sparked across its surface, the tang of a storm filled the air.

Sim swallowed. "No harm done," he said to Yuanel as Lihon re-sheathed his sword.

"Next time let him blunder through it," Sevaani said. "If he lives he might be more careful in future."

Sim scowled at her.

"Are Amarians always so quick with their swords," Erika drawled. "Or are we just lucky?"

"You might be thankful for the speed of a Blay Shon's blade if those dogs catch up to us," Jaric said.

Above them, the scrabbling of claws grew louder.

"Did your mistress give you a key?" Iana asked.

"Yes." Yuanel pulled a fist-sized disc from her pocket.

"Gods!" Sim said. "Is that real?"

"What do you mean, 'real'?" Iana arched an eyebrow.

"It's the largest piece of ivory I've ever seen!"

"It's not ivory," she said. "It is a *tresilian*."

"Like sunstones?" Darien moved closer.

"A sunstone is a *ci'nar*, a product of the Artificers of the Ciralys," Iana corrected. "This was made by the Sahrin."

"Can she use it?" Darien asked as Yuanel held the ivory-like disc at the centre point between both doors.

"I would presume, given she has it, that she can use it," Iana replied.

Sevaani and the princess were both watching their guide while Lihon, Jaric and the knight stood at the base of the ramp, peering up with swords drawn.

Sim took a step towards Kaiel as Jaric called out. "They're here!"

The hacking bark of the dogs answered. Red-black beasts, similar to the ones that had attacked them in the inn, came bounding around the curve of the spiral ramp. Their steel-sharp claws clicked on the dusty stone, long spiky manes flaring out behind them as they jumped off the ramp and charged towards the group.

Lihon moved, twisting his blades, and slicing through the splayed spikes of the dog that attacked him. Its barks became squeals of pain, but its momentum carried it forward, and the Blay Shon pivoted to bring his swords around, one after the other, clean through its torso, severing its spine.

Sim unsheathed his short sword, his hand clammy. He stepped back a little, letting Kaiel's bulk shield him. He glanced back to see Iana had positioned herself in front of Yuanel and Sevaani, and the disc that had been in Yuanel's hand was now floating before the door, slowly brightening with a red light.

"You might want to hurry," he called to them.

"Let me do it!" Darien pushed the woman aside. "I can see the runes." The light within the *tresilian* faded, and Darien lifted his hand to it, eyes closed.

The screeching slide of steel against scale, and dull, wet grunts came from behind. Sim winced, but Darien didn't turn, and the sinking *tresilian* steadied, brightening again.

Someone cried out behind them, and a hair-raising laugh echoed across the room.

The *tresilian* suddenly shone a brilliant red. Lines of energy flared out from it in radiating circles of spider-like runes that travelled around the door clockwise and counter clockwise. The ivory-like artefact flashed, and the runes faded. The door opened.

"Oh, well done!" a lilting voice cried. "And to think those fool Ciralys would waste a talent like yours."

Sim spun back around. On the ramp stood the Shol'mas priest who'd been at the High Conclave that morning. The man's hood was now pushed back, and fine black hair floated around his shoulders. Golden light shone from eyes set in a pale face of startling beauty.

"Priest," Iana said.

He gave a mocking bow. "Do be careful." He gestured towards Darien. "He's going to faint."

Kaiel dashed over to catch Darien just as he slumped forward; the *tresilian* clattering to the floor.

"I thought the Shol'mas and the Ciralys didn't get on?" Sevaani said.

"We don't, as a rule," the priest agreed as he walked down the ramp. "But this Scion needed assistance to fulfil his ambitions, and my Lady of Flame obliged."

He pointed at Darien. "Opening himself to that much *Asai* at this stage in his training was not wise." Golden eyes sparkled. "But I am impressed. Not that I expected anything less, given my Lady's interest in your party."

"Stay where you are," Iana said. Lihon and the others fell back, swords still drawn. The corpses of the daemondogs lay bleeding out on the floor.

"But I've gone to such trouble to find you. And you've killed my dogs." He grimaced. "Well, not *mine*. Horrible things. Always with that hideous bark."

"Why are you here?" Iana demanded.

The Chosen Priest stepped off the ramp. "I have come for the Awakened."

"Through the doors," Iana told them calmly, but Sim lingered, watching the priest.

"Now, Sim," she said again, and Jaric pushed him back.

Sevaani and Andraste both followed quickly, and Kaiel carried Darien draped over his shoulders.

"Oh, don't leave just yet," the priest said. "My Lady has plans for you."

"Erika," Iana said. "Go."

The knight turned her head.

"Your duty is with your Ardhel," Iana told her.

"Oh, my dear," the priest said. "It has been a long time since any of the Ciralys, let alone the Shaluay, had anything close to resembling the power to oppose my Lady. You don't even have the Estay Matrix."

"I do not have the Matrix, it is true," Iana said. "But I am a student of history."

From around her waist, beneath her gold belt, she took a long chain of dark, rusted metal, its fine links aglow with a fell-green iridescence.

The priest stilled. "I sense corusite," he hissed.

"Yes, you do." Iana flicked the chain like a whip and spoke a sharp word. The chain fell to the ground between them and then rose like a snake, its end swaying as though scenting the air.

"You wouldn't dare." The priest took a step back.

As though it had been waiting for movement, the swaying chain shot forward, and the priest let out a screech.

"Run!" Iana herded the rest of them through the doors, Lihon pulling them shut behind them.

Dark stone walls enclosed them. Iron sconces on the walls were empty, and arched doorways on either side led to darkness.

Behind them, the screaming diminished. Stone steps took them deeper into the bowels of the Spire, the structure of the lower corridors unchanging as they passed more doors and tunnels branching off the main hall. Black iron bars sealed off access to some of the galleries and passages, others were open, and even more were covered with strange runes. Dust carpeted the flagstone floor, and cobwebs hung across the passage like curtains.

Sim's chest was burning when they arrived at a low-ceilinged hall that led to another set of closed doors. "Great," he said, breathing hard. "Is this one locked too?"

Yuanel went to the door while Iana brushed by Sim to kneel at Darien's side, taking his face in her hands.

Sim watched as the Shaluay bowed her head, her rings glowing green, lines of light moving across the surface of the plain bands. Suddenly Darien pulled his head back and wrenched himself from Kaiel's support.

"What are you doing?" he gasped.

"I might ask you the same thing!" the Starbinder returned angrily. "What possessed you to engage a *tresilian*?"

"What?" Darien said, somewhat dazed.

"You have had little to no training! You are no further along in your understanding of *Asai* than someone newly Tested, and you just opened yourself to an artefact of the Sahrin?"

"I could see what she was doing –" he gestured at their guide, "and it wasn't fast enough."

"Fool!"

Darien turned away.

"Look at me! I understand you are upset that your plans have come to naught, but artefacts of the Summoners are not toys. No-one knows what they can do! Even the Ciralys Artificers barely understand what they are creating. You were in danger of Blinding yourself!"

Darien flinched.

"Oh, yes. That you understand. You almost joined the ranks of the Erlain without the Scion needing to lift a finger!"

"What does it matter?" he spat. "I am not going to be a Ciralys anyway!"

"There are other –"

Yuanel cried with triumph, and the door opened.

"Gods, what's that stench?" Sim said as putrid air wafted into the corridor.

"Is that the sewers?" Andraste asked, her eyes wide. "You're not leading us into the sewers!"

"Did you have another way out?" Sim rolled his eyes.

"But the sewers of Serjat..." She trailed off.

"Enough, children," Iana said sharply. She glanced one more time at Darien then walked to the door.

"Way out, Mistress," Yuanel said.

"Then let us see." Iana strode forward, and they all followed her through the door.

Beyond was a large circular room with a domed ceiling. Tall pillars edged the walls, and in the space between each pair sat a great stone chair. Thrones. There were nine thrones, eight identical in white marble, and one, at the middle point, made of black, glittering with flecks of gold. To the side, between a pair of pillars, a set of steps led down to a small alcove with a closed gate of rusting bars.

"Look," Sevaani said, pointing at the floor.

Sim stared.

"The Crowned Raven," Andraste said.

A giant mosaic, streaked with dust, gleamed dully on the floor.

Hundreds, thousands, of tiny tiles had been placed with intricate precision to depict a raven in flight beneath a coronet of nine tines. The same raven as that etched into the ruby on the ring in his pocket.

And the raven that had been carved into the keystone above the entrance to the sewers.

Andraste stepped onto the floor and wiped the sole of her shoe across the edge of the crest. The dull, steel grey of the tiles revealed a vibrant blue, and the raven gleamed like obsidian as the dust was brushed away.

"Amazing," she said, staring at the mosaic. She gestured at the thrones around the room. "It is said that the Nine once actively sought the wisdom of the Ciralys, but no-one ever saw them speak to each other. Do you suppose this was the room they held their councils in?"

"The Nine?" Sevaani said. "The ones who ruled before they became the Eight?"

"Yes." Andraste stared back down at the crest beneath her feet. "But that's only been in the last fifty years or so. Before that, there were Nine. Eight Highlords, ruled by the Raven Lord, the holder of the Undercity."

"The Undercity?" Sim's voice was strange to his ears, and he cleared his throat.

"Serjat is divided into eight fiefs. Each Highlord of the Eight holds one of those fiefs. But the Raven Lord held the world below the city. The home of outcast warlocks, acolytes of the cult of the Blue Mask, and crime lords and their gangs," Jaric said.

"They were ruled by a thief?" Sevaani wrinkled her nose.

"The Lords of Serjat recognised power. All rulers must, and all cities have unsavoury elements, despite our best efforts," Andraste said. "The Raven Lord was the most powerful man in Tremor-Salaya."

"But there are only Eight Lords now?" Kaiel asked, frowning.

"The Eight decided they could rule the Undercity as they did the surface, so they had the Raven Lord and his family murdered." Andraste pointed at the crest beneath her feet. "You can see the signs of the Raven all over Serjat if you look," she said. "But no Tremor-Salayan will ever speak of the night the streets of Serjat ran with blood."

"If we are done with the history lesson, can we go, please?" Darien said.

Yuanel was already at the gate, playing with another lock.

"She can't possibly have a key for every door in the Spire," Erika scoffed, watching the Amarian.

"Looks like she does," Sim said distractedly as the gate opened with a screech. Why did his father have the signet ring of the Raven Lord? It *was* the signet ring, wasn't it?

"What was that?" Darien said, his head whipping around towards the hall.

"It was just the gate, Dar," Kaiel said.

"No. Listen!"

Sim raised his head with a frown.

"I don't hear –" Erika was cut off as a shrieking howl came from the corridor behind them.

"The priest," Iana said, grimly.

"I thought you killed him!" Sevaani cried.

"It's hard to kill a Shol'mas," Iana said, a frown on her face.

"The priest is a Shol'mas?" Kaiel's mouth dropped open in surprise.

"Each Chosen Priest is imbued with a part of the essence of the Lord or Lady they serve. I fear my actions may have brought the full attention of his mistress upon us."

"Oh, that was clever," Sim drawled.

"Watch your tone, Borderlander," Lihon warned.

The howling rose beyond the doorway. In the darkness of the corridor, all Sim could see was a dull red glow as a hot wind rushed over them.

Orange cinders floated on the air and Sim took a step back. "Fire? Is that fire?"

"Get through the gate," Iana said. She cupped her hands around the star sapphire at her neck.

"What are you doing?" Lihon demanded. "You can't use the Wells. You don't have the Estay Matrix!"

"I must," she said. "It is the only way to get out."

"He's not worth it!"

Iana shook her head fiercely. "He might be the only one of us who is. We cannot survive what is to come without him!"

Lihon gritted his teeth and turned stiffly towards the others. "Move. Now!"

Another wave of heat blasted out of the corridor, and Sim could smell the rank stench of singed flesh.

"Where are you?" came a sing-song call from the growing red light beyond. "I didn't know we were going to play. And you cheated; I wasn't ready. But I am now!"

Flames flared, licking the wall of the passageway and outlining the silhouette of the Chosen. His shadow stretched tall before him, right leg dragging behind, and his long hair twisted in the air like snakes.

Darien pushed past Sim, jolting him out of his stupor, and he turned, running for the gate. Water dripped somewhere in the darkness, and the fetid air was almost as bad as the smell of burnt flesh behind them.

"Can she stop it?" Jaric asked as Lihon backed towards the opening.

"Perhaps." The fury in the Blay Shon's voice was gone, replaced by ice. "But I question the price she will have to pay to do so."

Iana stood in the middle of the chamber, facing the doorway as the priest limped into the room. Gone was the elegant man who had stood behind the Scion of the Ciralys. The silks that clothed his body were in tatters, the pale skin that showed beneath was blistered, and shadows danced across his face, his golden eyes now glowing red like smouldering coals.

"Where are your friends going, little witch?" the Chosen hissed. "Are they leaving you all alone?"

"What do you want?"

"My Lady wants the sting of corusite gone from Her servant's flesh!" Pillars of flame roared up behind him. "She wants the bitch who brought us such pain to *bleed*!!" A manic scream exploded from his mouth, only to end as abruptly as it had begun.

"And She wants the Child," he said softly. "Give me the Child."

"You cannot have him," Iana said.

The Chosen Priest laughed. "My Mistress is Kirana, Lady of Flame. And She can have anything She wants!"

The pillars of flame lashed forward, like two great whips, and Iana flung up her hand, a whirlwind of pale blue light erupting before her.

Fire met ice in a tremendous crash, and the priest fell back, crouching on his haunches like an animal.

"You cannot stop me, witchling," he hissed.

"Yes, I can," she said and raised both hands again.

Blue-white light seared Sim's eyes, and he spun away. Howling winds followed the light. The Chosen was smashed against a marble pillar, his mouth opened in a scream smothered by the wind, and the fires winked out all around them.

"The stars." Behind him, Sevaani's voice quaked with awe.

"What do you see!" Lihon spun around. "Tell me!"

"I see stars, blazing all around her!"

The Blay Shon searched Sevaani's face for something, and then he turned away.

The priest fell to the floor with a thud as Iana's light went out. Fear crawled across the man's face as he stared up at the Starbinder in her violet gown, the cora'stone at her throat pulsing with light. The shadows had fled from him, and his face looked like a skull covered with wax paper.

From the tunnel came a wet gurgle and Yuanel slumped forward, sliding off a black blade. A giant, horned head moved into the flickering light.

"Back!" Sim cried out in warning as the Korda'var roared.

They all stumbled back up the steps into the chamber, Lihon and Jaric pulling their blades as the Korda'vari followed.

Sevaani screamed, falling as the large clawed hand of a Korda'var grabbed her ankle. Before her scream had died, Kaiel jumped forward, sword flashing, and severed the beast's hand from its forearm. It roared again, and Kaiel brought his sword back up, taking off its head.

"*No*!" the Chosen Priest screeched. "The Child is *mine*!"

More Korda'vari pushed their way out of the sewers and into the room, the stone plates on their arms and chest glistening wet in the light. Bodies piled before Lihon as he spun his blades. Kaiel and Jaric stood with the Sithapian knight, while Andraste, a short sword in her hand, stood behind them.

A flash of orange made Sim shield his eyes, and he fell back as a roaring inferno exploded over the mouth of the tunnel.

Kaiel and the others were thrown off their feet, and Darien staggered, lowering his hand, and collapsing to his knees.

"Dar!" Kaiel scrambled over to his brother.

"I *can* wield *Asai*," Darien said in a whisper.

"What did he do?" Erika demanded. "Isn't he untrained!"

"I do not –" Jaric began, but the priest's shriek cut him off.

"You!" the priest cried, pointing at Darien. "You are the one!"

"No!" Iana raised her hand, but a pillar of fire fell upon her.

"You are the one!" The Chosen Priest's hands moved in a whirl, and a rope of black shadow lashed forward, wrapping around Darien's neck.

The Priest yanked, and Darien was wrenched off his feet, his hands scratching at the shadow rope around his throat.

"No!"Kaiel screamed.

"Look out!"Andraste cried. Sim spun as still more Korda'vari spilled out of the tunnel, their cloven hooves stomping on the burnt bodies of their dead.

Captain Daynar and Erika backed away from the entrance, and Lihon rolled Iana on the stone floor, dousing the flames that covered her.

The Korda'vari didn't rush forward but fanned out from the tunnel. Sim backed away. They weren't acting like Korda'vari usually did.

A man in scarlet robes stepped out from behind the Tainted.

Sim had never seen one his life, but he knew exactly what that man was, what he had to be.

A Bloodlord.

The creature was ancient. Its eyes were sunken holes in a leathery skull. Black-red runes were carved on its cheeks like wounds that hadn't healed, and blood dripped from them onto the neck of the half-moon collar that fanned out behind its bald head.

The Chosen Priest screeched in rage, and a bolt of light, as bright as the sun, shot over Sim's shoulder towards the Bloodlord.

Squinting, Sim could make out the Bloodlord, still standing, smiling a hideous, toothless grin of black gums. The creature raised his hands, ringed fingers like claws and crimson lightning lashed out at the Shol'mas' Chosen, smacking him back into one of the stone thrones and shattering it.

"Dar!" Kaiel cried out again as Darien, still caught by the shadow rope, was dragged along also.

"Release the boy!"

Sim choked back a hysterical laugh as Iana stepped into the centre of the room. The dust had shifted from the floor, and the crest of the crowned raven gleamed beneath her feet.

"His blood will set my mistress free!"The Chosen's eyes flared, and he kicked broken masonry away as he climbed jerkily to his feet. He pulled a glass dagger from his belt and dragged it through the air. Light blazed in a line behind the knife, and a howling wind filled the room.

Behind him, the whir of Lihon's twin jisanas rose in the air. Sim turned. The blademaster faced the Bloodlord. Two blades of red steel rose to meet the Blay Shon, stroke for stroke, while Captain Jaric and the knight fought the Korda'vari.

"I won't let you have him," Iana said.

"You don't have a choice!" the priest hissed.

"But I do." Lady Iana raised her hands.

The cora'stone on the torque around her neck began to pulse, and in the air above her, points of light appeared like stars.

"No!" the priest screamed, his image shifting as though two people stood in the same space. "The Wells are broken!"

"I am a Firstbinder of the Stars." Now it was Iana's voice that made the hairs on the back of Sim's neck rise. It was distant and vast. "The Wells heed my call."

The Chosen Priest wailed in terror. He dived through the rift as the points of light above Iana began to fall like a rain of hailstones.

The hole created by the Chosen Priest buckled. The lines of light that defined it snapped apart, whipping around the room like a lash, cutting through stone.

Sim scrambled back, looking for safety as one throne after the other toppled, sliced in two. There was a great crack. He raised his head in horror as the ceiling split.

Iana raised her hands in the air again, and there was an enormous explosion.

The world turned, and Sim's eyes filled with light. He was being twisted inside out, and a roaring filled his ears.

Then everything went black.

CHAPTER THIRTY-ONE

A Turning Key

DARIEN GASPED AND opened his eyes. Orange light flickered in the darkness. He tried to sit up but was pinned to the ground. Heart beating wildly, he struggled to shift himself out from under the weight atop him.

Ciralys Telaq's voice rang in his mind: *A Ciralys cannot retain his connection to* Asai *if he is not centred. Passion is needed in all things, but the beast of man must never rule the mind of the Awakened.*

He took a deep breath, then another and closed his eyes. Long practice brought calm and *Asai* blazed in his mind's eye like a sun. Silver and warm, it filled him like water filling a jug. Bitterness at his rejection by the Ciralys threatened to shatter his calm and he pushed it aside with effort, focusing on the physical, seeking to ground himself. His lip throbbed where Kaiel had punched him – *punched* him! He ran his tongue over his swollen lip, prodding the rough edge of split skin.

Kaiel had never hit him before. Never.

His throat burned and he lifted his hands to run his fingers over the tender skin at his neck. There was no swelling from the shadow rope, but its touch lingered. A quick cataloguing of his other aches and pains reassured him that nothing was broken.

He opened his eyes once more and focused on his surroundings.

There was a crackling to his left, and groans and voices from somewhere behind him. Relief washed over him that he wasn't alone, and he tried again to move the weight from his chest – he could just make out the blond hair of his brother. Anger flared, quickly followed by shame. He managed to wiggle himself free, but as he pulled himself upright, Kaiel slid, and Darien realised they were on a slope. He grabbed at Kaiel, halting his movement, his brother's chest now pinning his legs.

Darien remained frozen, heart racing as around them rocks and soil shifted.

Above them the Sormelene Span shone in the clear night sky, stars blazing around it – they were obviously no longer underground. It had only been afternoon when they fled into the lower passages of the Spire. The flickering orange light came from small fires scattered around a… a mountainside? Large, shadowy pieces of masonry lay across the terrain, and he recognised the pieces of broken stone on the slope around them as the thrones from the chamber. He shivered as an icy wind howled over him, silently thanking Lady Iana for the coat he was wearing.

He felt Kaiel move.

"Dar!" he called, and the ground beneath them shifted as he made to get up.

They both slid a foot or more before slamming against a large boulder.

"Don't move!" Darien warned.

"Where are we?" Kaiel asked, thankfully keeping still.

"I don't know," Darien said. "On a mountain."

"A mountain?" Kaiel sat up. "But we were underneath the Spire!"

"I said don't move!" he cried as more rocks slid away, crashes echoing in the darkness below.

"Kaiel? Darien?" Captain Daynar's voice came from above.

The scent of burning pine was strong in the air. Firelight illuminated thin trees clinging to the slopes and outlined the captain as he peered over the short drop to where they were wedged.

"Are you all right?" He wasn't shouting, but his voice was loud in the darkness.

"Captain! Where are we?" Kaiel got to his knees.

Darien let out an involuntary hiss and grabbed Kaiel's arm. His brother stopped moving again, but the block of stone they rested against didn't shift, and he let go of Kaiel.

"I do not know, Kaiel," Jaric said. "Can you stand up? We can pull you up to the rest of us."

"Take Dar first," Kaiel said, helping to hoist him up the steep slope.

Jaric hauled him up, and Darien stood on somewhat unsteady legs, brushing dirt from his trousers as Captain Daynar reached back down for Kaiel.

They were on a ledge of broken stone that was unnaturally straight – flat, like part of a road. More fires burned in scattered branches, steaming as snow melted and hindered the fire's progress.

He looked over the rest of the group. Lihon was a shadowy bulk sitting across from him with Iana's head resting on his lap. Sevaani was kneeling beside them, evidently checking her over. A groan to his right identified Sim. Beyond him, Erika gathered branches into a makeshift fire pit, while the princess stood beside her, staring at the night sky.

"I don't understand," Andraste muttered. "The stars are wrong. Look."

Darien glanced up and searched the stars for the twin pointers of the Herald in the east, but they were not there. Frowning, he scanned the sky and found what he was looking for to the south-east, far from where it usually sat in the heavens. Even the Span was closer, as though it sat higher in the northern sky.

"We are in the Eastern Realms," Lihon said from his position supporting the Shaluay.

"What?" Andraste spun on him.

"I recognise these stars; they are the skies of northern Amaria."

"Do you know what happened? How we got here?" Darien asked.

"I was fighting the Bloodlord; then I came to over there." Lihon pointed towards the edge of the stones.

"Will Lady Iana be well?" the princess asked.

"I don't know," the blademaster said stonily.

"Oh, my head," Sim groaned from behind them. He stood, his arms wrapped about his lean torso. "Where are we? It's freezing!"

"We do not know," Captain Daynar said as he and Kaiel joined them.

"We are somewhere on the Eastern Half," Andraste told them, her voice tight.

To the west, a howl rose in the silence.

"Korda'vari," Sim said, spinning around to peer into the night.

Andraste scoffed. "That is one thing we do not have to worry about. There are no Korda'vari in the Eastern Realms."

"Oh, really?" Sim raised an eyebrow as the howl rose again, like a knife scraping glass. "I'm certain that's not a wolf."

"But... how?" The princess was pale in the light of the Span.

"It is Korda'vari," Jaric said. "Put out the fires."

"We need the warmth!" Erika protested.

The captain rounded on her. "Korda'vari have poor night vision, but if they have a fire to guide them, they will come. Without it, they would need a Lloth'var to direct them."

"How do you know there is not one of those out there too?" Andraste asked.

"Because I did not see one under the Spire," Jaric said, scattering Erika's fire with a booted foot.

"Under the Spire. You mean they somehow came with us?" Andraste stared at him in disbelief.

"Why not?" Jaric drew his sword. "You are the one who said there are no Korda'vari on the Eastern Half."

"If Lady Iana could just whisk us across the world, why did we have to spend a month hurling the contents of our stomachs into the Nemisdrillion Sea?" Sim asked.

"She did not do this," Lihon said.

"Was it that priest? The Chosen?" Sim grabbed Darien's arm.

"How would I know?" Darien shrugged him off.

"I saw what you did in the chamber of the bone drake," he said, arching an eyebrow. "Your master taught you more than you let on."

Darien's blood went cold, but he managed to shake his head.

"That would mean the Bloodlord is here too," Andraste said to Jaric, ignoring Sim. "Unless you killed him, Lord Lihon?"

"I did not," the blademaster said. "Our battle was interrupted."

"It is said that only the greatest of warriors can stand against one of the daemonspawn," Erika said, awe tempering her tone. "Their powers are said to rival the greatest of the Ciralys before the Sundering."

"I would like to know where it came from, and why," Jaric interrupted. "Their kind has not been seen since the rise of the Imperium."

Darien thought of the Bloodlord, of Bertha in Glass Bay but held his tongue.

"The Ciralys and the Covens claim they were wiped out." Andraste moved closer to Erika and peered out into the darkness.

Jaric grunted. "And how would they know? They have not surveyed the greater part of Dal'mere in centuries; all their attention is focused on the Borderland catacombs and any other ruin they can strip of skystones or artefacts. They would have had no idea what was happening at Halaron."

"Do you?" Lihon asked sharply.

After a moment, the captain grunted. "The Borderlands have been quiet until recently. But that in itself means nothing, given all that has happened." He glanced at the princess and fell silent.

The final branches, still alight with flames, hissed into darkness as Sim dumped handfuls of snow over them.

"Take care to stay on the road," Jaric said.

"Who'd put a road up here?" Sim muttered under his breath, moving back into the middle of the cracked and broken stones.

"It is close to the turning of the day," Lihon said. "The sun will rise in three hours, maybe four."

A cry echoed across the mountain, animal in tone, but the rage it held made Darien's blood run cold. He couldn't contain his shiver.

"At least they don't have a Lloth'var with them," Sim said after a moment. "Just that Bloodlord."

Kaiel grunted in agreement.

"Who *are* you people?" Andraste muttered. "How can you possibly know these things?"

"We're Borderlanders, Your Highness," Kaiel said as if that explained everything.

With the flickering light of the fire gone, Darien's night vision improved, and he turned east to stare over Sevaani's head. The ground they stood on was uneven, as was to be expected on a mountainside, but there were some strangely flat stretches. Slabs of tiles, from beneath the Spire, he supposed, lay scattered all around, but they rested atop weathered paving stones that must have been here before they arrived.

He tracked the path as best he could in the night's light; missing stones made dark gaps, and the side of the mountain fell away, leaving a ridge that headed east.

"If there was a Lloth'var with them, the bulls wouldn't be making a sound," Sim was telling Andraste.

"We should move back," Jaric interjected.

"Why?" Kaiel asked. "What's wrong?"

"I am not confident the Korda'vari are as far off as they sound," the captain said. "We are obviously in a mountain range, and noise moves strangely in the heights."

"Couldn't this just be hills somewhere?" Sim suggested.

"The air is too thin," Jaric explained. "But let's hope we are not as close to Amaria as Lihon thinks." The captain looked south, over an ocean of darkness. "If we are *in* Amaria itself, and we are caught, we will be made slaves."

"What?" Sim said.

"Amarians allow no other race beyond the outer walls of the capital city, Shi'a Li'ang, or the trade port of Saurin'sha on the Nemisdrillion Sea. Any foreigner found outside of those two cities is made a slave," Andraste said.

Another howl split the night.

"That was closer," Sim said unnecessarily.

"The Korda'vari *are* closer than we'd thought."

"Lady Iana!" Sevaani's cry rose behind them. "Are you all right?"

"I'm fine," Iana said, and Darien felt a grudging admiration as she pushed herself upright.

"You should not have engaged the Starwells!" the blademaster said to her and Darien was surprised at his vehemence.

"I had no choice; I could not let the Chosen take the boy." She got to her feet. "Where are we?"

"We think we are in Amaria," Sevaani told her.

"The Eastern Half?" she lifted her head to the night sky.

"I do not understand how we got here," Andraste said leaving Darien's side to stand before Iana. "But I need to get home. If I am gone for any length of time, my uncle will have me declared dead."

"We are likely here because of the portal the Chosen was opening, but I can't return us to Serjat the same way." Iana took the blademaster's hand and rose. She swayed for a moment but held up a hand before Lihon could speak. "I am fine," she said. "The Chosen was using his connection with the Shol'mas Kirana to open a portal. I had no choice but to engage the Starwells to counter him. The energies raised from the Wells must have disrupted it."

"A portal,"Andraste repeated."Is that like a Ciralys Gateway?"

"It is a lost art of the Summoners that has none of the restrictions the Gateways are bound by,"Iana said.

"No more questions,"Lihon said.

Iana smiled."Don't fuss so."

"You attempted to access the Wells while more than half of them are silent, and the Estay Matrix is still lost.You are lucky to be alive."

"You could have died?" Sevaani asked. Darien eyed Sevaani as she pulled her shawl tight around her shoulders. Had she dreamt this too?

"But I didn't die,"Iana said."None of us did."

Another howl split the air, closer than before.

"Korda'vari?"The Starbinder turned to Lihon."Here?"

The blademaster nodded, his topknot swinging.

Darien dropped his hand to the pouch at his side as the others talked in circles, closing his fist around it. He couldn't feel the shard Telaq had passed him, but it reassured him to clutch at the cloth. The sheer sides of the mountain peak rose above him, and the glow of the Span lit the snow, leaving long shadows over the broken road. He let his gaze follow the road to the east, where it stretched off the mountainside in a narrow line. To either side of the ridge, dark shadows mingled with grey as the road continued, leading to a wall on the other side. At least it looked like a wall, in the dark of night it was just a shadowed mass, but there was an edge to the line that spoke of architecture.

His pulse quickened as he made out slender fingers of stone – towers? – rising into the night sky behind the wall.

"They're coming!" Sim's cry startled him and echoing roars of the Korda'vari erupted from the western slope of the mountain as their shadowy forms burst out of the treeline.

Kaiel and the others raised their swords and rushed to defensive positions.

"We are trapped!" Andraste cried. She wasn't scared. She was angry.

"Can you do anything?" Sevaani asked Iana, her hands grasping the edge of her shawl tightly.

"I can try."

The Starbinder raised her arms, the sleeves of her indigo dress falling back to reveal her obsidian-like bracers. Glowing glyphs appeared in the air before her, and her fingers danced over them, pushing some aside and rearranging others.

Darien watched her carefully; he could sense no *Asai* being used and did not recognise the symbols she employed. What power did the Shaluay use that did not arise from the Light of the Eye?

She levelled her hands at the Korda'vari. As she closed her hands into fists, glowing rings of blue-white light shot through the air with a hiss.

The rings sped through the space between the men, crashing into the dark forms before them. Darien stared in shock as light flashed in silent explosions at each hit, and Korda'vari screams rose as they went flying. It was *Asai* but not. What did the Shaluay wield?

"I can do no more," Iana said, lowering her arms. "I used too much energy in the Spire."

More Korda'vari, large hulking shadows, rushed to fill the gap and swords rang again. Bestial grunts and snarls merged with the wind and Darien saw Erika fall back with a cry.

Andraste tensed beside him, but the knight got back to her feet and re-joined the fight, her left arm dragging.

He looked around for something to use as a weapon and grabbed a branch, black in the snow. He yelped as his hand closed around it dropping it before he'd fully straighten, his palm stinging from the burn of a recently doused flame.

"There are too many of them," Andraste said. She had drawn two short swords.

"You can't join them," Sevaani cried. "You're a princess!"

"It is better than standing here waiting to be overrun!" Andraste's response was sharp but without heat. "I have been trained in swords since I was a child. Lord deOrlay was my first blademaster."

"And he would not forgive himself if something were to befall you trying to help them," Iana told her.

"I have to do something!" the princess said.

Iana looked around. "There has to be a way down from this mountain."

"Back there," Darien said. "This ... road heads out over a ridge."

She shook her head. "We can't be pushed to the cliff."

"It leads to a… a city or some such. Look." He pointed. "See the wall?"

"Are you sure?" Iana pressed.

"I cannot see anything," Andraste said. "There are no lights."

From the Korda'vari came a roar and then their grunts took on the rhythm of chanting. Darien's blood ran cold as he sensed *Asai* from within their midst. In his mind, the csitargon stirred. It wasn't *Asai* he felt. It was *Des'maadr*. "He's here."

"Who?" Iana turned to him.

"The Bloodlord." Darien stared intently at the dark mass of heaving monsters, the glint of moving swords flashing like pale lightning. Then beyond them, a pair of red, glowing eyes blinked in the darkness.

"There," he yelled, but the Korda'vari moved again, and the eyes disappeared.

"Go now!" Iana pushed them behind her.

Darien tried again to catch a glimpse of the Bloodlord, but Sevaani grabbed his arm and pulled him to the ridge. The mountain ledge fell away, and half the road seemed to disappear before them down the sheer black side of the mountain.

"Are you sure this is safe?" Sevaani yelled, the wind tearing at her words.

"We do not have a choice!" Andraste yelled. Crouching, she eased her legs over the side and lowered herself down. Darien and Sevaani followed suit. Iana and Sim came quickly behind them, with Jaric, Kaiel and Erika close behind. Lihon was lost in the darkness, but Darien was sure the Blay Shon was holding the Korda'vari back with his whirling swords.

The wind rose across the side of the mountain, and Darien was forced to crouch, grabbing at the edges of the blocks of stones that protruded from the road.

"Come on!" Andraste called. They cautiously moved out, struggling against the wind.

"Sevaani!" Darien heard Kaiel yell behind him. "You have to move!"

"I can't!"

Darien looked over his shoulder as Sevaani screamed and threw herself to the stones, her skirts and shawl streaming in the wind as it blustered over them. "I'll fall!"

He'd never known Sevaani to be scared of heights, but then in the Borderlands they'd never been higher off the ground than the third storey of the High Keep – and not all citadelfolk had been to the top of that!

Darien's stomach twisted. The wind pushed at him. The stone seemed to move under him, but he couldn't tell if it was loose or if it was just the wind. He looked up and saw Kaiel crouching on the block, one hand hooked over the edge to anchor him as the wind tugged mercilessly. Darien watched his brother turn side on to the howling wind and reached for Sevaani.

"Take my hand!" Kaiel worked his way around Sim and grabbed her. She flung herself at him. Panic flooded Darien. They were both going to go over the edge.

But Kaiel caught her and waved them all forward."Go!"he cried, and Darien forced himself to breathe. He began to move again, crawling behind Andraste, an unknown drop on either side of them.

It took forever to get halfway across. Darien had no idea how far the ridge ran; the half-light of the Span and the shadows of night played havoc with his judgement, but the wall he had spied from the ledge was growing taller in the sky the closer they came.

Looking back again, he could make out the dark bulk of Korda'vari milling at the edge of the mountain's ledge. Lihon was already halfway across the ridge-road when one of the Korda'vari fell, as though pushed from behind. It landed face-first on the ridge and rolled over the side with a scream that vanished as quickly as it began. The next Korda'var was more careful, and Darien could make out the red eyes of the Bloodlord in their midst.

Darien froze as those eyes met his own, and the daemon in his mind rolled in anger.

"Keep moving!"Sim's shout broke him free of the Bloodlord's gaze, and he loosened the grip of his aching fingers on the edge of the block and stepped forward.

Every time they slowed, they lost ground.

"No, Kaiel. I can't!"Sevaani sobbed.

"Wait." Darien glanced back again as Kaiel disengaged her arms from his neck.

"Just let me get over this side, and I'll help you across,"Kaiel called out to her.

The fool was going to get himself killed!

With gritted teeth, Darien turned away, concentrating on moving himself. The Bloodlord couldn't catch him. He didn't want to live his life as a slave to a daemon. He needed to focus. The ridge would have been hazardous even without the wind doing its best to send them over the side. Before him, one of the great paving stones had fallen away, and he gingerly felt for footing on the rock beneath, looking for a steady perch to reach across the gap.

The wall at the road's end was just ahead of him; Andraste was already standing on another ledge.

His stomach clenched as he pushed himself across, all caution replaced by the blinding panic of reaching the next paving stone without falling. He landed on the block of stone, his stomach feeling as though it had dropped from his body as the stone moved beneath him, but it held firm. He couldn't help the whimper that left his lips, but he pulled his weak, shaking legs up under himself.

How was Kaiel going to get Sevaani across that?

With his heart in his throat, Darien scrambled forward, making room for Sim and looked back. His half-brother leant over the divide and swung himself across the short gap. Kaiel edged ahead as a strong gust of wind barrelled into him, nearly knocking him off the ridge. But his hold was firm, and Darien watched him wait for the wind to pass before pulling Sevaani across to him. Darien closed his eyes briefly in relief, cursing Kaiel for his heroics.

Darien continued across the remaining length of the broken roadway, and onto the smooth and sturdy ledge that lay before a massive wall of everstone. In front of them was an enormous octagon gate, closed to the world.

Andraste stood in the shadowed recess, her white gown giving her a spectral appearance."There is no way in," she called to him.

"What?" he stepped forward.

"It is a dead-end!" Her shoulders slumped.

"No, it can't be!"

"We are trapped!" she said, hitting the stone gate ineffectually.

Darien wanted to scream in frustration. Taking a breath, he traced a rune in the air. With a flick of his Will, Darien filled it with *Asai*, and a small ball of pale light flickered into being above his hand. He had been told by Master Telaq not to make use of the cants he had been taught – to do so would go against all tradition, and the Ciralys would frown upon anyone unsanctioned using their lore – but those were consequences he no longer had to worry about.

The ball of *Asai* illuminated a smooth wall of black everstone. There were no openings or cracks to indicate where it might part, and there was no place for a key.

"Get rid of that light!" Sim hissed, coming up behind him. "Could you make us any more of a target?"

"The Korda'vari know where we've gone, Simeon," Iana said coming to stand beside Darien. "It makes little difference."

Darien stifled a curse. He would *not* die here. There had to be a way in!

"Look at those markings," Iana said.

He inspected the edge of the wall. Along the inside of the octagonal recess, on the stone at each edge, was inscribed a single rune. They were unadorned, and only the shadows cast by his light made them visible against the obsidian-like stone.

"What are they? Can you read them?" Andraste asked as Jaric, Erika and Lihon climbed off the ridge onto the platform.

"No, not without taking more time than we have." Iana shook her head.

"Then we have to make a stand," Jaric said.

"How long will that last?" Erika stared across the ridge at the approaching Korda'vari.

"As long as it must," Lihon said.

"Here they come." Kaiel raised his sword. The steel of the blade shone in the light of the Ring and battered hard against the club the Korda'var raised in defence. Jaric and Lihon moved to support him as Kaiel swiped his blade back around and slashed the Korda'var's chest open. The daemonspawn fell from the ridge and was replaced by another.

Darien turned back to the gate. Those runes *must* mean something. He turned his attention inward and let the Light of the Eye fill his senses. *Asai* flooded him, it coursed through his veins, filling his lungs.

To his eyes, the runes on the gate began to glow. They floated before him; anchored to the stone they were carved on, but also trailing into the air as though they existed in more than one dimension.

Behind him, the clang of steel on steel and the cries of his companions faded into the background. He traced each rune with his mind. He felt along their shape, tracing their curled edges. Still, he could not discern their meaning as they twisted beneath his regard.

More cries came from behind him, and sweat beaded his forehead. Firmly, he pushed his panic aside.

He studied the runes intently, and in his mind, he suddenly felt the daemon reach for *Asai*.

The silver light of *Asai* flared violet against his sight, and the eight runes stretched, reaching out to a ninth that appeared before him in the gate's centre. The ninth rune faded as quickly as it had come, and the others continued to twist in their place as he stumbled back, his focus lost.

The cries of the Korda'vari were louder, and Sevaani's screams were shrill against the roar of the wind. He snarled at his failure and opened himself to *Asai* once more.

This time the runes blazed as he filled himself with power. He lifted his hand. He didn't know what he was doing, only that it felt right. Touching his finger to the space in the centre of the gate, he dragged it down as though he were writing on the wall.

Asai filled the line his finger drew, and he blinked in surprise.

He moved to the middle of the wall and sketched the rune he'd seen.

It had eight lines that reached out to each of the runes around it, and it began to glow.

And as it glowed, it drew *Asai* through Darien.

He sucked in a breath as a trickle of Power became a torrent.

The rune he'd drawn hooked itself into his being and pulled. He couldn't stop it. *Asai* was filling him to bursting, straining his ability to contain it safely. The energy that raged through him was like nothing he'd ever imagined, and his panic was burnt away as his gaze was filled with Light.

But just as he felt as though his mind would burn, the flood stopped and the rune he'd drawn flared black, light shining around it. Across the closed gate runes of gold and azure, in tiny octagon tiles, appeared. One by one, they collapsed upon each other in a cascade, and the everstone gate disappeared.

"It's open!" Andraste cried. "How did you open it?"

Darien swayed on his feet, reeling. Hands grabbed him just as his knees gave way.

"Quickly, through the gate!" Iana called, and someone dragged him across the threshold.

CHAPTER THIRTY-TWO

Isae'eldar

"MOVE BACK!" JARIC shouted, pulling Kaiel forcibly from the ledge.

Kaiel breathed hard, lungs straining. There was splattered blood across the front of his shirt, and the arms of his coat gaped open from cuts, the wind stinging his exposed flesh. His sword arm was tight, the muscles aching from use.

"Kaiel! Get through the gate!"

He stared. The recess behind them was no longer dark with shadow; Iana and Sevaani were already passing under the opening. His stomach tightened, panic flaring at the sight of Sim dragging Darien.

Steel rang behind him, stopping briefly as a Korda'var was knocked from the ledge. Then began again as another took its place.

He stumbled across the platform; his eye caught by the white glow of Andraste's over-robe.

"What are you doing?" he asked, breathing hard. "We've got to go through!"

She didn't turn. "I will not retreat while one of mine still fights."

The light of the Span traced the lines of her face. He shook his head. "It's her duty to protect you. You're not helping Erika by staying out here and putting yourself in danger." He grabbed her arm. "Come on!" He pulled her through the opening into a large square bathed in the ghostlight of the night sky and the gurgling sound of falling water coming from a fountain at its centre. The others were crowding at its far side, a street stretching out behind them.

"Lihon, hurry!"

Kaiel turned as Jaric called out.

On the other side of the octagon gate, the Amarian's swords spun in a whirling frenzy, the steel flashing in the moonlight. Erika stumbled back towards them before Lihon finally dashed across the platform.

"The Bloodlord is coming!" he yelled.

But as the Blay Shon passed through the gate, the opening faded away, and the wall returned, shutting the daemonspawn out.

The night fell silent but for the howl of the wind and the thumping of his pulse.

"Are you hurt?" Erika grabbed Andraste by her shoulders. "Why did you wait? You could have been killed!"

"What kind of ruler would I make if I fled at the first sign of danger?" Andraste shook off her knight's hands.

"A living one!" the knight snapped.

"Erika –"

"It is my place to die for you!" Erika interrupted her. "Just as it was Renar's place to die for you. If you do not live, then our home falls to your uncle!"

"How am I going to get back home? Renar died for nothing!" In the silence of the square, her voice was shrill, echoing among the silent buildings that surrounded them.

"You are alive, Andra." Jaric had come up behind them. "And as long as you live, their lives were not given in vain. Men and women will die for you. It is their place and their privilege, and you dishonour them if you make their sacrifice for nothing. You were raised in the court of the Rose Throne, do not tell me that you have forgotten this so easily."

Tight-lipped, the princess turned on her heel and stalked away.

"She will be well," the captain said. He put a hand on Erika's shoulder as the knight made to follow her. "She just needs time."

Erika pulled away from him. Nodding sharply, she walked off in the other direction, and Jaric sighed. He offered Kaiel a grim smile. "And you?" he asked. "Are you well?"

"Yes, Captain," Kaiel said, and Jaric grunted.

"We are a little past my being your captain, Kaiel."

Kaiel was saved from answering as Lihon joined them.

"Will that keep them out?" Jaric asked, nodding at the wall that was back in place, sealing the city off from the outside world.

"Iana might know better than I." The Blay Shon shrugged. "But it looks like it will hold unless the Bloodlord can bring it down."

"It is possible," Iana said, joining them. "It would depend on the strength of the daemon the Bloodlord is enslaved by. Unless I have missed my guess, this was built by the Sahrin, and their citadels have ever been impervious to easy entry."

"Then how did we get inside?" Jaric asked.

"That is an excellent question," the Starbinder murmured, her eyes on Darien.

Kaiel turned to take in his surrounds. Floating wisps of light made the stone of the city glow. Some buildings had significant cracks in the walls, and traces of shadow spread across them; others had collapsed, stone littering the buckled roadway beneath them. Spurs of dark rock had erupted through the pavement, suggesting the city had once been on flat ground, not atop a mountain, and beyond the spurs rose slanted towers of sparkling crystal and stone.

Kaiel suppressed a shiver as the dark spaces of arched windows, and tall doors suddenly seemed like eyes, watching their every move.

"Here, Kaiel," Sim called, getting up. "Look after your brother, I dragged him inside here; you can do the rest."

Kaiel gave a start, panic flaring. He'd forgotten all about Darien.

"Dar? Dar, are you all right?" His brother was lying on the paving stones, Sevaani by his side. He crouched.

"I'm fine." Darien nodded.

Kaiel sighed in relief. "What happened to you?"

"Your brother opened the gate," Iana said.

"He did?"

"Yes." She eyed Darien speculatively. "A most remarkable feat."

"Why did the Ciralys reject him if he can do that?" Sim asked.

"Indeed," the Starbinder murmured.

Behind them, a dull thud came from the closed gate.

"We should move," Lihon said, appearing beside them. "We need to find shelter until morning."

"Simeon," Iana said. "Would you help Lihon scout?"

Sim eyed the dark buildings and shrugged, his hand going to the hilt of his short sword. "It seems pretty empty."

"It is not, look." Jaric pointed to a street, heading east. A dark stain glistened in the light, laying a trail on the paving stones.

"Is that blood?" Sevaani took a step forward.

"We should avoid going that way," Sim said.

Lihon surveyed the empty street. "We can discover who or what that belongs to in daylight. Come," he said to Sim, who followed the Blay Shon in the opposite direction.

Andraste returned to the group, her eyes dark and face pale. "Is this place a Dreamhold?"

"An Isae'eldar. Yes, I believe so." Iana gazed around. "Look." She walked to a large statue that loomed over the square. At Iana's approach, the figure began to glow from within, its misty crystal lighting the night more brightly than the moon, the Span or the wisps hanging in the air. The alien beauty of the carving was vibrant, for all that the crystal was riddled with cracks, and one arm had fallen to shatter on the ground, its pieces sparkling.

"I've seen statues made by the Summoners before," Sevaani said, "but never like this."

"You have?" the princess asked, her surprise evident. "We have five intact everstone statues in the palace in Sith'sara; how have you seen statues like this in the Borderland Wilds?"

"The Borderlands are full of wonders," Jaric said. "The citadels were built by the Sahrin after all."

"I did not mean –" Andraste broke off, and Kaiel was sure she was blushing. "I did not mean to offer you insult," she said to Sevaani.

Sevaani opened her mouth in surprise. Kaiel was sure she had never expected to be receiving an apology from a princess before. Or was Andraste a queen? He didn't know.

"That's fine, ah... Your Highness." Sevaani rallied, offering a quick bow of her head.

"Please, it is only fair you call me Andra." The princess smiled faintly, then cleared her throat. "Isae'eldari, Dreamholds, are believed to be impregnable. All recorded instances of their discovery have been of explorers seeing them on peaks, and in mountain ranges that rose during the Sundering. But no-one has ever been able to reach them; even gryphons will not fly to them. How are we going to get out?"

"I do not know," the Shaluay said, and another thud came from the gate.

"We need to get away from this door. Come, Dar," Kaiel said. "Do you need help getting up?"

"No," Darien protested, but grasped Kaiel's proffered hand just the same, as Sim ran back into the square.

"We've found a place we can shelter in," he said. "A tower. Sort of. It's just up this street."

The others gathered themselves and followed, the light of the crystal statue fading behind them.

—•—

The tower was a four-storey structure of crystal and everstone that slid diagonally into the sky. Each floor held a single open room, with stairs to the next running along one wall. Most importantly, there was only one entrance.

After a brief discussion, Lihon and Jaric set themselves up before the stairs on the third floor to stand watch. Kaiel and Erika had protested they could take a turn as well, but the captain and the Blay Shon had refused, claiming the morning was not that far off and that they should get some rest while they could. The others spread around the open room. The furnishings were not as hardy as the stone and crystal around them. Wood crumbled under careless fingers, and chairs lay in broken heaps, while tattered ribbons of fabric hung on the walls.

Exhaustion called Kaiel to sleep, but its embrace did not claim him for long. The dawn found him at a shallow balcony as the sun rose, its light setting the graceful towers around him alight like jewelled fingers of flame. The absence of birds to greet the sun was markedly strange.

"I can't believe it is morning already," Erika said, coming up behind him.

"Yes," he said, and his stomach rumbled, loudly. The knight laughed, clapping him on the shoulder.

"I'm hungry too," she agreed with a smile.

"Well, at least there's water in the fountain."

She grimaced. "But is it safe to drink?"

"It's running, so I guess so."

"That gives me pause," the knight said. "How can a fountain still be running so long after the Sundering?"

"Where the Summoners are concerned, it does not surprise me,"

Jaric said, joining them. "In the Borderlands there are still walls and roads that look as though they were erected yesterday."

Erika grunted. "It's strange to hear you speak so knowledgeably of a realm at the other end of the world."

"Things change," the captain said.

"Yes, they do, Your Grace." Erika looked away, gazing out at the city.

Jaric stared at the knight's back then turned to Kaiel. "I am going to examine the trail we saw last night. Do you want to come?"

Kaiel nodded.

"We will be back soon," Jaric told Erika, and she nodded tersely.

They exited the tower into the cold morning air, and Kaiel shivered. The stone building offered no real warmth, but it had sheltered them from the breeze that whistled down the streets. His new leather coat should have offered him some protection, but the cuts on the arms provided easy entry for the chill air. He was embarrassed at the state of the clothes Lady Iana had purchased. They were the finest he'd ever worn, and he'd ruined them in less than a month.

To the west, the mountain they had been deposited on rose above the city wall. It reached farther into the sky than he had expected, having imagined in the dark of night that they had been on its peak. Snow covered its sloping sides in a white mantle, but the sky was clear of clouds.

"I never expected to see Andra again," Jaric said as they made their way down the street.

Kaiel paused, studying his captain. Jaric was the same man he'd known all his life, his face strong, lines around his eyes and the dusting of silver in his black hair the only indication of his age. He was the man he'd always been, but now there was a difference in his bearing. As though he stood straighter, his manner more confident, more commanding.

No, that wasn't true. The captain *was* just the same as he had always been.

"Are you really a lord?" he asked.

"Does it matter to you if I was once the Rion of Orlay?"

"I... I don't know where that is."

Jaric chuckled. "Would that make a difference?"

"No," Kaiel said. "But that title doesn't mean anything to me."

"What if I was the High Prince of Ebron?"

"Well, I know who that is." Kaiel grinned.

"Borderlanders," Jaric said, not unkindly.

"You're a Borderlander too."

"Am I? I have trained the Rangers and led them in defence of Hanore, but I am still an outsider."

"Doesn't matter," Kaiel insisted. "I mean, yes, to some people, like the Nolins and old man Sam, it might, but to the rest of us, no. You're not an outsider at all."

"It might be easier if I was," Jaric sighed.

"What do you mean?"

"Kaiel, I was a Lord of Sithapia, Prime of House deOrlay; I was a friend and councillor to the Ardhel and an uncle to the young woman who is now its rightful ruler. I left Sithapia, choosing a voluntary exile under a cloud of scandal. I found a place in Hanore where I was needed, where my skills could be put to good use, and my past was unlikely to find me. I was happy after a fashion." His face was unreadable. "Now, I am conflicted. I am duty-bound to honour my commitment to Hanore, but my past reaches out, and I cannot help but believe the Elder Gods are moving in Their Dance. Andraste needs me."

"And we don't?"

"The Borderlands do not hold with the ties of the Houses, and another will have taken my place as captain already. The people of the citadels are hardy and honest like that, whereas the Houses and Dynasties of the Realms will play at bloodsport behind closed doors, and those who say they are your friend to your face will stab you in the back as soon as you turn away."

"What can you do to help her now?" Kaiel asked. "It seems to me the worst has been done."

Jaric gave a rough laugh. "The worst? She still lives," he said. "More can yet be done."

"What are you going to do?"

"I do not know," Jaric admitted. "It might be better if I never return to Hanore. Especially now that people from my old life know where I am."

"The Princess?"

"And Erika," Jaric grunted. "She has a right to bear me ill will." He looked around, then pointed at a street ahead of them. "The trail should be over here."

They walked into the square, the morning light shining on the crystal statue of the one-armed woman, the gate behind them still whole. And closed. Jaric crouched, studying the stains they'd noticed the night before.

"It's not heavy bleeding, but it's left a good trail," Jaric said.

"But what left it?"

"That's the question," the captain agreed. "Let's see how far it goes."

They followed the trail along the east road. Daylight revealed the buildings around them to be of various jewel tones that dazzled Kaiel. Before he'd seen the walls of the catacombs under Sonyth, he'd never known that everstone could be any colour other than white… or off-white and turning black in some places.

Though the mountain heights held the Isae'eldar from the ravages of explorers that visited the citadels, it had not protected it from time. Through crumbled walls, Kaiel eyed the interiors of buildings and towers. On other structures, roofs had gaping holes where tiles had disappeared, presumably fallen within, and the crystal walls and windows had cracked. But their most exciting discovery were the gardens.

While the everstone held firm against the encroachment of weeds, the gardens and small parks that surrounded the dwellings overflowed wildly; almost all of them containing trees with fruit ripe for the picking amongst intricately wrought gazebos of verdigris bronze.

He pointed the trees out to Jaric.

"We should take some back with us," Jaric said. "Do not eat anything until Lady Iana has seen it first, though."

"But they're just apples, aren't they?" Kaiel peered at the red fruit hanging from the nearest tree. "And over there are oranges!"

"We need to be cautious, Kaiel," Jaric warned. He nodded at the road. "The trail heads that way."

Ahead of them, the street opened onto another square, revealing tower after crystal tower, each taller than the one before, marching towards the centre of the city. Bridges linked the tower heights like gossamer webs shining in the morning light, and at their centre, taller than all the rest, stood a single crystal spire traced with white and gold everstone.

The trail they followed crossed the square, leading directly to the base of the central tower and up deep steps to an open archway at its base.

"What now?" Kaiel asked.

"We wanted to see where the trail led," Jaric said. "We found it. Now we go back to the others."

"Don't you want to see what's inside?"

The captain raised an eyebrow. "Not by ourselves," he said. "This looks like some sort of meeting place, the centre of the city. I do not doubt that Lady Iana will want to see it."

"Why *did* she help us?" Kaiel asked, the question bursting from him. "I'm grateful, but why is she getting involved?"

Jaric grunted. "Ask a Ciralys that question, and they'd tell you she was interfering. Trying to catch you on a hook for some scheme she has only half thought of."The captain met his eye."By Garnavaar, lad, I do not know. This business of you being the Scion of House Taaren'th is strange."He shook his head."Right now, you could do with all the help you can get, and if that comes from her, then I say you take it." Jaric cocked his head."You do not trust her?"

"No,"Kaiel said, then shrugged."I don't know. Dar doesn't trust her."

"Your brother is slow to trust anyone,"Jaric commented.

"He has his reasons."

"Was that the first time you had hit him?"

Kaiel stumbled."What?"

"Your brother has been on edge since we left Sonyth, and could do with cultivating some maturity," Jaric told him. "The punch you gave him was akin to a slap; you pulled it so hard. It would not have hurt, had it been harder."

Kaiel looked down. Punching Darien was not something he was proud of.

"You have nothing to be ashamed of. I have known both you boys all your lives; I am not a stranger passing judgement on him. He is a talented young man, but at times his arrogance would not be out of place in the palaces of any Realm."Jaric sighed."It might be harsh, but the Ciralys' rejection of your brother will do him good."

Kaiel laughed, disbelieving."How? He hung everything on joining them. He'll never go back to Hanore, but what else can he do?"

"Your brother will be fine once he gets out of his sulk. There is a whole world of opportunity waiting for a young man with a brain. If he wants to learn to wield the Light of the Eye, he can seek out the sorcerers of the Crescent Cities, or even what remains of the exiled Magi of the Shepherd Kings in northern Sithapia, though they are reclusive to be sure. But what are *you* going to do?"

"Me?"

"Yes, you.You were trying to stop Darien from going to Isoliere, then changed your mind back in Glass Bay and were going to try out for the Tal'desai. That plan is dashed. You have spent some time training the first forms with our Blay Shon on the ship, but you will not be able to go to the Black Sands to study further. The Amarians only let their own people into their Realm, unless you are a Shaluay. What are you going to do?"

"Well, after the Trials I had thought to go to Jaroff and join the Bronze Guard," Kaiel said.

Jaric grimaced. "I would advise against that."

"I know." Kaiel paused. He looked back over his shoulder again, but the street was empty.

"You could come with me," Jaric said.

"To Sithapia?" Kaiel quickened his step to catch up.

"If I return with the princess, I will most likely have Orlay forced back upon me, although that will not be easy. You would have a place in House deOrlay guard if you wish it."

Kaiel stared at the captain in shock. To be offered a place within a House was something he had never imagined would be a possibility after he'd failed the Kas'tirien Trial. He'd expected that work as a mercenary would be all that was available to him if he didn't want to be a Ranger. And having Rolen swaggering past every time he came back to visit was something he couldn't have borne. But he couldn't accept Captain Jaric's offer. Not when Darien was left dangling in the wind.

"If your brother wants it, he can find a role in my House also," Jaric said, eyeing him.

"Thank you, sir!" He bit his lip, considering. "I'll have to speak to Darien, though. I'm not sure what he's going to want to do."

"That is as it should be. Just know you are both welcome, and should Darien have other plans, you are still welcome without him. You are a good man, Kaiel, and a worthy soldier. Given time, you could rise high."

Kaiel could only grin.

"We should take some of this fruit," Jaric said, walking over to one of the trees in the many overgrown gardens, and Kaiel suddenly recalled where they were.

"The princess is right, sir. How are we going to get out of here?"

"I don't know, son," Jaric said. "But we got in, so there has to be a way out."

CHAPTER THIRTY-THREE

Convergence

"WE ARE IN the Daicremore mountains."

Darien was exhausted. He wanted to close his eyes and sink his head into his hands. Instead, he took another bite of the apple Kaiel had brought back.

It tasted like ash.

"Where?" Sim said around a mouthful of orange.

"The mountains between Amaria and Kia Norma," Darien muttered. He closed his eyes. It might have been better for him to have remained ignorant of the world than to study every book he could get his hands on. These mountains were effectively a wall that rose during the Sundering, closing Amaria off from the rest of the new continent, called the Eastern Half. They were barren of all but the hardiest plants and trees, offering no purchase for road or trail. All who had attempted to cross them had turned back or perished.

And they were somewhere in the middle of them.

But the throbbing of the mindstorm from wielding so much of the Light pushed aside any fear of their predicament. *Asai* had raged through him to such a degree he had almost Blinded himself. He didn't even know what sphere the Light he'd wielded belonged to. How could he do what he'd done last night and *still* fail the Ciralys' Test?

And the rune, when he'd seen it, had been inert. He shouldn't have been able to see it at all. No Ciralys could see inactive runes; only the Sahrin could do that.

His stomach churned, and he put the apple down.

"That's right, Darien," Iana said. He blinked. He'd almost forgotten the conversation going on around him.

"How do we get out?" Andraste asked. "The Daicremores are impassable!"

"We will leave the same way we arrived," Iana said.

Darien lifted his head. "How do we manage that? It was the Priest who was doing… something. Wasn't that what brought us here?"

"You said the trail of blood led into the tower at the centre of the Dreamhold?" she addressed Jaric.

The captain nodded.

"There is one other who was in the transfer with us we have not yet seen," Iana said. "The one who opened the portal."

"The priest?" Sevaani said.

"Yes." Iana nodded. "The Chosen of Kirana opened a portal to come here."

"And your working disrupted it?" Darien asked.

"I believe so. The energies I raised in our defence must have caused a backlash and dragged us through the portal as well."

"And the Chosen is here?" Andraste looked thoughtful.

"The Chosen Priest may be dead," Iana said. "That fraction of themselves the Shol'mas imbue their servants with is, I believe, what we faced at the end. It was trapped within his body by the corusite chain I set against him. But it makes sense that the Chosen would be here also."

"What's corusite?" Sim wiped orange juice off his chin with his sleeve.

"The cages the First put me in back at Glass Bay were made of corusite," Kaiel said.

"It is a mineral found in skystones," Jaric said.

"And it makes the wielding of *Asai* impossible. Well." Iana pursed her lips. "For a Ciralys or any other mortal wielder. The Chosen of the Shol'mas contain a sliver of their master within them. It is this that grants the Chosen their power and offers the Shol'mas eyes – or a body – to slip behind at any time they choose. The corusite could possibly prevent or interfere with a Shol'mas withdrawing from a priest's body if he died. Perhaps the Lady Kirana brought him here because there is something of the Sahrin that can free her from the priest – *if* she is trapped?"

Darien's hand clenched and unclenched around the pouch that carried the shard as the Starbinder fell silent.

"So, if we follow the blood, we'll find the prie– the *Shol'mas*?" Simeon asked, his voice flat. "Why would it help us. It was after Darien and he – *we*, are stuck here at its mercy."

Iana gave a small shake of her head. "We may find we are in a position to bargain with her."

Darien lowered his gaze. He'd worked open the ties of the pouch, and his fingers brushed the crystal hidden within. It was almost warm to the touch. He shook his head, dismissing the fancy. Maybe that was what the Shol'mas wanted? That daemon in Serjat, the Vak'nar, had wanted it. Though how it knew he had it, he couldn't guess. Maybe he could buy their lives with it? But did he dare give it up?

"Forgive me, Lady Iana, but I am hesitant to offer the Shol'mas anything." Captain Daynar pushed himself off the wall he leant against.

"Your concern is understandable," she said, "but you must trust me if we are to get out of here."

Darien said nothing as he watched the group.

"Very well." Andraste looked around at them. "We do not have any choice."

"I can't see any other way out," Jaric said at last. "But why is this Shol'mas so interested in Darien?"

"You said the possessed bone drake spoke of a mistress?" Iana's violet eyes caught the morning light. "We know that in the age that followed the Sundering, prophecies arose speaking of an Empyros' return. '*When the Bronze Spear returns, He will come again*'." She caught Darien's eye. "If the daemon's words were true – and that is always a concern with their kind – it seems to me, its mistress sought to stop those prophecies from coming to pass." She looked around the group. "What better way to seek out the bloodline of the last Empyros, than to hold the weapon linked to them? These tools of the Sahrin always seek the blood they are bound to, and the next Empyros, when he comes again, is prophesied to find it." She shrugged. "But this is all conjecture."

"Bronze Spear?" Sim said. "It was a trap to identify the heirs of House Taaren'th and kill them? That's why they're after Darien?" He frowned. "And Kaiel?"

"Yes," Iana agreed.

"House Taaren'th? The Empyros?" Andraste said incredulously. "This is all very interesting if you enjoy Evay tales, but *I* need to get out of here."

Jaric clenched his jaw. "Her Highness is right. We *all* need to get out of here." He clasped a hand on Kaiel's shoulder.

"Then we need to find the Shol'mas – or its priest," Iana said.

"Why would it help us now?" Darien asked.

"I don't know," the Shaluay said, her hands on her hips. "We can but exhaust all our options."

That made sense. Darien nodded to himself, and raised a hand to his forehead as the motion throbbed behind his eyes.

"Can you walk, Dar?" Kaiel asked, leaving the captain's side and coming over to help him up.

"I think so," Darien said and stood, only to sway on unsteady feet. His brother caught him around the shoulder, steadying him. Embarrassed, he offered Kaiel a grateful nod."Thank you."

"It's what brothers are for," Kaiel said with a smile, and they made for the stairs and the street below.

The morning sun had cleared the eastern peaks, and the coloured everstone of the city gleamed so brightly that Kaiel had to squint as they emerged from the tower.

He shielded his eyes, and saw the princess turn her face away.

Two days ago that would have made him uncomfortable, but now he and Sevaani had spoken... well, he didn't mind so much at all. But they needed to get off this mountain first.

His hand tightened on the hilt of his sword. If he didn't need the Chosen Priest, or Shol'mas or whatever *it* was, alive, he would have its head.

Everyone thought Darien was the one it was hunting, but he had been the one to use the spear. He was the one it must have been after. He had killed the bone drake, or it's body at least.

And if he'd had the spear back in Serjat, the Chosen would have been dead!

"Kaiel."

He looked up at Sim's soft call.

At the top of the street, Jaric had stopped. They were at the square in the heart of the city. Kaiel's skin pebbled as he took in the daemons guarding the entrance to the tower. Daemons that had not been there when he'd scouted the area a mere hour ago.

They stood on four clawed, insect-like legs, and rose nearly seven feet in height. Black chitin armoured their elongated torsos, marked with luminescent white designs that leaked black smoke like steam.

Great arms ending in wickedly clawed, three-fingered hands, were topped with spike-like protrusions that erupted from their shoulders. Horns mirrored the spikes and rose from skulls inset with four eyes, and gaping maws filled with razor-sharp teeth.

Mok'zul daemons. He recognised them from books he'd studied with the Kas'tirien. But what were they doing here?

Lihon gestured, and he crouched, joining the others.

"This is not surprising," Iana murmured.

"Not surprising?" Sim said. "I don't recall you mentioning more daemons when you said we should go look for the Shol'mas!"

"We have found the priest's mistress," she said softly, ignoring his ire.

"Kaiel!"

He edged up to the front of the party at Jaric's terse call.

"I want you to stay with Lihon," Jaric said. "Erika and I will head down the other street and work our way around so that we can come out the opposite side of the square. Once there, we'll signal you, and together we'll rush them."

"They're Mok'zul," Lihon said.

Kaiel nodded. "He's right."

"I know." Jaric was grim. "The rest of you stay back. We will be hard-pressed with these."

"You believe you can defeat them?" Andraste asked, incredulity staining her voice. "The Mok'zul are the elite of the Daemonlords' guards. You might as well fight a wyvern!"

"Captain Jaric defeated a Lloth'var under Sonyth," Kaiel said defensively.

"I'd expect nothing less of the former Grand Marshall of the Gold Rose," Erika offered, a strange mixture of grudging admiration and pride in her voice.

"A Lloth'var?" Lihon offered Jaric a bow of his head. "*Rai'u,* Gold Rose."

"And honour to the Blay Shon." Jaric returned the bow. He turned back to the others, "We have no choice here. We either fight them or stay. Which would you prefer?"

"I will assist as I can." Iana moved up to Lihon.

"Captain," Sim grabbed Jaric's arm. "I have this. It will help." In his hand, he cupped a small grey clay orb.

"You still have these?" Jaric stared at him in horror. "I thought you said you had left them at Sonyth?"

"Well, yes. I did say that." Sim gave a half-grin. "It's just a small one. I was saving it."

"How we got all the way here without you killing –" Jaric stopped himself with a visible effort.

"It's a *small* one," Sim protested. "But it should work."

"Then you come with me." He pointed at Kaiel and Lihon. "When we get to the other side, move around to the tower. As far back as you need to be out of their line of sight. We'll wait for you to get in place and then Sim will throw his egg."

"What's that supposed to do?" Erika demanded.

"At the very least it will distract them long enough that we have a greater advantage," Jaric said. "It packs quite a punch."

He kept close to Lihon as they crept around the edge of the square, passing through overgrown gardens, and behind the collapsed walls of buildings that lay scattered like broken eggshells. Kaiel's heart was racing, sure that at any moment the daemons would notice them, but they remained as still as statues, their red scales dark in the shadow of the tower.

Taking up his position, Kaiel concentrated on controlling his breathing as time stretched interminably. A bare two minutes had passed until Jaric and Erika were at the mouth of the street across from them. The captain motioned with his hand, and Lihon turned to Kaiel.

"Are you ready?" the Blay Shon asked.

"Yes." Swallowing, he took a deep breath, forced his body to relax, and waited while Lihon signalled back.

Jaric, Erika and Sim moved to a wall of ruins, edging up to the south side of the tower. Kaiel counted twenty heartbeats, and then Sim threw his egg.

It landed on the stairs between the Mok'zul and exploded. Azure flames unfurled like the blue petals of a *kainis-ris* rose after a storm, and a wave of force knocked the daemons to the ground.

Lihon moved as soon as the orb exploded, his jisanas singing as he engaged the closest daemon. Kaiel followed close behind.

The daemon, despite its size, regained its feet quickly, sweeping its clawed hand at Lihon who leaned back out of reach. Kaiel stepped to the side to avoid tripping over the blademaster, and was suddenly facing the enraged Mok'zul.

The daemon roared, a chittering hiss that reverberated like a chorus of agonised voices. He found himself screaming back. His sword lashed out, the steel blade gleaming. It slammed into the metal-hard chitin, and he drove his weight behind the blow, sliding the sword forward. He ducked under the creature's guard before bringing his sword back around, slicing across its exposed side.

A screech filled the morning air as the sword scraped along the chitin. For an instant, its companion froze. Then Lihon was beside him, pressing the advantage. His jisanas spun faster than the eye could follow, pushing the daemon back as it tried to gather itself and match the blademaster's attack.

"Get down!" Iana called out, and Kaiel dropped to the ground, years of training coming to the fore. A white-gold streak shot over his head, leaving a stinging trail of heat in its wake.

The Mok'zul roared again, and the stone beneath Kaiel trembled.

The daemon was impaled on a great lance of golden energy that burned Kaiel's eyes to look at. Black blood stained its edges and dripped from the wounds inflicted by Lihon's jisanas. The daemon roared as the lance of energy dissipated, and pushed itself up to lunge forward. It caught the blademaster with its clawed legs as it lashed out blindly.

Kaiel yelled as Lihon fell back and he was suddenly facing the daemon warrior alone.

He fell into the first stances of battle. He brought his sword up to catch the daemon's wild slash, turning it out of his personal sphere and opening the creature to attack. Keeping his centre, he moved forward and brought his sword back down, almost over-balancing as the blade shockingly cut through scale and sank into the flesh below.

The daemon roared again, and a surge of energy rushed through Kaiel's right hand, the wound on its back tingling and hot. The sword almost jumped in his grip, and the forms he was still learning began to flow as though he'd been practising them for years.

The daemon thrashed as Kaiel severed a claw from its hand. Blood pounded in his ears, and he pressed forward, pushing the daemon back. Surrounding sounds faded, and the sword pulsed with a strange energy.

He cut the Mok'zul, and his arms thrummed, the back of his right hand felt like it was on fire. Energy seemed to charge his sword, and it *pulled* him forward, spearing itself through the daemon's black chitin and sinking into its heart.

The daemon toppled to the ground, its weight yanking the sword from Kaiel's hand.

Sound rushed back, and he moved his head, dazed.

Beside him, Jaric and Erika still fought the remaining daemon.

A hand on his shoulder made him spin around, and Lihon's silver eyes bored into his. "Are you hurt?"

"No." Kaiel shook his head.

Lihon grunted, letting him go and pushed past him to the others. Breathing hard, Kaiel bent to retrieve his sword. He hesitated only a moment, then grasped the blade and pulled it out of the dead daemon.

He turned to re-join the fight, and as he approached, the remaining Mok'zul went wild.

Its arms lashed out like Lihon's swords, and Jaric crashed to the ground. It ignored the flurry of blades from Lihon, its chitinous armour sparking as steel clashed against it. Black blood dripped to the stone around them. The Mok'zul raised its head to the sky, bellowing an ear-splitting cry as though calling for aid. Lihon jumped in front of Kaiel and swiped his blade across its exposed throat. On any other being such a cut would be fatal, but the daemon's scale was harder than plate mail, and only a thin line of black appeared behind the blade on the red throat. The Mok'zul twisted, its claws smashing into Erika, knocking her off her feet and onto Lihon. They both went down in a tangle of limbs. The creature made to lunge past Kaiel. He blocked it, wielding his sword like an axe as he hacked into its shoulder.

The daemon bellowed, its arm swinging out to strike, but Kaiel ducked under the wild blow, yelling his own defiance back at it. It tried to turn, pushing towards the doorway as Kaiel's sword moved again.

He held the hilt tight with both hands as the sword – pulsing with a strange, dark silver glow – dragged him behind it. He slashed the blade across the daemon's back, the blade-sharp spines jutting down the centre, cutting his arms as his sword passed between them. The pull of the energy racing through his body and along the blade, and the fiery burn on the wound under the last of Shany's ointment, strengthened as the sword sunk deep, dragging Kaiel even further forward.

The daemon bucked and the spines, as sharp as cut glass, speared Kaiel's torso. He cried out in pain as the Mok'zul collapsed under its weight, with him on top of it.

Hands pulled him off its back, and he groaned, trying to sit up.

"Stay down, son." Jaric's voice was hoarse.

"The daemon –" he gasped.

"It's dead," the captain said. "Lie still."

"My sword?" He tried again.

"It's here." He recognised Erika's voice as the knight brought the sword over to him.

"Simeon," Iana called, kneeling by his side. "Help me." She ripped Kaiel's shirt open.

"Just relax and enjoy," Sim whispered in his ear with a grin, but Kaiel could tell from the wild light in his eye that he was worried.

"Erika, Jaric," Lihon called them from somewhere to his right. "We need to scout inside."

Erika squeezed his shoulder and got up.

"Don't move," Iana told him as she put her hands over his torso. "The spine of some daemons can be poisonous. I don't want to lose you from a couple of scratches."

"A couple?" Sim asked. "He looks like a pin cushion!"

"Simeon," Darien sighed, leaning over his other side. "You're not helping."

"Dar," Kaiel protested, moving to get up.

"Lie still." His brother pushed him gently back down.

A green glow from Iana's hand drew his attention, and an emerald coloured glyph appeared in the air above his chest. It sank into his torso and cold exploded over his body. He shot upright, pushing away the hands that tried to keep him down.

"Gods, what was that?" he groaned.

"Kaiel, you should take a moment," Iana said, getting to her feet.

"I'm fine." He eyed her suspiciously. "Thank you."

She sighed. "Very well. None of the spines punctured a lung, and the healing will burn out any toxins." She stared at him. "You will be sore tomorrow, and you need to eat as soon as possible."

Kaiel took a deep breath, his limbs still tingling with cold. The sun had barely moved in the sky, the fight lasting no more than a few minutes. Patches of Sim's egg still burned, and the white of the nearby everstone was streaked with black blood.

"Are we going to wait out here all morning?" Sim asked.

"You want to follow them?" Andra looked inside the tower entrance.

"If they get into trouble, how will we know?" Sim spread his hands. "We'd be better off going in than staying out here and wondering, wouldn't we?"

Before anyone could answer, an explosion came from the city behind them. The ground trembled, and in the distance smoke rose into the air.

"What was that?" Sim shouted.

"The gate," Iana said.

Sevaani looked up the street. "You mean –"

A howling cry filled the air.

"Korda'vari!" Darien hissed.

"Into the tower!" Iana commanded.

"But what if there are more daemons in there?" Andra said.

"Move!" the Shaluay called, and she led them through the looming entrance of the tower.

CHAPTER THIRTY-FOUR

Strands of Prophecy

DARIEN'S SKIN PRICKLED as he entered the tower, and he swept his eyes around the room. Light fell into the circular chamber from an unseen source, and ten tall pillars of sparkling light – one for each of the Elder Gods, he supposed – circled the room. Tiles of silver, white and gold spread across the floor, depicting the Seal of the Eye of Eternity – its beauty marred only by the trail of dried blood splattered across it, leading into the room beyond.

"It is said that the mark of the Eye first appeared on the hand of Quanare," Iana said, looking down as she crossed the mosaic. "It was she who first linked with an empyrean and deciphered the writings of the Ancients, laying the foundations of the Sahrin's power."

"We don't have time for a history lesson," Sim said. "The trail leads this way,"

Darien followed, his eyes tracing the graceful artistry. The presence of *Asai* was strong in the tower; he reached out to find it, only to stumble as the scar on the back of his right hand flared in sudden pain.

"Dar." Kaiel was behind him, pulling him upright.

"I'm fine," he said. "I wasn't watching where I was going."

"Gods," Sim said, coming to a halt at the archway to the next chamber.

His brother forgotten, Darien pushed forward. A vast chamber spread out before them. Shafts of pearlescent light fell from… somewhere, onto a glowing pool in the centre of the enormous hall. A lush carpet of grass covered the floor, and trees with green, blue and mauve crystalline leaves grew around the pool's edge like sentinels. Their branches moved in an unfelt wind, filling the air with chiming, while wisps of light floated between their branches.

"I don't see Captain Jaric," Kaiel said beside him. "Or the others."

"Maybe they went on ahead?" Andraste suggested.

"I don't think there's anywhere else to go," Darien said.

"What is this place?" Sim breathed.

"It is a Hall of Reflection," Iana came up behind them. "Here, the Sahrin held counsel and communed with the empyreans."

"Really? And what are they when they're at home?" Sim asked.

"Sim!" Sevaani said in a scolding tone, but Darien could tell she was as distracted by the sight before them as he.

"The empyreans are beings who dwell in the Light of the Eye of Eternity," Lady Iana said. "It is the Sahrin's ability to link with these creatures, to call them to our plane, that has humankind calling them Summoners."

"How do you know that? I've never heard of them before," Sim gave a half shrug.

"You doubt the word of a Shaluay?" Andra arched an eyebrow.

"Until three months ago, I'd never even heard of the Shaluay, *Your Highness*," he said, then gestured at the room. "No-one's been here since the Sundering. How would she know what it is?"

"Because the Shaluay have more knowledge in their cora'stones than the Ciralys have in all their libraries in Isoliere," a voice said from the pool. "Isn't that right, Firstbinder?"

"Who's there!" Kaiel shouted, raising his sword.

"Who indeed?" This time the voice came from beside them. "I am hurt that you don't remember me."

Darien stepped past his brother and peered into the room. From his resting place by the pool, the Chosen Priest of Kirana rose from the ground. Gone was the grace that marked the man when he had approached them in the bowels of the Spire. Clumps of hair had fallen from his scalp, and his flesh was withered like cracked leather stretched thin over a frame of bones.

"And now you come to cause me more trouble." He sighed. "I left you, and you follow me like fleas on a garis hound. What am I to do with you now? My Lady will not be happy you have found her Sanctuary."

"Left us?" Andraste said, her voice ringing in the hall. "You ripped us from Serjat and dumped us on the side of a mountain!"

"I did?" the priest's eyes widened, then grimaced as though the expression caused him pain. "The side of a mountain? How did you manage to get in here, then?" The priest looked at Darien. "Of course, the Blood of the Spear. But which is which?" He staggered towards them. "I hope you don't expect me to be grateful that you saved me the trouble of finding you again. Your arrival here may save me the flame of my Lady's displeasure, but I am still suffering from your foul metal!"

"So, Kirana's essence has left you," Iana said thoughtfully. "If a Chosen no longer possesses that part of his mistress that marks him as 'chosen', does that make you just another priest?"

He snarled at her, but Iana ignored him, casting her gaze around the room. "Our companions came in here before us. Where are they?"

"I sent them away," he said, his eyes glittering. "I did not wish to be disturbed while I recuperate. Did you know the only thing said to heal as well as the Shaluay's Genome Looms, is an Alenori Pool?" He gestured at the water.

"Where did you send them?" Iana pressed.

"Well now." The priest cracked a smile, his face a ghastly rictus. "I have something you want, and you have something I want. Perhaps we should trade?"

Darien's jaw tightened, and he swallowed.

"Kirana wants Darien and Kaiel," she said. "Why?"

"How could you not know?" the man hissed, his eyes narrowing. "The Mark of the Eye blazes and you remain blind! The Bronze Spear revealed itself before my Lady's oldest servant, and only one bloodline could bring it to do that. The rising of the Empyros is the key to my Lady's freedom!"

The priest straightened and glared at them all. Then he began to speak in a twisting language, the words slipping from Darien's ears before he could comprehend them. A passageway opened on the grass behind the pool, and a rushing wind escaped into the hall. A pair of obelisks, one of white everstone and a matching one of black, rose to flank stairs that led down.

Darien gave a start as his brother, his arm like a bar across his chest, pulled him back.

"Is that where Lihon and the others went?" Iana asked. "Where does it lead?"

"To the sanctum of the Highlord of this domain," purred the priest.

"What in the Void is he talking about?" Sim muttered.

"He means the daemon that possessed the bone drake," Darien said.

"From beneath Sonyth?" Sim said, staring at the fissure. "We killed it!"

Iana shook her head. "I don't believe you did."

Outside the tower came a bestial roar.

The Chosen jerked back. "Korda'vari," he snarled. "You have brought another's servants here?"

"Not we," Iana said calmly. "You, or the Shol'mas Kirana, conjured a rift that clashed with the energies of the Starwell. The resulting backlash brought here all who were in that room beneath the Spire."

"No! My Lady holds her plans as sacrosanct." The priest flung a burnt hand out at them. "You have destroyed me!"

"We didn't bring them here!" Sim shouted, already running across the grass, Andraste, Kaiel and Sevaani behind him.

The Chosen Priest screeched like a cat. Wind rose in the chamber, the wisps of light that floated in the trees snuffing out like candles. The floor rumbled, and around the hall, enormous eggs burst from the ground in showers of grass and soil. Gleaming pure white, the shells cracked, hatching fully grown Mok'zul into the room.

"Stop them!" the priest cried. "Stop the Korda'vari!"

Darien was jerked forward as Iana grabbed his wrist, pulling him towards the obelisks. "Quickly. We must find Lihon and the others!"

Around the edges of the room more Mok'zul hatched, and marched towards the entrance as the first Korda'vari burst into the hall.

The daemons met them with a fury, and Darien spun around in shock as a blood-curdling scream came from the priest. His heart pounded, and his chest tightened with fear as a pillar of fire erupted around the Chosen, flinging him into the air – though he did not burn.

"Lady!" the priest cried, his voice a scream of agony. "I am your vessel. Save me!"

"You have failed our Mistress." The deep voice came from all corners of the hall. "And now *Golakresh* desecrate sacred ground!" The tower shook, and the pillar of flame roared around the priest's body.

"I brought you the Blood! I did as you asked!" he screamed.

"And where are they?"

A presence washed over Darien studying him with an attention so vast he could perceive it even without opening himself to *Asai*.

"*Imanarg*!" the voice roared in outrage and Darien staggered back.

The crimson-clad figure of the Bloodlord entered the Hall.

"*You brought an* Imanarg *here*!" thundered the disembodied voice of the daemon who had possessed the bone drake.

"Great One, I did not!" the priest cried. "It was them! It was the Shaluay!"

"You are no longer of use to me," the daemon said, "but your body is."

The room went dark, and a red light like the glow of a furnace lit its edges, cast by the twisting pillar of fire. The Chosen screamed again, and the nauseating stench of burning flesh filled the air as the pillar's flame constricted.

On the other side of the room, a laugh rose above the cries of the fighting daemons and the Bloodlord stepped forward. The Korda'vari surged with renewed vigour around him, but for each of the Mok'zul that fell, two Korda'vari were slain.

"Darien!" Iana cried, her hand on his shoulder. "Come!"

But his eyes were riveted to the figure of the Bloodlord. A sword, a red line of light, unfurled in the creature's hand. It brought the blade up as a daemon stepped in his way, and with a flick of its wrist, he sliced the Mok'zul in half and stepped past the spasming remains without a glance.

An alien fear welled up inside Darien, and he felt the csitargon suddenly pushing against the wards containing it in a wild panic.

Cold terror had him stumbling after Iana.

Behind them came a massive blast and the ground rocked. Darien cried out, falling down the stairs.

"Darien, get up. We must run!" Beside him, Iana pulled him up by the back of his coat. He winced, the palms of his hands stinging where the skin had grazed away.

He looked around, disoriented. They were on a wide path that curved between dark walls. Light came from stones embedded in the ceiling and cast sharp shadows over intricately carved depictions of men and women that followed them on the walls.

The corridor shuddered.

"Quickly, we must find the others!" the Shaluay said.

"Iana!" from down the path Lihon appeared, running towards them

"The Korda'vari have entered the city," she told him. "Is there another way out?"

"There are many passages." He gestured. "But you must come. We have found something."

Again, the ground shuddered, and a roar of rage followed as the corridor trembled. *Asai* blazed behind his mind's eye and he staggered as the shockwave battered his psyche. Kaiel grabbed him, and this time he didn't shrug him off.

"That can't be good," Sim muttered.

"The fight is over," Iana said, looking back towards the stairs.

"Who won?" Kaiel asked.

"Does it matter?" Sim yelled as they ran down the twisting path. "They both want us dead!"

As they made their way deeper beneath the tower, ornate statues in lighted alcoves tracked their progress. Each was mounted on a raised dais of onyx. There were men and women, the insectoid Xious'bisan, reptilian Liss, even a winged Aerynaian.

"This place is making me nervous," Sim growled.

"*This* is making you nervous?" Andra's breath came short. "What about the fact that we are trapped in a Dreamhold with monsters out of legend?"

Darien ignored them both as the presence in his mind whirled restlessly. He spun around. There was nothing behind them, but he could sense the Korda'vari like a twisted shadow on the light of *Asai*.

That was a new ability, and its sudden manifestation scared him as much as the csitargon in his head did.

The path turned again, and they came upon a set of shallow stairs that led down into a small hall with channels of water bordering the edges of the room like canals, the water rushing to the far end to fall away into the darkness beyond.

On the large, platform-like floor between the canals, were four white caskets edged in gold. Atop each was a suit of silver kharidium armour, the gauntlets grasping the shafts of obsidian halberds, glittering in the light. At the end of the room, on a balcony that reached out past the falling water, was a golden casket.

And in the room's centre, Jaric and Erika stood before a pillar of light.

"Void take me," Sim said. "Look at this place!"

But Darien paid scant attention to their exchange, his eyes drawn to the everstone floor and the runes engraved upon its surface. Line after line filled the tiles from the base of the stairs to the dais with its gold sarcophagus. He knelt to inspect the inscriptions.

"Can you read it?" Sim asked him.

"No, I can't." He stood and brushed his hands, the abrasions on his palms tingling.

"This is no script of the Sahrin," Iana said. "These are much older."

"You know it?" Darien faced her.

"I recognise some." She moved past him; he bit his tongue and followed. "It is the language of the Ancients."

Jaric and Erika turned as they approached. The pillar was blinding to look at, but there was something about it that tugged at the back of Darien's mind. It wasn't the csitargon that had stilled as soon as he entered the room. It was something else.

"You found them quickly," Jaric said to Lihon.

"They were already on the path," the blademaster said, and quickly related what Iana had told him.

"Can the priest stand against a Bloodlord?" Jaric asked.

"He is no longer the man who chased us beneath the Spire," Iana said distractedly, studying the pillar before them. "The daemon that possessed your bone drake has him."

She ran her hands over the light, but some force prevented her from reaching into it. "How strange."

"Is it solid?" Sim stepped forward.

"Don't touch it, Sim," she admonished.

"You just did!" he said but folded his arms across his chest.

"It is not solid." She peered into the light again. "There is a ward around it, preventing anyone from seeing what it hides."

"Shouldn't we be looking for a way out?" Andraste asked.

"There is no way out."

Darien whirled at the voice. On the stairs behind them stood the daemon-possessed body of the priest, flanked by Mok'zul.

Cracks criss-crossed the blackened flesh of the body, and liquid flame moved beneath it like blood.

The ringing of swords being drawn filled the chamber as Jaric, Lihon, Erika and Kaiel stepped in front of the group. Darien took a deep breath as fear flexed in him. He was more than happy to hide behind his brother now.

Coward!

"You have chased these young men far, daemon." Iana's voice rang in the chamber. "You cannot stop the turning of the stars."

"There are no stars in the Void but those of Queen Di'shana's making." It smirked and walked down the stairs in a jerking motion. "Soon enough there will be no stars here, either." Behind him, the Mok'zul followed, spreading out either side of their master.

"I am of the Shaluay," Iana said. "I know the prophecies of which you speak. And I know that prophecy is not so easily turned aside."

Something touched Darien's shoulder, and he gave a start. He turned around, searching the room behind them, but it was empty. The glowing pillar caught his attention, and he stared. There was something *inside* the light.

"Then you would know it was a Shaluay who betrayed the Empyros," taunted the daemon, but its voice came from so very far away. "Your kind are like a pestilence, always poking and prying and demanding to *know*. Then know *this*. Your order's betrayal has stripped this world of those who might defend it. We will not be defeated again!"

"What is it talking about, Shaluay," Captain Jaric demanded, his voice icy.

Darien wanted to listen, but he could not turn away from the pillar. Its light had dimmed; he did not need to blink or shade his eyes from its brightness. He peered closer.

"Do not believe its lie, Rion deOrlay. Betrayal has ever been a tool of daemonkind," Iana said. "They revel in subterfuge and misdirection. It was no Shaluay who betrayed the last Empyros of the Sahrin to his doom. It was a daemon."

"Humans have ever been arrogant!" The daemon's voice was a distant snarl, but the room trembled. "When the Great Keystone of the Summoners was broken and the world shattered, your Seers were struck by a vision, were they not? The Saviour and Destroyer would be born again. The Child of the Moon, the Blood of the Spear!" The orange-red light of flame flickered across the room. "Your order has tried to rid the world of the bloodline of Summoners since the Sundering. All to prevent a new Empyros from rising. How many Sahrin have the Shaluay abducted over the centuries? For if an Empyros does not rise, the other half of the prophecy, the return of Di'shana, blessed be Her name, cannot be fulfilled. If there is no Empyros then the prophecy dies before She can claim your world!"

Heat washed over Darien's back, the light across the floor flaring red. It was like two people dwelt within him. One part of his mind was cataloguing the daemon's words, while the other tracked the runes that twisted, white upon white, within the pillar of light; he could almost grasp them. *Almost* understand them. *If they would just stop moving!*

"Iana, I warn you," Jaric said. "Is this why you joined us? To get your hands on Kaiel and Darien?"

"You doubt me?" Iana's voice cracked across the room. "It was I who worked to save Darien from this creature in Serjat, almost to my death. Do you think I did so only to kill him later? Daemons deal in lies, you foolish man. You can trust nothing it says!"

"Captain, no," Sevaani cried out. "She's here to help us!"

"Control yourself, Sithapian." Lihon's voice was cold.

"The Shaluay have no plans to kill anyone," Iana said. "The Empyros, the Summoner who can meld with the Empyrean called the Phoenix, *must* rise once more to stop the Des'maadrian Di'shana and the threat of the Void!"

"Prophecy is a fragile thing, words on the wind. And one *human* alone cannot stop my queen!" the daemon roared. "We watched as the Summoners fought and died according to our plans, as the continent of Athmay was rent asunder, and the world weakened. No humans will stand against our conquest again. And when these boys die, so too will your hope of salvation!"

Iana laughed scornfully. "You are no general of the daemon hordes. You are a csitargon and have not even found a live host in which to consolidate your footing in this realm. You, little daemon, are less than a footnote in whatever plans your queen may have. Your lies will not turn us against each other!"

"Enough of this foolishness!" the daemon spat. "Kill them!"

The Mok'zul gave a hissing roar in response, but Darien could not move. It was all he could do to look over his shoulder.

"Sim!" Kaiel yelled behind him. "If you have any more surprises for us, now's the time to use them!"

"I don't! All the eggs are gone!"

"That one touched the spear!" The possessed body of the priest pointed at Kaiel and the daemons surged forward.

The Mok'zul had surrounded Kaiel and Captain Daynar, claws clashing against swords as they surged forward. Kaiel and the captain had set themselves back to back against the onslaught. Lihon tried to reach them, but more daemons jumped into the fray, throwing themselves against his whirling swords.

"Stay behind me!" Iana cried.

"You cannot save them!" The daemon-priest's voice boomed over the fighting. "The line of Varos Korin'ad will die!"

Darien turned back to the column. It was as if he was called by the runes moving within it.

Without thinking, he reached into the light. Where Iana had been stopped, he was not, and the pillar vanished, leaving a block of black everstone, an altar, behind.

"Impossible!" the daemon screamed.

Darien fell back as the noise of the chamber rushed over him. He could move again! He turned around, his hand dropping to the dagger at his waist.

"You shall not have *The Tome of Ascension*!"

"Sim!" Iana whirled around. "Take this!"

She pulled a spear from one of the nearest sarcophagi and thrust it at him. "Use the blade to pry a lid off one of the caskets!"

"What?" Sim cried. "You told me not to touch anything!"

"Do it now!"

Darien watched in confusion as Sim took the spear, working the blade under the lid of the casket.

The daemon-priest roared, and Darien covered his face with his hands, nearly blinded by the explosion of flames from the body it inhabited. He fell back beside the everstone altar, and his gaze fell upon its surface for the first time. The top was smooth, devoid of any of the runes that were carved into the stone of the floor. On it lay a book with a clear, diamond-like gem, just smaller than the palm of his hand, embedded in the cover.

"I've got it!" yelled Sim, and the lid of the sarcophagus crashed to the floor.

A wail filled the room, and the Mok'zul swayed, dropping their weapons and clutching their heads. Around them, above all five sarcophagi, wraiths coalesced like living shadow. One, above the sarcophagus whose lid Sim had pushed off, reached out a transparent hand towards Sim, and he jumped back, but not before it brushed his head.

Sim screamed, falling to the floor, and the other wraiths began to move. Darien stared while Sevaani dashed past him and grabbed one of Sim's arms, dragging him away from the phantom, towards Darien and the altar.

"Help me!" she called, but a wraith loomed behind her. Darien turned away in terror, his legs trembling and the cold stab of shame piercing him. He stumbled over the stone altar in his haste, and his eyes fell upon the book resting on the block of everstone.

"Disturbing the dead will not save you!" the daemon-priest called.

"The shades of the Ala'sendi are protectors," Iana said. "They guard the tombs of the Sahrin against defilers."

"Then you've sealed your fate," the daemon sneered.

"The Ala'sendi are not sentient," Iana continued, more calmly than Darien believed possible. "They are drawn to that which woke them. That which opened the sarcophagus."

Darien looked over his shoulder as the Starbinder snatched up the spear Sim had used and hurled it at the still-stunned Mok'zul.

The shades converging on Sim turned as the weapon struck the body of the closest daemon.

As one the shades vanished, only to reappear across the room, surrounding the daemons. Reaching out, they sunk non-corporeal hands into the remaining Mok'zul, and the daemons began to scream.

Darien looked away from the sight, and again his eyes were drawn to the book on the altar.

The *book*.

The Tome of Ascension.

He reached out and touched its edge, his hands shaking in disbelief, only for the tome to crumble to dust in his hands.

"No!"The cry was pulled from the depths of his being.

"Dar!" Kaiel stumbled over to him, now free of the Mok'zul, sword still raised."Dar, what's wrong?"

He ignored his brother and grabbed the jewel that had fallen from the tome's cover. He clenched his hand around it so hard its facets bit into his palm. With an effort of will, he stopped himself from hurling it across the room. Instead, he dropped it into the pouch that held the shard Ciralys Telaq had given him.

"You will all die!" the priest's voice boomed in the chamber.

The shades were gone, the Mok'zul they'd touched lying lifeless on the ground.

Flames suddenly engulfed the possessed priest, burning like a funeral pyre, consuming every inch of the body until there was nothing left.

But the flames did not die.

The ground rumbled, and the five sarcophagi exploded in a shower of stone. Bones from within flew into the air, while the bodies of the dead daemons heaved in clouds of blood and gore as slivers of chitin joined them. The fire grew, the bones churning in a whirlwind, spinning impossibly fast before finally slowing to hang in a macabre reconstruction of a daemon's horned skull. Red flames burned in place of eyes.

You will not leave this room alive.

"It's in my head!" Sim sat up, struggling to his feet.

"The stars turn, daemon," Iana said, and Darien saw her shift her stance, raising her arms and exposing the bracers over her wrists."You will not stop us!"

The daemon screamed, and they all staggered back.

The blazing eyes of the bone-skull turned towards Kaiel and Darien.

You will not fulfil your destiny!

"Dar, move!" Kaiel pushed him aside as a torrent of flame spewed from the construct.

The heat was scorching, and Darien's nose filled with the stench of burning hair. He braced himself against the annihilating flames.

But they didn't come.

He looked up and stared. In his brother's hands, somehow, was the Bronze Spear.

Around them, a river of fire splashed harmlessly to either side of a shield of air. Darien could hear Sevaani screaming and Captain Daynar calling his brother's name.

The daemon's roar shook the walls. Its jaws opened impossibly wide. A great rushing filled the chamber as air was sucked in, and red-orange cinders flared between them.

"No!"

Darien went cold as his brother screamed his defiance. Kaiel's face was marked with blood and sweat and fury as he hefted the Bronze Spear, pulling back his arm. Darien couldn't breathe.

Asai flowed around Kaiel like a silver river, a pure energy that coruscated along his arm and across the length of the spear, gathering at its tip so quickly it was like a line of blue-white light.

"What are you doing?" Lady Iana stared at Kaiel in horror, and the Blay Shon pulled her back as Erika threw herself in front of Andraste.

Kaiel was wielding *Asai*.

Jealousy erupted through Darien, and the ice at his core exploded into a furious rage. All his life things had come easily to Kaiel. Friends, achievement, inclusion.

But *Asai*? *Asai* was Darien's. That was the one thing he had that his brother never could have. Never *would* have.

With an incoherent scream, Darien flung a hand towards Kaiel. The shard at his waist exploded with the Light of the Eye, flooding his mind and fire shot like a blazing rope at Kaiel.

"Kaiel, look out!" Sim warned.

But the torrent of molten *Asai* didn't touch Kaiel. Instead, Darien watched it shift, twist and then wrap around Kaiel's hands as it pulsed, joining the power cascading across the spear.

Then Kaiel threw the spear at the bones.

Darien barely noticed the spear sink into the skull construct's open maw or the fire blazing around them that was sucked in after it. His jealousy fled as shock – *guilt* – at what he had tried to do slapped him in the face.

The spear pulsed with a brilliant light within the skull.

Darien frowned. Kaiel hadn't closed his connection to the Light of the Eye. *Asai* was still flooding through him like an open floodgate.

Panic tore him from his stunned stupor. "Kaiel! Stop!"

"What is happening?" Jaric demanded.

"Run!" Iana screamed. "The water! Get under the water!"

Lihon grabbed Sevaani's arm, hauling her off her feet as Erika turned to Andraste.

"No. Get the boy!" the princess gestured at Sim still on one knee.

"Andra –"

"Do it!"

Darien turned back as another rushing sound filled the tomb. *Asai* called by his brother wrapped itself around and through the bones of the daemon's construct. A wave of sound exploded from the nexus point somewhere within, and energy erupted after it.

He was vaguely aware of Captain Daynar launching himself at Kaiel, just as another body barrelled into him, knocking him into the shockingly cold water of the canal.

The impact caused the air to burst from his lungs, and he gasped, choking, as water rushed to fill them.

Orange and yellow light lit the icy stream, and scalding heat followed as the water grasped him in its swift current.

Then he was tumbling off the edge and falling into the darkness below.

CHAPTER THIRTY-FIVE

The Saviour and Destroyer

KAIEL CAME BACK to himself, gasping for breath, gagging as water filled his mouth and nose. Shadows gave way to a light, and scalding heat soaked through the icy chill as quickly as a spark of flame consumed an oil-soaked rag. He was moving; his body was being pulled through rushing water. He panicked and kicked his feet beneath him, then suddenly he was falling.

Air rushed around him, and someone was screaming.

Light from below drew some fraction of his attention. There was a flash as something, *someone,* fell through a glowing ring of light above a wet cavern floor littered with jagged rocks. Another flash and someone else disappeared, following the torrent of water that thundered around them.

The ground rushed towards him.

He was too far out to make it through the ring. He was going to hit the ground.

Light flashed, and his stomach lurched.

The breath left his lungs as he landed on his back. He did not stop moving. The raging torrent dragged him down over smooth, worn stones. Light flickered around him, dazzling him, and the back of his head ached from its impact on the rock. Then he was cast into the open air again, as the water gushed out the side of a mountain.

Daylight blinded him, but he had the impression of grey stone cliffs and the blue of the sea across the horizon. As he hit the water, air was pushed from his lungs once again, and saltwater filled his mouth. He struggled for breath, taking in more water, panic rising as he lost sight of the surface in the turbulence. He thrashed wildly when a hand grabbed as fistful of his hair, pulling him up.

He broke the surface with a gasp, choking and spluttering.

"Easy, Kaiel!" Jaric yelled from behind him. "We have to get to shore!"

He tried to take in air and vomited water, his nose stinging.

"Calm down!" Jaric shouted. "Kick your legs under you slowly; it will help keep your head above the water."

He did as directed, kicking suddenly heavy legs. His knees ached, and his thighs burned, as though he'd run to the top of the Keepers' Towers in Hanore without pause. His back ached from the hard slap against the water's surface. There was more splashing to his right, and he looked across to see Lihon swimming, one arm around an unmoving Simeon.

"Over here!" Iana called.

Jaric pulled Kaiel's arm, turning him towards cliffs that rose from the water like a wall.

He moved his head from side-to-side, looking for Darien until the captain barked at him again.

It didn't take long until they reached the grey stone cliffs that circled the bay, the sea swelling around them and pushing them against the rocks. The waterfall they had plummeted from thundered into the sea, the noise like that of one of the storms that swept out of the Deadlands in winter. Kaiel pulled himself up onto a rocky ledge and collapsed, his arms weak, his chest billowing as he panted for breath.

After a moment, he pushed himself upright as Jaric helped Lihon and Sevaani drag Sim onto the ledge.

"Where's Dar?" His voice was hoarse, and he struggled to his feet.

"He's not here," Jaric said.

"Where is he?" Panic whirled through his sluggish thoughts.

"I don't know," Erika said, her voice rough. "Andra's gone too."

The knight sat behind him. She wore just a white cotton tunic over dark leather trousers, her tabard and mail missing. She lifted her head from arms crossed over her knees, her face sporting a large yellow bruise that was already turning black, her brown hair plastered to her skull.

Looking at her, Kaiel became aware of every bump and bruise he had suffered himself but pushed the pain aside.

"They went in the other canal," the knight said. "I saw them falling, but we went through that circle of light and ended up here. I don't... I don't know what happened to them."

"No." Kaiel shook his head in denial. "No!"

"Kaiel," Sevaani said behind him. "Sit down."

"He can't be dead!" He turned and gripped her arms. "He can't be!"

"No-one said they were dead, Kaiel," Iana said firmly, taking his wrist and pulling his hands away from Sevaani.

"I saw the bottom of that fall." He met her eyes. "The rocks –"

"There was a second portal," Iana told him. "We just need to find out where that took them –" She stopped, her eyes on his hand. "Kaiel." Her voice was light, but the grip on his wrist tightened.

"Wha–?" He looked at his hand. Shany's ointment was gone, washed off he supposed, and the scar it had hidden was visible. Had it grown? The single crescent line now began to curve down as though spiralling back on itself, and another moved outside to encase them both. But no, that wasn't possible. "It's just a... just a scar."

"It's more than that!" The Starbinder stared at him as if she had never seen him before. "I thought it was Darien," she said. "I thought he was the one."

"The one what?" Kaiel asked, then wished he'd kept his mouth shut. His stomach twisted.

She laid a finger on the scar. Kaiel flinched, and she dropped her hand."The Mark of the Eye," she murmured.

No. He wasn't a Summoner. He *couldn't* be a Summoner!

"Fat lot of good it will do him if he is a Summoner," Sim groaned. "We're in the middle of nowhere. Also –" he pointed at Kaiel, "your brother tried to kill you back there."

"What?" Kaiel turned away from the Shaluay. "Darien wouldn't do that."

"No! No, Kaiel." Sim shook his head vehemently. "I *saw* him. I saw what he did. The look on his face. For some reason, that spear saved you. And where in the Void did you get that from? I thought you left that in the Borderlands?"

"I did," Kaiel said. The spear had just appeared in his hand; he remembered raising his arm as though he could stop the daemon-priest with will alone, and it was just there. Like he'd *summoned*...

"Well, I saw him," Sim continued. "He would have killed you if he could!"

"Leave it, Sim." Kaiel didn't want to think about it.

"We have to find the princess," Erika said, oblivious to what was happening around her.

"That is the Nemisdrillion Sea," Lihon said looking out across the bay.

"Are you sure?" Jaric joined him.

"These are the Daicremore Mountains." The Blay Shon stared up at the tall cliffs. "And the sun has not yet reached its zenith. The only body of water west of the Daicremore is the Nemisdrillion."

"Those mountains stretch across the coast for leagues!" Erika said. "What are we supposed to do? Swim?"

Jaric sighed. "If we have to, we have to. We cannot stay here."

"A boat will come," Sevaani said.

"But when?" Jaric shook his head. "It could be days or weeks. And we would need to be able to signal them."

"My cora'stone can send what is effectively a flare at night," Iana suggested. "But again, there is little point if no-one is around to see it."

"No," Sevaani said, more insistently. "You don't understand. A boat *will* come."

Jaric turned to look at her. "You have dreamt it?"

Sevaani nodded. "But the light is wrong. I think it was morning."

"You think?" Sim muttered. "And were we all alive to be rescued?"

"Not helpful, Sim," Kaiel said.

"Yes," Sevaani said, ignoring Sim's doubt. "Yes, we were all alive. I don't think it will be long. There was no sense of… of starvation."

"You dream true?" Erika asked, looking at Sevaani intently.

"I believe the girl is a Dream Seer," Iana said. "But she is untrained."

Erika got to her feet. "And Andra," she asked urgently. "Did you dream of her? Where is she? Is she still alive?"

"I… no. No, I didn't… dream of her, or Darien." Sevaani shook her head, blonde hair gold in the sunlight.

"She is *untrained,* Erika," Iana said. "Until that changes, her dreams will come randomly."

Sevaani looked at the Shaluay. "I will be able to dream about what I want?"

"In time," Iana said.

"Well." Jaric looked across the ocean. "For now, it will have to be enough that we know we will get out of here."

"That's not what she said." Sim ran a hand through his wet hair.

"What do you mean?" Kaiel asked.

"She said a boat would come. Did we get on the boat? Did it rescue us?"

Sevaani straightened and looked at Sim. "I dreamt of the boat,

Simeon. I dreamt it for a reason. You should hold that hope in your heart."

Kaiel blinked. He'd never heard Sevaani speak with such confidence.

"'Hope in my heart'?" Sim stared at her. "We'll need more than hope to get out of this."

"Enough, Simeon," Jaric said. "A boat is coming. We will take that for now and pray to the Elder Gods it will be here soon."

"Well, we have fresh water coming out of that." Sim hooked a thumb at the waterfall. "And I have my pack, which I filled with fruit from those trees in the Dreamhold."

"We should be sparing with that food," Lihon said, still eyeing the cliffs around them. "We could be in for a long wait."

Darien cried out as he slammed into the slippery funnel of stone at the bottom of the waterfall. Stars exploded behind his eyes as his head hit the stone a moment later, pain lancing through his skull. The rushing roar of water filled his ears.

A strong current grabbed him, pulling him along at speed. He struggled for breath, swallowing water as his lungs tried to fill themselves. Water-smoothed rocks rushed by as the torrent carried him on, his body slamming along the sides of the tunnel, buffeted by the water enveloping him. As he was dragged around, changing direction, his torso bobbed above the torrent, and he tried desperately to retch the water he'd swallowed. Then the tunnel dipped, and he was heading down. He shot out of the dark into blazing sunlight then was falling again.

Sky, water, and the distant impression of land spun as he fell. There were rocks somewhere beneath him, he was sure, and he had a moment of panic before he crashed into more water, his body stinging as though he'd been slapped with a brick wall.

The roar became a muffled bubbling, and his heartbeat hammered in his ears. His body sank through the water. Down…

Panic jolted through him, and he kicked weakly, disoriented. Light. There was light. Up. Above him. Moving farther away. He was sinking. He tried to move his arms, but the water was so heavy. He kicked again. Barely moving. His lungs burned. Spots peppered his vision. He couldn't...

No!

He *reached*.

Asai filled him. Its silver light blazed across his mind's eye. Around him, the water churned.

Within two heartbeats, his head was above the water, and he was gasping for breath, taking great gulps of air.

Beside him, another body crashed into the water in an explosion of bubbles and whitewash.

They didn't come back up.

He waited, still trying to catch his breath.

There was no movement in the water below him.

"Light blind me!" he spat Sim's favourite curse.

Taking a breath, he dived into the cold, dark water, and collided with a body rising beneath him. The collision was soft, a bump, and he grabbed a handful of wet robes and dragged them up to the surface.

Gathering every scrap of strength he had left, he kicked until he broke the surface. Panting, he continued to kick his legs to keep his head above water, hoping that whoever was beside him was able to float because he was done.

It took him a moment to recognise the person he'd pulled up was Princess Andraste. He twisted looking for the others but the water – the lake – was empty. Wincing, he raised a hand to his head. The light of the sun shot through his eyes like a white-hot poker. He spat water and tried to get his bearings.

Behind him, in the north, mountains of grey stone crossed the horizon, and a waterfall poured from impossibly high cliffs above. From the shore, a dry wind scoured his face.

"Darien?" The princess's voice was strained. She coughed. "Where are we? Where are the others?"

He looked around again, his stomach tightening with fear.

"Darien?" Andraste repeated.

"I don't know," he said, his exhaustion taking the frustration out of his voice.

She was silent. In the distance came the cry of a bird he didn't recognise.

Where was Kaiel? Where was his brother?

And with that came images of Kaiel wielding Asai. He froze, trying to reconcile the memory. He had… he had attacked Kaiel. He'd wanted to kill him and something – the shard? – had helped him.

He stopped paddling and slipped in the water.

"Darien!"

In a panic, he kicked and got his head back above the water. "Come on," he said, starting for the western shore.

Tall trees with deep green leaves, not the firs or leather leaves he was used to, grew beyond the lakeshore. They stood close by the cliffs but thinned as they continued south, as though hesitant to leave the edge of the mountain range. To the south-east, farther along the shore, he could make out a green stone building of broad, sweeping roofs, stacked one upon the other, each successive roof smaller than the one below, reaching into the sky like a tower.

He staggered out of the lake and collapsed onto the dirt. A moment later, Andraste joined him. Darien rolled onto his back, sucking in deep breaths of the arid air. The earth beneath him was hard, but it felt good against his bruised back.

"Thank you," Andraste said.

She'd pulled her wet hair back from her forehead, and though her white robes were no longer pristine, she still held an air of authority. "You saved my life in the lake." She gestured behind them. "Thank you."

He eyed her. She had none of the cloying helplessness Sevaani played to, and none of the defensive self-possession of Meg. She was, he supposed, more like Prince Alesandr. Blood.

"You saved mine in the Isae'eldar," he said. "I pay my debts."

"How... practical of you."

He stared at her, but there was no mockery in her tone. She returned his stare evenly.

He looked away.

"Do you have any notion as to where we are?" she asked.

"No. I don't remember much after you pushed me into the water. Where did the others go?"

Andra sat up. "They jumped into the other stream. I thought we had exchanged one death for another when we went over the edge. The ground was littered with stalagmites. But there were two... circles, of light. The waterfall we fell from went through one, and they all fell through the other."

"It was a portal?"

"I have no idea what it was," she said shortly. "Or where Erika is. But I need to get back to Sithapia."

"You'll have a long way to go for that," Darien said. "I believe we're still in the Eastern Half."

She sighed and slapped the ground in exasperation.

Darien looked away; he had his own concerns. His entire life had been turned inside out, and now even his brother could wield *Asai*. His stomach twisted. Surely Kaiel hadn't *really* done that. It had to have been the spear.

The spear.

Where had *that* come from? The cursed thing would be the end of them both. Unless... he paused, his mind scratching a possibility.

Footsteps on dry leaves and the jingle of metal made him sit up. The world spun, and he groaned.

"Darien." Andra's voice was strained.

Head pounding, he peered out of one eye.

The tree line ended where they had crawled out of the lake, and before them rolled an empty plain of pale, dry grass.

To the east, in the direction of the pale green tower, stood ten men in green cotton tunics, under cuirasses of stitched, black leather squares. Their skin was blue.

Amarians.

The guardsmen moved to surround them, silver eyes watching them without expression.

His dizziness vanished.

Behind the soldiers, pale-skinned, round-eyed men knelt beside the poles of a palanquin. Each had a shaved head, and the left side of their scalps were covered with an intricate blood-red tattoo.

Slaves.

The guardsmen parted to allow a man in the silks of a Blay Shon through. The man's face displayed an old scar that ran through his left eye – Darien blinked as he recognised him as one of the blademasters who had been in attendance to the Shaluay Ambassador in Serjat.

The Blay Shon regarded them coldly, then bent and grabbed Darien's right hand. He dragged his thumb across the scar, his lips curling. The blademaster let his hand go and spoke in an unfamiliar language to the men behind him.

Darien inspected the back of his hand. His skin tingled. Shany's ointment no longer covered the scar, and the mark on his hand had grown, stretching to curve around in a sinuous line, like the letter *s*.

A pair of guardsmen stepped forward, and Darien was hauled to his feet by one. The other man pulled the princess up beside him.

"What is this?" Andraste asked.

"I don't know," Darien hissed, his voice hoarse.

"They are *Amarians*," she said. "Take your hands off me. Is this how you treat strangers?"

There was the slap of a palm meeting flesh, and Andra cried out.

Darien bit the inside of his cheek, not daring to protest.

The Blay Shon stopped before the palanquin, and the curtains moved as the blademaster spoke.

A voice answered, but Darien couldn't quite hear the words.

The Blay Shon bent at the waist, then pulled the drapes aside, exposing the woman within, and Darien stared as he recognised Shaluay Arais.

"You are trespassers in the land of the Black Sand," the old ambassador said. She spoke in the common tongue, as she had when Darien had seen her in the Spire. "By the law of the Empire, you are slaves to be claimed by the first House to find you." A wind rose around them, the dead leaves on the ground rustled like a watching crowd.

She looked at Andraste. "You are now the property of the Nimora. And you –" an aged finger pointed at Darien. "You, Child of the Moon, are to be taken to Arleth'taur."

The Star Cradle. The great citadel of the Shaluay, in the heart of the Black Sands. He wasn't being made a slave like Andra?

The Shaluay leant back, and a slave lowered the silk curtains, hiding her from sight once more.

Darien jerked in surprise as the guardsman holding him snapped a collar around his throat, then gasped as the cold sank through his skin. Fever chills broke out across his body, nausea rolling in his gut.

The cold at his neck burned, like red-hot needles, piercing his skin. As the light of *Asai* vanished from his mind's eye, he screamed.

The night seemed to be longer than the day when it finally fell.

Lady Iana had sent flares of light into the night sky at regular intervals. They were bright as bonfires and drifted slowly to the water.

"What's the point of that?" Sim asked. "We know a ship is coming. There's no need to send up flares, or whatever that light show is."

"We know a ship is coming," Iana agreed, "but we don't know why. The weakness of foretelling, or dreaming, is that we rarely know why the things dreamt happen. Consider this my attempt at giving it a helping hand."

Sim hadn't said anything more.

The sun had risen slowly, and Lady Iana had continued to cast flares into the sky until she'd deemed the sun too bright to continue. The sky brightened long before the shadows cast by the mountains at their backs had shrunk, tucked under the cliffs as they were. It had to be close to midday but one minute could easily feel like ten, stuck on this rock.

Kaiel groaned as he stood, his body bruised and battered. He'd slept on hard surfaces regularly since leaving Hanore, but this rock was the most uncomfortable he'd experienced. Hopefully, Sevaani's ship would appear soon, and they could find passage to somewhere with a bed. Although, he'd need to find something to hide the scar on his hand. At least until it faded more.

It *was* just a scar from that wound the Malkidem gave him in the Trials. Lady Iana was mistaken to think it was anything else.

Then why did Shany warn me to hide it?

"Okay, Sevaani," Sim said from the edge of the boulder. "I take it back."

"What do you take back, Sim?" she asked, lifting her head.

"We have company." Sim pointed out across the bay.

"A ship?" Erika stood, joining Sim.

"Ships," Sim corrected.

Around the south-head of the cove, four… five… six ships, and more sailed into view.

"That's not right," Sevaani said, and Kaiel looked at her.

"What's not right, child?" Iana asked.

"I only saw one ship in my dream." Sevaani gestured at the ships sailing into the mouth of the cove. "And it came from the north."

"Who cares?" Sim said. "It was a dream. Lots of dreams don't make much sense." He waved his hands in the air. "Over here!"

Kaiel saw Sevaani's frown. "It was just a dream," he said.

"It was a *true* dream, Kaiel. This –" She pressed her lips together. " – is not what I dreamt."

"I believe you," Iana said from Kaiel's other side. "But you have much to learn about your gift, and Dreaming is an exacting discipline, even for those to whom it comes naturally. You dreamt of ships coming to this place before we arrived and now, they are here. We would be foolish to disregard this opportunity."

Iana raised her hand to the sky, and Kaiel saw the black bracer the Shaluay wore flash with light. The pulse of light lasted no longer than a second, but he had to shield his eyes against the brightness.

"Well, that will draw their attention," Erika said as Kaiel blinked furiously to clear the afterimage in his vision.

"It was only one ship," Sevaani muttered, crossing her arms over her chest.

The ships sailed further into the cove, more coming up behind them until there were twelve that Kaiel could count clearly. The lead ship was a massive three-decked vessel with matching masts of black sails.

"Are these ships from Glass Bay?" Jaric asked, frowning.

"Possibly," Lihon said. The Blay Shon stood behind Lady Iana. "But Glass Bay is not the only haven for corsairs on the Nemisdrillion."

The lead ship dropped anchor and Kaiel could see people, a lot of people, crowding its deck and looking towards them.

Sim had stopped waving his arms. "I get the feeling something's not quite right here."

"Like what?" asked Erika.

"I don't know," Sim muttered. "Something."

A small boat was lowered over the side of the lead ship, and six men climbed down a rope ladder to board it. Within five, maybe ten minutes, the men in the dinghy had crossed the distance between them.

"Ho' strangers!"

Kaiel noted the men in the boat had their hands wrapped around the hilts of the short swords at their waists. He reached for his own, surprised he hadn't lost it in the ride through the waterfall and counted his blessings. The spear was gone, cast at the daemon-priest but maybe it would appear again if he needed it. The skin across the back of his neck prickled at the thought.

"Hello!" Jaric shouted as the sloop neared.

"Was it you, sending up those flares?" asked the first man, a burly sailor with more grey than brown in his hair and beard. The men wore undyed woollen shorts, their chests and feet bare, skin dark from the sun.

"Yes," Jaric said before anyone else could reply.

"Could see 'em clear to Malsa." The man eyed them as the sloop came closer.

"You're from Malsa?" Jaric asked.

"No, not rightly," the sailor admitted. "But we been past there not two days ago." He looked around. "Where's ya ship? Did it sink?"

"Can we speak with your captain?" Iana stepped forward, the cora'stone at her neck flashing in the sun. The man's eyes fixed on it.

"You're Shaluay." It was an accusation.

"I am."

One of the men behind the speaker leant forward and whispered in his ear.

The speaker's eyes narrowed, looking over each of them in turn. He frowned and replied to the man who'd whispered. The sailor shrugged, eyeing Iana again before nodding vigorously.

"Is there a problem?" Jaric asked, and Erika got to her feet.

The man spat into the water. "Would ye be the Lady Iana?"

"You have me at a disadvantage," Iana said. "Do I know you?"

"Nah, milady." The man's eyes went back to Kaiel before returning to her once more. "Me name's Fen. How about we get ye lot up to the captain's ship. She'll be right happy to see you."

Kaiel noted the man's tone, but he brushed his doubt aside. He had more pressing things to worry about.

"What is the name of your captain?" Jaric asked, jumping into the sloop as it stopped against the cliff.

The grey-haired sailor grinned, showing a mouth full of blackened teeth.

Rock sharks circled as the boat neared the black ship and Fen told them the shiver had been following them since they left Malsa. Sharp-edged fins that flashed in the sunlight cut the water ominously, and Sevaani pressed herself against Kaiel's side.

Once, he would have been happy at that contact. That she must have forgiven him the wound he inflicted on her brother. But somewhere along the way the feelings he'd held for her had changed.

"Don't mind them sharks, missy," Fen said. "They ain't much for jumping. Not like tiger sharks."

Sevaani hid her face on Kaiel's shoulder.

One of the sailors at the bow hailed the dark ship as they reached the rope ladder. Fen directed them up one at a time, while two other sailors took long poles with sharp hooked spikes on the end, and jabbed them into the water.

Fen flashed a black smile at Kaiel. "Just ta be safe."

Kaiel tried to ignore the sharks and focused his energy on climbing up to the deck of the big ship. Easily as large as the warship in the harbour of Serjat, if with fewer decks, this one was filled with people who stared at them in suspicious silence.

Men and women were dressed in a riot of colours. Some were shirtless, their bare skin tanned and gleaming, wearing trousers cut short on the leg and working at ropes and mending nets. But there were many more people, men, women and children who were not dressed for ship work, milling around the deck and staring.

At the back of the crowd, Kaiel spotted Lord Danyl, the First's majordomo. The man's eyes were sunken and black, and he still wore his fur cloak, though it looked burnt in places. He stared at them as though he'd seen ghosts and ducked away.

"Who are this lot?" bawled a painfully thin man with a hooked nose.

"It's them, Maris! It be the witch and her daemonspawn!" Fen had pulled his short sword and was joined quickly by the other men who'd been in the boat, surrounding them.

"Maris?" The man was so gaunt, Kaiel barely recognised the man who had led them out of the swamp to Glass Bay.

"Get the First Captain!" the corsair yelled, and a deckhand broke away from the crowd to go below deck. "Looks like our nets brought us a bad catch," he spat, eyeing them without a trace of friendliness.

Iana stepped past Kaiel, only to have Fen's sword pressed to her chest. "What is going on, Maris? Why are you all here?"

"Don't ya speak to me like we're friends!" the first mate snarled. "Corwyn gave ya passage. Shared food and water with ya!" he spat at her feet.

"We were given food, water and passage, which we paid for," Iana said, without blinking at his hostility.

"So speaks the witch. The First Captain was right about ya. If she speaks again, cut her throat. I won't be having her casting no spells on us!"

A grunt came from behind. Kaiel looked over his shoulder to see Lihon struggling under a net, while two other men looped more ropes around him.

Maris stepped up to him. "Ya sword, Borderlander," the man hissed, his breath foul in Kaiel's face. "Now!"

"Do it, Kaiel," Captain Jaric said. With great reluctance, Kaiel handed his sword over to the corsair.

"Truly, Taluun is looking upon us," came a familiar voice and the ragged men and women parted for Nataya Desrin. "It fucking took him long enough!"

Her steel-grey hair had been cropped short, and she wore a black armband on a crimson silk blouse. The First Captain of Glass Bay leant heavily on a cane, her face marked with burns, and approached them. The Var, Grazat, was at her back, a poorly healed wound and burn scars where his left ear used to be.

"Well, Bloodborn," she spat at Kaiel. "I warned you that if you brought trouble to Glass Bay, I would hunt you down. As chance would have it, the Great Lord of the Ocean himself has seen fit to deliver you!" Her eyes burned with a fever that made Kaiel shiver.

"Nataya, what is the meaning of this?" Iana said.

The old woman's eyes flickered, narrowing with hatred. "This is retribution!" she spat. "I warned him! I told him if he brought trouble to us, he would pay. And what trouble came. A Prince of Aldania. Looking for you!" She pointed a bony finger at Kaiel, her scarred face twisted with rage. "And you were not there to be given to him, were you? Oh no –" She circled him. "Your trail led him to us, so we paid the price. He brought a fire that could not be quenched! And while parents tried to save children, his men cut them down. *My* people. My *granddaughter*!"

"Oh, Nataya," Iana said, sorrow in her voice.

"Be silent!" Madness whirled in the old woman's eyes. "You brought this on us. Ruined us. Just as you ruin everything!"

"My lady," Kaiel said, stricken, his chest tight. "I am sorry. I would never have come to Glass Bay if we'd believed His Highness would follow us all the way."

"He wants you, boy," she told him between clenched teeth, her face crammed with hate. "He demanded we tell him where you went. And we did. *I* did! But it was not enough. He set the boats alight with a fire that burned on water! Do you know how many people we lost to those flames?"

Kaiel stifled a groan. Sim's eggs. Alesandr had taken them in Sonyth. Zaria… no!

"Yes, he wants you," she muttered. "But he is not going to get you."

Kaiel swallowed. "Truly, milady, I never meant for any of this to happen. Thank you."

"Do not thank me." Her smile did not reach her eyes. "He is not going to have you, because you have a greater role to play."

He glanced over his shoulder at the others. "I don't understand."

"Let me tell you," Nataya said, and this time her smile was more a snarl. "We survived, we lucky, *lucky* few because the Lord of the Deeps willed it so." She gestured over the expanse of the sparkling ocean and the packed ships around them. "His children follow us and they hunger for blood. It is now within our power to appease their appetite." There was a murmur from the crowd.

Over the First Captain's shoulder, some of the people offered him feral grins, but most just watched without expression. Maris's face was wooden, but he shouted orders to the sailors behind him. The crowd moved, and a long piece of wood was extended off the side of the ship. A sword was pressed against Kaiel's back.

"Your prince cannot have you," Nataya continued, eyes bright. "Because the rock sharks will." She addressed the crowd on the deck. "He walks the plank!"

"Nataya." Iana's voice was as cold as a winter storm. "Don't be rash."

"This is not rash," the older woman said. "I have thought long and hard as to what I would do if I ever saw you again." Kaiel jerked his head back as she spat in his face. "Walk!"

The steel at his back pressed hard, the point digging into his skin. He stumbled as a hand pushed him to the edge of the ship. The plank of wood extended before him. It was too narrow to walk on, the blue-grey of the water stretching out beneath. Sweat rolled down his face.

"Mother!" a voice cracked over the assembly.

"No!" Nataya screeched. "They die!"

Around them, men, and women in the red of the Trident Guard took up position, and Corwyn Desrin strode onto the deck. Unlike Maris, the man looked exactly as he had when they'd left him on the docks of the lower city two days ago, but his eyes... Kaiel couldn't meet them. Instead, he took in the unrelieved red he now wore.

"What do you think you are doing?" the captain of the *Crow* asked calmly – though there was no mistaking the menace beneath his tone.

"They have fallen into our hands!" Nataya rasped. "It is the will of Taluun!"

"On these ships, *my* will is the only one to order executions. Maris!" He turned to the man. "I have had enough of you undermining me at every turn. My mother is no longer First Captain, *I* am."

"Corwyn, I –" Maris began, but Corwyn's dagger lashed out, gutting him.

"No!" Nataya screamed, but the Var beside her wrapped an

enormous arm around her shoulders, holding her back. "They killed your daughter!"

Corwyn caught Maris as he fell, and two Tridents grabbed him, pulling him upright.

"Throw him over. As my mother has invoked Taluun already, it will not do to let his children go hungry."

The guards dragged the screaming man to the plank Kaiel had been about to walk, and unceremoniously threw him over.

Some of the crowd, children amongst them, ran to the rails. A splash cut off the screams, and a thrashing rose from the water before dying away.

"Grazat," Corwyn barked. "Take my mother below. She needs her rest."

"They killed your daughter!" Nataya screamed at him. "They deserve to die!"

"Alesandr Niskeri killed my daughter," Corwyn said coldly. "You will not get your petty revenge by trying to manipulate me. *I* am First Captain now. Remember it, or you can join your pet overboard."

Nataya screeched and flung herself at him, but the Var picked her up like a child and bustled her through the open hatch, the survivors of Glass Bay watching on in silence.

"Untie them." Corwyn gestured.

"Corwyn," Iana said as she was released. "What month is this?"

"Is that all you have to say?"

"It is important. You only left us at the lower port two days ago."

Corwyn's eyes narrowed. "I don't know what Shaluay game you are playing –"

"She speaks the truth, corsair." The ropes around Lihon fell away before the men could remove them. Two daggers gleamed in his fists.

Corwyn looked them over. "It's Ralten."

"Ralten?" Sim hissed. "It was Deson yesterday! What happened to the last two months –"

Iana cut Sim off with a raised hand. Looking at Corwyn, she bowed her head. "I am truly sorry for what has befallen you and your home."

Corwyn watched them, his eyes flicking between Iana and Simeon. "I do not hold with my mother's obsessions," he said at last. "But you will be off my ship as soon as we get to the next village on this forsaken coast."

"I understand, of course," Iana said. "If you can take us to Jardin –"

"The next village!" Corwyn barked. "The sooner you are gone, the safer we will be! Thank the stars you worship that my mother saw fit to educate me in the Realms. Few else here would grasp that something larger is at play. They'd have thrown you overboard and been done with you, but I am wary of what follows in your wake. I will not tempt the Father of Storms further."

Tension crawled through the air. "Very well," Iana said at last. "The next village will suffice. If we could use a cabin while we wait?"

"Use mine and stay out of the way. Others on this ship regard you in the same light as my mother does." His eyes scanned the watching crowd. "And I don't have eyes everywhere. We leave tomorrow, once the water stores are replenished."

A deckhand stepped forward and waited for them to gather themselves before leading them below deck.

Iana left the cabin quietly, careful of her steps. Water lapping against the hull and the occasional creak of timber were the only noises so late in the night. She made her way through the darkened corridor, climbing the ladder to the ship's main deck. She paused in the shadow of the hatchway, the cool breeze off the ocean tracing her face. Seeing no movement, she exited the passage and made her way to the forecastle, climbing to the deck above.

A sailor sat watch at the front of the ship, gazing across the water. Closing her eyes, Iana gathered herself and breathed out. Had he been watching, the sailor would have seen her form shimmer, the ghostlight of the moon shifting around her, making her almost translucent as she faded between worlds. Wraith-like, she made her way forward until she stood directly behind him. She lifted her right hand, and the amethyst stone on the ring of her little finger gave a single pulse, the violet light dancing over the back of the sailor's neck.

He slumped forward silently, and the light shifted around her once more as she stepped back into the physical plane. She caught the man by the shoulders and eased him to the deck, wrinkling her nose at his unwashed odour.

She then poured rum from a bottle she had purloined from a chest in Corwyn's cabin across the sailor's mouth and shirt. She tipped the rest over the side, and then placed the empty bottle in the comatose sailor's hand.

Stepping back, she surveyed her handiwork, then looked over her shoulder. The sailor at the opposite end of the ship was still, a huddled shadow, unaware of what had transpired.

Turning away from the lower deck, she reached her hands up to the torque around her neck and removed the cora'stone. She shifted the gem until she found the facet she sought then pressed the tip of a finger to it, holding it there until a light flared at the stone's heart.

The Shol'mas had shown their hand and a power that had not graced the Broken Continent since the Sundering had been used to destroy the csitargon. She had found a descendant of Varos Korin'ad and a Summoner. He had not yet come into his full power, but the flames of his pyre were kindling, and they would lead him to the mantle of Empyros, she was sure of it.

She stared into the cora'stone and let her awareness sink through the geometric fractals that formed the gem's interior, merging with its matrix.

Cold and blue, the glow of the stone was subtle, unobtrusive. The light at its heart blinked in a steady rhythm.

High above the Nemisdrillion Sea, amongst the twinkling stones of the Sormelene Span, a light flared and began to blink in response.

The End of Book One of
The Eye of Eternity.

GLOSSARY

Alay'thias (ah-LAY-thee-as): The Elder God of the Sun, called the Sunlord by some. He is the son of Li'aria.

Alesandr Kelam Niskeri (Ahl-es-AHN-der kel-am Nis-kair-ee): Fourth son of the current King of Aldania.

Andraste duCerin (Ahn-DRAHS-TAY doo-SER-in): Princess of Sithapia, Ardhel in-waiting.

Ang: A young Sola'var of Hanore; friend to Kaiel and Simeon.

Ants: see *Xious'bisan*.

Ardhel (ARD-hel): Sovereign or monarch; the person who holds by life tenure and hereditary right, the chief authority over the Realm of Sithapia and its people.

Arleth'taur (ah-Leth-tor): 1. High Asairic for Star Cradle. 2. The Citadel of the Shaluay, located in the Black Sands desert of Amaria.

Arac'diem (AH-RAK-dee-em): A daemon the size of a foal, it has the body and legs of a spider and torso that resembles a human child.

Arais Minashi (AH-ray-is Min-ASH-ee): Shaluay Ambassador to the Ciralys in Serjat. Former teacher of Iana.

***Asai* (AH-saI):** The energy that manifests all creation and the language that gives it shape. The Eye of Eternity is perceived as the font of Asai.

Women see the energy as a gold light and men see it as a silver light; it is not known why this is so, as it is the same energy.

Asp Knight: see *Brotherhood of the Asp.*

Aspirant: A person who is in training in the Palace of the Eye to become a Ciralys. It is the first rank of a Palace initiate, beneath that of the Awakened.

Athmay (ATH-may): A continent broken into the Eastern Half and the Western realms by the Sundering.

Awakened: Men and women who are in training in the Place of the Eye to become Ciralys. They have passed their Aspirant training but are not yet full members of the order.

Black Sands, the: A desert in Amaria extending across the majority of the realm; so named for the colour of its sand.

Blay Shon: An Amarian blademaster, trained by the Shi-Kaan Monks and considered without equal in their mastery of the sword on the Broken Continent.

Bloodlord: A wielder of *Asai* who willingly enters, or has thrust upon them, a symbiotic relationship with a csitargon daemon to gain power they would not normally have access to.

bone drake: An undead dragon.

Borderlanders: People who dwell in the Borderland Wilds, predominantly in the Three Citadels.

Borderland Wilds, the: Untamed lands that run between the eastern edge of Aldania and the western side of Dal'mere.

Breanta Toranth (BREE-ahn-tah TOR-anth): Wife to Malik Toranth, aunt to Kaiel and Darien.

Bronze Guard, the: A mercenary company based in Jaroff and often retained by the Carbinah.

Bronze Spear, the: 1. A *tresilian* artefact crafted for Varos Korin'ad, leader of the Sahrin. 2. The symbol of House Taaren'th and the Clan of the Bronze Spear. (*Also see* Ne'ronsylari)

Brotherhood of the Asp: Personal guardsmen of the royal House of Aldania, considered to be among the deadliest hand-to-hand combat fighters outside of Amaria.

cant: The formulaic vocalisation of *Asai* to produce a specific result or effect.

Carbinah (CAR-bin-AH): An Aldanian office of governorship appointed by the Royal Court in Dainyaia to the Borderland Wilds. A Carbinah is appointed for a term of four years.

Chelim al'Korat (CHEY-lihm ahl-KORE-aht): Sky Lord of the Second Circle of the Ciralys.

Chosen: A Shol'mas priest partially imbued with the essence of the Lord they serve. They are identified by motes of golden light flickering across their eyes.

***ci'nar* (Sy-nar):** A Ciralys artefact, created in imitation of the Sahrin's *tresilians*. The majority of *ci'nar* can only be used by a Ciralys attuned to the same Sphere as its creator; some few *ci'nar* can be used by anyone such as keystones, speakstones and sunstones. The manufacturing of these is controlled by Ciralys Artificers.

Ciralys (Si-RAH-LIS): Wielders of *Asai*, the order pre-dates the Sundering during which time they were assistants and administrators to the Sahrin. They consider themselves to be the rightful inheritors of the Sahrin's lost knowledge and authority. They are unable to summon empyreans.

Circle: A society within the Ciralys Order. These societies are neither philosophical nor political –although Circles undertake political manoeuvring. There are five Circles, and each one represents one element – or Sphere – of *Asai*. Each Ciralys belongs to the Circle that represents the Sphere they have a natural affinity to. The colour of the skystone rings of their Khaderneous medallion indicates to which Circle a Ciralys belongs.

Colum (COL-um): Captain of Glass Bay's outer guard.

cora'stone (COR-RAH-stohn): The stone in the neck torque of all Shaluay Starbinders, linking them to the Starwells and the Swarm.

corusite (COR-RAH-syt): An ore extracted from skystones. If placed against the skin, it prevents wielders of *Asai* and *Des'maadr* from using their abilities and causes great pain and illness.

Corwyn Desrin (Cor-win Des-rin): Son of the Nataya Desrin, father of Zaria, Captain of the Black Sail ship the *Crow*.

***Crow*, the:** Foremost ship of the Drowned Blades.

Cryndalene, the (crin-dah-LIN): An artefact pre-dating the Sahrin, that served as a seal upon a gateway in Nemis'draal, a city of the Ancients.

Crystal Spire: A large crystalline tower built by the Sahrin and located in Serjat. Chapterhouse of the Ciralys in that city.

daemon: A denizen of the Abyss.

daemon cat: see *Dycinion*.

daemondogs: Considered a lesser species of daemon, these dog-like creatures have limited intelligence and are tenacious hunters. Under the command of a higher daemon, they can temporarily obtain a humanoid form.

Daemon Hunter: See *Kas'tirien*.

Daicremore Mountains (DEY-cre-mohr): An impassable mountain range in northern Amaria that rose during the Sundering, effectively closing all access to Amaria via land.

Dainyaia (Deyn-YAY-yah): The capital city of Aldania.

Dal'mere (DAHL-meer): High Asairic for Deadlands. An area of south-eastern Athmay that was destroyed at the end of the War of the Summoners. It is home to the remnants of the Korda'vari Hordes and is characterised by poisons and roaming packs of daemons. The Veil between worlds is weak here.

Darscene Caves (DAR-seen): An abandoned mining site in the Borderland Wilds that the Kas'tirien used as their base of operations in the years after the Sundering. It is now the testing ground for those initiates seeking to become an apprentice to a Daemon Hunter.

Darien Toranth (DAH-ree-en TOR-anth): A young man from Hanore. Younger half-brother to Kaiel Toranth.

Deadlands: see *Dal'mere*.

Debrov (De-brov): Proprietor of the Sea Lion Inn in Glass Bay.

Des'maadr (Days-MAH-der): The energy that dwells in the Void. The antithesis of *Asai*.

Des'maadrian (Days-MAH-dree-en): Rulers of the Void and its daemonic inhabitants.

Deson (Dez-ON): The twelfth month of the calendar year and the first month of winter.

Desolation, the: An inconsolable feeling of sorrow, loss or grief that comes upon the Var that cannot be lifted. This emotion was the root cause of the fall of the Var Imperium.

Dobard Hay (Boh-BARD HEY): A veteran member of the Hanore Rangers.

Dreadlord: Giant daemons from the deeper planes of the Void, they are said to be amongst the most deadly of the Des'maadrians' minions and are driven by rage and bloodlust. Their bodies resemble that of dragons, with four legs, wings and a spiked tail but their upper torsos are humanoid in form with a broad chest, two arms and a horned head. It is believed to have been centuries since a Dreadlord last manifested on the mortal plane. The boneswords of the Kas'tirien are made from their remains.

Dreamhold: see *Isae'eldar*.

Drowned Blades, the: The corsairs of Glass Bay.

Dycinion (Dy-SIN-ee-on): A daemon cat that was released into Sobia during the War of the Sundering. It is highly intelligent and has a scorpion-like tail that paralyses its prey so that it may feast on living flesh. Its blood is acidic and burns the skin and can even damage metal.

Ebron (Eb-ron): Largest city on the east coast of Aldania, ruled by the High Prince of House Sarentis, vassal to House Niskeri.

Eight, the: The eight members of the council that rules Tremor-Salaya

Elder Gods: The elemental deities whose complex dance forms reality.

Empyrean (em-PI-ree-en): Beings that dwell within the Light of the Eye of Eternity.

Empyros, the (em-PY-ROS): 1. The Sahrin who bonded with the Phoenix, the most powerful of empyreans. 2. Title of the leader of the Sahrin.

everstone: A seemingly indestructible stone-like material created by the Sahrin in all their constructions. The secret to its creation was lost during the Sundering.

Exile Point: see *Glass Bay*.

Evay (eh-VEY): A reclusive, long-lived humanoid species native to Sobia, the Evay are natural wielders of *Asai* and deadly blademasters. Their culture is ancient and highly advanced but hidden from humanity.

Ewyn Salimarath (EH-win Sah-lihm-AH-rahth): Earth Keeper, leader of the First Circle of the Ciralys.

Eye of Eternity, the: 1. A nebula of five entwined rings that form an eye in the sky that is visible at night. This nebula is theorised to be the centre of the universe and the font of *Asai*. 2. A tattoo of light, identical to the nebula of the same name that floats on the back of the right hand of any man, woman or child who can learn to wield *Asai* and to summon the empyreans, or daemons.

Feldar Quaylin (FEL-dah KEE-lin): A scout of the Bronze Guard.

Feraan Hilenz (Fer-AHN Hi-LENS): Prime Councillor of the Crystal Spire.
First Captain: Leader of Glass Bay, elected by the Captains of the Drowned Blades; while the tenure of a First lasts as long as they live, the natural term of their life is often cut short by assassination.

Garnavaar (GAR-na-VAR): The Elder God of Earth, consort to Tarin.
Golakresh (GOHL-ah-kresh): Daemon tongue for Korda'var.
Glass Bay: A remote enclave of exiles, criminals and corsairs on the north-eastern coast of Dal'mere. Ruled by the First.
Grazat (Grah-ZAHT): A Sola'var in Glass Bay.

Halaron (HAL-ah-ROHN): A volcano in the depths of Dal'mere, said to have been the site of a city of the Sahrin.
Hanore (HAHN-or): A Sahrin Citadel on the Borderlands built during the War of the Summoners; now home to families who wish to live free from the Houses of Aldania.
Hedge Right: A tradition begun during the Age of Chaos that allowed Witch Covenant apprentices to join the Ciralys, thus bolstering their depleted ranks.
High Asairic (haI AH-saI-rIk): The language of the Sahrin now spoken only by scholars, some nobles, and the Ciralys. It is claimed that this is the language of creation and is needed to wield Asai, yet speaking the language alone does not affect reality itself. Its structure and meaning are somewhat fluid as the runes of Asai are multi-dimensional; thus, words and phrases may have different meanings, depending on the context.
Horde, the: The name given to the Varian forces tainted by *Des'maadr* during the War of the Summoners.
Hyla'var (HI-lah-var): The scholar, artisan and mystic caste of the Var. They are slender and tall, have elongated faces, pointed ears and slanted eyes.

Hyriax (HI-ree-ax): A sphere, or aspect, of *Asai* as identified to correlate to the element of fire. Ciralys who are naturally attuned to this sphere have ruby-coloured skystones.

Iana no'Rylak Sabay (Ai-yah-NAH Noh-RY-lak SAHB-ai): A Shaluay Starbinder.

Imanarg (IM-an-AHG): Daemonic tongue for Bloodlord.

Isae'eldar (AI-say-EL-dar): Sahrin for Dreamhold. These are Sahrin cities seen to sit high in mountain ranges that rose during the Sundering. These are often impossible to reach, and those that can be are unable to be entered.

Isoliere (AI-soh-lee-EHR): The independent city-state of the Ciralys, one of only two cities to survive the Sundering at the end of the War of the Summoners.

Ivy Throne: The seat occupied by the King of Aldania.

Jakora, House (JAH-koh-rah): A High House of Tremor-Salaya.

Jaric Daynar (JAH-rik DAY-nahr): Captain of the Hanore Rangers.

Jaroff (Jahr-OFF): Former capital of Aldania during the rule of House Taaren'th, now a back-water trading post at the south-eastern edge of the Realm.

Jisana (Gee-SAH-nah): A long, slim blade with a slight curve, forged by the Shi-Kaan Monks for the Blay Shon. Created with techniques learnt pre-Sundering, the blades will not nick, bend or break unless their owner falls in battle.

Joram Banhere (Jor-AHM ban-HEER): Spirit Seer, leader of the Fifth Circle of the Ciralys.

Kaiel Toranth (KY-el TOR-anth): A Daemon Hunter applicant from Hanore. Older half-brother to Darien Toranth.

Karlon Bahlestian (KAHR-lon Bah-LEHST-ee-ahn): Scion, leader of the Ciralys.

Kas'tirien (KAHS-tir-ee-en): An order with origins in the War of the Sundering, these men and women wander the edges of Dal'mere to ensure no daemon escapes into the Realms ruled by humankind.

Keeper: A rank within the Witch Covenants of Aldania.

Keeper Shany (SHAH-nee): Keeper of the Citadel of Hanore. Also see, Shanaya dyn'Tian.

Keeper Terias (TEH-ree-AHS): The Keeper of Sonyth.

Khaderneous, the (KAH-Der-nee-OOS): 1. High Asairic for the Eye of Eternity, similar in shape to the nebula of the same name. 2. The symbol used as the emblem of the Ciralys.

Kharidium (KAH-ri-dee-um): An iridescent metal of various colours, similar to dragonscale, forged by the Xious'bisan. Kharidium is lighter and stronger than steel and highly favoured by the Blood for the making of weapons and armour. Also referred to as *Ant Forged*.

Korda'var (KOR-dah-VAR): Those Sola'var who followed the Sahrin sworn to the *Des'maadrian*, Di'shana. They have been tainted by *Des'maadr* and regressed in intelligence, growing armour-like scales of stone upon their bodies and daemonic horns on their heads. They are also called *Tainted*.

Kirana (Ker-AHN-AH): Shol'mas Lord of Fire.

Ley Hub: A everstone platform that acts as the entry and exit point of Ley Path.

Ley Path: see *Renimor*.

Li'aria (LEE-AHR-ee-ah): The Elder Goddess of Fire.

Lich: An undead being who has used *Asai* to unnaturally extend its life.

Light of the Eye, the: 1. Also known as *Asai*. 2. A title of the Scion of Isoliere.

Lihon Tang (Lee-HON TAHNG): An Amarian Blay Shon.

Liss: A saurian race native to Hetar.

Lloth'var (LOHTH-var): Those Hyla'var who followed the Sahrin sworn to the Des'maadrian, Di'shana. These are the battle leaders of the Horde. A melding of Hyla'var and daemons, they are devastatingly fast and have heightened reflexes. Though they can differ in appearance, they are all tall, have pale white skin, and cloven hooves in place of feet. Also called *Tainted*.

Malik Toranth (MAH-lik TOR-anth): Brother of Mar'ee Toranth, uncle of Kaiel and Darien Toranth.

Malkedim (MAWL-ked-Im): A solitary daemon of fire, this denizen of the Void is largely bestial and often used in the vanguard of the Des'maadrian Hordes.

Mar'ee Toranth (Mahr-EE TOR-anth): Mother of Kaiel and Darien Toranth.

Maris (MAH-ris): A corsair of Glass Bay.

Massarle (MAH-sarhl): The capital city of Tomassia.

Master of the Swamp: A Shol'mas Lord imprisoned within an ancient tower in the Sukmaanai Swamp.

Meghara Carhrin (Meg-HAH-rah Cahr-IN): Orphaned apprentice to the Hanore Keeper.

Mok'zul (Mok-zool): a powerful daemon with four legs and chitin-like armour, they are often found as captains in daemonic legions.

Nataya Desrin (NAT-ay-AH Des-rin): First Captain of Glass Bay.

Ne'ronsylari (NAY-rohn-sil-AHR-ee): 1. Sahrin for Bronze Spear. 2. A *tresilian* artefact crafted for the war leader of the Sahrin during the War of the Summoner, pre-Sundering.

Nemisdrillion (NEM-is-DRIL-EE-on): 1. The sea that divides the Eastern and Western Realms of Athmay. 2. A Realm that sunk beneath a new sea due to a shift in the continental plate during the Sundering.
Niskeri, House (Nis-KEH-ri): The royal House of Aldania, leaders of the Clan of the Iron Boar.
Noman: A human under the possession of a daemon, or allied to, the daemons of the Void.

Ohrin (Oh-RIN): The third month of autumn.
Orlay (Or-LAY): A city on the east coast of Sithapia.
Orthias (Or-thee-AHS): The font of all elemental force, considered the first of the Elder Gods.

Palace of the Eye: The principal seat of learning for all Ciralys, located in Isoliere.
Prime Councillor: Head of the Ciralys in the Crystal Spire, second in authority to the Scion.

Raetlia (RAYT-lee-ah): A trading post between Jaroff and Ebron.
Ralten (RAHL-ten): The first month of spring.
Renimor, the (Rehn-ee-MOHR): 1. High Asairic for White Road. 2. A roadway that exists outside of the material plane, allowing those who walk its path to travel much faster than those in the world outside.
Rhodri duCerin (ROH-dree doo-SER-in): Son of Torimun.
Rion (REE-on): A Sithapian hereditary title ranking immediately below a prince.
River Asp, the: A major waterway of Aldania that stretches across the Realm from Dainyaia to the Borderlands.
Rocend Arbenuto (Roh-SEND AHR-ben-oo-toh): A Ciralys of the Fifth Circle.

Rolen Etine (Roh-LEN EH-tyn): Son of the Steward of Hanore.

Rowin Bruday (Roh-WIN Broo-DAY): A Captain of the Bronze Guard.

Samantra (Sah-MAN-TRA): Elder Goddess of the Moon.

Sander: A derogatory term referring to an Amarian.

sareis (Sah-REES): A game played by two people in opposition, each with 24 pieces on a board of octagon titles.

Sarnorn (SAH-nohrn): The Shol'mas Lord of Justice, brother to Sevaani.

Saviour and Destroyer, the: see *Empyros*.

Scion, the: The elected leader of the Ciralys. A political rank comparable to that of a monarch.

Serjat (Ser-JAHT): Capital city of Tremor-Salaya.

Sevaani Etine (Sah-VAR-nee EH-tyn): Daughter of the Steward of Hanore, sister to Rolen. She dreams things that come to pass.

Shadowstealer: see *Lloth'var*.

Shaluay Starbinders (SHAH-loo-ay): An order of historians, healers and seers who use Starwells as the source of their power. Pre-Sundering they held a high position as advisors to the people in place of the Sahrin.

Shanaya dyn'Tian (SHAH-nai-ah din-TEE-ahn): Keeper of Hanore, one of the three Borderland citadels. Mentor of Darien and Meg.

Sharenesh (SHAH-REN-esh): The Elder God of Water, father of Taluun.

Shepherd Kings, the: The rulers of the Darvelanian Empire.

Shi-Kaan (Shee-KAHN): An order of Amarian monks who practise a martial art and philosophy based on Sahrin doctrine. Their temple is located in the south-east corner of the desert of Black Sands.

Shol'mas (SHAOL-mass): A title referring to beings of immense power which appeared to humans after the Sundering, claiming to be messengers of the gods.

Shrine: A structure or place consecrated or devoted to an Elder God.

Sith'sara (SITH-sah-RAH): Capital city of Sithapia.

Sithapia (Sith-AP-ee-ah): North-western most realm of Athmay.

Skreet: A small, scaled monkey-like daemon that infests the Sukmaanai swamp. They are carnivorous and territorial.

Skystone: Debris that falls from the Sormelene Span. Said to be formed of manifest *Asai* and highly prized by the Ciralys.

Sobia (Soh-BEE-ah): The planet on which the continent of Athmay is located.

Sola'var (SOL-ah-VAR): The builder, worker and soldier caste of the Var. They are physically large and strong, and both sexes often exceed 6 foot 5 in height with pointed ears and slanted eyes. The males are characterised with baldness.

Sonyth (Son-ITH): One of three Sahrin citadels on the Borderlands, built during the War of the Summoners; now home to families who wish to live free from the Houses of Aldania.

Sormelene Span, the (Sohr-mel-EEN): The band of crystalline rock that orbits Sobia.

Spheres: Those individual parts of *Asai* that have been identified as attuned to the element of an Elder God.

Spirit Seer: The elected leader of the Fifth Circle of the Ciralys.

Starbinders: see *Shaluay Starbinders*.

Starwells: Constructs scattered across Athmay that are utilised by the Shaluay. Little is known as to their function other than they do not utilise *Asai*.

Steward, the: The elected leaders of the citadels in the Borderlands who hold their position for life. The Stewards of Hanore have been elected from the same family for five hundred years.

Sukmaanai (SOOK-mahn-ai): A large swamp in northern Dal'mere.

Sundering, the: The event that 'broke' the continent of Athmay. This is believed to have occurred at the end of the War of the Summoners.

Sunstone: A *ci'nar* that glows with a light brighter than candles or torches.

Taalren (TAHL-ren): A Kas'tirien from Hanore. Former mentor to Kaiel Toranth.

Taaren'th, House (Tahr-enth): A High House, they were the descendants of Varos Korin'ad and led the Clan of the Bronze Spear. They ruled Aldania after the Sundering until House Niskeri overthrew them.

Tainted, the: see *Korda'var* and *Lloth'var*.

Tal'desai (TAL-de-sai): The elite guard of the Ciralys.

Taluun (Ta-LOON): The Elder God of the Sea, son of Sharenesh.

Tarin (TAHR-in): The Elder Goddess of Nature, consort of Garnavaar.

Telaq (TEE-lak): Ciralys of the Third Circle, a long-time advisor to Prince Alesandr Niskeri, teacher of Darien Toranth.

Tear of Scrying, the: A *tresilian* artefact held by the Fifth Circle of the Ciralys, said to give the holder the ability to perceive the future.

Tears of the Eye: see *Skystones*.

Temple: A building dedicated to the worship of a specific Shol'mas Lord; maintained and populated by that Shol'mas Lord's priesthood.

Three Citadels, the: Three Sahrin citadels built during the war of the Summoner, on the edge of what was the Atresian Plains. Now occupied by the descendants of refugees who wish a life free of the rule of the High Lords of the Realms.

Tome of Ascension, the: A codex written before the Sundering that compiles the Sahrin's knowledge of the High Asairic runes.

Tore (TOHR): A Sahrin citadel on the Borderlands, built during the War of the Sundering; now home to families who wish to live free from the Houses of Aldania.

Torimun duCerin (TOR-ee-MUHN doo-SER-in): Prince regent of Sithapia, uncle to Andraste.

***tresilian* (TREY-sil-ee-AHN):** An artefact formed from *Asai* by the Sahrin for a specific purpose and usable by any sphere. Most were lost during the Sundering and are highly valued by Isoliere. The closest the Ciralys can come to replicating these are the ci'nar.

Tusked Skreet: A skreet set apart by its large size and deadly tusks. Characteristically solitary by nature compared to its brethren who live in packs.

Vak'nar (VAHK-nahr): A species of daemon that uses hypnosis and mind control to kill its prey. It can pass as human in shadow and in twilight. They are often used as scouts for the daemon hordes.

Var Imperium, the (VAR): The first civilization to rise after the Sundering. Ruled the Hyla'vari Congress, it provided stability and order in the vacuum left by the Sahrin.

Var, the (VAR): Varian term for people, or person.

Varos Korin'ad (VAH-rohs KOR-in-AHD): The last Leader of the Sahrin. At the time of the Sundering, he was the Empyros. Also see *Empyros*.

Vash'kiri (VASH-keer-ee): The Aldanian order of gryphon riders.

Vasharviel (VASH-ah-VEE-ehl): Elder God of Air.

Void: The dimension from which *Des'maadr* and daemons originate.

voidspore: A *Des'maadrian* virus that links a host with a daemon and either enables possession or feeds the daemons the host's life force.

War of the Summoners: The civil war between the Sahrin who followed the Elder Gods and those who swore themselves to the Des'maadrian, Di'shana, that occurred approximately four thousand years ago.

Wielder: A person who can see and direct *Asai*.

wielding: The act of using *Asai*.

witch: A wielder of *Asai* who does not follow the teachings of the Sahrin.

witchborn: A human who is born with the ability to perceive and wield *Asai*.

Yuanel (YO-UN-hel): Half-Amarian aide to the Shaluay ambassador Arais.

Zaria Desrin (ZAH-ree-AH Des-rin): Daughter of Corwyn Desrin, granddaughter of Nataya Desrin.

ACKNOWLEDGEMENTS

When I first started writing (many years ago) I imagined that I wouldn't need any help to get this novel completed and fit for publishing. Little did I know. Writing may well seem to be a solitary profession, but there are often a number of people behind the scenes.

My alpha readers: Christine Polec, who read the original manuscript – unedited – way back when, and whose enthusiasm has never waned. My gratitude knows no bounds (I hope you are not to disappointed with the changes I've made!). And Wade Wright, you didn't read the original manuscript, but I have come to consider you an alpha reader none the less (especially considering how many versions of it you did read!).

And my beta readers: Tamara Allcock, Sean Crow, Martin Le Roux, Karen Miller, Sylwia Niwczyk, Zena Shapter, Stephanie Tall, Susan Walkerden and Aidan Walsh. And to those who have read the manuscript more than once: Marcus Herniman, Chris Rosser, Craig Slater, Stephanie Smith, John Timmony and Kathryn Wardle – you have all read different versions of the novel, and your insights, the consideration you have shown, and the time you have given up to read my work is very much appreciated.

And lastly (but never least) my editors: Abigail Nathan and Amanda J.

Spedding. My thanks feel far too inadequate an offering for the assistance you have both offered me at different stages of this project, yet I offer them none the less. Without you both I would still be reworking the same old sentences and thinking *'one day I will publish this, one day…'*

ABOUT THE AUTHOR

Mark Timmony was born and bred on Sydney's Northern Beaches. He's wanted to write for as long as he can remember and has several notebooks filled with illegible scribblings from childhood to prove it. The desire to write led to work as a bookseller and he spent almost a decade working as a genre specialist in Sydney. *The Blood of the Spear* is his debut novel.

You can find Mark online at marktimmony.com

CPSIA information can be obtained
at www.ICGtesting.com
Printed in the USA
LVHW050401311222
736049LV00004B/1005